Oregon Breeze

Oregon Breeze

*Love Is Stirring Hearts
in Four Inspiring Stories*

BIRDIE L.
ETCHISON

BARBOUR
PUBLISHING

BIRDIE L. ETCHISON lives on the Washington Coast but knows a good deal about Oregon's Willamette Valley, the setting for the majority of her books. She loves to research the colorful history of the United States and uses her research along with family stories to create wonderful novels.

Finding Courtney

With love ad thanks to my Round Robin friends:
Colleen, Elsie, Gail, Lauraie, Marcia, Marion,
Pat, Ruby, Sandy, and Woodeene.

Chapter 1

Courtney Adams was late. She hurried into the choir room and grabbed her robe.

"Hey, what's up?" her best friend, Tina, asked, turning to give her a hug. "Thought you were sick or something."

"Listen, we need to get together sometime. Maybe after church?"

Tina smiled. "Sure. If I can talk Mike into waiting."

Courtney frowned. Of course. She was constantly forgetting that Tina was married now. They'd been close friends for so many years, sharing everything that happened in their lives. All that had changed drastically after Tina married a year ago.

The organist was playing the introit, and the choir sang as they came into the sanctuary. Courtney pulled the robe down over her skirt, adjusted the collar, and straightened her long, dark hair with her hand. She hoped she looked okay.

Harmonizing with the sopranos, she quickly got into place and walked down the aisle. She caught a smile from her mother and a wink from another friend. Tina's husband beamed at his wife. As often happened, Courtney got a lump in her throat when she saw her best friend with her husband. They had such a wonderful relationship, and she couldn't help thinking and hoping and wondering if someday she might find that perfect someone, too.

As the music ended, the choir assembled on the chairs off to the side of the pulpit. Courtney scanned the audience. She had a bird's-eye view and could spot a visitor in a second. Her gaze came to light on a young man with immense shoulders and a smile on his face. He sat in the second pew. Her breath caught. Funny, but he had looked up just as she saw him, and they stared at each other for a long moment. She looked away as Pastor Sam asked for a show of hands of visitors. Each Sunday morning he passed out bookmarks to visitors—crosses made by the Women's Guild.

A hand shot up, and Courtney looked at the stranger again. "And where are you from?" Pastor Sam asked.

"Right here in Portland," came the answer. Courtney's heart skipped a beat. *Silly,* she admonished herself. *You know how you really feel about dating, so stop looking. Stop thinking that it might be possible for you to find someone, to be happy. It will never be possible, not until you find your birth mother.*

The other newcomers were lost to Courtney, though she usually paid careful attention. She felt a finger poking her ribs, and she realized they were standing to sing the first anthem, "O, For a Thousand Tongues to Sing!"

She could have sung that in her sleep. She'd always been in a choir, starting out with the junior choir. She couldn't remember a time when she hadn't attended a church, a time when she hadn't trusted and believed in the Lord. She had accepted Him as her personal Savior at a young age—her mother, that is, her adoptive mother, Alice, had recorded it in her *Seven-Year Baby Book*. Nobody could have asked for a more wonderful parent. And her father, God rest his soul, had been there for her, attending her games, taking her to swim lessons, always her best and loudest cheering section. She had been devastated when he died of a sudden heart attack two years ago. And Alice had been bereft, but they'd turned to the church, as always, and been uplifted.

Courtney wasn't sure when it first hit her, but one day she railed at God about not being able to find her real mother. She'd made every effort, sending letters, getting help from the library and the Internet, but so far had come to a dead end. Why wouldn't God let her find her mother? Would it be like Tina said, that she might find her and discover she didn't want to be found?

Courtney found out that was sometimes the case when she talked to a counselor about it. "Some birth mothers have not told their families about their pregnancy or about giving their child up. A grown person suddenly appearing on their doorstep can put a strain on a marriage and the relationship with their other children."

"But I have a right to know," Courtney had replied. "I need information about my medical background." Tears formed in her eyes as she remembered the year she was fifteen and had to drop out of high school. Her symptoms had been so weird. She had been exhausted every hour of every day. She could hardly eat, had no appetite, and though she wasn't in pain, she was listless. Her throat was raw and her side was tingly.

"Mono," the doctor had said at first. The tests came back negative. Then the numbness started; there were more tests, and an MRI ruled out multiple sclerosis or a brain tumor, but no diagnosis had ever been made.

"We'll fight this," Alice had said. "You're strong. Healthy. I know God can heal you."

And she had gotten better. Not immediately; she suffered through six months of being weak and nauseated. Then the symptoms left as fast as they had appeared.

"But what if it happens again?" had been Courtney's question. "I need to know what my birth mother had, if this is something that was passed on to me."

Alice had been helpful and understanding when Courtney said she wanted to find her birth mother. "I think I would feel that way also, dear. But," and her mother had enfolded her in her arms, "I think Tina is right. Your real mother may not want to be found."

"And if that's so," Courtney had said as she flounced across the kitchen, "then I'll accept that. I won't bug her. Believe me; I know when I am not wanted."

"Your father and I have loved you from that first moment you were placed in our arms."

❧

"Are you daydreaming, asleep, or what?" Tina was yanking on her robe. It was prayer time.

"I was just thinking."

"That's obvious," Tina whispered behind the back of her hand.

Courtney glanced up to find the stranger gazing at her again. She trembled. *Who is that gorgeous hunk?* Tina wrote on the margin of her bulletin.

"How should I know?" Courtney said.

"And what's he doing here?"

"Maybe he's my brother."

Someone kicked the back of her chair. Courtney looked straight ahead, stifling a giggle. Sitting next to Tina meant sharing notes and thoughts. They'd done that when they were younger, but now they were supposedly mature twenty-three-year-old women, a bit old for passing notes.

She looked up and the man smiled, then winked at her. She felt the color flood her cheeks. She tore her eyes away, hoping nobody had noticed. She knew, however, that her mother would have; she was that perceptive, and there would be questions once they got home.

When the service was over, and after she removed her choir robe, Courtney took longer than usual to fix her hair. She brushed it high on each side and secured it with gold clasps. Tina was always bugging her about cutting her hair, but so far she liked it just fine this way. She could French-braid it, wear a George Washington ponytail, or wear a high one like she had when she was in grade school. If she felt extra young, she wore two ponytails.

"Are you coming or what?" Tina stood in the doorway, her short hair in place and an impatient look on her round face. "Sometimes you are slower than slow."

Grabbing her handbag, she joined Tina on the way down the back stairs to the fellowship hall. "I had to fix my hair again," she finally said.

Tina stopped and looked down at her friend. "You wouldn't have that problem if you'd just get it cut."

Courtney felt her insides bristle. "Did I say it was a problem? You said it; I didn't." The last thing Courtney wanted was to feel out of sorts today. Her mind kept going to the stranger and how he had smiled and nodded at the sermon, how his gaze kept meeting hers, how he'd actually winked. No, today felt good. Today she could put aside some of her concerns. Missing her father. Wondering, again, how to locate her birth mother. Why was it so difficult for her when others had found lost ones in a day, sometimes even hours?

Tina had said something. Courtney knew it by the exasperated look on her face, and she'd missed it because she'd been daydreaming.

"I repeat," Tina began again, "your mind isn't receiving messages this morning."

Courtney turned and hugged her friend. Tina had always been plump, but now with her advancing pregnancy, she had become a round butterball. "I'm so excited with the baby coming and all. Guess I got to thinking about how you must feel about now."

There were others on the steps going down, so the two girls paused and Tina glanced up. "I can't get used to the kicks. I think I have a soccer player in there."

As they entered the already-filled hall, the smell of coffee made Courtney's stomach growl. All she'd had that morning was a quick cup and a day-old doughnut from the bread box.

"Hey." Tina pulled her close, nodding at one corner. "Isn't that the new guy over there? You can't miss him; he's so tall."

Courtney's heart zigged, then zagged. Yes, it was him. She felt like she was back in her freshman year when she'd had her first real boyfriend and they'd attended all the football games. Rick. Funny. She hadn't thought of him for years until now. Perhaps it was the height.

"Knowing you, you'll be over introducing yourself—" Tina was interrupted when Mike appeared, took her hand, and pulled her toward the refreshment table.

"I'll talk to you later," Courtney said to her friend's retreating back. Of course, if Mike had his way, he'd have her out the door in nothing flat. The baseball playoffs were coming up, and Mike was a baseball fan.

"Hey, Court, did you sign up for next Saturday's soup kitchen?" Karen was at her elbow, clipboard with dangling pencil in hand. "I think I need just two more."

"Sure, Karen. Put me down. You can forge my name."

Courtney continued along. One thing for sure, the church needed a larger fellowship hall. She wondered if there wouldn't be talk about an expansion in the near future. Relocating was out of the question, as members of the administrative board had already vetoed that idea. But they had the parking lot, and the owners of the next two lots had offered to sell in the event the church voted on adding a recreation hall.

She found herself in the stranger's corner. Finally. Courtney had always been good with words—could talk her way out of a traffic ticket, had talked her English teacher into giving her an A- instead of a B+ on a test. That ability had put her on the high school debate team, and Parkrose had taken first place at state competition the first time ever. But suddenly she felt awkward as her eyes met the stranger's. How could she be tongue-tied now? He was the first to speak as he held out his hand and took hers. She immediately felt the warmth, the strength in his handshake.

"Hello. I'm Steven, Steven Spencer. And you are?"

She felt color rise to her cheeks. "Courtney. Adams."

He still held her hand, and she found herself liking it very much.

"Do you want some coffee?" He smiled, revealing two dimples. "I decided to wait until the line dwindled down."

"I'd love some, but you are the guest. I should be the one offering to get yours—" She was babbling and she never, ever babbled—not even when she was a baby.

"Nonsense. We'll both go get it. You lead the way."

Courtney wove through the crowd, nodding at this one, pausing to hug another. Steven almost ran into her once but stopped in time.

Finally they both had coffee—black—and a chocolate brownie each. "I was led to this church this morning," Steven said. "Just thought I'd tell you that."

She felt mesmerized by his intense look. "Led? And just how do you mean?" She had a picture of someone putting a collar around his neck and leading him down the street to the church with the loud bell. So many churches had stopped ringing the bells ten minutes before the service. She was glad Parkrose Community had not.

"A voice told me to come here."

He was joking. She knew it. Courtney was often gullible, but not this time. "And you want me to believe this." She took a deep sip of her coffee, burning her tongue.

His dark eyes flashed with humor. "No. I am serious. Honest. A voice told me it was time I found a church to attend on Sundays. The voice just happens to belong to my grandmother."

"Oh." Well, that explained it.

"The only problem being Grams has been gone for nine years now."

Courtney nearly choked on the brownie. He reached over and touched her shoulder. "Are you okay?"

"I don't believe in voices," Courtney said. "Only God's voice."

He grinned now. How many expressions could one face have? "Oh, I believe in God's voice, but sometimes He has people to send important messages. Do you not believe this?"

Courtney found it difficult at the moment to know what she believed. She glanced away and noticed the fellowship hall was clearing out. People usually mingled for just a few minutes before heading for home. Obviously Mike and Tina had left already.

"I suppose you need to go." He was talking again, not waiting for her answer, but she wanted to give him one.

"I believe God delivers His message to many people, and I must admit I've heard voices leading me, helping me make a decision." She smiled and felt herself relax.

"Say, would you like to get lunch somewhere?" He looked expectant. "And if not now, perhaps another time?"

The coffee was gone, and she turned to set the cup down. "I have a standing date for lunch after church with my aunt Agnes in Gresham, but thanks."

Karen came over with the clipboard. "I can't get anyone else to sign up. Know somebody else, Court? Someone I may not know of?"

Karen was as tall as Courtney was short. She held the clipboard out to Courtney to read, but her eyes were on Steven. "Hi." She smiled. "Karen Martin."

"Steven Spencer. And what's this for?"

"Our soup kitchen Saturday morning. We take turns serving. The young adults have it this coming week. The men's group serves one week, the guild another, and the youth group one."

"This Saturday?" Steven smiled. "Sure, I'll do it."

Before Courtney could suggest a name, Steven had grabbed the clipboard and penciled his name in. "Ten o'clock? No problem."

"You didn't have to do that, but it was nice of you," Courtney said after Karen left.

"It's time to get involved in the community—"

"Is that something else the voice said to you?"

He laughed. "No. Actually, it was my own voice saying it the minute Karen said she needed one more person."

"It's fun. You'll like the people. So many walks of life." She was rambling again, and she didn't want to ramble in front of a stranger. Yet Steven didn't seem like a stranger. In some ways she felt she had known him for a long time. Funny how some people affected you that way.

"Listen, I'd better let you get on with your visit. Gresham's a few miles out there. I'll see you on Saturday, if not before." He handed her a card and removed another from the inside of his suit coat pocket. "I need your phone number."

She took the card. "Steven R. Spencer, Computer Analyst." The office was located in the downtown area. Her heart skipped another beat. In fact, he was located just four blocks from the law office on Fifth and Market where she worked as a legal assistant.

"I have a card, also." She dug into the side pocket of her purse. Bob, her boss, had had the cards made for her, insisting that everyone must have a business card these days.

"I'll call you."

She nodded and watched him until he disappeared back up the stairs. She hoped he might turn around and look, but he didn't.

Courtney helped clear the table and made her way into the kitchen, where her mother was washing cups.

"Are you almost ready, Mom? You know Aunt Agnes. She'll be waiting and wondering why we took so long."

Alice Adams smiled and placed the last cup in the drainer. "I'll get out of this apron and be with you in a jiffy. Oh, by the way, wasn't that the new young visitor I saw you talking to?"

Courtney's cheeks flushed for what seemed like the fifth time that day. "Steven? Yeah, he's new, but you already know that."

"You certainly were attentive, or was it the other way around?"

"Oh, Mom. You know how I am." But this was different. She hadn't felt this way ever. Her mother would like nothing better than to see Courtney married. How she'd love looking forward to a grandchild. But Courtney couldn't let herself dream about marriage, a child. Not yet. There were things she had to know about herself first. Stones to uncover. Medical facts to be discovered. She loved her adoptive mother with all her heart, and she'd been even closer to her adopted father, but she had to know who she was. It was that simple. Janelle Landers was the name of her birth mother. And Janelle Landers must be found.

With sweaters slung over their arms, Courtney and her mom went up the steps and out into the golden sunshine of the Sunday afternoon.

Chapter 2

Steven walked the three blocks to his beat-up Ford. It needed a paint job, but it still ran and got good gas mileage. The kid he had working for him—just hired—had a new souped-up Trans Am, but Steven didn't want the payments that came with a new car. He was happy with his old heap. He paused, struggling with the driver's door. It stuck, and he always had to use extra force. As he crawled in behind the wheel, he looked around for the first time in a long while. The interior was tacky. It never bothered him before, but now he imagined picking up Miss Courtney Adams and asking her to get into the rust bucket. Suddenly the Trans Am was looking good. Perhaps he could rent it from Jeff for a night.

The sun was more than beautiful today; it was gorgeous. As Steven drove west toward Portland downtown proper, his mind was filled with the hymns sung that morning, the preacher's message that seemed to speak right to him, and the smile from an angel who sang in the choir. An angel named Courtney. "Wow, Grams, when you hit me with something, you really hit me," he said aloud. "I hadn't realized how far I'd strayed from church or from meaningful things in my life."

Ordinarily he would have stopped by the deli on the corner, but he didn't feel like eating and didn't know what he'd order if he did. Surely he could find a crust of bread in the house, a bit of peanut butter, and enough coffee to make a pot. So he went straight home.

His apartment was small but adequate. The walls were bare, as if he'd just moved in yesterday, when in fact he'd moved to Portland over a year ago and had rented this apartment the first day. It was the only one he had looked at. It didn't matter if he had a view—way too costly—nor did he need a large living area. He never planned to entertain, anyway. A kitchen, bed, and closet were the basic needs.

He started a pot of coffee, then went to the bedroom and opened his closet. It had plenty of room inside. He owned one good suit, the dark one he'd worn today. Grams had told him when he bought one for high school graduation, "Buy black and you'll not be sorry. You can wear it for weddings and funerals, as well. Waste not, want not, Steven."

"Yeah, Grams, you taught me well. I find it difficult to buy another suit or a car. But not hard to let my heart be taken by a certain dark-haired girl with twinkling eyes."

He hung the suit jacket next to the three dress shirts: two white, plus the light blue he had almost worn. For some reason he had chosen the checked one and the aqua tie. He had thought they matched, but now as he looked in the bedroom mirror, he decided they did not. Maybe he was color-blind and hadn't realized it until this minute. Nobody had ever helped him be color-coordinated. He wore tan Dockers to work each morning and usually a favorite navy blue V-neck sweater, sometimes a red sweater, and on occasion a sweatshirt. Jeff had complained about the sweatshirt. "Not presenting a good image," he said.

When had he become so frugal? Suddenly he wished he had nicer threads, a new couch, and a few paintings on the wall. He changed into his Dockers and a sweater and went back to the kitchen.

The coffee was finished, but the bread had mold on it, so he threw it in the sink. This meant he'd have to go to the deli unless he ordered a pizza. Half now, half tomorrow. *Waste not, want not,* rang through his head again.

He flipped on the TV. Baseball, *Hercules,* a preacher pounding the pulpit, and an ice skating show. Not much on Sunday.

He eased into a chair and grabbed his day planner. He never thought he'd be one to plan his days, but he found it invaluable once he'd gotten the hang of it.

The week was busy, but next weekend was open. Clear. He jotted down the words, *Soup Kitchen, 9:30 A.M.* Courtney had said ten, but Steven always arrived early, allowing himself time for getting lost or finding a parking spot.

He closed the book and wondered what it would be like to work next to Courtney. Would he be handing over the rolls or ladling up soup? Maybe he'd be in the kitchen washing up things. That would be okay. Grams had taught him to cook—not that he did so anymore. She'd also taught him to wash dishes and vacuum floors. "Men need to know how to do all things in the house," she'd said. "You never know when your wife might be sick or have a baby or something."

"What if I don't get married?" he'd asked. He was ten then, a tall, skin-and-bones, freckle-faced kid. Somehow he could not ever imagine marrying, thinking people rated marriage far higher than it deserved.

"You'll find someone one day and you'll wonder how you could ever feel so wonderful inside. And when that day comes, you'll want to commit, but be patient, Steven. Patience is a virtue, as the Lord tells us in the Good Book."

Patience. Steven had been patient most of his life. It was always the other guy who got the girl. He'd loved once in college, but he had been too backward, or so his roommate said. "Man, you see someone you like, you gotta make a move. You can't expect them to be aggressive. Some are, but those you may not want."

"Choose a Christian girl, and you'll be blessed many times over." That had been Grams's advice a few hours before she'd died. It was as if she knew she had to give him all the advice she had inside her. And Steven had soaked up the words, filled his mind with her presence, remembering the crooked smile he loved and the feel of the leathery cheek—soft, yet wrinkled from years of work in the sun. She'd been a true farm wife, never wanting to leave the Redmond ranch but having to when she had become ill. She'd hated the year she lived in the central Oregon town of Bend, yearning for the wide open spaces and wishing she still had the energy to raise cattle.

He had cried that night—cried because he missed her so much and because he felt he could have done more to make her happy. He had been expected to take over the ranch when he got out of school, but he didn't want that kind of life—and because he hadn't taken over, Grams had had to leave her beloved ranch when she became ill. The city called to him, and though Grams said she understood, he doubted that she really did.

Steven strode to the refrigerator to look inside once more as if something would miraculously appear on the shelf. Bare. Totally. He decided then and there to go grocery shopping. Big-time. He could suddenly taste Grams's pot roast with potatoes and carrots surrounding it and the dark gravy that bubbled in the little pot on the stove. He'd get greens for making salad, and flour, sugar, baking powder—all the ingredients for making biscuits.

As he walked the ten blocks to the nearest store, he wondered, *What is wrong with me? Why did I walk? Now I'll struggle with the bags getting back to the apartment.* But the sun was still out, and a slight breeze blew in from the Willamette River. Summer would soon be over, and fall in its brilliant colors would grace the hills on the opposite side. He loved fall the best—always would.

The cashier flashed him a warm smile and asked, "How are you this afternoon?"

He nodded. "Fine, thanks," he responded. As he headed out the door with two bags filled to the brim, he wondered if she was just being friendly or if he could have asked her out and had her accept. Courtney's face crossed his mind again. He had to see her before Saturday. How could he possibly wait that long? He wondered if she liked baseball. There was a Portland Rockies game on Wednesday. He laughed as he remembered asking his last date if she would like to see a game.

"I'd be bored out of my tree," she had said. Did he dare ask Courtney? Yet, wouldn't it be time to discover what she liked now before he became more interested?

He unlocked the downstairs door and took the stairs to the third floor.

The food halfway filled his refrigerator and one cupboard. Satisfied, he made a tuna fish sandwich with a slab of cheese on top and sprouts on top of that. And lots of mayo.

Next he'd go to Lloyd Center Mall, to the tall men's shop, since he always needed extra-long sleeves and length in everything. Had he ever been short? He couldn't remember a time. Even when he'd played Little League and later joined Babe Ruth, he'd been put out in the field because his long arms could catch the fly balls.

He turned on the rest of the ball game, though it was the Yankees playing Cleveland and he was a National League fan, mainly the Cardinals.

After finishing his sandwich, topped off by another cup of coffee, Steven left for his second shopping trip of the day.

And the Lord said on the seventh day ye shall rest rang through his mind as he headed for the Ford. *Rest. How does one rest? Does one spend the day in prayer? Reading the Bible? Attending the evening service? Bingo. Of course. They must have an evening service. Wasn't that when the youth groups met? And if youth groups met, wouldn't the young adults' group also meet?*

He found the bulletin in the front seat and looked at the back at the announcements. Evening service was at 6 P.M.

He would be there, but first things first.

Minutes later, Steven was in the mall and suddenly felt like a child in a toy store at Christmas. The men's store had never held such fascination for him. He bought two pairs of casual slacks, different colors than the usual tan (Jeff would be surprised), a couple of tees, and new socks. Invariably, he lost at least one when he washed clothes each week. Someday he'd run an investigation to see where lost socks went. There had to be a sock heaven somewhere. He also purchased a lightweight jacket and two dressy shirts, one a burgundy silk (Jeff really would think he'd taken leave of his senses), and a casual shirt with a button-down collar.

"Well, Grams, I hope you aren't turning over in your grave. I just spent $350 and didn't even buy a suit or a pair of shoes!" he muttered as he walked to his car.

This time the door of his old Ford annoyed him more than usual. He hit it twice before it opened. Maybe the time had come to consider buying a newer model—not brand new, but something more serviceable. He could hear Jeff's voice now. "A man of your means needs a better car, if you don't mind my saying so."

As Steven made his way west on Multnomah and across the Broadway Bridge, he felt good. Lighthearted. He had food. He had clothes. He had a girl. Well, maybe he had a girl. It was a bit early to get his hopes up.

After traveling the three flights, his arms loaded down for the second time that day, he filled the hangers in his closet and put the socks in the top drawer. The new clothes looked good.

He opened a soda and reached for the phone.

"Jeff, I know this is going to sound crazy, but can I rent your car for one evening?"

"What say you?" The TV blared in the background, and Jeff was chewing on potato chips or something equally loud. "Man, you want to rent my car? Are you okay, Steven?"

Steven laughed. "Yes. I just need something better than mine tonight; probably three hours tops."

"Man, I'm not heading out, so you can have it. Just be sure you don't park too close to anybody. People aren't too careful about opening their doors and dinging the one next to them."

"I know. I'll take care of your baby; never fear."

After jotting down the address, Steven made another sandwich, a fried egg this time with a dab of ketchup and a ton of butter. It was the only sandwich on which he didn't use mayo.

He flipped on the evening news, saw that it was disastrous as always, and flipped it right back off. He'd rather read than hear about someone shooting someone else. The forecast was for an overcast morning. He had always liked to know what the weather was going to be.

As Steven paced his apartment, not knowing why he was doing so, he surveyed the bare walls again. A Renoir print would go well on the one wall, and of course, a Monet. He should go to the galleries in town and select a local artist as well. Classics were great, but he liked to support Portlanders, too.

That would mean another shopping trip. Then he'd think about the car. This meant his checking account would dwindle, but he had his mutual funds and the stocks to fall back on. Business was doing fantastically well, so why not spend it? "You can't take it with you, Steven, but you need enough to live on. Spend wisely."

"Well, Grams," he sat back down in his favorite chair, putting his hands behind his head, "do you think I spent too much today?"

He showered for the second time that day, then decided to go casual for the evening service, wearing his new button-down shirt with his Dockers and the light jacket.

Steven thought about why he'd come to Portland. He had left central Oregon, where he'd lived all his life and liked the weather better since it rained less, but decided to move to a larger city for his expanding business. Portland seemed about right. He'd give it two years, then if he didn't like it, he could move to Seattle or maybe even south to California. He now knew why God had led him to Portland and why Grams had made him realize he needed God in his life again. He needed to get involved in a church—meet good people. Well, he had, hadn't he? He'd found the right church on the first try.

Humming, he took the stairs rather than the elevator to the ground floor and to the garage where his car waited.

He pounded the door twice. "Sorry, ol' friend. You're going to sit over in front of Jeff's house for a bit. Man, are his neighbors going to wonder what happened to him." Smiling, Steven roared out of the underground garage and headed back across the river for the third time that day.

Chapter 3

Courtney rolled the window down as they traveled east on Powell. She could have taken the freeway and her mother asked why she had not, since she liked to arrive at least by one.

"I just want to go the slower way today, if that's okay."

"Of course, darling. I'm just along for the ride, anyway."

Courtney reached over and squeezed her mother's hand. Aunt Agnes was Alice's older sister and had lived alone for the past five years. The sisters always reminisced about losing their husbands and about being widows, while Courtney usually sat and worked on a rug she was hooking.

"I do wish you'd come to live with me," her mother said to Agnes, as always, the minute they arrived. "You know how I dislike rattling around in that big old house."

"Then sell it and come live with me."

"In Gresham?"

Courtney smiled as she threaded blue yarn onto the large needle. She had the litany memorized. Neither sister wanted to move, though they loved each other dearly. Agnes had not had children either and had looked into adoption, but nothing ever came of it. Courtney had grown up without cousins since her father had been an only child. It was a lonely existence, though she'd never wanted for a thing. "God has His reasons for what happens," her mother always said. Courtney believed with all her heart in the goodness of God, in how He wanted only the best for her.

"Our girl has met a young man," her mother was saying now. Courtney looked up, her mouth falling open.

"What did you just say?"

Aunt Agnes smiled. "That you met a nice young man and—"

Courtney set the hook aside. "Mother's letting her imagination run wild. I only met Steven this morning."

"Mark my words; he'll be back for the evening service."

"Oh, sure. Right."

They had the usual lunch. Aunt Agnes liked tomato soup and grilled cheese sandwiches. For dessert there was a fruit plate, which in recent years included kiwi fruit and shortbread cookies. When the Girl Scouts had their cookie drive in March, Agnes bought two dozen boxes and put them in the freezer for use the rest of the year. There would be six cookies on the plate. Two apiece.

For some unexplainable reason, Courtney could only eat half a toasted cheese.

"But, dear heart, you always eat a whole sandwich with your cup of soup," her aunt protested.

"I told you she's in love."

"Mom!" Courtney felt like a small child with the two discussing her as if she weren't in the room. She never had liked that game.

"It's about time you thought about marriage," Aunt Agnes said, clearing the table of soup cups.

"I can't yet and you know why, Auntie."

"Of course. But I don't think you're going to find your birth mother. If the good Lord wanted you to, you would have by now."

Courtney felt a stabbing sensation run through her. It could be true. Prayers were always answered but sometimes not in the way one had hoped.

They left at three. This never varied, either. Aunt Agnes had her nap at that time, and Courtney and her mother returned home to a house that seemed cold and empty now. Even when her father had been alive, only the two of them had gone to see Aunt Agnes. "That's for you women," he had said. "You three have such a good time visiting and having lunch. I'd just be in the way." They'd all gotten together for Thanksgiving and Christmas and for birthdays, but not Sundays.

"I wish I didn't believe what Agnes said, sweetie," Courtney's mother said as they headed back home, "but you must admit she has a point."

"I'm not giving up." Courtney knew there was an edge to her voice, but she couldn't help it. They'd discussed this endless times, and though Alice agreed that it was something Courtney should do, she couldn't help letting her doubts be known.

"What if you are thirty and you aren't any closer than you are now?"

"Is thirty the magic number now? I'll be an old maid if I'm not married at thirty?"

"Don't sound like that." Her mother's voice got choked up, but Courtney plunged on.

"Mother, I love you dearly, but you must let me do what I must."

"But the Internet search has shown nothing. Not even a trace."

Courtney pulled into the driveway and pointed the garage-door opener. The two-story Cape Cod was the sort of house she wanted someday, should she ever marry. It was roomy, yet had such a homey feel about it. It had the same white paint and green trim her father had painted it with two years ago, just before his heart attack. The south side where the hot afternoon sun hit was peeling in spots, but she doubted that they could ever paint over it.

"I know I should have had some news by now, but that doesn't mean I give it all up."

Her mother got out of the car and headed for the small door leading into the kitchen. "I just hope you know what you are doing, honey."

"I do, Mom. I do. I know God is behind this search. I've never been more sure of anything in my life. And just this afternoon, while sitting out at Aunt Agnes's, I realized what I must do next."

"What is that, dear?"

"I'm going to Illinois, to the small town where I was born. Surely I can find someone who knows something there."

Her mother looked almost shocked. "You don't mean it."

"Yes, I do."

"But what about work?"

"I have time coming. Remember, I didn't take the two weeks of vacation this year. Bob will let me go."

"Are you sure?"

"Mom, he owes me."

"Bob is also interested in you. Don't forget that."

Courtney groaned. Her mother was intuitive. Courtney had never mentioned that he'd asked her out. She liked her boss, but knew she couldn't like him in that way. He didn't know God, and what's more, he used people to his advantage. She could never, ever fall in love with a man like that.

"I'll be sure to give Bob plenty of notice."

"Oh, honey, maybe I should come with you."

"No. Mom." They were in the kitchen, and Courtney poured a cup of coffee and put it in the microwave. "I know that might be a good idea, but it's just something I must do myself."

"Are you sure you'll be all right?"

Her mother was frightened of several things, and her fears had become more apparent since her husband had died. She didn't like to be alone, nor did she like the dark. Courtney had suggested she get a dog, but she'd vetoed that idea. Courtney knew that she was thinking about being alone now and that the thought terrified her.

"You could go out to spend some time with Aunt Agnes. Why don't you plan on doing that?"

"Oh, honey, I don't want to impose."

"Impose? Your own sister?" Though Courtney had never had a sister, she'd often longed for one and wondered what it would have been like to have a sibling, someone to share her ups and downs with. That's why she and Tina had remained such good friends.

"I'll call Fran over at Country Travel first thing in the morning and see if they have any specials coming up."

"You're assuming Bob will let you off. . . ." Her mother's voice trailed off.

"If he doesn't, I quit."

"You wouldn't!"

"Watch me."

"Well, you have your inheritance from your father. That could hold you over for a while, but surely—"

"Mother, I know I won't get fired. What's more, if he did fire me, I know of another place where I could work. Don't worry needlessly. What did God say about the birds of the air? 'Look at the birds of the air; they do not sow or reap or store away in barns, and yet your heavenly Father feeds them. Are you not much more valuable than they?' Matthew 6:26."

"I know, I know. I never worried like this until your father died."

Courtney stopped, put her cup down, and drew her mother close. "I don't want you to be concerned about me. I'm old enough to take care of myself."

"A mother never stops being concerned about her children," Alice said through her tears. She looked out the window into the backyard. The grass was green, the trees were green, but she missed the flowers her husband had always planted. He had such a way with a garden, but the small plot where he grew cabbages and tomatoes was bare and brown. Bare and brown just like her heart.

Chapter 4

Courtney and her mother arrived at church at five minutes to six. The piano played "Let a Little Sunshine In, Let a Little Sunshine In." Courtney hummed as she moved into one of the back pews. The view was better from the back, though her mother preferred the front. But Alice never moved because she liked sitting with Courtney, especially since she couldn't sit with her on Sunday morning when Courtney was in the choir.

"See? I told you." Her mother tugged at her arm. "He's here. That nice young man you talked to after church today."

Courtney's heart lurched. Could her mother be right? Should she be reading more into the depth of those pale blue eyes? She knew her face was flushed, so she touched her cheeks and willed the red to disappear.

"He's talking to Rod."

Rod was also single and had had an eye on Courtney since they were kids in junior high. Courtney thought of him as a brother and had told him so on more than one occasion.

"Look, dear. He's spotted you!"

"Mother," Courtney said under her breath. She felt like a small child on her way to the first day of school, with her mother hovering.

The three-member ensemble got on the stage and set up the sound equipment. This was Courtney's favorite part of the service. This and testimony time. The evening message was always short—ten minutes tops.

She glanced at the corner where the teenagers sat. They passed notes now, just as she and Tina had. Tina. Was Tina here tonight?

Courtney made a quick check, her eyes meeting Steven's. He waved, and the next thing she knew, he had left the pew and was making his way to her side of the church.

"That's one nice thing about him," her mother whispered her way. "He's on time. That's a true virtue; believe me."

Courtney squirmed. Of course her mother would say that. Courtney had struggled with being on time all her life. What would it be like to arrive early? She grinned at the thought.

He came down the other aisle and moved in next to Courtney. "I hope you don't mind if I sit here with you."

With no tie and what appeared to be a new denim jacket, he looked more casual. She liked the clean smell of him and moved to make room, when what she wanted to do was stay right there in that spot. Alice Adams leaned over, extending her hand. "So nice to have you attend evening service."

"Yes," Courtney added. "I didn't think I'd see you until Saturday."

He smiled, and once more she was disarmed by the way his whole face looked, the eyes dancing, almost as if teasing her. "I go in for things in a big way. Once I'm committed, that is."

Suddenly Courtney realized she knew very little about him and wanted to know more. A sinking feeling hit as she knew she couldn't tell him much about herself.

The first song began, and Courtney's voice rang out. She could feel Steven's eyes on her, and she tried to hear his voice, but heard nothing but her mother's.

After the song, he nodded. "I'm glad I sat by you. Your voice warms my heart."

It was the second time she blushed that evening. *Why is he having this effect on me?* she wondered. *Nobody has ever made me feel like this.* She stared straight ahead, afraid to look in his direction, afraid of what she might do or not do. She'd probably forget where she was.

Testimony time was longer than usual, but Courtney didn't hear much. She clapped and smiled at the appropriate times. Then Steven stood.

"I've been looking for a church home," he said. "Been in the city for a year. I feel at home here and will definitely be back."

Cheers rose, and hearty clapping filled the sanctuary. Evening service was always so informal. Courtney loved it, but her mother sometimes frowned. "Imagine playing 'Autumn Leaves' for service," she had humphed last week.

Steven sat, and Courtney had a sudden impulse to reach over and take his hand, but common sense held her back. *Oh, Lord,* she prayed inwardly, *this man is going to mean a lot to me. I can tell. Give me a calm spirit. Please.*

After the service, they milled toward the door. "It's a nice night. Could I give you both a short ride to the ice cream store over on Division?"

Alice looked almost shocked. They'd never gone out for ice cream after the service.

"You two go on. I can drive the car home, Courtney."

"But I want you to come also, Mrs. Adams."

Alice looked flustered. "I—well, I don't know."

"Of course, Mom. C'mon. It'll be fun. It's a warm night, and who wants to go home?"

"Why don't you take your car home and I'll follow?" Steven suggested.

The ice cream store buzzed with activity, but they found one booth in the front and sat. Courtney doubted she could eat. The two-mile ride over had been interesting. The car was nice, a Trans Am. She knew her mother was thinking that Steven must make good money. She'd hear all about it when they got home.

And then he spoke.

"Just want you to know this isn't my car. It's an employee's. He loaned it to me for the night."

"Oh," Courtney managed. But inside she wondered, *Why is he telling us this? Why would he feel the necessity to borrow a car? Is his own car a disaster?*

As if reading her mind, he went on. "My car, something I cannot seem to part with, has a problem with the doors. The passenger door refuses to open, and the windows won't roll down."

Alice laughed. "Sounds like the car Courtney's father and I first owned."

Steven ordered pistachio nut ice cream, two scoops in one of the fancy dishes, and Courtney had her favorite chocolate/peanut butter, but Mrs. Adams ordered a waffle cone with vanilla.

"Vanilla? You sure, Mrs. Adams?" Steven stared at her in disbelief. "With all these flavors, you choose vanilla?"

She nodded. "It's my favorite, and they simply cannot improve on it."

Courtney wondered what she would put in her journal when she got home. *Tonight I had my first date with Steven, and Mom came along.*

On the way home, they chatted about the community, why Portland was a good place to live, and how long the Adamses had lived in the suburb of Parkrose.

When Steven pulled into the driveway, Alice invited him in. He walked them to the door and stepped inside for a few minutes but didn't stay. "Tomorrow is going to be horrendous, as Mondays always are. Everyone who has had problems with their computer will have called in. Last week I had twelve calls on the machine."

"Oh, my, but that's a good problem to have, yes?" Alice remarked.

He nodded. "Yes, the business is doing well. I've also obtained a few accounts from large businesses in the downtown area, so that helps with expenses." He headed toward the door and Courtney followed.

Courtney walked down the sidewalk to his car in the driveway. The summer night was warm with a thousand stars beaming down on them. He took her hand impulsively.

She smiled, liking the warmth, the firmness of his large hand holding hers. "I love this time of day. It's almost magical."

"Yes." He stopped walking. "You know, your hair is beautiful with stardust in it."

"Why, thank you." Courtney used to feel embarrassed at compliments, but her mother told her, "All you do is thank the person. Works every time."

"Courtney, I don't know what is happening to me, but it's as if you're right in the middle of it and I need to know now—is there someone else?"

Wow, was all she could think. *One day, Lord. This is all happening in one day. How can that be? Is it right? Is it good?*

"There is no one right now," she finally said, her voice almost lost in the sounds of evening.

"I'm glad." He let her hand go. "I want to see you before Saturday. If you like baseball, I thought you might go to a Rockies game with me on Wednesday."

"I love baseball," she murmured. "I used to play when I was in grade school."

"Really? What position?"

"Catcher."

"That's the toughest position of all, if you ask me."

"Taking the gear on and off was the worst part."

"I played center," Steven said. He looked thoughtful. "I'm working on getting a men's softball team going, but we won't be playing until next year. Hey, I really must go. And thanks for going for ice cream."

Courtney watched as he dipped down low enough to get into the Trans Am. She tried to stifle her grin but couldn't. Steven waved and then he was gone. She stood in the glowing moonlight and looked at the sky. "Things have never happened this fast before, Lord, but I have to be careful," she whispered. "No way can I get serious with anyone until I know who brought me into the world. I just hope Steven understands that."

And with a deep sigh, she moved toward the door of the Cape Cod.

Chapter 5

Steven whistled all the way back across the river. He usually dreaded Mondays, but Monday meant he was that much closer to Tuesday, and Tuesday was next to Wednesday, and Wednesday night was the game. In the meantime, he'd concentrate on work and dream about things that might happen. *It's just too soon,* he kept thinking. *You can't fall for someone that quickly.* Yet hadn't he heard about love at first sight?

"That's your emotions speaking," Grams would have said. "You're letting your heart rule over your head and common sense."

He ran up the three flights and wasn't even panting when he got to 306. The bare walls screamed out at him. Yeah. He had to go shopping for art—and soon. Maybe Courtney would like to accompany him. *Let's see.* He had the ball game Wednesday, soup kitchen on Saturday, and church Sunday. Saturday afternoon was free. A perfect time to browse through art galleries. He'd ask her at the game. And with that settled, he slipped into the recliner and dozed off while catching just half of the major league baseball scores.

∽

Courtney floated into the house. Her mother was making noise in the kitchen. They really had not eaten much before church, and the ice cream only whetted her appetite.

"Mom?"

"I'm just fixing a little something. Come sit and talk to me."

Courtney pulled out a chair. The inquisition was about to begin. It had been this way when she'd dated Rod that one time. Then Lanny. And Rick. All just good friends, yet Alice always asked and always watched while Courtney talked, as if thinking this one could be the right one.

"I'm not asking any questions," Alice said as she placed a plate of crackers and peanut butter on the table.

"Now there's a switch," Courtney said, biting into a cracker.

"I don't need to, dear."

Courtney turned and stared. "Don't *need* to?"

"I have my ways of knowing. God gives me a nudge when I'm right, and I have this feeling about this young man. So polite and caring."

"Don't forget good looks, Mom. Looks are so important to you."

"I never said that."

"Didn't have to."

Grabbing a plain cracker, Courtney held it in her mouth a long while. She'd never forgotten the experiment in eighth-grade science. She could hear Mr. Arnold's voice now. "If you hold a saltine in your mouth for several minutes, the salt changes to sugar."

"What are you doing?" Alice asked.

"Eating a cracker."

"You're not listening to me."

"I can't get serious; you know that."

"Oh, dear. Not that. Please don't say this. It upsets me so much." Alice jumped up from the table and put the teakettle on.

"If you drink tea, you'll be up all night. You always complain the next morning."

Her mother nodded. "I know, but tea is soothing. It relaxes me."

"So one negative and one positive and the positive wins out. Good for you, Mom." Courtney pushed her chair back.

"Are you going to sit with me for a bit?"

Courtney pulled the chair back to the table. "Sure. For a bit. Tomorrow is a workday for me, though. Bob will not be in a good mood."

Alice stirred a scant teaspoon of sugar into her tea and held the cup up under her nose. It was apple cinnamon, her favorite.

"I just want to discuss this search thing."

Courtney sighed. "Mom, we've been over it before. You know how I feel, and you just have to accept that."

This time she did leave the table, glancing back once at her mother leaning over, trying to hold back words she so wanted to say.

Courtney came back. "Good night, Mom. It's been a wonderful evening, but I'm going to go soak in the tub. Hope that's okay."

"Of course, and good night, darling." Her fingers held onto her daughter's hand a bit longer than usual, then let her hand slip away. It was so difficult letting a child go and losing a husband.

"I'll have coffee on bright and early."

"You don't need to. I can catch some on my way to work."

"No, I like to do it."

And so it went. Every evening was similar, yet tonight was different for Courtney.

She turned her stereo on, reveling in the sound of Vince Gill's "If You Ever Have Forever in Mind." Letting the water run high, she hummed as she added three capfuls of lavender bubble bath. Tonight she'd be extravagant.

Later, as Courtney slipped under the thick quilt, she thought first about Steven's penetrating gaze, then his crooked little grin, and smiled.

Work was laborious, as it often was on Mondays. Bob seemed more attentive than usual.

"You're looking good, Courtney." He ran a hand through his dark hair. "Yeah, for a Monday you're looking extremely good."

Courtney looked out the window. "Thank you," she responded. Again she thought of how this was often the only answer one could give.

He came over and touched her shoulder. "How about going to dinner with me after work?"

"Work and pleasure don't mix. Didn't we discuss this before?"

"They can if I say so."

Courtney had always sensed that Bob liked her. When she'd first come to work, he'd invited her to lunch, and she'd refused.

"I just want to get to know you better," he had said then. He'd reached over and touched her face ever so briefly. It had made her uncomfortable.

When he asked her out again and she still refused, he seemed almost angry.

"Mr. Jenkins—"

"Bob," he interrupted, "Bob, please." His dark eyes met hers, and she looked away. "Is there someone else?"

"Not exactly."

And there hadn't been then. Now there was Steven.

He stalked back into the room and dropped another stack of letters. "I thought you seemed extra attentive today. You can't blame a guy for trying."

"Perhaps you'd like to come to the young adults' group at my church. We have a good time and do worthwhile things," Courtney said. "You could meet some nice women."

He looked at her through dark, narrowed eyes, as if he couldn't believe she'd suggested such a thing. "Listen, I had all the church-going I needed as a kid. No, thank you." He left before she could respond.

"Oh, Lord," Courtney prayed, "help Bob to know that no means no."

He acted rather frosty the rest of the day, and she didn't finish the work until six, an hour later than usual. A bit despondent, she dug Steven's business card out of her purse. What if he was still at work? Somehow she needed to see a smiling face about now.

Courtney applied lipstick and ran a brush through her hair before locking the office.

Sunshine, warm and golden, hit the changing leaves on the rows of trees lining Park Avenue. She liked walking the park blocks in the fall.

Steven had left, but a kid that looked entirely too young to be working there jotted down her name. "He'll see this first thing when he comes in the office." He grabbed a jacket. "Hey, did you say Courtney?"

Courtney smiled. "Yes."

"Hi, I'm Jeff." He held out a hand.

"Trans Am Jeff?" she couldn't help asking.

He nodded. "Yeah, that's me. And I know about you, too." He grinned. "Man, will Steven be mad that he missed you."

Courtney went out the door he held open for her.

"It was just a whim. To come here, I mean."

They rode the elevator down. "I like what Steven's been doing."

"Doing?"

"Yeah. New duds, for one. Says he's looking for another car, too."

Courtney didn't know what to say, so she said nothing.

"Hey, can I give you a lift?"

"That's okay. I took the Max in."

"No problem, but Steven wouldn't like it if I left you stranded. Riding the transit is okay, but don't you get tired of all the stops?"

"Yeah, but it's cheaper than downtown parking."

"Let me take you home. I'll even drive slower than usual." He grinned again.

Finally, Courtney agreed and followed him to a small garage a few blocks away. She did like the Trans Am.

"Steven will be pea green with envy when I tell him I met you and gave you a lift."

Courtney and Jeff had a nice talk, like old friends, as he fought the late-evening traffic. "This is why I don't drive," she said. "I hate the traffic."

Alice was on the porch sipping a tall iced tea when they pulled into the yard. "That wasn't Steven," she said as Courtney turned to wave good-bye.

"No. That's Jeff, Steven's employee. And he insisted on bringing me home. Said Steven would be furious if I was left stranded."

"Well, dear," Alice leaned up for Courtney's kiss on the cheek, "your life has suddenly become more interesting."

Courtney didn't mention Bob's asking her out. There were things mothers didn't need to know.

"How'd you run into Jeff?" Alice asked, following Courtney into the house.

"I went to Steven's office."

Alice frowned. Never, ever would Alice have gone to a man's office, nor would she have called one on the phone.

The phone rang, as if Courtney's thinking about it caused it to ring.

"Courtney?"

She trembled at the sound of his deep voice. "Yes?"

"Jeff just called me on his cellular and said you'd dropped by the office." There was a long pause. "I hate it that I missed you and can hardly wait for Wednesday. We have good seats."

"I'm so looking forward to it."

By the time she and Steven exchanged pleasantries, Alice had set the table and removed a casserole from the oven.

"I need to go. Call me tomorrow."

As she replaced the receiver, she wondered why her heart was pounding so hard. Everything was moving fast, way too fast.

Chapter 6

Courtney dressed casual for the baseball game—her first date with Steven, if she didn't count the ice cream after church. She decided on jeans; a pink shirt with pearl buttons, giving it a western look; and a matching denim jacket, one on which her mother had sewn a butterfly patch. After tying her dark hair back with a silver clasp, she looked for her favorite baseball cap.

The cap was from the old Portland Beavers' team that used to play in Civic Stadium. Her father took her to at least half of the games each season, and one year he caught a fly ball. The ball, autographed by the batter, sat in a prominent place on top of her dresser, right next to the cap.

She looked forward to seeing the Portland Rockies play. It might sound like a funny place to go on a date, but she loved sports—any and all sports. Once she'd gone with a guy to a Trail Blazer basketball game and ended up explaining the plays and why fouls were called. Courtney knew this wouldn't be the case with Steven. Last night she'd discovered they had another mutual interest. Monopoly. He'd once stayed up all night playing. That seemed a bit excessive, but one could get caught up in the game. She hadn't played since the nights when Tina used to stay over.

She hummed one of her favorite songs as she put away a stack of clothes from a chair beside the bed. Why had that song come to mind? She sang out loud:

> "I love you Lord, and I lift my voice
> To worship You, O, my soul, rejoice.
> Take joy, my King, in what You hear,
> May it be a sweet, sweet sound in Your ear."

Courtney had the run of the upper story since her parents slept on the main floor. Her bedroom faced the front of the house. Her mother's old sewing room was tucked back in a corner at the top of the stairs. The other bedroom was the one Courtney used to dream would belong to her sister. Every year until she was ten, she had asked for a sister for Christmas and for her birthday. Then she had given up and settled on a dog. Ruggles had died just last year, and so far she hadn't replaced him with another. Not that one could ever replace a dog.

An oak bed with a high headboard dominated the center of the spare bedroom. A matching dresser sat under the dormer window. A photo was on the opposite wall—a ballerina in a pink tutu. Courtney had wanted to dance, to be elegant and dainty, but one needed long legs to be graceful, so her dreams of being a prima ballerina soon faded.

Leaning against the bank of pink-fringed pillows, she spoke aloud. "Mom, you wanted another child so bad. I wonder why you and Daddy didn't adopt again."

Courtney had always known she was adopted, but it hadn't mattered when she was small. She'd been told the story countless times of how her parents had picked her out of all the other babies. She later discovered that wasn't the entire truth, but knew they had told her that to make her feel more special and loved. They'd heard about a young girl who could not keep her baby, and they had offered to adopt her child.

"We paid for her hospitalization and doctor and gave her some money to get back on her feet," her mother had explained.

"What did she look like?" Courtney had asked.

Alice had looked surprised at the question. "Honey, we never met her. A lawyer took care of the proceedings."

"But didn't you care? Didn't you want to know what I would look like?"

Her mother had taken her hands, pulling her to her bosom. "We just wanted a baby. We would have taken you if you'd been sickly, handicapped, or multiracial. We'd tried for five years, and the doctor said I'd never conceive."

Courtney had pressed on, but her mother really didn't know anything about the family or their background. Maybe it wouldn't have mattered, but a girl at school knew her birth mother, and they got together twice a year. Her friend had curly hair, just like her birth mother. What Courtney wouldn't give to know just that much.

"You are so precious to us," Alice had said. "You've seen the birth certificate and the little gown you were wearing after you were born."

And Courtney had. They were tucked into the large trunk in the sewing room. She went often to look at the birth certificate, reading it as if it would suddenly give her a clue to her real identity. The homemade gown had a pink crocheted edging at the bottom and at the wrists. It was packed in clear plastic to preserve it. She often thought of the mother who had made this nightgown for her baby.

"If you really must continue searching, you may need to go back to southern Illinois where you were born," her mother had finally suggested. "Maybe you can find out something there. Your father was stationed at Scott Air Force Base and got out of the service there so we could return to Oregon."

Courtney had held her mother close. "Mom, I do need to go there. Please understand. I love you very much but need to find this out."

Alice had pulled the hair back from Courtney's face. "Of course. I always knew the day would come when you'd want to know."

She thought about her father. She missed him so terribly and wondered why it had never been as imperative to find her real father as it was to find her birth mother. She recalled that half year of illness. Weakness had overtaken her body, and she had been tutored at home. Tests, hundreds of them, it seemed, had been taken. Nothing. Lots of things were ruled out. Diabetes. Multiple sclerosis. Anemia. Mono. Epilepsy. She had none of the symptoms for epilepsy, but the doctor was thorough. Then, miraculously, with everyone at church praying for her, she started back up the road to recovery. Soon she was her old self, her energy restored. She returned to school that fall and even played basketball when the season started.

"It's amazing," Dr. Bell had said with a shake of his snow-white head. "I can't explain it, but there are a lot of things I cannot explain. Guess I have to say it's an answer to prayer." He patted Courtney's shoulder.

"She's well again, and that's the main thing," Alice Adams said. "Our prayers were answered."

At first Courtney had been hesitant, fearful that the illness would return, but it did not. And soon she relaxed and let life happen again. Yet in the back of her mind, questions remained. What if she did get sick again? What if she was a carrier of whatever this disease was and it could hit her unborn child, should she marry in the future? No. She could not, would not, let the matter rest. She must find out about her medical background—must find her birth mother to get the answers.

It had been anything but easy. Every door slammed in her face. The Internet, which most said was helpful, did not help with her search. That was when she knew the only thing left to do, the only stone unturned, was to return to the place of her birth.

❧

Courtney heard a car in the driveway and looked out the window to see an old black car pull up. She laughed. Steven was right. It was in despicable condition, yet she had to admire someone who would even drive such a car, let alone pick up a date in it. No wonder he had borrowed his friend's Trans Am last week for the trip to the ice cream store.

The doorbell rang just as Courtney descended the stairs. She opened it before her mother did, though her mother always said a woman needed to keep a man waiting for at least five minutes.

"That's lame, Mom!" Courtney had retorted. "I don't think it appears too eager; it shows you are considerate."

So much for that discussion.

Steven smiled and started to step forward. Courtney wondered if he was going to put his arms around her or what. He stepped back and removed his baseball cap, holding it in his hand, seemingly more nervous than Sunday night after church.

"You look like you're ready for a baseball game," he finally said.

"I am." She removed her cap and hit his. "The Beavers here."

"San Diego Padres here."

"We don't match."

"I know, but who cares?"

Alice appeared and held out her hand. "Nice to see you again, Steven. And I do hope the Rockies win."

"You could come along, if you wanted," Steven said.

She laughed. "Me? No. I'm not the sports enthusiast my daughter is or the one my husband was. You two go and have a good time."

Courtney thought about Steven's willingness to include her mother in their plans. It showed a thoughtfulness she hadn't found in most men. He had been taught well by someone. She knew little about his growing-up years or he about hers. That would give them things to talk about for at least two more dates.

The stadium was nearly full. The Portland Rockies had loyal fans, though they were just an A-team. Courtney discovered that Steven liked the center bleachers best for a good, all-around view. If the game got tight, they'd move over closer to home plate.

"Popcorn before we sit?" Steven asked.

"Later," Courtney said. "I had a late dinner."

"Me, too."

He led the way, turning back to capture her hand, and they found the perfect spot and sat—but not for long. Courtney was out of her seat more than she was in it.

"Do you always get this excited at ball games?" Steven grinned. He was clearly amused by her enthusiasm.

Her face flushed suddenly. "I hope I'm not embarrassing you."

"Hardly." He studied her profile, thinking how much he enjoyed seeing someone having fun. Courtney was the type one could get to know easily, one you could enjoy being with. He never wanted the night to end. "I happen to like girls who are athletic."

"And I like *men*," she said, "who like sports."

At the seventh-inning stretch, with the score tied at 4, they decided to get popcorn and peanuts and two colas.

"Let's drive around after the game," Steven said.

"It'll be dark," Courtney said. "Does that matter?"

"No. How about going where we can see the city lights?"

"I know the very place," Courtney said. "There's a fantastic view. You won't believe it until you see it."

"Okay. Sounds great."

The Rockies won in the ninth, a stolen base on an error by Spokane. As they trickled out of the stadium, Steven stopped to buy two hats. "So we can match," he said, putting one on Courtney's head.

"Hey, thanks! I needed a new one. It's a long way to my spot, but on my end of town."

"Lead me on."

They drove across town and started driving up a large hill.

When they came to the closed gate, Courtney let out a disappointed, "Oh, no. I should have known. Of course they close the gates at dusk."

"A cemetery?" Steven sounded incredulous.

"It's Willamette National Cemetery, and my father is buried here. You can see out west over the entire city, and the view is fantastic. He has a very special spot."

Steven stopped the car. "You miss him very much, don't you?"

Courtney nodded, not daring to meet Steven's gaze. "He was a special man, a special father. We had no idea his heart was bad. The doctor said he undoubtedly had had symptoms, but he'd ignored them."

"Men hate doctors."

"So do some women." She grinned as he reached over and took her hand.

"I think I could spend the night here, just listening to you talk about your family and your life. You definitely have an effect on me, Courtney." He pulled her a bit closer. She felt herself leaning, afraid to let her guard down, as he was affecting her, also. No longer a teenager who had to worry about a dark night on a hill with a romantic moon beaming down, she suddenly felt vulnerable.

"I don't know a thing about you." She pulled back, though she hadn't wanted to. "What were your growing-up years like?"

"Grams ran it all. The ranch. The house. Me. But nobody ever minded. She was loving and special, sort of like your father was. You could depend on her. You knew she had your best interests at heart."

"How long ago did you lose her?"

"I was off to college, my freshman year, when the call came from a neighbor. It was the longest, most painful two-hour drive I ever had to make."

"From?"

"The University of Oregon."

"It's a nice campus. My father graduated from there. We went to sing once with another youth group."

"I played guitar in a band on weekends."

"You play guitar?" Courtney was immediately interested. "I had no idea you played. We've been looking for someone for our meetings. Just a few songs before the actual meeting starts."

"It's been a long time." His arm went around her, and he pulled her close again. "I think I could pick it up again pretty quick."

"Oh, Steven, I'm sure you could."

He started to lean toward her, but she pulled away. "Let's not start something we don't want to stop."

"You're right." He thumped the steering wheel. "I agree." An awkward silence followed.

"I'm looking forward to working in the soup kitchen," he said finally. "Not sure if I'll be of any help, but I'll give it a try."

"There's nothing to it. Scoop up the food. Smile at the customers. Tell them God loves them."

"You preach to them?"

"Not really preach. Some don't say anything, but I like to tell them how I feel about them and how I know God feels."

"You're pretty amazing, Courtney."

"No, I'm not." She met his gaze. "I think I'd better have you take me home." Her voice trembled, and she felt all quivery inside. She thought she'd been in love with a boy once, but never, ever had she felt like this. And from the way Steven looked at her, she knew he was feeling the same thing.

"I don't want to wait until Saturday. Do you suppose you could meet me on Friday for dinner? You're not far from the main downtown area. How about Brewster's?"

"Yeah. I'd like that."

He drove down the curvy, windy road toward town and back on to Ninety-second.

"I'll even buy."

"It's a date," she said, turning on the car radio to see what kind of music was playing. She found a George Strait ballad and started singing along.

"I like to hear you sing."

She looked over and smiled. Too soon, they were at Courtney's home. They said a quick good night, and she disappeared into the house.

Driving home, Steven whispered a prayer. "Thank You, Lord, for giving me a little push in the right direction—and thank You for Grams, too."

Chapter 7

Brewster's was the best place in town for ribs. They also had a great salad bar and terrific atmosphere. Steven needed to unwind. It had been a horrendous day.

Courtney left the office ten minutes late because Bob asked her to answer an e-mail that had come through at five.

She sighed. It seemed that no matter how hard she tried, she was always late for appointments and dinner engagements and barely on time for church service.

By the time she'd walked the four blocks to the restaurant, her hair was windblown. She entered the rest room, applied a touch of pale pink lipstick, and brushed her hair out. She pulled it back and put clips on each side.

Brewster's buzzed with activity as usual. It was a crazy, interesting place. Each table had a small tub of peanuts. People cracked the peanuts, throwing the shells on the floor. The décor was the fifties, which was the rage in Portland right now. Her mother loved going to anything that catered to her age group. She'd have to bring her here sometime. Of course, the peanut shells underfoot might bother her.

Steven had a table in the back and waved her over. He stood when she walked up. "I thought you might have forgotten," he said, looking intently at her.

Forget? How could I possibly forget? She thought the words, but stopped herself from blurting them out.

He helped her with her chair while she ran a hand through her hair. It was a nervous habit she had tried to break in the past. "Sorry I'm late. It's all Bob's fault."

Steven grinned. "I hope you asked for a raise."

"Not hardly. He's struggling, you know."

"As we all are."

She took the menu and ordered a cola from the waitress. Steven was all business at times, and she wanted to just forget work. She would much rather he talk about himself or about his hobbies. "Bob is in no position to give me a raise," she said.

Steven suddenly reached for her hand. "Sorry. That's none of my business."

She smiled reassuringly at him as the waitress set down her cola. "I'll have my usual," she told the waitress. "Unlimited salad bar." Salad bars were her thing. It seemed she could never get enough greens. Her mother used to kid her, saying she was half rabbit. As a teenager she could visualize that; but which half was the rabbit?

Steven grinned. "If I never looked at another salad, I'd be only too happy. I need something more substantial. I'll try the soup of the day, then an order of ribs."

He cracked open a peanut and handed it to her. "Aren't you going after your salad?"

She took the peanut. "In due time. I'll wait until closer to the time when your ribs will be done."

He leaned forward and grinned again. "You think of everything, don't you?"

Her gaze locked on his. "Perhaps. Is that a bad trait?"

"Hardly."

"Steven," she started, then paused, not sure when this discussion needed to take place. She decided now seemed like a good time. "Do you know that I'm adopted?"

He glanced up, his face revealing nothing. "No, I didn't."

Courtney leaned forward. "It affects the way I think and plan, and I just thought you might like to know."

"Have you always known?"

She nodded. "From the first."

"And you felt?"

"Happy to be chosen. To be loved and cared for by two wonderful people."

"And now?" Steven wasn't sure why, but for some reason he knew her answer was going to involve him.

"It's just that I need to find out about my background. I've been searching for the past four years."

The soup came, steaming with a pleasant fragrance. He picked up the spoon, never taking his eyes from Courtney's face.

She touched his arm. "I hope you don't mind if I ask a blessing first."

His face turned red. "No, of course not. Sorry I didn't think of it."

After she had offered the blessing and he had burned his mouth on the first spoonful, he asked why there had been no results after all that time.

"I don't know. It's been ultra frustrating."

"I assume you don't mind talking about this—"

"Quite the contrary. I *want* to discuss it. It helps." She met his level gaze while toying with the straw. "In fact, I'm planning on a trip to the town in Illinois where I was born. I'm leaving in two weeks."

"Leaving?" he choked, then sat there with a dismayed look on his face.

"You're not saying anything."

"I guess I don't know what to say. I'm not wanting you to go, if that's what you're wondering about."

She looked away, realizing she didn't want to be away from Steven, either, and for a second doubting she really needed to go. But it was because of how she was feeling about Steven that the quest had become even more crucial. How could she even think of a permanent relationship when she didn't know what she was bringing into it?

"I never knew my mother and barely remember my dad," Steven said then.

"But what happened?" She'd always heard that everyone had problems; you just thought you were the only one.

"I think I mentioned at the ball game about Mom dying, and Dad, unable to stand the loss, took off. Thank God I had Grams and the cattle ranch in Redmond."

"But how'd you get into computers?"

He pushed the empty soup bowl aside. "Because I didn't take to farming and cows and riding the range, to Grams's dismay."

"Oh, really? I can see you now, roping one of those little dogies."

"And how do you know about *dogies* if you've never lived on a ranch?"

"I read books, you know." She was teasing him now. Steven was too serious. Courtney had grown up with a father who teased constantly. It was good in a way. Perhaps. She tended not to take things seriously and had gotten in trouble on her first job when she told a customer the hamburgers were made from the best ground buffalo.

Courtney got up and walked toward the salad bar. "Just wanted to see how gullible you are," she called over her shoulder.

"Men are supposed to do the teasing," he said when she returned with a plate heaping with salad greens, tomatoes, cucumbers, green peas, cheese sticks, sliced boiled egg, and blue cheese dressing in a mound on top.

"True," she said. "That's how it works most of the time."

They talked about the week coming up and when he could see her again.

"Choir practice is Thursday at seven. Why don't you join the choir?"

"If you heard me sing, you wouldn't ask that question."

She stabbed a crouton. "You're going to play guitar, and that's more important than the choir any day."

The ribs came, stacked high on a platter. He grabbed his fork.

"Want to take in another Rockies game?" Steven asked when he'd finished the last rib.

"I'd love to."

She felt comfortable with him. He was also the first date she'd ever told about her background. She felt herself liking him more and more but wasn't sure about his commitment to God. She could not fathom being linked to someone who did not share the faith with her.

The evening ended too soon, and she lingered a bit longer than usual in his car.

"I'll see you tomorrow morning?"

"I'll be there." He leaned over and kissed her cheek. "Thanks for a fun time."

Later that evening, long after the house was straightened and she had decided what to wear the next day, she thought of Steven. She loved how his eyes crinkled up on the edges when he smiled at her. She also liked the way he was a gentleman and didn't assume she wanted his arm around her. He hadn't tried to kiss her yet, and that meant even more. Most men wanted more, so much more, on a date. She liked his old-fashioned manners.

Courtney came back downstairs to spend some time with Alice. She had volunteered at the local hospital that day and often wanted to talk about her day.

"I met a woman today who found her mother after a lengthy search." Alice leaned over and touched Courtney's arm. "She says you need to do it."

"Do it?"

"Go to Illinois."

Courtney leaned over and hugged her mother. "Thanks for telling me this. It's almost like a sign."

Her mother nodded. "That's what I thought, dear. A sign that God is with us and will help you and keep you safe."

Long after the house was quiet and Courtney lay looking out the window at the stars in the sky, she thought again of Steven and what this could mean should she find her birth mother. "Thank You, God," she prayed, "for caring so much about us. About me."

And then, with another thought about Steven linking his arm in hers, she finally closed her eyes.

Chapter 8

Courtney had wondered more than once if someday she might not come across a relative. The fact that her adoptive parents had left Illinois, coming west to Oregon, made the possibility "extremely unlikely," as Tina put it.

"You worry about things that probably won't happen, and I never worry about things when I probably should," Tina said.

The two had met early Saturday morning, grabbing a quick cup of coffee and a cinnamon roll at a café a few blocks from the soup kitchen.

"I'm not worried, just thinking about it," Courtney retorted. "By the way, how are you doing?" Her hand touched the firm round shape of Tina's stomach. Somehow she couldn't even imagine how it must feel, having someone grow inside you.

"Good," Tina said, slathering more butter on her roll. "The weight is good, but if I have very many more mornings like this, the pounds will pour on."

"It's so good to see you," Courtney said. "We never get together, except at church."

"I know."

Courtney leaned forward. "You remember the new guy at church on Sunday?"

"The one you kept looking at all through service?"

Courtney blushed. "Yes."

"You're seeing him, aren't you!" Tina's face lit up. "I could tell he was coming on to you."

"He signed up to help at the soup kitchen. We've had dinner at Brewster's, went to a Rockies game, and also drove up by the cemetery, and had ice cream, and—"

"Whoa, girl!" Tina rolled her eyes. "Is this fast or what?"

"Oh, I know, but something tells me he might be the right one."

"What does Alice think?"

"She likes him. He's always asking her to come with us."

"And your search?" Tina had polished off her roll and dabbed at her face with her napkin. "What's happening about that?"

Courtney looked serious. "I'm leaving for Illinois sometime soon."

"Leaving? You can't leave now."

"Yes, I can. It's the only way I'll ever find myself and know about my background."

"And what if Mr. Right doesn't want to wait?"

Courtney leaned back, pushing the roll aside. She wasn't hungry now. "That's a problem, all right."

"I'd think twice. Like I've said before, it doesn't take having a baby to be a mother." Tina pushed her chair back, placing the side of her hand over her midsection. "Everything sits right here." She grinned. "Just you wait, missy. One day you'll be able to experience this, too."

"I want to experience that, you know. And as far as Alice, I've always considered her my real mother. She loves me. Yet somewhere," her voice broke, "somewhere a woman gave me up to be adopted. Did she want to do that, or was she coerced into giving me up? Was she happy to be rid of me, or does she lie awake at night, stare at the moon, and wonder where in this vast universe her little girl is?"

"Do you still carry that picture in your wallet?"

"You mean the one with Mom and me in matching red, white, and blue bonnets?"

"Yeah, that one."

Courtney dug it out and handed it over. "It always reminds me of how much I've been loved and how much I have to be thankful for. Sometimes I ask God to forgive me for wanting to find my birth mother. Something just pushes me on."

Tina looked at the photo. "I love the smug smile on Alice's face." She looked at her watch. "We better get a move on."

Courtney grabbed the bill, and the two friends made their way to Northwest Third Street, making plans for a shopping trip after the kitchen was closed.

Tina took her volunteer duties seriously. She started setting out the bread and cookies. "Yum, potato soup," she said, taking a spoon and tasting it. "Has lots of bacon and onion in it, too."

"You can't go wrong on potato," Courtney said. She set the bread on a plate with tongs beside it. Someone always served the food. If they didn't, some took more than their share and others did without.

"Someone brought several of those boxes from Costco," Tina said. "Look. The cookies are frosted."

"They look good," Courtney said, grabbing one, though she wasn't hungry.

"I thought the new guy—what's-his-name—was coming."

"It's Steven," Courtney said. "Steven with a *V*."

"Well, I wonder where he is, Steven with a V," Tina said. "Looks like he isn't going to make it."

Courtney's heart sank. Something must have come up.

"It's time," Tina called. "C'mon, Courtney, stand by the bread."

The door opened, and the people started pushing through. Most had on well-worn clothes that smelled from not enough washing. With hair hanging in strings, some in dreadlocks, they shuffled to the table. Most wore smiles and mumbled thank-yous.

Courtney had finally gotten used to this part, but it was difficult. The first inclination was to invite people home to have an honest-to-goodness bath, to look in the closet for an old sweatshirt and pants to give someone, or to offer a decent bed for the night.

"You can't do that," Tina said. "How would you know which one to choose? How do you know you can trust them?"

" 'Inasmuch as ye have done it unto me,' " Courtney had started reciting the familiar passage.

"I know. We are doing what we can and, for the most part, the people have their little community right here and would not fit in with so-called regular life."

The line finally dwindled and then Gerta came in. Gerta, a perceptive and talkative old woman, had once been a psychologist. "I know people," she always said. "Can tell an honest person when I see one." She also liked to think she could make predictions.

Gerta flashed her toothless, happy grin. "So? Did my prediction come true from last month?"

Courtney looked puzzled as she tried to remember what Gerta had said. "I don't remember."

"You were going to meet a man," Tina said. "I remember that much."

"I meet lots of men," Courtney said.

Gerta laughed. "Ah, but I did not say that. And from the look in your eyes, I see you are thinking of a certain someone."

Courtney busied herself refilling the butter dish, preferring not to respond.

"Trust me; I will come in one day and you will not be here. You will be off with your young man on a honeymoon."

"Oh, Gerta, dream on," Courtney said, hoping someone else would come in. And when she looked up, someone did. Steven. Her heart caught in her throat. Tina looked up and saw him at the same time.

"You're late," Tina said. "We're just about ready to wrap it up."

"I brought carrots. All peeled." He set a huge bowl of carrots on the table. "Surely someone will want them." His gaze found Courtney's.

"What happened?" Courtney finally asked.

"Got hung up with a problem. It was a rush call from a large business firm. I thought I'd finish in plenty of time."

Gerta, who had started off with her tray, stopped and looked back. "See?

Didn't my prediction come true?"

Courtney knew it was coincidence. No way could Gerta know how she felt about Steven.

"I'll help clean up. That's permissible, isn't it?" Steven asked.

"Another crew is coming on for the cleanup," Tina said.

"Then I'll stay and it'll all get done that much faster."

Courtney felt him looking at her as she busied herself with the empty bread plate.

"I want you to go gallery shopping with me. Do you have the afternoon free?"

"I—have plans," Courtney started, but Tina was there, pushing her gently. "We can go another time. I really should get home to finish cleaning out the room for the baby's crib."

Courtney couldn't remember putting anything away or wiping the table off or waving good-bye to Gerta as she shuffled off. Steven had come. And she laughed as she saw him with rolled-up sleeves, proceeding to wash the soup pot. Her heart told her again that he was the right one. There was no doubt about it now. She knew, just as she knew she was God's child and He had her interests at heart.

"I'll be ready to go shopping whenever you are," she called from the doorway.

Chapter 9

Courtney helped Steven select a Monet print, a water scene in greens, blues, and purples entitled "Cape Martin," for one wall in the living room. For the opposite wall, they chose an Eric Wiegardt watercolor called "Sign of Spring," featuring the side of an old building with ironwork and a hanging basket filled with blue and red flowers; it was a nice contrast to the Monet in color and style. Wiegardt was a Washington State artist, and that was close enough to be local. A humorous Norman Rockwell for the bathroom concluded the purchases, though Steven wanted a glass creation for his coffee table.

"Think I've extended my budget for the month," he said, taking Courtney's hand. "And thank you for helping me choose."

"What else do you need to do?" Courtney asked as he put the wrapped paintings in his car.

"I think it's time for fun now. There's a bluegrass concert playing tonight down at Waterfront Park. Let's take a picnic lunch and a blanket and go. That is, if you like bluegrass."

"If it's a picnic and an outdoor concert, it wouldn't matter what was playing," Courtney replied.

After picking up fried chicken, potato salad, and two large sugar cookies at a corner deli, they joined the large crowd at the park along the Willamette River.

"The last vestiges of summer," Courtney said, hugging her knees up under her. The sky was a powder blue, and the early evening breeze came in from the river, cooling them off.

Steven nibbled on his cookie. "I like being with you." He reached over and took her hand.

"Thank you," Courtney murmured. "And the same to you."

"I want to see you tomorrow and the next day and the next."

Courtney met his steady gaze and wanted to say the same thing, but there were too many unknowns in her life just now. How could she commit to Steven?

⸙

They continued to date as summer blended into fall, and Courtney kept putting off her trip. Each week Steven played his guitar, and one night he opened up the Sunday evening service with "Amazing Grace." Courtney's voice lifted high and strong with the rest of the congregation, the volume increasing as they sang the last verse:

> "When we've been there ten thousand years,
> Bright shining as the sun,
> We've no less days to sing God's praise,
> Than when we first begun."

That night Steven made a public declaration of his faith. He did not like making speeches but had a few things he wanted to share with his friends at the community church.

"I have led a happy life and been blessed many ways by God. He gave me Grams—God rest her soul—when I lost my parents at a young age. She was instrumental in teaching me right from wrong, reading me God's Word, and seeing that I attended Sunday school. Yet my faith until now has all been lip service." Steven glanced around at the faces of the people listening to and watching him. "I didn't realize that one does not go to heaven by works, but by faith. And I have faith and believe that God sent His Son to save me, to make me whole. And I just thank this congregation for taking me in and loving me and caring about me. My favorite scripture is from Proverbs 3:5: 'Trust in the Lord with all your heart and lean not on your own understanding.' "

He sat down amid cheers and claps. His face wasn't even red, and he felt much better after his testimony. Courtney reached over and took his hand. Her gesture made him realize how much he loved her, how much he wanted to make her his wife.

"Let's go celebrate afterwards," he whispered in her ear. He had something for her and could hardly bear to wait.

She nodded and squeezed his hand again.

Courtney thought she'd prepared herself for what seemed inevitable. She wondered if women usually sensed when a man was about to propose. For her, it was as if God told her the first time she'd seen Steven sitting in the second pew that this man was going to become very important in her life.

They raced to the Ford, hand in hand, with Courtney giggling. She studied his profile, liking the good strong jawline, the way his nose angled perfectly, the short hair, his ears not too large, yet not small. She had his facial features memorized. She loved Steven. It had always been there, perhaps, but a sudden feeling of love so overwhelmed her she could hardly breathe.

"Where to?" he asked. "You're my guide, you know."

She kept looking at him and didn't answer.

"What are you looking at?" His hand reached over.

"You." Her fingers reached up and touched his chin. "But we'd better get out of the parking lot before everyone talks about us."

"I repeat, where to? We need to talk. Do you know a place that's on the quiet side?"

Courtney nodded. "Donovan's. It's not far. We could sit in one of the back booths. Then later I want to go up to Rocky Butte and look out over Portland. It's the best place for stargazing. The first time Mom went out with Dad, it was on the back of his Harley and they went up to Rocky Butte."

"*Your mom?* Alice rode on a motorcycle?"

Courtney laughed. "Yeah, my mom. I somehow can't imagine it, either, but I guess she was adventuresome then."

"I've never owned a motorcycle," Steven said. "Never wanted one. I was more into tractors than trucks."

"Then old, rundown, beat-up cars," Courtney added.

"Now don't make fun of my car. It might just hear you and stop running."

The little café on Skidmore was busy, but Courtney said it was always busy. She promised they made the best hamburgers, so that's what they ordered.

"I brought something along," Steven said, putting his cola down. "It's been on my mind and heart for several days, and I can't wait a second longer." He reached inside his pants pocket and brought out a small, velvet-covered box. Courtney held her breath.

"Go on. Open it."

Courtney hadn't expected anything like this. "Steven! A ring! I had no idea." It was a beautiful, oval pink stone in a platinum setting. "It's beautiful! What kind of stone is this?"

"Alexandrite. It belonged to my grandmother."

"Oh, Steven." Her breath came out in one long swoosh. "I couldn't possibly accept this. It's a family heirloom, and I'm far too careless with things. You just don't know."

"No." His tone was firm. "I want you to have it. I want you to be my lifetime partner, Courtney. I love you. Surely you know that by now." He took the ring from the box and gently placed it on her finger. "For always. You and me. You, me, and God."

She looked at him through sudden tears. "I love it, Steven, and I love you, too, but I'm not sure that I can say yes."

"Because of the trip to Illinois to find your birth mother."

"Yes, I'm leaving soon. I told Bob already."

"I want to go with you."

"No, I must do this on my own." She started to take the ring off, but he stopped her, taking her hand in his.

"No," he insisted, "it's yours. I want you to have it, no matter what. For always. I want you to wear the ring. I also want to help."

"I appreciate that more than I can say."

"Grams gave me this on her deathbed," he told her, his finger going over the stone. "She said when I found the right woman that I'd know, and I was to give it to her to wear with as much pride and honor as Grams had always had."

"And I will wear it with pride," Courtney said.

Later they drove up to Rocky Butte and looked out over the beautiful star-studded sky.

So far their dates had been with others, except the ball game that first night. Movies, playing tennis, the drive out to Multnomah Falls—all with Tina and Mike or the group as a whole. They'd been careful not to be alone as Courtney admitted right off that she didn't believe in relations before marriage. And it could be tempting. She thought of the paper of abstention she'd signed back in junior high after attending several Wednesday night meetings, all about staying chaste until marriage.

They sat on the stone fence, Steven's arm slipping around her shoulder. "This is my kind of night. My kind of girl."

"Oh, Steven. I wish I knew who I was. I wish I'd had success before now. You must understand why I have to go to Illinois. Not even my love for you can stop me. In fact, that's the reason I'm more determined to find out. I must find myself. What am I bringing into this relationship?"

"You're bringing love, caring, and a beautiful attitude. What more could a fellow want?"

Their eyes met and held. Then she pulled away ever so slightly.

"To know something about his wife, the mother of his children, to know about her background."

"Obviously it's more important to you than to me."

"How can I totally commit?"

"Totally commit?" His gaze burned into hers, never leaving her face.

"I mean like marriage."

"Of course marriage is uppermost in my mind."

"Oh, Steven, I know. It's just that I *must* know this first before settling on a date or making plans. . . ." Her voice trailed off.

"But you will keep the ring?"

"Yes, Steven." She held it up, letting the artificial light catch the sparkle from the gem. "It's almost too beautiful to wear, though."

"You think it's better stuck in a safety deposit box where nobody can see it?"

"I'm leaving for Illinois end of this month," she said. "I gave notice to Bob on Friday."

"I see."

"You know how I feel about it. This isn't a surprise."

"Please let me come with you."

"Steven, you can't. You have a business to run."

"So?"

"This is something I must do on my own. I don't even want Mom to come."

"How about Tina?"

"Mike would have a stroke. Besides, there's the baby."

"I don't like you going off alone to someplace you've never been before."

"I'll take my cellular, call you every day, sleep only in safe, well-lighted places. Not talk to strangers—"

"Stop!" He held his hand up. "I think you have it covered."

They left, and Alice arrived home as they did. Courtney rushed over and held her hand in front of her mother's face. "It's a ring, Mom. An engagement ring."

"Oh, darling, that's wonderful." She hugged Courtney, her eyes meeting Steven's over the top of Courtney's head. She stood a good six inches taller. "I am so happy for both of you. Come on in, Steven. This calls for a toast!"

"I really must go, Alice. Busy day, big contract tomorrow." He came over and hugged his mother-in-law to be. "It's been a busy night."

Courtney watched as Steven's car backed up and until his taillights disappeared around the corner. She watched with a happy, yet heavy, heart. She had hurt him; she knew she had, but she had to be aboveboard with everything. It was just the way she'd always been.

"Courtney, dear, aren't you coming in?"

Courtney stared into the sky, thrilling to the cascade of stars that covered every square inch of it. Her life had suddenly taken on a new dimension. Soon, very soon, she prayed, she'd be an old married woman like Tina. But first things first.

The time had come. Tomorrow she'd make the plane reservations.

Chapter 10

Once Courtney made up her mind about something, there was no changing it. She *would* go to Illinois. She *would* begin the search on foot. Alice was adamant that she, too, should go.

"I'll worry about you every second you're gone."

"Mom, you've always worried about me, and here I am, age twenty-three, healthy and strong—"

"And strong-willed, I might add."

"You wouldn't want me any other way."

Alice sighed. "No, I guess it wouldn't be you. I swear you're more like your father every day." They both laughed.

"You always used to say that when I was little. It's probably the first thing I have written in my diary."

"And it was true."

"But who knows who I take after?"

Alice stood, putting her shoulders back. "You know what they say about children. The first five years are the most formative. It doesn't matter who gave birth to you; who raised you gave you the principles you now live by."

"Oh, I know that, Mom. Truly I do." Courtney leaned over and hugged her mother hard. "I have never forgotten that, as well as the nights you were at my bedside when I was sick. No mother could have given more. No mother could be loved more."

They clung to each other, tears mingling.

"I don't want to see you hurt."

"God is with me."

"And Steven? Why not take him up on his offer? He says Jeff can run the business for a few days."

"And what if it takes the whole two weeks? It could, you know."

She held up the ring. It was still unbelievable that she was wearing it. It sparkled on her finger. She'd never met Grams, but she knew what a wonderful woman she had to have been. Not only was Steven goal-oriented, precise, methodical—all things Courtney was not—he was tender, gentle, and considerate. And that one fact made him dearer to her than she could have ever thought possible.

"Women, the gentler sex," he had said, almost jokingly, just the night before as they had sipped malts at their favorite ice cream store, the place where their relationship had started. Of course, church was where it really began.

"I don't think of myself that way, but I do know that God intends for the man to be head of the household, and if that makes woman the gentler sex, so be it."

"I still want to tag along, for moral support, if nothing else."

"I have to do this, Steven, and until I get some answers, I cannot set a date for our wedding."

He reached out, touching the side of her face. "I am trying to understand, really I am, but it's difficult. I cannot imagine you being so far away, where I can't get to you in ten minutes as I can now. What if you don't find out anything? Or," he added, his brow furrowed, "what if you find out something you don't want to know?"

"I'll handle it when and if that occasion arises. God is with me; don't forget. He's brought me through many things in my life; He won't desert me now."

They had discussed Courtney's illness on the second date. Steven had understood since he did not know his own mother, but at least he knew who she was and therein was the difference.

"I'll miss you."

"And me, you."

"And you'll call every night?"

She smiled, taking his hand again. "Absolutely every night. At 8:00 p.m., as you requested. Keep in mind it will be ten there."

"What if you run out of time and you reach a dead end?"

Courtney nodded. "I've thought of that possibility many, many times and will cross that bridge if and when I get to it. I like to think positive about this."

He held her hand up, gazing at the ring. "It sure looks better on your finger than it did sitting in that box."

"I love it, but I've told you that a dozen times."

"At least."

She closed her eyes, wondering if this was really happening. She thought of Bob's parting shot yesterday.

"Come away with me, Court. We'll go to the West Indies or Fiji or wherever you want. Just the two of us. I'll take you away from this. I'll love and cherish you forever."

She'd almost burst out laughing. How could he even say such things to her when they'd never dated, never talked about important things as she and Steven had? Bob was in love with the idea of being in love. His so-called passion was big and important to him, but he didn't know God and didn't comprehend why God was front and foremost in her life.

"You won't find your birth mother," he'd said.

"I don't want to hear it."

She had set a sheaf of papers on his desk. "I'm sure the temp will work out well."

Courtney thought, as she gathered things from her desk, that she might not come back. Oh, she wouldn't leave him in the lurch, but she doubted that she could ever really work for him again. She now wished she had taken extra schooling so she could be a full-fledged legal assistant, have her own office, and not have to take orders from someone like Bob.

The parting had been anything but amiable. Bob had grabbed at her, as if making a last-ditch effort to keep her from going.

"I love you, Courtney. I have since the day you walked in that door."

"Yeah, sure."

"You don't believe me."

"You're right; I don't."

"If you had given me half a chance, I would have proven it."

"I'll be in touch, Bob."

❧

Now she was surveying her room, wondering if she'd packed enough clothes. Would they be suitable? Would she be too warm? Or would it be cold there now that fall had come?

She pulled the flowered curtain back and stared out the window.

So many times she had done this over the years. Somehow she wondered if things would ever be the same again. She could see her mother selling the home and moving in with Agnes. Courtney wondered if she could bear this home going to a complete stranger who didn't know all the secrets, all the laughter, and all the tears that had been shed here. To her, a house was a home, a holder of emotions and memories. Many wonderful memories had been made here.

She heard his car before she saw it. The old Ford. Steven said he was still shopping for the "best buy." But she admired that in him. It was one of his good qualities.

"I might have a better car when you get back," he'd said last night. His breath was warm on her neck, and she knew he was about to kiss her. They'd been careful not to be alone for long because desire mounted inside them, threatening to take over.

"I kind of like this car," Courtney had said.

He'd looked incredulous. "You do?"

"Sure." She grinned. "I have to go in through your side and it's rather difficult to crawl clear over, so as long as I get the seat belt fastened, I'm okay, and I'm closer than if I got in on my side."

He'd laughed then. "You make me so happy, Courtney; I can't believe it. God is so good. I've been praying for the success of this trip."

She'd touched his lips with her cool fingers. "I know you have, and I thank you for it."

They had parted, but now he was here, taking her to the airport. Once she arrived at Lambert Airport in St. Louis, a good fifty miles from the area she'd go to in Illinois, she'd pick up the rental car, then be on her way. She could hardly wait.

Alice had been crying, though she tried to put up a brave front.

Courtney took her mother into her arms. "Mom, I am coming back. You know that, don't you?"

"What if your real mother wants you to stay?"

"I won't stay. What do I know about Illinois? Besides, I have two people right here I love more than life itself. And second, *you* are my real mother." She leaned over and kissed Alice's cheek.

"I just wish you weren't going alone."

"Are you worried about protecting me or worried that I really would choose to stay?" Somehow Courtney couldn't quite believe that would be something her mother would worry about, but Alice was known for her fidgeting and worrying ways. Her husband had chided her about it more than once. His last words to her had been, "Don't worry."

"Every time someone tells me not to worry, something terrible happens," Alice said now. "Remember your father—"

"I know. I was thinking that very thing."

Steven came back for the last small bag and took Courtney's hand. "Come. We'd better get to the airport."

She smiled. They had more than an hour, but Steven felt better if he arrived early. Someday that flat tire might just happen, too.

"I feel like your mother," he said once they were in the car, after the last, frantic wave at Alice. "How can I live without you for two weeks?"

"I may be back in a week, you never know."

"At least I'll hear your voice."

Courtney halfheartedly watched as Steven drove through the midafternoon traffic. He had insisted on parking and seeing her on the plane and would wait until it took off, then would go back to the office. She would feel safe just knowing he was praying for her, along with church members and, of course, her mother. She did hope—oh, how she hoped— this trip would bring the desired results.

Chapter 11

Steven watched until the airplane was a mere speck in the deep blue sky. He felt a tremendous loss, one greater almost than when he'd left the hospital after Grams died. What if Courtney didn't come back? What if the plane crashed? What if she had a change of heart after finding her birth mother? These discoveries could be tragic. While Courtney thought she would have the answers and could now go on with wedding plans, the news about her origin might put her in a tailspin. Depression was a big possibility.

The touch of her lips on his burned inside him. He could feel her warmth, her embrace, the smell of her. He didn't want the feeling to go away, but it would fade and then he'd just have the memory.

The sun rolled behind a cloud, and the blue sky suddenly darkened. The weather often changed that fast here in the Northwest. Steven made his way down from the observation deck. It was out of his hands now. It had *always* been out of his hands. God was in control. How many times had Courtney said that? And she believed it with her whole being. He'd never seen such a determined, positive person. Her upbeat spirit lifted him each day, and now she wasn't here, and he was going to have to come up with his own method of survival.

As Steven made his way back to his car parked in the economy lot, he pondered over his new situation. Two months ago he'd been rattling along with his life as it always had been. Grams had taught him the work ethic. He used to be happiest after putting in a ten-hour day. There was always something new to learn about computers, and Steven learned it well. He was high in demand already, after just his first full year of owning his own business.

He slipped behind the wheel of the Ford, knowing a car would be his next purchase. His closet held new clothes, his refrigerator was at least half full, he had fantastic art prints and one original. Now for the wheels. Courtney liked the old car. "It has character," she'd said more than once. "Wait and be sure you get a good deal. Read the ads, Steven. Something will come up. Probably a little old widow selling her husband's prized possession after his death. We had our Sunday car and then Dad's work car, and later I got the hand-me-down car."

Strange how so much of Courtney had woven into his life. His every thought was of her and something she had said or done.

He opened the day planner before starting the car. The soup kitchen was coming up this Saturday. Of course she wouldn't be back then. He'd offered again to work. There was a question mark in the margin. Did he want to coach the Boys' Club basketball team? There was a need, and since he liked the game and had played in school, he knew he could. But could he take the time? It was an unanswered question.

As he merged onto I-5, he thought of God and the verses that had become special of late. "Surely I am with you," from Matthew 28, kept going through his mind. "Yes, Lord, I realize You are with me, but why did You bring this person into my life, then turn it upside down by this burning desire of hers?" Yet even as Steven mouthed the prayer, he knew he would not have fallen so hard for Courtney if she'd been any other way. Fluff she was not. She cared about real concerns. She wanted to make the world a better place. She was kind. Gentle-hearted. Grams would have loved her to death. At that thought he almost rear-ended the car ahead, whose driver was talking on a cellular phone.

"Better keep my mind on the business at hand," Steven muttered aloud. "It's going to be a long two weeks."

Jeff looked up when he entered the office. He had two large rooms filled with old computers and parts. Jeff was good. He just needed direction.

"Hey, man, you better get to work. That new video place over on Morrison just called. Just wanted to remind you about their system being down."

"Oh, no, forgot about them. What'd you tell them?"

"That you were gone for the morning."

"I'll get over there later. Right now I have to—"

"Send out invoices," Jeff finished the sentence.

"Oh, man, I forgot."

Jeff left to answer a call. "See you whenever."

Steven nodded as he looked at the stack of invoices. He was glad he'd be busy this day. He was hoping for a complex problem, something to take his mind from his loneliness. And if it was bad now, what would it be like two and three days from now? That's when the plan began formulating.

He thumbed through the stack of papers on his desk. He needed a secretary. Maybe he should look into that—the sooner the better. He didn't like this part of owning your business. He was one of the best computer consultants in Portland, but that didn't mean that people paid him on time or that their checks didn't bounce. He needed to get the invoices out if he was to have money coming in.

But he couldn't get his mind off Courtney. Her eyes were mesmerizing to him, taking over his every waking moment. He tapped the pencil on his desk. At first he'd considered that this might not be love; but whatever it was, he was definitely caught up in the moment.

He leaned back, propping his feet on the desk. "Unchained Melody" played on the little radio Jeff always had on. He would have turned it off, but the melody took him back to another year and another girl, one he'd almost fallen in love with. But Grams had said, "Finish college first, Steven; then think about the girls."

And so he had. He'd graduated summa cum laude, only Grams wasn't there to congratulate him. Nor was his real father, who couldn't be found for any reason.

At three o'clock he had the invoices ready to mail, and he headed for the video store.

The system was down, really down. As Steven began testing, he lost track of time and soon it was past five and he hadn't eaten.

"Mr. Spencer?" Becky, the company receptionist, peered around the corner. "Would you like me to bring you something to eat? We have a great restaurant right next door. Their soup of the day is minestrone with beef. I can bring it here, or you could go over with me. I was just getting ready to have dinner myself."

It was irregular, but he agreed to go. He was hungry, having skipped breakfast in order to get Courtney to the airport an hour ahead of time. He followed Becky out the door.

The small café, a mom-and-pop type, had lots of soups, and he picked a potato, cheddar cheese, and bacon chowder, along with their house specialty rolls.

He sipped his coffee, then looked up to find Becky smiling at him.

"Do you always get so intense when you work?"

Steven shrugged. "Don't you?"

"Not hardly."

Her smile was nice, and she had a soft look that made him think of Courtney. "I like my work. I love a challenge."

She stirred cream into her coffee. "I can tell."

The waitress brought his soup and Becky's salad.

"I know this may sound weird, but I was wondering if you'd go somewhere with me tonight."

He nearly choked on his first spoonful of soup.

"I guess there is someone, then?"

Steven found it difficult to look her in the eye now. "There is. I'm engaged."

The conversation shifted to noncommittal-type things such as weather, whether an earthquake would hit in the next year, and so on.

"Let that be a lesson," Steven told himself later as he headed back to the office after the problem had been fixed. "Realize that if a woman looks at you with a smile, it might be a come-on." He laughed. Courtney would have thought the whole thing amusing. She probably didn't have a jealous bone in her body. He had been mortified at first, but then felt somewhat flattered.

Jeff looked up from a computer he had torn into and smiled. "That call turned out to be simple. She didn't know how to turn the computer on. Man, you get all the good jobs. I get stuck here with the phone and walk-ins."

"Next time you can take all the calls," Steven said. "Yeah, that's a good idea."

❧

It was after seven when Steven left the office and headed across the river. No way could he go to his apartment tonight. He had to get out and do something. Quite by habit, he later realized, his car headed toward Parkrose and Courtney's house.

Alice was just cleaning up the dinner dishes when she answered his knock. "Steven! What a pleasant surprise!"

He grinned as he entered the familiar house. "Seems my car wouldn't go in any other direction."

They both laughed. "I've already eaten, but there's leftovers. Some chicken and potato salad. If I'd known you were coming, I'd have waited to eat."

He waved her away. "Already ate, but thanks."

"Did Courtney get off okay?"

He nodded. "On time, too. Miracle of miracles."

"You understand why I couldn't go?"

"Yeah, I think so."

"How about a cup of coffee?"

"Yeah, sounds good."

As they sat at the kitchen table, they talked of Courtney.

"She's going to come away brokenhearted, I just feel it."

Steven nodded. "I've been worried about that, also." He reached across the table to cover her hand with his. "She has to do it. She'll never forget about it. God must want her to know. I think her prayers will be answered, and she will find her birth mother. It's just a matter of when."

Alice kept stirring her coffee, though there was no sugar or cream added. "It's difficult for anyone to understand who has never gone through it, but I love her as if I had borne her. She was so tiny and, after one look, I knew this was my child. I'd love her till death."

"Most adoptions are that way, I've heard."

"I used to worry she would one day want to find her mother, that she'd forget about us—Carl and me—but later I knew Courtney would never leave us. The bond between the three of us was tight. And God has been present every second of Courtney's life. I've never believed anything more."

"I know." Steven put the cup down. "I miss her so much. I guess my job is to keep super busy while she's gone. I'd like to take you out for dinner one night and maybe a movie?"

Alice wiped away tears that trickled down her cheek. "You know you already have become a son to me, the son I never had but wanted. I can't tell you how much it has meant to have you come into our lives. And, yes, I would certainly like to do both whenever you can work it into your schedule." She smiled. "You're the one who has a schedule. Me? I'm flexible."

Steven was glad later that he'd gone. Both were missing Courtney. Both loved her to the depths. And together they could be unified and pray that she have her heart's desire.

He didn't tell Alice about his plans, mainly because he wasn't sure when he'd go. He'd wait a few days. Jeff would get his wish and get the house and business calls. He could get a temp to answer the phone. Then he thought of Alice. Why not? She would probably enjoy working for a few days. She could answer the phone and check the appointment book. He'd ask her when he saw her at church on Sunday.

Alice couldn't have been happier to have Steven drop in. He was such a nice boy. He reminded her of her brother, who had died at a young age, before he married. She hadn't thought about Anthony in years. If only he'd lived, Courtney would have probably had cousins. Or if Agnes had been able to have children, there would have been cousins. If Courtney's life had been fuller, maybe she wouldn't have had this urge, yet Alice knew that wasn't the only reason. Courtney felt the need to discover her medical background before marrying Steven and having children of her own. But what if she discovered a terrible disease? What if her father was a criminal? Would that affect her in an adverse way?

Alice checked all the doors and windows, making sure everything was locked up. The fear she always felt at being alone consumed her, and she broke out into a sweat. She wished she didn't have this fear, but ever since she could remember, she'd been afraid once night fell. She picked up her tatting. It was an old sewing project, and she hadn't worked on it for years, but for some reason, the tiny stitches comforted her now. That and God's presence and the fact that Steven was helping to fill the void left by her loss of Carl, her husband of nearly thirty years.

That night Alice's prayers were as fervent as always, but they were filled with praise. Praise to her God for answering most of her prayers and for giving her such a full, wonderful life.

"Some people never have it this good, God," she said as tears slipped from her eyes. "I thank You for Your goodness to me all these years. And if it pleases Thee, please be with Courtney and help her in this quest. Amen."

The moonlight shone through the bedroom window, and Alice forgot her fear. For the first time in a long while, she was alone in the big old house; but she felt God's presence there, and she knew she never had been alone and never would be again.

Chapter 12

Courtney made her way down the aisle to find her seat, stopping to wait for passengers to place luggage in the overhead bins. She finally got to Row 16 and discovered she had an aisle seat. Across from her was the older lady she'd noticed at the airport being hugged by a young woman with dark eyes.

"Now, Mama, don't be afraid," Courtney had overheard. "You got here in one piece and will return just fine."

Courtney had shivered without knowing why. She'd had eye contact with the two for a brief moment before Steven put his arm around her. There was just something about the young woman's smile and the older woman's face.

Courtney leaned back and closed her eyes. She hadn't slept a wink last night and had hoped to catch a nap once they were in the air. She'd brought a book, her journal, and a poem she'd started a few months ago, but knew she probably wouldn't do anything. She always had good intentions, but she couldn't concentrate. It was more interesting to watch others on the plane.

She thought again of Steven and his insistence on staying until she was in the air. Knowing him, he had stayed until the plane was but a speck in the sky. She felt his presence now, the way his arms felt around her, the touch of his lips on hers. God had been so good to bring Steven into her life. And he was patient. So far he was willing to wait, to hold off the wedding until she found answers about her past. What if the answers weren't here? What if she discovered something terrible? A serious health defect in her family? What then? Would Steven consider marrying and adopting? Yet even as she thought it, she knew what Tina would say.

"How do you know what the background might be of a child you'd adopt? Seems you'd have the same worry, my friend."

Courtney hadn't seen Tina much lately. Large in the final trimester of her pregnancy, Tina preferred staying close to home. Then, too, Steven took up every spare moment Courtney had.

Steven. What a wonderful person. And Bob. He wasn't ready to give up; that much was apparent from yesterday's conversation.

"I don't care how you feel about this Steven; I'm not out of the running, nor am I about to give up," he had said.

"I'm wearing a ring, Bob. That's pretty conclusive," Courtney had responded as she shuffled papers on the desk, wanting the moment to pass. She hated confrontations, and Bob was definitely a confrontational type person. *Most lawyers are,* she'd decided.

"People change their minds."

Courtney wanted marriage. Alice wanted marriage. Tina was praying it would work out. And Aunt Agnes. She couldn't forget dear Aunt Agnes. Bob was the only one who opposed it, and that was understandable.

She'd packed light for the trip. Most towns had Laundromats, and she wanted to take her one suitcase aboard the plane. She'd heard far too many tales about lost luggage that was never recovered.

A rental car would be waiting for her at Lambert, and then she'd drive east, across the Mississippi River, over into Illinois, then to the small town where supposedly her mother had lived and borne her.

Courtney had notes and names and a list of towns in the general vicinity. *I'll start with Belleville, then work my way east to the various townships.*

A voice interrupted her thoughts. "Are you going on a fun trip, my dear?" the older lady asked, leaning forward.

"It's business."

Courtney looked at the lady sandwiched between two men who were apparently on business since they were both tapping away on laptops. Something about the woman made her remember how frightened of flying Alice was. Just like this stranger. She could reassure her and even pray for her. She couldn't help it that she wanted to help others. It was just the way she was. It was one thing Steven said he loved about her.

When the flight attendant came down the aisle, Courtney asked if the lady could sit next to her since the middle seat was vacant.

She smiled. "Sure, why not?"

"I'm so glad you thought of this," her new friend said, buckling in. "I'm Dorcas Whitfield."

"I'm Courtney." She extended her hand. "Glad to meet you."

"That's a beautiful ring, my dear."

Courtney smiled. "I'm engaged to a man in Portland."

"And he didn't accompany you?"

Courtney sighed, remembering the endless conversations. "He wanted to come, but it's a trip I must make alone."

"Sounds pretty mysterious to me."

"Well, Dorcas, it's something I need to do. And where are you from?" Courtney asked, wanting to change the subject.

Dorcas smiled. "I reside in Illinois. Clancy, to be exact. My eldest lives in Salem, Oregon. I suppose you know where that is. I'm going home, where my other two children live. I've lived in Clancy almost all my life."

Clancy. Courtney's heart spun. That was the name of one of the towns she was going to. What if she was sitting next to a relative? Wouldn't that be a true God-coincidence?

"I may be going to Clancy, myself."

"You, dear?"

"Yes."

"Clancy's awfully small. If you're going for a visit, I'd know the person. I know everyone there. Small-town stuff, you know." Her blue eyes twinkled. "Tell me the name."

Courtney hesitated. *Should I tell Dorcas?* she wondered. *What harm will it do? And possibly some good could come from it.*

"Actually, I do not have a definite name. I thought I did, but the name I searched for on the Internet brought me no results, so now I am studying a definite year and will try to find out about what happened in 1976."

"Seventy-six. The bicentennial year?"

Courtney smiled. "Yes. One and the same. It's the year I was born."

"And what are you looking for, exactly?"

"My birth mother." There; it was out. She hadn't wanted to talk about it, but perhaps this would be an answer to her lengthy search.

"Birth mother," the lady repeated. She leaned toward Courtney. "You want to find your birth mother?"

"Yes. I have no idea what her name is because we figure there is a false name on the birth certificate. My parents adopted me when I was two weeks old."

"Oh, my, oh, my. That's a tough one." She frowned as if trying to remember what happened in 1976. "I don't believe there were any girls expecting then, at least not unmarried ones. And I assume your birth mother was not married, or she wouldn't have wanted to give you up."

It hit Courtney then, a possibility she'd never, ever considered. Perhaps her parents *were* married but could not keep her. What, then? Didn't responsible people still give up children they knew they could not raise?

"Honey, you come to my house when you hit Clancy. In fact, you can ride with me and my son. There should be plenty of room."

Courtney smiled. "Thanks, but I have a rental car waiting."

"Oh, of course. Everyone reserves everything these days. I'm so far behind; feel like I should be on the Pony Express, not a plane."

The FASTEN SEAT BELT sign went on, and Dorcas suddenly blanched.

"This is my absolute most dreaded part of the trip. I told Sonny I wanted to take the train, but he said, 'No, Mama, the plane is faster and safer.'"

Courtney took her hand and closed her eyes. "I'll say a prayer for a safe landing, Dorcas."

"Oh, child, you do that." Dorcas refused to open her eyes, nor would she look out the window. The wheels came down with a heavy thud, and Dorcas squeezed tighter.

"It's okay. We're here. We've landed."

Dorcas opened her eyes and let go of Courtney's hand. "Thank God for yet another miracle."

As passengers made their way up the walkway into the airport, people waved and rushed forward. Courtney felt the lump in her throat again as she missed Steven. When she went home, back to Portland, he'd definitely be there. And she'd rush into his arms and probably cry like the woman ahead of her was doing. Oh, to be loved. It was surely God's greatest gift to man.

Courtney saw her seatmate grab the hand of a tall, dark-eyed man, and then she was introduced.

"This young girl prayed for your silly ol' mama. Her name's Courtney, and she's going to come see me in Clancy."

Courtney detected a slight frown, then Sonny nodded. "Of course, Mama. You found another stray, did you?" He turned and smiled at Courtney. "No offense, ma'am."

Smiling back, Courtney answered, "No offense taken. I'll be most grateful for a friend in town."

"And you must come for an authentic southern dinner."

"Southern?"

"Of course. You'll be in southern Illinois, you know. We do things the southern way, honey, not like those northerners do."

Courtney hadn't realized, had not dreamed, that there would be a cultural difference between the north and south part of Illinois. If her mother knew this the two short years they lived here, she had never mentioned it.

She took the card Dorcas handed over, promising she'd call the minute she hit town.

It took forever, but at last Courtney had her car, a spiffy red Chevy, and was headed east. A map lay open on the seat beside her. The air-conditioning was on. It was hot, a muggy kind of hot she wasn't used to.

When she crossed a bridge into Illinois, she realized this had to be the Mississippi. The river was not at all what she'd expected. After the clear, green-blue of the Columbia and Willamette Rivers, she thought the mighty Mississippi would be even larger and possibly greener. A thin brown stream wove under the bridge she crossed. The land seemed flat, and she wondered where the mountains were.

"Steven," she said, thinking of him for the fiftieth time that day. "I wish you were here. Maybe I should have let you come after all."

Chapter 13

Courtney pulled off the road into a small rest area for people like her who had to study a map. She was thankful Alice wasn't along. She'd be scared to stop like this. Courtney checked the locks. She was safe.

She opened up the map and studied it. Already she was tired and looking for a motel. It had been a long trip, and she had hardly slept last night. Okawville had her favorite motel, but she didn't want to go that far. Besides, it was out of the way. Belleville was the county seat, and she'd start her search there first thing in the morning.

There were so many villes. Everything ended in "ville." And the towns were small, according to her map.

Folding it up as she knew Steven would, precise and with the folds in the right place, Courtney laughed. *Funny I should think of that now,* she thought. *But when don't I think about him? Is this going to work? What if I miss him too much? What if I can't find anything?*

She looked at the address on the card Dorcas had given her. Suddenly she couldn't wait to see her again, couldn't wait for a friendly face. Courtney wasn't scared, as Alice would have been, but she was lonely. Dreadfully lonely.

With the car air-conditioner turned off, heat poured into the car. It was hot, different from cool, moderate Oregon. She grabbed a tissue from her purse and dabbed at the perspiration on her forehead.

Courtney started the car and signaled to get back on the road. Such a flat area; already Courtney missed the green-forested hills, the sight of Mount Hood on a clear summer day. She'd drive by Scott Air Force Base, where her father had been stationed. She planned to take photos to show her mother, who hadn't been back to the area since they left when Courtney was three months old.

A motel on the outskirts of Belleville with a café next door looked nice and handy. She'd get dinner, call Steven at ten, then relax. She trembled at the thought of talking to him. She missed him more than she'd ever thought possible, and she had left Portland just nine hours earlier.

Landers, Landers, Landers went through her mind as she unloaded her suitcase and overnight bag. Alice said the young girl's name was Landers. The first thing she'd do was look at a phone book.

No Landers were listed in Belleville or any of the other nearby towns. Landers couldn't be spelled any other way. Janelle Landers was the name on the birth certificate.

Courtney changed her clothes and put on a pair of tan slacks and a short-sleeved yellow cotton sweater. Thank goodness she'd included some cooler clothes. Her mother had been right.

The café was small but adequate. Courtney studied the menu, ordering a Cobb salad with extra bacon and a roll. That'd do her.

She read the local newspaper while she toyed with the avocado. It wasn't fun to eat alone. Maybe she wouldn't wait until ten to call Steven. She needed to talk to him now.

The girl bagged up the remaining salad and took Courtney's money.

She went back to the motel with M&Ms, the leftover salad, a newspaper, and a local advertising circular. It listed houses for sale and rent; she wondered what it cost to live here in Belleville, Illinois.

The room was stuffy because she hadn't left the air-conditioner on. It was going to take some time to get used to the weather here.

Steven answered on the first ring. "Honey. Courtney, are you okay? Was the flight all right?"

A warm spot inside her expanded. How she wanted to be with him this very moment, put her head against his chest. "Everything's fine, Steven. I'm fine. And you?"

"Missing you."

"Ditto."

"Dropped by your mother's—"

"Already?"

"She was more than glad to see me."

"Well, of course. I told her to stay with Aunt Agnes, but she didn't want to."

"I love you," Steven said huskily. "I just know these next two weeks are going to take forever."

"Maybe I'll find my mother tomorrow."

"And if you do, you'll want to stay and visit. Catch up on family things. Meet your cousins and so on."

"If and when I find her."

They talked about a concert he had tickets for in November and the soup kitchen, which she'd miss.

"I'll tell Gerta hello for you."

"And don't listen to her ramblings."

"Oh? That I am the luckiest guy in Portland to have found my true love?" He chuckled. "No; I think I can handle that."

Courtney hung up with Steven's closing words in her ear. "Good-bye, my sweet love."

Was she making a mistake? Did it really matter what her mother might have had or what medical horror her ancestors had? Steven would marry her anyway. He'd said so more than once. And if they had a child with an afflic-tion, he said they'd love it anyway. Maybe more so.

She turned the TV on and back off just as fast. In the silence of the room, she curled into a ball on the bed and sat staring into space. An image of what her mother might have looked like burned bright in her mind. Always she was pretty with blond hair. A round shape. Her smile would tell Courtney how much she was loved and how much she hadn't wanted to give her away.

Laying her notes out on the bed, she studied the map again. The search at the courthouse could take most of the day. The historical society was also a good place to begin as well as the library.

She'd wait a day, then call on Dorcas. She'd been so kind, though she'd acted a bit strange when Courtney mentioned the year 1976.

The next morning seemed cooler as Courtney, dressed in jeans and a red blouse, headed over to the café for breakfast. She had parted her hair, pulled it back, and put a large barrette in the back.

She hoped she didn't look too much like a stranger. She had an idea this place was almost like Clancy, where everyone knew everyone else.

After two cups of coffee, scrambled eggs, and an English muffin, she packed up her notes and headed out. She'd stay at the motel tonight, then decide if she wanted to stay in another town.

As she headed into Belleville, she wondered how old her birth mother was, if she knew the Lord at all, and also if she had not wanted to give up her child. If not, why did she? Courtney could not imagine in a hundred thousand years giving up her own flesh and blood, and she knew Alice would have been behind her 100 percent, urging her to keep her baby. They were like that. Not all parents were supportive, though.

What if she'd run away? But where would she have gone? If none of the relatives would take her, she'd have had to stay in some small rundown room and work nights and leave the baby with a sitter. No, probably her mother had traveled the only road she could.

The midday sun beat out of the sky when Courtney descended the court-house steps. Dead end. No Landers. They said a child hadn't been born in the county on July 8, 1976. No births recorded. Period.

It was lunchtime, but she couldn't think about food. Not now, not when she knew she had so much to do and possibly not enough time. Maybe she should have brought Alice. Alice could have searched in books and looked on microfiches. Yet Courtney knew her mother would fidget and act all nervous. It was better this way.

The library was small and smelled of old books. Courtney loved the smell of books, newspaper, and new leather. She took a deep breath and walked up to the main desk.

"No computers for our users' help," the plump, dark-haired lady said. "All we have is the old card catalogue. We're looking to be computerized by mid-2000." The librarian smiled. "Is there something I can help you with?"

Courtney explained part of her mission, and the librarian looked interested. "I'd suggest looking through newspapers. The newspaper morgue is in the basement."

Courtney spent the rest of the afternoon going through the 1976 papers. A lot had happened in 1976. It seemed every town had a celebration of some sort, and some had small parades to commemorate the Bicentennial. What a year to be born!

Still no Landers. There were two births registered the day before and one birth the day after July 4, but nothing for the seventh, eighth, or ninth. Courtney jotted down the names, adding them to her long list of possibles.

"We're closing," a voice said at her elbow. "Perhaps you can come back tomorrow?"

"Oh." Courtney jumped. "I didn't realize it was so late."

She hurried up the stairs, thanking the librarian, who was closing up the desk.

"Do come back, dear. And if I can help in any way, let me know."

"Dead end," Courtney muttered as she went to her car. "This is impossible." She wondered then if Dorcas might have some ideas of how and what to look for next. If her mother had registered under a false name, she'd never find her. How could she?

The evening breeze felt good on her skin. The library was air-conditioned, the basement almost clammy. She liked seeing sunshine, hearing cars, and seeing people walking. She was in civilization again.

The car was warm as she headed toward Scott Air Force Base. A guard stood at the gate, asking her mission.

"You don't know anyone here? You have no ID card or reason for coming on base?"

She shook her head.

"Ma'am, I hate to tell you this," he leaned down and looked at her skeptically, "but we don't issue passes to just anybody. You must have a sponsor before I can let you on. Do you know anyone stationed here?"

"Heavens!" Courtney cut him off. "I don't need to go on the base if it's going to create a problem. I was just curious." She held her camera up. "I'd take a few photos for my mother. My father was stationed here in the mid-seventies."

"I'm sorry, but that's not a good enough reason."

"I understand. No problem." Courtney waved, then turned the car around. She'd get a photo of the gate with the name on the sign. That would have to do.

She headed back to the motel and to the café. Maybe she'd try a chicken-fried steak tonight. And mashed potatoes with cream gravy.

The café was busier tonight, and a Garth Brooks tune belted out from the jukebox. Something about, "This is your song."

The steak was okay, but she couldn't eat all of it. Again she took a doggie box to add to the one from the previous night. She'd dump them out when she left in the morning.

Because it was too early to call Steven, she decided to take a drive through the countryside. She passed through one, two, then another town. Strange, but nobody seemed to be outside, nor were any of the businesses open except the local taverns on the corner. It was nothing like the hustle and bustle of Portland. Finally she turned and made her way back.

Steven answered before she heard the ring.

"Honey, you're late!"

"I am?" She glanced at her watch. "It's just nine thirty."

"I wanted you to call me at seven our time."

"Oh, right."

"I've been a basket case today."

"You have? But why?"

"Nothing's gone right. Jeff finally figured out the configuration on this program."

"I'm sorry."

"When did you say you were coming home?"

It was not a good conversation, and she felt guilty for leaving. She looked at the ring on her finger. It reminded her of a better time coming, of hope for the future, of Steven's love. His words had not helped.

"Call me in the morning," he finally said. "I know what the arrangement was, but I need to hear from you twice a day, not just once. Call at nine your time."

Courtney promised she would, then hung up, her heart aching. How could she go on like this? Not eating right. Her mind always thinking of Steven. Maybe something would happen tomorrow.

She flipped on the TV and half-watched *ER* while she did the word search in the newspaper.

Chapter 14

Dorcas was happy to hear Courtney's voice and gave her explicit directions to her home. "You'll be here for dinner, then?" she asked.

"What time?" Courtney asked.

"No later than six, honey. Is that okay with you?"

"Oh, yes. Sounds fine," Courtney answered.

"And you feel free to come at any time, you hear?"

Clancy, similar to the other towns in the area, was small with one main street of businesses. A funeral home with stucco falling off, three taverns, a Methodist church, a Catholic church with a high steeple that tolled the hour with loud chimes, a grocery store, and a small drugstore were the extent of it. George Washington Grade School was in the middle of town, and a small park with a baseball diamond was at the far end. A new settlement of homes was north of Main Street. Courtney headed out there and drove down the blocks, where small saplings were planted in each yard. Children played in the street, but moved as she drove slowly past. Of course they stared. People knew she didn't belong here.

She headed back out of the housing area and back through town. She dug out Dorcas's address—12 Birch Street. She'd passed Birch already. It was in the old part of town. She decided not to stop just yet.

The midday sun had given way to late afternoon heat as Courtney drove out of town and headed to the next one. Cornfields dotted the landscape. What she wouldn't give for a small soft drink. Maybe she should buy a cheap ice chest and just carry cold drinks in the car. She'd never imagined it would be this hot the end of September. The grass was brown, and the birches back in town were shedding leaves.

Five miles later she came to Breese. Funny names for towns. Probably family names. She stopped at a drugstore and asked if there was anyone named Landers living nearby.

"Landers?" The tall, buxom lady shook her head. "Child, I'd know if any Landers ever lived here. Lived here all my life, never been any farther south than Mascouta nor more north than Renton."

"You haven't been to St. Louis?"

"What do I need that big town for?"

Courtney smiled and paid for the local newspaper and a package of gum. It was past lunchtime, almost dinnertime, and she needed food.

She went back inside and asked where she might eat.

"Go on up to Renton. They got two cafés there, honey. Here you have to go to the tavern, and they do make the best fried chicken of anyone I know, but then I don't know many people outside of this here area."

Courtney thanked her and hurried to her car. Fried chicken sounded really good, but she figured Dorcas would cook that for tonight.

It was now hot, a scorching heat, and Courtney thought it was because there were no trees to lend shade, at least not once you were out on the main drag. She missed the tall firs from home. The only kind she had seen here were short and scrawny looking, although there had been a few oaks in the middle of town.

What do people do for entertainment? she wondered. So far she hadn't even spotted a theater or a bowling alley. In Belleville there were both, but not here. Not in the small towns. It would be strange living in such isolation.

She found a small café and ordered a chili dog and fries. She observed the locals laughing and joking, but nobody paid any attention to her. It was as if she were invisible.

She drove back to Clancy and pulled up in front of a tall, narrow house set amongst a grove of trees. It was painted mauve and had a burgundy trim. A fence surrounded the house, and a gate was unlocked. Courtney held her breath as she ventured up a sidewalk that had obviously recently been replaced. The grass was brown and thin in spots, but a few shrubs were blooming under the bay windows.

She hesitated, then pressed the old-fashioned buzzer.

The door swung open, and Dorcas threw her arms open. "My little Courtney! I'm so glad you came."

Dorcas had a pot of tea brewing and a plate of hors d'oeuvres waiting. She chuckled as Courtney came in and looked around.

"You didn't expect a refined home in a Victorian setting, now did you? Not here in farm country."

Courtney hugged the older lady and glanced at her surroundings. Large photos in oval frames decorated one wall. Wainscoting was throughout the living and dining room. A settee was in one corner with a Duncan Phyfe table and end tables.

"It's just too beautiful," Courtney exclaimed, clasping her hands. "I feel as if I'm walking into a room from *House Beautiful*."

Dorcas chuckled. "I consider it a compliment. Now come, let's have a cup of tea, then I'll show you the rest of the house. Sonny can't make it for dinner, so it'll just be the two of us, but that's okay. That man keeps way too busy, if you ask me."

"A workaholic," Courtney said. "My father was that way, too."

Courtney sipped the tea and smiled. "Very good. And I like the smells coming from the kitchen."

"You may find the guest bedroom especially interesting," Dorcas said. "Let's go now." She led the way up a long flight of stairs with a highly polished banister. "And, yes, you may slide down the banister, if you so desire."

Courtney laughed. "Were you reading my mind?"

"Perhaps."

"Please excuse the dust," Dorcas said, running her finger along the floorboards. "I used to have a maid do all of this, back in the days when I entertained. We had a book club going and a tennis club. Mr. J., my husband, never liked to entertain, so I just had women come in. Once when I mentioned the DAR, they almost ran me out of town."

Courtney chuckled. She couldn't quite imagine the scenario and found it difficult to believe that this was Rebel country. Not that she didn't have empathy for those who fought so hard for the South. After studying both sides of history, she felt the South had just cause for their grieving. But that was a subject she usually avoided.

"This is the room where I want you to stay, should you choose to stay overnight in Clancy."

"It's wonderful!" Courtney clasped her hands, falling in love with the guest bedroom with its high ceiling, wainscoting, and huge four-poster bed with flowered canopy dominating the center of the room. A fireplace took up the west wall.

"This used to be a sitting room, but I decided to use it as a full-fledged bedroom, and the offer is open to stay for as long as you'd like."

"Oh, my, no, I couldn't do that," Courtney gasped. "It's so very kind of you, but it would be an imposition, though you might say not."

Dorcas walked over to a photo on the armoire. "Here. I want you to look at this picture."

The frame was exquisite, with curlycues and an angel with wings in one corner. She looked at the eyes staring back at her. "Is this someone who fought in the Civil War?" The suit looked military. But it was the bold look, the piercing stare of the eyes, that shook her.

Dorcas cleared her throat. "Now you will accept my offer. Now you will understand."

"Understand?" A chill raced up Courtney's spine. "What do you mean?"

"If I'm not mistaken, the man you are staring at is your great-great-grandfather, and he fought in the Spanish American War of 1898."

Courtney nearly dropped the picture. "But—how—what—I don't understand—"

"It's a long story. Come sit in the next room while I tell you about it," she said.

"Jeremy Johnson, the man in the photo, was my grandfather. He had gone to Texas, then up North, and ended up fighting in that war. When he came home to Massachusetts, he married into the prosperous Eddy family. My father was his eldest child, and after my mother died of TB, my father left Massachusetts and came here. Why he landed here, I'll never know. I was a young girl of sixteen and soon met and married my husband, God rest his soul. It was a happy marriage; we had four children."

"But, how—"

Dorcas leaned forward and took Courtney's hand. "I'm getting to that part, and it will help you, but not in what you really came to find out."

Courtney started to open her mouth but closed it again as Dorcas continued.

"Our eldest son was born with a hole in his heart. Money was no problem as I had funds set up in a trust by my grandparents, and Jonathan's father owned half of this county."

"And your son is my father and you're my grandmother?" Courtney had started to piece it together.

Dorcas held her hand up. "Don't get ahead of the story, my dear. There's much to tell."

"Jonathan Jr. went to some of the best hospitals in the land. Johns Hopkins was one, and I know you've heard about the wonderful work and research they do. Our son had an operation, back when it was just an experimental type thing.

"He came home," Dorcas went on, "and started living a normal life."

"Normal, meaning he went to school and stuff like that?" Courtney interrupted.

"Yes. More than anything he wanted to play basketball, being tall and lean, but the doctors said no, he could not."

Dorcas removed a small white handkerchief edged in lace and dabbed at her eyes. "He was such a smart, but stubborn, boy. He was probably my favorite, being sick and all. Mothers have a way of favoring a firstborn and especially one who is ill."

"He died, didn't he?"

Dorcas nodded. "Yes, my dear, he did. When he was nineteen."

"I'm so sorry. But how do I fit into this picture?"

"A month after his death, we received a letter from the Watt family. They lived two towns over. Perhaps you've been to Darby?"

"No, I haven't—but I searched the records for the entire county and found nothing."

"That's because you're asking for Landers, and it isn't Landers that you want to know about, but Watt."

Leaning forward, Courtney gasped, "You mean I'm part of the Watt family?"

Dorcas nodded. "Yes, you are. So, it was providence that put us on the plane together. Do you believe in fate?"

Courtney shivered. "I believe that God allows certain things to happen, and this must be one of them."

"Our son disobeyed and played basketball at the gym when we didn't know about it. It was there he became good friends with Miller Watt. Miller, a wild boy, had a sister with an affliction we later learned was epilepsy."

Courtney cried out, "No, I don't know if I can bear to hear all of this. Not yet."

"You're right. This is too much to assimilate all at once. I debated about bringing it up, but you seemed so desperate to find your family. But let's go downstairs and have some more tea. I'll let this sink in before going further."

Tears rolled down Courtney's cheeks, and she couldn't stop them. She was an illegitimate child, though Pastor had said there were no illegitimate children, only illegitimate parents. Still, her parents had not married, since one was rich and the other from the wrong side of the track. And her mother had had epilepsy?

For certain she could not hope to marry Steven now. How could she, knowing this? How could she risk having a child with that disease? She'd been spared, as the tests had ruled out epilepsy, but it probably had just skipped a generation, which often happens.

Dorcas was fussing around in the kitchen, and Courtney sat huddled in the large Chesterfield chair. Its long arms and seat seemed to enfold her, holding her close. Suddenly she wanted Steven here with her, and her mother. Alice would know what to say and do. Alice would assess the situation and ask more questions, but Courtney was too numb to even think straight. It was far more than she could assemble at once.

She refused the tray of appetizers and held the teacup so hard she feared it might break.

"I cannot be absolutely certain, child, that you're my granddaughter, but the facts indicate this."

"My mother was definitely a Watt then, not a Landers?"

Dorcas nodded. "That part of the picture is the hurting part, Courtney."

"But I must know! I have to know!"

"Sherry Watt was such a cute little thing. All eyes and a big smile. She was in the same grade as my Jill. They weren't friends, but in a small school and area, everyone knows everyone else. The Watts lived in an old rundown house at the edge of Darby. Her father didn't own any land around here; just worked for others. He was dishonest from all I've ever heard about him. I'm sorry about this part, but his daughter Sherry was smart. Cute as a button. I think she had another name, but I can't remember it just now. I hired her one summer to clean house and wash windows."

"Do I look like her at all?"

Dorcas smiled. "Perhaps your build more than anything, but I see my son's eyes in you. I had that feeling sitting next to you but didn't know why or how it could possibly be. I had to think about it before telling you this. Surely you understand my reasoning."

"What happened to my mother?"

"Her father put another name on the birth certificate, I heard, so she could never be traced. I'm sure it was all her father's doings. He was mean and ugly, if I do say so myself. Everyone stayed clear of him then."

"So that's why I couldn't find any record of it."

"I'm sure Emil would have made sure it was a false birth certificate. He may have falsified the date, as well. He knew how to take care of things."

"What happened after I was born?"

"They moved in '79, I believe it was."

"And went where?" She had to know.

"Not sure, honey. When Sherry had you, the family insisted she give you up for adoption. They were barely making ends meet as it was. And they knew she'd have a crazy child." Dorcas shook her head. "They were superstitious. Not sure where that came from, but they thought she was crazy; they didn't accept the doctor's explanation about the epilepsy being controlled with medication."

The knot in Courtney's stomach grew until it clutched her so hard she could hardly get her breath.

"I think we shouldn't go on. You are positively pea green."

Courtney began sobbing, and once the avalanche started, she couldn't hold the tears back.

Dorcas was there, holding her to her bosom, rocking her gently as one does a child. Courtney was her grandchild. She didn't care how she'd come to be; the important thing was that she was hers, and she had loved her from that first moment. Yes, God had answered her long-ago prayer to know what had become of her son's only child. She'd lain many sleepless nights, regretting that she hadn't done more, hadn't searched for her grandbaby.

"Did my father love my mother?" Courtney choked out. She had to know.

Dorcas brushed the hair back from damp cheeks. "Darling, I know he did. I saw the romance unfold before my eyes and should have done something to nip it in the bud, but I didn't. We wanted him to go to college—he was behind, of course, as the illness had kept him out of school for weeks at a time. We tutored him, but still held him back a year."

"If he loved my mother, that's all that matters," Courtney said, her heart suddenly swelling with the love she felt for Steven. "I was a love child, at least."

Dorcas nodded, loving Courtney for her gentle smile and her loving, tender manner. "I know you're right, child."

"But," Courtney pulled back, "I still must find my mother."

"It's not going to happen, honey, but I've said enough."

"You don't think I can find her because they moved? But now I have the proper name and someone can help me."

"Perhaps so. I wish I could help more. They left the old house—it's still out on the main highway about nine miles from here. They moved on when it was condemned."

"You mean you don't know where they went?" It was too much; she convulsed into sobs again. "But I must find her."

Dorcas wished she had some answers, but she didn't, and Courtney's pain became her own.

"Honey, I want to call your adoptive mother. She needs to be with you now. Or your fiancé?"

At the thought of Steven, Courtney's head shot up. "Oh, no, I couldn't let him know. I have to break my engagement."

"But, why ever, dear?"

"Because of my past, my family, the people I came from."

"If he loves you, that is not going to matter one whit. Your family are the dear people who adopted you and taught you and loved you and made you who you are now."

Courtney believed that; she'd always been told that; but something hurt so deep inside, she didn't know how she could marry. Not now. Probably not Steven. It would take time to heal.

"As you already said, if God didn't want you to discover this, He wouldn't have made sure we were on the same plane, sitting next to each other. He wouldn't have led Steven to your church; He wouldn't have given you such loving, supportive parents."

Courtney glanced up. "I think I want my mother, Alice, to come. She may not fly; she is fearful of planes."

"That's fine. She can take a bus and come right here to Clancy, believe it or not."

Courtney dialed the phone number and waited for her mother to answer. The answering machine clicked on after the fourth ring.

"Mom, it's me, Courtney. I want you to come. I need you." She recited the number. "I've found my father, at least."

As she replaced the receiver, the tears began again. She'd found one link to her heritage, and she was so grateful. Finding her father was wonderful, and to think that Dorcas was related—but what about her mother? Her mother was more important—or was she?

Chapter 15

Alice came home from a full day of learning her part-time, eight-hour-a-day job exhausted. Never, even in the early days of marriage, had she worked more than part-time. Her volunteer work was six-hour days, but that was different. She could leave at any time. Still, she was happy to do it—happy to help Steven out and happy to have her mind on something besides Courtney.

She went straight to the refrigerator and opened a can of 7-Up. Sinking into the recliner, she took a long sip, then turned on the news. Every bone ached, yet it was a good feeling. If she could just stop worrying about Courtney. She'd always been a worrier; Carl had chided her about it more than once, and later Courtney scolded her. She'd had an uneasy feeling about Courtney all day, not knowing why.

Alice closed her eyes and listened to the latest weather report. She knew she would drift off before finishing the soda, but that was okay. There was nobody to cook dinner for. Nobody to entertain. Her last thought was that she was glad Steven had asked her to take over as receptionist for the five days he planned on being gone to be with Courtney. She would have liked to be with her child, but it was more important that Steven go now.

It was a surprise when he'd said he'd booked a flight out that weekend. "I just have to do this, Alice. She may not understand; she might be miffed at first; but I'm praying she'll be happy I'm there."

"And I'm sure she will."

The doorbell wakened her suddenly. It was Steven, his face filled with anguish. "I'm leaving earlier than expected, Alice."

"What's wrong?" Panic seized her. "It's my baby. What's happened to Courtney?"

"She wants you to come, and maybe you should, but I want to be there with her and I—" His face was white.

"Sit, Steven. Relax. Tell me what this is all about." Alice had always been good in emergencies. All that time when Courtney was ill and they hadn't known what was wrong, hadn't known if she'd ever completely recover, Carl had come apart, but she'd been the stalwart, calm one. Of course, God had been her mainstay—not that Carl didn't believe, but he hadn't been able to let go and let God take over. She was now being pressed into service again.

"I can make coffee. Or tea."

Steven shook his head. "I couldn't swallow anything right now."

"She called you, you know."

"She *did?*"

"Did you listen to your messages?"

Alice gasped. "I didn't even check. I was so tired and thirsty; I just went straight to my favorite chair."

"That's fine. I think that's the way it was meant to be. When she didn't find you home, she called my voice mail, and I got the message just a few minutes ago."

"What happened?" Alice grabbed his arm, fearful of what she might hear.

"She's found her father's family."

"Her father's? What about her mother's?"

"She wasn't clear on that point, but whatever, she's deeply upset, and I'm flying out first thing in the morning. Couldn't get a flight out tonight; they're all booked up. Some business convention in St. Louis."

"And you want me to go?"

"If you want, Alice. I can shut down the shop or just put on the answering machine and let Jeff handle the most important calls." Steven paced the length of the living room and back again. "She didn't ask for me. She wants you, but I must go, and you do what you think best."

"She wants me to come?"

"Go listen to your machine."

Alice played the message back and heard a frantic voice, so unlike Courtney, who always was in control of everything. Even in her illness, she'd been brave, certain she would be okay. And she had been. But this was something new. Different. Something she had no control over. And she had asked for Alice. Not her fiancé, but her mother. And if Carl had been here, she would have asked him to come, too.

She listened to the message twice, her hand gripping Steven's.

"I can't fly, Steven. I have such terrible fear of flying. If I go, it would have to be by bus. And it would take two days at least. She needs someone *now.*" She put her hand on his shoulder, and then he had his arms around her, hugging her hard.

"I'm going. Maybe you should come, too, even if it is by bus."

"Steven, I'll be more help if I stay and answer the phones for you. I learned all I needed to today. Just knowing that Courtney wants me to come means more than words can say."

"I'm sure Courtney will understand."

Alice nodded. "She knows my fear of flying. She'll understand, all right."

After Steven left, Alice replayed the message. This wasn't Courtney's voice at all. She sounded so—shattered. Her baby was frightened.

Alice went to the sewing room at the top of the stairs and pulled the trunk out. She lifted the lid.

Inside was the scrapbook she'd kept from the moment Courtney came to them. There were albums, too, but this particular scrapbook contained all the baby congratulation cards, then the early birthday cards.

The baby book was another treasure. She would never have not kept a record of all of her precious baby's doings.

"What if someone comes to take her away from you?" her sister Agnes had asked once, before Courtney's first birthday. "You know that happens."

"I'll fight them for her."

"Would you, Alice? I think not."

They had been fortunate that that hadn't happened, and soon they relaxed, knowing that Courtney would always be their child.

Alice removed the first pair of tiny shoes, the gold locket with a photo inside of Mommy and Daddy, the christening dress and the white lacy bonnet. She'd kept everything, preserving them in a large plastic bag. Someday Courtney might want them for her child.

Courtney had loved looking at her special clothes and her baby book. There was the locket of hair in a small envelope; her first haircut, it said on the envelope. There was a photo of her taking her first steps in the Mary Jane shoes.

She had taken ballet at age four, and Alice remembered the tutus she wore and the recitals for two years. She was always the shortest and the most clumsy. But it hadn't mattered.

Courtney had always asked about her real mother and father, wondering if she looked like them.

Alice opened the baby book. Had Courtney's mother wanted her? Had she loved her while carrying her? Somehow Alice thought so, since Courtney seemed so content as an infant, and there were facts now stating a mother's feelings mattered while she carried her child.

She held out her favorite photo, taken when Courtney was six and just starting school; her hair was in long curls, her smile wholesome. "My little pixie," Alice murmured. "I love you, my little pixie."

❧

Steven left, driving like a maniac back across town, praying all the while that Courtney would understand, that she would talk to him once he got there. A fear deep inside made him think otherwise, and he so hoped his gut feeling was wrong. . . .

He packed light. Even if he stayed five days, he could wash his clothes somewhere. He didn't want to take the time to check his baggage or have to wait there for it to come down the baggage chute.

He'd called ahead and would have a car waiting, a small compact. If only it weren't so far to Clancy, where she was staying.

Courtney was in pain. Steven knew her well enough to realize that. She would never have called asking for Alice to come if not. Nor would she have called him on the pager unless she was desperate. This was her problem, and she'd find the solution, she'd said more than once in the days before leaving for Illinois. Why hadn't she at least given him a clue? He had nothing to go on, only guesses, and what if she didn't want to see him? He had to take his chances. He loved her. He knew God had brought them together—thanks to Grams—and he wasn't going to bow out now. It didn't matter what she found out; they'd weather it together—stand united. Wasn't that what it said in the Bible? The apostle Paul's words came to him, but he couldn't remember from where. It was something about it not being good for man to live alone. Steven, not always filled with such determination, would fight this one. He'd fight to the end, if need be. Courtney belonged to him, and he didn't care about her background. They'd fight it together.

Sleep wouldn't come; he knew it wouldn't, so he tried to get interested in the late-night movie. It didn't work. Nor did the latest Grisham novel grab him. Music filled the background, soft listening music so he wouldn't bother the other tenants, though he thought the building was well insulated.

Finally he relied on a few passages from the Good Book. He'd marked them earlier after a discussion with the pastor. They calmed him down as he finally drifted off, only to hear the alarm ring at five.

Jeff had been only too happy to drive him to the airport. He let him off at the entrance. "Take it easy, man. You'll have a coronary if you get any more riled."

"Take care of the little guys, too, not just the corporations," was Steven's parting shot. "Do what you can, but get some sleep and food, also."

"Hey, man, I'll be okay. This is my chance to prove myself."

The car roared off, and Steven rushed down the aisle toward Gate 18. He had to go through the metal detector booth, but that was quick. Two pairs of pants, two shirts, and two of everything else was all he carried on.

Once he was on the plane, Steven got comfortable, hoping to catch up on some shut-eye once they were in the air.

You are doing the right thing, a voice seemed to say as he buckled in.

"Grams, is that you?" he said aloud.

"Were you speaking to me?" a voice said on his right.

"Oh, no, just talking to my Grams," Steven said.

The man's eyes widened. That took care of that. No small chitchat now. The man thought he was crazy, for sure. What if he'd said he was having a conversation with God? What might have happened then?

Steven's dreams were of Courtney, the white dress she'd wear down the aisle, the candle they'd light together, indicating the life they'd share, the promise to serve God, to let Him be head of their household, then the kiss after the minister said, "I now pronounce you man and wife." And then the wedding night when Courtney would be his, only his. Then the children they'd have.

The attendant's voice wakened him. "Sir, do you want a cola or a cup of coffee?"

"Coffee. Yes. With cream and sugar, both."

He never used cream and sugar, but this occasion called for it.

"You looked pleased," the man to his right said. "You were smiling. Must have had a good conversation with Grams."

Steven leaned forward, letting his seat snap back to an upright position. "You don't know the half of it."

Over coffee, the two men chatted, and Steven was glad he had talked to the man. It made the flight seem shorter, and he'd made a friend, in spite of his talking to his grandmother.

He had a rental car waiting, but it took forever to find the car rental place, then way too long to sign his name. *What was the point of calling ahead with the necessary info?* he wondered.

With a map at his side, he drove out of the airport and toward Illinois. With luck, he'd be there by one. He didn't have this Dorcas's address, but in small towns, someone would know. He'd ask at the first business establishment he came to.

As he hummed along with a gospel song on the radio, his heart jumped in anticipation of seeing Courtney again, of being able to comfort her, to reassure her that he was with her no matter what and always would be.

Chapter 16

Courtney slept fitfully that night. The bedroom was wonderful. It was the sort of room she would have hoped for in a bed-and-breakfast. The feather bed—she'd never slept in such a thing before—seemed to swallow her in its soft depths. She could have stayed here forever—here where her needs would be met, where she didn't have to think about what had happened in the past.

She'd also never slept in a canopy bed before, and it made her feel like a princess. Long, lacy curtains hung on all sides, offering semi-privacy, considering one could see through the lace. She didn't like them closed; it made her feel too hemmed in.

It was too warm for a fire, but she longed for flames to mesmerize her, to take her away from the discovery of the evening before.

As morning's rays splashed across the bed, the sunbeams dancing, Courtney grabbed her robe and pushed her feet into slippers.

She walked across the room and picked up the photograph. Her great-great-grandfather's eyes—if indeed her birth story were true—bored into her very soul. God had been good to bring Dorcas into her life. She belonged to someone now. She should be content knowing that much, but it was what she didn't know that had kept her awake most of the night.

How would she find her mother since she'd moved away? And how about other relatives? She must learn more about her mother, more about her physical condition. Would anyone even want to talk to her should she find them? Would they deny she was part of them? She'd heard of that happening. She couldn't understand why, but birth mothers often didn't want to be found. Oregon had passed a law saying the records should be open for all to see, but four birth mothers had filed appeals against that law, and so far the records remained sealed, just as they did in most other states.

Courtney wondered why Alice hadn't called back. Had she not been home? Had she gone out to stay with Agnes? She should have called Aunt Agnes instead of Steven. Steven wouldn't understand the turmoil she felt now. She loved him so much, but how could she expect him to understand. How could he possibly want to marry her now?

She lay back on the bed, burying her face into the soft folds of the comforter.

A large leather-bound Bible sat on the small nightstand. She hadn't noticed it before and wondered if Dorcas had slipped it into the room while Courtney soaked in the huge clawfoot bathtub last night. The tub was huge, big enough to hold two people, and her thoughts returned to Steven and what it would be like to be married to him. *Enough of those thoughts,* she'd chided herself. It wasn't meant to be.

The smell of coffee drifted up the stairs. Of course Dorcas would be up early. The morning sun had already heated up the house. There were no mountains or high hills to offer shade. No clouds to cover it. It would be a blazing, hot day. After breakfast she would call Aunt Agnes and see if her mother was there.

"Good morning, Courtney!" Dorcas called out, turning from the stove and coming over to hug her guest. "My, don't you look pink-cheeked this morning. You must have slept well in the feather bed."

"It's heavenly."

"Sit. I'm making pancakes from sourdough starter a cousin brought me from Alaska, oh, about twenty years ago now."

"The same starter?"

"Oh, my yes. And it makes the best, most tender pancakes you've ever sunk a fork into."

"I need to call my aunt Agnes. She might know why Mother didn't answer my call last night. They'd discussed Mom going out there. Both are widows now."

"That's a good idea, but why not eat first?"

Dorcas didn't tell Courtney about the call she'd received that morning— Steven calling from the airport, saying he was on his way, but to please not tell his fiancée.

Dorcas gave her a choice of bananas or grapefruit to eat first. Courtney chose the bananas and soon finished the fresh, sliced bananas topped with real whipped cream. Then Courtney ate four pancakes, immersing them with Dorcas's homemade syrup that was good and full of maple flavor.

The kitchen was large and airy as morning light filled the room and Courtney's heart. Today was going to be special. Perhaps her mother was already on her way. Perhaps she had pushed aside her fear of flying and would arrive sometime that afternoon.

Dorcas tried to detain her, but she had things to do, places to go. Soon Courtney was in the red rental, zooming down the long driveway back toward town.

She talked to the lady who ran the small gift shop. Dorcas had said she might have some information.

"And you're who?" The pleasant-faced woman seemed guarded. "I don't give out information to just anybody."

Courtney had to relate the entire story for what seemed like the hundredth time. "I really need to find my mother, so if you know anything about the Watt family, I'd be ever so grateful." She also told her about staying with Dorcas, but did not mention that Dorcas was probably her real grandmother.

"I knew Mrs. Watt. I knew her kids, but they took off and nobody has heard from them since. Unless—" A thoughtful look crossed the wide face.

"Unless?" Courtney didn't like prompting people. "Unless what?"

"There was a cousin. One twice-removed, I believe. A cousin from the mother's side."

"And?"

"She lives over in Darby."

"Darby?" Courtney knew that would be her next stop for sure now.

The lady pointed east. "It's the township ten miles over. You'll go through Reese first."

"Do you have her name?"

"No, can't say that I do. She married, of course, and the only thing I know is Lois. Yes, Lois was her given name."

"Oh, thank you, thank you so much."

Finally, she'd found something to follow up on. Racing to her car, she heard a horn honk and figured someone thought she was racing across the street in front of them. She stopped when the horn blasted again as a voice called her name. She paused, her heart pounding as she recognized the voice. But it couldn't be. Steven had a business to run. He wouldn't have come all this way in hopes of finding her.

But he had.

He stood, leaning against a small white compact, waiting to see what she would do.

"Steven?" And then she ran across the street and into his arms. The tears began, and he held her tight, smoothing the hair back from the sides of her face, saying nothing. Sometimes words weren't necessary. Touch was more important. Presence was also important. Words would come later.

"I missed you so terribly," he finally said when the sobs had ceased. She now had the hiccups, so he held her arm up as Grams used to do when he got hiccups. That made her laugh as she looked at him through her tears.

"But why did you come?"

"Did you really expect me to stay away?"

The sun shone on his face, and Courtney felt the fierce longing she always felt when she looked at him.

"I guess I expected you to honor my request."

"You called Alice."

"She's my mother, Steven, and I suddenly realized how much she means to me and this whole quest, and I just needed to see her."

"But not me."

"I didn't say that—"

"No, not exactly."

"So you're here because?"

"Because I wanted to come. Because you need me. Because I care about you. Because you are part of me. Because Alice doesn't like to fly. But mostly because I love you."

She broke away and looked into his deep, craggy face. "Oh, Steven, I can't marry you now. I just can't. Not after the things I'm finding out."

"We'll discuss it over a cup of coffee. I see that little café is open."

"I have to get to Darby."

"I'll go with you."

"You can't." The smile left her face, and his heart nearly stopped.

"Why not?"

"As I said before, I must do this on my own."

He took her hand, but she pulled away.

"Steven, I just can't think about marriage. I can't even discuss it now. It's not good that you came."

"You didn't feel that way a minute ago."

"I know. I was so—well—relieved to see you."

"And you love me."

"Yes."

"Then I want to go. Isn't that what love is about? Isn't that what God intended? That we share one another's burdens—make them lighter? I don't understand why you don't understand that concept, Courtney." His voice sounded hard.

"Steven, I'm sorry you spent that money and came all this way for nothing."

"Nothing is for nothing. I'll never believe that."

She turned, walking away from him. "I don't expect you to understand."

"And I don't. That's for sure. I won't let you go, if that's what you're thinking. I won't give up. I'm not one to run home and to give the ball back. I will fight this, Courtney. I don't care about who had you, what they were like, what medical problem they had, if they were in prison. None of that matters. Not one bit!" His voice had risen, and a person across the street stared.

"Shh—" She put her hand on his lips.

"I won't hush. You can't make me. You go ahead to where it is you're going, and I'll just follow you in my little rental car. I'll follow you today. Tomorrow. And the next day and the next."

Courtney squeezed her eyes tight. She couldn't cry again. Not here. Not now. Not on Main Street in town. Not in front of Steven. There had already been too many tears. She couldn't succumb to them again.

"Come on. Let's discuss this inside the car. Yours or mine?"

She said nothing, but followed him back across the street, slipping into the seat and watching as he made sure she was safely in before closing the door. The warm, soft interior made her suddenly laugh, the first time since she'd left Portland.

"What?" He looked puzzled, as if he couldn't believe she'd be going from tears to laughter.

"It's rare that you hold the door open for me, considering you can't even open the passenger door on the Ford."

"You're right. It felt good, now, didn't it?"

She smiled. "Very good. I'm sorry, Steven, for acting like this, but I feel strongly about it, and you just have to understand."

"I'm trying. Believe me, Courtney, I'm trying."

"You need to head east, since you're so insistent. But you're staying in the car, should I find this Lois, who may just be my cousin."

"Will do."

And he meant it. He didn't care what the conditions might be. As long as he could be there for her, to lift her up, to pray with her, to cry with her, or to rejoice. It didn't matter. God had not put her into his life to suddenly snatch her away. He'd never been more sure of anything in his entire life. And with a self-confident smile, he put the key in the ignition and headed out onto the street, going in an easterly direction.

Chapter 17

In a matter of minutes, Courtney filled Steven in on her father and how her mother had worked at the Whitfield home.

"She was just a maid, Steven. And she fell for my father. Of course he couldn't marry her. He was ill, too. We could have a child with a hole in its heart."

"What is Dorcas like?"

"She's wonderful, Steven. She wants to see me again and would like to meet you."

"She called me, you know."

"No, I didn't know."

"It's probably just as well."

The afternoon had cooled off as a gentle breeze blew in from the west.

"Shall I shut off the air-conditioning?" Steven asked, noticing Courtney's hair flying in the breeze. She had opened the window after he had started the car.

"Yes. I much prefer the fresh air, even if it smells like corn and harvesting and cows and things."

He laughed. "It does smell different than the exhaust fumes in Portland. Kind of nice for a change. Brings back memories of Redmond and home and the ranch."

Courtney looked thoughtful. "It must be wonderful to know exactly where you are from and who your mother was, and even though she died, you know who you are. Oh, Steven, I don't know why I'm doing this." Her mood shifted. "I'm so scared of what else I'll find."

"I know, honey. I know."

"But do you?"

"Well, I think I do." His hand reached over to cover hers. "I know nobody can know unless they've gone through it. I never knew my parents, but at least I knew who they were, faults and all."

"That's just it. Not knowing and wanting to know, yet afraid to find out. Afraid of rejection. Of not being loved."

"You'll always be loved by those who know you and consider you their own flesh and blood. You know that, honey. Nobody could love you any more than Alice."

At the thought of her mother, the woman who had nurtured her all these years, tears came to her eyes again. "I'm tired of crying, Steven. I refuse to cry anymore."

"Then don't." He slipped an arm around the back of the seat. "I think we should sing some praise songs. Won't that help?"

"Yes!" She belted out one of her favorites, her voice drifting off into the winds as they tootled down the highway:

> "Heavenly Sunshine, Heavenly Sunshine!
> Filling my soul with Glory divine,
> Heavenly Sunshine, Heavenly Sunshine,
> Jesus is mine!"

"I don't know that one," Steven said after she'd sung three choruses.

"I learned it before I knew how to talk yet. It's always been a favorite on a day when the sun is shining. We don't sing it much anymore. Maybe I'll request it at a Sunday night service."

"I like it, too. Sing it again."

And so she did, her voice even higher and louder than before.

"Praising God always makes me feel better. Why did I let myself get so worked up?"

"It's understandable."

"I still can't marry you, though. I need to think about this. There's just too much going on."

Steven's face dropped as he turned away, not wanting to say the words that had popped into his mind. Patience. God was teaching him patience in many things, this being the most important right now.

"I was hoping we could set a date. Alice is eager to start planning a wedding." Steven looked straight ahead. "Could we maybe discuss that possibility?"

A town loomed up, and he slowed to twenty-five.

"I need time to sort this all out. You said before that you understood."

"I'm trying, really, I am, Courtney."

"There's something sinister in my background. I can't just ignore it."

"Sinister?"

"Yes; my grandfather was not a nice man."

"In what way?"

"He lied to my parents, for one thing." And then she was telling him about how her folks had paid for hospitalization and for Sherry to get on her feet.

"I probably have the same in mine. We can't all be perfect." But even as he said the words, Steven felt a sinking sensation. She wasn't going to let this go. Maybe never. Maybe Courtney wasn't the right one for him after all. If so, there surely would be some indication. Some sign. Maybe he'd been wrong in coming here. Yes, she did need time, and he had interfered, blundering in where and when he wasn't wanted. He should have insisted that Alice come, even if it was by train or bus.

"Background is important," she said.

Steven didn't reply.

"I am sorry, but you can at least talk to me."

"I guess everything's been said, Courtney. I shouldn't have come. I see no recourse but to leave on the first flight I can get out of St. Louis." He stopped the car and turned it around. "I'll take you back to your car."

"But we're almost there."

His jaw was taut. "No, it's better this way. You're absolutely right. I should never have come. You didn't ask me to. I just thought. . ." His voice drifted off.

"Steven, don't be angry with me." She looked at him expectantly, but he still stared straight ahead.

The five-mile ride back was soon over, and he pulled up behind her car. She glanced over, but he wouldn't look at her.

Her mouth went tight. "Maybe you want this back then." She twisted the ring off her finger and put it on the seat beside him, then yanked the door open. Without a backward glance, Steven backed up and made a U-turn and headed west. He didn't even kiss her good-bye. He wasn't able to trust himself to do just that, not when he wanted so much more, something he now doubted he could ever have.

Courtney stomped over to her car and flung the door open. "Let him be that way. It's better that I know now than later." She slid into the seat of her small red car, wishing she had called Steven back, wishing now she had told him she needed him and wanted him here with her, but she couldn't do it. She thought of the alexandrite. Why had she given it back? That was the end of the end. Now Steven was angry, or was it a hurt reaction? She didn't blame him. Her mood swings were unbelievable. One minute singing praises to God, the next fear and doubt. Yes, most of all doubt. Doubt about a future that might not be hers to enjoy.

The scenery was the same, the weather the same, but a chill raced over her as she knew she couldn't have done it any differently. How could she marry Steven knowing what she did about her family? No-account people. A grandfather who was mean and not liked by any of the people in town. He'd made her mother work. He'd probably made her give up her baby. He couldn't have known God and could not have reared Courtney right. She knew she should be thankful for Alice and Carl, for the love they'd bestowed on her, the home she'd always had. How different things might have been. Yet could she turn her back on her family should she find them? Perhaps they needed to know God. Perhaps they would listen to her. She'd never know until she found them, until she discovered who and what they were.

She passed through Breese and saw the next town was five miles east. Of course. All the townships were five miles apart, no matter which direction they went.

Courtney had to pull over once because she couldn't see through her tears. *How silly of me,* she admonished herself. *I got exactly what I asked for.* And it was true. All her life she'd known what she wanted and gotten what she wanted. Sometimes it happened instantaneously. Sometimes it didn't. When the illness struck, she'd prayed for healing. Her parents had prayed for healing, and the entire church prayed that the doctors would be guided into finding the right answers. She'd had to wait. She'd learned patience in that six-month period. Like her birth father, she'd been tutored and had kept up with her class. She'd later graduated salutatorian. Yes, God had given her a decisive mind, apparently unlike her mother. From what she'd heard thus far, she was more like her father's side.

She pulled back onto the road. Such light traffic. It was a treat to drive down the highway from small town to small town. An occasional car passed. Those who did come along wanted to go much faster than her fifty-five.

She tried to swallow the hard knot in her throat. Why had she not taken her ring back? Why hadn't she asked for it? She really should never have taken it off. She loved Steven with her whole being. She knew she did. He had to understand. He'd agreed with her plans in the beginning. But he'd wanted to orchestrate; he'd been insistent on coming, and when she said no, he ended up coming anyway. But Alice hadn't, and that was the tender side of him that had come, that had wanted to be with her, and that had left his business to come to be with her. So it seemed he really didn't understand after all.

Another car beeped and drove past her, a car full of teenagers in a hurry. "Hey, lady, why don't you get a horse?" came the call. One kid made an obscene gesture, and Courtney felt sudden fear. She was out where nobody could help her should someone decide to pull her over. Her body could be tossed so easily in the cornfields. The harvest was over, but the stalks stood tall and, though dry and brown, held their own.

She clicked on the radio, searching for a Christian radio station. She must get her mind off of such gruesome thoughts.

Darby came into view. A couple of buildings stood in haphazard fashion, leaning toward the ground. A small grocery store and a post office were on the right. A café with a peeling sign was directly across the street. Courtney pulled into the post office lot. The postmaster might know someone named Lois. It was worth a try.

"Lois? No last name?" The woman smiled. She was the postmistress of the small town. "Pretty hard without a last name. I know of two. Lois Johnson and Lois Oberthauff. What age would she be?"

"I think older. Maybe twenty years older than me. Someone in their mid-forties."

She nodded. "That'd be Oberthauff then. She's out of town about half a mile. Turn at the first road out of town and go left. The road dead ends at their house."

"Oh, thank you. And wait—I want to send these postcards. I need stamps."

Courtney dug out the cards she'd picked up earlier for Tina, Steven, and her mother. She'd send Steven's even though she'd seen him. The knot came back.

She thought about getting a quick bite to eat, but the place didn't appeal to her, though she'd discovered that often the smallest places had the best food. She knew she wouldn't be able to swallow anyway. It was just that way.

Courtney followed the directions and traveled extra slow on the potholed dirt road. She imagined it would be hard come winter if they had rains like the rains back home.

The farmhouse was old but well kept. The lawn was green and trimmed with a huge hydrangea bush in full bloom at one side. A row of bright yellow marigolds bordered a front flower bed.

The house, painted white with red trim, made her remember how the Cape Cod at home had once had red shutters like this. Awnings were on the left side of the house, shading it from the sun's rays in the evening. The right side also had awnings.

Courtney pulled into the far side of the U-shaped drive.

A door opened before she got out of the car, and a robust woman came down the steps.

"Hello. You lost, miss?"

Courtney held her handbag tight, walking toward the woman. "I think not. The postmistress in Darby directed me to your home."

"Oh. How can I help you then? I don't recognize you at all. . . ."

Courtney stood in front of the woman, searching her for some sign of similarity. The high cheekbones? Shape of face? Color of hair?

"I'm Courtney Adams. I have reason to believe you might know my birth mother."

The woman's face blanched as if she'd seen a ghost. "Your birth mother?" she repeated.

"Yes. I have papers to show you and conversations to discuss. I really need to find my mother for medical reasons. I hope you can help."

"Come on in. I'll put on some water. We have an hour before Mel comes in for his meal. He's a bear if I don't get it on the table at the dot of twelve."

"I understand."

The house was well kept and picture-perfect inside. Crisp curtains fluttered at the windows. Western furniture upholstered in bold blue plaid dominated the room. A Western painting hung on the wall over the fireplace mantel. "The Heartache's on Me" by the Dixie Chicks sang from a radio, probably in the kitchen.

"This is a lovely room," Courtney said.

"Well, sit while I bring us something to drink. Coffee or tea?"

"Coffee, please. No sugar or cream."

She took a deep breath, trying to decipher if the woman knew anything. She was hospitable, kind, as many were toward stranger; but had there been recognition, a glimpse of something in those eyes?

"Now tell me who you are and exactly what you think you know and what led you here."

Courtney began from what she knew about her birth, the adoption in Belleville, her parents moving back to Oregon, the desire to find out her background after the illness, and meeting Dorcas on the plane and finding out who was probably her father.

"I see why you are interested in finding your roots. It can be very beneficial in some cases." Lois stirred her coffee vigorously. "I may be able to help, but I'm not sure I want to."

"What!" Courtney suddenly jumped up, nearly spilling her coffee. "How can you say this?"

Lois sighed. "There is no concrete proof, for one thing, so why give you info that could be wrong?"

"But I want to know anything. Maybe I'm grasping at straws, but that's better than knowing nothing." Courtney sat back down. Outbursts were uncalled for and so unlike her. Just as tears were.

"Your mother may be my first cousin. Our mothers were sisters."

"Oh, Lois, I need to know where she is. I want to talk to her just once; even on the phone is fine. I just have to know something about her. If you have a photo maybe—"

"I have one photo. That may sound strange, but our families were not into taking pictures. My aunt Bernice married a no-good-account poor farmer. Emil knew nothing about farming or making a living. He—well, no need to go into all that just now."

"But I need to know everything. Please, oh, please." Her eyes welled up with tears again. "My mother, your aunt?"

"Courtney, I'd let you see your mother, but it's quite impossible."

"Is she living in Europe? Australia? Where?"

Lois stood then and walked over to the window, looking out. "Your mama loved you. You need to know that."

Courtney's heart jumped. "I was loved? I heard that the house was condemned and that my family moved on. I'm hoping you know where."

"Yes, the place was condemned and is barely standing." Lois paused, as if searching for the right words. "You were born in my husband's mother's house."

"Oh, my." Getting closer gave Courtney a heady feeling. "I thank you so much, and if I could come back after lunchtime, that's fine. Right now I'd just like to walk around on the grounds where my mother once lived and played."

"And died."

"*Died?*" Courtney could never explain the sinking sensation she felt at hearing the news that she would now never see her mother face-to-face. Never would there be a hug, a kiss, an exchange of facts over the years. No declarations of love. How could she stand it?

Chapter 18

H ow—did she die?"

Lois looked away, tears filling her eyes. "Your mother died three years after you were born, three years after her beloved baby—you— were taken from her arms."

"She didn't want to give me up?"

"Not hardly. She loved you more than life. If you only knew how many lovely things she made before you were born. Lacy little sacques, nightgowns, a crocheted bonnet with pink ribbons—"

"I have one of the nightgowns with pink crocheting." Courtney swallowed hard, thinking of her mother painstakingly making such beautiful things for her.

"She knew you'd be a girl. She saved some of the money she made from keeping house for the Whitfields and had my mother buy flannel so she could make a blanket. We bought the flannel in Belleville. She hid everything, not wanting to rile Uncle Emil any further. She also hoped her father might change his mind, might let her keep you; but he was afraid you would have the same affliction, and he couldn't stand to have another 'crazy' in his house."

"A 'crazy'?" She shivered. Wasn't that what Dorcas had said, too?

"He was very superstitious and thought she had the devil in her. Many a times she was beaten. It was because of this she started going out with boys, boys she knew would never marry her, but would love her, even if only for an hour." Lois hesitated. "You have no idea how much this hurts to tell you, how I've kept it inside me all these years. The only pretty part of the picture was the fact that a childless couple adopted Vannah's child and gave her a good home—"

"Vannah?" Courtney said the name twice. It had a nice sound, a different sound. Then she remembered Dorcas had called her Sherry. "Maybe we're not talking about the same person. I heard she went by Sherry."

"Oh, that. She lived in a dream world and thought Sherry sounded more romantic. The family called her Vannah, her given name."

"I need to know how she died, all the details, if you don't mind." Courtney looked at her ring finger. The imprint was there as Steven's engagement ring had been on her finger for two months. She had had to give it back. How could she keep something so precious, so wonderful, when she had no right to it? She was just plain, common white trash.

"The important message is that your mother loved you with all her heart and soul. She was forced into giving you up, but believe me, that was far better than the life you would have had under the Watt roof."

"If only I'd known her. The photo you mentioned?"

"It's in my special album upstairs. I'll go fetch it. I also have something else for you."

Courtney set her cup down. The coffee was cold, but it was wet and made it so she could swallow. "I very much want anything my mother had or made."

Courtney waited as doors closed and a shuffling noise ensued. Then the footsteps came back down.

"Here it is." She bent over Courtney while she looked at it. "This is me on the right and my brother on the left. Your mother, shorter than us, is in the middle."

Courtney held the photo as a combination of joy and love welled up inside her. Her birth mother. What a nice smile. She felt her own mouth. Yes, she had her mother's mouth. Very definitely.

"You look some like her. Same build, and yes, your mouth is the same. But you are so refined by comparison. Happy. With a confident air. All things Vannah never knew in her short life."

Boots stomped outside, and Lois jumped up. "I forgot the lunch, but it'll just take a second to microwave the soup. Excuse me."

She looked at the photo again, wondering if Lois had found the other object she'd mentioned. She'd take anything, even a silly drawing from second grade. Voices sounded, and Lois tried to appease the deeper voice.

"Not that soup again, Loie. I was hoping for a couple of your thick sandwiches."

"It'll just take a second, Mel."

And then he was in the living room, staring at her. "So? You've come looking for your heritage, have ya?" A short, broad-shouldered man looked at her out of intense brown eyes. Courtney felt a fear rush over her and grasped the sides of her chair.

She stood. "I'm Courtney Adams and my mother was—"

"I know who your mother was. I knew about you, too."

"Mel, the sandwiches are ready," Lois called out.

"I'll be there in a minute." He strode over in stocking feet and touched her chin. "You look like your mother. Very much so."

"You knew her, too?"

"Of course. Everyone knows everyone in Darby. My dad bought this land from the Shermans, who had rented it to your grandpa."

Courtney's head spun. It was all so confusing. How could she ever keep things straightened out?

"We used to run around. Your mother's brother, me, Lois, and a few other kids." He looked serious. "That was a long time ago now. Nobody knew for the longest time that Vannah was pregnant. She kept it well hidden."

"Mel, don't you think—"

He waved Lois away. "That's the one thing about being my own boss. My time's my own."

"Yes, but—"

He thumped the table and glared. "Wrap it up. Or, better yet, ask our guest to have lunch with us."

Courtney wished she could just disappear. She sensed hostility between this couple and didn't want to be caught right in the middle of it, nor did she want to be the cause of it. Perhaps she should come back tomorrow.

"I—really should probably go."

"I can meet you at the bakery in town tomorrow morning," Lois said, a bit too anxiously, Courtney thought. "We can talk more, and I'll give you the few things I kept. Since we were cousins and all, it was decided I should have her belongings. And one such gift is something I know she'd want you to have."

Courtney hurried out of the farmhouse and down the steps. Yes, meeting at a restaurant was a much better idea. She felt relief, yet fear, and she wasn't sure why. Surely God wouldn't have had her come all this way for nothing.

The blistering sun shone down on her back, making her glad to be in the car and moving again. She thought she saw a face at the curtained window but couldn't be sure.

She drove around until hunger forced her to drop in at a small drive-in in Okawville, the largest town outside of Belleville. She sat in the cool corner of the small café and chewed on French fries. Her search had all but ended. She was free to go home tomorrow. Or the next day. If Lois would just keep in touch. And if she could tell her where she could find other members of her family. This was all so new to her. The idea that she had cousins and maybe aunts and uncles. But her mother was dead. Her dream of being held, being told she was loved, would not come true now. Epileptic. Her mother had been taunted for her disease, made to feel she was unworthy of love. If only Courtney could have seen her just once and told her she loved her, thanked her for giving her up to a loving adoptive couple.

"Ma'am, are you okay?" a voice was at her elbow. "I asked if you wanted anything else."

Courtney looked at the young girl with pimples on her face. "I—no—that is, I am just fine and don't need anything."

"Refill on the soda?"

Courtney nodded. "Yes, a refill would be nice."

She found herself thinking about meeting Lois tomorrow.

❧

Steven drove faster than the speed limit as he headed back toward the city.

He'd had enough of farm life. Enough of this countryside, the cornfields, and the searing heat. He couldn't wait to get back to Portland and back to work—so he could forget. Yet a voice made him stop and think.

Patience. All of God's children need to learn patience. It's truly a virtue.

He thumped the steering wheel. Patience be hanged. He'd been more than patient. He'd been loving, waiting, yearning, wanting, and hoping. Yes, above all, hoping that Courtney would find what she was after and that she'd be able to get on with her life—their life—and want them to make a life together. He loved her so very much.

Sometimes you have to let things go, free them.

He'd freed her all right. She wasn't his, perhaps had never been his. Why had it taken him so long to figure it out? Courtney didn't want marriage. Not now. At least not to him. He felt the ring in his jeans pocket. He'd never give it to anyone else, though he hoped God would lead another woman his way—and soon.

An impossible hurt consumed him.

Belleville was out of the way, but he felt the need to go to a larger city, get lost, and think about things. He already knew there'd be no flight to Portland until morning. He called Jeff, who said things were fine. No big problems yet. And Alice was working in the office, handling calls as if she'd been there all the time.

"I'll be back tomorrow, Jeff. Think you can hang on until then?"

"Courtney?"

"Don't ask."

"Okay, man. Just thought you might plan on staying another day or so. We're doing okay. People don't mind waiting. I even helped one lady with a problem over the phone."

"Good for you, Jeff. You get a raise."

There was a chuckle at the other end. "I knew you'd say that."

Steven hung up and pulled into the nearest restaurant. It offered steaks on the billboard, and somehow he felt like eating a ten-ounce medium rare. And then he'd find a motel and watch a movie before going to sleep.

But he couldn't get Courtney out of his mind. As he picked at his salad, he missed her so much—wanted her with him. The waitress had a nice, warm smile and gave him the idea she'd be happy to see him when she got off. He might not have thought about it twice, but she mentioned the time her shift ended. He'd never been into picking up women, but the idea got to him now. Maybe he could put Courtney from his mind.

She was waiting outside the restaurant when he left. The night air was balmy, almost sticky.

"Could you give a girl a lift?" she asked.

"Sure. Hop in."

They chatted while he drove the miles to her home. "I suppose you think I sidle up to all the men."

He grinned. "The thought had occurred to me."

"Well, I don't. It's just that you looked so lonely and sad, and I don't like to see a nice man like you sad."

"I have reasons."

"You aren't from around here, are you?"

"No. I'm here on business from Portland, Oregon. I go home tomorrow."

"No chance of staying or perhaps coming back?"

He pulled up at the house she'd pointed out.

"No, I doubt I'll ever be back here."

"Just thought I'd ask. No harm in asking, now, is there?"

He waited while she got out of the car, and then she leaned over. "I thank you for the ride and the conversation. If you get lonely enough, you know where I live now."

Steven pulled back onto the main road and sighed heavily. He could have had a date. He could have forgotten about Courtney for one night, but something compelled him to move on; a voice seemed to say that this was not right, and he knew it wasn't. Grams would have been mortified. *Give Courtney time,* the voice said. *She just needs time.*

What was the rush, anyway? He'd waited this long without a soul mate; he guessed he could wait a while longer and make sure he found the right one. God would nudge him when he needed to make a move. Even so, he'd never give the ring to anyone else. It was Courtney's ring. It would always be Courtney's ring. Somehow he figured Grams would understand.

Chapter 19

Courtney, who usually ran late, was right on time, but Lois was already there, leaning against her car. A small box was on the hood. Courtney waved as she hurried over. "You're early."

"Farmers get up early," Lois said with a half smile. "Mel left on a business trip to St. Louis. I have the whole day to relax and talk to you."

Courtney felt exhilarated. "I say let's get some coffee and maybe something to eat."

"I've eaten," Lois said, "but I'll have one of Hilda's cookies. She bakes the best."

The bakery, with a long room extending along the west wall, was nearly vacant. Tim McGraw sang from a small radio perched on a shelf.

They took their coffees and went to the far corner. Courtney ordered a cinnamon roll, lightly warmed, and Lois got a chocolate chip cookie.

Courtney scooted across the booth. "I am so excited about this. I could hardly sleep."

"We're cousins, you know," Lois said. "I never, ever thought this day would come."

Nodding, Courtney looked pleased. "Cousins. You have no idea how good that sounds to me. I've always dreamed of having a cousin."

Lois smiled. "I have lots of cousins but rarely see any of them. Everyone has moved on to greener pastures, as the saying goes."

"I can hardly wait to see what you brought."

Lois's green eyes sparkled. "I don't have much, but what I have is yours."

"Oh!" Courtney was so taken back, she could scarcely speak. "I would be happy to get anything."

Opening the box, Lois handed over a crudely painted picture. "I have no idea why or how I even got this. It was in Vannah's personal belongings, the few things Aunt Bernice didn't keep."

Courtney studied the painting, the kind kids paint in first grade. Her mother loved blue, as there was dark, light, and medium blue splashed across the now-stiff paper. A yellow sun peered out of one corner. A green tree was in the middle with red apples in the branches. A girl sat in a swing, her legs stretched out. She held it up. "Do you think this is supposed to be my mother?"

Lois nodded. "Yes, I'm sure it is. Most kids do self-portraits or family members at that age."

The waitress came with the huge cinnamon roll and several pats of butter. "And here's a carafe of coffee." She smiled at Lois. "How're you guys doing, anyway? Seems I never see you."

"Fine, Kristi, just fine." She turned to Courtney. "This is my long-lost cousin, Courtney."

"Hello." The young woman smiled broader than before. "Pleased to meet you. Are you from around here?"

Courtney shook her head. "Afraid not. I live in Portland, Oregon."

"Oregon!" Her eyes widened. "Goodness, but you're a long way from home."

Lois stirred cream into her coffee. "Yes, she is. In fact—well—I have to look into this, but she might be related to you, also."

"Go on now!"

"I'll let you know after I think about it for a minute," Lois said.

"Are you sure about that?" Courtney asked, suddenly more interested in the young waitress.

"Listen, I declare, everyone is related to someone in this area. We don't have many people moving here, and so many stay on, so cousins marry cousins, and what do you know? More cousins."

"First cousins?" Courtney asked.

"Oh, I'm sure not. First cousins can't marry, as you must know."

Courtney buttered her roll and took a small bite. Her heart raced so much she could scarcely swallow. It was almost too much for her to comprehend. Family. How she'd always longed for family besides Aunt Agnes and an uncle she never got to see.

"You're not married?" Lois asked then, glancing at Courtney's now-bare finger.

"I was engaged."

"Was?"

"Yes. We broke up just yesterday, just before I arrived at your house."

Lois set her cup down hard. "You mean he's from around here?"

"Oh, no. He's a native Oregonian and just followed me here."

"He did? Now *that* sounds romantic."

Courtney felt a small tug at her heart. Maybe it sounded romantic, but their parting words had been anything but romantic.

"He doesn't understand my quest."

"Quest?"

"Yes, quest. My mission to find my birth mother."

"Well, you've found her, so what's the problem now?"

Courtney took a long sip of her coffee. "It's just that I cannot marry without knowing my mother's medical background, and I am so hoping you can answer some of my questions."

"Then what?"

"I'll know if I should marry or not."

Lois leaned forward. "My dear cousin, one can always marry, no matter what. Perhaps you should not have children; that's your decision."

"This is true, but I *want* children. Doesn't everyone?"

Lois shrugged. "Mel did not."

"No? And?"

"We've never had any."

Courtney didn't know what to say. She'd just always felt that life wouldn't be complete without having two or three babies.

"So, back to why you must know about your mother's health. Do go on."

Soon Courtney was telling her about the mysterious illness and how she'd had a series of tests with nothing conclusive.

"Did you have seizures?"

Courtney recoiled, remembering that night, just as if it had been yesterday. Waking in a sweat, she'd twisted and turned, and soon Alice had been there with cold cloths, wiping her forehead. And then she'd convulsed, and minutes later she was wrapped in a heavy blanket and on her way to the emergency room of Woodland Park Hospital.

"I do not have epilepsy. That was ruled out. My convulsion happened because of my sudden rise in fever. The doctor said that was not unusual. It's never happened again, and he said probably it won't."

Lois nodded. "Then for sure you do not have epilepsy."

"But what if I'm a carrier and my child is born with it?"

"And what if your child is born with cystic fibrosis? Or with muscular dystrophy or contracts leukemia when he's two years old like my friend's child? Don't you realize everything is a risk? Nobody can be assured, just as you might get hit right out in front of this bakery and die on the spot."

Courtney shivered. "I know, but—"

"No, I don't think you know."

"My mother definitely had epilepsy?"

Lois nodded. "She didn't go to school on a regular basis. She had grand mal seizures. The seizures scared everyone, and most of the kids shunned her. It was awful for her."

"And her parents?"

"You probably heard from Dorcas Whitfield that they were superstitious."

"Yes, I did."

"That's why she couldn't keep you." Tears welled in Lois's eyes. "Such stupidity. I cannot imagine carrying a baby for nine months, then being forced to give it up."

"I always wondered how my mother could give me up, or why—"

"Well, wonder no more. She made all those baby things for you, hoping to see you wearing them, hoping that her father would reconsider. Of course he had the final say in everything that went on in that family."

Lois set the drawing aside. "I also have a photo of the family, without Vannah. Who knows where she was."

Courtney studied the faces of the people standing in a yard, a big, old house in the background. Lois pointed to the tallest person. "That's Emil. And George. Miller. Your grandmother Bernice, and the baby, Clyde."

"My mother was the only daughter?"

"Yes, which was just as well. Emil needed boys to work the land, to farm. Vannah could do nothing some days. The least bit of stress caused her to have a seizure."

Hundreds of questions ran through Courtney's mind. There was so much she wanted to know, needed to find out. Her mother had been sickly all her life? What might have happened if she'd gone to a doctor in Chicago or a large city? Someone who specialized in epilepsy?

As if reading her mind, Lois continued, "A doctor was suggested in St. Louis. That's closer than any other large city here in Illinois, but Emil said they couldn't take the time or the entire day lollygagging when nothing could cure the seizures—"

"Not cure, but control," Courtney broke in.

"I know, honey. Believe me, Aunt Bernice did everything she could to try to convince her husband otherwise."

Courtney felt sick suddenly. Perhaps it was the cinnamon roll. Too much, too sweet on an empty stomach, but she knew it was far more than that. "If only he could have been persuaded."

"You might have grown up here? You might have had Emil's hand on your backside not once, but twice a day? Is that the kind of life you are missing now?"

Courtney winced. "I never thought of it like that."

"Well, you should. Emil was a *mean* man. The boys left as soon as they could when the house was condemned."

"I heard he was mean."

"Yes. The landlord, who turned out to be my father-in-law, didn't want to fix the house up. The only way to get Emil out was to have the county say it wasn't fit to live in. And it did look pretty bad."

"Where was my mother?"

"She died the month before."

Courtney refilled her cup with coffee. This was the part she had to know but wasn't sure she wanted to know now.

"How did my mother die and where was she?"

Lois took a bite of the roll Courtney had pushed to the edge of the table. "I'll just have a taste since you're through."

"Sure, go ahead."

"Vannah must have had a seizure as she was coming downstairs that winter morning. Whatever—she tripped and fell headfirst."

Courtney shut her eyes tight as it soaked into her mind.

"She was dead when the ambulance arrived."

"Dead from the seizure?" Courtney asked.

"I don't know if it was the fall or the seizure. No autopsy was performed. You had to know Emil. The EMT, a friend of Mel's, said she had a broken neck."

Tears slid down Courtney's cheeks and onto the table. "I can't believe something could happen like that. And nobody even cared!"

"Yes, people cared." Lois touched her hand. "Believe me, a lot of people cared about your mother. A lot of us loved her."

"But why couldn't someone do something?"

"You just didn't cross Emil, nor did you interfere with someone else's business. A schoolteacher tried, back in fifth grade I think it was, and Emil had her fired."

"But he couldn't do that."

"Oh, yes, he could and did. It's not what you know but who you know, and someone on the school board apparently owed Emil a favor."

Courtney felt the tightness expand in her stomach. It was too unbelievable. "I just wish I could have known her."

"She was gentle, Courtney. And just in case you're wondering, she named you before they took you from her arms."

"She did?"

Lois handed over a sheet of paper. "Here are some scribblings I found in a notebook. She wasn't sure which one to choose, so she wrote down several names. Isn't it strange how she liked names starting with *C?*"

Courtney took the paper and stared. Her name wasn't among the list, but there was Carole. Chastity. Camille. Catherine. Chelsea. Candy. Charlotte. Cynthia. Then one was circled. Cerise.

"Cerise?" Courtney exclaimed. "That's a color. It's deep to purplish red. I think it's French."

"It was your mother's favorite color. They buried her in a dress my mother made special for her. It was cerise with a white lace collar."

"Courtney Cerise," Courtney said aloud. "That's going to be my new middle name. I think it only fitting, don't you?"

"Would you like to go to the cemetery?"

The breath caught in Courtney's throat. "I—never thought of that. Of course I want to."

"And we can drive out by the old house."

"It's still standing?"

"Oh, yes. It's just five miles beyond my place and about three from the cemetery. We'll do the cemetery first.

"I'll give you the diary she kept. You can read it on the plane ride back to Portland."

"I won't be able to wait until then," Courtney said. "I'll read it today. Tonight."

Kristi brought the bill and both hands reached for it. "Let this be my treat to my newfound cousin," Lois said. "If you want, you can buy lunch later."

The sunshine bore out of another clear blue sky as Courtney followed Lois to her car. She'd insisted on driving, since she knew where to go. They made arrangements to leave Courtney's car parked around back in the alley.

"I have to buy flowers," Courtney said then. "A bouquet to put on the grave."

"There are no florists here or in the next town. We farmers just don't buy enough to keep them in business."

"What about the store? We could go and buy a flat of marigolds—"

"Not this time of year, but we can pick some of mine."

And so they did. They were short-stemmed, but the bright orange was beautiful. There was one purple hydrangea left on the bush. "Almost as if God wanted my mother to have her favorite color," Courtney said.

Lois nodded. "It's a nice touch."

They got back into the car. "It's not far. A small plot out at the edge of Darby. If you didn't know to turn, you'd miss it altogether."

"What did my grandmother do when Vannah died?"

"Aunt Bernice went into deep depression, hon, the likes of which I've never seen. She blamed Emil. I know that's why they left the county, and with the house being condemned, there was nothing holding them here."

The cemetery was less than an acre in size, and Lois went directly to the plot. There was no headstone, just a marker on the ground.

Courtney fell to her knees. She'd so wanted to meet her mother face-to-face, hold her close, tell her she loved her; but there was no mother, only someone buried in the ground. Someone under this marker with her name and birth and death dates etched lightly on the concrete, twenty-one years ago.

Courtney traced the letters with her fingers: *Vannah Louise Watt, Born March 31, 1960, Died April 5, 1978*. Courtney arranged the small bouquet just right, making a circle around the stone.

"She was eighteen and six days," Lois was saying. "Eighteen and an unhappy, lost soul."

"Did she know God?"

Lois smiled. "Funny that that hasn't come up before. Yes. She did. All the kids attended church, and Vannah accepted the Lord as her Savior one Sunday morning a couple of years before she got pregnant with you."

"Thank You, God," Courtney said, realizing she hadn't thanked the Lord for leading her to this cousin, to this small plot in a cemetery that contained the remains of her mother.

"Let's go to the old homestead," Lois suggested.

Courtney got up from the grave, brushing dried grass from her knees. "Yes, I'd like that very much."

The house, once tall and magnificent, was a weather-beaten gray as if it had never seen a coat of paint. Windows were broken out. Rotting steps led up to a porch that ran along the entire front of the house. It, too, was caving in.

Courtney hopped out of the car and ran up to the steps.

"I don't think I'd go in there," Lois said, appearing at her side. "You could fall right through the floor."

"I have to go inside, Lois. I wonder if the steps around back are sturdier."

"Let's go see."

Courtney hurried around back, stepping over brambles, thistles, old lumber, rusty cans, and hubcaps. "Yes, these steps are better." She was up the steps in no time. It was imperative she at least look inside the house.

The rooms were bare except for dust, cobwebs, an old broken-down table, and stacks of newspapers. The late morning breeze blew through the broken-out windows. Then Courtney spied the staircase.

"The bedrooms are upstairs?"

"Yes. Your mother's was at the west end of the house." Lois took one look at the decaying steps and said she'd be outside. "I'm going to have a sneezing fit if I stay in here any longer. Be careful and walk on the outside of the steps."

"I'll just be a minute," Courtney replied.

Slowly, deliberately, she climbed the stairway, her hand clutching the railing. It was this stairway her mother had fallen from. Sadness welled up inside her. If only things could have been different.

Her mother's bedroom had tattered shreds for curtains hanging from one dingy window, the only one still intact. Courtney figured the bed would have been in the middle of the room. This was the room she'd been born in, the room her mother stayed in, slept in, dreamed in, and cried in. She'd also read here and wrote in a diary.

Courtney closed her eyes, saying a fervent prayer. "Lord, thank You for bringing me here. Thank You for letting me be in this room. And if my mother's in heaven, let her know I love her and wish I could have known her."

She took one more look before backing out of the room. If she came again, the house might be gone. She wondered why it hadn't already been torn down, but God knew of her need to see it, to walk up the steps to this room.

Lois was leaning against the car door, fanning herself. "You look like you've just seen a ghost."

"No—spirit," Courtney responded. "I've just been with my mother's spirit." She brushed damp hair back from the side of her face. "Thanks, Lois, for bringing me here. You have no idea what it means to me."

The older woman slipped an arm around Courtney's shoulder. "I'm glad you came to Darby."

"I am, too. I want to keep in touch," Courtney said. "I really do."

"And I with you."

"Perhaps you can come to Oregon sometime."

"Honey, people around here do not travel. I've never been farther west than the arch in St. Louis or farther east than Germantown."

"Oh. Then I will come here again."

"With your husband, I hope."

Courtney felt the fear again. "I don't know about that. He must be thoroughly disgusted with me. I returned the ring. He'll find someone else."

"Maybe not." Lois headed back to the car. "I'm betting he'll forget all that and be more than ready to give you the ring back."

Courtney wondered if he was worried about her, if he had flown back to Portland and gotten in touch with Alice. She hoped Alice wouldn't be upset. She owed her mother so much. Her life had been easy and filled with love and tenderness. How fortunate she was. She'd never realized just how much until now.

"I think you should call your—what did you say his name was?"

"Steven. Steven Spencer."

Lois smiled. "Courtney Cerise Spencer. It has a good ring to it, don't you think?"

"I'm still not sure about having a baby—"

"That's a decision you can make later."

"Later?" Courtney looked away. God was good. God had answered many prayers. He'd healed her that time eight years ago from the illness. He'd given her loving parents. He'd helped her locate her mother and her family. He'd brought Steven into her life. He'd given her a good job. She'd had her father's presence for the first twenty-one years of her life. Why couldn't she trust God with this one last thing, to give her a healthy child to love?

And then it hit her. What if the child wasn't healthy? Did that matter? She thought of a family at church who'd had a Down syndrome child. Little Billy was the love of everyone. He was so loving and good-natured that people couldn't wait to see him, and when he had wanted to be an acolyte, Pastor Sam had agreed. "He will do a fine job," he said. And so he had. They just made sure his shoelaces were tied before going down the aisle, then Pastor suggested buying him shoes with Velcro.

Courtney looked over at Lois. "The fear I've felt is gone. I can't explain it, but suddenly I know that, no matter what, I would love any child God gave me."

"Just as your mother loved you with all her heart and soul."

They drove back to Darby and sat and talked before ordering sandwiches back at the bakery. "I wish you the very best, Courtney," Lois said, "and by all means, call that young man of yours and apologize." She got into her car and waved as she backed out of the parking lot.

Courtney smiled, for she intended to do exactly that. On the seat beside her, a small box held all the treasures that would be dear to her the rest of her life. They would be passed down to her children and their children.

She wondered about Steven. What would she say? Would he forgive her? Or would he have given up and moved on with his life? She couldn't blame him if that was the case.

Pulling over, Courtney removed the cellular phone from her purse. Her fingers trembled as she started to dial the familiar number, but a tap on the window made her jump. She turned to look into the face of Melvin. He wasn't smiling.

Chapter 20

Courtney was shocked to see Melvin. Had he been waiting for her? If so, why? Dressed in jeans, a clean white shirt, cowboy boots, and a rumpled hat, he motioned toward his truck. Courtney's heart tightened. *This might not be safe,* ran through her mind. What would she do if he suddenly drove off with her? She didn't like the dark, brooding eyes. Yesterday he had looked angry enough to hit her, and his disposition apparently hadn't changed.

"Hello," she finally said.

"I need to talk to you. Now."

He flung the passenger door open. She hesitated only a second. One didn't argue with a command like that. She prayed that it would be all right.

"I'm not sure if I—"

"What? Want to go with me?" He smiled. "Not much like your mother, I see."

"What do you mean by that?" *What did Melvin have to do with my mother?*

He helped her up into the high seat, closed the door, and hopped in beside her but didn't turn the key.

"I have something to say, and I ain't going to say it twice. What you do is up to you, of course."

"Does this concern my mother?"

"None other." He stared out the window, carefully avoiding her gaze.

"I'd known Vannah all my life. She was just there. One of the kids. Like the other girls. But she wasn't like the other girls." He paused, as if needing to catch his breath. "Not at all."

"What was she like?" Courtney reached over, touching his arm. "I want to know. I *need* to know."

He turned and scowled. "Why do you think I'm here?"

Courtney leaned back and sighed. "I have no earthly idea. All I know is that you seem to be angry with me—"

"Because people shouldn't go nosing around."

"You mean because I asked Lois about my mother? Because I am trying to find out who I am, you are holding that against me?"

"I know you mean well. Maybe I'd be doin' the same thing." He removed his hat and rubbed the top of his head. His hair was sparse and turning gray.

"You're not going to tell me—"

"I might if you'd stop interrupting. This ain't easy for me, believe me. Please hear me out. It'll only take a minute if you keep quiet."

Somehow Courtney wondered if this was going to be one of the longest speeches he'd ever made.

"I think your mother was one of the sweetest girls I'd ever known. I loved her, and that's the God's truth."

"Loved her?"

He turned and scowled. "I asked youse not to interrupt."

"Sorry."

"I told my pa one night that I loved Vannah, and I thought he'd come unglued. Said I had to start thinking about more important things like farming and learning how to find a wife that'd be a help to me."

Courtney leaned back, the knot in her stomach growing tighter.

"I knew that Jon was no good for her. I tried to warn her, but she was in love with that guy, his car and all. Then, too, she saw him every day, working over in that big, fancy house. She didn't know how I felt about her because I couldn't tell her."

"When she turned up in the family way, she came to me, begged me to tell him. Well, I did, though I knew it wouldn't do one bit of good. His ma wouldn't let him marry her, just as my pa wouldn't let me even date her. Sure enough, I told Jon, but ol' rich boy wanted no part of it."

"And what did you do?" Courtney couldn't help it. She had to know.

"We never thought anyone would come a-looking. We heard that the baby had been adopted by an air force couple, and they were moving out of the area."

"Alice and Carl. My parents."

"Whatever." He still wouldn't look in Courtney's direction.

"But why come and tell me this now? You could have said it yesterday."

"Oh, no, I couldn't have."

"Why not?"

"Because Lois don't know."

"Lois doesn't know what?"

"That I loved Vannah with all my heart and soul. I never tol' her. Never intended to. What's the point? And I asked Lois to marry me a month after your mother died, but I never, ever forgot Vannah, and I doubt I ever will. I should have stood up to Pa, taken her away, done something."

It was suddenly clear. Melvin had loved her mother. He'd wanted to marry her, wanted to raise another man's child. Was it because of this that he did not want children?

"I will never speak of this to Lois or anyone, I promise."

"Good. You can leave now. No need to talk to Lois anymore." He turned and made her look at him. "Do you want some money? I ain't got much, but there's some saved that Lois don't know about."

Courtney couldn't believe he'd ask. Why would she take money from this man?

"I don't need money to keep me quiet."

"Here. I want you to have this." He pressed an envelope in her hand. "I've kept this all these years but want you to have it."

Courtney took the envelope and started to open it.

"No. Wait until I'm gone. Then look."

He hopped out of the truck, came to her side, and opened the door. "You know, you have her hair. Definitely. It's long and shiny, just like hers was. It really took me back when I saw you standing there in the front room."

Before she could answer, he jumped in behind the wheel, and the truck sped back down the highway toward home. Melvin could have been her father. He wasn't, but he'd loved her mother; and just knowing that someone had loved her like that meant more than anything. Her hand touched her hair. Her mother's hair. She had her mother's hair.

She thought of Steven. If only she could talk to him now, feel his arm go around her protectively. If only. Her life seemed to be filled with if onlys right now.

Courtney went back to her car and got in. "Oh, God, thank You for letting me know this about my mother. And now, please help me to know what's right; give me some answers."

Her fingers clutched the envelope close, but she would wait to open it until after she called Steven.

Chapter 21

Courtney had to work up the courage again to call Steven. Finally she dialed his cellular number and waited. He answered on the second ring, almost as if he had been waiting.

"Steven?"

"Courtney? Are you all right? Where are you? Can I come to see you?" His questions came out like bullets hitting a target.

"Courtney?" he repeated.

"I don't know where to begin," she finally answered, her fingers gripping the receiver hard.

"It doesn't matter. Can I come to be with you?"

"But you're too far away. I mean, you went back to Portland—"

"Wrong!"

"You didn't go back?"

"I'm in Belleville. I just couldn't leave, Courtney. I don't care if I lose the biggest contract in Portland. No way could I desert you now."

"I don't know what to say." Her heart thudded so loudly, she was certain he could hear it over the wires.

"Say nothing unless it's 'I love you, Steven.' "

She laughed then. "That's the easiest part. Forgive me?"

"There's nothing to forgive. Now, where are you?"

"Back in Clancy."

"Sit tight. I'll be there. Should only take thirty minutes, forty-five tops."

Courtney decided to stay in the little park at the edge of town. Steven's voice had warmed her heart and her spirit. She didn't deserve him. She'd never deserved him. But, then, she didn't deserve to be God's child, either. But, thank goodness, her being saved did not rely on what she deserved.

With trembling fingers, she opened the small box Lois had so lovingly put together for her.

A few poems were on top. She read them with tears in her eyes. The first rhymed, and as Courtney read, she felt the grief her mother must have felt as a young, frightened girl.

> *A little baby I now carry*
> *Though I can never marry*
> *I pray she or he will always know*

How much I cared, but could not show
O little child, I cannot keep
Surely you know how I weep
To another home you will go
But it was not my idea,
No, never my idea

Courtney could read no more. With tear-filled eyes, she laid the poems at the bottom and removed a small, leather-bound green book. *Five-Year Diary,* it said in gold letters.

Dare she open it? Could she bear to know what her mother's thoughts were? Her fears? She sat as afternoon sunlight poured through the window of the car. She prayed. She talked to her mother just as if she were in the car with her.

The diary was worn, the edges tattered. The writing was clear and written in a childish scrawl. Courtney's fingers touched the words. Precious words she would read. Soon she would know her mother; and as she looked again at the faded snapshot of a laughing child in the middle, her heart tightened. Just one touch was all she'd ever wanted. But it wasn't to be. This had to be enough.

Papa has never understood me. He hates me. I'm only a burden, and now I am bringing another burden into the world.

I can feel my baby move inside me. It's like magic. I put my hand on the bulge, and it kicks back. I love my little baby so much.

Courtney shut the book. She couldn't read anymore. She took the small envelope and carefully removed the purple ribbon. It was frayed on the edges as if it had been tied and untied many times.

A woven ring of white daisies dried to a fine powder was inside. Her mother had woven this bracelet of daisies for Mel? It had meant so much to him, he'd kept it all these years, yet knew how important it would be to Courtney, Vannah's child.

She wrapped it back and retied the ribbon. Such love he had felt and still felt. Could she feel that deeply toward Steven? Somehow she knew he cared for her in that wonderful way.

Courtney closed the diary. She'd read more later. She could only take so much at one sitting. "If only things had been different," she said out loud. "If only you had been allowed to keep me, Mama, but God in His infinite wisdom wanted me to belong to someone else. To bring love and laughter to a home. And you, Mother, did that. If it weren't for you and your unselfish desire to give me to others, Alice and Carl would not have known such happiness.

"What you did was the ultimate sacrifice. Just as our God gave up His Son. None of us can know how that must have felt, not unless we were there."

A tap at the window made her jump. Steven's face loomed bigger than life as he motioned for her to unlock the door.

"Honey! Oh, honey." Then she was out of the car and into his arms. "I've been so worried. I couldn't sleep last night. Just kept praying I was doing the right thing. Then God gave me peace of mind. It was as if He was saying, 'My son, didn't I tell you to be patient? You must learn patience.' "

"Steven, I wouldn't blame you if you never wanted to see me again."

"Hush. I don't want to hear that." He lifted her chin, his mouth touching hers with a gentle kiss. "There. I just prayed I'd be able to hold you one more time, kiss you once more."

"I'm not afraid anymore, Steven." She raised her eyes to his. "It's all so wonderful. I can hardly wait to tell you."

"Shall we go somewhere or just sit in the car?"

"I feel more comfortable here."

"Okay." He came around to the passenger side.

An hour later, completely spent, Courtney leaned against Steven's shoulder, liking the feel of his arm around her, liking the smell of him, the words he'd spoken. It didn't matter that she hadn't known her father. It never had mattered.

"I haven't told you everything," Courtney said then.

"There's more?"

"Of course."

"Start in then."

She took a deep breath. "You know how worried I've been about having, well, you know, a family and all?"

"Yes."

"Lois told me that nobody ever has any guarantee, and God laid it on my heart that no matter what, you and I'd love our child, even if she or he were epileptic."

"Oh, honey, I've said that all along. Besides, there have been so many advances in medicine this past decade that our child would never suffer as your real mother did."

"Do you suppose I should call Mom and tell her we're on our way home?"

"Yes." Steven removed the box from his coat pocket. "But after this is back in place."

The stone shone as he slipped it back on her finger. "Here to stay this time, right?"

"Yes, Steven. Here to stay."

He lifted her face for a kiss. And then another.

"There's something we have to do before we leave."

"And that is?"

"You have to meet Dorcas. My paternal grandmother."

"Lead the way."

Dorcas invited them in, and Courtney told her all that had happened. "I'll write you," she said. "I want to keep in touch."

They clung together, and Dorcas handed her a small box. "It's just a few things I thought you might like for keepsakes. A few photos of your father and a small quilt I made for him."

Courtney wiped away the tears gathering at the edge of her eyes. "Thank you so much. I love you." And they clung together again.

"You take good care of her for me," Dorcas said. "But I know you will. I'm just sorry for all that happened, my child. I hope you understand and can forgive me." Her eyes watered as she recalled how sick her son had been. "I couldn't bear to see him marry anyone at all. It was as if I knew he wouldn't live long here on Earth."

"It's over and done with," Courtney said. "I'm just glad I got to meet my real father's family."

She left with Dorcas in the doorway, waving.

And as the sun slipped behind a low layer of clouds, the couple held each other's hands while they skipped down the path toward the car.

Epilogue

Mrs. Alice Adams and the late Carl Adams
request your presence at the marriage
of their daughter
Courtney Cerise Adams
to
Steven Andrew Spencer
Saturday evening
December 18, 1999
At half past seven at
Parkrose Community Church
Reception following in the church fellowship hall.
RSVP

There. The last one is sealed and stamped," Courtney declared, "except this one that I must deliver in person."

"Gerta?" Alice looked puzzled. "Who is this, dear?"

"She's from the soup kitchen. You'll love her, Mom. She's a very sweet old lady and a good friend."

"Oh?" Her mother looked even more puzzled as she added her envelopes to the towering stack. "Any friend of yours is a friend of mine."

"The wedding of the year," Aunt Agnes said.

"And it will be. Yes, it will be." Courtney's eyes were shining.

"Mom, you sure you don't mind my changing my middle name legally to Cerise?"

"Of course not, darling. Now let's look at the beautiful wedding dress again."

"Gladly."

Alice removed it from the protective plastic bag. "It's just too beautiful."

Courtney held the full-length white taffeta gown to her cheek. The scoop neckline would show off the lovely necklace of pink Chinese sea pearls, a gift from Aunt Agnes. A double-tier veil, long white gloves, and dainty white satin slippers made the ensemble complete. White orchids and stephanotis made up the bridal bouquet. She'd seen a picture in a floral catalogue and knew that was what she wanted.

"If Dad were here, he'd make some comment such as, 'What a lovely gunnysack. Too bad they didn't have such things when your mother and I married.' "

"I miss him so much, Mom."

"I know, dear. So do I. But you can honor his memory by having the best marriage ever."

"I'm just glad I found some of my family," Courtney said.

Alice hugged her. "Yes, you finally *found* Courtney."

"Not that I was really lost."

"But you thought you were."

Courtney thought back to the six months when she was ill, how she'd asked God to spare her life because she had lots of living to do. "And I want to wear a white wedding dress and walk down the aisle and look longingly into the eyes of the man I will spend the rest of my life with," had been her prayer.

And God had granted that request.

The Sea
Beckons

With love and blessings to my five granddaughters:
Tawnisha, Jennifer, Samantha, Laura, and Tabitha

Chapter 1

Alice Adams sat in the office waiting for the phone to ring. It had been a slow morning, as Wednesdays often were. Two stacks of envelopes were ready to mail. One stack was invoices for the month of May for Spencer Computer Consultants, and the other was an advertisement for a sale on good, used computers. The back room had computers on the table, in all corners, and one chair held an old daisy wheel printer.

"Totally obsolete," Steven had said, "but you never know. We may be able to use some parts."

Alice glanced at the clock. Courtney, her daughter and only child, was at the obstetrician's office for a checkup and an ultrasound to determine her baby's gender. Alice preferred the old way of waiting until the baby's birth to know the sex. It was something to look forward to, but then nobody had asked her. She went along with whatever Courtney wanted. And one good way to look at it was she would know what color sweater to knit. The baby was expected November 21, a month before Courtney and Steven's first anniversary.

She was glad they had wanted a baby right away. Nothing could have made Alice happier. She'd so longed for a baby when she and Carl had first married, but it wasn't in God's plan. After several miscarriages, they'd decided to adopt, and Courtney was that child. Now Alice would be a grandma, and she could hardly contain her excitement.

Jeff whistled out in the hall. She knew it was Jeff because he always whistled "Puff the Magic Dragon." He was her son-in-law's right-hand man, and she was quite fond of him. He had a nice sense of humor and was respectful. So many young people weren't these days. But at fifty, Alice was "out of touch," as some put it.

"Hey, Mrs. Adams. I mean, Alice! I found a customer when I was at Maxson's." She had asked him to call her Alice, but he usually forgot.

"Oh, really?" She smiled. "As if you needed to drum up business."

"Yeah. My friend's father is visiting, and his laptop stopped working. I have it here. He'll stop by later this afternoon to pick it up."

Steven didn't need more customers; he was far busier than he wanted to be. He had put an ad in Sunday's Help Wanted column, looking for a second employee. Jeff had decided he wanted Saturdays off, imagine that. And of course Steven wanted to spend more time with Courtney and the baby, who would soon join their family.

The phone rang. Alice leaned over, catching it at the end of the first ring.

"Spencer Consultants—"

"Mom, it's me!"

Alice drew in a quick breath. "So you know what the baby is and everything's okay?"

"Yes, we're having—"

"No, don't tell me," Alice interrupted. "I want to wait until I see you in person. Maybe we can have a cup of coffee. Or is it orange juice you're drinking these days?"

"Mom, what say we take a walk over by Meier & Frank during your lunch break?"

Alice chuckled. "That doesn't have anything to do with the fact that they have one of the largest baby departments, does it?"

"Mom, no! Of course not. I don't suppose Steven is there?"

"No, honey, he has that job over on Swan Island. Said he'd be gone until five or so."

"I wish he could have come to the doctor's with me, but we'll celebrate tonight."

Alice looked out the window at the view over the Willamette. The river was still high from spring rains. The river ran through the downtown area, going north and south. A jet ski zipped by. Later in the day, pleasure boats would fill the water. A barge now moved slowly past. Usually offices with a view would be too costly, but Steven got a good deal because he knew the owner and was on his payroll to keep all his computers up and running.

"I'll meet you in an hour on the corner; that is, if Jeff will let me leave then."

Jeff's head shot up at the sound of his name. "I bet you and Courtney are going to buy out the baby store."

Alice tried to look shocked. "Jeff, how could you possibly think such a thing?"

She told her daughter good-bye. Jeff was writing on a business card and now held it up. "I say the baby's a boy!"

"You have a 50 percent chance of being right."

"Yeah, so I do." He bent back over the laptop.

Alice took a moment for a silent prayer of thanks. Thanks that Courtney had carried her child this long. It was a good indication. But since Courtney was not her natural child, there was no reason not to believe she'd have a full-term pregnancy.

She straightened her short salt-and-pepper hair and rose to get a cup of coffee. So much had happened in one short year. God had answered many prayers. If only Carl were here to feel this joy.

"There. I had an idea that would be it." Jeff cut through her thoughts. He was in the workroom, a large room with one big table and several smaller tables, all containing computers in various stages of being fixed.

"It just needed a good cleaning where the plug goes in. People never think about it. It's sort of like cleaning the earwax out of your ear. Here, call Leighton. He can pick it up anytime."

Jeff handed Alice a card. *Leighton Walker. Oysterville, Washington.*

"Oysterville? What's he doing here?"

Jeff shrugged. "Here on business, I guess. All that I know is he's an oysterman."

"An oysterman?"

"You know what oysters are. Someone has to grow them."

"They don't grow them, do they?"

"It's quite a process. You don't dig them like you do clams or fish for them like other seafood."

"I didn't know." She dialed a local number. A deep voice answered immediately.

"This is Alice at Spencer's Computer Consultants, and I have Mr. Walker's laptop ready."

"Yeah, that's me. Now that's what I call speedy. You say I can come pick it up now?"

"Anytime, Mr. Walker."

She gave directions to the downtown office. She wondered if he would arrive before she left to meet Courtney.

She had just reached for her lightweight jacket after adding lipstick to full lips—her Carl had always said she looked like she was pouting—when the knock sounded. Instinctively, Alice adjusted her skirt and collar. It was a nervous habit. She always wore a tailored suit to the office, though Steven said she could dress casually.

"Yes?"

"I'm Leighton Walker. Came to pick up my laptop."

Alice shivered unexpectedly as a pair of deep brown eyes met hers. It was as if in that second, Carl was smiling at her. He was the same height as Carl, a good six foot three. At five-nine, Alice felt more comfortable around tall men. But it was the crooked smile that made her face flush.

"Is there something wrong?"

He looked puzzled, and Alice had to laugh. "Oh, my, no. It's just that you remind me of someone."

"I'm not from around here."

"I know." She held up his card. "It says right here you're from Oysterville."

His frown disappeared as he appeared to relax. "Good deduction."

Jeff stuck his head around the corner. "It was like I thought. Just needed a cleaning."

"Well, Jeff, I sure appreciate this. Most places take a week or more. How much do I owe?" Leighton removed a wallet from his back pocket.

"Ten is fine."

"Ten? That's nothing."

"Only took me ten minutes." Jeff plugged the laptop in. "See, it comes right on. No problem."

Leighton extricated a ten-dollar bill and handed it to Alice. She was already writing him a receipt.

He folded it and placed it inside his wallet. A woman with a smile stared out of the top picture in the picture part of his wallet.

"Who do I remind you of?" he asked then.

Alice felt the color rise to her cheeks again as she looked away. "My late husband, Carl."

"Oh."

She nodded and pushed her chair in. "Yes. It's been five years now."

"I know about loss. I lost my daughter three years ago. Cystic fibrosis."

"I'm sorry to hear that."

"Hannah lived longer than most with CF because of her stubbornness. She was so determined and fought the illness with everything she had. She was the youngest of my five."

"Five!" The word slipped out before Alice could stop it.

"Five? Yes." He looked at her with a perplexed expression. "Does that surprise you?"

Alice smiled inwardly, thinking of how long she had wanted just one child. What a blessing to have two, but five? She wondered if she could have handled five.

"I just have one. Courtney," she said finally.

"I guess five sounds like a lot. And believe me, it is when they all get together." A shadow crossed his face for a fleeting moment.

"And where are your children now?"

"Two live on the peninsula. Luke, my oldest son, helps me run the sea farm up in Oysterville. Tom teaches math in the high school, and John lives here. Not sure about my youngest son, Aaron. He's off somewhere, doing his own thing."

And who is the mother of these children? Alice wanted to ask.

As if reading her mind, Leighton added, "My wife died some years ago now."

"I'm sorry, but your children are a blessing to you."

"For sure."

He handed her a card that showed the peninsula, a long, thin strip of land surrounded by the Columbia River, Willapa Bay, and the Pacific Ocean. "I live about as far north as you can go. It's beautiful there."

Alice wanted to talk longer, but needed to leave. "I'm sorry, but I'm meeting my daughter and better not be late. She's having a baby, my first grandchild, in less than five months."

"Hey, congratulations!" His eyes crinkled up on the end as he held the door open. "I'll ride down in the elevator with you."

Alice had heard of people falling in love at first sight, but she'd never believed it was possible. She didn't believe it to be possible now; yet there was something, a magnetism between them. His eyes seemed to smolder, his gaze meeting hers head-on. This was one of those times when she missed Carl.

Missed his comforting arms, holding her close, the feel of his strong body, his thick, muscular shoulders. Why was she feeling this way now? And why was this man staring at her? She knew he was, though she hadn't met his gaze again. She hadn't dared. She could imagine what Courtney would say about all of this.

"Here we are." The elevator door opened, and he stepped out, waiting for her to exit. "Alice, isn't it?"

She nodded, her face burning again, almost as if she were embarrassed.

"I have not looked at a woman since Hannah's death, but something inside me is urging me to ask you out. Could I drop by and take you to lunch tomorrow since today is taken up?"

"I haven't dated, either," she heard herself saying. Her hand went to her hair. "I don't think I should start now."

"This is irregular, I know, and you don't know me, but trust me when I say I don't go around asking women out. But sometimes you just want to talk to someone over a lunch of clam chowder and breadsticks."

Alice laughed then. "Clam chowder? How did you know that's my favorite?"

He shrugged. "I didn't. That's good, isn't it?"

"I suppose it is."

They were out on the sidewalk, though Alice couldn't remember walking down the hall to the main door of the building.

"I'll walk with you to where you're meeting your daughter, if that's okay."

Alice fell in step with the attractive man, unable to believe she had talked to him as if he were an old friend.

"How about if I stop by at noon tomorrow?"

Then she remembered. She wasn't going in tomorrow. Steven planned on being in the office all day, so Alice had the day off.

"I'll be at the hospital. I volunteer mornings."

"Well, maybe another time when I'm in town."

He looked so disappointed that, without thinking it over, Alice blurted out, "I could meet you at one o'clock. Say, the library."

He had impulsively taken her hand, just as Courtney walked up the block.

"Mother?" Courtney said, as if she couldn't believe this was her mother standing on a street corner of downtown Portland with a man. A nice-looking man.

Alice smiled as Leighton stepped forward, extending his hand.

"Hello, I'm Leighton Walker, a client, and you're Courtney. Congratulations on the baby. We were just talking while we waited for you."

Courtney finally shook his hand. "I—that is—thank you." She looked imploringly at her mother, but Alice said nothing.

"We're having lunch tomorrow. Do you want to come?"

Courtney was silent.

"It's probably not a good idea," Alice said, breaking in. "I don't think—"

"I'll be waiting at one. The library steps."

They watched while he turned and disappeared around the corner of Fifth and Madison.

"And now, are you going to tell me about the baby?" Alice reached over and pushed a tendril of hair from her daughter's cheek, eager to change the subject. "If only your father were here to rejoice in this awesome occasion."

Courtney narrowed her eyes. "Mom, Dad *is* here. I feel his presence a lot. Now, are you going to tell me who that man is?"

"His son is Jeff's friend, and he's here visiting, and he came in and, oh, I don't know. It all happened so fast—"

"Mother, you don't even know him. I'm sure Steven would feel as appalled as I am right now."

"What!" Alice's voice was almost shrill. "I'm not a child. Why should you feel appalled?"

"Mom, it's a different world now than when you dated Dad. You can't trust people."

"I can trust my own instincts, and I know Leighton Walker is a very nice man. Now, are we going to go shopping or what?"

But even as she said it, Alice knew the conversation would not be about the expected baby, but more about her lunch date.

Chapter 2

Leighton Walker hurried up the block, his long strides full of confidence as he thought of the woman he had just met, the look of near shock on her daughter's face. Well, he felt that same shock inside him now, although a different kind. He liked this woman. Her voice had a happy sound. Or was it her laugh? She was going to mean a lot to him; it was as if God had opened a door, and this time he wasn't about to slam it.

He had made the trip to Portland to woo potential customers. He'd opened the Sea Gifts Store the year Hannah died. Now customers could come in and buy six or a dozen fresh oysters. He also had canned and smoked oysters and offered oyster stew. It was something he'd always wanted to do. Just last week he'd added a variety of spices and books by local authors. Things were selling well.

Oysters were a succulent treat to most, but Hannah had disliked them. "One thing about oysters, Daddy," she'd said after a night of a bad attack, "you either love 'em or hate 'em."

He had held his fragile child close. *Oh, Lord, help me to face the inevitable.*

Hannah had lain back down. "Daddy, I know you are praying. I can always tell." She giggled. "You get that furrow in your brow, and your mouth relaxes."

"Is that so?" He pulled the covers up under her chin, thinking once again how much she looked like her mother, Nancy. Nancy with the laughing eyes, dimples, and mischievous grin. Nancy, whom he had known all his life.

He wondered why his heart had suddenly lurched at the sight of the tall, lean woman with dark eyes and short curly hair in the computer office. Had it been the depths of her eyes or the smile that filled up every inch of her face? He'd not seen a smile like that in a long, long time.

Without a second thought, he'd felt a nudge and had spoken to her about lunch. *It was crazy,* he thought now as he leaned back in the chair. He always stayed at John's high-rise apartment when he came to Portland. He had come to try to sell his line of canned oysters to two of the main seafood restaurants in town. He had two appointments this afternoon. How would it come out? A peace and sudden warmth filled him. If it worked, it did. If it didn't, it didn't. Leighton had learned at a young age that one had to roll with whatever life gave you. When his child was born sick, he turned to Nancy with a nod.

"We'll love her, Nance. Cherish her and protect her and do what has to be done."

"Easy for you to say," had been her comeback. She looked up at him out of listless eyes. "I prayed so hard for a girl. I didn't think I had to pray for one to be healthy." She turned away. "I didn't think God would be so cruel, Leight, to send us one with an affliction like this."

"God is never cruel."

"He was this time."

"No, Nance, you have it wrong."

It had hurt to see her unwilling to accept the challenge, to care for the baby who so needed her mother's loving touch.

Nancy had tried for a year, then left. Luke, at twelve, did not understand at all why his mother moved out of the house. The other three seemed to take it more in stride. She met them after school and took them for ice cream, or they'd walk the beach. But she didn't come home to see Hannah, nor would she answer Leighton's calls.

They had never divorced, though he knew she dated other men. Then she left the peninsula and sent notes and cards to the boys. Again, she did not include Hannah.

She had died by her own hand three years later. He'd prayed for her soul, knowing she had been tortured and couldn't have been in her right mind to do such a thing.

He'd been alone twenty years, throwing himself into his work. His children were his whole life, especially after Nancy left. He had tried to be both mother and father. Then Aunt Rita came to help out, and he'd been thankful. She had pounded Hannah's back when the mucous was so thick she could not breathe. Together they worked and prayed for the frail child. Aunt Rita invented games that were quiet, read a multitude of books, they fingerpainted garish orange and purple pictures, doing whatever was needed for her small, sick niece. Recently he'd heard about new treatments and lung transplants for CF patients, but the news had come too late for Hannah.

Back at John's apartment, Leighton looked out at the view of Mount Hood, a glorious snowcapped peak. His heart swelled nearly shut. So many things had happened in his life. At eleven, he'd been miraculously saved after a sudden squall and his canoe capsized in the bay. He'd disobeyed by going out alone without permission. After clinging to the canoe for an hour, he'd been rescued by a crabbing boat. The spanking he expected was not administered by his father or mother. Two things he remembered from that day: his mother who couldn't stop crying and his belief that there had to be a Supreme Being who took care of small boys who did foolhardy things.

When his sick daughter was born, Leighton had dug in his heels and coped. Then Aaron strayed from the fold, and Leighton had no idea where he was now. The boy, a happy-go-lucky child, had made everyone laugh. He had more of Nancy in him than Leighton ever realized. Each day began with a prayer for Aaron. And, of course, his other three sons. God was the main force in his life.

God was there, Someone to cry out to, to pray to, to lean on in tough times. But never had he thought of another helpmate. He'd been making it okay, hadn't he? Then today he met Alice.

"Lord, have You given me a sign today? Are You telling me I should pursue this woman? I can't believe I had enough nerve to ask her out for lunch."

He thought about the verse in Psalms that said, "Great peace have they who love your law, and nothing can make them stumble."

The phone rang, breaking through Leighton's reverie. It was John.

"Dad, I have tickets to the Pops concert tonight, but I'm driving down to Salem. Haven't found anyone who can use them. How about you?"

"What would I do with two tickets?"

"You must know someone else in town."

Leighton's mind flashed to Alice. She seemed to be the type that would enjoy a concert. "Yeah, I'll take them off your hands."

"Good. I'll drop them by before I leave."

Leighton sat back and wondered if Alice would agree to the concert. This seemed more like a date than lunch tomorrow.

He'd been out of practice so long. He smiled. He'd never practiced even back in the beginning. He and Nancy had attended the same church, the youth group, and went on all the functions. They just sort of started dating when they were both seventeen. And nature had taken its course. He had never looked at another woman, not really looked. Friends tried to pair him up after Nancy's death, but he was too busy with work and taking care of his kids. There'd been no one, unless he counted Cora.

He showered and took his one good suit from the hanger. He had wondered about dressing casual for this meeting with the restaurant owners but decided against it. He might be a beach bum, but he didn't want to look like one.

An hour later, he sat across from the man who signed on the dotted line for his next order of oysters, then Leighton talked about the new products. "You can sell the canned oysters right in the restaurant. Offer them some of our new spices. Soon your customers will be clamoring for them."

They rose, shook on the deal, and Leighton left, his head held high. "Wow, Lord, that one was easy. Now, if my phone call to Alice comes off as easily."

He was back at the apartment. The screen on his laptop, a purchase of just two years ago, sat staring at him. Fish of all sizes and colors bobbed up and around on the screen, mesmerizing him. He started to dial the number, then hung up.

"Ah, why don't I just go ahead and call? If she says no, the sun still rises tomorrow morning."

Alice had gone home, and he got Jeff.

"She just works mornings most of the time. If it looks like a busy week, like after an ad comes out, Steven asks her to come in for the whole day."

"I suppose it's against protocol to give me her home phone number."

There was a pause. "Well, I suppose not. You are a client, after all."

Seconds later, Leighton was once more dialing a number. On the third ring, an answering machine kicked in. Of course. She probably hadn't gotten home yet. He'd call again in an hour or so.

～

Courtney finally told her mother she was carrying a boy.

Alice hugged her close. "I'll like having a grandson. Of course this means Jeff wins. He said it was a boy."

"I can't wait to see Steven's face. He's going to rush out to buy a football. Just you watch."

They meandered through the baby department, and Alice bought fuzzy blue sleepers, blue receiving blankets, and a quilt that was definitely for a boy. "Isn't this fun?"

"I won't have enough room in the apartment if you buy like this every time you get close to a store."

Alice nodded. "You're right. Let's call it a day."

After calling to check with Jeff, Alice decided to go on home. She had things to mull over, baby clothes to look at again, a lunch date for the next day.

An hour later, after taking Max, the local transit, to Parkrose, Alice lugged her purchases to her car. She often stopped at the grocery store but wanted to go straight home today.

The light blinked on her telephone as she dropped the packages on the bed.

"Who would be calling?" she said aloud, her mind always going to Agnes, her sister.

A male voice boomed into the room. "Leighton Walker here. We met earlier today. I'm the one with the ailing laptop."

She trembled as she glanced at her face in the mirror over the dresser. "He's calling me? But why?"

"Have two tickets for the Oregon Pops concert tonight. Just wondering if you'd go with me. Don't know anyone else in town and thought it might be fun. I'll call you back around four."

A Pops concert. She loved the group. And she hadn't been to a concert in years. She couldn't return the call, as he hadn't left a number. She hoped he wouldn't ask someone else.

She looked in the kitchen for leftovers. There was a chicken drumstick and a bit of the Jell-O left from Sunday. That would do. She put water on for tea when the phone rang again.

"Alice?"

"Hello, Leighton." It seemed funny to address him by a name that sounded as if it should be his surname, not his first. "I got your message."

"And?"

"I think it would be wonderful. How did you know I liked the Pops?"

"I didn't, but it just occurred to me that we might like the same kind of music—the mellow kind you can hum along with. I don't care for what my boys listen to."

"My thoughts exactly."

"Should I go casual or dress up?" he asked now. "Seems I don't have much choice between a suit and Levis."

"Well, I hear from Courtney that anything goes. I'd say casual."

"Good."

"And I have just the outfit to wear," Alice added.

Alice had a skirt in mind. It was a flowered challis and hit her midcalf. She'd wear a solid pink top and jacket. She loved challis. The material was soft and made her feel young—not that she'd been thinking about feeling young lately. Her heart was doing strange flip-flops. What was wrong with her? This was a casual acquaintance. One didn't get all excited over friends, now, did they?

Her hands ran through her short hair. Well, there wasn't much to do with her hair. One style and that was it. That was probably good. "Lord, You sure dish up surprises. A date for tonight and a grandchild on the horizon. Not sure I can stand so much excitement.

"And, Lord, I sure hope I know what I'm doing. I don't want anything serious to happen, so is it wrong to look forward to going out with this man? Is this part of Your plan for me?"

As Alice looked in the mirror at her flushed face, she thought of Carl. It was as if he were smiling, urging her on. It had been a long time since she'd felt a man's arm on her shoulder or held hands. It looked like that was all about to change.

Chapter 3

After talking to Leighton, Alice decided on a lingering bath with lavender-scented bubbles. She usually didn't take time for such luxury, and she intended to enjoy every minute.

Leaning back, she let the day's happenings go through her mind. It had started out as a typical early summer day at work. She was happy for the job. It got her going each day. She now had something to look forward to. Not that she didn't see Courtney and Steven, the main focus of her existence, but it wasn't the same with Courtney out and safely ensconced in her own apartment.

"You have an adjustment to make," Agnes, her dominating sister, said one Sunday a few weeks after the wedding. "You aren't the center of Courtney's universe these days."

It was true, though Alice did not consider herself to be an overbearing parent or a demanding one. And she knew from talking to other mothers that once a child was married, they lost contact. That wasn't going to happen to her. Not ever.

She reached for a towel. At times her loneliness was overwhelming, almost more than she could bear. It was at these times that she turned to a few of her memorized Bible verses. She knew she would never be alone. God was there to sustain her.

A man in her life? Alice didn't think so. That would be too big of an adjustment. Besides, this man did not live in Portland, and to move elsewhere was quite impossible.

The phone rang as Alice started to dry her hair. She grabbed it before the answering machine went on.

"Alice? I know this sounds ridiculous, but do you have plans for dinner?"

"I. . . Well, there's a piece of chicken left over from Sunday."

"Why don't I stop by early and we'll go to Jake's? My son said it's one of the best places around for seafood."

"Your son's right. Jake's *is* good, and I think dinner would be lovely." Alice couldn't remember the last time she'd had dinner at Jake's, and certainly it had not been with a man.

"It's settled then. Now, if you'll give me directions to your house."

"I'm out here in Parkrose. You have a bit of a drive, and the traffic is bad. Don't go the freeway. I'd take the Burnside Bridge and come east on Sandy."

She replaced the phone and checked her face in the mirror. Pink cheeks. Yes. Courtney called when Alice had one foot in her panty hose.

"Mom?"

"Hi, honey. How're you feeling? And what did Steven say about having a boy?"

"Steven is thrilled. Oh, Mom, he brought home this huge teddy bear. It's just darling."

"No football?"

"No, but I'm sure that's next."

"Listen, dear, I really want to talk, but I have to get dressed in fifteen minutes. Think I can make it?"

"Fifteen minutes? Mom? This isn't water exercise night."

"I'm going out to eat and then to the Pops concert."

"Oh, did you finally talk Agnes into going to the Pops?"

"I'm going with Leighton."

There was a long pause, and Alice knew she wouldn't get off the phone before Courtney had an explanation. And even if she hurried, she wouldn't quite be ready for the now-earlier dinner date.

"Mom, I can't believe this. It's almost bizarre, so unlike you."

"His son had tickets, and rather than see them go to waste, Leighton invited me. And since we're both hungry and there are so many good places to eat downtown, we're having dinner first."

"Are you sure Jeff knows him?"

"Call Jeff."

"Well, you should be able to judge character, I guess. What did you say he did for a living?"

"He's an oyster farmer from Oysterville."

"An oyster farmer?"

"Yes. That's what they call them, I've been told. They grow them and export them to San Francisco and other areas. He's just in town on business."

"Oh."

"Honey, I'll tell you all about the evening tomorrow."

Date. Imagine. She'd thought the word *date.* After hanging up, Alice felt all giddy again. She couldn't believe the feeling that raced through her. She'd never thought about going on a date, much less feeling this way about anyone. Carl had been her whole life. And their romance was tame. In fact, her best friend, Todi, had asked if this was really the guy she wanted to spend the rest of her life with.

"Yes, and why do you think not?" They'd stopped after the youth meeting for Cokes at their favorite hideout. Todi drove an old, beat-up Chevy, and she stared out the window with the green door that didn't match the gray body.

"When I fall in love"—Todi rolled her eyes—"I want to see sparks and feel butterflies in my tummy and expect to be with him every single minute."

"You know Carl's off on that two-week program, or I *would* be with him."

"But you don't talk about him constantly, and you rarely glance at your engagement ring, and—"

Alice remembered now, after all those years, of shushing Todi up, then wondering later that night in the sanctity of her bedroom if she really did love Carl, asking God if this was the right mate for her.

Maybe they had not had a whirlwind courtship, but it had been good and solid and strong. Never wavering. She thought of a scripture she had marked in her Bible: "Be on your guard; stand firm in the faith; be men of courage; be strong. Do everything in love."

Besides, Todi was. . .well, Todi. How many mothers would give a child that name? Todi's mother was eccentric. Todi got a car on her sixteenth birthday and passed the driving test the same day. She drove all around, and her mother never asked when she'd be home. She liked to pretend she was lost, and Alice, being gullible, believed her. Todi was crazy, doing things Alice could only dream about, but Alice loved her like a sister.

Todi. Alice picked up a silver picture frame from the dresser. Todi had the ever-present impish smile. Her hair had turned gray before she lost it. Chemo had not stopped the cancer, and Todi died at the young age of forty. Alice swallowed hard and replaced the photo. Todi had taught her how to love life and to laugh. Agnes, Alice's serious, stalwart sister, would never have ridden a motorcycle, especially not with someone she had just met. But Todi had dared Alice to do that as she jumped on behind the friend of Carl's. Together they rode up to Rocky Butte and looked out over the city, with its twinkling lights.

Alice wondered how she could have done that, been so trusting with a man she had skated with twice. Yet she had put her trust in the man with the dark eyes, just as she was putting her trust in another man three decades later. A man with a trusting smile and a winning way. She had never told Agnes about the motorcycle ride, just as she wasn't about to tell her about tonight and her date with Leighton.

Alice and Carl had had a good marriage. They'd traveled while he was in the air force, then come back to Portland to settle down. The Cape Cod was the first house they looked at, the perfect neighborhood for the family they'd have. Except the babies didn't come. After endless prayers, Courtney was a wonderful gift from a woman who could not keep her baby.

Alice brushed a tear aside and slipped her outfit on, then the flats. She liked casual.

Had she ever thought of finding someone else? Not really. She was happy with things the way they were, happy to bask in Courtney's romance and now the expected baby. She didn't need to focus on a man. Did she?

The outfit fit her curves well. She looked sideways in the mirror. The water exercise classes had firmed her muscles, made her slim. But the most wonderful gift was the energy she had. And working for Steven had made her energy even more boundless.

Alice was applying a makeup pencil at her left eyebrow when she heard the car in the drive. One thing she'd always liked about this house was that she could hear someone coming down the driveway. She quickly penciled the other eyebrow, deciding the lipstick and blush could wait until she'd answered the door.

Leighton didn't get out of the car. Alice looked out the bedroom window and saw him sitting, waiting. He was early. Maybe he was the type that didn't like to be early and would wait until it was six.

She quickly added a touch of pink gloss and a bit of blush to her cheeks. She was ready now. If he didn't come to the door in a minute, she'd go out.

The bell rang just as her hand touched the knob.

She opened the door and smiled. He was breathtakingly handsome in the Levis and a buff-colored sports jacket. His hair was salt and pepper with a neat, trim cut but long sideburns. His eyes, a deep brown, looked at her with an almost little-boy look. Their gazes met and held.

"Alice." He stepped forward and took her hand. "You look absolutely beautiful, and I'm so glad I thought of dinner."

She took her eyes away long enough to motion him in. "We could have a cup of coffee or something, but perhaps we should get going. Jake's can be crowded, even on a weeknight."

His hand lingered on her shoulder as he helped her with her wrap. Why did she feel so tingly? She was simply having dinner with the man.

"I think what we're doing is absolutely mad."

She looked up and saw he was serious. "Mad?"

"My asking you out, not to count the way I am feeling right now as I look at you. Alice, I haven't thought of a woman in so long. I'm totally out of practice. I don't know what to do or say. I'll be inept. You'll laugh at me."

Alice laughed then. Well, he'd given her permission, had he not?

"See?"

"I was thinking the very same thing just before you arrived. As I was dressing for this occasion, my daughter called. She thinks I'm behaving like a teenager, and quite frankly, I believe I am, too. If only my best friend, Todi, were here, I'd ask her what she thought."

"Todi?"

Alice smiled. "We were inseparable all through high school. And she said I didn't love my first husband madly enough."

"And did you?"

"I loved him, I guess." Alice didn't go on to add that she had never felt this way, so vulnerable, so wanting him to kiss her that she had to shake her head to make the thought go away.

"I was mad about my first wife, but she didn't feel the same. Or maybe she did at one time. I'll never know now." He glanced at his watch. "We'd better go or we'll be late for dinner and the concert."

They walked side by side up the walk, and he opened the car door. Alice swallowed again, wondering if Todi could see her from her vantage point in heaven.

The car was nice. Clean. As Alice stole a sideways glance at Leighton, liking his strong profile, she sensed this would be the first of many such dates.

Chapter 4

They were early, but Jake's had a long line of patrons waiting.

"Maybe we better go somewhere else," Leighton suggested. "I don't like rushing through dinner." He wondered if she felt that way, too. Apparently she did, as she immediately turned and walked back toward his car.

"I agree. If we have to wait thirty minutes, we could be late for the concert. Let's go down on the river." Alice smiled. "I know this new place, and it just might be that everyone hasn't caught on to it yet."

Alice directed Leighton down Burnside, then south on the Naito Parkway, which went along the river. Another turn and they pulled into a parking lot. The river was busy with boats and barges, and a gentle wind blew, sending Alice's hair flying. She directed Leighton down a flight of wooden steps that would take them to the floating restaurant.

"This is wonderful," Leighton said, taking her arm and helping her down the steep steps.

"I've been here just once. The seafood is terrific, and it's fun to watch the activity on the water."

"We don't have a floating restaurant at home. Can't do that with a change in the tide twice a day, but you'd like some of the places we do have. One of my favorites is on the bay. The Ark has a great menu."

Alice was delighted she had picked a place Leighton obviously enjoyed. Not everyone liked dining right on the Willamette River. The Newport Bay was well moored and moved very little, even when a barge went by and caused high waves to lap at the base of the restaurant. A man on a jet ski rode by, waving at the people on the deck.

Leighton's dark eyes met hers. "I'm glad you thought of this place. I'll have to see if John's come here yet. I love the water and the action on it."

Alice smiled, remembering a time when her husband had bought a boat. It had been used mostly for cruising up and down the river in the summer. Courtney had learned to water-ski, and for that they often went to one of many lakes in the area. Those relaxing summer days brought back many pleasant memories.

"Did you ever water-ski?" Alice asked.

"No, have you?"

"Yes, I learned how one summer, and we skied several years until Carl sold the boat."

"I suppose I'm too old to try it now."

"Well, I sure wouldn't want to try again. Probably wouldn't be able to walk for a week," Alice said, as they both burst into laughter.

"Do you realize how nice it is here with both the Willamette and Columbia Rivers?" Leighton asked. "Not to mention Mount Hood in the distance."

Alice nodded and sipped on her root beer. "But aren't you surrounded by water on the peninsula?"

"Yes, but it's quiet on the bay. A few crabbing boats and a canoe now and then. That's about it. I'd like you to see it sometime." He forked a shrimp out of the cocktail sauce. "I've wondered about living in the mountains, but I'm not sure what I'd do there. Oystering is pretty much in my soul."

Alice wanted to say something charming and witty but knew she didn't have to worry with Leighton. It was a safe, comfortable feeling, so uncanny, since she didn't even know the man. She was attracted to him, just as he showed signs of being attracted to her, and she liked that very much. It was a good, yet exhilarating, feeling.

"What are you thinking about?" Leighton asked. "You can't smile in such a charming way and not let me know what you're smiling about."

Alice decided to tell him the truth. Why not? They weren't kids anymore. She set her fork down. "It's just that I feel as if I've known you forever, and it's strange."

He grinned. "I tend to affect a lot of women that way."

It was a joke, she knew. His eyes gave him away with a twinkle of merriment. "Obviously, you say that to all the women you date; is that what you mean?"

"Yep, you've got my number." He turned serious then. "I've had few dates since Nancy's death. It was such a disaster, I swore off dating and just took care of my family and my business the best I knew how. But there is a woman I sort of thought about dating."

Alice wanted to ask more about this woman, but decided it wasn't any of her business. She leaned forward. "Your business sounds pretty successful."

"It's been working so far."

The waitress arrived with large bowls of clam chowder, which Leighton said he could never get enough of. "I like trying chowder everywhere I go. I have my favorite spot back home, which I can't wait to take you to. There's a gorgeous view of the ocean, and it has its beauty and charm just as your river does here."

They paused for a short blessing, each saying their own. Alice felt even more impressed by this tall, homespun man she'd barely met.

They lingered over dinner, Alice taking time with the lobster, dipping each bite in drawn butter. Leighton seemed amused until he glanced at his watch.

"Isn't the concert at eight thirty?"

"Yes. Surely it isn't that late."

"No, but we'd better go, though I know it's just a few blocks away."

Concerts were held downtown in a complex of entertainment theaters and concert halls. They arrived just as the lights dimmed.

The first song, in honor of the Fourth of July, was George M. Cohan's "Yankee Doodle Dandy." Everyone stood, cheering. Men saluted the huge flag on stage. Alice and Leighton covered their hearts to show respect.

"I was too young for World War II or the Korean conflict, but I joined the ROTC in high school," Leighton said.

Alice felt the warmth of his hand covering hers, as a trio ran out on the stage and sang "Don't Sit Under the Apple Tree." Alice hummed along, then stopped as she realized her voice was carrying. Leighton leaned over. "You can hum in my ear any old time you want to. I don't mind at all. In fact, I'd join you, but I would scare everyone out."

Alice wished the concert would never end. She couldn't remember the last time she'd enjoyed anything so much.

It was after ten when their clapping brought the performers out for a second encore.

Leighton insisted they go for desserts at a place his son had told him about. "John said I wasn't to miss it. That it was definitely a must."

"I'm still full," Alice protested, but seeing the firm look on his face, she gave in. It was a way to make the evening continue.

"We can split one, then," he said.

The restaurant was cozy and great for intimate dining. They settled in a back booth and ordered two black coffees and a thick slice of lemon soufflé pie with two forks.

"Alice, I find myself wishing I didn't need to return to Oysterville. I want to stay, want to take you out again, want to—" He paused. "I guess what I'm trying to say is I enjoyed the evening and hope you did, too."

She felt her heart beating faster, keeping time with the thoughts in her mind. How could this be happening? How could she be feeling this way? It made no sense. Here she'd been going along in life, thanking God every day for her many blessings, and was He now telling her there was more that He wanted her to have?

"You're not saying anything." Leighton leaned over and touched her hand. "I hope I haven't said too much. I tend to level with everyone right off. The kids always know where they stand with me."

"Quite the contrary. It's been wonderful, and I was just thinking the other day I couldn't have anything more wonderful happen. Now this."

They left the restaurant and strolled down past Pioneer Square, where another couple walked, seemingly oblivious to everyone. A full moon shone down from a dark sky. Leighton took Alice's hand as they climbed the steps toward the street where the car was parked.

"Everything looks so different at night," Alice said. "I haven't been downtown this late since forever."

She wanted the moment to last, but knew it would in her mind and heart.

"I suppose I better take you home, though I don't really want to."

"Nor do I want to go."

"We have to be careful. I feel like a teenager who can't be left alone with you for more than a minute."

They laughed at that thought as they got into the car and Leighton headed back across the river. Lights danced on the water, and the Morrison Bridge dazzled them with the pink and blue lights.

"I love the city at night," Alice said. "I like it where I live, but there's just something magical about being downtown at night."

She'd thought once of having an apartment in the downtown area, but it hadn't seemed practical. Besides, she liked the Cape Cod in Parkrose. There were memories there. Space. And love. Lots of love and laughter echoed from the rooms. How could she ever leave a place she loved so much?

"You're a happy person," Leighton said as he pulled into her driveway. "You have no idea how much that means to me."

"Your wife wasn't happy?" After saying it, she wished she could take the words back, certain that Leighton would not want to talk about the past.

He looked away. "Nancy wanted things she couldn't have. It didn't matter what I did; it was wrong. God knows I tried."

Alice touched his arm. "I'm sure you did, Leighton. Some people can't be happy. I like the old saying of Abraham Lincoln's: " 'Most people are about as happy as they make up their minds to be.' "

"For years I blamed myself for the breakup of my marriage and home. And later, when Nancy, when she ended it all, I took on more guilt. How can someone ever know another's agony?"

"I'm glad you told me. Being the typical curious female, I would have wondered about it. I'm sorry she took her life. That must have been hard on your children."

"They hadn't seen her much those last few years. Luke took it hard, though."

"And so here you are now, and you're probably wondering why."

He leaned over and kissed her forehead. "I know why I'm here, and I believe God led me to you. And now I better go before I kiss you again and you find yourself inviting me in."

Long after he left, Alice stood by the window looking out into the dark night. The entire evening was like a dream. The food had been great, though she hadn't been able to eat much. The concert was lighthearted, and they'd laughed a lot. And later the dessert and stroll had ended the night.

It was midnight. She hadn't been up this late for years. And the funny thing was, she couldn't call Courtney and tell her about it. Oh, for a good friend like Todi. She'd just have to write it in her journal for posterity. And she'd always remember this one night of fun and feeling like she was loved and desired.

Leighton had said he would return soon. In the meantime, he wanted her to plan on a visit to the peninsula and to his Oysterville. Could she do that? Should she?

Yes, she would go. She wanted to go. And as she turned and saw the blinking light of the answering machine, she wondered how long ago Courtney had called.

"Mom, you should be back by now. It's eleven thirty. I checked and the concert was over at ten thirty. Where are you? I'm worried."

Alice laughed as she kicked her shoes off. Funny how the tables could turn. Here her child was worried about her as if she were a little kid. Maybe she'd better call. If she didn't, Courtney might call the police and report a "missing mom."

She laughed again as she reached for the phone.

Chapter 5

Leighton met Alice at the library the next afternoon. He had offered to pick her up, but she'd said it was quicker to ride the Max in. She had another place picked out.

"It's a quaint place on Broadway. One of my favorites." She smiled. "It has great fish and chips and a nice salad bar."

He took her hand, and she leaned into him as they walked down a few blocks. The sun had finally decided to shine after a morning of an overcast sky.

"Do you realize it would take a month of having lunch to hit all the good spots?"

He grinned. "Sounds good to me. You have more to choose from than I do at home."

Alice didn't want to ask but had to know. "Are you going back today?"

"Yes, after my appointment. I'll go to John's and pack my few things and get out of town before rush-hour traffic."

"I suppose all this traffic seems strange to you." Alice sipped her soda.

"This is true. I can go to the four-way stop in Ocean Park, and if there's a car ahead of me, that's news."

After a trip to the salad bar and splitting an order of fish and chips, Leighton glanced at his watch. "My stars, how did it get so late? I have thirty minutes to make it to the northwest side of town."

"You'll make it. Relax."

"I like being early, though."

"You should be."

Not that Alice was late for appointments, but she'd learned it rarely did good to be early, since it seemed she always had to wait.

When Leighton signaled the waitress for the tab, Alice offered to leave a tip.

"Don't even think about it. It was my idea. My treat." As he walked her to the Max stop, he said, "I'll call you."

"Let me know when you get home. And I hope the restaurant places a big order."

His last glimpse was of her waving from the back of the train as it headed east.

❧

The owner was most cordial and open to Leighton's new products.

"People eat out, enjoy a dinner of oysters. They want to take something home. It could be a memento of their trip, or for local patrons, it might be something to

142

eat later, to extend their pleasant evening."

"Yes, I know what you mean." The young man, a Mr. Nelson, younger than Leighton's sons, leaned forward. "The Original Taco House has their salad dressing and salsa for sale in a showcase just inside the door. I understand they sell a lot of both items." He nodded. "I'll take a case each of smoked and plain oysters and a dozen of the spices. I doubt that they sell as fast as the oyster products."

Leighton stood, and the two men shook hands. "I'll see that it's delivered within the week."

Leighton could have Ken, his deliveryman, bring the orders in, but he just might deliver the products himself. It would be a first, to be sure. He didn't come to Portland often. Usually, he couldn't wait to leave the traffic noises, the sound of sirens, loud boom boxes, the general sound of people rushing. He missed the quiet peninsula, where people did things in their own good time. Each day when he picked up his mail, he chatted with Casey, the postmaster. He knew everyone at the store. He was friendly to the tourists who frequented his small business. They were used to instant gratification, and he didn't act as if it was an affront to wait on them, as some merchants did.

"Dad, you're semiretired," John said every time Leighton came to town. "You have a crew working for you. What's your hurry?"

Leighton always came up with the same answer. "Son, when you're away, the boys will play. I need to stay on top of things. You know how I feel about that."

It was true. Just as every household needed a boss, an authority figure, a business needed the owner present. But it was also because Leighton had to get away. It hadn't changed in the ten years he'd been coming in on business. Until now. And all because of Alice. She made him realize he *liked* having someone there. Someone to talk to. It was a good, yet uncertain, feeling.

He hurried back and changed from his suit to casual wear for the trip home, then packed his toiletries. He stood at the window of the high-rise, looking once more out across the Willamette River. On a clear day, Mount Hood was visible from fifty miles away. He'd wondered what it'd be like to ski on those runs or to snowboard, which was the current rage. Not that he kept current. If he did, he'd be in-line skating down the sidewalk. In his day, it had been roller skates, and every Friday night he and Nancy had gone to the skating rink at the camp in Ocean Park.

Change that thought. Now you not only have to watch out for roller blades, but skateboards, too. He had been nearly mowed down by one the day he arrived.

Once outside, he looked at the sky. Rain clouds. Soon the mountain would disappear from sight. It rained a lot in Portland. It rained a lot in Oysterville. Even in June it rained. And December, January, and February. Leighton was used to it. While elsewhere people shoveled their walks in winter, people here wore raincoats, rain hats, and carried umbrellas.

His car was on the blue level of the parking garage. He paused in the entrance and thought about going back inside and calling Alice to tell her about the big order, to say he would miss her. Tell her he missed her already. But he was too old for love. Leave it to the young kids to find their one true love. Leighton would bask in his work, his four grandchildren, and his sons.

Leighton got as far as the approach to the Morrison Bridge and turned abruptly on Third Avenue. There must be a pay phone booth nearby. Most large towns had phone booths on every corner. Then he spotted one. He'd have to park in a zone with a parking meter, but he had change. He always carried change. Yes, a cell phone would have been nice about now, and he could hear John lamenting, "You have a laptop, Dad, but won't get a cellular phone. What if something happens on the road?"

So far nothing had.

He dug out Alice's phone number and dialed, hoping she'd be there. If she'd stayed downtown, they could have taken a drive, stopped for coffee somewhere, or just walked in the City Park Blocks. It was his favorite place in the downtown area.

"Leighton? I thought you'd be long gone by now."

Did he catch a hint of surprise? Delight in her voice? He swallowed, not wanting to sound ridiculous, wondering what she might say.

"I'm heading out and just wanted to say good-bye again." It sounded inane, but he felt compelled, felt as if God was pushing him that way.

"How did the appointment go?"

"The Ringside placed the largest order so far."

"Leighton, that's wonderful! How encouraging."

He had a sudden irrepressible urge to touch her, to hear her laugh. "I'm going to miss you." The words were out, and he couldn't snatch them back.

"I'm going to miss you, too."

He could visualize her soft blue eyes, the funny little half grin she did a lot, and wondered at the thump, thumping of his heart. "It's crazy, isn't it?" he said. "Us two oldsters acting like a couple of kids. I hope you know this is so unusual for me."

She laughed, and the sound warmed his heart. "And unusual for me," she murmured. "Yes, crazy but nice. Courtney thinks I've lost my mind."

"I'll call you when I get to Oysterville." The noise from the traffic made it hard to hear, and besides, someone was waiting for the booth.

"Good-bye—oh—and Leighton, next time you come to Portland, I want you over for dinner."

"I'll count on it."

He replaced the receiver. He'd wanted to say more than good-bye, but what? He stepped out of the booth, put the slip of paper in his pocket, and headed back to his car. Man, but her voice sounded good!

He'd be thinking about their times together, dreaming of when he'd see her again, thanking God for giving him hope, for making his heart light again. And now he had a dinner to look forward to.

～

Soon Leighton was out of the traffic and winging his way west. He stuck in his favorite tape, *Fiddler on the Roof,* as he drove over the familiar miles to the peninsula. He had the songs memorized. The boys laughed at him, though he remembered when they were young and he put the tape in, they'd sing along. Especially Aaron.

He hadn't told Alice about Aaron, why he'd run away, the problems they had. Didn't most families have problems? Kids ran off all the time, and Leighton figured when Aaron was ready to come home, he would. There wasn't much Leighton could do about it. Once in a while Luke or Tom mentioned their brother. Cora brought his name up often.

His thoughts went to home and Cora. She hadn't crossed his mind until now. She'd be at his house, have it all clean and shiny, and dinner in the oven. She had loved Aaron, but that's because she'd taken care of him when he was young, after Aunt Rita died. If the truth were known, Cora spoiled Aaron. She'd also been good with Hannah and had suggested once that perhaps Aaron left because he couldn't stay and watch his sister die.

"Hannah may live for a good many years," Leighton had argued. "Nobody knows how long she has."

Cora shook her head. "Leighton, the child is dying. Right before our eyes. Don't pretend when pretending is no good. You're only fooling yourself."

She'd been partly wrong, and he was partly right. Though she grew weaker and could do less, not even walk down the road to pick up the daily paper, Hannah had lived two more years.

He thought again of Aaron as he sang, "If I were a rich man." Aaron, eyes wide and innocent, had asked, "But, Daddy, aren't we rich?"

He had leaned over, ruffling the child's sandy blond hair. "We're certainly not rich, but we're not poor, either."

Had he not given him enough attention? With worry over Hannah and her taking so much of his time, Aaron had been ignored more than the older boys. Leighton hadn't meant to ignore him. God knew how much he loved him, just as he loved all his children.

As for Nancy, she kept everything inside her. Unable to voice her feelings about how she felt, she had not leaned on God for help, nor had she sought help from a doctor. The boys had come along, one every two years. She'd been a good mother. A caring mother. Yet he had failed her. He had not given her enough attention. It seemed that his love and attention were showered on his sons from the time they were toddlers right until they went off to school. Then Hannah was born, and Nancy cried all the way home from Portland after they'd seen a specialist, loud sobs that tore at Leighton and made him want to stop the car, pull her into his arms, and tell her it would be all right.

"We can handle this, honey," he'd said instead, looking over at his young, distraught wife.

"I wanted a perfect child. All our other children are perfect."

"God knew we would love her anyway and take extra-special care of her."

"I don't want that responsibility."

As if on cue, Hannah woke from her car seat in the back. Whimpering, she waited for her mother's arms, but Nancy didn't budge.

"Do you think she's hungry?" Leighton asked. "I could pull over so you could nurse her."

"And then watch while she throws up everything?"

"Oh, honey, don't be like this."

She hadn't faced him the day she left, but he found a note on the dining room table.

Please forgive me for being weak. I know you will find someone to help with Hannah, someone who can hold her and give her the love and attention she needs. That person just isn't me.

"But what about our sons?" Leighton had said to the still, empty room. "What about Luke, John, Thomas, and Aaron? They need a mother. And I need a wife." He'd anguished long into the night, unable to sleep. The thought came to mind that God didn't want him to fear, that He wouldn't give him a larger burden than he could bear.

He had blamed himself, though friends and family said he'd done everything he could. Yet he knew he had not.

When Cora moved up to Oysterville and offered to keep house and cook and mother the Walker children, Leighton had seen her as an answer to prayer.

Cora was indeed a godsend. She loved horses and the outdoors, and the boys took to her right off. She didn't seem to mind caring for a child who coughed constantly and needed to be pounded. She loved to cook, and he'd often find freshly baked cookies when he returned from the cannery. Always there was a pot of stew or chowder or a roast in the oven. Leighton knew he couldn't have survived without her.

Cora had a big heart, and once he sensed she cared for him in that way, but he didn't look at women or think about marrying again. He just couldn't.

He wondered if Cora would be there as he stopped and picked up his mail. Often she was gone when he got home from work, but it might be different today. She would want to know how the trip went and if he'd sold anyone on his new products.

Her car was parked in the usual spot under the trees.

Chapter 6

Leighton's heart sank. He'd expected Cora to be here, yet he wasn't prepared for what he needed to say. He liked having her here. He had always known she wanted more, but though he was fond of her, he hadn't made any moves. And now after meeting Alice, it was as if a whole new world had opened up. He couldn't quite explain it, but he knew he wanted to see Alice again. Somehow he needed to convey this to Cora.

He didn't have a chance to retrieve the spare key from under the hedgehog foot scraper before the door flew open. Cora, hair pulled back with a dark green ribbon, smiled expectantly.

"So? How did it go? Did you sell the oysters? I thought you were *never* going to get here. I made dinner hours ago—" She paused, her eyes meeting his level gaze. "I suppose you stopped at Hump's or somewhere on the Oregon side."

"It went better than I expected." He tossed his jacket over a chair. "Everyone I met was receptive to the idea and placed an order."

"But that's wonderful!" Her eyes shone. "You don't seem too excited about it."

"Just tired."

"Of course. Come on and let me heat you up some dinner."

He moved past her, wondering how to broach the subject. He never had been one to mince his thoughts. Besides, Cora knew him well. She understood his moods, his concerns for his family, the business. She was special, but he couldn't think of her in a romantic way.

"Is something wrong?" She leaned over and smoothed dark hair back from his forehead.

He moved. "Cora, I don't feel like talking tonight."

"I understand. I'm far too chatty at times. It's my worst fault." She grabbed a hanger out of the hall closet.

Groaning, he knew this would be far worse than he'd ever anticipated.

"I had a problem with the laptop and had someone look at it."

"Is it fixed?" She looked at the small case that held the computer. She'd thought it was a frivolous expense at the time and had told him so.

"It's fine now. It wasn't serious."

"Then you should be feeling good about everything." She looked at him expectantly.

I am, oh, I am, but how can I tell her?

"I cleaned out the refrigerator. It was getting pretty gross."

"Thanks. I appreciate it."

"Leight, you're acting kinda weird. Is John okay? Have I done something?"

"John's fine. Portland's fine. The car runs fine. I'm fine. It's just that, well, when I took the computer in, this woman was there and we had lunch today."

Her eyes narrowed. "You mean—" Her voice fell. He turned and gently held her shoulders.

"I wasn't looking for anyone; you know that. I told you years ago when Nancy first left that I would never love anyone again."

"But now it's suddenly different?"

He shook his head, knowing he'd said too much, had hurt this woman whom he knew had strong feelings for him. "Things happen, you know, things you can't explain. Things just sort of clicked."

He thought Cora would say something, but she stood, staring out the window at the bay, her voice barely audible when she did speak.

"I've waited for you, Leighton. I thought that someday you might grow to love me. I know your likes and dislikes. I could run the business, if need be. The boys respect me. I. . . What went wrong? I can see that loving you was a mistake."

"It's never a mistake to love someone, is it? And I can never repay you for helping with Hannah and the boys and the cooking and cleaning. You did far more than I ever paid you for. And you're such a wonderful friend." He wanted to continue, but her voice cut through him.

"Friend? That's all this has been? Just friendship?"

"Oh, Cora, I never promised you anything, did I?"

She sat on the small love seat that looked out over the bay, staring into space, watching the trees that swayed in the gentle breeze.

He had hurt her deeply. He had always been afraid he would hurt her in the end. How could he not, when he didn't feel the same for her?

"I should have let you go," he finally said. "You needed to find someone to love, to marry, to have a child with."

"I couldn't, Leighton. Not feeling the way I do." She raised her face to his, the hint of tears in her blue eyes. "I could never, ever give you up. It's that simple."

She rose and walked to the other end of the living room, her hands touching the keys of the old upright. "What's she like, Leighton? Is she young? Beautiful? *Charming?*"

He slumped into one of the old easy chairs that filled one corner of the large room. "I can't even describe her to you. It's strange, I know. She has a lilt to her voice. Doesn't that beat all? The one thing I keep thinking about is her voice and how it sounds."

He also remembered that she was tall, her figure was rounded, and she had brown hair. Her eyes were blue, but he wasn't even positive about that. But when she talked, he had listened. And her words, the expression, the inflection in her voice had captured his attention.

"You fell in love with a *voice?* I find that difficult to believe. And what does she think about you? You've said how you feel about her but nothing about her feelings."

He didn't want to have this discussion now. Of course, he never wanted or liked discussions. Especially not with a strong-willed woman like Cora. She seemed to read things that weren't there or to hear something he hadn't said.

The room was dark now, as it often was on cloudy days. She stood at the piano but did not play. She was a good pianist and often played songs she knew he liked, but she only touched the old, polished wood. He should never have led her on. He hadn't really; she had led herself on.

"Is she coming here to visit?"

"I don't know."

"You didn't ask her?"

He sighed. "As a matter of fact, it was mentioned, but I doubt that she would come right now. Her daughter is expecting her first baby, and Alice has just the one child. She probably wouldn't leave her now. It's far more likely that I'll go back to Portland."

"How old is she? And I suppose she's thin." Cora had been so sure if Leighton had ever found someone, it would be a younger, more alluring woman. She, for all her good points, had bad ones, the main one being her weight. She had tried diets, a hundred or so, but nothing ever worked.

Leighton turned the small reading lamp on beside his chair. "I don't know her age, but she's definitely older. Courtney is twenty-four or so."

"You met her daughter and all her family?"

"Just the daughter. It's her husband who owns the computer business, and Alice works part-time for him."

"*Alice,*" Cora said with a sneer.

"You'd like her. She's quite personable."

"I just bet." Cora reached over and grabbed her purse. "I am not giving up, Leighton. I waited this long and will wait longer. She won't want to move here. Just you wait and see."

Before he could answer, she'd turned and gone out the front door, slamming it behind her.

Her words stunned him. He had not wanted to talk about Alice. His feelings were so new, so unexpected; he didn't know what he felt or what she felt. Cora had been a friend all these years. If something was going to happen between them, wouldn't it have happened already? How could he make himself feel something that was not there? Would she want someone who did not love her in return? Somehow he could not believe that.

Cora had been engaged once and moved to Cathlamet, a small town on the Columbia River. No one had been more surprised than he was when she came back home to Oysterville. She changed jobs from teaching English to running a bed and breakfast. Then she came to care for his family when Aunt Rita died.

He hadn't meant to hurt her. It wasn't his way. He should have known what was happening long before this. After the boys were gone and Hannah had died, why had Cora stayed on? Had he asked her to? Funny, but he couldn't even remember now.

Leighton sat awhile longer, his mind moving forward. Tomorrow he'd check with Luke, see how things had been in his absence. Luke was essentially the boss, hiring and firing, keeping track of production numbers, making sure everything was in working order. Leighton was a figurehead more than anything. He'd put in a good many hours in the field and in the cannery. It had been hard with Hannah so sick. He'd taken off early to relieve Aunt Rita in the earlier days, as a baby needed constant attention, and it was too much for just one person.

In the morning he'd make out the new orders, adding the restaurants to his database. For now, he needed to call Alice and let her know he had arrived home.

❧

The day after Leighton left, Alice called Steven.

"I want a modem so I can get e-mail." Leighton had told her last night that his son was installing the program, and he would be able to write to her every day, maybe even twice.

"Alice, I asked a couple of months ago if you wanted to go on the Internet and you said no."

"Changed my mind."

"This guy you met doesn't have anything to do with that, does it?"

"A person can change her mind, yes?"

"I'll do it on Sunday. Can't get to it before that."

"Sunday's fine."

❧

Steven was there when Courtney and Alice returned from Gresham and the customary visit and lunch with Agnes.

"How's it going?" Alice asked. "I'm so eager to use it. You'll leave the directions, right? I tend to forget things."

"Yes, of course. It's installed. I'll show you in a minute." He pulled Courtney close, nibbling the back of her neck.

"I have this tape I want to watch," Courtney said. "It's about natural childbirth."

"In a sec, okay, hon? I need to show your mother how to bring up her mail."

They walked back to the office, and Steven handed Alice a slip of paper with her password. "Don't tell anyone the password. And here's your address. You can change it if you want."

"I'm Alyce?" She stared at the paper.

"Your name was already taken, so you have to choose another spelling. Sorry. Now you are *Alyce@pdx.com*. Be sure you don't put a period after the com, though, okay?"

Alice nodded as she brought up an empty document. "Just a minute." She looked in her letter file for Leighton's e-mail address.

"Why don't you send a card?"

"A card?"

"Yes. Some Web sites offer free electronic cards. They have music, too. And there are all sorts of categories."

Alice nodded. "That would be fun."

After sending a *Just thinking of you and here's my address* card, Steven showed her how to log off the Internet. "You want the line to be free for phone calls."

As if on cue, the phone rang, and Alice grabbed the extension.

"Leighton! I just sent my first e-mail message." She giggled.

"Hey, great. I'll send one back. Talk to you online soon."

"Wait. Are you still coming next Thursday?"

"Yes."

"I'm thinking about you," she said.

"And me, you."

"I have to go. Courtney's yelling from the living room."

"Mom?" Courtney bolted up and shut off the VCR. "Was that Leighton on the phone?"

Her face felt flushed. "Well, yes."

"And he's the reason you got online."

"Yes. E-mail is going to be fun and a lot cheaper than the telephone."

"Okay, let's look at the tape." Steven pushed the START button.

Courtney lay flat on her back, her hands placed on the small mound that was the growing baby. Steven nodded. "We may as well practice now. See how it works."

The tape showed various exercises and ways to breathe. Steven leaned over, breathing along with her.

"Seems you don't need that quite yet," Alice said.

"You're right!" Courtney rolled to a sitting position. "Mom, I'm worried about you. You can't be serious about getting involved at this time in your—" She stopped as if knowing she'd stepped over the bounds.

"At this time in my life? Was that what you were going to say?" Alice walked past her daughter and into the kitchen, where she put the water on for tea.

"Oh, Mom, I didn't mean it the way it sounded." Courtney was at her side, hand touching her shoulder. "It's just that I worry about you. I'd hate to see you get hurt."

Steven stood in the doorway, his lanky form filling the space. "Courtney has a point, but I also think your mom isn't the type to go off half-cocked with some guy she hardly knows."

"Exactly!" Alice turned, teabag in hand. "I find Leighton attractive. He's nice. Attentive. All things I'd forgotten about since your father died."

"But Daddy was your whole life."

"And life is for the living, seems I remember hearing once," Steven said. "I think you should see this man. I know John, and if his dad's even half as nice, you can't go wrong."

"But, Steven," Courtney implored, rolling her eyes, "he lives at the coast. How can Mother even think of letting this go any further?"

Alice turned the water off and got out her favorite ceramic cup, a colorful red, green, blue, and yellow one that her sister, Agnes, had made years ago in a ceramics class. She dipped the bag up and down more times than usual, willing herself to say the right words, if she, indeed, needed to comment at all.

"He seems very nice, and that's all I'm saying about it." Steven left the room, while Courtney, never backing down from a discussion of any sort, put her hands on her hips.

"Mom, you don't know a thing about him. Is he a believer?"

"As a matter of fact, he is." Alice hummed as she dumped a teaspoon of sugar into her cup and stirred.

"Mother! You don't use sugar in your tea."

Alice just smiled.

"I cannot believe this person has affected you this way."

Alice rummaged around for something to go with the tea, but could only find saltines. She wasn't in the mood for crackers.

"Your father was methodical, Courtney, and I'm afraid you take after him."

"He wasn't my father, so there's no way I could 'take after him,' as you say."

Alice felt as if she'd been punched. Courtney had to be upset to come out with that statement. Because she was adopted, any traits she had were not inherited, but some she had developed over the course of years by watching and doing by example.

"You know what I meant," Alice said. She fought off the sudden tears that threatened. Nobody knew unless they had tried to have children how it felt, how wonderful it was when you finally could adopt, and how it was on that first day with the tiny bundle in your arms. She had never forgotten the feeling and felt thrice blessed now that Courtney would be bringing a child into the world. Soon Alice would feel that thrill all over again, even though the child wouldn't share her bloodline.

"Mom." Courtney put her arm around her mother. She had to lean up to do it since she was short and her mother stood a head higher, even in stocking feet. "I didn't mean to hurt you. I'm just concerned, that's all. Just like you were when I went to Illinois in search of my birth mother. It's okay to be concerned, isn't it?"

Alice let out a sob and turned to pull her daughter close. "Of course it's okay to be concerned." Alice dabbed at her cheeks with a tissue she'd found in her pocket. "Just don't try to be the boss."

At that, they both laughed, and Alice took her tea into the living room. Steven had rewound the tape and started it over.

"Steven, honey, it isn't going to happen for five months," Courtney said, wrapping her arms around his neck.

He pulled her down and kissed her cheek. "I know that, Court, but I'm going to be the most ready father there ever was."

Minutes later, Alice was back in the kitchen, checking the pot roast and getting the drippings ready for gravy. Preparing the Sunday meal always brought back the memory of that first night when Steven returned to the second service and came to sit beside Courtney. Alice had known then that something was happening between the young couple, and here they all were less than a year later.

"God certainly works fast sometimes," Tina, Courtney's best friend, had said that afternoon after the wedding when they were all eating wedding cake and talking about the couple.

"Yes, He does," Alice said. "And when one follows Him completely, there's no mistaking what He's given."

Now as they sat around the table, they held hands, and Steven asked the blessing.

The meal was quieter than usual. Afterward, Alice shooed the two out of the kitchen so she could clean up. She needed time alone to think about Leighton more clearly, to wonder, to question, to marvel at the pounding of her heart at the mere thought of him. Even now she could smell the woodsy scent of his cologne.

Maybe it isn't good for man to live alone, she mused as she placed the last plate in the dishwasher. Maybe God wanted her to be with Leighton. This could be His plan for her. The big problem was in convincing Courtney that her mother just might need something else besides loving her daughter, son-in-law, and expected grandchild.

She slipped into her bedroom and looked at her flushed cheeks. It was strange, this feeling that engulfed her. Yet he did live far away. How could they possibly see each other that often? And she could never—no, absolutely never—think of moving to the coast. It would be too far from her precious family.

Yet she dreamed of him, wanted him to think of her, wanted to see him again. How could she possibly wait four more days?

Chapter 7

In the two days since he'd come home from Portland, Leighton found his life had returned to a semistate of normalcy. But he had more bounce in his step and a reason for getting up in the mornings. He'd take his cup of coffee and the binoculars and sit in the love seat.

The bay was calm, the tide in, and the beauty of the sunrise caused his heart to swell. He'd never tired of looking out over the water to the Willapa Hills in the distance and watching while a crabber came up the bay. Crab was plentiful in the bay, but the crab pots were set out only for certain months, and the season had just begun.

God had been good to this little spot, this forgotten finger of land next to the ocean on the west, the bay on the east, and the Columbia River on the south. He loved the clean air and took a deep breath before downing his coffee and heading to work.

It wasn't even six yet, and the morning was nippy. He pulled a cap on before hopping into the truck.

Luke had left a note on the office blackboard.

Dad, I'll be late today. Lisa has an appointment with the doctor, and I said I'd go with her.

Leighton erased the note and wondered what was going on. Lisa was never sick. And if she was, she wouldn't need Luke to go with her. Unless. . .

Soon the first shipment would be brought in for sorting. Four workers would work on the line for two hours, have a short break, then work until noon. He'd go into the store, check supplies, and make sure there was enough for the weekend. Tourists were arriving in droves. If it wasn't for them, business would be slow, but he sure wished they'd learn to drive the speed limit. It was a complaint of all old-timers.

For some reason, Alice's smile flashed through his mind. Would she fit in with this operation?

Stop, he commanded himself. He didn't really know her. One dinner, a night out at the concert, followed by a lunch was not much, yet he felt comfortable around her.

The phone rang. It was Luke.

"Dad! I knew you'd be there."

"What's up? Is something wrong with Lisa?"

"No, it's just the usual."

"The usual? Could you be a bit more specific?"

"You know. It happened to you enough times."

"No, I don't know." He didn't realize he'd raised his voice until one of his workers looked over.

"We're having a baby, Dad."

"A baby? I thought you said three was enough."

"Well, things happen and there you are."

"Don't worry about rushing in. Take your time, Son. We're doing okay. No problem."

Luke started stammering. "I understand you met someone."

"You've talked with John, then."

"No. Not John. John and I never talk. You know that. It was Cora."

Cora. Of course she would be talking about it. That's the way it was here. Everyone knew everyone else's business. Cora would have people in her corner, and he'd be classified an A-1 jerk for not asking her to marry him.

"Don't believe everything you hear."

"Dad! Don't you think I know that?"

"Cora and I had words. Haven't seen her, but that's okay. Her bossiness gets to me. She doesn't own me, after all."

"Still, she thought she had a chance that someday you'd get over Mom and—"

"That's what I mean," Leighton interrupted. "I got over your mother long ago. I just don't want to risk getting hurt again."

"Is this Alice nice?"

"Luke, would I like someone who wasn't?"

"No, I suppose not. Guess I can trust your judgment."

"Thanks for the vote of confidence. Alice is a city gal. I doubt that anything will come of it." Yet he found his heart pounding at the thought of her.

"Some city gals want to be country gals."

"How's Lisa feeling?" Leighton had always been adept at changing the topic of conversation. Nancy had accused him of dodging the issue at hand more than once. And perhaps he did.

"Yucky about now. She hopes to get something for the nausea."

"Are you two happy about the baby?"

"Yeah, Dad. Of course. Why wouldn't we be?"

Leighton let his breath out. Nancy had hated each pregnancy. He wondered now why they hadn't been more careful. Two children would have suited her better than four sons and a sick daughter.

"Just wondering."

"Lisa loves children. She's not like my mother."

Of course Luke knew about his mother. He'd been twelve the day she packed her bags and left them.

"Why don't I take you guys out to celebrate tonight? We could try that new place in Long Beach. I hear it has good food."

"Sure. I'll check with Lisa. Gotta run."

Leighton mused how the only time he had a real conversation with Luke was on the phone. They could be in the same building, outside checking lines, or sharing any number of tasks and not say more than two words. At work they were there to work. The phone was for communicating.

He couldn't help but think about Luke as he replaced the receiver. He had always been sensible. Forthright. No man could have asked for a better son. He could rely on him to make the right choices, and he seemed to have a natural business sense. He was a lucky man. Neither Tom nor John wanted anything to do with the oyster business.

And Aaron. Leighton felt deep regret about his missing son. Was Aaron happy? Was he even still alive? He had so hoped in the earlier days after Aaron ran away that he'd call and say he was on his way home. Then he hoped he'd just call to say he was all right. Was he living out of a suitcase, or had he found a good job?

Kids. And wives. Sometimes a man was lucky and got a loving wife and kids who made him proud. Nancy. Why hadn't he suspected the problem with Nancy, that she had depression? He'd thought he knew her before they married. Why hadn't her dark, dancing curls, her laughing blue-gray eyes given him some small warning? He loved her so, but his love didn't matter, didn't help. It just hadn't been enough.

Leighton turned the lights on and inspected the bins where the oysters were sorted and shucked. State law required that the bins be washed with a bleach solution at the end of each day. If they had been cleaned properly, he'd smell it. He leaned over for the telltale scent.

They were fine. He went to the back and checked supplies. He'd have to make a trip across the river on Thursday. Of course, if he was that far, he could just turn the car east and keep going until he arrived in Portland.

Alice. He couldn't get her face out of his mind. Was it because it had been so long since he'd been with a woman? Could it be that God was guiding him in this direction? How did one ever know for certain? As with everything in life, there were risks. Could he risk getting his heart broken?

Chapter 8

Leighton dreaded waiting even a few more days to see Alice. It was as if he now questioned how he felt about her and wondered if she would look at him in that same way, her eyes showing interest. Being apart was not a good idea. On the downside of fifty-three, it was as if life were passing him by. As a young man, he'd felt he had forever, but now he knew it wasn't true. Nobody had forever. Only through the grace of the Lord Jesus Christ did anyone have eternal life.

He also believed that one could make or break their happiness. He had broken it once and felt he wanted to try again. He *needed* to try again. He was sorry about Cora. She had stopped by once to pick up a jacket she'd left. She'd straightened the papers in the living room, clucking her tongue over the condition of the kitchen.

"You do need a woman to take care of things." She put her hands on her hips. "Why don't I just come once a week?"

"I don't think that will be necessary." He paused for a long moment, as if searching for the right words. "Cora, more than anything I'm sorry for hurting you. I hope you believe that."

She held out a small box. "Photos. I had them at my house. Just kept forgetting to give them to you."

He took the box and thanked her. "I don't remember you taking pictures."

"Yes, well—I gotta dash. See you." She left with a half wave.

Lifting the lid, Leighton saw that the pictures were scattered; no organization here, which surprised him. Cora, being so efficient, would have had them in an album. Then he saw the bits of black paper on the back. She'd taken them out of one of those old photo albums, but why hadn't she left them in there?

The box of assorted photo albums was in the hall closet. He looked on the bottom shelf, but they weren't there. A small picture was under spare blankets. It was of Nancy and him when they first married. Had Cora taken the albums, then decided she'd better return the photos? But why would she take the pictures out of the album and not return it?

He went back to the living room and sifted through the photos.

A laughing Aaron and Hannah looked back at him in the picture on top. Tears came to his eyes. His children. And he didn't know where one of them was. Hannah was in heaven, but Aaron? Where might Aaron be?

There were the boys fishing, horseback riding, a picnic up at Leadbetter Point, picking oysters, the cannery after it had been rebuilt. A photo taken at

Thanksgiving and Christmas. Then he realized that none of the photos were of him. Had she kept those? But again, he wondered why. It didn't make sense.

He set the photos back and paced across the living room. Had Cora taken other things? If so, how would he know? He didn't keep track of dishes, knick-knacks, or anything like that.

Cora was a needy person. She needed to be needed. He was sure of that. Not only was she intelligent, she was clever and steadfast. Loyal. She would make some man a very good wife. He just wasn't that man.

He put the photos back in the closet and wondered why Cora had taken them home. Surely that must be what happened. He'd have to ask her about it sometime.

✑

Alice was thrilled with e-mail. She checked the mailbox first thing in the morning, and there was always a letter because Leighton rose early. She answered right off, though she figured he wouldn't be home to check until that evening.

He sent crazy cards with messages. She sent cards back.

One day they'd written five times and talked on the phone once.

"Just have to hear your voice, you know," Leighton said.

"And I like hearing your voice, as well."

"How's Courtney doing?"

"Just fine. I think they have the entire nursery furnished and a stack of clothes in the chest. It's her old chest that she painted a pale blue. And I've got the small downstairs bedroom turned into a nursery."

"Sounds great. My son Luke and his wife are expecting. This is the fourth for them."

"Oh, my."

"I guess we like big families."

"So do I. I would have had one more after Courtney, but the good Lord didn't look at it that way. Two possible adoptions fell through, then I just decided it was too heartbreaking to get my hopes up only to have them come crashing down."

"So now you will have grandchildren to enjoy."

✑

Over the next few days, Alice went through the motions of living. Courtney laughed at her inability to sit still.

"I've never seen you like this, Mom." She shook her head. "I guess it's true—the old adage that anyone at any age can fall in love."

"I never said I was in love—"

"You didn't have to."

"I know perfectly well that life will go on as before if I never see Leighton Walker again."

"It's just that he captured your heart whether you want to admit it or not."

"Maybe you're right, sweetie. I wasn't looking. You know that. But he's so interesting, and the fact that he believes in God—well, that makes him even more special."

"So you said before, and praise God for that," Courtney said. "I always said that I hoped you'd find a good Christian man, should you ever start looking for someone."

"And that's the weird part. I wasn't—"

"Looking," Courtney finished her mother's sentence. "Yes. It just happened. It's all part of God's timing. Like Steven and me. What if he hadn't come to our church that Sunday morning?"

"Exactly."

Alice poured them each another cup of tea. Courtney had quit drinking coffee in favor of herbal teas, which wouldn't hurt her baby. "I have a surprise for you," Alice said.

"A surprise?"

Alice brought a large shopping bag in and began taking out the contents. "Little undershirts. And here's two pair of shoes that you wore when you were little. And of course this yellow bunny sleeper is precious. Remember how you used to call it your bear? Your father kept saying it's a bunny, but you insisted that it was a bear."

Courtney held the clothes close. "Mom, these are so special. I'll treasure them."

Long after Courtney had left, Alice wondered what she was going to do with her hours. She simply could not sit still, and she had cleaned out the closets, put new shelf paper in the kitchen, and had filled three boxes to give to the disabled veterans' group. Should she offer to work another day in the office or volunteer more hours at the hospital? She could get involved with the literacy program. But would she be able to concentrate on anything? Her mind wandered, and the little thread of excitement that coursed through her veins was still there. She might do more harm than help.

As if in answer to her flitting mind, the phone rang. Leighton's deep voice seemed to fill the whole room.

"I'm leaving in the morning. Not much point in waiting another day. How does that sound?"

"I can have dinner ready. I'll put in my famous oven Swiss steak. It's delicious. You'll love it. I'll ask Courtney to bring a green salad, and there's a pie in the freezer made from last year's rhubarb."

"Sounds like a plan."

"Be careful, Leighton." *I couldn't bear if anything happened to you now,* she wanted to say, but didn't.

After hanging up, she immediately dialed Courtney. "I know you just got home, but how about coming for dinner tomorrow?"

"I was just there, Mom. Why didn't you ask me then?"

"Because I didn't know it then. Leighton just called and will be here at dinnertime. I really want you to get to know him, and Steven hasn't even met him."

"I'll call Steven and get back to you."

It was a done deal, and now Alice would clean and buy the beef and other ingredients. She wondered if his son was as bothered about his sudden romance as her daughter was. It seemed silly when she thought about it. Why wouldn't Courtney be happy that she'd found someone? Then she and Steven wouldn't need to worry about taking care of her in her old age.

Two trips in less than ten days. And more messages than she could count, plus phone calls. She'd say she was being pursued.

And on that happy thought, she grabbed her purse and headed out the door for the closest grocery store. She had all night to wait and wondered what she'd find to do.

Chapter 9

It was nine o'clock before Leighton got out of Oysterville. Ken loaded the cases of oysters on the old Chevy pickup. The company owned a delivery truck, but he didn't want to take it. It was better to leave it for Luke in case something came up.

"Dad, you're driving this into Portland today?" He scratched his head. "Why? It's far cheaper for UPS to deliver, or let Ken take it or even me." A broad grin crossed his face. "Oh. Got it! Finally came to me. I'm thick at times, you know."

Leighton hit his knee with his cap, as if there were dust to shake off. "Yeah, well, I just want to make the trip. I made another appointment at a place Alice suggested."

"If you're finding new clientele, that's a good enough reason. And guess I should have suspected that, with you wearing a white shirt and tie." He leaned over and flipped the tie with his hand. "Of course the cap's gotta go."

"How's Lisa doing? Getting over the morning sickness?"

"It isn't going to work," Luke said, rolling his eyes. "You can't change the subject on me."

"Okay, okay. I'm going in mainly to see Alice. Is that what you wanted to hear?"

"Yeah, guess it was. So when is she coming here so we can all meet her?"

"ASAP," Leighton said. Hearing raised voices inside, he pushed past his son.

Luke often hired Mexican-Americans, but the local men, who had lived on the peninsula all their lives, resented others coming in and "taking over our jobs," Olson, the spokesperson, said. Sometimes a fight developed between the two races, and Luke had to reprimand them. Just last week he had fired two trouble-makers, and it looked as if he might have to do that again. It probably wasn't the best time for Leighton to leave. He'd always run a smooth operation and resented that there was more trouble these days. Some of the younger Anglo men were lazy and didn't want to work. They then picked on the "Mexies," as they called them, for making them look bad.

"Do you want me to take care of that?" Leighton asked as the voices inside grew louder.

Luke headed for the door. "No, I'll handle it. You go on, and I'll see you when you get back."

"You'll let me know if anything else comes up?"

"And how will I do that, Dad?"

Leighton held up a cell phone. "Forgot to tell you, but I bought this yesterday. Here's the number."

A smile crossed Luke's face. "I don't believe it. You finally did it. First e-mail and now a cell phone. Welcome to the twenty-first century, Dad."

Leighton gave him a high five and strode over to the truck. The last time he'd taken the car, but if they went anywhere, Alice would have to drive or settle for the ole Chevy.

As he drove down Sandridge, he passed by Nancy's parents' old house. He still got a funny feeling when he remembered the times he'd knocked at the door, shyness overtaking him. He had always kept in touch for the boys' sake. They were the only grandparents left now. He swallowed hard, wishing his parents were still alive. His mom would have liked Alice.

He made a left-hand signal to turn onto Highway 103 when a honk sounded. He looked on the opposite side and saw Cora. She honked again. He honked back. She pulled a U-turn and came up behind him, using her flashers. Was something wrong? Had Luke sent her after him? No, she was heading north. He pulled over, and seconds later she hopped out.

"Where are you going with all those crates?"

"Making a delivery." He avoided her gaze, though he could feel her eyes scrutinizing him. He expected her to say something about the tie, but she didn't. She just stood with hands on hips.

"It wouldn't be to Portland, now, would it?"

"Sure is."

"I don't suppose you want company."

He couldn't believe she'd suggest it. Wouldn't that look ducky to drive up to Alice's with Cora in tow?

"I'm staying over at John's. He's just got the one spare bedroom."

"You could easily make the trip in a day."

Why is she doing this? She knows about Alice. Why act as if she doesn't? She's never before asked to go to Portland.

"Cora, I really must go. I have an appointment with a restaurant. Sorry. Maybe another time."

She stood at the side of the road, arms now folded. "Sure, Leighton. And you're not going into Portland for any other reason."

"I didn't say that—"

"It isn't going to work; you know it isn't."

"I'll find out then, won't I." It was a statement more than a question. "And I really need to get going."

She went back to her car, made another U-turn, and headed back north. He wished she hadn't seen him. What was she doing at the south end this time of morning? It seemed a bit odd. And why had she confronted him? This wasn't like Cora.

Thirty minutes later he was on the main road going east. He played *Fiddler,* but it didn't make him laugh as it usually did. A heaviness hung over him, and he was having trouble shaking it.

The closer he got to Portland, the more he thought about Alice. Had he set himself up for disappointment? What if she really wasn't interested, now that she'd had time to think it over, and she didn't know how to tell him? This was probably all a dream, and he'd wake up to find himself back home in bed, with the blankets on the floor.

The traffic thickened as he approached Portland. A layer of haze hovered on the horizon, and a headache started at the base of his neck. He never knew if it was from anxiety or the exhaust fumes. Today he willed the headache to leave. He wasn't going to let anything interfere with his time here.

The new restaurant was in the northwest section of downtown Portland. He found it just fine and presented the idea as he had the other times.

"Yes," the manager said, "I've noticed how some of the restaurants have the display case close to the door and cash register. It *is* a good idea. I'll try it."

After receiving the signature on the dotted line, Leighton hopped back into his truck and put the order on the clipboard. Ah, one more reason to come into town.

Now he had to make the deliveries. He soon discovered he wasn't as young as he used to be and wondered why he hadn't remembered a dolly. Fortunately, they had one at the second restaurant. By the time the last delivery was made, he felt a strong twinge in his lower back. He pulled up to a drive-through espresso shop and ordered a cold latté. It was already three o'clock. He'd head out to Alice's now, but there was one more thing to do.

The night they'd walked, he'd noticed a florist shop up on Fifth. Now he walked out with a bouquet of pink roses. He wasn't sure why he'd picked pink, but she'd worn a pink top that night, and it made her cheeks even rosier. Red would mean more serious intentions, and yellow didn't seem right. Pink was the best choice.

It was going to be four o'clock before he got there, and he knew he'd be caught up in traffic, but he headed out.

Alice answered the door quickly, as if she'd been there waiting. Her eyes widened when she saw the roses.

"How did you know that pink was my favorite color, Leighton?" She hugged him then.

"Just a guess. You look really good."

She wore an apron over beige slacks and a pink-striped top. She hugged him again before heading to the kitchen to find a vase. "I worried that you were either late getting started, got lost finding the restaurants, or were caught in a traffic jam." Her cheeks were flushed, matching the roses. She kept holding them out to admire.

"None of the above," he said. There was no way he was going to tell her what really happened, with Cora stopping him. "I don't believe it. Here I bought a cellular phone and meant to call you, but plumb forgot I had it."

"You need a cell phone when traveling on the road. I'm glad you have it."

He watched as she poured water in a tall cut-glass vase, then added a few grains of sugar. "This is supposed to make them last longer." She put one stem in at a time instead of stuffing them all in at once, as Leighton would have done.

A voice sounded in the hall, and Courtney entered the room. "Oh, Mom, roses!" She bent over and smelled them, then turned to Leighton. "How nice to see you again." She held out her hand. "And the roses are beautiful!"

He took her hand. "It's nice seeing you again, too. And when is the baby due?"

"Before Thanksgiving." She smiled. "Figures. It's a boy, and boys like to eat. My friend Tina's baby is nine months old, and Isaac eats constantly."

"Guess you know what you're in for," Alice said, not taking her eyes off of Leighton.

"My eldest son and his wife are expecting, also. I think he said around New Year's. It's their fourth."

"Fourth?" Courtney seemed as surprised as Alice had when Leighton mentioned he had five children.

"Maybe in time for a tax deduction," Alice said, checking the oven.

"Mom, I'm going to walk over to see Mrs. Rogers. Haven't seen her since I found out I'm carrying a boy."

"Yes, honey, that's a great idea. You know she'll be delighted to see you."

Leighton watched as the short girl stepped into sandals and went out the door.

"Was her leaving deliberate?" Leighton asked.

"What do you think?"

"I think she didn't want to be around in case I came up and slipped my arm around you and pulled you close and kissed you." He bent down and kissed Alice's forehead, her cheek, then her mouth.

"Hmmm," she said, "I could get real comfortable doing this," and she kissed him back.

"Yes, but we don't know each other yet."

Alice laughed. "You know you're right. I keep forgetting that."

"Things don't happen this fast," Leighton said, meeting her steady gaze. "And I'm not sure I should be left alone with you."

"But the food is cooking—"

"Have you ever heard of shutting a burner off?"

A car horn sounded, and Leighton jumped. "Saved by the horn."

They were giggling like two schoolkids when Steven entered the house. "I left early because it's been one hectic day. Honey? Alice? Where is everybody? I know the company's here."

A blushing Alice met him as he rounded the corner. "Courtney's over visiting

Mrs. Rogers. Nice to see you, Steven, and glad you came early." She hugged him.

"Oh, hello. You must be Leighton." He held out his hand, and Leighton shook it firmly.

"Yeah. The one with the rusted-out truck."

"Oh, it is? I didn't notice."

"Gets rusty at the coast, you know." Leighton was giving him the once-over, just as he knew Steven was doing the same.

"You have no idea how I've looked forward to meeting you. Jeff keeps saying you're an okay sort of guy, and I like to believe the best about people. But Courtney keeps worrying about things, and I didn't know what to think."

"And now?" Alice asked.

"Don't put him on the spot," Leighton said. "Wait until after we play a game of Scrabble. Alice told me it's your favorite pastime on a Sunday afternoon."

"You play?"

"Not really. I mean, it's been a long time."

The evening was pleasant. Leighton had two helpings of Swiss steak and a salad and two pieces of rhubarb pie. He didn't dare tell Alice that he hadn't been eating as well since Cora didn't come to cook. Besides, he wanted her to know he liked her cooking. That was important to most women. Not his sons' wives, though. They both preferred gardening to cooking. But then Alice was old-fashioned.

"Time to play Scrabble," Courtney said once the dishes were cleared off the table. "I always win, but I might be nice to you." She grinned.

She wasn't nice to him, and Leighton came in last. "That's what happens when you raise boys and end up playing Battleship, War, and Fish."

"Fish!" Steven laughed. "I remember talking Grandma into playing that."

"Let's play," Courtney said. "I'd love to."

It was after ten when Leighton said he'd better get over to John's. "He doesn't even know I'm coming."

"And this is how a cell phone is handy," Alice said. "You could have called him while you were on the road."

He left Alice standing in the doorway. He wanted to kiss her, really kiss her, good night, but opted for a brush of his lips across her cheek. She took his hand again and held on to it as if she didn't want him to leave, either.

"I think we'd better go," Courtney said, walking up behind her mother.

"Everyone's leaving at once," Alice said. "I'm going to be lonely."

Leighton wanted to come back after that remark, but knew he couldn't. "See you soon," he called. "I'll send you a late-night message from John's."

"I'll be waiting."

He opened the truck door when she came running out. "I forgot to thank you for the roses again." She looked into his face. "They're beautiful."

"You're most welcome," he said, a lump coming to his throat. He had to go. It was imperative.

It was a long, lonely ride back across town, and he was glad John was there. He needed to talk to someone. Anyone. The feeling he'd had since he'd first met Alice only intensified tonight, and he knew he was definitely falling in love with her.

Chapter 10

Alice spent a restless night. She had wanted to spend more time with Leighton but was glad Courtney and Steven had come, happy that they liked him. In her book, the evening had been a smashing success, especially when they laughed as they played Fish. She knew Courtney would be full of questions and comments tomorrow.

Checking to make sure the burners were all off, Alice caught the scent of roses. She looked at them and marveled at their fragrance, their beauty. She'd have to take Leighton to the Rose Test Gardens in Washington Park. That was definitely on the agenda.

She checked her e-mail, and Leighton had sent a message, as he'd promised. She laughed at the two polar bears hugging.

"Yes, it was a wonderful night," she wrote back. "Courtney didn't say, but I know when she likes someone. You made an impression with her. As for Steven, he's easygoing, so no problem there. Will I see you tomorrow?"

"I'm leaving at five," he wrote back. "Sorry, but when I talked to Luke, he said he thought I'd better get back as soon as possible. There are two men who both want to be boss. It's a long story. I'll explain it sometime."

"I hope it isn't anything too drastic."

"Not anything I can't handle."

"Good night and sleep tight," had been his last message.

Alice slept with those words going through her mind. Sleep tight. No chance of that, not with a hundred thoughts racing through her mind. She knew what Todi meant now. She had not felt this way about Carl. It was entirely different. Did that mean she had not loved him as much? She knew that wasn't true.

She turned on the small lamp beside the bed and read one of her devotionals. It was the one for Wednesday, the day she first met Leighton. "Don't shut the door on new happenings. Rejoice in what God sends your way."

"So, Lord, there is more to life than getting old alone. More than living through the life of your children, anticipating grandbabies. I welcome the challenge."

Leighton sent a greeting card the next morning. Alice printed it out.

At eight he called from Astoria. "Just checking in. I kind of like this phone, but I won't call in traffic."

"I hear the police are cracking down on cell phone users," Alice said.

"Are you going into Spencer Consultants?"

"Yes, Steven said he wanted me there in the afternoon."

"I'll call you tonight, then."

❧

Leighton arrived at the cannery when the first shift was still there. "I understand there've been problems lately, and I want you to know I won't tolerate it. If you don't want to work here, fine. There's the door. I'll give you a week's severance pay. But if you do want the job, then you're going to need to get along with the others. No taking sides. As far as I'm concerned, we're all Americans and we work together. Period. Any questions?"

Nobody raised a hand. "Good. So get to work. And come to me with problems, understand?"

Luke met him outside. "Dad, I think it might work. They listen to you, you know."

"It *has* to work, Son. We've never had this happen before, so let's just not put up with it. Be firm."

He left later to check on the stock in the store and to add the new order to his computer. Alice kept flitting through his mind. He had a plan and would call her tonight.

❧

"I know one thing, Alice," he said when he found her at home. He had decided to call because he wanted to hear her voice. It soothed him.

"What's that?"

"It's your turn now."

"My turn?"

"Yes. Your turn to come visit me. Bring the kids. I'd love it, and so would my sons."

"I'll definitely plan on it, but I'm not sure about Courtney. I think she wants to stay close to home just now. Some expectant mothers don't like to get more than twenty miles from the hospital."

"Good plan."

"And did you resolve the problem at work?"

"I hope so. I had a talk with the troublemakers. I told Luke we just had to pray for peace among our workers. We can't let things fall apart now."

"I've been thinking about you, about wanting to see you again."

"Yes, I've been thinking, too," Alice murmured.

"I need to see you soon. Real soon."

"Before next weekend?" She gripped the receiver, as if it were trying to get away.

"Yes. And I don't want you to worry about driving. I'll send the Bay Shuttle. And Trudy can put you up at one of the most elegant bed and breakfasts you've ever seen."

"Who's Trudy?"

"A shirttail cousin, but I'm not sure whose shirttail."

Alice laughed. "How wonderful it must be to have cousins and lots of aunts and uncles. I never had a big family, and Courtney wished she had a cousin when she was growing up."

"Will you come, then?"

"Yes, I'd like that."

"Fine. When?"

Alice mentally calculated that Steven could do without her. The answering machine could pick up calls, and she didn't need to be at the hospital this week. One call could get someone else to take her shift. She wanted to go immediately. But would that sound too eager?

"I'd like you to come tonight, but I know that isn't possible."

That was all the encouragement Alice needed. "I can be ready tomorrow morning."

"Tomorrow it is." Leighton's voice had a sudden lightness. "I'll check the Bay Shuttle's schedule, then get back to you."

Alice clasped her hands as she stared into the growing darkness. He wanted to see her again. He felt the same way she did. And at that thought, she jumped to her feet and hurried to the bedroom. What should she take to the beach for a few days' vacation? She had clothes piled on her bed when the phone rang again.

"Mel, the driver, will stop for you tomorrow at noon. I'm meeting you in Seaview, as we'll have a few hours for sight-seeing. I'll show you the south end before going to my end of the peninsula and Oysterville."

"Sounds wonderful. I'll be waiting." She gave him her address and directions from the airport, where Mel would be coming from.

Back to the packing. She should take a dressy outfit in case they ate out at an elegant place. Her high-heeled gold sandals and the new pantsuit she'd wear on the shuttle bus. She wanted to look nice when she arrived, as there'd be no chance to change.

When the phone rang, she figured it was Courtney, but it was Leighton again.

"I didn't tell you all that I had on my mind."

"Oh? What is that?"

"That I think you're the neatest lady I've met in a very long while, and I can hardly wait until you get here."

"In the meantime, there's e-mail," Alice murmured.

"Yes, there is. Sleep well tonight. We're going to hike, and I want you to be in good shape."

After the conversation, she tried to get into the novel she'd been reading, but kept reading the same sentence over and over again. Finally, she put the book aside and grabbed her journal.

"Lord, You wouldn't have allowed me to be in this position if You didn't love me and want what is best for my life."

A couple of verses from Hebrews 11 made Alice smile. "Now faith is being sure of what we hope for and certain of what we do not see. This is what the ancients were commended for."

Alice read the verses again and felt tears form.

"Lord, you know I have faith, and because of that faith, I am reassured that this is a step You'd have me take."

She closed her Bible and reached for the phone. She better call to let the kids know she would be gone for a few days.

"Mother, are you sure about this?" Courtney said. "Don't you think you should slow down? Let things simmer for a while?"

"Simmer? What do you mean, let things *simmer?* It's already simmering."

"I mean *wait.* Don't rush into anything."

"I'm not rushing. And as for simmering, it's been doing that since the moment I saw him."

"Okay. I just hope it's going to work out."

"If God wants it to, then it will. I'll call you from there. Here, let me give you Leighton's e-mail address so we can keep in touch that way."

"Okay, Mom. Have fun."

"And that's exactly what I intend to do," Alice said as she replaced the receiver. "I'm having an adventure, for sure."

Chapter 11

A lice had changed her mind a dozen times about what to take on the trip. Leighton had warned her that the weather was changeable.

"It can be a nice summer day, seventy degrees or so, then the ocean breezes blow in, and it gets foggy and damp."

She had been to the coast many times in her life, but always on the Oregon beaches. She always took older clothes, baggy jeans, sweatshirts, and holey sneakers. But she was meeting Leighton and wanted to look nice.

She packed a pair of blue shorts and a favorite jean shirt with embroidered bears on the pockets. It was the dress she couldn't decide on. Should it be the long flowered crepe or the dressy navy blue linen?

She couldn't believe that he'd insisted on having the Bay Shuttle pick her up.

"But I can drive," Alice had protested again.

"No. It's farther than you realize. You'll hit Chinook, think you're there, then you have the whole peninsula to drive. I'm talking twenty-five miles here."

The shuttle would take her to Seaview, where Leighton would be waiting. "I'll be there before you will, and we'll see the south end, the fishing boats, and the lighthouses, then come on up to my end of the world."

"Lighthouses?" Alice asked.

"Yes, there are two."

"I love lighthouses," Alice said then. "I have a lighthouse collection."

Alice decided on nice butter yellow slacks and a matching jacket, with a lighter shirt. It had been a birthday gift from Agnes.

She wore a gold bracelet, gold rose earrings, and a matching locket. High-heeled sandals completed her outfit. Now all she had to do was wait for the knock at the door. He had assured her that the Bay Shuttle had only the best drivers, and she'd be in good hands.

It was as if her life passed before her eyes while Alice waited. This was turning a new page. She'd thought she was near the end of the book of her life. She'd accomplished many things, and God had blessed her many times over.

She checked to see if her Bible and book of devotionals were in the smaller bag. They were.

Alice heard a car outside. She peeked out the window and saw a young man hop out and head for the house.

"Ms. Adams?" He held out a hand. "I'm your driver. My name's Mel."

She nodded. "I'm ready, Mel." She suddenly felt uneasy without knowing why. "Let me check the burners one last time."

He chuckled as he took the two bags and headed for the small van.

"I remember reading a joke in *Reader's Digest* once," Mel said once they were on the road heading west. "This woman always thought she'd left the iron on, and she and her husband'd have to turn around and go back to check. Then one year, as they were driving down the freeway, she said she knew she'd left the iron on. Her husband stopped the car and went to the back where everything was packed. 'Nope! You didn't. Here it is.' And he held the iron up for her to see."

Alice laughed. "That's a good one."

"And a smart husband," Mel added.

Alice leaned back against the cushion and envisioned Leighton coming to meet her. What would they say to each other? Would they be awkward? She felt like a girl, not the mature woman she'd always projected.

"Have you been to the peninsula before?" Mel asked, breaking into her reverie.

"Never."

She wanted to say she'd like anything if Leighton were there, but instead said, "Do you know Leighton Walker, the man I'm meeting?"

Mel met her gaze in the rearview mirror. "Alice, everyone knows everyone there, especially people like the Walkers, who've been in the oyster business since the beginning of time. Leighton's a community leader, too, and that means a lot to a small place like the peninsula."

"Oh. I suppose I should have guessed that."

"I worked for him one time at the cannery."

"And how was that?"

"Good job, but I don't like smelling like oysters all day. You'll see people walking around in tall rubber boots in town, and you'll smell 'em a mile away."

Alice laughed. "I can hardly wait." She leaned back, then remembered the bag by the front door.

"I forgot my hat!" she blurted. "And my tennis shoes. Oh, no."

"Too late to worry about that now. Besides, there are places to buy things like that. People always forget something. Usually it's a jacket in the summer. They expect it to be hot all day, and it just isn't."

Alice was the only one on the Bay Shuttle, a rare occurrence, according to Mel. "We've gotten so busy with the shuttle that they've added another van."

They chitchatted for a while, then Alice read a book. She also enjoyed the scenery along the way.

"We're getting close to the Astoria Bridge. Surely you've been across it."

"No, I can't say that I have." Alice's breath caught as Mel drove around a curve. Suddenly there they were, high up over the Columbia River, with water in every direction as far as she could see. She shivered. "This reminds me of the suspension bridge at Canon City, Colorado. It scared me half to death when we walked across it. At least I have the safety of a car."

"Yeah, that right? This is one of the longest single-lane truss bridges ever built. Now we're almost level with the water. Isn't that a spectacular view?"

"It's gorgeous," Alice said, her stomach settling down. "It reminds me of a ride they had at the old Jantzen Beach Amusement Park I went to as a kid."

They were soon across the river and on solid road, passing through a tunnel, the town of Chinook, and finally, Seaview.

"I see Leighton's Chevy," Mel said as he was waiting to turn left. Alice felt her heart thud madly. There was Leighton, standing next to his truck, long and lean in Levis and a plaid shirt, a cap on his head, as if that would hold back his unruly hair.

She didn't remember getting out of the van or realize that her luggage had been put in the back of Leighton's truck. All she could do was watch him, his manner, and the way he smiled, and she knew. Knew that her life would forever be entwined with his.

He pulled her close briefly, then, hand in hand, they went to the truck. "I didn't think you'd ever arrive."

Alice felt her cheeks flush. "Mel made good time."

"You know what I meant. I'm sure he did. I came thirty minutes early just in case he made even better time. I regret I don't have the car, but it needed a brake job. I'll pick it up tomorrow."

"It was a lovely drive, and I sure don't mind riding in a truck."

"And it's a lovely day. We're not always so blessed with sunshine." He helped her into the truck, his hand lingering on her arm. "Luke had a fit when I said I was picking you up in the old Chev."

"I like the truck. I can see even better."

"You always look at things from the positive angle, don't you?" Leighton leaned over and impulsively kissed her cheek. "I like that."

"I never thought about it."

"It's true."

He thought of Nancy, who complained daily, and of Cora, who got cranky at times.

"Let's go for our sightseeing drive. We'll get out and walk to North Head Lighthouse, then go over to the restaurant I was telling you about."

"Whatever you have planned is fine," Alice said. "I'll enjoy every moment."

"What did your daughter say about your coming?"

Alice laughed. "Courtney didn't say a whole lot. She worries about me, though."

"As a good daughter should."

"And your boys?"

Leighton shrugged. "They knew you were coming, and that's about it. I don't tell them all my business, just as they don't tell me all of theirs."

"Sounds typical of the male gender."

"Don't go getting all stereotypical on me."

Alice stole a look out of the corner of her eye. "It's true and you know it."

"You'll meet Luke at the cannery tonight. We'll drop by before closing."

Alice thought of Courtney's words. She didn't want Leighton to know what she'd said about getting hurt. That was like fishing for a commitment, and she was far from wanting to do that.

Golden sunshine, a true gift for the day, filled the truck. When Leighton rolled his window down, Alice sniffed the ocean air. There was nothing like it anywhere.

"I hope you can stay several days," he said.

"I'm not sure. Do I have to know now?"

"Of course not."

"I can stay two days, anyway, if you want me that long."

Leighton turned and met her gaze. He'd just pulled into the parking lot and shut the engine off. "If I want you—"

"Company should never stay more than three days, my mother always said. I don't want you to tire of me."

"I won't, and I sure know that Trudy won't."

They walked down the winding path that led to the lighthouse. Through the thick growth of trees, Alice caught glimpses of a sandy beach, waves splashing up, and dots that were people.

"Benson Beach. Where the campers go," Leighton explained. They stopped, and he held her hand gently. "We can go there sometime, too. There's so much to do."

The lighthouse was around the next bend, and Alice drew in a sharp breath. With a red top, it stood like the commanding beacon it was.

"We can tour it."

But Alice didn't tell him about her fear of heights or that she hadn't once flown in an airplane. "I'd like to stand down here and just watch the ocean, if that's okay."

"Remember, I've been here many times. It's your call."

They leaned against a chain-link fence and looked south then north. The water was a china blue, the waves white and fierce. A wind picked up, and Alice breathed in. Leighton's hand still held hers, tighter now.

"It is beautiful. Like Paradise must be."

After the drive back into town, Leighton pulled up next to a large building. A sign beamed from the third floor.

"Here's where you'll get the best clam chowder ever."

As they looked out on the water and watched children running from the waves, Alice savored the chowder, stirred her iced tea with a straw, and wondered if this was just a dream. She could hardly wait for Courtney and Steven to come here, also.

"Look, a car's getting towed," Leighton said. "People forget how difficult it is to navigate in soft sand. They're always getting stuck."

"Do you drive on the beach?"

"Sure. Always have. We could go, but the tide's in, and it's best to wait until later, when it's out."

The waitress came, offering them dessert menus.

"The Columbia Sludge Pie is awfully good," Leighton said, but Alice knew she couldn't eat another bite. She'd been like this, eating so little ever since that afternoon they'd met.

"We can come back later for dessert," she said.

"Sounds fine to me."

Moments later they were outside, walking the boardwalk that ran above the sand, still affording walkers a view of the water and all the activity.

"I can see why you love it here," Alice finally said. "Such a far cry from the city."

They drove what Leighton called the back road until they reached Oysterville.

"The whole town is on the historical social register?" she asked. That sounded pretty important.

Leighton nodded. "Sure is. It was a booming town in its day. Back in the late 1800s and up until 1920 or so. Had its heyday, so to speak, but that was almost a century ago. Now we have the old church that has vespers during the summer and weddings with receptions in the old schoolhouse. And every year before Christmas, there's an old-fashioned party with more food than you could possibly try, a Santa, gift exchanges, and drawings for various products from local merchants."

"It's breathtakingly wonderful! After living in the city, I had no idea such a place could even exist."

Leighton pulled up in front of a Victorian house painted a creamy beige with a forest green trim. "This is it! My abode."

Alice stared in fascination. Huge trees bordered the front yard. The grass was thick, green, and lush. A picket fence outlined the property.

"This is where you've always lived?"

"Since I was two."

"It's wonderful."

The bay was at full tide, and Alice drew in deep breaths. "I love it!" She looked over at Leighton and saw an almost bemused look on his craggy face. "What? Are you laughing at me?"

"Leighton!" A voice called from the open doorway of the house. "I have dinner ready." A short woman with dark hair pulled back into a tight bun looked at Leighton, then noticed Alice.

"I didn't know you were bringing a guest."

Alice felt her face go hot. Who was this person standing on the porch, acting as if she owned the place? As if she belonged to Leighton or perhaps he belonged to her?

"I'm Alice Adams." She stepped forward and offered her hand. "I've never been to Oysterville, and it's a wonderful, delightful place!"

The woman frowned, then took Alice's hand. "I'm Cora Benchley. I've been housekeeper, cook, nanny—you name it—for the past fifteen years since Aunt Rita died."

Alice felt the smile freeze on her face. This was the woman Leighton had mentioned that first night at the restaurant, and she definitely looked as if she owned the place.

Chapter 12

Alice felt uncomfortable as the woman scrutinized her. Had Leighton known she would be here? She obviously felt she belonged, and it was as if Alice were trespassing on her property.

Leighton, also feeling uncomfortable, finally found his voice. "Cora, why are you here? I hadn't planned on eating at home tonight."

"I like to cook. You know that." She swept her hand toward the immense porch. "It's simple fare. A pot of clam chowder, thick with clams and chunks of potatoes, bacon, and lots of butter and cream, just the way you like it. There's also hot corn bread. And I made a blackberry crisp from berries I picked last summer and put in the freezer. Besides, Leight, you left everything in an absolute shambles."

Alice swallowed hard. This woman clearly knew what Leighton liked to eat, and it appeared she pretty well ran the place. She also probably knew that Alice was coming but had decided to ignore the fact.

"Are you staying here, my dear?" Cora asked then with the slightest hint of sarcasm in her lilting voice.

"Oh, I don't think so," Alice said, once she found her voice.

"Leighton?" She turned to face him.

"No, Cora. She'll be over at Trudy's bed and breakfast. I thought that was much more appropriate. I just brought her here to see the place and Oysterville. We're going by the cannery before it gets dark to see if Luke is there."

"So you won't be eating?" Her face showed her keen disappointment.

"Actually, we had dinner at the Lightship."

"Ah, well, the chowder is better the second day, anyway. As for the corn bread, I'll just take it home with me."

Alice wanted to disappear. This had not happened very many times in her life, but this was one of them. Why hadn't Leighton told her about the woman who kept his house? She surely had designs on him—no doubt about it—and as was so often with men, Leighton now seemed flustered about the whole thing.

"Am I going to meet your boys?" Alice heard herself saying, not liking the uncomfortable silence.

"Boys?" Cora looked perplexed.

"Not tonight," Leighton said.

"Oh, I assumed they were coming since Cora cooked and cleaned."

Cora whirled around. "I don't tend to the boys now, but Leighton still needs looking out for and caring. A whole lot of caring."

Alice took a deep breath. "I'm sure he does," she said, suddenly wishing she wore Levis, as Cora did, feeling out of place in the dressy yellow slack set.

"Listen, I think we'd better get on over by the cannery, then I'll take you to Trudy's."

Cora hurried to the kitchen, and seconds later the sound of the refrigerator door opening and closing told them that the dinner, so carefully prepared, was now being put away.

"It was nice meeting you," Alice called out as Leighton held the door open, his hand brushing against her shoulder. She jumped aside.

"Same here," the voice called from the kitchen.

"She knew you were coming," Leighton said in a low voice. "She also knows I told her I didn't need her working for me anymore. She's acting like she's taken leave of her senses."

Alice knew why Cora had acted like that, but she didn't dare say so. She walked down the steps, careful not to trip in the high heels. *How inappropriate,* she thought for the second time that day, *to bring such footwear to the beach.*

"Forget the way Cora acted. Don't let her ruin your visit."

"I'm not sure what to think."

Leighton scowled. "She's an old friend. Nothing more. She just likes to run things. Always been that way."

Again, Alice didn't comment. Men could be so blind.

"You'll love the bed and breakfast," Leighton said, slipping his arm casually around her shoulder. Alice wanted to lean into him, wanted to feel the safe comfort of his arms, but she couldn't. Especially now that she knew about Cora. There was more to Leighton than she first thought.

"Cora means well," he said, as if reading her mind. "She gets a bit bossy. I've put up with it over the years, and that's why I said something to her the other day."

"She loves you," Alice said. "It's very clear."

"Loves me!" He looked perplexed again. "Now, why on earth would you think that?"

"Oh, Leighton. If she's been keeping your house and taking care of you for a long while, she's not about to give it all up now."

"She's a friend. She knows that. I've always paid her for her work and the cooking. It isn't as if it's gratis."

"Cora wants more than money."

"That's nonsense!" He closed her truck door, and soon they were driving north again. The cannery was closed down for the night, which he thought strange. "I'll look into it tomorrow. Besides, it's late and you need to get to your place for the night. 'Tomorrow is another day,' as my mother used to say."

Alice nodded. She was tired. They'd done a lot, and she'd been busy since six in the morning. It was time to relax and kick off these ridiculous sandals. Tomorrow she'd buy a pair of sensible tennis shoes. She'd noticed a store back in

Long Beach that must sell them.

"I've had a wonderful time," she said as the truck now headed south. "I'm looking forward to doing more sight-seeing tomorrow."

"And so we shall." He slipped his arm around the back of the seat.

"Tomorrow is going to be a wonderful, beautiful day," Alice murmured. "I can hardly wait."

They drove up a long, winding driveway that was wooded and secluded, then pulled up in front of a huge house with three stories. "This is it!" Leighton said.

"It's a mansion!"

"With a view. And the best cook you could ever hope to meet."

"I won't tell Cora you said that."

Leighton's face grew serious. "That's enough about Cora."

He led Alice to the sitting room that overlooked the bay. The tide was in, and it looked peaceful and serene—a sea of glass with the hills in the background. A formal parlor was to her right. An older man sat in a burgundy wing chair, reading a magazine. He nodded. "Nice night, isn't it?"

"Yes, it is," Leighton said.

Trudy appeared, drying her hands on a blue-and-white-striped apron. "Leighton, you've brought your guest. I'm so glad this was a slow weekend. No festivals, fairs, or parades." She laughed, and Leighton chuckled.

"Apparently a lot goes on around here in the summer," Alice said.

"Oh, yes," Trudy said. "From Memorial Day until the end of September, I'm usually filled to capacity. But I love it!"

Leighton set Alice's suitcase down.

"How about I give you the complete tour in the morning?" Trudy said. "Perhaps you'll want to sit out in one of the Adirondack chairs and watch the sunrise."

"I'll be back over for breakfast," Leighton said. "I'll let Trudy show you to your room." He leaned over and kissed Alice's cheek.

"Yes, do come early," Trudy said. "You know how you like my cranberry-orange muffins." She hugged him impulsively.

"Is eight soon enough?"

"Better make it seven thirty."

The two watched as Leighton strode toward the door and left without looking back.

"Come, dear, let's go to your room on the second floor. I'll carry your luggage. I'm quite used to it, you know."

Alice followed Trudy up the winding staircase, with its highly polished oak banister and wide, deep steps. Trudy paused in front of a door with a whimsical sign that read GARDEN ROOM.

"Here it is. It's perfect for one guest. You still get a queen-sized feather bed, though."

Alice looked at the large four-poster bed with a slatted headboard and a blue-and-green gingham cover. A nightstand with a pitcher decorated a table in one corner. The drapes were pulled back with a sash that matched the comforter.

"It's so lovely; I hate to muss the bed," Alice said, noticing the private bathroom to the left. "I'm going to just love it here."

"Nothing's too good for Leighton. Heaven knows that man's been through a knothole twice."

"Everyone must know Leighton," Alice said.

"Oh, my, yes. It's a small town, you know." Trudy patted Alice's arm. "It would take some getting used to for a city gal."

"You seem to know Leighton so well. Are you related?" Alice said, remembering that Leighton had referred to Trudy as a shirttail cousin.

"Cousins twice removed, I think, but I've never figured it out. I've known him since the day he was born. His parents were of fine stock. They don't come any better than the Walkers."

Alice knew she shouldn't ask, but she had to know. "I suppose you know Cora, then?"

"Cora Benchley? Oh, yes." Trudy leaned over and fluffed up both pillows. "She's had her eye on Leighton since she returned from Cathlamet. I expect that's been at least fifteen years ago now."

"I know she's in love with Leighton."

Trudy nodded, then met Alice's steady gaze. "Yes, I'm afraid that's the truth of it. Though Leighton is absolutely blind to it. That's a man for you!"

Alice wasn't sure how to respond to Trudy's statement. "I'm going to sleep well in this room," she said.

"Glad you like it. Leighton chose it because it looks out over the bay. In the morning, you'll have the most beautiful sunrise you've ever seen."

She leaned over and turned down the gingham quilt. "If you need anything, just let me know, okay?"

She closed the door behind herself, and Alice was alone for the first time since early morning. She needed time and space to function. A time for prayer and meditation at the end of the day helped her gather her thoughts. It also helped her face any problems that had come along.

Cora. Was she a problem? Perhaps not. Cora loved Leighton, and he probably loved her but couldn't see the forest for the trees. Alice was just a friend, and though she got tingly at his touch, she knew nothing would come of their friendship. How could it, with the distance between them? Surely he had realized that by now. And yet. . .

She opened her suitcase and chose a long floral dress with cap sleeves. It would do for lounging, and she'd probably wear this to breakfast in the morning. Leighton. He had more than one woman who loved him. What on earth did he see in Alice? She knew nothing about the oyster business. She didn't know his children nor his late wife. She hadn't even brought proper clothing to the beach. And here she had to pretend to know about this life.

Alice sat on the edge of the bed, loving the soft fullness of the quilt. A small bathroom was off the bedroom, and the bathtub looked inviting—especially when she saw the bath oils and huge, fluffy towels.

After a long, leisurely soak in the huge claw-foot bathtub, Alice sat on the edge of the bed and thought about all that had happened in the past four days. It seemed impossible. How could she, Alice Adams, be in this situation? She had led such a simple life in the years since Carl's death. Now she was embarked on something that almost frightened her. Could she cope? Did she even want to?

She dried her hair with the big, thick towel, then brushed several strokes. Her journal and Bible were the only things left in the suitcase. She wrote in her journal when things troubled her, and this was beginning to trouble her. She had no right to come, to step in and take over for a woman who loved Leighton, who had obviously loved him since his wife died. Maybe even before. How could she fight that? Did she really want to?

She opened the Bible randomly and a highlighted verse jumped out at her: "Teach me your way, O Lord; lead me in a straight path."

"But, Lord, do I want to follow? How do I know? How can I know this is the right step? And what about Courtney and my grandbaby-to-be? How can I think of leaving them, should it come to that?"

She slid under the soft comforter. Tomorrow was going to be another day like today had been. Something told her she'd better get a full night's sleep so she'd be fresh and ready. But would she ever really be ready to step in and be Leighton's helpmate? Is this what God expected of her?

She closed her eyes and prayed: "Not my will, but Thy will, Lord. Help me to know what You'd have me do, what You want me to be. Amen."

181

Chapter 13

Cora was waiting when Leighton got home. Somehow he knew she would be. The house was dark except for a faint ray of moonlight.

"Leight—" Her voice broke.

He turned the lamp on beside the recliner.

"No. Shut it off, please. I can sit in the dark and think, just as I can sit in the dark and converse."

"Okay." He sat in the chair, almost afraid to go any closer.

"I've known you a long time."

"Yes," he said finally.

"It's a long time to put into a relationship that is clearly going nowhere."

"Now, Cora. That's just it. There has never been a relationship, not to my way of thinking."

"You took me out to dinner that one time."

"It was your birthday, if I remember right."

"Yes, well, Mama warned me that things were one-sided." She laughed. "And you know what? My mother was right. But I'm stubborn. You saw me training that horse that wouldn't let a soul near it."

"Yes, you were fantastic with that Morgan. Cute little filly, wasn't she?"

"Yes, she was. I fit in here. I know everyone. The peninsula is my life. Yours, too. I also know that you like just a touch of starch in your shirts, you eat dinner at six most nights, and you prefer the turkey stuffed with bread dressing instead of corn bread." She laughed then. "Remember when I put oysters in and nobody would eat it?"

He remembered only too well. Cora, who hadn't been with them long, burst into tears and refused to eat dinner.

"We have memories, and that's what you build a relationship on." Her voice grew louder. "Not some person you meet one time and get all excited about."

Leighton nodded. "You're right. There is something to say for continuity."

She got up from the love seat, moving a dining room chair over next to the recliner. He knew she wanted him to reach out, to touch her, to say he'd been wrong, that he'd reconsider. But he couldn't do what she wanted.

"Cora, you're right about a lot of this. And maybe I need advice, but you're not the one to ask."

"It hasn't stopped you in the past." Her voice came out stilted, not sounding like her at all. "We can still be friends, can't we?"

"I suppose we can. You know I love the peninsula. The bay. My house. The oysters. My life here in general. How can I give this up and move elsewhere?"

"Heavens!" she blurted out. "Why would you even consider such a thing?"

"I'm not sure. It's just that sometimes I feel lonely, and life is short when you get right down to it. God never gave us any guarantees about how long our time is here on earth."

"That He didn't."

"I've thought about my child, my little sick darling who died in my arms. I think about my boys and being there for them, and hoping against hope that Aaron might come driving into the yard someday."

"And he just might."

"But there's a missing link, and I may have found what I didn't know I was even looking for."

Cora jumped to her feet. "Why can't *I* be the missing link?"

When he said nothing, she kept the ball rolling. "It's okay to be friends first. All the books and articles say that."

Leighton sighed. How had he gotten into this conversation, anyway? She didn't understand. She would never understand. Love couldn't be forced, and what he felt for her was only gratitude. Appreciation. Admiration.

"Maybe Alice isn't the right one. I don't think she wants to upset the apple cart any more than I do. We both have our lives in different places. Yes, we enjoy each other's company and, yes, we do seem to have a lot in common, but maybe it isn't enough. Who knows? I certainly don't have the answers."

"What exactly are you saying, Leight?"

He leaned forward, putting his head into his hands. "I think I've just come to realize that I need, or maybe I should say *want,* a helpmate. Alice helped me see that. Here I've been so caught up with raising my kids and the job taking every spare minute. Now it's as if I never had time to enjoy life."

"And so you and she are enjoying life?"

"No, that's just it. I'm not sure about her and me. It's just an awareness that made me understand my needs."

"So what I said is right. We can build a relationship. It *is* possible. I've always been here; you know that."

"Yes, I know. And I appreciate all you've done—"

"Appreciate?" She paced across the room.

"Yes, appreciate." He could feel her breath as her face got closer. "I think I'm going to date for a while."

"Oh. That's what this is about. You want my advice about dating? Is that why you're telling me this?"

"Well, yes. As a friend."

"Leighton Walker, I think you are probably the most stupid man I've ever seen. Have you listened to anything I've said? Have I ever meant anything to you at all?"

"Cora? Why are you yelling?"

"Because I'm tired. It's been a trying day, and I'm going home!"

She spun around and banged out the door before he could even rise.

The gravel spit as her car turned and headed out the winding driveway.

Leighton sat in the darkness. Cora didn't understand how it was. He did not love her. How could he pretend something he did not feel? Pretense never had worked for him. He knew women did it all the time, but not men. Maybe he should talk to Trudy. She might listen to him without getting angry.

He did not move. There was nothing he wanted more than to sit here and to think about his life. It was dark out now, and an occasional light from a car on the highway across the bay and on the road to Bay Center sparked like a firefly. Not that he'd seen fireflies, but he'd heard about them. And someday he might see a real one.

Finally he rose and paced across the room. His mind was in a turmoil. He knew he did not love Cora. He also knew how he felt around Alice. She made him feel like singing, and it had been a very long time since he'd had that feeling. Was that wrong? Or had God been waiting to show him there could be joy in life, and why didn't Leighton just reach out for it?

❧

Cora sped down the driveway and back toward town. Her house was north of Leighton's on Stackpole Road, but she wasn't going home. She could not go home. She had to talk to someone, and as she often did when problems hit, she'd find her cousin, Meredith, and ask her advice. Of course, Meredith would agree with Cora's mother that she had given enough time and energy to this relationship. Tonight's conversation only backed that up. But how could she give up the only man she'd ever loved?

The darkened house made Cora consider just leaving without their talk, but she couldn't. She knew there would be no sleep for her tonight.

She grabbed the key from under the pot of petunias and let herself in. "Meredith? It's just me. Put away your gun."

"Cora?" a sleepy voice called from the bedroom, then a woman appeared in the doorway. "What are you doing here this late?"

"It's only ten."

"But I have to get up and go to Astoria at seven tomorrow."

"I know and I'm sorry, but you're the only one I can talk to."

"Not Leighton."

"Well, yes, as a matter of fact—"

"Listen, Cora, you've never listened to any advice I've given you, so why should I think you'll listen now?" The tall, buxom woman turned on a small light and put the teakettle on.

"Because I just might listen this time."

"Yeah, sure." She pulled a chair out and eased into it. "I think you should move away from here. Go as far away as you can so you won't be tempted to come back every weekend."

"Away? Where, pray tell?"

"How about Bar Harbor, Maine?"

"Maine!"

"You like the water, so you'd have water there."

"But that's over three thousand miles away!"

"And that's what you need—distance."

Cora got up and took the singing kettle off the burner. "No. Maybe I'll go visit Aunt Joan in Virginia."

"I don't mean visit."

"I can't start my life over. I'm forty-two!"

"I know how old you are. I'm just a year behind."

"You're not married yet."

"And I'm not pining for a man who will never, ever love me, either."

They had instant coffee, jelly rolls, peanuts, and everything else Meredith could drag out of the refrigerator.

"I haven't had a night feast like this forever," Meredith said.

"Not since the last time I got you out of bed."

The two were still talking at midnight. Meredith, who was even more organized and opinionated than Cora, had it mapped out. Cora would call the travel bureau and get the first plane heading out of Oysterville. She would look for work in Virginia, and she would not have contact with anyone here.

"If separation doesn't make him realize how much he misses you, nothing will."

Cora would not tell Leighton she was leaving. She'd leave her house empty, take a suitcase of clothes, and Meredith would feed her cat. What happened when Leighton found his refrigerator without food would be his problem, not hers.

"I think this is a wise move," Meredith said. "Though I'll miss you something fierce."

"You can come visit."

"Yeah, I suppose I could do that." Meredith, who taught school, was out for the summer and usually planned at least one trip over her vacation.

Cora hugged her good-bye and headed for home. Now she could sleep. Or could she?

The best-laid plans ran through her mind as the clock turned to one, two, then three. Finally, she got up and put some music on. The Dixie Chicks sang "Once You've Loved Somebody."

She wasn't sure what she would do, but neither Virginia nor Bar Harbor, Maine, was the answer. She could never leave and admit defeat. Never.

Chapter 14

A morning sunrise awakened Alice, its brilliance summoning her. For a moment she forgot where she was. With sudden delight, she jumped from bed and looked out the window at the sky in explosive reds and oranges. She'd never seen anything like it. Of course, the fact that she never was up at this hour might have something to do with it. It wasn't even six o'clock yet.

She padded to the bathroom and looked in the mirror. Her eyes were puffy from sleep. Obviously she had slept well, not waking once, though she had been sure she would. It had been so quiet. No sounds of cars zipping by, no sirens in the middle of the night, no lights or phone calls. Silence. Golden silence.

Alice opened her journal and wrote a few lines at the top. "I'm ready and waiting for whatever is to be."

Her Bible devotional was surprisingly just what she needed to hear. "Consider it pure joy, my brothers, whenever you face trials of many kinds."

"I don't know if I'm being faced with trials, but I am ready for whatever this day brings, for whatever You want me to do."

The scent of coffee came up the stairs and entered through the register. Warm air also came through the intricate metal register on the floor. Alice had not felt chilled, but the warm air was nice.

Alice opened the door to the deck just off her bedroom and slipped outside. It was cold. Brisk. She grabbed the small throw blanket at the foot of the bed and wrapped it around herself as she watched the changing sky from the Adirondack chair.

She had two choices for the day. The beige silk slack set, totally not right for here, or the long jumper that would be better and more suitable. She decided on the jumper, a pink blouse with a touch of lace, and the sandals that would be replaced with tennis shoes.

Now Alice smelled something baking. Probably the cranberry muffins. There was a tap on her door as a cheery voice called out, "I have coffee if you'd like. I don't expect Leighton until seven or so."

Alice hopped up from the chair and opened the door. Trudy came in with a tray laden with not only coffee but a plate of fresh fruit. Mango slices, grapes, apple wedges, and blueberries.

"Just to tide you over."

"But how did you know I was up?"

"I heard the floors creak. I shouldn't have told you my little secret." Trudy beamed as she poured a cup of coffee. A tiny pitcher contained cream, and a small ceramic pig was filled with sugar. "I bought this from a lady who comes from North Dakota each summer and sells her pottery at our local Fourth of July festival. Isn't he charming?"

Alice nodded and poured sugar into a spoon. "I must get one of these." She knew Courtney would love it, since she had just started collecting pigs.

Trudy beamed. "I just so happen to have a few extra. I like to keep small gifts on hand to give my guests as a remembrance of their stay at Trudy's Bed and Breakfast on the Bay."

"The coffee is wonderful and the fruit a real treat."

"I'll leave you to your own devices. Come down when you're ready." Trudy looked elegant in her white apron that fit over a green-and-white-striped pinafore dress. Everything about this trip was elegant.

Alice sat, sipping her coffee, and looked out at the bay. So beautiful and quaint and quiet. How could she not want to stay here? But, of course, she was thinking about things that probably wouldn't be, anyway. Leighton had a relationship with that Cora woman, who obviously adored him and his family. How could Alice look for a future with him? Besides, it was too early to think about such things. She had come to spend time with him and sightsee, and that's what she was going to do.

She left half of the fruit, put on the sandals, and took the tray back downstairs. A girl of ten or so was in the kitchen cutting wedges of toast.

"Good morning," she called out when Alice brought the tray into the kitchen. "I'm helping Aunt Trudy."

"How many other guests are there? It's so quiet; I thought I was the only one."

"We have three other rooms filled. Newlyweds, someone celebrating their anniversary, and a lady by herself, like you."

Alice walked out onto a deck that ran across the entire back of the house. A goose called to his mate in the distance. Such a peaceful setting. Courtney and Steven would have to come here to see the beauty of this place. Perhaps it could be an anniversary gift.

She sat in one of the lawn chairs, drawing her feet up under herself. She felt as if she could stay in this same spot all day. How fortunate to have met Leighton, and how amazing that he brought her here to share this with her. How could she ever go home again?

"There you are!" Leighton stood over her, leaned down, and kissed her cheek, just as he had last night. "I'm early, but Trudy called to say you were up, and so here I am."

"Oh, Leighton." She felt all breathless. "This view is heavenly. Thanks so much for bringing me here."

"I thought you would like it."

"Trudy brought coffee and fruit to my room, and I slept through the whole night. I can't even remember the last time I did that."

She knew she was rambling, but she felt comfortable with this kind man and the way he was looking at her, all smiles. Did he feel the same toward her?

"We'll eat one of Trudy's breakfasts fit for a queen, and you may not want to eat the rest of the day."

Alice chuckled. "I'm already thinking that. How can I eat more?"

They sat watching the bay and the sun behind the hills. The silence was comfortable, as if they knew no words needed to be spoken.

Leighton spoke first. "Your face shows your pleasure, and that brings me such satisfaction. You have no idea how much."

"Where are we going today? One thing I need to do is buy a pair of tennis shoes. I thought at that store back in Long Beach."

Leighton nodded. "Yes, I suppose those shoes wouldn't be good for hiking to Cape D. It's an uphill climb, and tennis shoes would definitely give you better traction."

"I left the bag with my old tennis shoes at home."

"We don't have to hike, of course."

"Oh, but I want to. I haven't hiked much since, well, since Carl died, but I do the aerobics at the pool, so I'm in shape."

His eyes twinkled. "And in good shape, I might add."

"Breakfast time!" A small silver bell rang from the dining area.

"Doesn't that smell good!"

Platters were filled with sausage, bacon, and slices of ham, along with a stack of pancakes and another of Belgian waffles. Plates of honey, jams, real butter, hash browns, and a spinach frittata covered the lace-covered tablecloth. The dishes were an elegant porcelain with a tiny red rose pattern.

"Who would have expected this at the beach?" Alice exclaimed. "Perhaps my gold sandals aren't so out of place."

A young couple entered the dining room, holding hands. They nodded. "Hi. We're here on our tenth anniversary."

"And this is my first time here," Alice said, looking toward Leighton.

For the next several minutes, a conversation was carried on, and Alice heard how life was in Flagstaff, Arizona.

"There are two things you must do while here," Leighton told the couple. He stirred sugar into his coffee. "Go to the north end to Leadbetter Point. It's like Cape Cod, I've been told, because it's flat, but it has more dune grass. If you have binoculars, take them along. There are more birds in that area than anywhere else on the peninsula. In order to get there, you'll go through the old town of Oysterville. That's also worth a stop."

"Which is where Leighton lives and owns an oyster cannery," Trudy added.

"The south end has more hills, good hikes, and a great panorama of the ocean. You can also see clear to the north end of the peninsula on a nice day. Pick up one of the visitors' guides from the newspaper office in Long Beach."

"I have plenty of guides right here," Trudy said. She fetched one from an end table in the parlor. "This can tell you lots of things to do and places to go."

The couple beamed. "Thanks so much."

Alice tasted the frittata and chose a slice of bacon and a muffin.

They all started eating, and it was quiet, but only for a few minutes.

"We'll be back," the young man said, pushing away from the table. "I won this vacation from my company, so time is limited. We can take in one of your suggestions, then we have to leave for Seattle to catch an early flight home."

"But this has been elegant," his wife said, a tiny woman no more than five feet tall.

"I can't eat another bite," Alice said, folding the napkin and setting it on her plate.

"There's always tomorrow," Leighton added. "I bet there will be something new to try then."

Alice went back upstairs for a wrap and her purse.

"We'll go to the store first so you can find some walking shoes," Leighton said.

Trudy hollered for them to wait a minute. Seconds later, she came back with a shoe box, and inside was a pair of blue deck shoes. "I thought you might be able to wear these. Someone left them here, and when I mailed her a note, she said not to bother with sending them back. They're brand-new."

They fit, and Alice thanked her.

Trudy handed Leighton a small white paper sack. "Just something else to take along."

"What's in that sack?" Alice asked, noticing that Leighton stowed it in the backseat.

"A box lunch."

"Packed by Trudy?"

"None other."

"She does everything so effortlessly."

He looked over and grinned. "That's just the way it appears. We're all laid back here on the peninsula, or hadn't you noticed?"

Except Cora, Alice wanted to say. Cora had managed to get a barb in, letting Alice know she would have a fight on her hands should she pursue this relationship. But Alice was enjoying herself. She wasn't going to let herself get serious about Leighton. His place was here, just as hers was in Portland. There was no harm in an occasional visit, and when he came to town, they could take in a movie, or she might fix a dinner of her famous baked chicken.

"You're smiling. What's on your mind?"

Alice leaned forward. "Oh, just thinking about life in general, realizing we never know what lies around the next bend."

Leighton reached over and covered her hand with his. "I think God likes to surprise us, don't you?"

"Yes, indeed, I do."

"Tomorrow we'll have to go to the vespers at the Oysterville Church. You'll love the service."

"Is that the church you attend regularly?"

He frowned for a moment. "No. There's only an afternoon service during the summer months. Other times I attend a community church, when my schedule allows."

Alice thought about her church and how much she would miss her friends, her daughter, the new baby, if she ever left. And there would be more children, because Courtney said she wanted a large family.

"There you go again. It's as if I'm not here. You keep thinking about other things."

"And that's rude of me. I'm sorry."

The ride down what Leighton called the back road was scenic, with large trees and woodsy areas. A house could be seen now and then, and if she looked close, she caught a glimpse of blue water from the bay, but it was mostly brush and foliage.

"I cannot imagine how I lived my whole life in Portland and never knew about this spot. I like it. It isn't commercialized, as so many of the beach towns are in Oregon."

"We like it that way."

"Are we going to Cape Disappointment now?"

"No, not yet. We'll go to Waikiki Beach while the sun's out. The weather is fickle here; it could be foggy and cold by noon."

"At least we don't need to stop at that little shopping center." Alice wiggled her toes inside the new blue deck shoes, which would be perfect for hiking.

Alice sat back again and felt her body relax. She wouldn't go off and think about things he knew nothing about. She would share just a bit of her life with him.

"The first time I hiked was in Florence, Oregon. I went with Todi. We went every year hiking to the lighthouse—the minute the trails were dry."

"Todi?"

"An old school friend. We were inseparable. Then I married Carl, and the air force took us all over."

"Tell me about Carl, if you can."

Alice felt sudden warmth. Of course she could. She liked talking about Carl and the wonderful years they'd shared, the day they brought Courtney home.

"I was married young. And you?"

"That's not fair." Leighton scowled. "This is supposed to be about you."

"I just wanted to compare."

"Okay. I guess that's fair. I married young, also. Nancy and I went all through school together, but we never dated until our last year of high school. Then, suddenly, things turned serious."

"I met Carl at a roller rink in Portland, so I hadn't known him forever, but things still went pretty fast." She thought about the motorcycle ride but decided not to tell Leighton about that.

"You kinda know when that someone is special, don't you?"

Alice nodded. "Yes, I believe you do." She touched his hand. "But your marriage didn't last?" Leighton had mentioned Nancy a few times but always changed the subject. She didn't want to press him now.

"It was because of Hannah. Or so I thought at the time."

"Hannah's cystic fibrosis?"

"Yes. I couldn't see us putting her in a home. That's what Nancy wanted to do. 'We can't raise her with four healthy boys,' Nancy said." He looked away. "I thought it was the very thing Hannah needed. To be around boys who were rambunctious and healthy."

"And she lived longer than some CF kids."

"Yes. And we tried different medications. It was our love that kept her going. I'm convinced of it."

Alice wanted to ask about Aaron but knew Leighton had no clue about his whereabouts. She decided one serious subject was enough for now.

Leighton pulled up into a nursery with a house on the bay. "This is my cousin's, and he said he had some rhodies I could plant."

After a brief introduction of Alice and his cousin, Leighton put the shrubs in the back of the truck and headed out again.

"I suppose you know everyone who lives here."

"Only those who've lived here over twenty years." He met her gaze, then both looked away.

"It's a good place to live, Alice. It was a good place to raise my boys and Hannah."

"The suburbs were good, too."

Leighton nodded. "I hope you don't mind, and I should have asked sooner, but is it okay if we have dinner with Luke and his family and Tom and his wife and kid?"

Alice paused. "I think that would be nice. I'd like to meet your sons."

"Good. Now that that's out of the way, we can relax and have a good time."

Chapter 15

Leighton chose the 42nd Street Café for dinner. "It's Luke's favorite, and it's closer to Tom's place. He has a summer job painting boats."

"Bet that keeps him busy."

"He likes it because it's close to home and he gets taken out on various boats during the salmon season."

The café was a cottage-style building painted aqua with a deeper aqua trim. The side yard was filled with white Shasta daisies and tall, slender pink holly-hocks. Alice marveled at the sight. The plants seemed more vibrant in color than they did at home.

"I kind of wish I'd at least met Luke at the cannery. Now I have two sons to meet."

He took her hand and led her inside. Bob, the owner, manager, and some-times cook, ushered them in.

"How's the oyster business doing?" He looked expectantly at Leighton.

"Just fine. Took orders for restaurants in the Portland area, and I guess it's time to get you on the bandwagon, also. This is Alice Adams. She's a friend visit-ing from Portland."

Bob smiled. "Happy to meet you. Hope you enjoy your dinner tonight." He pointed. "Our specials are written on the board in the front."

"We need a large table, enough for nine."

Bob shook his head. "I don't think so. Your son called, saying Lisa isn't feel-ing well, so the kids are staying home."

"And I wanted Alice to meet Lisa. Guess it'll just be Luke, Tom, and Mary, then." He turned to Alice. "Lisa's the one who's pregnant."

They were led to a table for six in a far corner. Alice admired the antique fur-nishings and was humming to a tune she knew from the CD that filled the room with soft music.

The sons and Mary arrived at the same time. Alice held her hand out, taking first Luke's hand, noticing how much he looked like Leighton: tall and broad-shouldered, with a thick thatch of dark hair. Tom was shorter but had the same brown eyes that twinkled as she turned toward him.

"Glad to meet you, Alice."

A small woman with a long braid and a wide smile held out her hand. "I'm Mary. And what brings you to the peninsula?"

Alice felt her cheeks flush. "I met Leighton a few weeks ago—"

"Four weeks ago, to be exact," Leighton finished her sentence. "And where is Bunkie?" He turned to Alice. "That's Tom and Mary's only child. She's a girl, a precocious five."

"She's staying for the week with my mother," Mary said. "I'm sure she'll have a fit when she finds out where we came to eat."

"So, now, what do you think of our little spot?" Tom asked, pushing Mary's seat up.

"I'm enjoying everything immensely."

Leighton held Alice's chair out. "I noticed Bob has the special seafood chowder. That's what I'm getting."

Soon two baskets of bread appeared, corn relish, and "our special marionberry-cranberry preserves," the young waitress said.

The evening was pleasant, the brothers sharing stories about the cannery when they worked there each summer and on weekends during the school year. Alice listened intently, wishing she could have known them then.

"I never liked it, though," Tom said, buttering a second slice of bread. "Man, I like this bread. What does it have in it, Mare? Dill?"

"I think so."

"Mary grows herbs and is making the spices Dad is selling in the store now."

"And I couldn't think of doing anything else," Luke added, putting a dollop of corn relish on his bread plate.

"That's what makes it special. Having someone working who likes the job," Leighton interjected. "It always works out for those who love and serve God."

The waitress took their order. Since salad came during the meal, Alice asked for a small portion, with blue cheese dressing.

"It just comes in one size, ma'am."

"Very well. I'll have the seafood chowder, since Leighton recommended it highly." She figured she might be able to finish a bowl of soup sooner than a full dinner. "What's in it?"

"There are three kinds of seafood in the chowder tonight. Clams, halibut, and salmon."

"You'll like it, Alice. I guarantee it," Leighton said. "If not, you can order something else."

"No, that sounds great."

Luke and Tom ordered steaks, and Mary ordered fried chicken. "It's because I can never get it right. I always get chicken when I eat here."

The salads came, along with cups of coffee for the men and Alice, iced tea for Mary. Alice left half of her salad and left the bread alone, though it looked delicious.

The chowder arrived in a wide soup bowl, with a dash of paprika and crushed parsley flakes.

"So, Papa, when is the due date?" Tom asked his older brother.

"Around Christmas, I'm afraid."

Tom grabbed another slice of bread. "Is this going to be it, or are you trying for a basketball team?"

"Three was supposed to be it," Luke said, his eyes all serious. "But sometimes God has something else in mind."

"Tell her we missed her," Leighton said. "I'll stop by with Alice tomorrow and bring her some flowers."

"Hey, Dad, that'd mean a lot to her."

Alice let Leighton finish her chowder, wondering how he could eat so much. And the boys like they hadn't eaten all day. Mary took her chicken home. She'd only eaten the potatoes and gravy.

"Dessert, anyone?" The waitress came and poured more coffee.

"Not for me," all chorused in unison. Alice couldn't have agreed more.

Once out in the parking lot, Luke and Tom teased Leighton about going to Portland to find a date.

"Yeah, Dad. We have women right here."

Alice felt a sinking sensation. Noticing her discomfort, Leighton took her hand. "Alice is a good friend," he said.

"Well, happy to meet you, Alice." Luke walked toward his car. "And we'll probably see you tomorrow."

Mary leaned over and hugged Alice impulsively. "Don't listen to anything they say," she whispered. "They're both protective of their father. It all has to do with Nancy, of course. They don't want to see him hurt."

Alice nodded. "My Courtney says the very same thing."

"If you get a chance, stop by and see my herb garden."

Leighton hugged Mary and each son, then waved.

"I'm sorry about what Tom said. He was just kidding. He's the practical joker of the family."

"You said I was just a friend," Alice said, looking at his profile as he pulled out onto the highway.

"Was that wrong?"

"Well, no. I guess not." She paused. "I think I'll enjoy vespers tomorrow."

"Ah, I recognize that tactic." He took her hand and squeezed it. "Good old changing the subject."

They laughed as they headed for the boardwalk, hand in hand, to watch the kites and the last bit of daylight escape on the far horizon.

⌒

Once back at the bed and breakfast, Alice used her calling card to call Courtney. Maybe she was being silly, but she worried about her and needed reassurance that her daughter was okay.

"Mom! I'm surprised to hear your voice. Is everything all right?"

"Yes, honey. Things are fine. I will be taking the 4:00 p.m. shuttle back tomorrow. Leighton wants me to attend the vespers at three, then I'm off."

"Are you having a good time?"

"A wonderful time."

"And?"

"And what?"

"Is this going to be a monthly occurrence? You go to the beach, then Mr. Walker comes to Portland once a month?"

Alice's heart pounded. She wondered if seeing each other twice a month would be enough, yet he'd said she was just a friend.

"Oh, nothing like that," she finally answered. "We're just friends, that's all."

"Mom, I don't believe that and neither do you."

"But, tell me, how are you doing?"

"I'm fine. Feeling more twinges in my back, but the doctor says that's normal for the second trimester. He said perhaps I should rest more often."

"You're sure you're all right? Did the doctor suggest another ultrasound?"

"Those things are expensive. I'm sure I'm doing what all pregnant women do, so stop worrying."

Alice always had worried. Carl used to give her a bad time about it. "Stop worrying, honey," he'd say. "If God cares for the tiny sparrow, one of the smallest of birds, think of how much He cares for you."

He was right. She always knew that, yet doubts sometimes came in, and worry replaced good common sense.

"I'll see you at evening service then, okay?"

"Sure thing."

Alice held on to the phone after Courtney's good-bye. She couldn't put her finger on it, but something wasn't quite right. Courtney's voice didn't have the usual lilt. Was she just tired, or had she and Steven had an argument? Courtney usually gave in because it was far easier to do so. She never had liked confrontations. Or could she be concerned about Alice's relationship with Leighton?

Alice sat on the edge of the bed and slipped out of her shoes. She was glad for the phone in her room, as it afforded privacy.

She felt exhausted, then going through all the happenings of the day, knew why. It wasn't as if she were a kid and could bounce back after two hikes and meeting new people and putting a smile on her face constantly. At least here, in the sanctity of her room, she could be herself.

A tap sounded on the door.

"Alice? I have a bit of refreshment for you." Trudy opened the door and entered with a small tray, which held a small pot of tea, two slices of biscotti, and a tiny dish of blackberry preserves.

"The blackberries grow wild here. We're surrounded by bushes. And I don't let any of my guests go hungry. By the way, I understand you like spiced apple tea."

Alice looked startled, then laughed. "That Leighton. Of course he told you!"

Trudy nodded. "That he did."

"As for going hungry, I know that's impossible here. Leighton and his sons eat like loggers."

"It's the salt air, dear. It gives you an appetite."

"Well, I may have a cup of tea and try one piece of biscotti, but I'm still full from my seafood chowder."

"There's a game of Scattergories in the parlor—if you're interested."

Alice brightened for a moment. "I love the game, but I need time alone. To reflect and write in my journal. Read a few scriptures."

"I thought so. You do look tired." Trudy paused in the doorway. "I thought you might like to talk, but I can see you just need peace and quiet. We still have tomorrow."

"Yes, we still have tomorrow," Alice said as she poured the apple-scented tea into a delicate china cup. "Or, as Leighton said earlier, 'Tomorrow is another day.' "

But after Trudy left, Alice wondered what her hostess might want to talk about. Was it something about Leighton, something that would concern her? Maybe she should have acted more interested. Now she'd wonder about it all night.

Chapter 16

The day had been full, and Leighton came home to rest up, to listen to his messages, to try to figure out what was happening to him. Alice, like a child, loved everything he showed her, every place they went. She was better at hiking than he was, though he hated to admit he was out of shape. He'd been having a problem with arthritis this past year, and it had bothered him when they climbed the hill to Cape D Lighthouse.

Alice had loved the finger sandwiches, fruit, and home-baked cookies Trudy had packed, and they'd enjoyed the surfers at Waikiki Beach. Meeting Luke and Tom for dinner had also gone well, until Leighton kiddingly said something about Alice being just a friend. Her conversation seemed clipped after that.

The answering machine held one message. It was Luke, saying he had two things to discuss.

Leighton grabbed a glass of ice water and sat on the love seat in front of the window before dialing. After they exchanged greetings, Luke got right to the point. "Dad, are you sure you want to get involved with someone who lives so far away?"

Leighton felt his heart soar at the mention of Alice. Of course, Luke would be concerned. It made Leighton feel good that his son cared enough to protest. At least he wasn't being ignored.

"Did you like her?" Leighton said, deliberately not answering the question.

"She seems fine. Kind of quiet."

"Well, what can you expect with you two bazookas talking most of the time?"

"Aw, Dad, I only see Tom once in a blue moon."

"I know."

"Anyway, I realize this person is not just a friend. I saw the way you looked at her when she wasn't looking and the way she looked back when she thought you weren't looking."

"Don't be ridiculous."

"It's never too late to fall in love."

Leighton cleared his throat. "And what was the second concern?"

"Whether we ship oysters to that place in Summersville. They haven't paid for the last shipment."

After discussing that problem, Leighton said he really had to go.

"I'm not letting this issue rest," was Luke's parting remark.

The sun had left the hills, and the room suddenly felt chilly. The house was big, too big for just Leighton. Cora enjoyed keeping it up, and he knew if he had said the word years ago, she would have moved in lock, stock, and barrel. But he couldn't marry for the sake of convenience. There had to be more to a relationship than that. Cora was beautiful. She had a glow about her at times that made him notice her, and once he had thought she might be the one. But she was also stubborn and a bit bossy. He knew if they married, she would run the business and the house and tell him what shirt to wear and how much sugar he could put in his coffee. He didn't want that. He rather liked being his own boss and had decided to keep it that way.

But then Alice had entered his mind—no—make that his heart. He hadn't wanted to let her in, but somehow she had come in, anyway. And now he didn't know if he could let it go any further. He didn't think she felt about him in that way, so why even be concerned about it? Besides, could two people their age really find happiness? At fifty-three, he knew he was set in his ways. He wanted things to keep on just as they had been. Why rock the boat, as the saying went?

He wondered what it would be like to come home to find her in the kitchen, rustling up dinner. Yet even as he thought it, he knew she was closely entwined with her daughter and son-in-law in Portland. He'd heard about one sister she only saw once a week. But Courtney was her whole life. And now there would be a baby. How could he expect her to give that up to move to far-off Oysterville? Even if she loved him, he couldn't ask it of her.

His heart sank at the thought of not seeing her. No, they would just be friends. Friends saw each other often. He could go into Portland more often than in the past. Or would it be easier to let it drop?

Leighton went to his recliner and sat back. He turned the TV on to catch the late news. There was something soothing about watching the news. With all the drive-by shootings, murders, and tornadoes going on, it made a person's problems seem small by comparison.

He closed his eyes and prayed that he would be content to go on with his life as it had been. There was nothing wrong with that, now, was there?

❧

Alice awoke feeling refreshed. It was an overcast day, a layer of clouds shutting out the sun. The smell of coffee had awakened her, but this time she wanted to go downstairs and offer her help.

"Did you have a pleasant sleep?" Trudy smiled as she adjusted a doily on the small table in the foyer. It held a vase filled with wildflowers from the nearby woods.

"It was perfectly wonderful. I needed that sleep."

"Tell me about your day yesterday."

Alice followed Trudy into the kitchen. "Where do I start? Thanks so much for the delicious lunch. We ate it while sitting on piles of driftwood at Waikiki Beach. We came back there after our hike."

"A nice spot, for sure, especially when the sun's out."

"Kids were playing in the water, digging in the sand, and we just sat and watched."

"Come on in and have a cup of coffee with me." Trudy motioned to a tall stool. "I'm mixing scones for breakfast and need some company. Sometimes I miss women's chatter."

The spacious kitchen, like everything else in the bed and breakfast, was tastefully decorated in shades of green and pink.

"This is such a lovely spot. I'm sure I'll be back."

"Perhaps you'll be back but not staying here. I predict you'll be the lady of the house out on 324th Place."

Alice's cheeks reddened. "Oh, I don't think so. If anyone is the lady of the house, it will be Cora."

Trudy looked up, flour on her hands. "If that were meant to be, Cora would be safely ensconced in the house now. Leighton has been lonely, but even he won't admit it. Cora has kept his house and made him think he's making it just fine alone, but what man doesn't want to find someone to share his life with?"

Alice sipped her coffee, mulling the words over in her mind. "I don't think Leighton is ready to let go of the past."

"You mean Nancy or Cora?" Trudy shook her head. "My dear, Nancy caused him more pain and grief than any two women could. I think what he needs more than anything is to forget Nancy and go on with his life."

"She took her own life."

Trudy nodded. "Yes, but she wasn't in her right mind. I don't know when or why or what happened, but she went from a capricious little thing, so full of life and happy, to a woman who was totally depressed. I think she was under medication in Seattle, but as people often do, I think she went off the meds."

"And she's buried there. Leighton told me that."

"Yes, even though her family has a plot in Lone Fir."

"Is that where Hannah is buried?" Alice had wondered at the time, but sensed that Leighton was uncomfortable talking about his child.

"Hannah is in the Oysterville Cemetery. There was somewhat of a heated discussion about whether she would be buried at Lone Fir with her mother's relatives or in Leighton's family plot. He won, which is as it should be. I can't imagine her family raising such a ruckus, when Nancy treated Hannah that way."

"As you said, Nancy couldn't have been in her right mind. A mother protects her child. She loves and nurtures it, just like a mama bear."

Trudy set the scones aside and pulled a chair out. "I want Leighton to be happy. I think you're the one."

"But we're just friends, Trudy. I admit I have strong feelings for him, but it's way too soon to guess what might happen. Way too soon to speculate on what would be good for him. Or me."

"And you're from the city."

"All my life. And I have my daughter and a dear son-in-law and a sister who is alone, just as I am. She's been widowed lots longer than me. And there's my church, my volunteer activities; but most of all my only child, Courtney, is expecting a child now."

"I understand. But there are volunteer opportunities here. Portland is less than a three-hour drive away, and if you could find happiness for yourself, don't you think you'd want that? And don't you think your daughter would want that for you, also?"

Alice felt excited at the prospect, but she also felt apprehensive. She couldn't even let herself consider it. Besides, there was Cora. Even though Trudy said she wasn't a worry, Cora was ready to fight, if necessary.

"Tell me about Aaron."

Trudy poured two more cups of coffee. "He's another burr under Leighton's saddle. Heaven knows, the man's had enough. Sick child, crazy wife, and a runaway teen."

"Has he tried to find him?"

"Hon, I can talk about Cora or Nancy, but when it comes to Aaron, I just don't know what happened or if Leighton's tried to find him. He's very close-mouthed about it. All I remember is that Aaron was the sweetest, kindest kid you'd ever hope to meet. He was so good with Hannah. I think he knew she was dying and couldn't hang around and watch it happen."

"It must have been awful for Leighton."

"The worst thing ever is to lose a child."

"Yes," Alice murmured. "I lost more than one."

The front door opened, and Leighton called out, "Anyone up yet?"

As Alice turned and caught sight of him in the entrance of the kitchen, her heart jumped, and she knew, *knew* in that minute that she wasn't falling in love with this man. He already had her whole heart—hook, line, and sinker.

Chapter 17

Hey, you two, since the others aren't up yet, why don't you take your coffee and go in the sunroom?" Trudy pointed to a room with windows facing south and east. Filled with plants of various sizes, it looked like a jungle. Two easy chairs faced the bay.

"Why are you up so early?" Alice asked Leighton as she followed him, coffee in hand.

He grinned. "I might ask you the same thing."

She sat in the paisley-covered wing chair, while he took the burgundy one. "I had a good night's sleep, yet more restless than the night before."

"Why is that?"

"I talked to Courtney right after you left. Says she's fine, yet I have this gut feeling that something is wrong."

"Maybe she's just missing you."

Alice set her cup down. "I suppose that could be. We're close. We've been separated only twice: when she went off to summer camp and when she went east in search of her birth mother."

"And she found her mother?"

"She found most of her family, but her mother had died young. At least, Courtney found her grave and took flowers there."

"That must have been tough."

"Yes, rather traumatic. But she came back with her mother's diary, photos, and a few pictures she had painted in school." Alice remembered how she'd felt when hearing the news. She'd hurt for her daughter, felt hurt that she would never know her mother.

"How long ago was this?"

"Just a year. Right after she met Steven. That's why it was important. She felt she needed to know her medical history before she could marry."

"No skeletons in the closet?"

Alice winced. "Well, I wouldn't say that. Her mother had epilepsy, and her father wouldn't take her to the doctor. He thought she had evil spirits. I don't know the whole story, but Courtney heard all she needed. Steven agreed there were no guarantees when carrying a child. And so they married."

"It's like with Hannah. We had no idea we'd have a sick child, especially not after four healthy boys. But there it was. Cystic fibrosis hits Germans more than any other race."

Leaning over, Alice touched his arm. "I'm sorry for your loss."

"Life goes on. About the search. How did Courtney manage to find her mother?"

"A people locator Web site on the Internet couldn't help, but that's because the birth hadn't been recorded. I suggested she go to the town in Illinois where we'd adopted her. She went from town to town and finally found someone who would talk."

"At least she knew where to begin."

"Yes, that helped."

"With Aaron, which I've been wanting to talk to you about, I have no idea where to start searching."

"Courtney might have some ideas. Haven't you tried to locate your son in the past?"

Leighton strode over to the window. How could he explain? In the beginning, he'd tried to find Aaron, but when Hannah turned worse, he'd concentrated on her health. Still, a part of him was missing, and he doubted he would ever feel whole until Aaron was found.

Alice came and stood beside him, slipping her hand into his. "I'm sure it's difficult to talk about. Not knowing is far worse than knowing."

"It's different for men," he finally said. "It isn't that we don't love our children, but we tend to treat sons different. Heaven knows how much I loved Aaron. He was just a happy-go-lucky kid and kept everyone laughing with his antics. Then he changed. Became sullen. Started skipping classes. I didn't know how to handle him and came down hard. Grounded him. He resented it and ran off. He was eighteen."

"Did you look for him then?"

Leighton looked away. "I thought he'd be back."

"I don't see it as any different with a boy," Alice interjected.

"Mothers are fiercely protective. Don't come near my child. Don't hurt my child. Fathers are there, but it's just not the same. We try to make them tough so they can go out and face the world. And that's what Aaron decided to do."

"I don't agree about fathers. Men put up this barrier, daring someone to break through, but down deep they're tenderhearted. Just like you. You're hurting far more than you let on."

"Yeah, that might be so. Still—"

"Still, what? A lost child is lost whether it's a boy or girl." She reached up and touched a lock of hair that had a mind of its own. He turned and took her into his arms and held her close. He liked the way her heart sounded against his chest, making him feel alive as old feelings came to the surface, feelings he'd kept deep inside, afraid to let out. Always there was the risk of being hurt. She let herself bask in the comfort of his arms, not wanting the moment to end. He moved away first.

"You've made me think about things, Alice. I know I must find Aaron. It's been too long, and I'm tired of waiting, hoping he'll come back on his own."

"It's good you've come to this decision. And if Courtney can help, I'm sure she'd be happy to."

Voices sounded on the stairway, and seconds later Trudy rang the breakfast bell.

The meal was scrumptious—scones with thick raspberry sauce, a fruit platter, and bacon and ham. A new couple had arrived the night before and sat on one side of the long oak table. Two elderly sisters chatted about the array of food.

At the end of the table closest to the kitchen, Leighton held a chair out for Alice.

"Here is my main dish for the morning!" Trudy proclaimed. "A sausage, asparagus, potato, and cheese medley. I hope you'll like it."

As Trudy cut huge squares, fragrant steam rose from the dish. Soon everyone had a helping. Alice looked across the table at Leighton and felt the color rise to her cheeks.

The sisters introduced themselves as Mattie and Geraldine.

"We feel out of place," Geraldine said. "Here's Cheryl and Ian on their honeymoon, and it's quite obvious from your faces"—she looked from Alice to Leighton—"that if you're not on a honeymoon, you should be!"

Alice blushed deeper. "We're just good friends."

"We've only known each other a few weeks or so," Leighton added.

"My first husband knew me one day before he proposed," Mattie, the younger woman, said. "I was sixteen, isn't that right, Sister?"

The smaller woman nodded while her sister went on. "Geraldine never married because Papa didn't like her intended, so here she is. I say if you find the right person, you should marry. Even if you have to run off."

Mattie, who monopolized the conversation, turned to Leighton. "It's time you started a new life, young man. I don't believe in fortune-telling, but I can tell things by looking at a person's face. You have a good, thoughtful one."

Now it was Leighton's turn to blush.

"I concur," Cheryl, the younger woman, said. "Good advice, Mattie. Life is too short not to go for what you really want."

"And what God deems is important," Trudy added, pouring everyone more coffee. "I ask God what He wants and expects from me each day, and usually I get an answer." She smiled at her guests. "This bed and breakfast came about because of an answer to prayer, a prayer that I'd find something new and a way to be useful in my remaining years."

They all clapped. "And a great answer to prayer," Alice said. "I've never stayed in a bed and breakfast, and I like the idea. You get to know people from all over."

"Now, if you'll excuse me, I must pack." She hurried up the stairs to gather her belongings. They wouldn't return to Trudy's before Alice had to leave on the Bay Shuttle.

When Alice came back downstairs, Trudy had another picnic basket ready. "You have so much to do. Enjoy this before the vespers service."

The first stop was the cannery and Leighton's new store with gift items. Customers could also order fresh oysters. Alice bought two jars of spice and a can of smoked oysters. "For Steven. The spices are for Courtney."

"Good choice," the lady behind the counter said.

Leighton opened a door and motioned Alice to go ahead of him. "Goodness, but there are hundreds of them," Alice said, watching four workers standing over stainless steel bins while they sorted mounds of oysters.

In a small office off to one side, Luke looked up from a desk. He nodded. "Hello again," he said as Leighton and Alice entered.

Amazed, she continued to watch the workers through an office window. "These oysters are shipped across the bay. There they're opened and sent back to us," Luke explained.

"We're not a full-fledged cannery, though I always refer to it as one," Leighton said. "But the bay is a good place to produce oysters, and they're in high demand, as I'm sure you know."

Alice followed Leighton through a back door. They looked out over the bay. The tide was out now, leaving mudflats nearly as far as she could see.

"Can we walk on the mudflats?" Alice asked.

"Not unless you have boots. It looks solid, but the ground is swampy."

"Who's that man walking out there, then?"

"That's old Charlie. He walks every day on the flats. Not sure why. It's just what he does."

Charlie looked up and waved. Leighton waved back.

Luke came out. "Lisa was disappointed she didn't get to meet you. Next time, we'll have you over for dinner."

Next time. It was as if he expected her to return. After last night, Alice thought Leighton's sons didn't like her.

She smiled. "I hope Lisa's feeling better soon. I'd love to meet your family."

A gentle breeze blew in from the bay, and Leighton put an arm around her. "Should I get your sweater from the truck?"

"I'm fine."

They headed to Leadbetter Point. Leighton parked the truck in a shady area, and mosquitoes buzzed around them in droves. Leighton withdrew a bottle of insect repellant from the glove compartment. "Lots more of these insects where we're going."

"Is it far?"

"Two miles to the ocean side and two back, unless we get lost."

"Leighton, you wouldn't get lost."

"It's been known to happen. I think there are a couple of people from Seattle still out there somewhere, wandering around. We just might run into them."

She hit his arm playfully and proceeded down the well-marked trail.

When they got to the ocean side, Alice ran onto the beach, exclaiming over the sand dollars. "I must take some home. They're beautiful." She held one up and let the sand pour out.

"I just happen to have a plastic bag in my pocket."

Alice looked at him, shaking her head. "You think of everything. Of course, you knew there'd be sand dollars here, didn't you?"

"Yes, I did. And I also knew you'd want to gather some."

Soon the bag was full of whole sand dollars, and Leighton led the way back. "Be sure to look for any signs of those missing people."

"Yeah, sure."

When they got to the truck, he took out a blanket and led the way down to the bay side. "I know the perfect spot for our picnic."

Fried chicken, potato salad, jam bars, and small cans of apple juice were in the basket. "A regular feast. Trudy thinks of everything," Alice said, taking a napkin after she'd finished eating. "That was delicious."

Leighton leaned over and wiped a smudge of jam from her cheek.

"It's time to go to vespers."

The service was wonderful. Alice loved the old church with its high ceilings and flowered wallpaper, listening to the matriarch of Oysterville giving the history of the church and area. The old pump organ had a unique sound, and Alice and Leighton shared a hymnal while they sang "Stand Up, Stand Up for Jesus."

Leighton leaned over and took her hand. "This is the last time we'll be together for a while," he whispered.

"I know."

"Unless I come back to Portland."

"Which you will," Alice said with a half smile.

When they stepped out into the afternoon, warm light had broken through the clouds. "It's sunny, now that I'm leaving to go home," Alice said.

"Speaking of which, there's Mel now."

Leighton retrieved Alice's bags from his truck, stowing them in the back of the van. He leaned over and kissed her forehead. "I'll send you a card. It'll be waiting when you get home."

She wished he were going with her now. Wished she didn't have to leave yet knew she must. He waved until the van turned the corner onto Sandridge Road.

"So? How do you like our peninsula?" Mel asked.

"I like it very much." She sighed. "Leighton's a wonderful person, isn't he?"

"The best. He cares about the community and gives far more than people realize. He also treats employees fairly."

"That doesn't surprise me." Alice already knew it didn't take much to love the tall, lean man.

"You'll be back," Mel predicted.

"Perhaps."

"No, you will. I'd bet on it."

She wanted to ask him about Cora but decided against it. She didn't want to gossip behind Leighton's back. It didn't seem right.

When Mel pulled into the driveway nearly three hours later, Alice expected to see Steven's car. It was almost time for the evening service. Even when they didn't come for dinner, they drove to pick her up.

"Just a minute, Mel. Will you wait until I check to see if everything is all right?"

Mel had her two bags and headed up the walkway. "You want to check in the house?"

She nodded as she unlocked the door. "I'm one of those people who are scared to go into an empty house after I've been gone. It's especially scary at night."

"I'll look in the closets and under the beds."

Alice could see he thought it was a laughing matter, but he humored her. She heard doors open and close. Then he was back. "Looks okay."

"I've been afraid since I was a child. Carl tried to talk me out of it, and I was okay for a while." She had looked under all the beds now. "After he died, I was worse than before."

The light blinked on the answering machine. She handed Mel a tip and thanked him for coming in to check things out.

"I'll be on my way now," he said.

"Thanks again, Mel."

"That's okay. I'd do anything for Leighton."

Alice closed the door and rushed to the phone. She hit the machine's playback button. Steven's voice cut through the stillness of the house. "Alice, we're not going to the evening service. Courtney's tired. She's okay, so don't worry. Call us when you get in. And I repeat, *don't worry.*"

Alice's fingers shook as she dialed the number. Courtney's voice answered right away. "Mom? I'm so glad you're home."

"I should come over right now."

"No, that isn't necessary. I'm okay. I just had a bad night; I think it was gastritis. I knew I shouldn't have eaten that Italian sausage and spaghetti yesterday."

"Sweetie, are you sure?" Alice thought back to when she miscarried, but it had always been in the first trimester. Courtney was far past that. "Are you sure you shouldn't go to the emergency room tonight?"

"No. I'm okay. I need to rest and didn't think it would be good to try to go to the evening service. I'm dying to hear all about the trip, so will I see you tomorrow?"

"You're sure you don't want to go in and be checked?"

"No. I'll call tomorrow if I still have the pain."

After unpacking a few things, but not all, Alice turned on her computer to check her e-mail. She had not one, but two messages from Leighton. She clicked on the first one.

> *I'm so glad you came to my corner of the world. I hope you had a good time. Luke and I were talking about you again. Seems you are my favorite topic of discussion. I miss you already.*
>
> *Leighton*

The second one was a card, but she didn't want to look at it just yet. She hit the RESPOND button and poured out her heart and worries to him.

> *My daughter is having abdominal pains. Remember when I said I didn't think her voice sounded right? I'm really worried. Thanks for the great time. I miss you already, too.*
>
> *Love,*
> *Alice*

Leighton never used the word *love*, and Alice thought it strange. It was as if he didn't like the word, as if it scared him. Perhaps she used it too randomly.

She hit the SEND button, then returned to finish emptying her suitcase. The phone rang. Grabbing it, she almost yelled a hello.

"Alice?"

"Leighton! I just read your message. You didn't get my answer already?"

"No. I just wanted to hear your voice. What is it? Is something wrong?"

She swallowed back the tears that suddenly threatened. "It's Courtney. She's having abdominal pains. I'm so afraid for her and the baby."

"Do you want me to come?"

"Oh, no. It's okay. I know you're busy."

"I'll come if you want me to. You shouldn't be alone when you're upset."

"No. Just keep in touch, okay?"

She hung up, and the tears ran down her cheeks. She wanted him to come, wanted him to be there. She needed someone to lean on, to assure her that things would work out. If only she could stop worrying, stop thinking the worst would happen. Carl had always chided her for jumping to conclusions.

Hurrying to the kitchen, Alice put the teakettle on. Perhaps a cup of tea would soothe her.

Then she saw the roses on the dining room table. Their petals drooped a bit, but the stems still stood straight and tall. Tears sprang again to her eyes. She thought of God and how He was there to lean on.

"O Lord, please hear me now. My little girl's in trouble. Don't let anything happen to her baby, I beg of You."

She sat with her head bowed, one pink rosebud clutched in her hand.

Chapter 18

Alice slept with the light on all night, something she did when worried. Light offered her comfort, just like the Bible on her nightstand. She thought of one of the first verses she had memorized: "Thy word is a lamp unto my feet, and a light unto my path."

She remembered going to Sunday school in a starched dress, knee highs, and black patent leathers. Agnes balked about going after she turned thirteen, but Alice accepted Christ as her personal Savior at a young age and attended the youth group and all other activities. She missed her parents now, wishing they had lived long enough to see Courtney marry.

Alice wondered if it was too early to call Courtney. She'd have a cup of coffee, then call.

No answer. Alice sank against the pillow. Courtney had gone to the hospital during the night, and Steven hadn't called her. She was sure that's what had happened. She dialed Steven's cell phone.

"Steven, where's Courtney?"

There was a long pause. "At home, I assume. I left less than an hour ago. She didn't answer the phone?"

"No. That's why I called you."

"She's probably in the shower. Try again. If she doesn't answer this time, I'll go home to check things out."

She dialed again, and Courtney answered. "Mom, I just got your frantic message. I'm sorry. Steven says I should take the phone into the bathroom."

"Honey, I was scared to death."

"I'm going in to see the doctor tomorrow because he's not going to be in the office today. But I feel fine now. No pains. I'm a little tired, that's all."

"Oh, praise God." Alice felt she could breathe again. "If you're feeling up to it, let's go see Agnes this afternoon."

"That's a great idea. I want to hear about Oysterville and all the things you saw."

Alice checked her e-mail before calling Agnes.

"Of course I want to see you," Agnes said. "Come for lunch. I missed the two of you yesterday. Just didn't seem like Sunday. And what's this about your going somewhere to see a man?"

Alice chuckled. "I'll tell you about it when we get there."

When Courtney was in the car, Alice studied her critically. "You look peaked."

Courtney adjusted the seat belt to accommodate her expanding tummy. "Mom, I'm fine. If I weren't, I wouldn't be going with you."

"Agnes is going to give me the third degree about Leighton."

"Of course she is. Isn't that what big sisters are for?"

"Exactly what did you tell her?"

Courtney grinned. "That I thought you were serious about this guy. Why else would you have gone all that way to visit?"

"Well, we'll deal with the topic, should it come up."

The subject came up after hugs and hellos.

"I can't wait to hear the news," Agnes said, "but since the soup's hot and the sandwiches toasted, let's eat." They always had the same meal. It was tradition.

As soon as they sat and offered a blessing, Agnes started in. "Please tell me you're not seriously considering remarriage at your age!"

"You think I shouldn't?" Not that Alice was contemplating it, but she wanted to see Agnes's reaction.

"What I think doesn't matter, but you're crazy, that's what! One doesn't go running off to who knows where on a whim. I know you too well."

Alice stirred her soup. "I distinctly remember you telling me once that I should think of marrying again."

"Well, I meant someone from your church, not some guy from another state."

"Oysterville's just one hundred and fifty miles away."

Agnes hadn't had a happy marriage. After her husband's death, she never considered dating again, let alone marrying. But she thought male companionship might be good for Alice, who seemed far more dependent and was lost without Carl.

Alice expected Courtney to join in the conversation, but she remained silent.

"It's way too far, considering your family is here." Agnes set a plate of shortbread cookies on the table.

Alice chewed on her toasted cheese as she tried to gather her thoughts. Agnes had been the forceful one, the one who got her way. Though she and Alice saw each other once a week, Agnes always sat like a queen on her throne, expecting her dictate to be met.

"Leighton is a very fine man, Auntie," Courtney finally said. "You should come to meet him. He brought Mom pink roses."

"Roses! Do you know how much they cost now?"

Alice nodded. "Courtney's right. He is very thoughtful—all the things you'd ever want in a man—"

"Hold on." Agnes raised her hand. "Just what are these attributes? Maybe we should make a list."

"Security," Courtney said.

"He's a Christian, and he's compassionate."

"How do you know that?" Agnes asked. "Seems you haven't known him long

209

enough to have that one figured out."

"Companionship," Courtney said. She'd often mentioned how much she and Steven enjoyed being together and felt free to talk about anything.

"He's nice-looking, though I don't count that as a must," Alice said.

"But he's taking you away."

"Oh, Agnes, we haven't even discussed that yet."

"If his job is on the bay, growing oysters and selling them, why does he come to Portland?"

Alice nibbled a cookie. "He has a son and business here, also." She suddenly remembered he had another order, and knowing how she had worried so much, he'd probably be back sometime this week. Her face got red. She needed to change the subject.

Alice leaned toward Courtney. "So, Agnes, what do you think of our girl here? Doesn't she look radiant? And she's really showing now."

Courtney pulled her jumper close to reveal the baby. "Six months, Auntie."

"And it's a boy?"

Courtney nodded. "Steven Carl."

"Steven Carl!" Alice cried. "I didn't know you'd picked out a name."

"We did. Just last night."

"I like it. After Daddy and Granddaddy." Agnes turned to Alice.

"And you're going to just leave, with the baby coming."

"Agnes, I am *not* leaving."

"Humph! I think you will."

Courtney went over and hugged her aunt. "Everything will work out, but we need to go now. It's been wonderful as always, Auntie."

Agnes stood in the doorway, waving, her body erect, her face dispassionate.

"Maybe Auntie is jealous." Courtney looked at her mother.

"I wondered about that. Visits with Agnes wear me out. She's too argumentative and looks for something to complain about. She wasn't always that way. We had fun when we were kids."

"Perhaps she wants to remarry, though she says she doesn't want to."

"She'll never meet anyone stuck in her apartment day in and day out," Alice said.

"Well, I say let's take it a day at a time. No sense in making hay if there's no grass in the yard."

Alice laughed. "I never heard that one!"

Courtney smiled impishly. "I just made it up."

"I love you; you do know that."

"Of course."

"And Steven's a lucky man."

"He knows that." Courtney stuck her chin up, then grinned. "I'm lucky to have him, too."

They drove along I-84, and Alice took the Eighty-second Street exit. "Do you want to go home or stop by the house?"

"Let's stop at your house first," Courtney answered. "I think I'll lie down for a nap, if that's okay."

Alice frowned. "You sure you feel all right?"

"Yes. It's just that I need more rest now." She leaned back against the headrest.

"Of course. And I'll check my e-mail."

"Mom, you're fanatical. I can't believe it!"

"Yeah, you've got that one right."

There were two messages. The first was from Leighton, saying he might be in town on Wednesday.

"Wednesday," Alice said aloud. "That's the day after tomorrow."

The second letter was from an unknown address. The message was chilling. "You don't know what you're doing or who you are fooling with." It was unsigned.

Alice felt sudden fear. Who would send such a message? It must just be some sick joke. Why would anyone wish her harm? She hadn't done anything to anyone. She thought of Cora. But, no, it couldn't be her. Even Cora wouldn't do something like that.

She jotted down the address from the letter, and after reading Leighton's message again, she printed it out.

Courtney was still napping, so Alice called Steven and asked him to come by for dinner.

"I'll be there no later than six."

She told him about the message.

"Alice, don't open any letter unless it's from a known address."

"I didn't know that."

"There're a lot of crazies out there, so just be aware. Leave the message alone, and I'll take a look at it."

Alice left the computer on and went in to make an apple pie, Steven's favorite. It was the least she could do for all his help with the computer.

Steven looked perplexed when he came into the kitchen. "Do you know a Meredith?"

"Meredith? No, should I?"

"I found a name from the server, but they can't tell me any more. I sent a message, saying we'd call the police if there was any more harassment."

"Harassment! One letter is hardly that, is it, Steven?" She quartered the apple, wondering who Meredith could be. She certainly hadn't met anyone named Meredith.

"Maybe it isn't harassment, Alice, but you can't be too careful." He looked at the apples in a bowl. "Are you making an apple pie, by chance?"

"Sure am. Now you must stay for dinner."

"You know how to drive a hard bargain."

Courtney cleared her throat behind them. "Hey, guys, don't I have any say in where I eat?" She grinned impishly. "I'm feeling better now. Sometimes sleep is all a person needs." She patted her tummy. "I just wish he wanted to sleep when I do."

Steven leaned over and kissed his wife. "Honey, you're beautiful right now. I love you so much."

Alice dumped the apples into the crust, wondering how she could even think for one minute that she might be happy living somewhere else. This was home. It would always be home.

Chapter 19

By mid-September, Leighton had come to Portland at least once a week, and Alice had gone to the peninsula twice a month. Courtney seemed to be fine with no more abdominal pain and was counting the days until her baby came. Now that she was in the final two months of her pregnancy, Alice didn't worry as much.

Courtney had collected every conceivable gadget and piece of furniture from a changing table to baby scales. Blankets, sleepers, socks, and rompers filled the chest of drawers. The Ladies' Guild at church had given a baby shower. Since she needed more space, Courtney found another dresser at a yard sale and was in the process of sanding it down. Steven promised to paint it.

The last time Alice had visited Leighton, they found a delightful baby book at Sweet William's, an exclusive gift boutique in Ocean Park. Courtney loved it on sight as she leafed through the pages.

"It's actually from Leighton," Alice said. "He saw it and insisted on buying it."

"I'll have to write him a thank-you note."

"I'm sure he'd appreciate it."

When they weren't together, Alice and Leighton e-mailed daily. She couldn't imagine life without him and thought he felt the same. Each time it was more difficult to say good-bye, yet nothing was brought up about a permanent relationship. He'd attended church with her more than one Sunday, meeting her friends, and she'd had dinner with Luke and his family. She'd also seen Cora again, and Cora had been cordial.

Each time Alice went to the peninsula, she stayed with Trudy at the bed and breakfast. She'd learned what to wear to the beach now—her warm gray hat with earflaps, jeans, and layers of clothes. Mornings were cool, but afternoons were often warm. It was hard to know what to expect.

Alice and Leighton had hiked on every trail from the south end to the north. He'd started teasing her, calling her a mountain goat.

"I don't mind being a goat," she said. "Suits me just fine."

Alice had come for the Beach Barons' Car Extravaganza.

"You're going to think of me as a permanent fixture," she said when she arrived at Trudy's.

"And that would suit me just fine." The older woman gave her a quick hug. "I enjoy the company."

The night before the car parade, Alice and Trudy sat on the front porch shelling peas.

"I guess I should be content with things the way they are. Why can't I just be happy to have Leighton as a good friend?"

Trudy raised an eyebrow. "You don't think you're more than just a friend?"

"Nothing's been said about making our relationship permanent. It probably wouldn't work, anyway."

"Of course it will," Trudy said.

"I could hardly expect Leighton to move to Portland. His work, his whole life is here."

"And you don't think he wants you to move here?"

"I suppose he does," Alice hesitated, "but I'm not sure I can leave my daughter and grandbaby."

Trudy shook the pea pods out of her lap. "I know I'm old-fashioned, but I say it's the woman's choice. If the man earns a living, she should go where he can make that living. I'm sure Leighton notices hesitancy on your part, and that's why he hasn't suggested marriage."

"He sends the cutest cards. Some are romantic, but he never signs them with love."

Trudy glanced at the road. "As I said before, Leighton's been hurt deeply. He doesn't want to risk another failure or a possible rejection."

"I'd *never* reject him. I know I love him. I knew from the beginning."

"It'll work, then, because I know he loves you, too. He's as much as said so to me."

"And what about Cora?"

"Cora has to find her own happiness. She clung to an idea too long. It's time for her to move on, and I think she's finally come to realize the futility of a life with Leighton."

"I wish we could find Aaron, too. I know how it hurts Leighton."

"Aaron will be found. I have every confidence that he will. It's just a matter of time." Trudy rose from the chair. "Let's go pick some wildflowers for the table and see if there's enough ripe blackberries for a cobbler."

"Are you sure Leighton's coming for dinner?"

"He said he was. Said he had a meeting with Luke, then he'd be right over."

Alice popped a ripe berry into her mouth. She made a face. It looked ripe but was tart.

Trudy laughed. "That's why you have to add lots of sugar. You just never know how many are really sweet."

❧

Leighton knew what he had to do. It wouldn't be easy, but some decisions weren't. He'd discuss his plan with Luke.

He found Luke overseeing the shipment of oysters. The truck was full. Ken, the driver, nodded. "Hi, Mr. Walker."

Luke held out the shipping ledger for Leighton to read. "What's wrong? I thought you were taking off for the day."

"We need to talk. Can you leave Tim in charge and come with me to get a cup of coffee?"

Luke frowned. Leighton never took off during the day, nor did he suggest coffee in the middle of the afternoon. "Sure, Dad. Whatever you want."

"Can you run this operation without me?"

The question threw Luke off-guard, and he stepped back. "Well, I think so, Dad—"

"No, you have to know. No thinking about it."

"Yes, I know what all you do, and I suppose I always figured someday you'd turn it over to me. I just thought it wouldn't be for another ten years or so."

"I'm putting you in charge now, but first we need to talk. I'll meet you at Jeanine's in ten minutes. I'll ask her for a back room so we can have some privacy."

Jeanine's was not the place he usually went. She made lattés with soy milk and did a lot of natural food stuff that Leighton wasn't into, but she had a large clientele and that suited Leighton's needs. She also made the best smoked turkey sandwich he'd ever tasted. Of course it was too late for lunch, so he and Luke would have to settle for coffee and a piece of her fresh rhubarb pie.

"Hey, how's the oyster business?" Jeanine asked when he got there.

"Doing fine, just fine."

"Where's that friend of yours that came in a few weeks ago with you?"

"Alice?"

Jeanine smiled. It was the kind of smile that lit up her whole face. "Yeah, guess that was her name."

"She's here now."

"Oh?" She looked as if she expected him to go on with more details.

"I'm meeting Luke," he said, ignoring her probing question. "Can we have that table in the back where you have the knitting classes?"

"Of course you can. What are you ordering?"

"Two coffees and two slabs of rhubarb pie."

"Just sold the last piece, Leighton. I have coconut cream, though."

"Okay. That'll do." He didn't really care what she had. He just needed to do something with a fork while they talked. Luke had never been easy to talk to. Quiet. Stubborn. He had a touch of his father in him.

Jeanine brought the coffees back just as Luke came in.

"For Pete's sake, Dad," he muttered after she left, "what's going on? We've never come in here for coffee before. This is the sort of place I'd take Lisa to."

"I know."

"So what's up?"

Leighton took a sip of coffee and watched Jeanine set a slice of pie in front of his bewildered son.

"*Pie?*" Luke said. "Now if you'd said we were coming for pie, that's a whole different thing."

"Shut up and eat," Leighton said. His voice sounded gruff, but his mouth turned up at the ends.

"Okay. I'm waiting."

"I hear you and Cora have been talking about me behind my back."

Luke almost choked on his coffee. "What?"

"She said you two and Tom had discussed my life, and all of you agreed I had no business getting interested in a woman who isn't from around here."

"Dad, now, that's not fair."

"What's not fair? That I'm calling you on the carpet about it, or that I found you out?"

"You know what I mean—"

"No, I don't. That's why we're here."

Luke played in the pie with his fork. "It's just that, well, Cora would make you a really good wife, so why look somewhere else?"

Leighton narrowed his eyes. "What if I'd told you that Lisa wasn't right for you? What would you have done?"

"Ignored you, probably." He dug in and polished off his pie in record time, then shoved the plate back. "I know it's none of my business, and it was Cora who brought it up. I just sort of agreed with her."

"Which gave her fuel for her cause." Leighton leaned forward. "Luke, do you believe in love?"

"Ah, Dad, of course I do."

Jeanine reappeared, holding up the coffeepot. "Yeah, refills would be nice," Leighton said. He knew she was wondering what was going on. "Not selling the business, Jeanine. Just want you to know that."

"Oh, good. I'm relieved to hear that." She smiled, then left them alone again.

Leighton picked up the conversation. "If you believe in love, as you say you do, and if you believe things happen for reasons and that God is the Supreme Maker and if we know what's good for us, we ask for His guidance, then you wouldn't agree with Cora. I don't love Cora, I've never loved Cora, and frankly, I doubt I'll *ever* fall in love with her."

"Okay, okay, Dad. Don't get hot under the collar. Keep your voice down. If you don't watch out, she might pop in at any moment. This is one of her favorite places to go, or didn't you know that?"

"No, I didn't. How would I know that?"

Luke downed his coffee and pushed his chair back. "So I said something I shouldn't, and I apologize. I have nothing against Alice, but she's a city gal. You know what happens to city gals. Look what happened to that appliance repairman,

Fred, when he married Rachel. He stayed on, but she moved back to Seattle."

"I know that, Son. And that's why I want you to take over the business in my absence."

"Absence!"

"I plan on being gone for a while. I'll keep in touch, and if there are any big problems, you can call me. I'll be just three hours away."

Luke shook his head. "You're not making sense. How can you leave something you've done your entire life? If you'd gone to the city, my mother might be here today—" His voice trailed off, as if realizing he'd said too much.

Leighton looked at his son, feeling the hurt return, the hurt he'd felt when Nancy first left, the hurt when he'd received the news of her death, the hurt when he heard of the note she'd left behind. A note that said she'd be buried in Seattle, not in the family plot on the peninsula.

Luke had also felt this hurt, perhaps more than the younger boys. He'd known his mother the best and had acted up in school for several months after she first left. He'd been old enough to remember the arguments when she'd begged Leighton to "get out of this godforsaken spot and move to Seattle or Portland. Somewhere else, *anywhere else!*"

Leighton tightened his jaw. "You're hitting low, Luke. Mighty low."

"Sorry, Dad. I shouldn't have said that."

"People change over the years. They grow; they learn to listen and to feel with their heart, not just their head. Perhaps that's the crossroads I'm at now. But it isn't going to be forever."

"It isn't?"

"No. I want to be up there for Alice, to be with her while her daughter's going through this pregnancy. It's important to her. She doesn't have a bunch of kids to shuffle through, you know. When you have just one, you look at them with a whole different perspective."

"Dad, I'll run the business. I can manage without you. It may take more time than I'm putting in now, and quite honestly, I don't know how Lisa will take it. But if it isn't forever, she'll understand. Just as I'm trying to understand how you can even leave the peninsula."

The two shook hands, then Leighton watched his son head back toward the cannery. He paid for the coffee and pie and told Jeanine that if she ever stopped baking pies, he'd move away.

He walked out, smelled the wonderful salt air, the clean air, something he would miss in Portland. But he couldn't have everything, could he? Alice needed him now, and he was going to be there for her if the city killed him. It wasn't as if he couldn't get away and come back down for a weekend.

He squared his shoulders, then took one more deep breath before heading to Trudy's.

Chapter 20

Alice returned home with Leighton's words running through her mind. What had he meant when he said things were going to work out? She had begged him to tell her what he was talking about, but he said, no, the time wasn't right. She guessed she'd just have to bide her time, but it wouldn't be easy.

Three days later, Courtney called with exciting news. "Mom, you'll never guess what!"

"You know I'm horrible at guessing games, so just tell me."

"I got a lead on Aaron. I'm calling Leighton immediately, or do you want to?"

"Oh, no, sweetie. You call him. You did the work. He's going to be beside himself with joy."

"I know. I just hope it pans out."

Courtney located Leighton through his cell phone. "There's an Aaron Walker in East Belfast, Maine."

"You're kidding! You really think it might be him? Do you have a phone number and an address?" Leighton's first thought was to fly to Maine and see Aaron face-to-face.

"No address, just this number."

"I'll take it."

Aaron Matthew. He felt a tight knot in his throat at the thought of his son. Missing. A runaway. Not one of those who heard the 800 number and called home to say, "I'm fine, Dad." No. That wasn't Aaron's way. And here, perhaps, he had been found, but did he want that? Leighton had hoped since that day five years ago when he left, that one day he'd open the door and there would be Aaron. Of course he'd throw his arms around him and call Luke and Tom, then John. There'd be rejoicing, just like with the prodigal son in the Bible. Leighton would want to share that special time with Alice. There was almost too much to think about.

What should he say to a son he hadn't seen for so many years?

Courtney said Aaron was working in a lobster pound in Maine. Who would have thought it? Leighton figured that Aaron would get as far away from the sea as he could. He'd never seemed to like the oyster business or anything about the water.

Leighton finally mustered enough courage to dial the 207 area code, then the rest of the number.

He got an answering machine. It wasn't Aaron's voice. Disappointment hit him, but he left a message, anyway.

"This is Leighton Walker, and I'm trying to reach my son, Aaron Walker. If I have the right number, will you please call home? Aaron, I love you."

Leighton didn't leave the house that day. He sat staring out at the bay. He couldn't e-mail Alice because that would tie up the line. Now he wished he had two separate lines as Tom had suggested in the beginning. When he remembered to use his cell phone, she wasn't home.

Leighton thought of Aaron as a toddler, at age two. Independent. Bullheaded. Here he was still, the captain of his own ship, balking at any suggestion his father made.

The next morning Cora called him before he left for work.

"I heard that you found Aaron."

"He hasn't called back."

"You can't just forgive him—"

"Cora, you always loved Aaron. How can you even think I'd turn my back on him? Surely you remember the story of the prodigal son."

"That's a parable."

"So? Jesus taught with parables. It's one of the most remembered and most cherished parables of all times."

"I don't think it's fair to Luke."

"I don't hear Luke complaining."

"No, you wouldn't. Luke doesn't make his thoughts known all that much."

"You're telling me that Luke would be unhappy if Aaron returns to Oysterville?"

"Yes, I am."

"Well, I'll just see about that," Leighton muttered under his breath.

Halfway to work, he stopped and parked alongside the road. Cora had done it again. Gotten him hot under the collar and all ready to pounce on Luke, then he remembered what had happened last time.

No way was he going to ask Luke how he felt about it. If Aaron came home, he could help Luke run the business. Having Aaron home would be an asset and certainly not the way Cora made it sound.

He called Alice on the cellular phone, saying he was sending a big bouquet of flowers to Courtney. "What does she like best?"

"Carnations. Any color. She just likes their fragrance."

"Carnations it is, then. I—" He hesitated. "I'll see you soon, I hope."

❧

In the middle of the night, Courtney awoke with a wet, sticky feeling. She groped for the lamp, gasping when she saw the blood. She shook Steven. "It's the baby! I'm losing the baby!"

He rolled over to the edge of the bed. "Honey, no." Anguish spread across her face as she pointed to her nightgown. He reached for the phone. "I'm calling the doctor."

"No, Steven. It's too late for that. Please just—" she gasped for breath—"take me to the hospital."

He found her jumper on the back of a chair, groped for the sandals under the bed, and grabbed a towel. He didn't remember getting dressed or bringing the car out front, but he helped Courtney, who was almost hysterical, into the front seat.

She lay her head back, a grimace crossing her forehead.

"I better call Alice."

"Call from the hospital," she said. "Oh, Steven, this can't be happening!"

Steven sped over the limit toward Providence Hospital. Thank goodness it was only five miles away. He prayed for a policeman to come along, but the streets were deserted. The car clock said 2:00 a.m.

"I know this is bad," Courtney whimpered again. "It shouldn't be happening. The baby must be in distress."

"Honey, we're almost there." Steven had called ahead to the hospital, alerting them to the emergency, and they were waiting with a wheelchair at the entrance.

"Steven," Courtney grabbed his arm. "Don't leave me." Her eyes were wide with shock.

"Honey, you know I wouldn't."

She began crying softly then, and by the time she was wheeled into one of the examining rooms and the doctor on duty came to check, she was openly sobbing. The doctor was young, and Steven hoped he knew what he was doing.

"Mrs. Spencer, please try to relax. We're here to help. I think you have a condition called placenta previa. Your chances of keeping the baby are good."

Courtney cried harder. "No, I know it's too late."

"Honey, please." Steven stroked her arm.

"How far along are you?"

"Seven months," Steven answered. He knew as much about the pregnancy as Courtney did. "It's our first."

"Did anything unusual happen today?"

"Oh, no. I take very good care of myself—"

"No previous miscarriages?"

"No."

"She's had a relatively easy time of it," Steven offered.

"Have you had an ultrasound?"

Courtney nodded. "Yes, back at the end of June."

"Everything looked okay then?"

"Yes, everything's been fine all along," Steven interrupted. His voice was harsh, but he couldn't help it. Why didn't this doctor *do* something?

"Honey, I better call your mother." He took his cell phone and stepped into the hall. Of course, Alice would be asleep, but if he waited until morning, she would be deeply hurt.

Alice answered with a sleepy "Hello?" but instantly came awake. "I'll be right there," she said.

Steven went back in and took Courtney's hand.

"Complete bed rest is a must if you're to keep the baby," the doctor was saying. "I've ordered an ultrasound so we can see how things look. It will show the extent of the condition, since there are various stages."

Courtney's face was pale, and her chin trembled as she looked from the doctor to Steven and back again. "But what happened?"

"It happens in one of two hundred pregnancies. The placenta is covering the cervix and it causes bleeding. Have you had contractions?"

"No."

"We'll know more once we see the ultrasound."

Alice arrived in a taxi, not trusting herself to drive in the middle of the night, especially not when she was upset.

Steven heard her voice in the hall and stepped out to motion her in.

"They've scheduled an ultrasound. Until then, we wait."

Alice bent over Courtney and kissed her cheek. She tried not to cry, but the tears welled up and spilled down her face.

"Honey, I'm so sorry."

"It isn't definite that she's losing the baby," Steven said. "The doctor says the bleeding might stop."

"Mom—" Courtney opened her eyes and reached for her mother's hand.

They were crying when the nurse came in and suggested that Courtney needed her rest. Courtney begged for either Steven or Alice to stay with her.

Steven left to get a cup of coffee from the cafeteria machine. He couldn't believe this was happening. Courtney had gone to the doctor on Monday. He said she was doing fine and had gained two more pounds. The baby's heartbeat was strong. Her color was good, and no swelling showed in her ankles.

He took the coffee black, though he usually put sugar in machine coffee. It was always so acidic, but this time he needed the bitterness to stay awake. It might be a long night.

Slouching in a plastic chair, Steven stared at the coffee. He loved Courtney so very much. When she hurt, he hurt. He knew how much she counted on having their baby, how much Alice had prayed. Now this.

"Lord, if I could do anything, anything at all, I'd do it in a flash. Losing the baby would be devastating for her. To discover her birth mother is no longer living, losing her father at a young age—this is enough. Don't give her any more."

He drained the cup, squashed it in his hand, and tossed it into the nearest receptacle. If only he understood things better. If only Grams—who'd raised him to be a believer—had explained that part to him. How did you protect someone you loved with all your heart? How did you keep bad things from happening to them?

A janitor, sweeping the floor, looked over. "Are you okay?"

Steven nodded. "Yeah. My wife's in emergency. Guess I'd better get back."

When he entered the room, Alice looked up with pain-filled eyes. Courtney appeared to be sleeping.

Dr. Blanton, the gynecologist, had come in. "The ultrasound shows it's what I suspected. The best condition would be if the baby stayed in the uterus a few more weeks, but if bed rest doesn't help and the bleeding continues, we'll need to perform a cesarean section."

Alice called Leighton from the hospital. For once she hoped the answering machine would pick up because she was afraid she might start crying when she heard his voice.

He answered on the third ring.

"Leighton, I had to let you know—Courtney's in the hospital." Then she couldn't talk.

"Alice? Alice, speak to me."

Steven, assessing the situation, grabbed the phone. He explained what had happened and that they had every reason to hope she could carry the baby longer.

Alice ran out into the hall to cry. It wasn't good for Courtney to see her upset. Besides, she didn't know what to do with herself.

Steven joined her in the hallway. "Leighton says he's coming to town."

"He can't."

"But he will." Steven put an arm around Alice. "Don't you know by now that men feel protective about the women they love?"

She looked up. "He doesn't love me."

"He doesn't? You mean he hasn't said it in so many words?"

Alice looked down at her knotted tissue. It was in shreds, and she dug for another in the pocket of her jacket.

"You think about it, Alice. If you start putting two and two together, you'll come up with the answer. Now, I must sit with Courtney."

Alice paced back and forth, wondering about what Steven said. She wasn't sure she loved Leighton, but if wanting him here now, if wanting him to share the ups and downs was any indication, she guessed—no—she *knew* she loved him and couldn't imagine not having him in her life.

❧

He never doubted that he'd drive to the city. It didn't matter that it was three in the morning; he had to go. And as he drove over the miles, he realized he had come to a crossroads. He'd battled it. Tried to look the other way. Did everything in his power to ignore the facts. Then when he'd talked to Luke and today when he'd heard from Aaron, things had come together. God's timing, he knew.

Alice was hurting, and he hurt because she hurt. He was in love with her. He'd tried to deny it more than once. He listened to people talking, his sons suggesting he cool it, that he look for someone closer, someone who understood what life was like in a place like Oysterville. And he knew it would be hard doing what he had to do. He'd mulled it over in his mind a hundred times, set his plan into motion by discussing the business with Luke. Now that Aaron was coming, they could work the business together. Maybe Aaron would like to take over the store operation, fill orders, and look for more products.

Now he couldn't wait to see Alice. As he sped over the miles, he slipped *Fiddler* into the player. He needed something to lighten up the situation, so he sang, "If I were a rich man."

Chapter 21

D r. Blanton suggested Courtney stay until morning. "I want you to be closely supervised. We have a wonderful staff here. They'll alert me should you start hemorrhaging again. And if you have even one contraction, I want to know immediately." He smiled as he patted Courtney's arm. "For now, stop worrying."

"Celia," he called to a nurse. "Put her on an IV. I don't want to take a chance of dehydration."

"Yes, Doctor, right away."

"When can she come home?" Steven asked.

"If all goes well, tomorrow. I'll make rounds around ten. I'll make a decision then." The doctor paused in the doorway. "Since there's plenty of room, we'll just keep you here. If things change, you'll be up on the third floor."

"There's only one solution," Alice said after Dr. Blanton had left. "Courtney should come to my house. I can take better care of her there. She can have my bedroom, since obviously she shouldn't climb the stairs."

"Mom, I can sleep in the nursery."

"No. You need the larger bed. I'll take the single bed in the nursery."

Steven nodded as he kissed Courtney's forehead. "We're going to have a fine, healthy son," he said. "And if he should come by cesarean, that's what will happen."

Alice hugged her son-in-law. "God bless you, Steven. I need someone with positive thinking right now."

"I just pray for no contractions," Courtney said. "It sounds as if that will be the deciding factor."

The nurse looked in. "Why don't you all try to get some rest?"

"Yeah. I can sleep sitting up," Steven said. "I've done that before."

Alice dozed fitfully as she sat to one side of the bed, while Steven sat in the other chair, holding his wife's hand.

Someone cleared his throat from the hall. "The nurse told me where to find you."

Alice jerked awake and saw Leighton. Smiling, she rushed to his side. "You came."

He put an arm around Alice. "Wild horses couldn't have kept me away. And I want you to know it's going to be okay. We have the whole peninsula praying. I called Luke before I left."

Tears formed in Alice's eyes. Leighton tightened his arm around her. "I thought you could use some support about now. So what does the doctor say?"

"We just have to keep her quiet and in bed," Steven said.

Courtney opened her eyes. "Thank you for coming. I always wanted to be lazy."

"Don't listen to her," Alice said. "She makes an awful patient, believe me."

"We're hoping she can go home in the morning." Steven glanced at Leighton. "Man, you look like you could use some coffee. I'll show you where the machines are, unless you want me to bring you some."

"No, I'll go with you."

"So how's it really going?" Leighton asked once they were out of earshot.

"I think we got a warning in the nick of time." Steven ran his hand through his hair. "The baby may have to be taken, but the doctor is hoping to wait a few more weeks, at least."

"This is so hard on Alice."

"I know."

Leighton found a cinnamon bun to go with the coffee. "What did they do, sprinkle a little cinnamon on cardboard?"

Steven laughed. "I see you haven't had much of hospital vending machine goodies."

Shaking his head, Leighton said, "No, not since my Hannah was so sick."

"Yeah, heard about that. I'm sorry."

"God doesn't shut the sun out every day."

The two men walked back. When Leighton was confident that everything was okay, he left for his son's.

As he drove across town to John's high-rise, Leighton wondered if he really knew what Alice felt. Would there be room in her life for him? Was he going to matter to her? He read something in her eyes, felt something in her touch, but was it enough?

"Lord, You know my prayer and I know You hear me. Help me to accept what Your will is in this. Help me to be there for Alice, but to be patient, too."

When John didn't answer the doorbell after several rings, Leighton suddenly wished that he'd remembered the key. The door finally swung open, and John stared. "Dad! What are you doing here?"

"It's a bit of a story. Can I come in?"

"Well, sure. I just wasn't expecting you to come calling at 7:00 a.m."

"Aren't you going to work?"

"Well, yes, but as you know, when you own your own business, you can be late sometimes." He rubbed his eyes. "I repeat, why are you here?"

"I drove in to be with Alice. Her daughter is in the hospital. She might lose the baby."

"Oh, no. That's awful."

"I'll be sticking around for a while. That is, if I can stay until I find another place."

"*Here?* You're moving to Portland?"

"I'm moving toward that, yes. I take it you haven't talked to Luke, then." Leighton slumped into the nearest chair.

"No, but I've been working late. Trying to get ready for the poinsettia orders. The biggest sale is the Friday after Thanksgiving."

"My son, we're both growing things. You flowers, me oysters." John went into the kitchen and poured water into a coffeepot. "I gotta have my caffeine. Then we need to talk."

"*Talk?*" It seemed like that was all he'd done lately.

"I think it's fine that you found someone to go out with you when you come to town, but why don't you leave it at that?"

Leighton eyed his second youngest son. "That's easy for you to say. You've never been married or even shown any indication you have anyone on the horizon. You obviously don't love someone."

"Dad, you went that route once."

"And does that mean I can't find love again because I'm *old*?"

"I didn't mean that."

"That's what it sounds like." Leighton poured himself a cup of coffee. "Now, do you have any bread to toast or cereal? I'm famished. I'm also finished discussing this."

After John left for work, Leighton took a short nap. Then he checked and discovered Courtney had been discharged. He headed over to Alice's, stopping first for a bouquet of pink roses and yellow carnations.

"Leighton!" Alice looked surprised yet pleased. "I'd hoped to see you again before you left." She went in search of a vase.

"Remember the decision I talked about the other day?"

She nodded. "Yes, but you were so secretive."

"I'm moving here. To Portland. I'll be staying with John for a while, maybe help him out with his business."

Her eyes widened. "What do you mean?"

"I want to be here with you. I've already talked to Luke about things, and he's willing to run the business."

"Moving *here?*" Alice stopped arranging the flowers. "Maybe we both better sit down."

"I've given Luke full reins in the business, for the time being. I need to be near you, to see you every day. I think we should get married." The minute he said it, he wished he could take the words back. This wasn't the best way to propose marriage. He hadn't been romantic at all. Now that he thought about it, he realized he'd never said he loved her. Her eyes looked almost glazed.

"What did you mean when you said you gave Luke full reins in the business?"

"I said I was going on an extended vacation from my business."

"You did this because of me?"

"Yes. Is that surprising?"

Alice's eyes filled with tears again. "I guess it shouldn't be, but it is." She reached over and took his hand. "I guess when God's guiding your life, nothing He does should be amazing."

"I love you," he said in a thick voice. "I've loved you since that afternoon I first saw you. I hadn't even been praying to meet anyone. It just happened, with God's timing. Sometimes He kinda zaps you when you least expect it."

"But you can't move here, Leighton. It wouldn't work out."

"Why not?"

Alice moved her hand. "I can't let you do it. If I agreed to this move, you'd regret it. The bay is in your blood. Your work is there—your home, the cannery. I can't let you give that up."

"My mind's made up. I'm going to do it."

"And I say it's wrong." Her voice rose as she looked away. She couldn't look him in the eye. Not now.

"Are you saying you won't marry me, then?"

Alice got up and walked across the room. "I guess I am, Leighton. I don't want to give up my home here. It's my life. My family. You know that, so it wouldn't be right for me to ask it of you."

"I'm offering it."

"Oh, Leighton, I think not. It seems we're at an impasse."

"That's it, then? You're giving up on the whole idea of us being together?" He stalked to the door. "I thought this was what you wanted, too. I guess I was wrong."

She didn't answer.

He opened the door, then turned around. "I'll be at John's if you want to call."

She watched as he hurried up the walk. She wanted to cry out for him to come back but couldn't. As tears ran down her cheeks, she knew God would help her get over this obstacle as well as all the others she'd had in her life.

~

Leighton drove to the nearest drive-through and ordered a cup of the strongest coffee they made.

"Maybe you want a double shot of espresso, sir."

"Make it a triple shot," he said.

He took the hot beverage, found a place with time on the parking meter, and stared at the Willamette.

"I've never wanted much, Lord," he said aloud. "I've tried to live a good life, be a good husband, father, son—not necessarily in that order. It seems things always happen to me, or as some would say, I've been at the wrong place at the wrong time. But you know, Lord, I wouldn't trade a day of it for anything else. I can't imagine not having had Hannah in my life or knowing Alice for these past few months. Maybe You'd have me go back to Oysterville and take care of my business, after all."

He finished the coffee and got out, putting the cup in the nearest trash can. Then he drove across the Morrison and on his way to John's to get his overnight bag. He'd never even unpacked.

Chapter 22

Alice felt like a displaced woman. She had given up her volunteer job, the position with Spencer Consultants, and worst of all, had sent Leighton on his way. It had been a week since he'd returned to Oysterville, but it seemed like months. He sent e-mail on a daily basis, but the phone calls stopped. And inside her was an emptiness, but she couldn't think about it. All concern was with Courtney and keeping her stress-free.

Courtney had settled into a routine, and though Alice felt her daughter was doing well, she knew that she worried about her condition.

"Mom, what if I lose the baby?"

"You're not going to, so there."

"Are you going to visit Leighton soon?"

"I can't now."

"I don't want to see you moping around."

"Have I been moping?"

Courtney leaned up on an elbow. "Yes, Mom, you have. And it makes me think about the scripture where it talks about a woman leaving her family and cleaving to her husband to build a new home. And that's what Steven and I are doing. Now you must build a new life for yourself with Leighton. We're going to be fine."

Alice felt her heart race at the thought. She hated that he hadn't called. She missed hearing his voice more than she'd ever imagined.

"I wonder if you shouldn't talk to the pastor about this to get some fresh insight."

Alice knew what her daughter was trying to do, but it wouldn't work. She'd decided that Leighton's place was in Oysterville, doing the work he loved, the work he'd always done. He'd be miserable in the city. After six months, maybe less, he'd be climbing the walls. No, she was certain she'd made the right decision by sending him home. He'd find someone. There was always Cora.

"It's better this way."

"Is it really?" Courtney set her embroidery down. Since she'd become bedfast, needlepoint and embroidery—which she'd put aside after marrying Steven—now came out of the sewing basket. "Don't you think God wants you happy?"

"Of course, honey. God wants only the best for His children. I've always believed that."

Courtney reached for a strand of blue floss and threaded a needle. "Then if that's true, don't you think He had a hand in your meeting Leighton like you did? He could have had his laptop fixed on a day you were volunteering at the hospital."

Alice nodded. "Yes, that's true."

"So I think it was ordained that you two meet and fall in love."

"Why couldn't I have found someone closer?"

Courtney set her work aside again. "I don't know. But according to the Bible, we're not supposed to know all the answers."

"I know that, honey, but I just can't even consider leaving you now."

"I think I understand." She reached over and took her mother's hand. "I wouldn't want you to. But I'm wondering if Auntie doesn't need to be doing something about now. She could come to stay with me for two or three days while you go down to the coast."

"I'll think about it."

Alice left the room then and got out the makings for cookies. She always baked when she had to work through a problem. She would make something chocolate, Courtney's favorite.

When she had the first batch in the oven and Courtney was napping, Alice turned on the computer. There probably wouldn't be any messages today. Should she send him a card? Yes, she wanted to do that. She'd tried to shut it out of her mind, but she knew she'd never forget the hurt look in his eyes or the way he'd turned and walked out the door, closing it softly behind him. She could still hear the sound of his car driving off.

She clicked on the letter icon and saw the number on the screen, announcing she had a card to open. She closed the door so Courtney wouldn't hear the music as she brought it up.

Dozens of colorful hearts were scattered across the screen. The message floated, and it was as if Leighton were in the room whispering in her ear. "I think of you every moment of every day and am still hoping you'll change your mind. Leighton."

She printed it out and added it to her growing notebook.

"Mom—" The door opened and Courtney peered in. "I thought so. You're checking e-mail, and I think the cookies are burning."

"Oh, no!" Alice raced down the hall, and the burned smell filled the kitchen. "I've never burned cookies in my life," she said, grabbing a pot holder.

"And you haven't been in love for a very long time," Courtney said.

"You go back and lie down, young lady!"

Alice scraped the burned rounds into the garbage and plopped into a chair. So much for concentration.

Courtney stood, arms folded. "Mom, I can't let you do this."

"Do what?"

"You know what I mean." She patted her rounded stomach. "I already called Auntie last night when you went to the store."

"You did?"

"Yes, and she can come. So you can get away and go back to the peninsula to see Leighton and get this cleared up."

"There's nothing to clear up."

"Mother, give me some credit for brains. You're in love with him, and he obviously adores and worships the ground you walk on."

"You can't say that."

Courtney looked exasperated. "And who made the trip here in the middle of the night? Ask Steven. See what he says."

"Agnes really agreed to come stay with you?"

"Yes. And I want you to go. I mean it. I can't believe it's over. I think you two need each other, though I admit I was a bit jealous at first."

"You were jealous? I just thought you didn't want me to marry again."

"I know. After mulling it over, I knew I was being selfish."

"Oh, honey, I had no idea."

"Now, Auntie is coming, so I think you have a trip to plan."

Alice's hopes soared. "You really think I should do this, and you don't mind having Agnes here?"

Courtney laughed. "Would I have brought it up if I did?"

Alice felt better after speaking to Agnes. "I can't say I agree with what you're doing, Alice, but I guess it isn't up to me to judge, now, is it?"

"I'll have the cell phone," she told Courtney, "so if anything should happen, I want to know immediately. That's why it's better if I drive my car."

She didn't think of how she hadn't wanted to drive the night she got news that Courtney was in the hospital. But now she felt everything was under control. No more spotting. No contractions. The last doctor's appointment had gone well. And Courtney stayed calm and had complete bed rest. This would give Agnes a chance to feel needed.

Alice decided not to tell Leighton she was coming, though she alerted Trudy that she would need her old room.

"Is everything okay with you two?" Trudy said.

Alice swallowed hard. "Well, maybe not exactly, and that's why I'm coming up. And, Trudy, I want to surprise Leighton."

"Okay, honey, whatever you think."

Alice packed just a few things, not knowing if she'd stay more than one day. Leighton might not want her anymore. Maybe he and Cora were a twosome. She certainly couldn't blame him. She didn't want to wait until morning but knew she must. It was going to be another sleepless night.

Chapter 23

The autumn day couldn't have been nicer or mellower. Alice was glad Courtney insisted on the trip. Things *had* been up in the air. She hadn't meant to hurt Leighton but knew she had. He'd risked his heart, and she'd all but shattered any dream he had of their building a life together.

She drove over the now-familiar route and stopped in Clatskanie for coffee and a break to stretch her legs. It was the halfway point. She liked to walk down by the river that ran through the town. Sipping her take-out coffee, she sat on a bench and contemplated her decision. She kept vacillating. One minute she was going to tell Leighton she'd changed her mind and she'd move to Oysterville and be his wife. The next minute she knew she could never do it, just as she could never expect him to move to the city.

A light breeze ruffled her hair, and she remembered the many hikes she and Leighton had enjoyed. He had always been so gentle, protective of her. How could she not spend the rest of her life with him?

It was two o'clock when she arrived at the bed and breakfast. After Trudy carried her bag up the stairs, Alice freshened up a bit, then got back into the car. She could hardly wait to see Leighton now.

Trudy came out, waving her hands. "Dear, I just wanted you to know that Cora's at Leighton's house."

"Cora's at the house?"

"It's not what you think, I'm sure. She just probably finagled a way to go help clean. I know her."

Alice felt a sinking sensation. If Cora was there, she certainly wouldn't welcome the sight of Alice. Maybe she'd better stop by the cannery first.

Luke was the first person she saw. His face registered shock as he hurried over. "Alice! What are you doing here?"

"I must speak with Leighton. We had words before he left Portland the last time, and I just need to talk to him."

"He's in the store. I'll tell him you're here."

Alice went back to her car, wondering if she'd find the right words to convey her regrets at hurting him. That had never been her intention.

Leighton walked out the door of the Sea Gifts Store and headed toward her. His gait was purposeful, and her heart knew at that moment how much she loved this man. How much she wanted to be a wife to him. She got out of the car.

"Alice? Why are you here? How's Courtney?" He looked concerned.

"Courtney's fine. The last checkup showed the baby is in good condition. They may do a C-section at eight months."

"But why are you here?" he repeated.

Alice felt compelled to gaze into his dark, haunting eyes. "Agnes is there. She'll do fine for a day or so."

"And then?"

Alice swallowed hard. "And then Courtney will have the baby, and—"

Leighton's gaze never wavered. "And then what? I'm waiting for that part. Do I move to Portland as I suggested, or are you coming here?"

"Well, I—" Again she couldn't find the words she wanted to say. Why was this so difficult?

"I can't keep going on like this. I'm the type of guy who needs to know point-blank where he stands. I know that the sun is going to come up in the morning and it's going to go down each night. I need to know if I can come home to the woman I love with all my heart and know she's there, body and soul, wanting to be with me and not pining away, wishing she were somewhere else."

"I'm trying to say what's in my heart." She wanted him to take her into his arms, to tell her everything was going to be all right, but he stood erect, staring at her, not saying what she'd hoped to hear. "I was wrong in sending you home like that. I hurt you, I know. I hurt us. I've come to apologize, Leighton. I can't get you out of my mind, and I just had to see you, to try to explain."

A car pulled up, and Alice saw it was Cora. Did she and Leighton have something going on? Had Trudy known and been afraid to tell her?

Cora rolled down the window. "Leight, I'm going across the river for that order. Did you have anything else to add to the list?"

She never said hello to Alice, as if she were invisible.

Leighton went over and leaned on the car. Alice wanted to disappear. Why had she thought this would work? She'd hurt him so much. How could this be happening? She'd loved and lost.

Alice started to get into her car, but he stopped her as Cora drove off.

"I have to know, Alice. No in-between for me. Perhaps it's better this way."

"Yes," she said woodenly. "Perhaps it is."

"How long will you be here?"

She swallowed hard. "I'll probably leave early in the morning."

She went back to Trudy's, holding the tears in check, but once she got to the privacy of her bedroom, she let them fall. Moments later, a tap sounded at the door.

"Alice? I have tea and some cranberry scones. Do you feel like company?"

"Yes, I do."

"So," Trudy said, setting the tray on the corner table. "I take it you saw Leighton."

"And Cora."

"You jumped to conclusions about Cora, I see."

"She's helping him run the show."

"Of course. That's what she wants. Are you ready to stand by and let it happen?"

Alice stirred her tea mechanically. "He wants an answer from me, an answer I don't have."

"What part of 'yes' don't you understand?"

"There are too many entanglements in my life. Leighton can't handle that. He as much as said so."

"Poppycock! He's trying to conceal the hurt. That man's been through a fog thicker than any I've ever seen hit the bay."

"Cora's the one who can help him through."

"May I remind you that he doesn't love Cora?"

"He can grow to love her."

"So you're giving up just like that?" The older woman snapped her fingers. "Frankly, I thought you had more starch in your backbone."

"Trudy, I just feel so overwhelmed."

"Leighton will be by. Later. Count on it. I think I'll make that meat loaf he likes so well."

Alice offered to help. She peeled potatoes, sliced onions, tore greens for a salad. She had to keep busy. It kept her mind from mulling over the situation.

They waited, but Leighton hadn't come by six, nor by seven. At seven thirty Trudy said they'd better eat. "I'll not call him. It's up to him. What I know is there's a hurting man out there, and he needs time, Alice. Just give him time."

⌘

Leighton, still shaken by Alice's presence, left work early. He'd had to restrain himself to keep from rushing to her, from taking her into his arms and telling her how much he loved her, how glad he was to see her. It had taken courage for her to come, for her to leave Courtney. And she'd done it. Why, then, had he been aloof? And why had Cora come at that precise moment? He'd seen the hurt in Alice's eyes and knew what she must be thinking.

When he entered the house, he glanced around, noticing the neatness. Cora had stopped by one day at work, insisting she needed a part-time job until something else opened up. He'd said she could come out twice a week to clean. She kept it dusted and vacuumed, and there were clean dishes from the dishwasher again. The refrigerator held dinners and leftovers from previous meals.

Fresh wildflowers graced the table. His daily newspaper was on the nightstand beside his recliner. The *TV Guide* was opened to the right day. Why hadn't he noticed this before? Why did it hit him now?

He changed into clean slacks and a shirt. A photo of Nancy sat on the chest of drawers in his bedroom. Not that he ever noticed it, but he supposed he'd kept it there for the children's sake. He never wanted them to forget their mother. He touched the glass covering her face. It was free of dust. That meant Cora had to have dusted in his room every day she was here.

He put the photo back and thought again about his life. In spite of the sorrow, there'd been lots of joy. Even with Aaron running off, Leighton liked remembering the youngest son with the lock of hair that hung down on his forehead, the laughing eyes, the stubborn streak that got him into trouble. It was that stubborn streak that keep him from calling. Then, too, he could have moved on. Would Leighton ever see Aaron again?

In the refrigerator he found spaghetti and meatballs and half of a lemon meringue pie. He'd have a bit of both.

The sun had left the hills, and the room suddenly felt chilly. The house was big, way too much house for just himself. Why was he staying on here?

Cora enjoyed keeping his house. But she was also stubborn and bossy. If they married, she would run every aspect of his life. He'd been taking care of himself, but then Alice had entered his life and his heart. He hadn't wanted to let her in, but somehow she had.

He heard the car in the driveway and knew it was Cora. He'd expected her to come. It was just her way, and he knew her ways far too well. He'd let her into his life, as well, and she'd mollycoddled him, making him think he needed her around.

"Leighton, I didn't think you'd be here." She was breathless, and he noticed she wore a dress, a frilly thing with lace.

"Then why did you come?"

She sat next to him on the love seat. "I guess I hoped you would be."

"Cora." He leaned forward. "We need to talk."

"Yes?" Her eyes shone.

"It isn't going to work, and you know it."

"What isn't?"

"You and me. Getting together. Marrying. Whatever it is that you want. I admire you tremendously, but I don't love you. I think we've been down this road before."

"It's that Alice!" She shot to her feet. "I don't know why she just doesn't stay in Portland. Everyone thinks we make a great couple. Ask Luke. Tom. Your daughters-in-law."

"It doesn't matter what they think. It matters what I think, what I feel."

"Alice doesn't know what a man needs. If she did, she'd have moved here by now."

He shook his head. "Alice is going through a lot right now. It's taking her time to sort things out."

"I'm not giving up, Leighton. I told you that before." She stood by the door, her hand on the knob. "I'll not come by until you call."

"Cora, will you wait a minute?"

She paused.

"Why did Meredith send Alice a threatening letter?"

Cora's hand fell at her side. "How did you—?"

Leighton chuckled. "Steven, Alice's son-in-law, told me. He e-mailed her and warned her about it being against the law to harass someone."

"It was just a joke."

"Yeah, sure."

"She doesn't deserve you, Leighton."

And you do? he wanted to say, but didn't.

"And another thing's been bothering me. Why did you take the photos out of the albums and put them in a box?"

She shrugged. "I just liked looking at all of you and, oh, I don't know why!"

"I'm sorry, Cora, but I've said that before, haven't I?"

"Yes, you have." She looked away. "I'm leaving now, but I'll wait for your call, and call you will. Alice isn't meant for this kind of life. Remember her coming in the first time in those ridiculous-looking gold high-heeled sandals? She won't survive. When you come to your senses, as Luke says you will, I'll be waiting. Remember, it's the little cottage at the end of Territory Road. The one with the white picket fence along the front."

He remembered, all right, but said nothing. The door closed softly, and her car started. Soon the sound died away. Leighton sat as if in a stupor and wondered why he thought he could ever control his life. For a man of fifty-three, he wasn't doing a very good job of it. As he watched the lights flickering from across the bay, he wondered what he was going to do next.

Chapter 24

After dinner Alice went to the Garden Room, her home away from home. Her heart was heavy. Leighton hadn't come. Nor had he called. That made his feelings clear. Sometimes love wasn't enough. Loving a person didn't always make a relationship work. She knew Leighton had loved his first wife, but it hadn't been enough. How could he risk it again?

She didn't belong here any more than he belonged in Portland. "Your life is in Oysterville," she'd told him. "Having coffee at that little corner café."

He had agreed, finally, and written in an e-mail, "Yes, I expect you're right. If I'd wanted to find someone, I would have looked here first."

It was the wisest move for both. How could either uproot a life? Alice thought about Carl and all the traveling they'd done while he was in the air force. She'd survived that, hadn't she? It had been fun then, packing up, going to a new location, never knowing what to expect. But she'd been young. At fifty, she considered things twice. No running into a relationship without thinking of possible consequences. Thank heavens she and Leighton were smart enough to realize that.

She felt a tear slide down her cheek and brushed it aside. She wouldn't cry. She'd leave first thing in the morning. There was no point in staying now.

Since she'd only brought one change of clothes, Alice didn't have much to pack. It would only take her five minutes. But while she put her few toiletry items in the small bag, she couldn't seem to stop the flow of tears. If Leighton loved her, he would have come over by now. They'd parted so badly. She could still hear the sound of his voice—so flat and clipped—when he'd left. A lump lodged in Alice's throat at the memory of her refusal. What she'd said hadn't been true. With every expression, every action, and every time he touched her, she wanted to be with him forever.

Alice set her suitcase on the floor, then reached for her journal. She wrote a few lines, then looked at the inscription of the day. "Consider it pure joy, my brothers, whenever you face trials of many kinds, because you know that the testing of your faith develops perseverance."

Alice turned to the first chapter of James. She'd always loved this verse. But it was what came later that spoke to her heart now. "But when he asks, he must believe and not doubt, because he who doubts is like a wave of the sea, blown and tossed by the wind."

The Bible closed as it slipped from her grip. "Lord, are You telling me not to have doubts? That I should believe in this possible relationship, that I should have done or said something to let him know how I truly felt?"

Trudy tapped on the door. "Alice, I'm having a bout with loneliness. Can you come and have a spot of tea with me?"

It had only been an hour since they'd eaten, and Alice knew it was Trudy's way of trying to make her feel better.

"I'll be right down," Alice answered.

Trudy was in the parlor. "I'm all caught up on the work around here, and there's not a decent program on the TV. Here. Have some shortbread. I just made them yesterday."

Alice laughed. "Guess you didn't want me to miss my sister. She always has shortbread on Sundays when Courtney and I go to visit."

She looked up and smiled. "That so?"

"Agnes is probably going to gloat and say she could have told me so. I mean, about this happening with Leighton."

"Sisters can be a blessing, but they can also be a pain in the neck," Trudy said. "I was never so blessed."

The two women chatted about their earlier lives and how they came to believe, how their faith had sustained them, and how they knew it would go on sustaining them.

"I would marry in a minute," Trudy said, "if someone should come along, but I firmly believe there is only one man for a woman. I had my one chance in a lifetime, and I thank God for the twenty-two years we had."

Alice had heard other women say that, but she didn't believe it. She felt there could be more than one match in a person's lifetime.

Trudy got up and closed the drapes. "What time are you fixing to leave tomorrow?"

"I think five would be good. I'll hit Portland after most everyone's gone to work. I hate driving in rush-hour traffic."

"I'll be up to make the coffee and get some muffins baked."

"No—" Alice reached out. "Please don't bother with that. I'll pick up coffee at one of the drive-thrus."

It wasn't a good night. At least not for sleeping. Alice loved the large bed, the fat feather pillows, and the view out the window. Leighton lived on the same bay that her room overlooked. A full moon cast a glow on the night's edges. She wondered if he might be looking out his window, gazing at the moon, also. Or had he already forgotten about her and was busy watching a favorite TV program?

She felt tears press against her eyelids, but she couldn't give in to them. She was returning to Portland, going home and awaiting the birth of her first grandchild. Life couldn't get much better than that.

❧

Alice slipped down the stairs at five o'clock. It was still dark and damp, while the first traces of dawn filtered through the tall firs. She was going to miss this quiet, relaxing place. By the time she reached the Astoria Bridge, the first glorious rays from the rising sun would guide her way.

Trudy was awake, and she handed Alice a small box lunch. "For the road, my dear. But do stop to stretch once. I'll be praying for you." The two hugged, and Alice quickly got into the car. She started backing out of the parking spot and nearly hit a Chevy truck.

Leighton! Had he come to say good-bye? She trembled as she pulled back into the spot. He roared into the driveway and was out of the truck before she had the engine shut off.

"You can't leave without my seeing you." The dark eyes held such intensity that her heart thudded.

"Get out of the car," he commanded, opening the door and touching her arm. "I didn't hold you yesterday, and I have to hold you just once more, to feel you in my arms, to just breathe in your fragrance. Oh, Alice—"

And then she was in his hard embrace, and the tears threatened again. This time she couldn't stop them, and as they fell against the wool of his coat, she felt his rough fingers brushing them away, then taking a handkerchief from his pocket.

"Don't cry. I can't bear to see a woman cry, especially not the woman I love."

"Leighton, we've been through this—" But his mouth got in the way, and she couldn't finish the sentence.

She felt herself melt against the thick chest and felt his hands in her hair, taking out the ribbon she wore. "I love you, Alice, and I'm not going to let you just walk out of my life. I know what happened yesterday, the harsh words spoken in Portland. I've gone over my doubts so many times, but I know where your heart is, and I also know that where you are, I've got to be or I'll die."

"Oh, Leighton, I love you."

"Oh, sweetheart. I love you, too."

"But—"

"Hear me out. I say we compromise. I'll help John out in his nursery a few months in Portland, then you come here with me for a few months in Oysterville."

"Do you think that would work?"

"We're at the age when we can make it work. Anytime you want, go down to be with your kids. And why not let Courtney and Steven have the house, and we'll use one of the spare bedrooms upstairs when we come to visit? I think it's a dandy idea."

Alice felt her hopes rise as she gazed into Leighton's eyes. She took in his strong, determined chin, his thick hair, and knew, yes, it would work because with God's help, they would *make* it work.

The front door of the bed and breakfast opened. "Will you two come in out of the cold?" Trudy yelled. "I have fresh coffee made and hate to see a pot go to waste."

Leighton shut Alice's car door, then closed the door of his truck. Arm in arm, they trudged up the steps and into the house.

Epilogue

O   h, Mom, I'm so excited at the prospect of going to Oysterville to see
         where you'll be living half of the year." Courtney's eyes were shining.
         "And the wedding will be beautiful."

"I haven't seen Leighton this happy since that morning at Trudy's when we
knew we wanted to build a life together." She looked pensive. "If only Aaron
would get in touch. Now give me that grandson so I can tell him how much his
grandmother loves him."

Steven Carl felt good in her arms. He was healthy, now weighing ten pounds.
In the six weeks since his birth, he had gained and progressed well, in spite of his
being born a month early.

"You are one lucky baby," she cooed against his soft cheek.

"Mom, getting married in the Oysterville Church is such an awesome idea!"

"I think so, and of course, Leighton does, too. He has far more children and
friends and neighbors there. The church here will throw a reception later."

Alice had to pinch herself every time she realized what was happening. In
December she and Leighton would repeat vows. The church would be filled with
bouquets of pink roses. A reception would be held at Oysterville's old schoolhouse.

Leighton was driving into town today. And together they would write out
their wedding vows. As Alice cut a picture from a magazine, she knew her wedding dress would be the most beautiful thing she'd ever owned. White velvet with
long sleeves and a scoop neckline. It would look lovely next to Leighton's tuxedo
with a pink cummerbund.

Courtney, in a long pink organza gown, would be the matron of honor, and
Luke would be his father's best man.

The telephone rang. It was Leighton.

"Is this the bride-to-be?"

Alice giggled. "I am, if this is the groom. Where are you now?"

"About five blocks away and can't wait to hold you in my arms again."

"Leighton, people will talk."

"Let them talk, anyway. You'd better be in the yard in about two minutes."

As Alice ran outside, she thanked God for answered prayer, for the happiness
that welled up. It was going to be a wonderful life.

Ring of Hope

To Ashley, Aurora, Tianna, and Isaac—
four bright stars in my life

Chapter 1

East Belfast, Maine

Deanna Barnes was preparing the Lobster Pound, an outdoor fresh-lobster restaurant, for the evening's festivities. A birthday party for twelve was scheduled, and GB, her brother, had reluctantly agreed to stay to help. Her daughter, Madison, clutched at her coat, looking up at Deanna with her dark brown eyes.

"You know, my part of the job ends when I bring in the day's catch." GB turned the water on under the lobster pots. "Maybe Dad should hire someone."

Deanna shrugged. "I suggested an ad in the local paper, but Dad doesn't want to. He thinks someone will just come walking up looking for work."

"Maybe they will. He's been right before."

Their father, Mick, entered the room as if he knew they were talking about him. "I've been praying for someone to come by and give us a hand around here. I think my prayers will be answered soon."

Mick, a grizzled old man with a head full of gray hair and a short beard, owned the Lobster Pound. He did the buying, hiring, and firing, and his word was the final say. He nodded now, looking from son to daughter, then granddaughter.

"Of course we'll manage," Deanna said with a smile. "We always seem to get by somehow." She hugged her father, hard. He sounded gruff, but there wasn't an unkind bone in his body. "We could advertise and have more parties if we had help; that's all I was thinking about."

"Help is coming." He stuck a cherry-wood pipe in his mouth and chewed on the end. He never lit it, but it was his comfort, his pacifier.

"Madison, you must sit at your little desk now and color or draw pictures. Mommy is going to be very, very busy."

"And I'll just get in the way?"

"Yes, honey. That's about it." Deanna had to look away, not wanting to see the girl's expression, her strong chin—both so like her father's. If only Bobby had lived. They would have all the help they needed. Who knew, when he'd gone to check the traps that afternoon, that a nor'easter would blow up? Storms were capricious here in Maine, and that had been a bad one.

The boiling pots were nearly ready; Deanna set out plates and silverware with tubs of butter and thick slabs of French bread. The tables and benches on the upper floor, where people ate their lobster, were clean, but she hadn't finished the floor and was ashamed that it had only been swept and not mopped. A sign overhead listed menu items, including crab, mussels, haddock, halibut, cod, and scallops.

She didn't hear the car, but GB did. "Someone just drove in. Maybe it's Dad's answer to prayer."

Deanna looked up. Soon the parking lot would be full. "Why do you say that? It's probably just an early customer."

"Just a hunch."

Their father had walked up the hill and was talking to a man who stood near a car that was a rust bucket if she'd ever seen one. The man was young looking, which meant he would be strong and full of energy. The two came down the hill, her father leaning on his cane, the younger man walking with a spring in his step.

"This is Aaron," Mick said, nodding toward the sandy-haired man. "He's looking for work. Do you think we could use him for a few days? Told him I hadn't gotten around to advertising. If it weren't for this ol' rheumatism, I'd be doing more. . . ."

Deanna looked up into the stranger's eyes and felt a sudden pang at his steady gaze. A person could tell so much from a person's eyes. She held out her hand. "I'm Deanna. Nice to meet you, Aaron."

"And you."

He wasn't from around here; she was almost positive. Just two words spoken, but she hadn't detected a Maine accent.

"This is GB, my brother, and my daughter, Madison."

"Maddy!" the little girl proclaimed.

"Maddy for short," Deanna said with a nod.

A bark sounded as a huge black lab bounded around the side of the Pound and stopped alongside Aaron. He sniffed Aaron's shoes, but the hair didn't go up on his back.

"Murphy here thinks he owns the place. He's anything but a watchdog and can't stand to be left out of a thing." He nuzzled Aaron's hand when he stopped patting the big dog's head.

"Yeah, I'd say you passed muster," Mick said.

"Where are you from?" GB asked, a frown creasing his brow.

"Been around." Aaron smiled. "Was working the forest, logging trees and sending them off down the Kennebec. Worked in a toothpick factory before that, and then in June I decided to hike the Appalachian Trail."

GB turned and listened now.

"Made it to Mount Katahdin," Aaron continued, "then back to this logging area."

"A logger and a hiker?" GB looked almost impressed—or about as impressed as he ever would look.

Deanna figured that explained the hiking boots, denims, and well-worn backpack. Still, she didn't think he was from Maine—not born and bred.

"Been wanting to do something else," Aaron said, shifting his gaze back to Deanna. "I like the water. I want to find work on a lobster boat."

"You have a license?" she asked.

"No." There was a slight hesitation.

GB crossed his arms. "Well, you must have a license to run a boat around here. And I already have a sternman, so I don't need anyone to help on the boat just now."

Another puzzlement, Deanna thought. If Aaron were from Maine, he'd know about restrictions for lobstermen.

"Sternman." Aaron repeated the word.

"You know. The one who baits the traps. Sis used to do it, but then she got married."

"You don't need help with the boat, GB, but we do need someone to help out here with the Pound," Deanna quickly added.

"Yeah, that we do." GB, a younger version of his father, frowned. "Say, I wanted to hike the Appalachian Trail but never got around to it. Where does it start?"

Aaron looked cautious, as if he knew he was being questioned for a reason. "Springer Mountain in northern Georgia. We can talk about it sometime, if you like."

Mick seemed oblivious to the conversation while Deanna continued to study the young man who had appeared, it seemed, in answer to her silent prayer.

"Deanna can show you what to do," said GB. "You decide. Stay and work here or move on. After one night of work, you'll have your answer." GB tossed his white apron into a bin in a corner of the room.

Deanna nodded. "That I can do. Been working the Pound a long while now. I could boil lobster in my sleep."

She realized that Aaron might be a logger, and that was fine and good, but he didn't know about lobstering. He couldn't fool her; he had come from somewhere else. Not that it mattered. They needed help, and if this was the one whom the good Lord had sent, then it would work.

Deanna pointed to the holding tank. Several lobsters of various sizes swam in the water. "People come here first, select the lobster they want. Someone, and I guess that could be you now, takes the lobster out with the net, then dumps it in the pot."

"How long does it take to cook?" Aaron asked.

"It varies. I'll show you what to do, how to test the lobster."

"Okay. I think I can manage that."

"Dad weighs the lobster, takes the money, and I get the plates ready, slice the bread, and melt butter for the lobster."

"But where do the customers eat?"

Deanna pointed. "The tables are all upstairs. You'll be running up and down these stairs all night. Guess it's good that you're a hiker. Otherwise, you probably couldn't do it."

She knew he was watching her as she started up the steps with a tray of napkins and silverware. Aaron carried another tray with supplies, which included a package of balloons.

The tables were picnic style, painted white with benches to match. The floor was wide, unpainted planks, with a view of the river. The Pound looked like a dock, tied down on the rocks at tide line. Several boats bobbed up and down in the harbor, with one heading in now.

"We get customers who come in on boats, tie up at the dock, and come over. Others arrive in cars. Tonight we're having a party, so if you want to blow up some balloons and tack them to the posts, that would help."

Deanna wished he would quit staring at her. He looked young, too young for her—if she was interested, which she was not. She had loved Bobby with all her heart and had no intention to marry again. At least not for a while.

"How long is the Pound open?"

"Most of the year, unless we have a severe winter. Our regular customers stop by for lobster, and we also do mail order."

"Uh-huh."

"Mommy!" Maddy's voice called from below. "Can I come up there?"

"No, honey. We're heading down."

Aaron followed her down the wide, deep steps, and she knew he was staring at her again.

"Do you think this is something you want to do?"

He nodded. "I like to learn new things, and as I said before, I've always loved the water."

"And where did you grow up?" She felt she had to ask.

"Does that matter? Do I not get the job if you don't know that?"

"You're not from Maine," she said, avoiding his steady gaze.

"No, I'm not. But I've lived here going on four years now."

"I see."

Mick walked over, holding his granddaughter's hand. "So what do you think of the place?"

"It's good." Aaron looked at the older man again. "I think I can handle the job."

"I 'spect you'll need a place to stay," Mick said.

"Well, sir, I do at that."

"The Seaview Cottage is down the road a piece," Mick said. "You're welcome to stay there for a bit."

"Dad!" The word escaped from Deanna's mouth before she could stop it. Her face turned red.

"What? Why not let him stay in the cottage? Been sitting there vacant long enough!" His tone was gruff, but Aaron just smiled.

"Oh." She looked at Aaron again and pulled back her dark, thick hair, then reached for a hair net. Her father was right, as always, but it was hard to think of someone sitting at the kitchen table or nestling in the bed. . . .

"Been sleeping in your car, I bet."

Aaron nodded. "Yeah, I have."

"You can help out tonight, then my daughter will have you sign a contract for the cottage—"

"I have no money," Aaron said. "That is, I won't until I've worked a few days."

Mick turned, took his hat off, and put it back on, eyeing Aaron all the while. "I somehow knew that, young man, but you can pay me the end of next week."

Deanna felt like saying more but realized it was time to get busy.

Aaron watched while Deanna picked out a lobster, as if she were choosing that one for her dinner. "Now you do it."

He caught the live lobster from the tank, using a wooden trap that set down inside the water. "Why do their claws have rubber bands on them?" he asked.

"Because they're cannibals," Mick said with a laugh. "They'd eat one another if we didn't keep them banded."

Then Deanna showed him how to cook one by dropping it into the pot of boiling water, then testing to see if it was done. "We throw them in alive; that's so people know that they are fresh."

"Seems kind of cruel."

"It is, but their misery is short-lived. Here now, watch. If you cook a lobster too long, they're tough. Meat's stringy. People won't be back if you don't serve good lobster." She gave Aaron a puzzled look. "A lot of our customers are tourists, you know." She stood back, as if surveying the situation. "I think you should just wait on customers tonight."

"Okay. Whatever."

Aaron blew up the balloons and made three trips up the stairs with butter, extra plates, and ashtrays. Since it was an open-air restaurant, people could smoke. Dress was casual. Aaron's first customers were from Pennsylvania.

"We saw the Lobster Pound sign from Highway One."

Aaron grinned. "That's what brought me here, too. This is my first night working here."

Another birthday party came, and Deanna watched while Aaron ran up and down the steps. He might feel it in his legs in the morning, but being a hiker, perhaps not. She wondered what it would be like to hike along for miles and miles. Not that she could ever hope to do that, not now that she had Maddy.

At last it was nine o'clock, and she turned off the OPEN sign.

"I'll like working here," Aaron said as Maddy peered out from around her mother's legs.

"You'll be busy, that's for sure," Deanna answered, turning to go behind the counter.

Aaron tossed his apron into the bin along with GB's. "I suppose I better start the cleanup."

"Don't you worry about the upstairs," Mick answered. "Plenty of time to get at it tomorrow."

"Are you sure?"

"Yup."

Deanna removed her hair net, letting the curls bounce as she walked.

"I like your hair," he said, and then his face reddened.

She felt her face flush, too, as she handed him a clipboard and a pen. "Thank you," she murmured. "This is the form Dad talked about. Just says that you will leave everything as it is now." Her eyes met his again. "It's pretty standard." She looked away.

Murphy came from around the side of the Lobster Barn, went up to Aaron, and pushed against his hand, wanting attention again. Aaron bent down and nuzzled the dog, then made a face. "You're wet!"

"He loves the water. All labs do. Bet someone threw a stick for him to fetch," Mick said.

"How long you staying?" Deanna asked.

"A few months, probably."

One dark eyebrow arched. "Then moving on?"

"Maybe longer. It all depends."

Deanna got that quivery feeling inside again. She didn't want to feel this way. Bobby had been gone only a little over a year.

"Here's the key. No need for me to go with you. The linens are in the closet just outside the bathroom door, and there are dishes and extra blankets in a cedar chest at the foot of the bed."

Aaron took the key, his hand touching hers briefly. "There's only one problem," he said. "Your father pointed north, but I don't see anything. You didn't give me directions."

"Just follow the path. It's around two bends, hidden in trees. Can't miss it."

"I'll see you in the morning then."

She hesitated before answering. "You could. . .come up to the main house for a bite to eat. I know it's late, but we get too busy to eat until now. Our main meal's at noon."

He frowned, as if thinking it over. "I'm kinda tired. Think I'll just unpack, shower, and go to bed. Thanks anyway."

Deanna watched while he walked up the hill to his car, hoisting a large duffel bag over his shoulder, then took off in the direction she'd pointed. A knot rose in her chest. She hadn't been inside the cottage for a long time, and she wondered if Aaron would find it to his liking. There were so many memories there. . . .

Murphy bounded down the path after him, but Aaron turned and pointed in the direction of the Pound. Her father was right. Murphy, as most dogs, was a good judge of character, and he definitely approved of the new worker. Deanna took Maddy's hand and headed toward the house.

Chapter 2

Aaron knew Deanna was watching him. He had wanted to ask why it mattered if he rented the cottage. Those brown eyes of hers concealed secrets. She had the child, so she must be married, but where was her husband? Away at sea? In the service? Maybe he'd find out later, but perhaps not. You couldn't tell about these people from Maine. They seemed to lock their hearts inside, not sharing with anyone.

He didn't want to think of how tired he was right now. Exhausted. And hungry. But soon he'd sleep in a real bed and hear the water lapping against the shore.

Aaron could hardly believe his good luck, but it had been like that since he'd first left his home five years ago. Jobs were offered him at the precise moment he was down to his last dollar. More often than not, he had a roof over his head. He'd known when he hit Belfast and saw the Lobster Pound sign that he would stop to see if they could use an extra hand. He'd worked on crab boats back in Oysterville. He loved the water. He knew the water, and the Lobster Pound sat at the edge of the river, which flowed into Penobscot Bay. This was perfect.

Aaron made his way down the path that wound around and through a copse of pine and birch.

And then he saw it. A weather-beaten cottage, small and cozy as he had expected, was built into the hill, with briars and brambles creeping up one side. He made his way through a tangle of spider webs, opened the door, and stepped in.

He dropped his duffel bag just inside the door. He'd get the trunk out of his car later. A round braided rug decorated the linoleum floor. The couch looked comfortable, and a small TV sat under the window hung with red floral curtains. Someone had lived here. That someone had made it look pleasant. It had to have been Deanna. She must have been married, because her last name was different from her dad's. The little girl, a tiny replica of her mother, had her mother's dancing, dark curls. Tonight he had wanted to touch Deanna's curls, but of course he had not.

Aaron opened the cupboard. There were pots, pans, dishes, silverware, more than he'd ever need. This would do just fine.

Behind a drawn curtain was a double bed. A quilt with a bright red tulip design covered the bed, a four-poster. He would put the duffel in the closet and unpack tomorrow.

He sat on the edge of the bed and removed his boots. He couldn't explain it, but somehow he felt as if he'd come home. It was strange, but after only a few hours, Deanna had caused him to grow introspective, to consider that maybe it was time to think about settling down. Yet, why wouldn't that settling place be Oysterville? Had it really been five years since he'd left on that cold, windy October morning?

hannah had coughed. The cough was worse this night than most times. Aaron had sat huddled on his bed, listening and knowing that his little sister was dying. Nobody wanted to admit it. Cora, their part-time housekeeper who had taken over after an aunt died, said, "She'll be okay in a week or so." And his father wouldn't discuss it at all. He'd go pound her on the back and take her to yet another doctor. The diagnosis was always the same. People with cystic fibrosis do not live a full life.

Aaron remembered Hannah's good days. Hannah with her big, big smile— the little girl he had loved more than anyone. They'd spent summers digging for clams, going with their father to check crab pots. There'd been hikes out to Leadbetter Point. When she could no longer walk to the road to catch the school bus, Leighton Walker had paid a tutor to come teach her math and English, the two subjects he deemed most important.

Aaron had gotten out of bed that last night and offered to make his father a cup of coffee, but his father had pushed the idea aside, moving past Aaron as he headed for Hannah's bedroom.

"Just go away, Aaron. There's nothing you can do!"

It had been true, of course. Aaron knew that, but if only his father had hugged him or looked at him as if he cared. But he hadn't, and Aaron went back to his room and thought about the plans he'd made a few weeks earlier. It was time to go. He made his bed, cleaned off the top of his dresser, and stuffed as many clothes as he could into the duffel bag. The Bible Grandma had given him was put in the bottom, along with a small photo album of family pictures.

The first traces of dawn were creeping over the Willapa Hills and casting shadows across the bay when Aaron slung the bag over his shoulder and headed out. And he didn't look back. Nor had he ever looked back since leaving Oysterville that morning.

Now, as Aaron lay across the bed in the small, neat cottage of his employer, he wondered if he'd ever stop feeling guilty about running off like that. He should have left a note, but he hadn't even done that. He'd had no idea of where he'd go. Seventeen, a year left of school, and a runaway.

It wasn't as if Hannah was the only family. There were three older brothers, Thomas, Luke, and John. But they had never been close, and he'd always just been the "little brother." Sometimes he talked to Luke, but then Luke married and was too busy to stop by.

Aaron opened his eyes and thought of Deanna again, how loving she was to her child and to her father and brother. The family was tight. He'd never known that feeling. Aaron's mother had left because she couldn't handle the role of mothering an extremely sick child. Later, she committed suicide in Seattle. He always wondered if he couldn't have done something, maybe tell her he loved her, and then perhaps she wouldn't have killed herself. The last time he'd seen her was when she waited outside his first-grade classroom and then took him out for an ice cream cone. If only he'd known. . .

He couldn't sleep, so he got up, found his food stash, and ate the last of the potato chips, then he looked to see if there was anything in the cupboards. A can of cinnamon, a box of soda, an old jar of instant coffee that had dried up at the bottom, and a package of assorted teas were on a top shelf. Five bags were left, so he put water on for tea. He much preferred coffee, but tea would suffice. He chose peppermint, and soon the smell filled the cottage. At least the cup kept his hands warm as he thought of the dark curls and the brown eyes. Again he wondered why she seemed protective of the cabin. Her sharp intake of breath happened when her father asked if he wanted to use the cottage.

Aaron rinsed the cup and went to the bedroom. Maybe he should just go ahead and unpack. Why wait? He opened the closet and saw a dress hanging at one end. Deanna's wedding gown. This had been Deanna and her groom's home; he was sure of that. It was her love he felt when he first stepped inside—a pleasant ambiance that soothed him. It had her touch. And he felt her presence. He knew she must be older; he had turned twenty-two just last week but felt much older and wiser than when he ran off.

Aaron turned on a small radio and listened to a soft-rock station. He had to sleep, as he was expected to work early. Fishermen never slept in, and neither would he. Tomorrow would be here before he was ready.

&

"Dad?" Deanna stepped into the living room. The TV was silent, but she could hear her father's gruff voice reading a book to Maddy.

"We're upstairs, Mommy. Grandpa's reading *The Cat in the Hat*."

"Okay, honey." *Weird,* Deanna thought. Usually her father would have a cup of coffee and the TV on, with Maddy playing house or making a fort for her plush animals.

Deanna opened the refrigerator and took out sandwich meat. They ate their big meal at noon, so the evening was usually a snack. Her thoughts went to Aaron again. No one since Bobby had made her heart pound like this, and thinking about Aaron now made it race again. *Silly,* she admonished herself. *You know nothing about him.* And that was what seemed so strange about her father inviting him to stay in the Seaview Cottage. *How could he?* she asked herself again. The man could be an escaped convict, someone who might rob them. The money taken in each night was fairly accessible; they'd never been worried about robbery before.

She chewed her lip, a nervous habit she couldn't control, as she set the pan on the stove. Funny that she'd think that about him. He definitely did not look the dangerous type. In fact, she was certain he was younger than she was. He had a little-boy quality about him that appealed to her father, but it was the depth, the loneliness in his eyes, that spoke to her heart.

Deanna put sandwiches on the table and microwaved a cup of coffee. "Hey, you two," she called up the stairs. "Wanna eat a bite?" She smiled as she heard the scuffling of feet on the floor and their affirmative answer.

Her father entered the kitchen first, with Maddy close behind. Deanna thought it the perfect moment to voice her reservations about Aaron.

"Dad, about the new help. . ."

"Now don't go a-gettin' mad at me." He pulled his chair out. "I know it was an impulsive thing to do, giving Aaron the Seaview Cottage, but it was as if God was nudging me, saying, 'Here is your worker. Trust Me. He's a good kid.' "

"Who's a kid?" Maddy asked, tilting her head.

"You are!" her grandfather said, pretending he'd nipped her nose off her face. "See, I got it right here!"

"You don't either, Grandpa! It's still here!" Then she started giggling.

After the blessing and she'd taken two bites of her sandwich, Deanna looked up. "Dad, I know we needed someone desperately, and I know God works in mysterious ways, but to offer him the cottage. . . Why, I haven't even—"

"What? Cleaned it out? It looks just fine to me and is going to look like a palace to a kid who's been working in the woods and living in his car. He's an honest one, Deanna."

"I like that man who worked for us today. . . ," Maddy said.

"Aaron," her mother said. "His name is Aaron."

"Ae-won."

"No. Air-un. You can say air, like the air you breathe, Maddy."

"Aaron!" she shouted.

"Yes," Deanna said. "Now eat your sandwich." Deanna wasn't too worried if her daughter didn't eat well now, because she always had food at the Pound for Maddy to eat.

Deanna looked at her father. "I invited him to eat with us," she volunteered.

"So you must think he's okay. Just don't want to admit it."

"Oh, Dad. It just surprised me. You know I've tried to go down there and take things out, but it's just too hard."

"Are there any cookies?" Mick asked, as if wanting to change the subject.

"Does a bear live in the woods?"

She poured a glass of milk, put two sugar cookies on a plate, and took them over to the recliner. "Here you go."

Turning toward Maddy, she said, "And you, young miss, need a bath before bedtime."

After Mick had gone on to bed and Maddy was sound asleep, Deanna sat in the living room. She liked sitting in the dark among the late evening shadows. As long as she could remember, the dark, whether it was morning or night, held a fascination for her. She could talk things over with God.

Tonight, her thoughts kept going to Aaron and where he was now. The cottage had been her home for two years. She'd sewn floral curtains for the kitchen, made pillows for the living room, and cross-stitched a Maine sunrise. The bedroom walls were painted blue because it was Bobby's favorite color. "The color of a summer sky," he'd once said, pulling her close that first night in their new home. And now Aaron would have that bedroom. In the closet he'd find her white satin gown wrapped in layers of plastic. There was no way he'd miss the dress.

Why was her mind wandering, thinking, dreaming? Her heart had pounded at the sight of the young man, but she admonished herself for even thinking that someday there might be another man, a soul mate. Yet she sensed Aaron was going to mean something to her life. She wasn't sure how she knew; she just did. A verse, Psalm 44:21, went through her mind: *"He knoweth the secrets of the heart."* She believed that with her whole heart and deep down knew that God often answered prayers in surprising ways.

Deanna thought of when she'd met Bobby and how fast they had fallen in love. They were young, "too young to marry," her father had said, but they married anyway. Four years of marriage, a child born that first year, and now a year since Bobby's death. It had been one of the worst "sneaker storms" to hit the Atlantic Coast, and he had asked her to go out with him to check the traps. Sometimes she wished she had, but then Madison wouldn't have had either parent.

She made Bobby a saint after he died, but she knew there had been a hint of unraveling in their relationship. He had not shared her faith, her love of God—and marriage meant being equally yoked. It also meant giving and taking.

She shook the thoughts from her mind. Maybe it was time to stop mourning Bobby's death, to move on; perhaps she could once again make a home for a man who would love her in return. Yet Aaron couldn't be that man. He was a drifter, a wanderer. She didn't want that. She had to keep reminding herself that physical attraction was not important—there were spiritual aspects to a marriage that really counted. God would direct her to the right person. Someday.

Chapter 3

Deanna rose at four as she always did this time of year. Usually she was rested and ready to meet the day, but just knowing that someone was in the Seaview Cottage made her night restless. Her father was right. It didn't make sense to leave the cottage empty. It should be used.

She filled the coffeepot. Her father expected his morning coffee, crisp bacon, scrambled eggs, and several thick slices of toast for breakfast. And there was always a pot of oatmeal. She could do this in her sleep. Thank goodness Maddy was still in bed and would not get up for another hour. These few minutes gave Deanna an opportunity to mull over the day and to have morning devotions. When her mother was alive, they would sit together at the oak table, hold hands, and pray for each other before their day unfolded. How she missed that. More than anything, she'd dreamed of running her home that way, too.

She pulled her hair back and tied it with a red ribbon to match her shirt. The dark curls sprang in ringlets, still damp from her shower. Aaron had noticed her hair. Silly. Here she was again, thinking of him. She set the slices of homemade bread aside, turned the coffee on low, and sat at the table, her head bent over her Bible. She read Proverbs 10:22: "The blessing of the Lord, it maketh rich, and he addeth no sorrow with it." Deanna jotted down a few thoughts in her journal: *"Patience, Lord—You know I need patience. Let me be happy with the blessings of my child, a father I adore, and a brother who causes me problems but is still my brother."*

❦

Aaron got up before dawn, found the granola bars in his duffel and the last container of orange juice. He gulped it down and then showered. He donned his heaviest pair of jeans, a T-shirt, a red flannel, heavy socks, and boots. When he stepped outside and felt the fresh, crisp air, he grabbed his stocking cap and pulled it down over his ears. Mornings were usually brisk on the water. Maybe he'd let his hair grow out, as he had last winter. He might even try a beard. He had planned walking along the water, but when he saw the light in the bigger house, he headed toward it.

He paused before knocking, hoping he wouldn't disturb anyone. Deanna answered the door, and his heart caught in his throat.

"I wouldn't have come, but I saw the light. Forgive me if I've intruded."

"I'm surprised you're up this early. But do come in! Why not have a cup of coffee and eat breakfast with us?"

"Oh, no. I just wondered if I should go down to the Pound and begin cleaning up from last night."

"Before breakfast?" Her eyes met his, but only for a moment.

"I've eaten."

"Oh." She looked disappointed.

The Bible lay open on the table. "You were reading, and I interrupted."

Deanna smiled as she closed her Bible. "Morning devotions," she said, as if she needed to explain. "I was reading Proverbs. It gives so many rules for life. Are you a believer, by chance?"

Aaron paused. "I—well—yes, I believe."

She wondered if he was just saying that for her benefit; yet there was a certain longing in his eyes as he looked at the Bible, as if remembering a time when he'd read the scriptures.

A shuffling noise sounded on the stairway, and moments later Mick entered the room. "Ah, the new worker. More than punctual, eh?" He stroked his beard and looked from Deanna to Aaron. "Throw a couple more eggs in."

"No, sir, I've eaten. I just wanted to get started cleaning the upstairs, or whatever it is you want me to do."

"Mommy!" a tiny voice called from the top of the stairs. "Can I get up yet?"

"Of course. Come on down. The oatmeal's ready."

"But I want Cap'n Crunch."

"Whatever." She looked over at Aaron. "Usually she sleeps longer, but it isn't every morning that two deep, baritone voices fill the house."

The little girl in a flannel nightgown and Donald Duck slippers soon wrapped her arms around her mother's legs and held on for dear life.

"Hi, Maddy!" Aaron held out his hand. "I'm sorry if I woke you up."

"No." She rubbed her eyes. "It was Grandpa."

"I sound like a foghorn, that's for sure," the older man bellowed.

She ran over and threw her arms around him. "I like your voice, Grandpa."

"I insist you sit with us; have a cup of coffee and at least some of Deanna's toast." Mick poured two mugs of coffee and set them on the table. "We have simple fare, but it's plenty and filling."

Aaron sipped his coffee, while Mick added cream and sugar. He offered them to Aaron. "No, it's strong, just the way I like it. And hot."

The older man talked while Deanna flitted back and forth from counter to stove, from refrigerator to stove. In moments she had tomato juice on the table, three plates, and two bowls. Bacon sizzled in a skillet, while she cracked eggs into a small bowl and whisked them. She could feel Aaron watching her, and she wondered what he was thinking. He certainly wasn't talkative like her father, and Maine people were known to be reserved. Not Mick Nelson's family.

Maddy slipped off her grandfather's lap after one small sip of his coffee and sat at the far end of the table on a booster chair.

"Maddy, would you put silverware and napkins around the table?"

"Yes, Mommy." She hopped down and went about her task as if she did this every morning.

"Lobsters is the way to go here in Maine," Mick was saying. "We get orders from all over the world. I'd say half the business comes from outside orders. Of course, summers it's the tourists. They're what keeps us going for sure."

"We were certainly busy last night."

"Do you like lobster?" Maddy asked, plunking a fork down on the napkin.

"I love them. And you?"

"They're okay, but I like peanut butter and jelly the best."

"You better not have her do any commercials for TV," Aaron said.

They all laughed and finished breakfast. It would be a busy day, and there were things to do.

Chapter 4

Aaron felt a warm, pleasant feeling inside. Deanna's cooking was better than Cora's. He hadn't been this full since the buffet he'd found in Bangor. He could tell Deanna enjoyed cooking. Some women, like his mother—what little he could remember of her—cooked because they had to. It was an argument he remembered hearing from early childhood.

"Cooking is a chore I detest," his mother had said. He remembered the fiery look in her eyes as she pointed the spatula at his father. "I'd never cook another meal if I didn't have to."

Funny that he should think about that now. He followed Mick out the door and down the steps.

"We have lots to do around here." The older man wore an old parka with hood and patches on the elbows. He hunkered down in an effort to keep the cold wind out.

"My son handles the boat now. I used to help on the boat, but he has a local lad now, and they bring in what they can. Some days are better than others."

"I wondered about going out sometime. You know, set the bait or whatever."

"GB is licensed. Maine is particular about that. I have other jobs in mind for you, son."

Aaron nodded. At home the oystermen and crabbers were also licensed. Why would it be different here?

"I'll be happy to do whatever you want. I did notice the building is in need of paint."

"We should have gotten that done earlier in the year, but if we get a good day between now and winter, we'll just do it."

Aaron nodded. "I can paint, clean up, and also wait on customers—whatever you want."

A voice sounded, and Maddy came running down the hill, as well as she could run. Bundled in a snowsuit, fur cap, and mittens, she looked delightfully roly-poly; Aaron stifled a laugh.

"That daughter of mine—she's overprotective. If Maddy has the slightest little sniffle, out come the winter clothes, and she'll check her forehead every hour on the hour."

Aaron sensed the older man loved his daughter and the grandchild more than he wanted to let on.

"She's all she has," Aaron offered then.

Mick leaned against the railing close to the pound box. "That's so. You know about that, do you now?"

Aaron nodded. "Yes. I guessed that there's no father around."

"He shouldn't have gone out in the boat that day. Crazy fool! He wanted Maddy and Deanna to go along, but Deanna wisely said no, that she'd heard a storm was brewing and she'd rather stay home with Maddy."

Maddy finally reached them and hugged her grandfather's leg. "Grandpa, Mommy says I can stay with her in the office until you go up to watch the news."

"That so?" He pulled the pipe out of his pocket and stuck it between his teeth. He did not light it, and Aaron wondered if he ever did.

"Grandpa, Mommy also said you should turn the heater on in the office."

"That's exactly what I had in mind." He reached down and grabbed her. She giggled and pretended she wanted to escape.

Aaron leaned over and tickled her under the chin. He remembered how Hannah had liked that at this age.

She smiled back and grabbed his hand.

"Are you two going to stand out here all morning and lollygag?" The voice was sharp, but the eyes held merriment.

"Oh. You here already?"

"Well, Dad, someone has to work. The books are done on the fifteenth of the month, and this is the fourteenth."

Deanna unlocked the door and turned on the light. "Brrr, it's cold, and it isn't even close to winter yet."

Maddy ran inside and turned the heater on. All it took was the push of a button.

"Mommy, can we go to the store today? I'm all out of Cap'n Crunch."

"There's oatmeal, Madison."

"Can I have raisins in it?"

"Of course."

Aaron glanced up and found Deanna's gaze unwavering. He smiled and felt that tug in his heart again. *Calm down, calm down,* he reminded himself. *This isn't to go any further.*

"Here are the jackets, hats, and boots that I mentioned earlier," Deanna said, opening a large oak door. "Help yourself."

"I'll buy a coat soon," he offered.

"No need." Mick stood in the doorway. "We got plenty of stuff others have left, so you might as well save your money."

Aaron picked out a heavy, navy blue pea coat; something about the navy blue with the emblems on the buttons appealed to him. Wool was always warm, and it held up well in stormy, wet weather. Of course, it would be warm in a few hours.

"I thought these work shoes would be okay. I wore them at the logging camp."

"Yes, they're fine."

"We really need the upper deck cleaned and disinfected," Deanna said. "It didn't get done the night before, and if we don't do it every day, it starts smelling pretty fishy."

"And the garbage also needs to be emptied," Mick added. "I think that should keep you busy for a couple hours."

"And maybe Aaron can pick up a few items at the store," Deanna suggested, looking at Maddy, who had found her box of crayons and a much-used coloring book.

"I wanna go to the store," she said, looking up with a green crayon in her mouth.

"Madison, get that crayon out of your mouth now."

The little girl dropped it and stuck out her lower lip. It was clear she was a mite spoiled and used to getting her own way.

"Well, I do wanna go to the store," she repeated.

"We'll see."

It was clear that the matter had been dismissed, at least for a little while.

Deanna looked at Aaron again and then pointed. "The cleaning supplies are in a closet upstairs." He could see that she was not one to waste time.

He went up, glancing back once because he sensed that eyes were on him. Deanna looked away abruptly, but Maddy waved a crayon at him.

The floors were messy. People obviously cracked their lobster with gusto, scattering shells everywhere. There were garbage cans for shells and another for soft drink cans, but still the table was smeared with melted butter, bits of lobster shell, and wadded-up napkins.

He would need hot water, plenty of soap, and a disinfectant, but first he'd clean off the tables and sweep up the mess.

This job reminded him of Oysterville. Who would have thought he would trade cleaning up in the cannery, where he cracked open oysters, for taking care of a lobster pound? Here he was more than three thousand miles away and doing the same type of work. He should have stayed at the logging camp. But then he would not have met Deanna.

It took an hour to empty the small garbage cans into the larger one and sweep the floor. Then, on hands and knees, he scrubbed with a stiff brush. The floor looked great when he finished.

"I don't think anyone has cleaned the floor like that since my wife died." Mick had climbed the stairs. Aaron hadn't heard him because the radio was playing downstairs.

"Did I do it right?"

"You sure did." The older man grinned. "The only problem is you have to do this every day."

"I know, sir."

"Mick. I don't go for the 'sir' stuff."

"Okay."

Aaron leaned back and poured a cup of coffee from the thermos Mick had handed him. The two sat at a clean table and looked out over the water.

"You know, I'm going to have to sell the Pound one of these days."

"You are?" For some reason Aaron could not imagine it being sold, just as he couldn't imagine his father ever selling the cannery in Oysterville. "But why?"

"GB doesn't want it. He has some notion about going to Massachusetts and doing something else. Deanna will go and get married on me and be raising more kids in some little white house with red trim, and I'm way too old to worry about it anymore."

"It should be kept in the family," Aaron said. "I don't think Deanna is going to leave."

"She can't operate the boat, bait the traps, and all that—"

"With help she could." Aaron set down his empty mug. "Have you asked her about it?"

"Don't have to. Women don't do those things."

"And why not?"

"She's got the kid, and that takes up a lot of her time. Now if I'd had more sons, or my wife had lived. . ." Pain momentarily etched his face. "Not that I'm not thankful for what the good Lord gave me."

Aaron picked up the bucket of dirty water and then set it down again. "I'd talk to her about it if I were you. Make sure what it is that she wants."

"To get married again. I know it. She's told me before."

"Maybe she's not ready for that."

The old man's eyes narrowed as he looked at Aaron. "How would you be knowing that when you just arrived here yesterday?"

"Because I think she still loves her husband. It's that simple."

Aaron thought of his father and how long it had been before he got his wife out of his mind. Aaron wondered if he had ever, in fact, succeeded. He never dated, never seemed to want to.

"I'll talk to her, but I'm in no rush about this. We have a good season coming up, and we ship our lobsters all over the world, you know. Thanksgiving and Christmas are busy times. Most people think about turkeys and hams, but we have our regular customers who order for the holidays."

"Dad! Aaron! Are you ready for lunch? I'm going up to the house to throw some food together."

"Yeah, sounds good," Mick answered. Then to Aaron he said, "Now, can you imagine that? How on earth do you throw food together?"

"With great care."

"Of course, it will be good. It always is."

Aaron laughed. "Well, I see I'm going to put on weight if I stay here very long."

The old man turned on the top step and almost glowered. "You are going to stay, young man, aren't you?"

"I said I'd stay a month, at least."

"A month! I'm going to need you longer than that."

Aaron grabbed the pea coat he'd left on the bench, having worked up a sweat while performing his job. "I won't leave you dangling," he said.

And as he walked down the steps, he knew he couldn't wait to be in the sunny, warm kitchen watching Deanna as she stood at the stove, then came to the table and said grace before they ate whatever it was that she had fixed. He might stay a long time, a really long, long time after all. . . .

&c.

It was after lunch and the dishes had been done when Deanna suggested they go on into town and get supplies. "We can drop the garbage off on the way."

"And pick up Cap'n Crunch?" Maddy asked.

Deanna laughed, and he liked the way her mouth turned up. He found himself wanting to touch her, wanting to grasp one of the curls, wanting to feel how soft she would be in his arms. He shook his head and reached for his lightweight jacket.

The afternoon was warmer, and he slid into the front seat of the car next to Deanna. She drove an old, dented Chevy, the car she'd learned to drive in, she explained to him as she backed around and drove up out of the driveway.

"I like to drive," she said then. "And you?"

"Yes, when I have dependable wheels."

"One can always take a bus—"

"I like to ride a bus," Maddy interjected in her chirpy voice.

"Yes, honey, I know you do."

"I get to ride the bus to Sunday school."

"You do?"

"The church we attend has a bus that picks up kids, and it works quite well."

"I'd like to go to church while I'm here."

"I think you'd like our church. It's small and friendly. I know most of the people, as we don't move around much in Maine, not like people out West."

"How do you know about people out West?" He felt he had to know.

"Well, look at you. I think you're from the West, even though you don't say. You just sound like it."

"Is that a fact?"

She glanced over and smiled one of those special, warm smiles that touched his heart. Again. "Yes, it is."

"Is that bad?"

She tilted her head as she pulled into the recycling center. "No, not at all."

"Mommy, why are you looking at Aaron like that?"

Her face turned a bright red, almost as red as the lobsters in the boiling vat.

"Because she likes me." There, he'd said it, but the words surprised even him.

"Everyone likes Aaron," Deanna said then. "I just know that about you."

Aaron wished, oh, how he wished. . . He would like nothing better than to go to his father and be welcomed with a hearty hug and a clap on the back, but Leighton hadn't even tried to find him. If he'd tried, Aaron could have been found. There were private investigators who did that sort of thing.

"Someday you must tell me about your family," Deanna said as she unbuckled Maddy from her car seat.

"Someday I might, but it's a pretty boring story."

"I bet it won't be to me."

A couple of heads turned as they entered the store, and Aaron smiled. It was a small town where everybody knew everyone. It was like that at home, too.

One young woman was particularly bold as she stepped up. "Hi, Deanna. Who's your friend?"

Deanna introduced him as Aaron, who now worked for the Lobster Pound. Aaron nodded, and they moved on.

"Dottie has always been nosy," was Deanna's explanation. "Don't pay any attention to her."

Maddy wanted to sit in the shopping cart, even though she was big, so Aaron lifted her up and set her on the seat.

"It's better this way," Deanna said then. "Now she can't grab food on the shelves."

"Tell me what kind of meat you like," she said after picking up the cereal, a gallon of milk, and two loaves of bread.

"I haven't been able to choose in so long, I don't know what to say. I like everything. I really do."

She selected a roast, a large package of pork chops, a turkey breast, and some ground beef. "I'm sure you'll get tired of lobster."

"Does your brother ever come over later?" Aaron asked.

"GB isn't much to mingle. He goes out way before light and comes back in, brings in the pots, and leaves. Seeing the catch of the day is something Dad still enjoys."

"Can you imagine ever doing anything else?" Aaron asked. If the old man wasn't going to ask, he would.

"Why, what do you mean?" She reached over and took a box of candy away from Maddy; she'd just been able to reach it by stretching her little arms out.

"Have you ever thought of living somewhere else, away from the Pound?"

Her eyes looked startled. "Why, no. Why would I?"

It was as Aaron figured. This was her home, her life. She had no intention of moving on, not even if a man came along and swept her off her feet. . . . Deanna turned and eyed him with a puzzled look. "Why do you ask?"

He wanted to tell her about the earlier conversation with her father but didn't feel it was right to do so. "Just wondering is all."

Maddy started reaching for a package of gum this time, and Deanna turned her around and made her sit up straight. Aaron was glad for the diversion. Why had he asked her anyway?

She paid for the groceries while Aaron stuck a quarter in a coin-operated mechanical horse and, after asking Deanna's permission, put Maddy on its back.

Her curls bounced as the little girl laughed with glee. She was an easy child to love. Her mother was even easier. And with a sudden fear, Aaron knew he was not going to like moving on. He was not going to like it at all.

Chapter 5

That second night, Aaron thought about his good fortune. He had a roof over his head, a job, and there was a woman with eyes that twinkled and a gaze he couldn't put out of his mind. It was the myriad of thoughts that tripped him up.

He thought of Jill back in Oysterville. They'd dated his junior year. She was cute, too, with eyes that captivated him, but that was a long time ago. Jill probably was married and had a baby by now.

As always when he thought of home, his mind went to Hannah. He had prayed, telling her that it would get better. It has to, he always said to himself. Things can't get much worse. He had prayed for a miracle, but it didn't happen. And because of it, he had run as far as he could go. He had not attended church in months, and God seemed very far away.

Aaron listened to the sounds of waves lapping against the shore, down the hill from the cottage. The smell, the feel of the place, reminded him of Oysterville—yet it was different. The bay here was calmer, though he supposed that when a storm blew up, the waves would toss and the wind would howl around the house. He remembered looking out his basement bedroom window at home, watching the aspens sway back and forth, their branches interlocked, the leaves in a frenzied state as they fluttered in the wind. Fir trees withstood the wind better, dropping a needle or two, as Willapa Bay was stirred to frothy waves of gray and blue. Sometimes he'd grab his long jacket and a stocking cap and run out the door, then tear off down the path to watch from the water's edge. In the earlier days, he'd taken Hannah with him. He didn't think his father ever knew about their night adventures.

Later, when Hannah grew more frail, he'd hear her coughing and knew she'd been awakened by a storm. Sometimes he went to her room and held her hand. Words weren't needed as they listened to the storm, wondering if the wind would die down by daylight. Usually it did.

Aaron felt his heart nearly squeeze shut. He should never have left her. How many times had he gone over the scene in his mind, knowing, wishing he'd been there for her. Why did people fear being around dying people when family and friends were what they needed the most? Would the guilt ever stop?

∼

Aaron opened the door to the cottage and slipped outside. He didn't have shoes but wore heavy wool socks and an old pair of slippers. He wouldn't go far, but he wanted to see where the path went that ran along the front of the cottage. The night was lit by a full moon, its rays shining on the water below. He breathed deeply of the night air, noticing the pungent smell of pine. Maine was called the Pine Tree State for good reason. The air smelled different from that in Oysterville.

He wore his jeans, grimy from a day of cleaning the mess on the upper floor. He wore nothing over the T-shirt. The night was cool, but he shivered once and then became accustomed to it. He'd become used to the cold winters in northwestern Maine. He breathed deeply again. Hearing a twig crack, he thought it was probably an animal on the path ahead. A light beamed up and down along the path, several yards to the north. Aaron ducked behind a tree, not wanting to be seen. The sounds came closer, the light illuminating the tree branches and shrubbery that grew along the narrow path.

And then he saw it was Deanna. She was dressed in a long coat, her hair bouncing as she hurried along the trail. The flashlight swung back and forth. She came closer, and he knew she might pick up his shadow or even his scent. Then he heard Murphy. The dog would give him away for sure, so Aaron stepped out.

Deanna stopped and gasped. He could barely make out her outline and couldn't see her eyes but sensed her fear.

"It's just me," he said. "I couldn't sleep, and it was such a beautiful night."

"Oh, my goodness, you scared five year's growth from me!"

Murphy bounded around the bend and wagged his tail when he saw Aaron.

"Do you often go alone on a midnight stroll?" he asked.

She set down the flashlight. "Oh, no. Rarely. At least not this time of year. Besides, as you can see, I'm not alone. Of course, Murph stops to sniff every bush he sees." She hugged the black Lab close.

Murphy nudged Aaron's hand. "Yes, I'm okay now. You've decided I can stay, is that it, fella?" He ruffled the dog's thick fur, and Murphy came back for more.

"Murph's not a good watchdog, but he'd protect me if anyone tried to hurt me." She hesitated for a moment, as if she couldn't think of what to say next. The silence was awkward as Aaron took a deep breath.

"I like late-night walks. Always have." *We must be alike in that way,* he couldn't help thinking.

"So do I." She nodded as she passed in front of him, then turned and looked back. "But morning will be here before we know it. Do stop in for breakfast. It makes Dad happy to have someone to talk to."

And what about you? Aaron wanted to ask, but the words stayed deep inside him.

He waited until she disappeared. Once, Murphy looked back, as if expecting Aaron to follow.

If he thought he couldn't sleep before, he definitely couldn't sleep now. Not with visions of bouncing curls and deep, deep brown eyes dancing through his mind.

Aaron thought again about the night he'd left home, carrying the duffel. He had no idea where he was headed. He just had to get away, and later he'd think about returning.

He'd climbed in back of a pickup that had stopped at a tavern, covering himself with a tarp. Probably the driver wasn't going far, but he'd ride for a few miles. Surprisingly, the truck headed south, then off the peninsula; soon it was driving over the Astoria-Megler Bridge. He was getting as far as Oregon at least. Maybe he'd take a bus. He had some money stowed in a sock at the bottom of the backpack. His shoes were almost new, and his jacket was sturdy and in good condition. He had one change of clothes and two chunks of Cora's corn bread left over from dinner the night before.

The truck finally came to rest in the driveway of an older home located in a neighborhood of what Aaron guessed was Portland or one of the city's suburbs. He waited for a few minutes, then threw off the tarp, climbed out of the truck bed, and headed off toward the glow of lights in the sky that he knew emanated from the heart of the city. He would ask for directions to the bus station as soon as he reached a business that was open all night.

The bus took him to Idaho. There were no questions asked. Nobody said, "Hey, kid, aren't you kind of young to be traveling alone?"

Aaron was so hungry by the time the bus arrived in Boise, he could have eaten a possum. His money wouldn't go far, so he'd need to look for work soon. He finally decided Boise was as good a place as any. And that's how he managed. He worked a few weeks here, a few there, then traveled north to Montana. He'd considered going south but had heard they were hiring cowboys in Montana, and he'd always thought about living on a ranch someday. It would be different from living with water surrounding you on three sides. He'd seen lots of mountains, tall trees, and a few lakes, but nothing that compared to the Columbia River, the Pacific Ocean, and Willapa Bay on the peninsula.

It turned out there were no jobs in Montana, so he stayed in North Dakota for a while, later moving on to Minnesota and then Wisconsin; and it was there that he stayed the longest, working on a dairy farm. He liked the owner, and the house was nice, with a bedroom all his own. He bought an old pickup with two hundred thousand miles on it, and one morning after thinking about Hannah, he knew he had to keep moving.

Not once had he written or called home, and the more time that passed, the more he knew he could not do it. His father would light into him for being disrespectful, and what was the idea, his running off and not even finishing high school? "What's gotten into you, anyway?" was the usual question thrown at him at every turn. His father, once a gentle giant, by this time seemed angry about everything and at everybody. Aaron couldn't help it that Hannah was sick. Didn't his father know Aaron loved Hannah just as much as his father did?

After the pickup, Aaron bought Levi's, wool shirts, underwear—all the things a young man needs for wintertime—and stashed them in a footlocker he'd found at a yard sale. He left Wisconsin, driving instead of hitchhiking or hopping freight.

Weeks before, he had mailed a money order to his hometown to subscribe to the local paper, the *Chinook Observer*, asking that it be sent to him general delivery at the small Wisconsin town. Later, he'd sent a change of address request when he settled for a few weeks. He had to keep track of things back home, though he had no intention of returning. At one time he had considered doing so, but now he knew he wasn't going to go home. Not yet. Maybe never.

In Michigan, Aaron worked in a car lot selling used cars, but he was miserable. He didn't have the ability to sell anything. The only good that came of it was that he traded the pickup for a car with fewer miles. A month later he drove into northern Ohio, up through Cleveland, and on to Erie, Pennsylvania. From there he traveled along the southern tier of New York. There he worked at an artist's studio.

Tammy had needed someone to do screen painting on T-shirts, and he liked the work. It was a beautiful little town on the shore of Lake Chautauqua, and he realized once again how much he'd missed the waters of home. He rented a cabin and decided to stay for the winter. And winter he did have, with blowing snow that almost buried the cabin. But even though he was cold, with the cabin never warmer than sixty degrees, he looked out at the lake with great fondness. He just might not leave here. Besides, Tammy brought him dinner almost every night, and she was an excellent cook.

Tammy had told him her daughter was away at college, but would be home for the holidays. Once again Aaron was included in a family's home. It didn't make him long for home, because he could not remember ever having a home with a mother and a father. His mother had taken off when he was four, and though Cora looked after the house, it wasn't the same at all. He suspected that Cora would have liked to marry his father, but Leighton dated no one and did not ever plan to marry again. He had told Aaron this one afternoon while they picked oysters and packed them in boxes for shipping.

"But maybe I would like a mother. Tom would; he told me so."

Leighton had shaken his head. "Sorry to disappoint you, Son, but I have no desire to travel that path again."

"Do you believe in God?" Aaron wondered later why he had asked the question, but he'd felt he had to know.

"Of course I do." He had leaned over and ruffled Aaron's hair. "I can see I've been neglecting you. What do you say we drive into Portland tomorrow? I need to pick up some supplies, and we can eat at that café down at the square and maybe go watch the boats come up the Willamette. How about it?"

It was one of the last good times they'd had, and one of the few Aaron could even recall. Christmas and other holidays were observed, but there was no joy in the celebration. His brothers seemed to draw toward each other, but all Aaron had was Hannah, and she was dying.

"Hello?" A voice had broken through his thoughts as he'd sat looking out over the lake. Aaron glanced up to see a dark-haired young woman standing at the end of the pier.

"You must be Shellie, Tammy's daughter."

"Yes, I am." She laughed, and he froze up, thinking how she sounded just like Hannah.

"I'm going to have a cup of tea. Would you like some?"

They'd been inseparable for two weeks; he'd even convinced her that a good coffee was better than tea any day. Then she left to return to college, though she said she'd write and be home again in two months. Aaron felt his heart soar and looked forward to seeing Shellie again. But after a week of feeling bereft, he decided he couldn't stay, that he would never let his heart love again. It hurt too much.

He left the next morning before Tammy and her husband awakened. He wrote a note and pinned it to the door, thanking them for their kindnesses and saying he hoped their business would continue to flourish.

Aaron traveled east, along the lower part of New York and then cut up through Poughkeepsie. He found a job in a newspaper office delivering papers; that lasted a month. He went up to Vermont and stayed a month, then crossed New Hampshire and headed into the northwest corner of Maine. He had done it. He had wanted to travel clear across the United States, and he had succeeded. His first job was in a toothpick factory, and there he stayed for a year. Then he got the logging job. It was good, and he enjoyed the outdoors work, hauling the boards by sled during the winter months, shipping them down the river once the ice floes broke up.

There were no more women that attracted him, but that was because he never smiled twice at anyone. Aaron moved on because a jealous coworker thought Aaron liked his wife. He didn't need that kind of trouble.

He wasn't sure how he ended up clear over on the eastern side of the state, but here he was, and it was the Lobster Pound that had caught his eye, prompting him to stop. Was it just two days ago when he arrived, found he liked it here, and wanted to stay?

And would he ever learn that women were to look at, talk to, but not to care too deeply about? It only caused heartache. His father had been right—who needed marriage? For that matter, who needed God? Hadn't Aaron done pretty well on his own these past years?

Aaron slipped out of bed and turned on the small bedroom light. He stared at the wedding gown again. A huge trunk was at the foot of the bed, but he didn't look inside. It was a good thing he didn't need more room, as this was the only closet. He'd been living out of his duffel for so long, he wouldn't know what to do with hung-up clothes.

Aaron guessed he'd just have to ask Deanna about the dress. It was too bad he wasn't looking for a wife, for he knew she'd be a good one. He thought of the little girl with the dimples and flyaway dark hair. He wanted to hold her close, as there was something about Maddy that reminded him of Hannah when she was younger.

Aaron pulled the sliding door shut. Deanna and her husband had lived in this cottage. They had come here after their wedding and had conceived a baby in the very bed he slept in. But the sea had taken him away. Well, it wasn't Aaron's responsibility to take away the look of loneliness he saw in her dark eyes when she thought he wasn't looking.

Finally he gave up the idea of sleeping and put some water on the stove, thankful he'd bought coffee the day before. There was nothing like a fresh cup of coffee at 3:00 a.m. Coffee was definitely an essential of life.

He looked at his reflection in the depths of his cup. Deanna came to mind again, and he tried to shake the thought. Maybe he'd better not stay here at all. It might not be a good idea, considering the way he was feeling. Not a good idea at all. . .

Chapter 6

Deanna hurried up the stairs and slipped into the house as quietly as possible. Her heart still pounded from seeing Aaron on the path moments ago, and she tried to ignore the way her mind raced. She hugged Murph impulsively and then went to the cupboard for his doggie treat.

She sat in the darkness again, though the hour was late and morning would come too soon. There was something about Aaron that puzzled her, and she wasn't sure what. His smile captivated her and made her feel alive again, like when she first loved Bobby. Now Maddy was the light of her life, and daily she thanked God for her precious child. She remembered hoping for a son to carry on Bobby's name, but Madison was the very likeness of her father, and perhaps one day she'd carry on his name with a hyphen for her new married name. But that was a long way off. . . .

The wind picked up, whistling around the house, a reminder of the changeable weather even in early September. Deanna reached for the afghan and slipped it over her shoulders. She had to go to bed; she would have to tell her mind to stop thinking. She wasn't ready for a relationship. It wouldn't matter how nice the person was. And the haunting look in Aaron's eyes told her he wasn't ready for one, either. They would just be friends. It was better that way.

Leaving her boots at the door, Deanna headed up the stairs. Her father's heavy snores filled the whole upstairs of the house. She'd gotten used to it but remembered that when her mother was still living, her mother wore earplugs to bed.

Maddy was curled into a ball, her thumb in her mouth. Deanna had given up trying to break her of the habit months ago. She didn't want her child sneaking around a corner to suck her thumb. And she'd thrown the pacifier away when Maddy wasn't even a year old.

She pulled the covers up under Maddy's chin and bent down to kiss her forehead. A swell rose in her chest as she looked at her child. Such a blessing. What a miracle a child was. How could anyone ever abuse children? It was beyond her comprehension. She got on her knees and said her evening prayers, asking for guidance, for safety, and for health for all. "And, Lord, if it isn't asking too much, I ask for GB to catch lots of lobsters tomorrow and on into winter."

Maddy rolled over, almost smacking her mother in the mouth with an outstretched arm, breathing that funny little catching sound. Deanna touched her soft hair once more, then tiptoed down the hall to her room. Maddy's room was the small one up under the eaves, a perfect room for a baby. Later, when she had more toys and dolls, she could have the larger room at the opposite end. They'd left the cottage after Maddy was born and came to the big house. Mick had insisted on it.

Deanna crawled into bed, but her mind wouldn't let her sleep. Her thoughts went back to when she'd first met her husband. He wasn't from Maine and had moved in with a brother. He came to church one Sunday, and later, they sat across from each other at the monthly potluck. He had been bold, almost brazen, from that first meeting. After they had their choice of pie, he asked if he could walk her home.

"If you want to walk two miles," she'd said.

"I don't have a car," was his answer.

"Oh." She assumed everyone his age had a car. "We could walk then. That would be okay."

And so they did. Shortly after that day, Bobby bought an old clunker. Once he had wheels, he came calling almost every night.

It had been a whirlwind courtship, and he asked her to marry him two months later, she found herself saying yes.

"You hardly know the man," her father had argued.

"You're right, Dad," she retorted, "but I love him, and he loves me, and that's all I need to know."

He sighed, looking up from the lobster trap he was repairing. "Your mother would have wanted you to have a wedding."

"Dad, I don't need a big, fancy wedding. Really, I don't care about it."

"Your mother would come back to haunt me if I didn't give you away in the proper fashion."

In the end Deanna had relented, and everyone in Belfast was invited to the wedding of the year. Could she help it if most of the townspeople—who had known her mother since Deanna was young—wanted a chance to see Deanna married in the church with a white dress and all the trimmings?

She had found the dress in Bangor but took it back when her father scratched his head after looking at the price tag. "Four hundred for a dress?"

"Daddy, I told you I didn't need a big wedding."

"But this is ridiculous."

"There isn't time to have one made." Geneva was the town seamstress, and Deanna had thought of her, but she knew it took time to design, cut out, and put together something as fancy as a wedding dress. Then there were all the fittings. But her father insisted she ask, and Geneva set everything else aside and had the dress made to fit Deanna's small frame perfectly; she did it in a week's time.

The scalloped neckline and tiny pearl buttons at the waist were what Deanna ordered. There was just a small train, no sweeping one, and the veil was simple and one that Geneva had on hand for another young girl who had changed her mind about marriage the day before her wedding.

The gown was still in the cottage. That was why she couldn't believe her father would offer to let Aaron stay there. She kept saying she'd bring the dress up to the house, maybe get a few other items, such as wedding presents—some she had never used—as well, but that time had not come. And now a stranger was living there.

She wondered if Aaron had noticed the dress. Yet how could he not? Surely he would be hanging up clothes, and the dress would be quite noticeable, even if it were pushed to the back of the closet.

Deanna closed her eyes, and it was Aaron's eyes, Aaron's smile, that floated through her mind, not Bobby's. Was she to the point of forgetting her husband, Maddy's father? Was it time to think of a father for Maddy? A permanent father? Her grandpa paid her a lot of attention, and when GB came around, Maddy clung to him like a lost lamb. Yes, she supposed Maddy needed a father in her life, yet Deanna had to be sure it was someone who loved Maddy as if she were his own, and how many men could do that?

There was a secret in Aaron's blue eyes. Had he left a loved one behind? And did he even have a home? If so, where? Maybe he was an orphan. He hadn't said, just stated that he was looking for a job and would do just about anything for whatever pay they could give him.

Deanna closed her eyes again and thought about her walk along the water's edge. She had walked every night after Bobby died, even in the winter. She'd lost weight and was just starting to fill out her clothes again. Now she was feeling like walking, and apparently Aaron was, also. Did people who stayed up at night have lots on their mind? Or if one went walking, did it indicate that there were things he or she was worried or concerned about?

Since she couldn't sleep, Deanna threw off the covers, turned on the small lamp across the room, and foraged through the top drawer for the photo album. Perhaps looking at Bobby would bring back a sense of contentment. It was worth a try.

⁂

Aaron sat, sipping his second cup of coffee, realizing that if he were to get up and go to work, he needed some shuteye. Finishing his coffee, he set down the cup and lay on the bed, fully clothed.

Once he was asleep, the dream came again. Hannah was reaching out and crying for him to help her, to pound on her back, to make her better.

"Hannah, I cannot help," he said. "Nobody can. One day you're going to heaven to be with Jesus."

Aaron woke up, his shirt wet with sweat, realizing it was that same dream, the one he always had when his life was in turmoil. Why had he come here? Why didn't he leave in the morning, tell them he'd made a terrible mistake, that he really must be moving on. He'd say that he had a dying uncle in Massachusetts or make some such excuse. Crumb, he didn't need to give a reason. He hadn't even unpacked his duffel bag. He could send money later to cover his lodging.

He had his jeans and his boots on when he realized he couldn't go. He didn't want to go. He would stay. Give it a month. He'd keep it casual. Nod hello, answer questions Deanna might have, talk to Maddy now and then, and of course, be friends with Murphy. One could not ignore a dog. They didn't allow it. They asked no questions, nor did they demand anything but love and attention. He could handle that. Yes, he could definitely do that. He'd stay. At least for now.

He undressed and crawled under the covers, where sleep came, and this time it was a peaceful, restful sleep. He slept until 5:00 a.m., when a ship's horn blasted from the bay, causing him to shoot out of bed, his feet slipping on the throw rug beside the bed.

Chapter 7

When morning came, Aaron wondered again what had led him to this particular lobster pound. There had been others farther north along the shoreline, and there would probably be more south, should he venture that way, which was his inclination. What had led him to go off the main road, driving down the winding road until he was in front of the huge white building with its inviting sign?

Had God led him here? He wasn't sure how he felt about God's leading. It seemed that some believed in God's provision and guidance far more than did he. And yet, he could never deny that it was God who had helped him through several situations over the past five years.

Deanna would be bustling around in the big house, but he didn't want to interrupt her time for devotions. She needed that to recoup. He wondered if she'd have scrambled eggs again, or would it be something different? It was Sunday morning, and he knew the family attended church. Should he go with them if he was invited?

He pulled back the curtain and looked out the window. Morning light was seeping through the clouds, but a layer of fog clung to the shoreline like hair on a dog's back. Typical weather for here, just as it had been back home. Many mornings, Aaron had walked to catch the school bus in the fog. Winters had been rainy, and he wondered if it also rained a lot here on the eastern seaboard. He hadn't seen much inland. Someone had told him it was warmer along the shore. Last winter it had snowed. It snowed and snowed and snowed some more, until he got sick of the stuff. That had been the winter of logging, a job he'd never thought he would like. And yet he had liked the logging camp and the men he worked with. Now he knew what it meant to log the woods—how one had to bundle up or freeze. At home you bundled up to keep dry; here it was to keep warm. He'd never been so cold!

A figure came up from the dock. GB. He'd stayed home yesterday and came early today to check the traps. Minutes later a horn sounded, and Aaron knew he had left for the day's work.

Aaron finished the last of his crackers and had a second cup of coffee. Even if Deanna had prepared a big breakfast, he'd still be hungry. Funny how it worked; you could make do with a few stale crackers, but let someone set a plate of ham and eggs in front of you, and you could wolf it all down in minutes.

He laced his boots, checked the stove, threw the cover up over the bed so it looked made, then opened the door.

It was only five. Hadn't Deanna said to come at six? That meant he had awhile to walk to the docks, wishing more than anything that he owned a boat, that he could go out and empty the pots, add more bait, and bring home the day's catch. Maybe he'd get to do that yet.

Aaron looked at the holding tank, watching the lobsters swim. They were actually ugly, and it wasn't until they were boiled that they became the beautiful red color. The counter where people ordered was ready for business, and the office was beyond that. Through the window he could see the sign up over the desk. It read:

> *The pessimist complains about the wind,*
> *The optimist expects it to change,*
> *The realist adjusts the sails.*
>
> William Arthur Ward

Aaron liked the saying. It was so true and totally appropriate for here on the coast. He felt he was a cross between an optimist and a realist. He wondered what Deanna was. Definitely not a pessimist. Perhaps GB was, though. He came across that way to Aaron.

He walked around the side of the building. It needed new paint. He had noticed that yesterday, but in the morning light it was more evident. Chipped paint on the east side due to the harsh winds—he'd heard this meant one had to paint just about every year. It was then he saw Deanna in the window of the big house. She was looking out, and he waved heartily. She waved back, and his heart did that funny little lurch it had done last night when he'd seen her coming down the path.

He took a deep breath, deciding to head up to the house after all. Maybe he could get a better perspective on what was expected of him today. Mick had not said much last night, just that he had plenty to do before the Pound opened for business.

"I need another pair of hands, son. These are old and arthritic." He held them up for Aaron to see. They were bent and gnarled, the nails thick and yellowed. He could see that those hands couldn't do much work. So he would be the hands and the legs, too, for Mick. Yes, he could do that. Now if he could just keep Deanna in the right place in his mind. . .

❧

Deanna had seen him walk down to the Pound. Hands in his pockets, hunched over, he seemed to be inspecting the side of the building. Maybe he could do the needed repairs, spruce the place up a bit, maybe even paint it—all jobs Bobby would have done had he lived.

At the thought of her husband, the lump returned to her throat. It was over, and no amount of wishing would bring him back. "You must get on with your life," Pastor Neal had said. "Life is for the living, Deanna. Perhaps there is someone out there who needs a wife and a child. I know God will provide. Just be strong in your faith."

She smiled, thinking of the verse she'd come across this morning. It spoke to her heart, and she had written it in her journal:

> *Thou hast turned for me my mourning into dancing: thou hast put off my sackcloth, and girded me with gladness;*
> *To the end that my glory may sing praise to thee, and not be silent.*
> *O Lord my God, I will give thanks unto thee for ever.*
> PSALM 30:11–12

It was Sunday, and Deanna looked forward to attending church. Maddy liked Sunday school, and she needed the interaction with other children her age. If Deanna had more time, she might have looked into a preschool for Maddy, but in reality, she felt safer keeping her at home with her. At least for now.

Would Aaron attend church with them? He'd mentioned doing so when they went to the store, so she would ask. He couldn't do any more than say no, and he just might say yes.

She walked away from the window, remembering how the young man had looked down on the dock, hands thrust in his pockets. It was time to get busy with breakfast preparations. She wondered if Aaron liked pancakes as well as her father and Maddy did. Maybe she'd make them special today. She had overripe bananas and nuts. This had been a favorite of her mother's, and Deanna loved making them for the family.

She was beating egg whites into a heavy froth when the knock sounded, the door opening slightly.

"Do you suppose I could come in and get a cup of your good coffee?"

She smiled as she waved him in. "I've got the coffee ready and am starting pancakes now. I hope you like bananas and walnuts."

Aaron grinned. "Our housekeeper made banana-nut pancakes, and it's one of my fondest memories."

Deanna almost dropped the spoon. "Are you serious? You're not just saying that. . . ."

"No, I mean it."

"I've never known anyone else who made them."

Their glances met, and Aaron wondered what it would be like to have Deanna whipping up meals in his kitchen. He decided it would be nice and something he'd never tire of.

"Would you like to attend our church this morning?"

"What about work? I have the upper deck to clean up before customers arrive."

She laughed. "Have you not heard that thou shalt rest on the seventh day?"

"You mean you don't open on Sunday?"

"Well, no, we do open, but not until three, so there will be plenty of time."

Aaron said yes, he would like to go, then helped set the table, since neither Maddy nor Mick was up yet. It felt good to be working in the kitchen next to Deanna. He liked the feeling. He liked her. He definitely had some rethinking to do.

Chapter 8

That first week was a learning experience. Aaron was the "gofer" at the Pound. Not that he minded. It was all work that needed to be done. Mick did what he could to maintain the place and kept busy mending broken traps, but there were days when he was "stove up" as he called it, and Deanna had taken over. This left her frazzled, as she wanted to spend time with Madison and also cook more, one of her favorite pastimes. Aaron worked hard, and consequently he discovered that he ate more.

He whistled now as he worked, cleaning up the restaurant on the top floor. He even had the steps clean and polished. The windows were the next things he tackled. It was amazing how people flocked to the Pound for a good Friday night lobster dinner. He'd met a lot of the local townspeople, along with travelers who had heard this was the place to stop for lobster. But he learned after that first night that they also served a variety of seafood, and Deanna had recently added chowders and stews to the menu.

And all the while, Aaron found himself pulled more and more toward Maddy and her mother. The child followed him around as he worked, and though Deanna called out suggesting that she should come down to the office to color or read one of her books, Maddy would beg to stay upstairs with him. She didn't get in the way. He rather liked the distraction.

One evening Deanna suggested a drive over to Stockton Springs to pick blueberries the next day. "It's the end of the season, and blueberries are Dad's favorite berry. He can get by with us gone for the morning. Let's get up early and take off by six so we'll have plenty of time for picking."

"Mommy, can I pick blueberries, too?"

"Of course. I have a bucket the right size for you."

"Mick will be okay?"

Deanna nodded. "Sure. We'll get back in time for me to fix Dad a good meal, and then later I'll make blueberry pies and put some in the freezer."

Her eyes sparkled as she spoke, and it was all he could do to keep from pulling her into his arms and running his hand through the thick thatch of curls. He looked away, then back again after he felt more composed.

"What if someone comes to the Pound?"

She grinned impishly. "We can put a sign on the door: 'Gone fishin'.' "

Maddy came up, dragging a doll by one arm. "Did you say we were going to go fishing?"

Aaron and Deanna both laughed as Deanna held her small daughter close. "No, honey. Not fishing. We're going to pick blueberries."

"And I get to go, too?"

"Of course," Aaron said.

That evening Deanna served pot roast from the midday meal, which Mick called dinner, and apple pie.

"I wish this was blueberry," she said to her father. She turned to Aaron. "You know that Maine is noted for its blueberries?"

She was teasing him now. Aaron nodded. "I picked blueberries last year. They grew wild in the valley there. The loggers laughed at me, but I loved them. Back home we have blueberries, but they are a larger berry and cultivated on farms. We call the smaller version a huckleberry."

"Well, Daughter, my plate is empty, and you know what that means."

Deanna cut another slice of apple pie, topping it with a dollop of whipped cream. "My father loves his pie more than anything."

"Can't argue with that. Go on, Son. Have another piece. There's more when this one is gone, right?"

Deanna cut a second slice for Aaron, as well, then gave Maddy a tiny sliver as, of course, she was clamoring for more, too. "There's enough for GB to have a piece if he wants one after bringing the boat in."

"You going somewhere?" Mick looked up, his fork poised in the air.

"In the morning, Dad. I told you, remember? Aaron, Maddy, and I are taking a short trip over to Stockton Springs to pick blueberries."

"When are you getting back?"

"In plenty of time to open up."

"Oh. Well, it isn't as if you two haven't worked hard this week. And the weather won't hold, that's for sure."

⁓

Aaron stayed up late drinking coffee that night. He thought of all the things he had not yet done, places he had not explored, and wondered if that was why he felt torn. Deanna kept coming to mind. He had nothing to offer and definitely felt marriage, which most women wanted, was not in the offing. Not now. Probably never.

The sky was dark with a low layer of clouds when Aaron stepped outside. Blueberry picking would be fun and a change of pace. He'd wear the only casual pants he owned. A bullet gray knit sweater would lend warmth.

He walked up to the kitchen, expecting to see Deanna bustling around. She was not. He opened the door and went in. There was no fragrant smell of coffee brewing or rolls in the oven. Was something wrong? Had he misunderstood? He didn't want to call out in case she was still asleep.

He thought about the morning newspaper and went back out to fetch it from the box at the top of the hill. He could go back and heat up water for instant coffee, too. He decided to go back to the big house.

Voices came from upstairs. One was Mick's, and he didn't sound happy. Should he go up to see if he could help? But what if Deanna was in her night-clothes? No, that would not do at all.

A voice called out. "Aaron? Are you there? I thought I heard the door close." She stood at the top of the steps, dressed in Levi's and a cherry red sweater, her hair loose and free.

"Do you need something?"

"It's Dad. I can't leave him like this."

"Why? What's wrong?" He started up the steps.

"He had a bad night and won't go back to bed. Someone must be here to answer questions, should anyone come, and I don't want him down there work-ing. It's just too hard for him."

Aaron was on the landing now, close enough that their shoulders touched as he started to move past.

"Well, I agree. He shouldn't be left. So what's the problem?"

"He says to go on; he wants us to have a good time."

"There are more days. . ."

Deanna smiled, stepped on her tiptoes, and impulsively kissed his cheek. "I knew that's what you'd say. I told Dad that. You're such a positive-thinking per-son, I knew you'd say we should just reschedule."

Maddy was in the hall and threw her arms around Aaron's legs. "I never thought you'd come upstairs," she cried, hugging him hard.

Aaron stepped back, as if realizing he was up in the confines of the old house. It was not right that he was here, and yet she had called out to him.

"I came to see your grandfather."

Mick's voice blustered from a room down the hall. "Drat and colored goat feathers! I can take care of myself! Been doing it ever since I was knee-high to a grasshopper!"

"Now, Dad. . ."

He was in the hall now, a robe thrown over long johns. "I insist that you leave me here. If I get worse, I'll call 9-1-1 or maybe someone from church. I say you need to go and pick those blueberries—have some fun. 'All work and no play makes Jack a dull boy,' as my mommy used to say."

Aaron stepped forward and put an arm around the old man's shoulder. "Mick, we can wait for our fun day. Really, it's okay. Placate Deanna. She would not have one ounce of fun if we left you behind feeling like this."

"Oh, you young whippersnappers! Think you got all the answers!"

"Grandpa!" Maddy tugged on his robe. "I think you'd better get dressed or go back to bed."

They laughed, and Deanna scooped her daughter into her arms. "You tell him, honey."

"I want Aaron to carry me downstairs." Maddy turned to face him.

"Maddy, you must get dressed first. Then I'll come up and get you if you meet me halfway," Aaron said.

The upstairs had unconventional ceilings, with eaves on each side and small windows looking out at the bay on the west side, the road out another, and due east out the third. A flowered carpet covered the floor, and the doors were old and heavy with old-fashioned ceramic knobs. A dim light was in the middle of the hall, lighting the area as best it could.

"That's right. You've not seen the upstairs before," Deanna said. "It's really quite charming. Dad has the largest bedroom; it used to be his and Mother's, of course. Mine is the next largest, and Maddy has a tiny room at this end. No bathroom up here, which makes it quite unhandy, but I love the house—I especially love it upstairs here."

And I love you, popped into Aaron's mind before he knew it was there. How could he think such a thing? He smiled and started down the steep steps.

"I'm glad we're not going; it wouldn't be fun if you were worried about your dad."

"And I would worry. I'll be down as soon as I lay out Maddy's clothes."

Soon warmth filled the kitchen, and the smell of coffee made Aaron's stomach growl. He watched while Deanna put water on for her father's oatmeal—he never went without a bowl of oats in the morning. "That's what's kept me alive all these years," he claimed.

Biscuits were cut with a round cutter and placed on a baking sheet. Eggs were taken out of the refrigerator and set where they wouldn't roll off the counter. He was supposed to be reading the paper, but for some reason he couldn't get past the headlines, which was something about a crash of three vehicles near the state capital.

"Dad is getting more cantankerous," Deanna said, turning around from the counter, an egg in each hand. "I have seen it coming for the past year or so. He wants his way. He forgets something, and then he seems to get mad at me when he forgets what I told him the day before."

"Aren't most older people that way?"

Aaron hadn't meant to be funny, but her eyes suddenly lit up in that way she had that made the thought come to mind again, *I love you, Deanna Barnes.*

"I've never been around many old people," she said, her face getting serious again. "Maybe a physical checkup would be the way to go, but he balks at that, too. Doesn't want to see a doctor when he can still get out of bed and walk and eat. He is as stubborn as they come!"

"Let it go for now. Maybe we can come up with a plan. Let me think about it."

"You'd do that?"

"Sure. Why not?"

"But he isn't your family. . . ." Her words hung in the air, as if she realized too late what she'd said. He knew she had avoided talking about family in the past, and he was glad for it.

"He's my family now," Aaron said simply. *All the family I have,* he wanted to say.

Before she could answer, Maddy called from the stairs. "Okay, Aaron. I'm ready now! You can come get me and give me a piggyback ride."

"You spoil her," Deanna said as he pushed the paper aside and started up the stairs.

And she's my family, too, he wanted to add.

※

Deanna started beating eggs. Just as her father always had oatmeal, he also insisted that eggs should be part of the breakfast fare. Not that she minded. She didn't pay much attention to cholesterol, but perhaps it was time he did. No, it was time to seriously consider a full physical checkup for her father. It was long overdue. In fact, she couldn't remember the last time he'd even gone to a doctor. If he got a cold, which everyone did in the middle of winter, he took his favorite over-the-counter meds.

She watched while Maddy and Aaron came down the stairs, Maddy's shrieks filling the house. Maddy was so adorable, lovable, and needed a father. She looked at Aaron, and the thought jumped to her mind: Could Maddy call Aaron "Daddy" someday? Would she like that? Deanna smiled as she whisked the eggs, then felt a hand touch her arm. She felt his presence, smelled his scent, without looking up.

"Yes?" she asked. But no more words came out as she felt his gaze meet hers, and she felt swept away with sudden longing. How could this be happening when she had loved Bobby so terribly much? How could she transfer those feelings to an absolute stranger she'd only known ten days?

"I said, can I help?"

"You can help me set the table," Maddy said, pushing past her mother to the silverware drawer.

"I'll get the plates and bowls," Aaron said, reaching around Deanna.

For as large as the house was, the kitchen was fairly small— at least the workspace. They touched because he couldn't help it, and it was as if an electric spark went between them. He stepped back, the plates firmly in his hands.

"I think I'll go read the paper."

"Coffee's ready. Go sit, and I'll bring you a cup."

Mick entered the kitchen, leaning over, his hand over his left side as if he was having a problem walking. "It's the weather. Cold is coming. That's what my hip tells me."

"But there is medicine you can take, Dad. Dr. Anderson would prescribe it for you, but you must go in first."

"Humph!" He held his favorite mug out for Deanna to fill with coffee. "I am not taking any of those things. They tell you if you have high cholesterol, don't take it. If your heart's bad, don't take it. If you are constipated, don't take it. . . ."

"Dad!"

"Well, isn't it the truth? I am not going to take something that has all those side effects."

Deanna looked at Aaron and rolled her eyes. "Still, it's something we should check into."

Mick humphed again and grabbed a piece of the newspaper. Deanna knew that as far as he was concerned, the subject was closed.

Maddy chatted while she put all the chairs around the table just so. Then they sat, and Deanna glanced at Aaron over the top of her coffee mug. He smiled and then turned to Mick.

"Maybe I should paint the south side. What do you think?"

"Think the weather's going to hold?"

"I could paint one section and wait and see if it dries before tackling more."

They left the house. Sunshine filled him with hope. It always did. So far, East Belfast had not had much rain, nothing like the fall and winter rains in Oysterville. But the snow would come; even here in coastal Maine, snow came and stayed.

Murphy bounded over, wanting a scratch behind his ears and a pat.

"Hey, boy, how are you this morning?" Already the young man and the dog had become fast friends. Murph wouldn't attack just anyone, but if someone started to harm his family, no telling what he might do, and Aaron knew the dog now considered him to be family. It was a good feeling.

After Maddy was bundled up, Deanna slipped on a coat and walked over to Aaron. "Thanks for being kind to my father."

"Kind?"

"Yes. . .you know." Her eyes met his, and once again the feeling came over him. "He's so cantankerous, but you seem to know how to deal with him. I am at my wit's end at times, but he listens to you. I know he likes you."

And confides in me, Aaron wanted to say. Somehow, with her standing here, close enough for him to smell the faint scent of violets, he wondered if her heart hadn't mended and she just didn't know it yet.

"I think it will be a great day for painting, and I'll try to get this one wall done."

"Thanks again," Deanna said before turning and going inside the office. Maddy didn't want to go with her mother, but Deanna insisted, saying that she would get paint on her, and it was hard to get it off.

It would be white, of course, and maybe he'd suggest a trim. Red seemed appropriate. Red and white. He knew Deanna liked red. And suddenly he whistled a tune from *Fiddler on the Roof,* which took him back to a time when he and his father had been pals. Back when his father had loved him and thought him special. *Will I ever know a time like that again?* he couldn't help wondering.

Chapter 9

Aaron didn't get much chance to talk to GB, though he wished he could discuss the day's catch. GB came in and put the lobsters in the holding tank while Aaron was busy with customers. He'd see Maddy there, peering into the carrier.

"What a day!" he proclaimed one Friday; he stopped when he saw Aaron watching. Aaron didn't know what he'd done to make GB angry, but he wore a scowl when he looked in his direction. He'd seemed friendly when he'd talked about the Appalachian Trail that first day. Maybe he was upset because Aaron had spoken about going out in the boat. As if he would take over GB's position. He had no intention of doing such a thing.

"You can't go out on this boat!" GB had said that afternoon. His expression was harsh. "You need a license. Those are the rules."

Mick stopped hauling and looked from Aaron to his son. "He isn't taking your place. Not at all."

But from that afternoon on, GB tried to ignore Aaron, so Aaron stayed out of his way. No point in riling him up more. He was glad GB went home after the day's work. Things were unpleasant if he hung around, and he never wanted to cause friction between family members.

The lobsters were dumped into the holding tank. Three large, five medium-size, and one that measured right on the nose—just large enough. "Seen better days," GB said. "But this will add to the mix."

He scowled again at Aaron. "Thought you would be gone by now."

"GB!" Deanna looked at Aaron as if wanting to see what his reaction would be. Aaron felt his face go hot but said nothing. It was often better to ignore people. If the old man needed an extra pair of hands, how could GB be against that? GB didn't help around the Pound, and Aaron worked at things Mick could no longer do. He wondered if GB knew how frail his father was.

"Don't listen to GB," Deanna said later, after GB had driven off in his pickup. "He thinks he's lord and master around here. Always has. He's such a crank at times!"

Aaron smiled. He understood only too well about brothers. At least Deanna only had to contend with one.

Aaron thought of GB a lot in the next few days. Mick seemed certain that GB wanted nothing to do with the business, yet his actions said otherwise. It appeared he cared very much what happened, and after Aaron had been in East

Belfast two weeks with no signs of leaving, GB brought it up one afternoon over cups of coffee on the upper deck. Customers hadn't arrived, probably wouldn't for another hour.

"Dad, I mean no offense, but since things will be slowing down soon, don't you think the three of us can handle the Pound now?" He looked at Aaron. "Not anything against you, but my father doesn't have that much money."

Mick's chin jutted out. "Don't talk about me like I'm not here." He pointed his pipe at his son. "And how much money I have or do not have is my business. Besides, Deanna says more help means more customers."

"Deanna knows nothing about it! She's searching for something else." GB shoved his cup aside and stalked down the stairs. At the bottom he turned and shook his head. "I repeat, we can handle it!"

Deanna came out of the office, hands on hips. "Just go home, GB, and leave us alone!"

"Fine. Maybe I'll just quit, and you two can figure out who is going to go out and bait the traps, dump 'em in, and go back later and haul 'em up! It isn't any party out there, Dee, and you, above all, should know that!"

Her cheeks went red, then white as she turned and ran up the hill to the house.

"That boy!" Mick said, pouring more coffee from the thermos. "He's like the lobster. He gets in the trap and then can't figure how to get out. He never has known when to just shut up. I think I know what's ailing him, but it's just too bad!"

"Maybe I should leave—"

"No, son. I'm still making the decisions around here and will continue to do so until they put me six feet under."

Aaron knew what the drift was now. If he married Deanna, there would be less money for GB. Well, GB had nothing to worry about. Maybe he'd tell him the next time he saw him.

Deanna had gone off in a huff the same time GB left. Aaron guessed she was at the house. He decided to go on up and see if he could help, but halfway to the house, a car pulled into the Lobster Pound. He joined the people halfway down the hill.

"Evening."

The couple smiled and held hands as they went in to pick out lobsters, then ordered from the restaurant window where Mick stood. "I'll get these cooked for you in a minute."

"Do you want me to handle it, Mick?" Aaron offered.

"Guess you better since Deanna is off at the house in a snit. Not that I blame her."

Aaron plunged the two lobsters into the boiling pot and timed it. The larger one had to stay in the water a minute longer. Mick got the butter ready, popped the French bread into the oven for a minute to heat, and got out the silverware.

"I could do this in my sleep," Mick said with a laugh. "But it's a good life; you know what I'm saying?"

Deanna and Maddy didn't come back to work, and Aaron and Mick managed just fine. It was a light night. One never knew what to expect in the restaurant business.

Later that evening, when the Pound had closed down and the light meal was finished and Maddy had fallen asleep, Aaron got up from the sofa where he'd been reading Maddy's favorite book, *Blueberries for Sal*. He watched as Deanna carried the sleeping child up the stairs.

He sat on the couch and realized the house was quiet and that he enjoyed the silence. Soon the TV would go on, but for now, both Aaron and Mick seemed content to just sit.

"Don't hurt her, son," Mick said, breaking the silence. "That's all I ask. Just don't hurt her."

Aaron was stunned. He said nothing for a long moment, choosing his words carefully.

"I would never hurt her intentionally."

Mick pulled his pipe out of his mouth. "I didn't reckon you would."

Aaron felt uncomfortable. He rose to his feet and nodded. "Busy day. Think I'll turn in early."

He had thinking to do. If he stayed here, he would never be good enough for Deanna, and if he weren't honest with her, Mick would have his neck. If he left without so much as a good-bye, he would forever see Deanna's dark, expressive eyes in his mind.

The night was nippy, a nippiness that one often felt on the bay during the winter. But it wasn't winter yet. Winter was three months off.

He got out the instant coffee, then decided to walk the path along the bay. He had walked it on more than one occasion but had not run into Deanna again, though he had hoped to.

Was Deanna still in love with her husband? Would Bobby always hold a part of her heart? And if so, why could he think of nothing but taking her in his arms and proclaiming how he felt? Not that marriage was in the bargain. He knew most women wanted marriage, and that was the scary part.

The water was calm, and as a sliver of moon shone out of the darkened sky, it lit the path. Murph was suddenly there, and Aaron wondered how long he'd been trotting along behind him. And what was he doing here? He usually stayed at the house.

Then he heard her voice.

"Aaron!"

He stopped and waited for her to round the bend and catch up. "What are you doing out here?" He took her hand in both of his and held it tight. "You're freezing!"

"I know. I should have grabbed my gloves."

She wore a jacket with hood and boots. "I always forgot my gloves when I was little, and Mom would despair over me."

"When did your mother die?"

She looked past him, as if she couldn't quite meet his gaze. "I was in tenth grade. GB had just finished college."

"Your father told me it was cancer."

Deanna nodded. "Yeah. She'd had it a long time but never went to a doctor; nor did she tell any of us about the pain or the lump in her breast. . . ." Her voice broke.

Aaron's arm went around her as he pulled her to his chest. She clung to him as tears rolled down her cheeks. Murphy tried to wedge his way between the two and whined.

"He doesn't like to see me crying."

"Dogs are like that—there when you need a companion."

"Oh, Aaron, I do need a companion. I never realized it until the day you came. There was something about your eyes, your manner, and I hoped you'd stay on."

"You did?" Her hood fell back, and suddenly his mouth was against the curls; he held her as tightly as he dared.

"GB had no right to abuse you that way today. When I came back downstairs from putting Maddy to bed, I saw the empty chair where you always sit, and I thought you were leaving." She lifted her face. "I knew I couldn't let you go. I mean. . .I really like you. I know something else, Aaron."

"What's that?" He wanted time to stand still. He wanted to keep holding her, loving the way she felt in his arms, the feel of her head against his chest.

"I knew I never, ever wanted a day to go by when I didn't see your face," she finished.

Aaron was stunned for the second time that day. He cared deeply for Deanna, but her words meant more than caring. Her words talked of commitment, of being together in a permanent relationship. He couldn't do it. It might not work, just as his parents' relationship had not. Yet, he wanted to keep holding her as he listened to the lapping waves of the Passagassawakeag River in the distance. She stayed against him, and he touched the curls. She was so soft and vulnerable.

"You're shivering, Deanna. You must go back."

"No, Aaron. Wait."

She leaned up and touched his mouth with her lips. He held her close again, returning her kiss for a moment before something made him move back.

"We can't be alone, Deanna. It's not a good idea."

"Yes, I know."

Murphy nudged his hand with his wet nose. It was almost as if he was saying, "It's okay; it's going to be okay."

Deanna stepped back. "I shouldn't have said any of that. I'm sorry."

Their gazes met again, and he wanted to tell her how he'd felt that first afternoon when he saw her with the sunlight on her dark curls, how he'd felt she was the most beautiful woman he'd ever seen. He said nothing, but instead whispered, "Never be sorry for expressing your feelings. Feelings are neither right nor wrong."

"You aren't moving on?"

"No."

"I. . ." But the words wouldn't come as she turned and ran in the direction of the house.

Aaron wanted to go after her but knew he shouldn't. Murphy looked at Aaron as if to say, "Well, aren't you coming?"

❧

Long after Aaron returned to the cottage, he felt something amiss in the house but wasn't sure what it was. Then he saw the space in the closet. The wedding dress was gone. When had she taken it? Earlier that day? Yesterday? And why? He glanced around. Everything else in the cottage looked the same. He sat on the bed, head in hands. Could he stay on now, now that she'd said all that? He felt love for her in his heart but couldn't say it. It was too soon. He couldn't commit. There was no way for this to be possible.

Aaron reached deep inside his large duffel bag and pulled out a tattered Bible. He had packed it that long-ago night in Oysterville but until now had not read it.

It still smelled of genuine leather. He looked at his name embossed in gold on the front cover. The Bible fell open to Psalm 34. He read there, "I will bless the Lord at all times: his praise shall continually be in my mouth."

Aaron thought about the things that had happened since he'd left his home. He'd made friends, held several occupations, gone hungry a few times, and was wet and cold on more than one occasion. He'd met Shellie in New York and a woman in northwest Maine at the toothpick factory, but he always left before things got tight. He could do so again.

But he didn't want to leave, and this realization bothered him more than he thought it would. He read more verses by the light of the small lamp beside the bed. It felt good to be in God's Word, and he remembered the times his grandmother had told him Bible stories, the ones he had heard in Sunday school as a boy. He felt the tightness in his chest. Should he run away again? Finally, Aaron closed the Bible and turned down the bed.

Chapter 10

Deanna felt like such a fool as she ran in the house and up the steps, hoping her father was still asleep. With tears stinging her cheeks, she peeked in on Maddy. She was angelic as her dark curls fanned her Sleeping Beauty pillow. Matching curtains covered the windows that looked out over the bay.

Leaning down, Deanna kissed her daughter's forehead. Maddy needed a father. Bobby had been a wonderful father, but God took him home and now here she was, acting like a lovesick widow needing a husband and wanting a father for her child. What must Aaron think?

She entered her own room and kicked the boots off. The pink, furry rug felt good to her stocking feet. How she loved this room, the one her mother had lovingly painted the summer before she died. The ruffled curtains were sewn on a Sunday afternoon. The bed was perfect for one or would do for two if they liked to sleep in spoon fashion. *Stop it*, her mind cried out. *You've gotten along just fine so far and will manage longer. If the good Lord wants someone to come along, He'll make sure you see the signs.*

She sat on the edge of the bed, and Aaron's face came to mind. His eyes sparkled when he looked at her as if he cared, really cared. How did one know if they should pursue a feeling or just let it drop?

Dear, Lord, I need direction, big-time. Please help me.

Bobby came in a dream that night. In the beginning she dreamed about him a lot, but it had been a long time now. His cocky smile that had warmed her heart in the early days of their relationship seemed to say, "You've got to make a life for you and Madison. Keep me tucked in your heart, but there's room for someone else."

Deanna rose in the morning with renewed hope. She wasn't sure why, but somehow she knew things would work out. She also knew that Aaron was carrying around baggage, something he hadn't shared with her—or anyone else, as far as she knew. What had happened to make a young boy move clear across the United States? It wasn't the usual situation. Kids ran away, yes. She remembered running off to a friend's house once, but when her friend's father said she couldn't live there, she'd returned home, words of forgiveness on her lips. If only Aaron would talk about his life, his childhood. She really knew nothing about him, and it was true what GB had said that first day: "He could be a thief or murderer for all you know. Don't be taken in with his innocent, boyish smile."

Deanna also knew that she was older, by a year or two. Not that it mattered.

Well, to some it did. Was that what really troubled him? Somehow she didn't think so.

It was time to put the coffee on and fix breakfast. She hoped Aaron would come in before her father got up. She wanted to apologize for what she'd said. She didn't want to take it back, but something about the look on his face made her know she shouldn't have assumed anything.

But Maddy woke up crying, and after she'd comforted her from what appeared to be a nightmare, Deanna heard her father in the bathroom. The day had begun whether she was ready or not.

❧

Aaron had choices. Didn't one always have choices? He could stay here, carry on as if nothing had happened, or he could suggest that Mick find another person to help with the Pound. And yet he couldn't always run off like he had in the past. Didn't there come a time when one faced up to facts? He had to grow up sometime, and maybe that time was now. Maybe Deanna did love him, and it was true he had this overwhelming urge to care for and protect her. And Maddy was a nice bonus in the overall picture. Who got Murphy? He was clearly Deanna's dog, but Mick loved the black lab, too.

He dressed and headed for the big house.

Deanna had her back to him when he opened the door. She whirled around, and he saw the hurt look in her eyes. He swallowed hard.

"About—"

"About?"

They both began talking at once.

"I spoke out of turn," she said. "Please ignore what I said."

"I—I. . ." But he couldn't get the words out of his mouth. She wanted to ignore it? She hadn't meant it? Were they just to be friends?

"Okay," he finally managed. He held his hand out. "Let's just be friends then."

The minute the words were out, he realized it was the wrong thing to say. She turned back, but not before he saw her face crumple.

Smoke rose from the fry pan, and she grabbed it, without a pot holder.

It fell to the floor with a resounding crash. "Oh!" she cried out, running to the sink and putting her hand under cold water.

Aaron picked up the cast-iron skillet and scooped the bacon back into the pan. Maddy had come into the room and cried at the sight of her mother's crying. Mick bounded out of the bathroom, as much as he could bound, and surveyed the mess in the kitchen.

"What on earth?"

"Oh, Dad, I never burn anything!"

"Nor do you pick up a hot handle! Here, let me see it."

Aaron watched as the older man scrutinized his daughter's burn, and then he was holding her close.

"I—I forgot something at the cottage," Aaron said, wanting to flee as fast as he could. Oh, he'd really solved things now, hadn't he!

"Just a moment, young man." Mick's voice boomed out. Maddy clung to her mother's leg, and Deanna had turned back to the refrigerator for more eggs.

"I don't know what happened here, but you're not moving on again. Not just yet. I believe you signed a rental agreement. . . ."

"Dad!"

But he was adamant.

"I understand," Aaron said. "I'm not leaving, just forgot my gloves on the table."

As Aaron returned to the cottage, he realized he'd really done it this time. Now he was not only an enemy of GB but of Mick, as well. So much for that inner voice. He'd hurt Deanna, and that was the last thing he wanted to do. He grabbed the gloves and headed back. "Well, God," he prayed aloud, "I'm wanting to listen to You, so You have to tell me what to do now. Do I apologize or what?"

While he waited for an answer, he had work to do, and it wasn't getting any earlier.

Chapter 11

Aaron need not have worried. It was as if nothing had happened. Mick didn't mention the incident, and Deanna smiled and appeared to be fine. Far be it from him to bring it up.

Two days later, Deanna said they had to pick blueberries. "It's now or never. Besides, Dad is doing better."

The drive to Stockton Springs was lovely, with a vivid show of autumn color. "This is my favorite time of year," Deanna said.

"Mine, too," Aaron responded.

"Well, I like audumn, too," Maddy announced.

They exchanged glances, and Aaron saw the twinkle in Deanna's dark eyes.

The field of blueberry bushes went as far as one could see. Soon they had been assigned an area and started picking.

Aaron couldn't believe how fast Deanna picked. Maddy was like the little girl in her favorite picture book. She ate far more berries than went into the bucket.

"Mommy, are you sure there aren't any bears around here?"

"No, darling. No bears. We're not in the woods or mountains. Besides, there are too many people picking berries just like we are. People tend to scare them off. Sorry to disappoint you, but no bears."

"We have bears back home," Aaron offered. "One night we heard this clatter-bang, and a bear had come right into the garage and overturned the garbage can."

"What did you do?" Deanna asked.

"A big bear?" Maddy asked, holding her hand high over her head.

"No, actually, it was a cub. We started closing the garage door after that."

"I want to hear more," Deanna said, dumping a handful of berries into her nearly full bucket. "C'mon. Tell me another story."

"Yes, tell us a story, Aaron!" Maddy echoed her mother's request.

Aaron put his bucket over for Deanna to help him fill it. He wanted to talk about his family someday, but not right now.

"Please, Aaron." Maddy tugged on his arm.

"Only if you pick more blueberries."

"I will, I will."

"My sister and I went blackberry picking once. Blackberries grow wild everywhere, and they have a wonderful flavor, but the seeds get stuck in your teeth."

"What happened?" Deanna persisted.

"We got lost."

"You did?" Deanna shot him a puzzled look. "But weren't you close to home?"

Aaron chuckled. "Yes, we were, but we went down this old logging road, and it stretched on and on. And then the mosquitoes came, and poor Hannah was eaten alive."

"Who's Hannah?" Maddy asked.

"My little sister."

"Little like me?"

"No, she was older." He looked away, thinking how much Hannah would have enjoyed this excursion.

"So what did you do?"

"I knew Dad would be worried," Aaron continued, so I stopped at the first house and asked them to call my father."

"Was he mad?"

"Oh my, no. Just worried, because we'd been gone half a day."

"I've never gotten lost," Deanna said.

"Have I been lost?" Maddy asked, popping another blueberry in her mouth.

"No, because I won't let you out of my sight."

Deanna stood and held her bucket up. "With my full one and your half bucket, we'll have enough to last a couple of months at least."

"Yes, we probably better get back to the Pound," Aaron said, dumping his berries on top of Maddy's. "I guess we have to concede that your mother is the best blueberry picker around."

They paid the blueberry grower and headed back.

⁓

The following week, the trio, plus dog and a picnic lunch, took another trip, this time to Camden Hills State Park. The scenery reminded Aaron of Leadbetter Point, the northern tip of the peninsula, a place he had explored many times over. He was itching to hike again. It was awesome to be out there alone with his thoughts. He might do the Pacific Crest Trail next. It ran from Mexico north into Canada.

Maddy clapped her hands in the backseat. "We're going on a picnic, a picnic, a picnic!"

"I'd say she's wound up," Deanna said. The car window was down, and Deanna's hair blew in the breeze.

They stopped and got out. The sky was a clear blue, the air warm. Maddy soon shed her jacket and ran around in circles. Murphy ran after a ball Aaron usually kept in his pocket. He turned to take the picnic basket from Deanna.

"I'll find a picnic table," he offered.

"Let's sit on a blanket instead. There's always a blanket in the trunk."

"Okay. Sure."

As the sun hit her hair and face, Aaron suddenly wanted to take her into his arms and just hold her.

"Aaron, do you see yourself going home one day?"

"I don't know." He looked away, not wanting to talk about it, yet wanting her to know. "I have three older brothers. Thomas, Luke, and John. My father held the family together after my mother died by her own hand when I was seven."

"Oh, Aaron, I'm so sorry to hear that. . . ."

"My father shut out happy things. Hugging times. Family picnics. If it hadn't been for my grandparents, we probably wouldn't have had Christmas. Then there was Cora."

"A family member?"

"No. Cora's just, well, Cora. She lives in Oysterville, and when marriage plans didn't work out, she needed someone to care for, so she took us motherless kids on, you might say."

Deanna smiled. "She's the one who made the banana-nut pancakes."

"Yeah, that's right."

Maddy ran up and grabbed Aaron's arm. "Come play Frisbee with me and Murph."

"Maddy, can you wait just a minute?" her mother asked.

Aaron touched her shoulder. "Hey, it's okay. We'll talk again later."

"Promise?"

Aaron crossed his heart. "Yes, promise. Now come on and play with us."

Of course Murphy was the best Frisbee catcher of the four. Sometimes he didn't want to give it up and played tug-of-war.

"I say we eat lunch," Deanna said, "then we can go on a short hike."

"A hike?" Maddy asked.

"Yes, it's like a walk," Deanna explained as she unwrapped sandwiches.

"Oh. Where do we go?"

"Probably down by the water and up through the woods," Aaron said.

"Not that we can keep up with a real hiker," Deanna said.

The lunch was finished in no time, and then they walked along one of the marked trails. Murphy had to be leashed, and he didn't like it, but he had to protect his family. They walked for a half hour, until Maddy asked to be held.

"Maybe we should go back," Deanna suggested.

"I don't mind carrying her," Aaron said, feeling the little head rest on his chest. By the time they got back to the picnic site, Maddy was asleep. Aaron let Deanna take her and lay her on the blanket.

"I like that little girl," Aaron said. Deanna smiled and shyly took his hand as they sat side by side on the far end of the blanket.

"I know you do, Aaron."

Aaron traced her fingers. They were long and graceful, and he wondered what a ring would look like on her left hand. It could be a ring of hope, because they both had hurts to get over. He pushed the thought out of his mind as fast as it had come.

"Aaron, do you think you might stop running one day? I truly wish you would call your father and tell him where you are. Even if you don't go back—and maybe you don't want to, or maybe you do—but just to let him know that you're alive would be the right thing to do."

He grabbed a blade of grass and tore it into little bits. "I know what you say is true, but I just can't. Not yet."

"You were just a kid when you ran away. Boys do impulsive things. Besides, you were hurting, and it sounds as if there was nobody there for you to turn to."

Aaron pulled away. Deanna didn't know about Hannah. He wondered what she would think then.

Another family came to the small wayside park, and their dog barked when he saw Murphy. Maddy cried out as she sat up and rubbed her eyes. "Where am I?"

"Honey, you're just fine. You're with your mother and me." He held her close and rocked her in his arms. She laid her little head on his shoulder and closed her eyes, as if aware that no harm would come to her.

Aaron's fingers went through the curls. She was so like her mother. A feeling of wanting to protect her rushed over him.

"Here is your sweater," Deanna said, leaning over. She brushed against his arm, and once again he had to control himself to keep from grabbing her and pulling her down on the blanket.

"I suppose we should head back," Deanna said, as if she had guessed what he was thinking.

"Yes. It's almost three now."

Deanna linked her arm through Aaron's, and he gently patted her arm.

"I suppose if I'm to move on, I need to do it before the first snow flies."

Deanna stopped walking, and the sunshine went out of her smile. "Yes, I suppose you should."

Maddy patted his face. "I love you, Aaron."

He hugged her. "And I love you, Miss Madison."

"Promise me one thing, Aaron," Deanna said then.

"What's that?"

"That when you go back to Oysterville and your life there, that you will remember us and write and let us know how you are doing. That isn't too hard of a promise to keep, is it?"

❦

Aaron wanted to say that he didn't want to go back, that he thought he would miss her too much, but he couldn't say that. She might misunderstand. She might feel obligated into loving him back.

"Of course, we'll keep in touch!"

They trudged back to the car, each with their own thoughts while Maddy chattered on, as if everyone was listening.

The light was on in the Lobster Pound, and two cars were in the parking lot.

"Are we late?" Deanna asked, looking distressed.

"No, I don't think so."

"I hope Dad's okay."

"Deanna, I think he can handle it. Don't worry."

She gave him a look as if to say, "That's easy for you to say."

Mick had butter melting in the large pan, had sliced the French bread, and had turned on the water to boil in the huge vat. He glanced up and waved. "So? Was it fun?"

"Yes, Dad. Are you okay?"

"Of course. Why wouldn't I be?"

"We aren't late."

"No, but a car drove in, so I came on down and got things rolling."

In no time Deanna had the plates out, the silverware set in the tray, and napkins stacked on a second tray.

"Was it a good day?"

"Excellent." That came from Aaron. "I know why people love Maine and cannot leave."

Deanna looked up, as if puzzled and wondering if he was referring to the place or the people. She said nothing. She turned toward her father.

"Dad, did you have your nap?"

"Yes, now will you stop your fretting?"

Orders were placed, and the people went to the upper floor, waiting for their lobster.

The night turned out to be more than mildly busy. Most customers were tourists spending the last few days of their autumn vacations.

"We read about this lobster pound and decided to try you out. Did you know there's a review on the Internet?" a family from Kansas asked.

"Is that a fact?" Mick shook his head. "Modern-day technology is something else!"

Aaron had offered to set up the pound with a computer and a better way to keep track of customers, orders, and figures for taxes, if nothing else. He hadn't known much about computers until he worked for the lumber company, and in a week he'd taken a crash course, as they needed to be computerized, but nobody was ready to do it. Aaron, being the last one hired, was elected to learn. And learn he did.

Aaron took two lobsters up to waiting customers, then hurried back down for another pair. It looked like it would be one of those nights when people kept coming in, and they'd use most of the lobsters out of the holding tank. Even though there were other items on the menu, most people wanted lobster. GB was ill and had not gone out since Tuesday; it was now Thursday.

When Aaron came down for at least the tenth time, Deanna reached over and kissed his cheek. "Just because you're so cute."

"Oh, yeah?" He briefly pulled her close with one arm, in a partial embrace, before releasing her and running back upstairs with yet another order.

They made several pots of coffee, emptied out the large ice chest full of sodas, and people still came.

"Must have been the glorious weather. Guess it makes people hungry for lobster," Aaron offered.

"Tail end of the tourist season," Deanna said.

"Some have heard about Deanna's homemade apple pie," Mick quipped.

"Dad! I don't make apple pie for the Pound."

"No, but I've been thinking it would be a good idea."

Aaron laughed, and soon Deanna, seeing the humor, joined in the laughter.

"Actually, it should be blueberry pie, though, not apple. Maine is known for its blueberries. Or maybe cranberry-apple."

"We grow cranberries in Washington State," Aaron said. "Not as many as you do here, but we're second in the nation."

"I thought you westerners harvested apples, not cranberries," Mick said.

"We do. But cranberries do well near the bay side, not far from where I used to live."

"You going back?" Mick asked.

Aaron removed another lobster from the vat and plopped it on a plate. "I don't know yet."

"You'll always have a job here," Mick said. "Just want you to know that."

And you'll always have a place in my heart, Deanna wanted to say. Instead she quipped, "Yes, you wash down those floors and tables better than anyone we've had."

She then wanted to kick herself for sounding so inane.

"And I appreciate your offer, Mick," Aaron said. "I guess I don't know what I want to be when I grow up."

Maddy, who was in the office and seemingly not paying attention, hopped down from the chair and came over with her opinion. "And when I grow up, I'm going to marry Aaron!"

When everyone laughed, she looked perplexed, as if wondering what she'd said that was funny. It was very real to her.

At nine the neon sign went off, and it was another hour of partial cleanup. As people left, all claiming it was the best lobster they'd ever had, Aaron knew he could be happy here. He'd never had a doubt about it. And he could be happy with Deanna and her child, and yet. . . Talking about his father and his family earlier had made him realize that he needed to take action, needed to talk to his father again, perhaps apologize and start over with a clean slate. That is, if his father were able to forgive him.

There was clam chowder and toast with honey butter for supper. After they'd all eaten, Aaron said good night. He needed more sleep than he'd been getting.

There were just too many things to think about, and his sleep had suffered. Soon he'd make up his mind about what to do, and then maybe he'd sleep peacefully.

"Aaron!" Deanna caught him at the bottom of the steps. "It was a wonderful day, and I just wanted to thank you."

"Ditto," he said, taking off his cap and looking in her direction. "We'll do it again. Good night."

His heart that had felt lighter suddenly went heavy. Deanna did that. With her sweet smile and kind words, he would think of how it would be to have her by his side, working together to perhaps build a house, to share their life, have a child or two to go along with Maddy. But he was in no position to offer her his pledge, his love, or any promises.

Once back at the cottage, he dug out his photo album, which had fallen to the bottom of the duffel bag. Not once had he looked at it in all these years since running off. He knew it was there, and that thought lent him comfort, but he had not been able to look at the photos. Not those of Hannah or of him and Hannah playing in the sand at the water's edge. Not the one, the only one, he had of his mother in a dark suit and a slight smile. She'd been going away that day, his father told him, going to Seattle where she'd start her life over. It had lasted three years before the depression got the better of her and she killed herself to escape, because she really was, in her words, "not a nice person."

Another photo showed the four boys lined up on the deck with trees in the background. There were also photos of his grandparents and a few of his father as a child. And one on his parents' wedding day.

It was his family, his beginning. He belonged there, not here. He would go back. He just had to make enough money to set aside, after paying rent, for a trip to Oysterville. He wasn't sure why it was suddenly clear, but it might have something to do with prayer and how he had asked God for answers.

Chapter 12

Deanna announced Friday morning that she was going out on the boat to check the traps since GB was still ill.

"He should go to the doctor, but he's stubborn like someone else I know," she said. Her father stuck his cherry wood pipe in his mouth and just glared. She invited Aaron to ride along as her sternman. She would empty the traps since Aaron wasn't licensed, but he could help by adding fresh bait. Maddy would stay with Velma Cole from church.

"But I want to go with you," Maddy protested, tossing her coat aside. "It's fun in the boat."

"You'd be totally bored," Deanna said in her firm, no-nonsense voice. "We're going to be out there until past your naptime. You can come another time."

Her lip stuck out. "Promise?"

"Of course I promise. We'll find something fun for you to do. Maybe rent a movie."

They dropped Maddy off, complete with a sandwich, banana, and two cookies in Deanna's old Cinderella lunch box. The little girl ran over to hug Velma Cole.

"We'll be back as soon as we can."

"No problem."

The sun beat down out of a cloudless blue sky, with a few wispy clouds on the far horizon.

"No storm today," Deanna said as they drove back to the Pound and hurried down to the docks. She couldn't help thinking about Bobby, though. Would the fear ever leave her completely?

The *Sylvia Ann*—named for Deanna's mother—bobbed up and down, as if waiting to be taken out to do her job.

They'd stopped long enough to put on rain gear and hats. Aaron held the boat while Deanna got in, untied the rope, and jumped in.

"Our buoys are green and white with a small ring of yellow. I think GB said there should be about fifty out there."

"Fifty!"

"Several are on one line, you know."

Well, no, he didn't know. Lobstering was definitely different than crabbing.

They jetted across the river and up the bay, wind blowing into their faces. Aaron sat up front with Deanna, thinking how cute she looked, so tiny and almost engulfed by her heavy rain gear. Surely they wouldn't need it today, but she said it was always better to wear it, as it often was blustery and rainy as they went out a ways.

"I think we'll come back with twenty lobsters," Aaron said then. "What do you guess?"

Deanna laughed, pushing a stubborn lock of hair back from her forehead. "I'll say thirty."

"Seems GB has been bringing in an average of twenty, at least since I've been working here."

"That's why we're going to get more, since the traps haven't been checked for a few days."

A row of buoys loomed up in the distance, and Aaron got the pulley and winch ready, but Deanna did the pulling.

"Rock crabs!" she said in disgust. "Toss 'em!"

Aaron threw them back into the water, then baited the empty traps and lowered them back in.

The next one held two baby lobsters. Aaron measured them after Deanna showed him how.

"Too small," he said, tossing them overboard.

The next trap held a female. "Look at the eggs!" Deanna said, pointing.

Aaron looked at the creature's underside, studying the minute particles. There were thousands of eggs.

"She's been marked." She pointed out the notch. "Someone has caught her before and put her back."

"You never keep the female, then?"

"Not us. Some have been known to scrape the eggs off and keep them. If they're caught, it's a heavy fine."

There was only one lobster large enough to keep. It went in the holding bin. Soon the pots were full of bait and lowered into the water.

"One lobster doesn't look very good."

"We've got a lot more to check."

A boat zoomed past, and Deanna waved. "That's Mr. Pendlebury. He owned a rival pound down the road apiece, but he retired last year and just likes to be out in the water every day."

He waved back as he went back toward the harbor.

More rock crabs were found in two pots, and one trap was broken. "Some conniving lobster figured out how to escape." Deanna laughed. "We'll get him next time! Dad can repair it."

Bottom fish, a huge hunk of seaweed, and a few other miscellaneous fish were caught. On the next to last trap in the string, ten lobsters were legal size, and keepers.

Aaron banded their claws so they wouldn't snap and dumped them into the tank.

"They're vultures. Vultures of the sea," Deanna said, looking back at Aaron. "When did you first go out on the water?"

They drifted along aimlessly now, the motor humming. "I was probably Maddy's age." She leaned back and gazed overhead. "I can't remember ever not being in a boat. It was more natural to me than riding in the car. The only time we rode in a car was Sunday on our way to church. How about you?"

"I wasn't that young, but I went out on a neighbor's crabbing boat when I was about seven."

Deanna opened the lunch sack and produced two thick meat loaf sandwiches, two pickles, bananas, and chocolate chip cookies. Seagulls soared overhead, swooping down as if expecting scraps.

"Gulls certainly are vultures," Deanna said, throwing her crust in the air.

"That's because you feed them."

"Well, they look pretty the way they zero in on the target."

"And fight over it. . . Hey, this is the same thing Maddy had."

"I know. That's what was in the refrigerator."

"I love your meat loaf."

"Why, thank you!"

They leaned back and finished their meal. Aaron was missing one thing: his harmonica. Many times he'd wished he had it with him, especially when hiking the trail. Music soothed him. He decided to tell Deanna about oysters.

"It wasn't that way with me. I mean, about growing up on a boat. Oysters are different than crabs or your lobsters. The crabbers go out in a boat; they set the pots and go back later to retrieve them. Oysters grow on strings that have been put down in the water. It's quite a process but not nearly as interesting as going out in the boat every day. You put on hip boots and work when the tide is out. When you come back in from working, you smell to high heaven."

"I guess we had oysters here in Maine once, but lobsters are the thing now."

"How long have you had the Pound?"

"Grandpa got a loan from the government right after World War II, and Dad took over the operation from him."

"And you will take it over next."

Deanna frowned. "I doubt it. GB will have something to say about that."

"What if he doesn't want to lobster anymore?"

"Oh, he will."

Aaron remembered Mick's words but dropped the subject, as apparently Mick had not yet talked to his daughter about his concerns.

"Was your childhood happy?" Aaron asked next.

"Oh my, yes. Very happy, except later on when GB decided he didn't like me."

"You were Daddy's pet."

"And the baby, so I got more attention. My father married late, and Mother didn't think she could have any children. Finally, ten years later, GB comes along.

They must have doted on him something fierce. He was eight when I was born, and you know the old saying, 'his nose got cut off.'"

"I had the opposite." Aaron leaned back against a boat cushion.

"Because you were the youngest?"

"Youngest boy, yes. It's not an enviable position, believe me."

"So I've heard."

"Mom had us boys close together, and Dad said she never wanted more than one."

"Why did she keep having babies, then?"

"I have no clue."

"A child should always be wanted," Deanna added.

Aaron nodded. "I couldn't agree more. When my sister, Hannah, was born, she was so sick, they thought she'd die before she came home from the hospital."

"Really? What was wrong?" Deanna asked.

"Cystic fibrosis."

"Oh, I know a couple from church with a daughter who has CF. We've prayed for the family many times." She touched his arm. "I had no idea, Aaron. I'm so sorry."

"Yeah. Cystic fibrosis is not fun. Some live longer than others, and Hannah did at that, but I don't call it living. Not the way it was the last year before I left."

"You couldn't stay to watch her die. . . ."

It was the first time Aaron had let himself talk about it, but there was something about Deanna that made him open up. She was a good listener. She acted as if she cared. And caring was something he had not had from anyone in Oysterville, not after the trips to Portland stopped. He'd not been in school then, and he enjoyed the time alone with his father. Cora had been kind to him. Cora, who had come to help out after his aunt died, then stayed on.

They finished lunch, and Deanna put the wrappers in a plastic bag. "I think we better be on our way, though I could stay out here the entire day. It's good to be on the water again. Good to drive the boat. And good to have such nice companionship."

"Ditto," said Aaron.

Deanna picked up speed, heading toward the next row of buoys bobbing in the water. The water was still calm, but clouds had moved in across the sky from the north.

"Do those clouds mean a storm?" Aaron asked an hour later as he cleared out the last pot. They now had an even dozen lobsters. There was one more row of pots to check. He couldn't believe it was two o'clock. The time had zipped by so fast.

"I think we'll get some rain, yes, but it's not windy, so I'm heading out for the next batch of traps."

Finally, they hit it big-time. Each trap had at least one lobster that was big enough to keep. "I'm keeping count, and so far we have twenty-five, so we both win," Aaron said.

"Wait! I forgot about one more. GB doesn't always put out this many, but I think I see our buoy in the distance."

They sped to the spot where she'd pointed, and there they were.

"Of course you had to win," Aaron said. "I concede."

"The odds were in my favor." She gave Aaron a playful swat on the arm. "Besides, I'm the owner."

Aaron didn't want the day to end. If he had his way, he'd be coming out every morning to set and check the traps. He loved the water, the smell of it, the wind in his face, the way the salt water tasted. He would never tire of this job.

"I can see you're enjoying yourself."

"It shows?"

"Oh, yes."

She reached over and took his hand. "I wouldn't mind having you for a fishing partner any day of the week. Too bad GB wouldn't trade off, but he won't. I just know he won't. And you'd need to be licensed, anyway."

"Maybe someday."

"Aaron, you could get licensed, you know. It's something to think about. That is, if you stay. . ."

Aaron said nothing. He did not know what he was going to do.

"You're a wonderful person," she continued. "You show genuine concern, and you're so good with Maddy. Murph adores you, and my father took to you right off."

"I hope you're pleased with our efforts of the day," Aaron said in an attempt to change the subject.

"Oh, I am." Her eyes lit up. "And how about you?"

"Very much so."

"I think that one lobster may be one of the largest we've ever caught. I'll have to see the measurements in the log Dad keeps."

A sudden wind gust gently rocked the boat; they were about two miles from shore. Deanna glanced to the north, her eyes widening.

"It's a squall. We must have relaxed too long out here."

"I didn't feel it getting cold or anything."

"Neither did I."

She pushed the throttle down, and the boat lurched forward, then stopped. "Oh, no. Something's wrong." She tried the engine again. Nothing.

"Do you have gas?"

"I'm sure we do. GB fills the tank the night before. Unless he forgot. . ."

Her eyes grew wider. "We've run out of gas before. We'll just need to paddle in, that's all." She handed Aaron an oar.

❧

The outline of the harbor was visible in the distance, and Deanna knew they could make it in before the storm hit if she didn't panic. It was a large craft, but if they both paddled hard, it was possible. She tried not to think about the pending storm and Bobby. But all the terror, the waiting, watching, and praying washed over her now like a giant wave, and she found her mind turning toward God, asking Him to let them return safely.

"Is this what they mean by a nor'easter?" Aaron yelled over the sudden sound of crashing waves.

"Yes!" Deanna yelled back. They were so close, yet made no headway with the paddling. It was as if the tide were pulling them out to sea.

"How about the CB?" Aaron asked.

"The light's off—I think the battery's dead!"

Another huge wave crashed against the boat, soaking them as water splashed over the hull.

"We need to bail," Aaron shouted.

"No!" Deanna shook her head. "Keep rowing. I can't manage both oars. Her arms ached, but she had to keep going. She thought of Maddy. Precious little Maddy. "Oh, Lord," she prayed, "please help us to get ashore."

"We'll make it!" Aaron shouted back.

She glanced at him, this young man she barely knew. Was he scared, too? *Trust Me,* a voice echoed through her thoughts. *Put your faith in Me. . . .* And she felt her body relax as the fear lifted from her spirit.

"Yes, we're going to make it," Deanna shouted back.

The rain came then, in slanting sheets, just as a light in the distance bobbed toward them.

"Someone's coming to help," Deanna said. Her hands were red and numb from the constant beating of the water.

"You out of gas?" a voice bellowed.

"Yes!" Deanna yelled back, taking a deep breath as another gust of wind hit. "Mr. Pendlebury, you're a godsend."

"I have an extra gas can. I'll try to pull alongside!"

Both boats rocked together, threatening to tear into each other as another gust of wind hit hard, but finally, Aaron grabbed the can. Soon the gas was in the tank, and the boat started right up.

"Phew!" Aaron said with relief.

"Thanks!" Deanna shouted as they headed toward shore—and home.

GB was waiting at the dock, his ample arms crossed, his long raincoat flapping against his legs. "Had a little trouble, I see," he said, shouting against the wind.

"You didn't fill the gas tank!"

"You should have checked," he yelled back. "Or Aaron should have thought of it, since you're a woman and women are known to get rattled."

"Just a minute, GB; that's not fair. I can drive this boat as well as you can, even if I haven't manned it since Maddy's birth."

"Still," he gave her a hand, leaving Aaron to fend for himself. "Still," he repeated, "seems you would remember that was the number-one rule."

"Oh!" She shot past him and on up the ramp. He could be so infuriating. "I'm going after Maddy," she called over her shoulder, shedding her rain gear and reaching for a towel.

Fuming, she sped over the miles to pick up her child. She'd been scared as memories of Bobby filled her mind, yet the water and boating were her whole life. Why hadn't she checked the gas gauge? And why hadn't she seen the storm coming? Life was precious to her now, now that she had a little one to care for. She would not take chances like that again.

Maddy came running when she heard her mother's voice.

"Mommy, your hair is all wet and yucky!"

"I know, honey. A storm blew in, and we ran out of gas. I thought I'd never feel the hard ground beneath my feet again."

"How about a cup of green tea?" Velma asked. "That should warm you up."

"Tea sounds wonderful." She eased into the nearest chair and pulled her child onto her lap. She caressed the dark curls, loving the feel of her chubby little body. Deanna didn't care if she got back in time to help at the Pound. Let GB do it, along with Aaron and her father. Besides, she didn't want to face GB again with his knowing sneer, his "I can't believe you did that" maddening grin.

"Did this boat problem just happen?" Velma asked, bringing the teapot to the table.

"Yes."

"I knew it," Velma said with a nod. "I felt led to pray around three. I didn't know why, but when God puts something on my heart, I stop whatever I'm doing and just pray."

"Oh, Mrs. Cole!" The tears began again, and this time Deanna let them fall.

The older woman held her close. "There now, you just cry all you want. Tears are cleansing, you know."

"Mommy, what's wrong?" Maddy hopped over and looked into her mother's face. Velma handed her a tissue.

"Mommy's just so glad to be here with you. Don't worry about me crying."

Soon Maddy had a small cup of tea, half cream and a heaping spoon of sugar. She dipped animal crackers in the tea and said, "Yummy!"

Velma laughed. "Doesn't take much to amuse a child."

"I like it when we have tea, Mommy," Maddy said, hugging her mother. "Oooh, you're still wet and cold."

"That's why I suggested the tea," Velma said. "There's nothing as refreshing as a cup of hot tea."

"But I really do need to go now," Deanna said, pushing her chair back. "What do I owe you?"

"What! You think I'd charge for taking care of my best friend's granddaughter?" Velma's eyes suddenly grew moist. "Oh, but I miss that mother of yours. Sylvia and I did the zaniest things together!"

"Oh, I know—yes, I know." Deanna hugged her hard. "And I miss her so, too."

"She'd want you to be happy, Deanna. You know that, right?"

"Yes."

"I think something is going on in your life right now, and I say grab hold and hold on tight."

Deanna wished she could believe Velma Cole's words. If only she knew what Aaron was thinking. If only she could see some sign of affection. His eyes told her he was interested, but nothing ever happened. And even though they were comfortable together—like today out in the boat—she feared it would go no further, and soon he'd be on his way again. She had to wait. What did it say in the Bible about patience? She had lacked it all her life, so maybe it was time she learned.

⁂

Aaron was in the open area of the Pound, watching the road, as if waiting for Deanna's car to appear. When she came down the hill, he hurried up and opened the door. "Are you okay? Is Maddy all right?"

"Yes, why do you ask?"

"Hi, Aaron," Maddy called from the backseat as she unbuckled her car seat.

"I thought you'd be right back."

"I was tired and wet and cold and was offered a cup of tea. I hope that was okay."

He stepped back, looking puzzled. "Have I done something wrong?"

And at that question, she turned and hurried up to the house, carrying Maddy like a sack of potatoes.

Why didn't I answer him? she wondered later. Why had she left him standing there with that near hopeless look on his face? Why had she burst into tears before getting into the sanctuary of the house? Why had the day turned out with her feeling stupid and inept? And had GB failed to put in gas on purpose, or did it happen because he'd been ill lately? Maybe she should give him the benefit of the doubt. As for Aaron, she'd apologize for her bad behavior when he came into the house tonight. She hoped he would still come and that he didn't carry a grudge. She couldn't bear for him to be angry with her.

Chapter 13

I decided if I ever got through that winter up north logging, I'd be able to survive anywhere."

It was late one night, and Deanna, Mick, and Aaron sat around the fire munching popcorn and halfway watching a news documentary on TV.

"I'd never survive a winter in the wilds," Mick said, moving closer to the fire. "The old bones wouldn't take it."

"Not that you'd ever need to worry about it, Dad." Deanna leaned over and patted her father's hand. The gesture was not lost on Aaron. He liked the way she catered to the old man, because it was done out of love, not duty. He wished, oh, how many times had he wished, for such a relationship with his father.

"I think my days in the wilds of winter are over, too," Aaron said, leaning back. "I like the comforts of a nice fire, a full stomach, and being able to put my feet up."

Evenings were often spent talking, reliving the past, as Mick liked to do, and snacking on something Deanna whipped up in the kitchen.

"Never logged," Mick went on. "Always wanted to try it, but I guess it will have to be in my other life now."

"As if you believed that," Deanna said.

Often the discussions led to religion. Aaron listened while Deanna espoused her faith, her belief in a higher being. Aaron wanted to ask why God allowed tragedies to happen, why he took a young child from a parent's loving arms, why he let a father drown at sea.

"God wants us to lean on Him," Deanna said, as if reading Aaron's mind. "Oswald Chambers said if there were no valleys, we'd never know the thrill of the mountaintop experience. Things happen because people are disobeying God's laws."

"Hey, I can relate to that mountaintop thing," Aaron said. "That's what I feel when I'm hiking."

" 'Love ye one another,' the second greatest commandment of all," Deanna added.

"And love the Lord your God with all your heart, soul, strength and might." Aaron grinned. "Did I get that in the right order?"

"I don't think the order matters that much."

Mick held up his empty coffee mug. "Just a tad more, honey. It's decaf, right?"

"Of course, Dad."

"Here, allow me." Aaron was on his feet, taking the mug and pouring a bit more for himself, as well. Comfort. Ease. Relaxation. He couldn't remember a time when he and his father, brothers, and Hannah had sat around the living room enjoying each other's company. It simply had not happened. Was it because of Hannah's illness? Perhaps it was because they didn't have a mother. But there was no mother here. Mick and Deanna talked, laughed, and debated, yet no cross words were spoken. Mick's voice rose from time to time, but Deanna was calm and collected. He wondered how she did that. Yet he knew she could get angry, remembering the day on the boat.

"How about your family?" Mick asked then, as if he'd been reading Aaron's mind. "What did you do of an evening?"

"Nothing like this," Aaron said. "We weren't into discussing things. We each went our own way. Hannah needed lots of attention, especially in the last few years of her life, so Dad spent every moment doing for her."

"And your mother?"

"My mother left the family when I was four or so. She's dead now."

"Oh, lad, I'm sorry to hear that."

Aaron drained the last of his coffee and rose to his feet. "Suppose I'd better get back to my place." He caught Deanna's glance and nodded. He didn't want to leave, but sometimes you had to do what you had to do.

❧

Long after Aaron left and her father had gone to bed, Deanna sat in the semi-darkness, wondering why Aaron was uncomfortable when talking about his past. Everyone had problems, and nobody was perfect. And sickness was rampant, at least in the families she knew. If he could just talk about it, he might feel better. He claimed to believe in God, but his actions didn't always show it. He was troubled, and she wanted to ease the pain if he'd just let her get close.

Still, thoughts of getting close to Aaron made her breath come in fast gulps. This felt different from how it had been with Bobby. Bobby had been her first love, and somewhere Deanna had read that first loves were unique. She was older now and, she believed, wiser. She was a mother and had been a wife; she worked hard. Her life had been good. The one thing she lacked, the thing she wanted more than anything, was to find someone with whom to share those precious moments, someone to trust and confide in, someone to love and to love her back. Was it going to happen one day?

She picked up the framed photo of her parents on their twenty-fifth anniversary, which was shortly before her mother's death. Even then the cancer was working on her, but she did not know it. Her mother looked so young and beautiful. Deanna had been only fifteen; GB was twenty-three. She wasn't one to complain, just as her father wasn't.

"You have your mother's gentle ways," her father often told her. "You're also pretty, but not as pretty as my Sylvie was. Nobody has ever been that pretty."

Her mother was a New Hampshire girl who had come to Maine on vacation.

She had met Mick at the Lobster Pound, where she and her family had a meal. Mick, fresh out of the navy after a six-year stint, ran it with his father, who had also been a navy man.

"I knew from the moment she first smiled at me that she was the one. I had to wait, though. She was too young, lived too far away. But we corresponded. And I was like a 'smitten puppy' as my father said."

Deanna never tired of hearing the story. She remembered Grandfather Nelson, also, though he had died when she was ten. She wondered what it would be like to wait five years for the person you loved. Could she wait five years for Aaron? Would it take him that long to find what he was searching for? Would he want to take her along, to be yoked with him for the rest of his life? She could settle for nothing less.

"You like him, don't you?" her father had said the second day after Aaron arrived. "I can tell, you know."

"Dad, he's such a nice man, but I honestly don't know what I feel right now."

"Don't hide your feelings, child. Go as the Lord leads you. He's guided you before, and He'll guide you again."

Deanna wondered why the words haunted her now. What she wanted was to bundle up and go for a walk, but she wasn't prepared to run into Aaron again. She put her feet up on the coffee table, thankful that Aaron had stumbled onto the Nelson Lobster Pound. God had led him here; she believed it with her whole heart. And God would turn his life around; she was positive of that, too.

The last flame went out, with only the embers remaining. It made her think of her heart and how it felt right now. Bereft, without Bobby. But Bobby was gone. It was time to move on, time to build another fire, just like this fire would be rekindled tomorrow evening. A passage of scripture from the third chapter of Ecclesiastes came to mind: *To every thing there is a season, and a time to every purpose under the heaven. . . . A time to weep, and a time to laugh; a time to mourn, and a time to dance.*

She had wept when her mother died and again when Bobby drowned. There had also been happy times. She'd beamed with pride when her newborn had been laid in her waiting arms. She'd laughed when her baby first recognized her face, when Madison heard her name and smiled, when she walked and talked and her hair turned curly. Mourning came with the deaths, but after mourning was a time to dance, a time to move on. Yes, it was time for her. Was it going to be time for Aaron, as well?

Deanna looked back at the embers and took the cups to the kitchen. Enough time spent on memories.

❦

Aaron wondered if God had put these thoughts about Deanna in his mind. He liked the way her eyes lit up when he entered the room.

The cottage was cold, but he didn't turn on the heat. He'd clean up and go to bed. Tonight he wanted to read scriptures. There was something she'd said that he wanted to see if he could find. He remembered hearing the verses before, something about everything in its own time. He wondered where he'd find it. He should have asked her. Somehow he knew she would know exactly what book it was in.

He read a few psalms, deciding he'd do the search tomorrow. And maybe he'd just ask Deanna, swallow his pride, and show his difficulty with remembering Bible verses. That was okay, wasn't it? Not everyone could remember where to find what. The Bible was a huge book. His mother hadn't believed, or she wouldn't have done what she did. His aunt had told him that people were never in their right minds when they committed suicide. Was that true? He wished he could remember more about his mother, but the main thing was the constant weeping. He could hear her, as his bedroom was directly below his parents' room. Loud voices always sounded before the crying began. Sometimes his father would leave, and Aaron would hunker down, wondering where his father was going and wishing he had stayed. Wishing his mother would stop crying. And wishing he wouldn't waken to hear Hannah crying, then coughing—always coughing.

The brothers, being older, worked in the oysters, and Aaron remembered going down to the bay when he was six or seven and being shown how to do it. He'd never liked the work, always wishing he could be in one of the crabbing boats that went up the bay to set out their pots. Why hadn't his father chosen that kind of work? It wasn't as messy.

Of course he hadn't known then that crabbing was messy, too. And hard work. Still, it was his dream to one day own a boat, to be respected as an upstanding member of the community. And if it happened, how would his father react? He knew his three older brothers didn't care. Nobody really did, so why should he return to Oysterville?

He thought of Cora, who had tried to be a mother. She'd be there when he returned from school, offering him a plate of cookies and a glass of milk. He also saw how she watched his father and had a feeling that Cora was there, not because of the kids, but because of Leighton. He wondered if his father even knew. And was she still there taking care of things, running the house and cooking meals, keeping the cookie jar full? He imagined she probably was.

He closed the Bible, glad he'd brought it, though he hadn't read it much in the past few years. Could he ever have a strong faith like Deanna and her father? Was that what gave them such peace, made them rely on, love, and care for each other? Was it what put the smile on Deanna's lips? What made her work hard and take care of things, then begin the whole process over again the next day? Faithful. That was a word to describe her. She was faithful to all—her God and her family.

He opened the curtain and looked out into the inky darkness. He liked the cottage. He wondered how the young couple had managed. It seemed small for two, but when you're in love, you want to be close. Would he ever find closeness or such solace?

Chapter 14

Mick announced one day in early November that he had decided to follow Aaron's earlier suggestion and get the Pound computerized.

GB protested. "Dad, we've been getting along just fine without it; why add an extra expense now?"

"What's wrong? Are you afraid you'll lose some of your inheritance?"

"Dad! That's not fair."

"Well, it's the truth, isn't it?" He chewed on his beloved pipe. "I want to go forward, and it bothers you. I say it's because Aaron suggested it. Right? Why don't you like him?"

"He's a no-account drifter."

Mick tapped his pipe on his boot. "He may be a drifter, but I dare say 'no-account' is way too harsh."

"What do you know about him?"

"That he's honest. I know he's a good, hard worker and that he's from the West Coast—a place called Oysterville."

"Why isn't he back there, working in the oysters, then?"

"That part I don't know."

GB shook his head. "Dad, it's going to cost you."

"I know that, Son. But we can get a Web site and take orders with the computer, and it sounds like a great idea. It isn't as if I just jumped in with both feet. Been thinking about it for several weeks now."

"Whatever. I'm going home."

Deanna was pleased when her father and Aaron came home with the computer. They'd gone to Bangor and looked around for the best deal.

"Right now we just need to get this baby set up."

"There's a desk up in the spare bedroom. I think the two of us can handle it." They carried the desk down and set it in a corner of the living room.

"I'll work on this tonight," Aaron said. "Won't take long to get you going. Then I'll give you both lessons."

Mick held up his hand. "I don't want a thing to do with it. Never liked machines."

"Now, Dad, you need to learn, too."

"I'll leave that up to you young folks."

Maddy was more excited about the large box she now had to play with. She crawled in with her favorite bear and blanket. "It's a playhouse," she called out.

"Can I color on it and make windows?"

Deanna laughed. "Of course."

Aaron had the computer up and running a few hours later.

"How do you know about computers?" Mick asked.

"I learned at one of my jobs. They had a computer, and I studied manuals and picked it up. Soon people were asking me to fix computers and printers."

"It's the up and coming thing for sure," Deanna said, sitting down and admiring the colorful screen saver. Maddy was enthralled with the bright colors in all sizes and shapes that kept moving about on the screen.

"I could look at this all day," Deanna said.

"And later on, if you want a change, I can put a photo of Maddy on it."

"You could?"

"Sure. It would be neat, I think."

Deanna learned the first few things she needed to know in order to use the computer—how to sign on and where to find different programs.

"It isn't a play thing," Mick humphed when he saw the Solitaire game on the screen.

"No, it's not. But she needs to learn how to use the mouse, and this is a good way to practice."

A few days later, they had an e-mail address, and the Web site was up and running. Now all they had to do was wait for orders to come in.

There were three orders the following morning. Deanna was impressed. "We might not be able to keep up with this, Dad. Here's an order from Oregon. Can you imagine? A business in Portland, Oregon, wants our lobsters."

GB had to go into the house and see the computer the next day. "Why isn't it in the office?" he asked. "Seems that is where you'd want it."

Deanna shrugged. "Maybe not. It's less damp and cold in the house. I can process orders and things after we close at night."

GB just stared at the screen.

"Here, you want to try?" Deanna urged him.

"Nah. I don't like computers. I don't like cell phones and all this other modern stuff." He turned and barreled out the door.

Aaron showed Deanna how to play another game that night. He told her to beware, because she could get hooked on it. Mick grunted from his easy chair. "Maybe GB's right. Seems this could be a boon, but it could also boomerang."

During the next few days, Deanna explored chat rooms, different Web sites, and e-mailed her cousin in New Hampshire. One day the Missing Persons link piqued her interest, as she hoped to find an old school friend, Lois Ann.

If Aaron hadn't set up the computer and included his name as one of the contact people, there never would have been a message from Courtney Spencer. Deanna stared in disbelief at the words on the screen:

I am seeking a young man named Aaron Walker. He just turned twenty-two. He comes from the West Coast—Washington State to be exact—a small town called Oysterville. Aaron knows a lot about oysters, as his father is an oysterman. He might mention having three older brothers and a sister who died of cystic fibrosis.

He is medium height, has sandy blond hair, and is a friendly sort. If you have any info, please contact me at this e-mail address.

Deanna felt fear rush over her. Fear like she always felt when she thought Aaron might move on. This Courtney had to be an old girlfriend. How else would she know this much about him?

Deanna stared at the message, reading it through two and then three times. She had to tell Aaron. He was at the Pound, getting it ready for tonight's customers. What would he do? Would he pack everything and get out of East Belfast first thing in the morning? What if she didn't tell him? He'd never know. How would he? He left most of the computer work up to her. She took the orders, answered questions, and was enjoying learning about chat rooms and other items of interest. Why had she gone into the Missing Persons link?

Deanna shut off the computer, doing it the way Aaron had showed her, and went upstairs to check on Maddy. The child clutched her bear tight, and the sight of her daughter caused a knot to rise in Deanna's chest. She should never have planned or considered about how it would be if Aaron were to stay, if Aaron fell in love with her, if Aaron would give up his earlier life and be content to stay here. The idea had crossed her mind many times in the weeks since Aaron came. And Maddy loved him. Murphy loved him, too. The big dog loved playing ball and being scratched. Mick had come to rely on the hardy young man. Only GB would rejoice if Aaron left. And leave he would if she told him about this Courtney. Maybe she could bring up the name casually and see if there was any reaction.

Deanna had never been devious in her life. Honesty was her middle name. Once, when a boy had shown interest in her, she'd refused to go out with him because her best friend liked him. No, she had to tell him. But perhaps she could wait a bit longer? That was deceptive, but not totally so. Yet all the while it was as if God were telling her she had to tell him, that it was important that someone reach him. It might not be a girlfriend after all.

Deanna bundled up Maddy when she finally awakened—a jacket and a scarf to keep the wind out of her ears. The wind was fierce this afternoon, and Maddy was inclined to get earaches.

Aaron was readying things in the serving area. "I think we're ready. Doubt that we will have any customers coming in from boats tonight. At least I wouldn't want to be out in this wind."

"I hope GB gets back soon."

"That's right. Shouldn't he be here in ten minutes or so?"

Deanna nodded. She had Maddy go to her little corner to play. Deanna was lucky that Maddy was such a good, cooperative child. She wondered if she ever had a boy, if he'd be mild and quiet like this. She also wondered if he'd have sandy blond hair and ruddy cheeks, or would he be dark-haired like her?

She couldn't not say anything. She just couldn't.

"Do you know someone named Courtney?"

Aaron stopped polishing the counter and glanced over. "Courtney? No, I don't believe so. Why, does someone named Courtney know me?"

A bit of relief went over her. She wasn't a past girlfriend. His face would have given him away. That was one thing she knew about Aaron, had known from that first day. Like her, he was honest. He could not outright lie; she was sure of it.

"Her last name is Spencer."

It was then that Deanna realized Courtney hadn't said where she was from. She could be from anywhere, be anyone. Just someone who liked to surf the net. Yet if this resulted in Aaron going home, returning to Oysterville, it might as well be a girl. He'd pack in a minute and be gone by morning's first light.

"Why do you ask?" Aaron repeated. He stood watching her, as if wondering what was wrong. "Who is this Courtney, and what does she have to do with me?"

She avoided his steady gaze. "You'd better go up and find out for yourself. She left a message on the computer, at the Missing Persons' site."

"She did? You mean someone, after all this time, has tracked me down?"

"Maybe she's been there all along—you just never went to the right place on the Internet."

"I suppose I need to go see about it."

He was off up the hill, throwing a ratty old ball for Murph as he went. Deanna swallowed back the tears. It couldn't be good news. It just couldn't. She hoped he'd find out soon. What if it was about his father—maybe he was dying and needed Aaron? She couldn't try to hold him here then. Fathers were important. She knew how she'd feel if something happened to her father.

Maddy showed her the picture she'd drawn, and Deanna broke down and cried.

The little girl looked up, her hand touching her mother's cheek. "Mommy, is my picture making you sad?"

"Oh, no, honey." She cried even harder as she clutched her close. "It isn't you, sweetie. It's just something else. Mommy doesn't feel very good."

That was true. Her stomach churned, and there was a pain, the pain of loss, in her heart. No way could she tell Maddy that her reason for tears was because she had drawn a small child at a table, a mother, and a father, and they were holding hands as they bowed their heads to say grace. A family. That's what Maddy wanted and needed: a real family.

❧

Aaron turned on the computer and went to the Internet. Five minutes later, he found the message. His breath stopped. Someone named Courtney was looking for him. He didn't know how old the message was or why she was looking for him, but it could be anything. My father. His mind went to Leighton, and he wondered if he could have had a stroke or a heart attack. He sat back, drumming his fingernails on the desktop. He had to find out.

He went into e-mail, typed in the address, and sent a message.

I don't know who you are, Courtney, but I am Aaron Matthew Walker, and I am from Oysterville. What does your message concern? Is it about my father, Leighton Walker? I'll give you the phone number where I am staying. I'm in Maine. Do call and let me know. Thank you—

Aaron Matthew Walker

There certainly could be more than one Aaron Walker, but he doubted that there would be another Aaron Matthew Walker. He waited a full minute before hitting SEND, then his message was on its way.

He turned the computer off and went back down the hill to the Lobster Pound. Strange how one day your life is one way, and you get up the next morning and it all changes. Of course he might not return to Oysterville. He liked it here. When Deanna asked about Courtney, he knew she feared it was an old girlfriend, but he honestly had never known anyone named Courtney.

Deanna glanced up, a look of mixed emotion on her face. "Did you find the message?"

Aaron nodded. "I'm sure it was someone who knows my father. I don't know anyone with that name."

"Maybe he hired her to search for you."

He shrugged. "Could be, I guess." But inside, he asked, *Why did it take him so long? And yet, maybe he has been searching all along.*

"I sent a message back, so we can check later tonight or in the morning."

"I hope it's nothing serious."

"So do I, especially since my car won't make it that far, and I don't have enough money for airfare."

"My father would loan you the money. I know he would."

"Let's just see if this Courtney answers tomorrow."

It wasn't an e-mail message but a phone message on the answering machine awaiting them when they went up the hill to have a late supper.

Deanna pushed the button as a man's deep voice filled the room.

"Aaron, is this the right phone number? Is this my son, Aaron Walker? I am confused, because the recorded message said something about a Lobster Pound. I'm looking for someone named Aaron. Are you there, Little Buddy?"

Aaron jumped to his feet and looked out the window. It was his father, all right. His voice hadn't changed a bit. He balled his fists at his side while the message went on—something about coming home and missing Aaron.

"Here's the number," Deanna said, handing him a sheet of paper.

"Thanks, but I do remember my own phone number. Nothing changes much in Oysterville, especially not phone numbers." He didn't have to look to know that she was chewing on her lower lip.

"Are you going to call?"

"I'll call, but not yet."

"I think you should call now."

Aaron frowned. "I have to think of what I will say."

Deanna felt the tears threaten again. That phone call, if Aaron made it, could change her whole life.

It was a few days before Aaron called. How could he explain his absence and lack of communication?

Aaron also put off getting in touch with his father because he knew it could change his whole life, and he wasn't sure he wanted to do that. Finally he went up to the big house and said he was ready to make the call to Oysterville.

The phone rang just once and then was picked up.

"Hello."

Aaron swallowed hard. "Dad? It's me, Aaron. Your Little Buddy."

"Oh, my. Alice was right. She said you'd call."

"Alice? Who's Alice?"

"A friend whom I hope you will meet if you come home. Her daughter, Courtney, thought about the Internet search. I didn't think it would work."

So that's who Courtney is. But who is Alice? "Dad, I have a job here."

"I figured as much."

"I'd like to come, but well, I can't just up and quit."

"Of course you can't."

"I want to see you."

"Oh, Aaron, how about Thanksgiving? Could you come to see me then?"

Aaron wondered how he could tell his father he had no money. Well, he couldn't. He just couldn't. As it turned out, he need not have worried.

"I'll send the money for a ticket. You find out the cost, and the money will be there."

"Dad, are you sure?"

"Never more sure of anything in my whole life. It's been too long, Son. We have some fences to mend."

"Yes, Dad, we do."

Aaron sat on the edge of Mick's bed and wondered what he would say. He knew the old man would understand, since he was a father. He wasn't sure about Deanna, but it was GB who would rub it in now. "See? I told you he was just a drifter. Well, good riddance, I say!"

Aaron walked back down the steps, listening to the sound of the late news on the TV and the clicking of keyboard keys while Deanna left a message for someone. He walked in and cleared his throat.

"Looks like I'm going to be heading back to Oysterville for Thanksgiving."

"Going to see your family?" Mick asked, looking away from the TV.

"Yes, to see my family."

"Who is Courtney?" Deanna had to know who this woman was who had turned her life upside down.

"She's the daughter of a friend of my father's, and she was certain she'd find me on the Internet."

"And she did." Deanna looked away. "One thing I know for certain," she said, "is that there is going to be one very disappointed little girl when you leave and one unhappy black lab."

"And I believe there's someone else who will feel the same way, though she won't admit it," Mick said.

"Dad!" Deanna's cheeks flushed pink.

Aaron knew she couldn't let him know what she really thought now, how she didn't want him to go. He wanted to tell her that he didn't want to go, either, yet hearing his father's voice had taken away some of the hurt, and he found himself eager and curious. Would his brothers be glad to see him, or would he be like the prodigal son, with the father eager to have a big feast while the boys resented all the attention he might get? It could be interesting. And yet, in spite of all the possible consequences, he found himself needing to find out, wanting to go home at last. Home to Oysterville. . .

Chapter 15

The trip across country was uneventful and definitely took less time than Aaron's cross-country trip to Maine that began five years earlier. This was his first flight. There'd never been a reason to fly before. He liked all of it except taking off.

"Thanks for flying with us today," a flight attendant said as she pointed out the safety measures. Something about her smile made him think of Deanna. Not that he'd ever stopped thinking about her. He really hadn't thought he would react this way. Her face, her smile, the way she touched his arm, haunted him, and he'd thought of little else during the flight.

Deanna had insisted on taking him to the Bangor airport. "No way am I going to let you take the bus there."

"I could, you know."

She sighed. "Of course you could, but I have to see you off."

They talked constantly on the forty-five-mile trip. Impersonal but important things. Such as, if he ever came back, he'd have a job. He knew that. Then they were there, and he told her to go home because she couldn't come down to the waiting area anyway, not with all the security measures now taken at airports.

"Promise to e-mail me," she said as he got his bag out of the trunk.

"I doubt my father has a computer, but I'll write," he called over his shoulder.

She suddenly was out of the car and running toward him. "Aaron, I'm praying for a time of forgiveness, for you to be one with your family again. We'll all miss you, you know."

Then he was kissing her and grabbing her for a longer kiss before leaving to enter the airport terminal. His last glimpse was of her waving and blowing him a kiss.

Aaron closed his eyes in an attempt to sleep. It didn't work. He then read the airline's magazine and ate the breakfast they brought, a muffin that tasted like cardboard.

He looked out over the wing of the plane. The late fall day was clear, then they went in and out of clouds. It was like magic. It became clear again, and he saw farmlands flatter than he could have ever imagined, then they passed over the snow-covered Colorado Rockies, Mount Adams in Washington State, and then Oregon's majestic Mount Hood. They started the descent to land at Portland

International. Would his father and brothers be there to meet him?

The landing took forever, but finally they were on the tarmac and taxiing to the gate.

Soon people popped up, retrieving their luggage from the overhead bins. Aaron had checked in his one bag, as it was too large to fit under the seat or overhead. Though unencumbered by luggage, he let others exit ahead of him. They seemed to be in such a rush. Maybe he should have been, too, but he just wasn't. There was this inner fear that his father would still be angry, that nothing would be resolved.

When he finally got up to the baggage area, a large sign greeted him, and a huge cheer went out: WELCOME HOME, AARON!

A sea of faces enveloped him, and then he felt his father's hug as he was pulled into the older man's grasp.

"I can't believe my Little Buddy has come home."

"Aaron, glad to see you again!" It was his brother, Luke, and children surrounded him. How many kids did he have, anyway?

"Son, I want you to meet Alice, my wife."

Aaron looked into the face of a laughing woman, and he held her proffered hand.

"Dad? You didn't tell me you were married."

"I wanted it to be a surprise."

Aaron was surprised, all right. As far back as he could remember, his father had never dated. Not once. Now here he was married. The warm smile made him feel good, though.

"Courtney, my daughter, the one who found you on the Internet, couldn't make it. Steven Carl, the baby, takes up a lot of time, but she'll be at the house, and we're having a big celebration tonight."

House? What house? They weren't heading for Oysterville now?

Aaron moved with the throng. The contingency was seven people. His father, Alice, his brothers—all three, and two of Luke's children. The wives had stayed home, for what reason, Aaron didn't know. And soon he would meet Courtney; Steven, Courtney's husband; and their baby. It was mind-boggling. To go from having nobody to suddenly belonging to a family again was going to be mighty strange.

Alice's house had been explained to him on the trip. She and his father lived in Portland part of the year, and the rest of the year they lived in Oysterville. That part alone was hard to imagine.

Aaron waited, knowing someone would ask the inevitable question: Why did you run off like that? But so far, nobody had. His brothers drove their vehicles, while he rode with Leighton and Alice.

"We have a wonderful dinner prepared. We will stay here for the night, then go home to Oysterville tomorrow morning," Leighton said.

"I want to e-mail Deanna—let her know I arrived okay."

"Deanna?" Both Leighton and Alice echoed the question.

"Yes, she's the daughter of the man who owns the Lobster Pound where I work. We're just friends."

Leighton and Alice exchanged glances but said nothing.

"Your father and I used to e-mail each other several times a day," Alice said then, playfully hitting her husband's arm. "It's the best way ever to keep in touch."

He didn't write when they first arrived at the house because it was pandemonium. He met Courtney, who had sent the e-mail message, and Steven, who owned a computer business, and got a glimpse of the baby. It was almost too much to comprehend.

"I need to send that message," Aaron said after a dessert of chocolate cake topped with vanilla ice cream. Apparently his father remembered his fondness for chocolate.

Aaron sat in front of the blank screen for a long moment. Why was this difficult? Why was he experiencing this sinking feeling when he thought of what Deanna must be doing now? Because of the three-hour time difference, she would have Maddy in bed and would be in front of the computer playing a game, sending a message to one of her old friends, or sitting in the darkness. He doubted that she'd find his message until tomorrow.

Deanna,

I arrived on time to find a throng of people with a silly sign welcoming me home. I didn't quite know what to say.

My father is married, and that was a shock. It'd be like your father suddenly getting married. You probably wouldn't know how to handle it. I'm having a problem with it, although Alice is nice, and my father seems happy. Alice has a daughter and a grandchild, so I have more than one to get acquainted with. Courtney, her daughter, is the one who first wrote.

As I sit here alone in this room, with noise pouring out from the living room and family room, I find myself wanting to be back in Maine, where it's quiet.

Just wanted to let you know I am fine. Hope you are the same. You can write to me if you want.

Deanna had checked her e-mail every ten minutes, hoping, oh so hoping, that Aaron would write. Her father had shut off the TV at ten, saying she was silly to expect him to keep in touch.

"I love you, Daughter, but sometimes you're not too smart when it comes to men."

"Dad, you don't know that. Aaron and I have something special. I believe with all my heart that God brought him here to us. He went home because he has some things to clear up, but I think he's coming back." A tear slid down her cheek. How could he forget their kiss? It sealed her thoughts and feelings for him, and she knew he had responded with the same. *At least that's what I'm praying,* she thought.

"See you in the morning," her father called, his footsteps clattering up the stairs. "I know the time is different there, but I wouldn't wait up too much longer for a letter." Deanna ran after him to give him a big hug. Above all, she wanted him to know that she loved him. After all, he was the only sure thing in her life, the bit of stability she needed.

The letter came at 11:00 p.m., Maine time.

She read it twice, looking for some small sign that Aaron missed her, that he maybe even loved her. He said he missed the quiet. That she could believe. He said she could write if she wanted.

If? Wild horses couldn't keep her from writing back. But she'd be careful. She couldn't give away her heart and what she felt. She had done so once, and Aaron had not reciprocated. She would not make that mistake again.

> *Aaron,*
>
> *You have no idea how glad I am to hear from you. I knew there would be a bunch of people to meet you. That's the way families are. Sometimes I miss having a big family, people to get together with for holiday dinners.*
> *But I have Dad and Maddy, and that's enough for now.*
> *Dad's gone on to bed, and Maddy has been down for quite some time. Murph is looking for you. I could tell when I came out of the house just before opening the Pound. He kept looking at the door, as if waiting for you to come, then stared down the path, thinking you might appear. If dogs could talk, he'd say he misses you!*
> *Do write again. I want to know how Oysterville looks and all your old haunts, old girlfriends, etc.*
>
> *Your good friend,*
> *Deanna*

She had to put in the part about girlfriends—let him know that she was aware there were other women vying for his love. She wanted to tell him, "Oh, how I miss you," and sign her letter "All My Love," but that wouldn't be right. Aaron had to come to grips with his life, what he'd run away from.

Deanna shut off the computer, then the lights, and tiptoed up the stairs. Her steps were not bouncy, for she wished that someone was going with her. Someone, she realized now, whom she loved with all her heart and soul. Not that she hadn't loved Bobby, for she had, but Bobby was gone, and she needed to get on with living. "Life is for the living," her father had said more than once.

She thought again about Aaron's letter. His father had married, and Aaron truly seemed shocked, yet wasn't that part of God's plan—that people would find each other and live together in harmony? But one needed to find someone they could be equally yoked with.

The bedroom looked as it always did, but for some reason she felt lonelier tonight. She wanted to be with Aaron now, wanted to meet his family, wanted to be in a loving family circle. Dare she hope that this might become a reality someday, or should she give up her dream and just get on with it?

She sat at her window bench and picked up her journal. There were several entries, all added since Aaron first came looking for a job.

"Do I lose hope, or do I hang on to what I dream about, what I believe and want and truly think might happen someday?"

A moon slid behind the layer of clouds, and Deanna closed the journal. Far away a young man sat with his family, and she couldn't help the tears that came and coursed down her cheeks. She just wanted him to be happy. That was the main thing. . . .

Aaron was given the guest room and left the party early. He was on eastern time, after all. He hadn't slept on the plane, though he'd thought he might, and last night had been a no-sleeper. *Deanna.* Why did her face keep popping into his mind? She had her life in Maine, and he would have his here. A crabbing boat was what he wanted. He'd do crabbing rather than oyster harvesting. He hoped his father would agree.

He pulled back the comforter, wondering if Deanna would find his message. Tomorrow he would check, but for tonight he would merely dream of her last impulsive hug, the way her lips had touched his, lightly at first, then with fervor. "Do come back as soon as you can. You will always have a job with us! Dad wanted me to tell you that."

"And I love you," Maddy had said before he left the house, throwing her arms around his legs. He'd lifted her high and then held the child tight. He had wanted to include Deanna, but she was looking out the window. He saw the tears before she turned away and knew she was crying silently now. But what could he do? He had to go, had to return to Oysterville. If he went back, he would go to her; he would let her know how he really felt. If, if, if. . . It was a short word but had such deep meaning. . . .

Chapter 16

The peninsula, this little corner of southwest Washington State, had changed. Aaron looked for familiar landmarks as his father drove through the town of Long Beach. Being a resort area, the usual entertainment area was intact: the merry-go-round, bumper cars, the Game Center, Cottage Bakery, then gift shops, restaurants, and a pharmacy on the corner by the light. Gone was the Book Vendor, where he had gone to pick up his girlfriend, Jill, who worked there on Saturdays.

"What happened to the bookstore?" he asked.

"Well, the owner wanted an art store to go in there, so that's what happened."

"No bookstores?"

"Oh, sure. There's still Sandpiper Books in the mall."

Alice turned around. "I imagine it seems strange to come back after five years."

Aaron nodded. He wanted to like her; she seemed nice, but it was going to take getting used to, her being his stepmother. He had heard the story of how they met when his father took a laptop in to be fixed. Alice worked in her son-in-law's office a few days each week and was there when Leighton came to pick up the laptop. One thing led to another, then she'd come to Oysterville for a visit, and that was that.

Deanna came to mind again. She was already getting ready for the evening's customers by now. He could see her bobbing back and forth, her dark hair dancing as she waited on each one and wished them, "Bon appetite!"

"Did you meet anyone in Maine? Besides Deanna?" Leighton asked, breaking through his thoughts. *How uncanny,* Aaron thought. It was as if his father were reading his mind.

"A few girls."

That answer was as good as any. He didn't care to discuss any of the women he'd met while traveling—especially not Deanna.

"Jill is single," Leighton said. "Just ran into her at the store last Sunday after church."

Aaron had thought at one time he might marry her. He'd been just a kid then, not even sixteen, but had wanted someone to love, someone to love him. Like most teenagers, Jill had not been ready to settle down and apparently still was not ready to settle down.

"She was married briefly to Lenny. Remember the kid who used to work for us on Saturdays?"

"Lenny?" Aaron tried to put a face to the name but couldn't.

"He left the peninsula shortly after the divorce. I have no idea where he is, but Jill is at Jeanine's, working part-time. It's close to winter, so things have slowed down a bit."

"How's the clamming?" Aaron asked then.

"We were open last month and the first part of November. People been getting their limit."

"I can't wait to see the house," Aaron said as they drove through Ocean Park on their way to Nahcotta. Then it was a straight shot down Sandridge and home.

"And Jolly Roger's is still canning oysters, I bet."

"Oh, yeah. Think the owner will retire soon, though—leave it to others to run."

"Just like you are doing," Alice said. She turned, and their eyes met briefly as the car headed north.

The huge Monterey cypress trees still stood like sentinels, forming a canopy high over the road. But a lot was cleared by Morehead Park, and the old barn was gone.

"What happened to the barn, huh, Dad?"

"Oh, they had to raze it. Just too dangerous to leave up without doing major repairs."

He was almost home. Home. The thought brought back memories, some painful. That last night here, with Hannah coughing on and on, his father hollering at him to just leave, to go away. And then his footsteps going to her room. He wasn't needed to help. Hannah's last words had been, "I'm going to be okay, Aaron," said between bouts of coughing.

Yeah, right, he'd thought. *When pigs can fly on the moon.*

He put the idea out of his mind. It was no good going over it. Heaven knows, he'd gone over it repeatedly since that night. Five years' worth of remembering, wondering, and wishing it had been different. Wishing he'd just stayed.

And yet, he wouldn't have met Deanna if he had.

"We're getting close, Little Buddy." Leighton put his arm around the back of the car seat and touched Alice's shoulder. It was these little acts of endearment that bothered Aaron, yet he knew this was silly; the problem was, he could not recollect a tender aspect to his mother and father's relationship.

Piles of oyster shells dotted the landscape, and then they were past Joe-Johns and making the little bend in the road. Aaron noticed numbers on all the mailboxes.

Then they were there. The house, large and silent-looking, had not changed. Of this Aaron was glad. The shake roof, the large stone fireplace between two windows, the spot where there had always been flowers that now had begonias still blooming in oranges, yellows, and reds. And then he caught a glimpse of the bay. The water, a clear, deep blue, seemed to go on forever. It was calm—no whitecaps today. Aaron couldn't wait to get the binoculars to see more.

"Dad!" He bounded out of the car, leaving his duffel in the trunk. He could get that later. "I can walk on the mud flats."

"Better get boots."

"Are they in the furnace room?"

"Same place."

Running into the garage, Aaron opened the door where they'd kept boots and extra coats and hats. A twenty-five-pound bag of birdseed stood on the floor. This must be Alice's hobby, he decided.

He pulled the boots on over his stocking feet and grabbed a hat, just in case the wind came up.

"I'm off!"

Aaron ran down the narrow road where his father drove the old truck, past the shed where he'd kept tools at one time, and crossed over onto one of the trails. There was the garden spot. Cornstalks stood and swayed in the breeze. Dad and his garden. He always had to have a garden. Aaron had liked everything but the zucchini.

He thought of Deanna again and the night she served sautéed sliced zucchini wedges. He'd eaten them and decided they weren't as bad as he recalled from when he was younger. No way would he not eat what she fixed.

When the tide was out, there were acres of mud flats. One could go clamming here, could dig for the small clams people loved. He would not do that. He just wanted to walk along and smell the clean air, feel the breeze on his face, and go back in time—to when he often walked here with Hannah tagging along. Aaron found a log and sat, looking out at the wide expanse of the Willapa Bay. Some things never change, he decided, and for that he was grateful. Some things do change, though, and that was what he needed to get used to.

It was an hour before Aaron headed back to the house. The smell of coffee filled the air as he slipped out of the boots and left them in the furnace room. He walked down the long hall toward the kitchen and living area.

A new floor had been laid. It looked nice. He stopped at the entrance of the small bedroom, the one that had been Hannah's. There used to be a blue carpet on the floor, as Hannah loved blue. Her small bed had butted up against one wall, and a dresser had stood against another. They were gone now, and the thought of his little sister coughing, getting sicker and sicker in this room, made him want to bang the wall. How could this be an office now? That meant every memory of Hannah was gone. He didn't even see a photo of her. How could his father just forget her like that? He wondered now, something he hadn't thought about until this minute: Where was his sister buried? Was it in the old Oysterville Cemetery, a place so close that he could go and visit her grave? He'd have to ask.

A computer sat on his grandfather's old desk.

Aaron went in and looked at the photos of his family members: Grandpa and

Grandma Walker, his mother's family, and cousins. These used to be in the hall. There was even a small photo of his mother on the wall by a photo of Hannah. The knot in his throat grew tight.

"Aaron? I thought I heard you come in." His father was there, slipping an arm around his shoulder. "Does it seem much different?"

"The bay, no; the outside of the house and the yard, no. I see you've cut down trees and cleared out some of the brush."

Leighton nodded. "Just to give us a better view." His father cleared his voice. "How about the house?"

"This was Hannah's room, and you took everything out."

"I saved it all. I moved it down to Luke's old bedroom."

"But why?"

Leighton's eyes filled with sudden tears. "I couldn't walk by every day and see her bed, the posters on the wall, and not think of her. It seemed better this way."

Aaron nodded, knowing he would have felt the same had he been here.

"Dad, what happened to Cora?"

His father's face looked blank for a long moment. "Cora has gone to Oregon. She's working for a hazelnut farmer there."

"Cora's left the peninsula? I find that hard to believe."

"Sometimes change is good for a person."

Aaron leaned over and looked at another row of photos, ones he didn't recognize.

"This is some of Alice's family. Her sister, daughter, son-in-law, and the baby, of course."

And then he saw the wedding picture, his father and Alice coming out of the Oysterville Church while people waved and threw rice at them. Only it wasn't rice anymore, but birdseed. It was the ecological thing to do.

"I can see you and Alice are happy," Aaron said.

"I didn't think it would ever happen to me," Leighton answered. "I never considered remarrying. When you botch up one marriage, you just think it's better not to try again."

Aaron leaned over the computer. "Dad, I'd like to send a quick message to my friend."

"Sure. And when you're finished, come and have some coffee while Alice finishes dinner. I think we're having clam fritters tonight."

"I should have brought you lobster. . . ."

"Lobsters would be nice, but that's okay," Leighton said. "You go ahead and send your mail, then we'll talk."

Aaron brought up the e-mail and typed in Deanna's address. He put that on hold and went back to the Internet, typing in Courtney's address, which he'd used to contact Deanna the previous night. There was a message:

Aaron,

> *Dad has not been well, but I think it's just the flu. He wouldn't go get a flu shot, though they offered them at the grange hall. He's stubborn, as you well know. I think a lot of men are that way.*
>
> *Maddy asks every day when you are going to come to see us. I made the mistake of saying you might come back one day, not to live here, but to visit. She picked up on that and won't let the subject drop. Murph is still looking for you, too. When we walk down the trail past the cottage, he stops and whines at the door, as if you were there and will suddenly appear and throw the Frisbee.*

Aaron reread the letter, looking for some sign that Deanna might miss him, too, but it wasn't there. The old man, the kid, and the dog missed him. He guessed that would just have to do.

He went back to his letter and told her this would be his regular address now. The other had just been for one night.

Deanna,

> *Hello. See if you can get GB to talk your father into seeing a doctor. He might listen to him.*
>
> *In some ways everything seems to have changed here, but in other ways, it is the same. The bay is calm and peaceful, and I walked along the mud flats. It's different here than at Penobscot Bay. I wish you could see it sometime.*
>
> *I can't get used to the idea of my father remarrying, but Alice seems okay, and she loves him. I can certainly see that.*
>
> *It's almost dinnertime. I hope to hear from you. Please give Maddy a big hug for me and throw the Frisbee a couple of times for Murph. Tell Mick I hope he feels better soon.*

> *Your friend,*
> *Aaron Walker*

Aaron reread his letter, visualizing Deanna sitting at the desk. It was almost as if she were in the room with him. He shut down the computer and went down the hall.

The table was set with new blue chinaware that Aaron had never seen. It had to be Alice's. There was French bread on the table already and bowls for salad.

There were several additions to the house—the new dishes, pictures and paintings on the walls, and a new easy chair—but the dining-room table and chairs were the same as he remembered, as were the love seat and couch in the living room. A baby grand piano with a glossy black finish sat in one corner. Hannah had been the only one who played it. He remembered her fingers running up and down the keyboard. "Such grace," the piano teacher said. "She has a natural talent for it, Mr. Walker."

"Then she will continue with lessons," Leighton had said. "She needs something to feel good about, and I can't think of a better thing than music."

Alice brought clam fritters and baked potatoes to the table. "This is it. Guess we can eat now."

After his father blessed the meal, Alice began passing the food.

"What are your plans, Aaron?" his father asked once the meal was over and they had taken coffee into the living room.

"I want to get my own crabbing boat."

"You have money for a boat?"

Aaron's cheeks flushed. "Well, not exactly."

"You've used your inheritance?"

"Yeah, Dad, guess I did. It costs money to travel, to pay for a place to stay, food—you know, the usual expenses."

"Yes, I do know."

"I suppose I should have saved that money for the boat. I shouldn't have left at all. I know that's what you are thinking."

"I didn't say that, Aaron."

"But you're thinking it." He expected his dad's jaw to tighten as it had in the old days. The steam would come rolling out his ears any moment now. But he got up from the table and sat on the old familiar love seat in front of the window, looking out at the bay and saying nothing.

"I had to go at the time."

"I figured that out."

"You didn't seem to want me here."

"What?" The voice rose just a bit.

"You told me to get out that last night. . . ."

"Is that what this is about? I told you to get out, yes, but I meant out of the room, for Pete's sake."

"I know, but I needed you, too, Dad, and there just wasn't enough of you to go around."

His father kept staring out the window. Alice took his hand in hers, then leaned over to kiss his cheek. "Your father has worried about you endlessly."

"Yeah, right."

"Aaron! You must show respect for Alice."

"I'm sorry," Aaron said, looking at her briefly.

"I don't want to talk about this now," his father said. "I think we need to wait, think over things, and discuss it at a later time."

"You mean sweep things under the rug like we always used to do?"

"No. I want to discuss it, but only when we are both calm and even-tempered."

"Whatever. Do I still have the same bedroom downstairs?"

"Of course. If that's what you want."

Aaron clumped down the stairs, refusing Alice's offer of apple pie à la mode.

He couldn't stick around. No way. It had gone as he predicted, except that his father had not blown his top like he had expected. He seemed calmer and definitely more at ease.

The bedroom was unchanged. As Aaron looked around at the same curtains at the windows, blue with sailboats, the light blue walls, and the four-poster bed with the fish design bedspread, a lump came to his throat. How could nothing have changed? It was as if he'd never left. Hadn't anyone slept here? Well, he supposed not, since his brothers were older and lived elsewhere.

Aaron looked at his old baseball mitt and ball. The team had signed the baseball after his home run in the playoffs. He held the mitt and lightly tossed the ball into it. That seemed so terribly long ago now.

Footsteps sounded overhead as he lay across the bed. He was tired—his inner clock was still three hours ahead. He supposed he should go and apologize. He should have thanked his father for sending the money, should have told him how good it was to be home, should have at least said, "I love you, Dad," but "I love you" had not come from his father's mouth, either. He thought of what was said at the airport.

"It's good to have you back, Son."

"I missed you, Dad."

"You're looking good, a bit taller."

It was superficial, not what Aaron had needed to hear. Not "I love you, Aaron." Perhaps those words would never be said. He was probably wishing for something that could not happen.

He remembered his duffel bag and went out the basement door and up the steps that led to the side yard. The duffel bag was out of the trunk and standing at the top of the steps going down. It was as if his father knew he would come this way and find his belongings.

Aaron slung it over his shoulder and headed back down and to the basement. He'd freshen up a bit, then go back upstairs and attempt an apology. Would his father accept it? At this point he didn't know. He couldn't be sure of anything. Too many changes, and he hadn't been here for any of them.

Chapter 17

The living room was dark, and Aaron thought his father and Alice had gone to bed. The conversation could wait until another time. He wasn't sure how his father would react when he said "thank you" and "I love you."

"Aaron?"

He jumped. "Dad? You sitting in the dark?"

"Yes. I enjoy watching the lights across the bay; gives me a sense of peace, of fulfillment somehow. Come sit beside me."

"Alice?"

"She's in the bedroom, reading. That's one of her favorite pastimes, and far be it from me to try to change her habits after this many years."

"Dad?"

"Yes?"

He saw the outline of his father's jaw, could reach out and touch him if he chose. He looked straight ahead, knowing it was more difficult to look at someone when you confronted them or offered thanks. He didn't want to get sidetracked now.

"How do you know when you are in love?"

The question surprised even him. It wasn't what he meant to say at all. How could he have asked it?

A low chuckle sounded from his father. "Somehow, I didn't think that would be the topic of conversation."

"Neither did I!"

"You did meet someone. The person you e-mailed earlier."

"I like her a lot, Dad. She's a beautiful, Christian young woman, raising a child by herself. Her husband was lost at sea. One of those quick storms that come up."

"Oh, I'm sorry to hear that."

"She writes how everyone misses me—not that I've been gone that long—but she doesn't say a word about her—you know, if she misses me."

"It's too painful, I suspect."

"Why? What do you mean?"

"Have you told her how you feel?"

"No."

"Then that's what I mean."

"She knows. I'm sure she knows."

"Not if you don't say the words. Women have to hear the words. I made that mistake with your mother; I should have told her every day that I loved her. It might have made a difference."

"Do you tell Alice?"

"I sure do."

"Sure do what?"

Neither had heard the feet cross the floor.

"I heard voices," she said. "I thought you were watching TV."

"In the dark?"

"I walk around in the dark." She sat in the rocker and rose as quickly as she'd sat. "I think you two were talking. Sorry I interrupted."

"It's okay."

"No. It's not," Alice said. "Good night, Aaron."

After she'd left, Leighton told Aaron about their courtship. "I knew the first time I saw her that she was going to become something special in my life. She had this laugh that was contagious, and I just liked her manner. But I had a problem convincing her at first. In fact, I gave up at one point but then went back to her house. I was on my way back home here when I realized I had to try once more. I had to make her see how I really felt."

"And she accepted it."

"No, not exactly."

"Not exactly? What do you mean?"

"She had a life that was full—her daughter, the expected baby, a sister, her part-time job, her volunteer work. She didn't need a man in her life."

"Oh."

"Yeah, that's hard to take when you want to become part of someone's life."

"Well, something must have happened to change her mind."

"I think God did it. Heaven knows, I said enough prayers."

"It isn't ever easy, I take it."

Leighton laughed. "You're young, Aaron. You have your whole life ahead of you."

"But if you know—"

"If you know, you need to step forward and make something happen. It won't happen on its own."

Aaron thought of the apology he'd meant to convey, but somehow he couldn't say it now. Why couldn't he say a simple "I love you" to his own father? If he couldn't do that, how did he think he ever could speak those words to Deanna or any other woman who came into his life?

❧

Deanna knew the cottage would be empty. Empty of Aaron's belongings. But it seemed his presence was here. He'd made the bed, swept the floors, and the curtains were still tied back. He liked it that way, so he could see outside better.

The hurt crept up her toes, through her midsection, and on to her heart. How was she going to forget him and go on with her life?

She looked under the bed, hoping there'd be a sock or a pair of shoes—something he'd left behind. There was nothing. She smelled the bedspread to see if his scent was left behind. He never wore cologne, so she didn't expect to smell anything, and yet there was a certain scent as she lay across the bed and let the tears come.

Deanna didn't know how long she'd been here at the cottage when she suddenly thought of Maddy. She'd left her coloring in the living room. How long had she been gone? Her father was there, but she wasn't certain he'd think before going outside and leaving his granddaughter alone.

She sprang from the bed, took one last look at the cottage, then headed down the path. Murphy was waiting and whined.

"I know. You miss him, too." She bent down and ruffled the dog's fur. "But he'll be back. I must believe that, Murph."

Deanna hurried back up the path to the house.

Maddy was still coloring, but looked up and smiled. "Mommy! I was looking all over for you!"

Deanna leaned over and pulled her child close. "Honey, I shouldn't have left you alone. Are you okay?"

"I drawed a picture for Aaron."

The hurt stabbed at her again. "It's beautiful, and in blues and reds, his favorite colors."

"When can I give it to him?" She looked up out of serious eyes, waiting.

"Honey, Aaron had to leave unexpectedly, but you know what?" And suddenly her heart lifted. "We'll e-mail it to him. We can send it as an attachment! I'm so glad we bought that scanner."

The door opened, and Mick came in. "It's kind of lonely around here, isn't it?"

"Yes, Dad, it is."

"He won't be back, you know."

Deanna felt the ache start again, deep within her. "No, I suppose not."

Her father looked at her for a long moment. "There'll be someone else, Daughter."

"But Aaron's coming back because he loves me," Maddy said then.

Deanna wished she could say the same. If only she could bank on that fact.

"That boy has a lot of thinking to do," her father said. "He'll straighten things out with his family. Then, if he is ready, and I repeat, if, he might come back, and you will have your answer."

Deanna chewed her lower lip.

Mick strode over and poured a mug of coffee. "I've said my piece, and I won't say another word about it."

Deanna leaned over and hugged the back of her father's shoulder. "I know,

Daddy." She rarely called him Daddy anymore, and he turned and held her tight for a brief moment.

Maddy had folded the colored picture and handed it to her mother. "It's for when you find Aaron."

And that night he had sent a message, and hope soared once again. Not that he said he missed her, but he let her know that he'd arrived okay, and if she was reading right between the lines, he missed all of them. It was a hope she had to hold close. Just maybe God had heard her prayers after all.

Chapter 18

T he first morning after returning to Oysterville, Aaron rose early, before his father or Alice. It seemed funny to get up before it was light out, but it wasn't four in the morning to him—his inner clock said it was seven.

He donned rubber boots, a hat, and a heavy jacket from the furnace room. It would be cold this early on the bay. It would be cold anywhere on the peninsula. It was the third week in November.

Soon his nose and eyelashes were covered with a light mist that was falling as he made his way down the path to the bay. He'd grabbed a couple of cookies from the cookie jar in the kitchen and took one out of his pocket. Peanut butter, one of his favorites.

He had something else in his pocket. He'd found it in a dresser drawer last night. Grandpa's old harmonica. Aaron played a few bars of "Amazing Grace." Music soothed him, as it had Hannah. Sometimes they played together, and "Amazing Grace" had been her favorite hymn. He wondered now if it had been played at her funeral. The knot returned to his throat.

He had been a coward. It was true. He should have stayed and spent what time he could with her. Had she missed him? He couldn't ask his father or his brothers. Nobody would know. Aaron thought of asking God for a sign. Was that wrong? He needed to know that Hannah had forgiven him, that, yes, she had missed him, but had understood why he couldn't stay.

He sat on an old log at his favorite spot and waited for the dawn to slip up over the Willapa Hills. It was an awesome sight on a clear morning. The mist had stopped, but he felt the spray from the bay as a gentle breeze rolled across the water. A crabbing boat, with lights on, went north, and he waved. He was certain the skipper couldn't see him, but he didn't care. He felt better about waving. Should he talk his father into helping him buy a boat? It might be two or three years before he could pay for it. Was it what he really wanted now?

The tide was going out, and soon he could walk on the mud flats again. They weren't pretty, but there was food in the mud. The sandpipers flew over from the beach side looking for shrimp barely discernible with the naked eye.

He played another tune, one his father used to whistle a lot, "There's Something About That Name." Aaron couldn't remember the words, but the tune stuck with him: "Yes, there was something about the name of Jesus."

Aaron played yet another tune that he hadn't thought of in a long while, "She'll Be Coming Around the Mountain." He'd heard Deanna humming it more than once, usually while the bacon or ham sizzled. It was probably because she was in a good mood or as she had said one morning, "I feel especially blessed today."

The choked feeling returned as he put the harmonica away. How could he make a new life when his thoughts constantly returned to the house on the hill and the woman in the kitchen, bustling around each morning feeding her father and daughter, and then later adding Aaron to the family around the table. She never complained and took things in her stride. He thought of Mick, who had treated him like a son, had trusted that Aaron would be good for the rent on the cottage. And GB. He didn't miss him, but he wondered if anyone really missed GB.

Another crabber went north. Aaron didn't bother to wave. The light was seeping through the trees now, and soon the sun would appear, adding its pinkish-red glow to the horizon. It was a sight he would never grow tired of. Yet there were gorgeous sunrises and sunsets on the East Coast, as well, and there was someone to share them with there. He thought of the night they had nearly collided on the path, the day they picked blueberries, the picnic lunch at the park on a blanket, with Maddy between them. Her hand felt soft in his callused one, and it hit him then that he could go on all through the rest of his life with this woman. Yet he had left, returning to the area of his birth.

"Hello. Am I intruding?"

Aaron almost fell off the log as he whirled to find Alice bundled in a long jacket with a blue stocking cap covering her head.

"I—that is—I like to come sit here."

"I bet you've missed it."

He swallowed hard. "Yes, I have. Do you always get up this early?"

"Usually not, but my heart has been troubled lately."

"It has?" He moved over so there was enough room on the log for Alice to sit. She sat beside him and looked out over the bay, clasping her hands in front of her.

"Aaron, I love your father with all my heart."

"Yes, I know. I can tell."

"Are you okay with the idea that he found someone after all these years?"

Aaron turned and stared at the woman beside him. She made him think of Deanna, except the hair wasn't right. And there were lines around her eyes and wrinkles here and there. "I am fine with it, and anyone can tell he loves you."

Alice hugged her knees close. "You really think so?"

"Yeah, I do."

There was a moment of silence, and then Alice spoke. "I didn't come to discuss your father or me. I want to know about you, Aaron. You're a true enigma if ever I saw one."

"I am?" He would never have classified himself in that way.

"Yes, you are. What's going on in that head of yours, I find myself wondering."

Aaron didn't want to discuss it, and especially not with someone he hardly knew. Yet she sat silently, as if waiting for him to say something, so he guessed he'd have to try to explain.

"You know about Hannah. . . ."

"Oh, yes. And I know how it tore your father apart because he couldn't do anything. I understand that so completely. I never was able to have children, and when my Courtney came down with a mysterious ailment when she was fifteen, I was grief-stricken, so fearful she would be taken away from me."

"Courtney is adopted?"

"Yes."

"I didn't know that."

"But back to Hannah. I am thinking you left because you and she were close, and you couldn't do anything to help her. . . ."

Tears pressed against his eyelids. "She coughed so much more; she couldn't go out to play, could no longer go to school. It was awful. And the last night I was home, my father—well, he didn't understand why I wanted to be with her. He asked me to leave and not come back."

"Oh, Aaron, he didn't mean never come back."

"I know that now."

She put an arm around him. "So you ran because it was the only thing you could think of to do."

"Something like that."

"But to never call, never write—that's what I don't understand. Your father not only lost his beloved Hannah, he lost you, as well."

Aaron felt the old hurt return as he dug his boot into the soft ground. Oh, he had words to say, words to defend himself, but nobody would understand, and especially not Alice or his father.

"You think he didn't love you because he didn't give you any time."

"He worked and worked, and Cora pretty much helped us out. And before that an aunt stayed with us." *All I ever wanted was for him to say he loved me, to put an arm around me. Was that expecting too much?* is what Aaron wanted to say.

"Do you suppose you two could make up? I mean, really make up. God teaches us to forgive. Not that we can completely forget, but we need to learn the lesson of forgiveness."

"I don't think he's forgiven me."

"Oh, I think he has. I know he has."

Alice stood. "This is one of the most beautiful spots I've ever seen, and to think I would never have seen it if it hadn't been for your father's laptop."

Aaron nodded. "I have always loved the bay. I like the ocean, too, but it isn't serene like this."

"Let's go have breakfast. Those cookies you took earlier couldn't have filled the hole much."

"You knew?"

"I heard the jar lid scrape just as I was getting up."

Aaron laughed. It had made a certain sound, but he'd never worried before about sneaking food out.

"I'm going over to see an old friend—thought I'd have breakfast there."

"Looking like that?"

Aaron shrugged. "Why not? I just look like an oysterman. It's pretty common around here."

"Do you want to use my car?"

He smiled. "Yeah, sure."

❧

Jill was pouring coffee when he entered the small café. She glanced up, her eyes widening in surprise. "Aaron Walker! Is it really you?"

He went over and gave her a brief hug. "Yep, one and the same."

"When did you get into town?"

"Two nights ago."

He watched while she made the rounds, then brought a customer's order. Finally, she came with order pad in hand. She looked the same, and it surprised him. He didn't know why, but he thought she would have aged. Her hair was long and blond, pulled back into a ponytail. He remembered asking her once if she would get married in a ponytail, and her answer had been, "Yes, and is that a proposal, Aaron?"

She had a trim figure, and her eyes were the same brown with hazel flecks. He had always liked her eyes.

"So? Are you back for good?"

"Yeah, I think so."

"Where were you all those years?"

"Here and there. Mostly in Maine, though."

"Maine! That's thousands of miles away."

"Yeah, I know. I liked it, though. Quiet. Sort of made me think of Oysterville."

"Are you wanting to go out or something? We could take in a movie down in Long Beach."

Aaron remembered the movie house. He and Jill used to go a lot when they were dating. It was either that or bowling.

The door opened, and he recognized both guys sauntering in. They'd all gone to the same high school, the only one on the peninsula. He waved, and then they were talking, asking him the same questions Jill had. He supposed it would always be like this. In a small town, people either didn't move away, or, if they did, they didn't come back. He had done both, so that made him unusual. Maybe that was what Alice meant when she said he was an enigma.

"Hey, let's go have a few beers tonight, shoot some pool at Doc's."

"It's still here?"

"Right on the same corner, man."

Aaron didn't want to say that he didn't drink anymore. He had at the logging camp, but it was too easy to let it take over your life. And he knew it didn't glorify

God. Now that he was searching for answers, it wasn't right to let drinking be part of his life.

"Thanks, guys, but Jill and I are going to a movie."

"You and Jill, just like before, huh?"

"Yes, just like before." Jill brought his toast. "Are you sure this is all you want?"

"This is fine." He didn't want to say he was hoarding his last bit of wages and wondered if he even wanted to spend money for movie tickets. He could hit his father up eventually or maybe ask Alice. She seemed more approachable.

"Just coffee," the guys said.

Aaron stayed long enough to say hello to another group of people he remembered from school days. One was a retired teacher, the other, the librarian.

"Are we going to the late movie?" Jill asked as she refilled his cup.

"Sure. What time? And you'll have to tell me where you live now."

She laughed. "Oh, I'm back home again, Aaron. Living with my mom. I was divorced a year ago and just didn't have the money for an apartment."

"Divorced?" He pretended he hadn't heard it already.

"Yes."

"Someone I know?"

"Maybe. He worked for your father once. We started dating after you left. He's gone now, though." She laughed again as she tossed her head. "No children, so I'm lucky there."

Aaron pushed his chair back. Married. Divorced. No kids. Jill thought that was the way it was supposed to be because her mother had been divorced three times.

"Say, do you still like that crazy musical, *Fiddler on the Roof*?"

It was Aaron's turn to laugh now. He had the tape in the car, the car he'd left behind in East Belfast. He hadn't remembered about it until now.

"Yeah, I still like that musical."

"I always liked hearing you sing along with it. You have a good voice."

Aaron thanked Jill for the compliment, finished his breakfast, and waved as he pulled out of the parking lot. He wondered if he should borrow his father's truck for tonight.

He drove through town and noticed Jack's Country Store. It was an icon in the area—had been there since he could remember. He went by the library and stopped at a resort where he had worked one summer mowing the lawn and keeping the grounds up. He had decided then he would never be a gardener. No, he was a fisherman, a man who loved the water.

His mind went to Deanna again. She was different than Jill. Though they hadn't gone out yet, he knew after a brief conversation that Jill was flighty, had no real goals. He almost wanted to back out of the date.

Mist began falling as he drove east, then north, heading for Oysterville and home.

Home. It sounded funny, not quite right. Would he feel at home again soon?

Chapter 19

Alice was in the kitchen making cookies. "Can't seem to keep the cookie jar full."

"Thanks for use of the car."

"Anytime." Alice glanced up. "Why don't you take it tonight and go find some friends?"

"You were reading my mind," Aaron said. "Actually, I visited an old friend, and she suggested a movie tonight."

"That should be fun."

"What should be fun?" Leighton asked as he padded into the kitchen looking from his wife to his son. "Been busy answering orders for oysters. Some from as far away as New York."

Aaron couldn't get over the fact that his father was retired now. It seemed strange not to have him leave for work in the morning. He also never dreamed his father would buy a computer, much less use it.

"Dad! I have an idea. I'd like to send some oysters to Mick and his family."

"The place where you last worked?"

"Yes. They'd enjoy getting oysters. And maybe they could send us a lobster. How about that?"

"Oh, I love lobster," Alice said. "I've read about the lobster pounds on the East Coast."

"Maybe you could go out and see firsthand," Aaron said. "That would be a good trip for you two to take. By the way, can I use the computer?"

"Sure," Leighton answered. "I'm going over to the store. Why don't you come, Aaron? I can wait a few minutes."

"I'll just walk down there."

"It's two miles."

"I can handle it."

Leighton leaned over and kissed Alice. "I'll be back in time for lunch. I wouldn't miss your clam chowder for anything."

Aaron found not one, but two letters from Deanna.

"Maddy says hello," the first one began. *"She's drawn you two pictures now. We all miss you."*

All? It was the first time she'd included herself in the "miss you" part. A warm feeling filled him.

The second message made him sit up.

"Dad's still not doing well. Not sure what it is. If I didn't know better, I'd say he was having heart problems, but he says, 'My ol' ticker is working just fine, thank you very much.'"

What could it be? Aaron stared at the screen, but instead of the words, he was seeing a crusty old man, as stubborn as they come, chewing on the end of his cherry-wood pipe.

He hit the RESPOND button.

"Do you need for me to come help?" Aaron wanted to ask. He wanted to, but how could he disappoint his father about Thanksgiving? His brothers, their wives, and the assorted grandchildren were coming, along with Alice's family, and he must be here for that. It was a combination "welcome home" and Thanksgiving meal.

"I'm going down to the Sea Gift Farms with my dad," Aaron typed out. *"A surprise is coming your way. Your father will love it! I pray for his quick recovery."*

Later, he wondered why he hadn't told her how much he missed her, how he couldn't get her smiling face out of his mind. . . .

❧

The store was different from what Aaron remembered, and he stared in amazement. The large room where workers sorted oysters had not changed, but there was an addition—a gift store. Canned salmon, sturgeon, and oysters filled the shelves. Various cookbooks lined up on a bottom shelf, and spices were on the counter in special gift baskets. Friday's bread had been baked and had sold out within an hour of coming in.

"Dad, this is looking good."

"How about working here, Aaron? You could manage the store—I've got one gal moving to Seattle, and my other helper is going back to school after Christmas. What do you think?"

Aaron hesitated. He had told his father that he wanted to be a crabber, that being on the water was important, was what he'd dreamed about since he was ten or so.

"Sleep on it," Leighton said. "Thought you could do this for a while until you get your crabbing boat."

Aaron met his father's steady gaze. He had remembered after all. "Yeah, Dad, you're right."

After shipping off a package of smoked oysters to Maine—he'd decided on smoked oysters because they didn't require dry ice—he wished he'd be there when the package arrived.

"Let's go have some of Alice's great clam chowder," Leighton said.

He rode back with his father, knowing it was time to ask about Hannah, though he felt awkward about bringing it up.

"Dad, where is Hannah buried?"

His father swallowed, staring straight ahead. "In the Lone Fir Cemetery, next to her maternal grandparents. It's off of Sandridge Road."

"Yeah, I remember. I want to go there."

"Yes, I think you need to see it." Leighton finally looked over at his son. "Perhaps tomorrow would be a good time for us to go."

~✑~

It was early when Aaron left for his date. He wore khakis and a navy blue wool sweater. He had an errand to run first, before darkness fell.

He drove down Sandridge, the "back road" as the old-timers called it. He stopped at Clarke's Nursery, buying a bronze chrysanthemum for Alice. It would look nice in the center of the Thanksgiving table. He also bought a small bouquet of carnations. Pink. Hannah had liked pink.

It was dusk by the time he reached the winding road to Lone Fir Cemetery. Maybe he should have waited for his father, but this was something he needed to do alone. Aaron felt a growing tightness as he drove up the small incline toward the spot. He remembered going here when an aunt died. Remembered the cold, rainy morning, standing beside his father while Hannah stood on the other side. It had been a short service with a song sung, scripture read, and the words of the pastor. They'd left immediately, as his father was worried about Hannah catching cold, as colds laid her up for days.

It wasn't cold today. It wasn't warm, either, just a typical gray November day, but unusually calm. He stopped at the top of the U-shaped drive and got out. He knew exactly where the family plot was and sauntered past a few other graves; all the while the tightness grew.

Then he saw it, and he gripped the carnation stems. He hadn't thought it would be this difficult. The gray marble slab looked newer than most. Aaron bent down and read the inscription:

OUR ANGEL
HANNAH ELIZABETH WALKER
BORN APRIL 15, 1984
DEPARTED OCTOBER 20, 1999
SHE WILL LIVE IN OUR HEARTS FOREVER

Aaron traced the letters of her name. Bending the carnation stems, he made a heart and laid them on the grave. Sorrow welled up inside. How could this be? She was too young to die.

"I loved you more than anything, Hannah, but I know your spirit is up in heaven with Jesus. This is for you, Hannah." He took out the harmonica and began playing "Amazing Grace." He played several verses, pausing more than once to wipe away the tears, then knelt down again. "I'm so sorry I wasn't there for you." He closed his eyes. "God, please forgive me, and take away this guilt. Draw me close, let me know and depend on You as Deanna does."

Aaron knew he wouldn't be back, but it didn't matter anymore. He felt cleansed. Free from sin and guilt. He would always have Hannah in his heart. Nothing would ever change that. Aaron got to his feet, thanking God for the peaceful, calm moment, as there wasn't even a breeze. As if in answer, a ripple of wind touched his face, then was gone. He smiled, knowing it was a sign of God's presence.

He walked back to the car, feeling lighter than he had in a very long time.

Aaron didn't want to keep the date with Jill, but he didn't want to call her to tell her he wasn't coming, either. Nor was he ready to go back to Oysterville. Perhaps the movie would be a good diversion.

He drove by the docks in Ilwaco, looking out over the boats in the slips. It was past fishing season, so the boats were idle. Two men drank coffee on the stern of one. He waved in passing. A new restaurant had opened, a coffee shop, plus a trendy little gift shop. There was a pizza parlor, but it had a FOR SALE sign in the window. That was too bad, as it would have been nice to pick up something after the movie. It also would have been nice to look out over the water as they sipped colas and ate pizza.

After leaving the docks, Aaron drove through town and up the hill past the old grade school, although it was now a middle school, then down the road past the high school. The mascot, a fisherman in a bright yellow raincoat, stood in front with a dilapidated old boat at the school's entrance. Everything looked the same. The concrete steps leading up to the school, the football field with its covered bleachers. Aaron swallowed hard, remembering how he'd gone out for football and hated it. The next fall he ran cross-country, and that was more to his liking. In the summer he played baseball. But mostly, he didn't care about school sports. He just liked to be on the water.

It was almost seven, so he drove back up the hill and toward the house where Jill lived. He wondered what Deanna was doing now and if Mick felt better today. Why couldn't he get the little family out of his mind? He knew Deanna, and soon she'd write a letter and include Maddy's drawings. She just did things like that.

The front door opened, and Jill's mother motioned him to come in.

"Goodness, it's been a long time, Aaron, but you haven't changed a bit." She smiled and touched his arm. "I think you have more muscles."

"It's from working," he said. "I was at a logging camp for a year. Now that's hard labor."

"What's hard labor?" Jill asked as she entered the room. She wore a short, tight skirt, and her hair was down around her face. He could never remember seeing her look like this. She walked up and hugged him. "You're looking good," she said.

He swallowed hard, knowing her statement required a response from him. "And you, too."

"You guys have fun. Catch up on the good ol' times," Mrs. Benson called with a wave.

"We do have time to slip into the Anchor Tavern for a quick beer."

"I don't drink beer," he answered.

"Don't drink beer?" She looked at him as if she couldn't believe what she'd just heard. "But everyone drinks beer."

"I'd like to stop for an ice cream cone. I noticed a new little store close to the gas station."

"Oh. Well, okay."

Aaron knew the evening would not go well. He hoped the movie was worth seeing. He also hoped that nothing was expected of him later. Not that Jill wasn't nice, and not that they didn't have a history together, but right now he was wondering why he'd agreed to a date. He didn't feel he belonged here, not anymore.

"We can walk on the beach or stroll the boardwalk," Jill suggested. "We don't have to see the movie. It's up to you."

"No, it's a comedy. Should be fun. We can walk later."

Aaron managed to make it through the evening. He laughed at the movie. He and Jill shared a big tub of popcorn, but when their hands touched, he felt nothing. Jill seemed more like a cousin or an old friend, not a girlfriend.

"You're preoccupied," she said when they got into the car. They stopped at the only place open and had a cup of coffee, though she suggested a tavern again.

"You've changed," she continued. "You're not like the Aaron I remember."

"I know."

"I suppose you want to take me home."

"Yes, I think so. Jill, I'm sorry. I just can't see picking up where we left off."

"There's someone else?" She leaned over and pulled his face down. "I don't want to see you leave a second time. You'll adjust. It just takes time."

"Jill, what we had once was good, but we were just kids then. I've grown in a different direction and so have you."

"It's because I suggested having a beer. . . ."

"No, it isn't that. It's just not going to work out. You and me."

After he walked her up the sidewalk, her mother opened the door and looked out. Of course she'd been watching from the window and had undoubtedly expected Aaron to either come in or to at least kiss Jill on the porch, but he'd hugged her briefly instead.

"Kinda early," she said as Jill rushed past.

Aaron drove home, his head whirling with thoughts. Maybe he didn't belong here. All he thought of was Deanna, the way she made him feel. He wondered if she would still be up when he got back to Oysterville. He doubted it, but he'd send an e-mail anyway.

❧

Later, Aaron sat in the office, thinking about Hannah again. He opened the bottom drawer, where he'd found his harmonica earlier. This must be the drawer his father referred to, the one where Hannah had kept her treasures. Under a stack of children's books, he found the small, leather-bound book with DIARY printed across the front in gold. Was this Hannah's? He'd never seen her writing in anything but the spiral notebook, where she jotted down poems. Where was it? He'd love to read some of her work now. Hannah's poems often rhymed, but not always. Aaron had memorized one:

IF I HAD ONE WISH

I wish I could run and play
I wish I wouldn't cough
And if wishes were roses
We'd all smell good.

He found a small box with stickers, barrettes, and a sand dollar they'd found on the beach one day. They often found broken ones, but this was a perfect, whole one, and Hannah had held it high. "For my collection," she'd said.

Aaron touched the diary, wanting to open it, wanting to read, but not daring to, as it was personal. Still, who would know? He opened the pages, flipping through until he came to the year and month he had left. His name leaped off the page.

"Aaron left last night. I thought he might someday. He's so worried about me, but I wish he wouldn't be. I don't blame him for going, though I'll miss him something fierce. But I know he will be happy wherever he goes. Aaron has a way of making people smile."

He gripped the small book, a lump coming to his throat at the memory. And now he knew she loved him, that she had forgiven him for leaving like that; she had even expected it. Yet why hadn't he been strong for her? Why, he was no better than her mother, who couldn't handle her child's illness.

The light came on, and his father stood in the doorway. "Aaron? I got up thinking I heard a noise. Is something wrong?"

Aaron lurched to his feet, the words pouring out. "Dad, I went to the cemetery earlier. I left flowers on Hannah's grave. It was wrong of me to leave when she needed me. Can you ever forgive me? Will you love me again like you used to when I was little and we'd take those trips to Portland?"

"What?" Leighton grabbed his son tight to his chest. "Aaron, I never stopped loving you, though it may have seemed like it. And as for forgiving, how could I not forgive you when God has taught us that forgiveness is one of the most important of all things?"

As the hurt of the past five years poured out, each spoke of things that had hurt, things they had not understood, and Aaron knew he was forgiven, and it was just like Alice said. He also knew that if he left again, it would be under different circumstances and for different reasons. Good reasons this time. He felt led to return to Maine, and Leighton would understand. This time he'd have his father's approval. But he couldn't tell him until after Thanksgiving.

Chapter 20

Preparations were made for the Thanksgiving feast. Alice baked both a ham and a turkey.

"Why both?" Aaron asked.

"Because we have eighteen people coming."

"Eighteen?" Aaron had counted sixteen.

"Well, we can't leave out dear Mrs. Endicott and her sister. They are all alone, and since neither likes to cook, I had to ask them."

Leighton nodded. "Definitely. Alice always thinks of things like that."

Aaron remembered the Endicott family that lived in Oysterville, but they had never been invited to dinner, let alone a Thanksgiving meal.

"I also asked my sister, Agnes, but she hates riding in a car this far, so I guess she will never see the beautiful peninsula or Willapa Bay."

Aaron wasn't sure when it hit him, but probably after everyone had arrived. Coats and hats were hung in both hall closets, Luke's kids were involved in playing a game of Risk on the card table, and the men sat and watched the football game while they waited for John to arrive from Portland. Aaron looked around, and in that house full of people, teeming with noise and loud greetings, he felt alone, adrift, as if he didn't belong here. He imagined a quieter Thanksgiving dinner in East Belfast. It would be Mick, GB and his wife, Deanna, and Maddy. Possibly her cousin would come from Farmington. And they just might ask Velma Cole, who took care of Maddy whenever the need arose.

There would be turkey, stuffing, homemade rolls, and fruit salad. "And we will have sweet potatoes," Deanna had said.

"And if one doesn't like sweet potatoes?" Aaron had asked.

"Then one only has to take a tiny spoonful, because a certain little pair of eyes will be watching to see what is done."

Aaron had laughed. "Oh, of course. A good example must be set."

Here in the Walker home, the children, the two younger ones, did not want to settle down. They had fun running up and down the basement stairs, playing tag. Alice had help in the kitchen from her daughter, Courtney, who had arrived the night before. Alice looked flustered. Clearly she wasn't used to such a large gathering, either. And Courtney, who didn't know what it was like to be raised with siblings, seemed unable to handle the noise.

"I have a splitting headache!"

Steven came up behind her and rubbed her temples. "Do you want some aspirin?"

"Yes, please."

The baby, Steven Carl, cried then, and Courtney excused herself to go nurse her child. "Mother, can I sit in your bedroom and just close the door?"

"Of course, sweetie."

When the table was set, with Leighton and Aaron's help, the dinner bell rang. When two of the younger boys didn't come, Leighton rang the bell again.

"This is a special day, a special dinner has been prepared, and we will all sit at these three tables together to partake of this food."

"But, Grandpa—"

"No buts. I'm the oldest person here, and because I am, I get to call the shots. There will be time for playing later. Now find a chair and sit so I can ask the Lord's blessing on this outstanding meal." He reached for Alice's hand. "Your grandma has worked very hard to fix this for us, and enjoy it we will."

Aaron listened as his father thanked the Lord for the food, the day, the family, the love that filled the room, and then all said, "Amen!"

He liked Alice's dressing, but he couldn't eat more than a couple of bites of anything. He never knew he would miss his friends in Maine so much. It was as if they were his real family, and these were people he barely knew.

He begged off from pumpkin pie, then reached for the telephone. E-mail was fine, but today, especially today, he wanted to call, wanted to hear Deanna's voice and talk a minute to Mick—and to Maddy, of course.

It was quiet when he heard the familiar voice. Of course their meal had long been over.

"Aaron!" She covered the mouthpiece, but he could still hear, "Dad, it's Aaron calling from Oysterville."

After talking to Maddy, he told Deanna that he wanted her to come visit his family. There was a long pause, as if she was deliberating, and then finally she spoke. "Aaron, I'd love to come, but I can't leave Dad just now."

"Is he still feeling bad?"

"It isn't just that. Who would take over for me?"

"Yeah, okay. You're right."

He hung up, thinking about what she'd said. Was she using her father as an excuse not to come? Perhaps she did not want to see him again. Yet how could he forget the lilt to her voice, the excited sparkle that he knew was dancing in her deep brown eyes as she talked, the way they'd kissed at the airport.

He sat in the office, which so far none of the children had discovered today, and closed his eyes. He had to decide what course his life was going to take. And he had better decide soon. . . .

Chapter 21

Do you think you'll return to Maine to work at the Lobster Pound again?" Alice asked a few days after Thanksgiving. She'd walked to the bay and sat beside him on the log. He had said very little the two weeks he was home. She knew he'd had one date with an old girlfriend, and though the girl kept calling and he would speak to her, he never went anywhere with her again. She'd known from that first evening, when they'd all been partying and rejoicing at the Portland house where Courtney now lived, that though he seemed happy to be home, his heart was elsewhere.

"Mark my words, Leighton, that boy is not going to be staying," she had said later that night.

"Nonsense," he'd retorted. "He's always wanted to be a crabber, and though I'd like him to work in the store, I'll go along with whatever he wants."

"I don't think he'll stay," Alice said again now. They sat on the deck, enjoying one last day of late fall sunshine. Aaron could be seen through the binoculars where he sat on his log. He was not moving, just sitting still and staring straight ahead.

"Maybe I should walk down and talk to him."

She'd put her hand on his arm. "He'll be up shortly. Let him be. He's thinking it all out."

"If he wants to return to Maine, I think he should do it," Leighton said. "Now that he's come home, we've mended fences; he can go back there. Maybe we'll take a second honeymoon and go meet this Deanna and her daughter."

"Or maybe we should offer to fly her out here."

"No. Can't do that. She's needed there, according to Aaron. Her father isn't well and the brother works, but doesn't help out at the Pound, and that's where the profit comes in."

Alice reached up and pressed a finger along the deep furrow on Leighton's brow. "Then why the worried look? If we're going there, you should be happy about an upcoming trip."

"I'm just not sure yet. Let's wait to see what Aaron decides."

Aaron had trudged back up the trail and to the house in time for six o'clock dinner. He said very little but answered his father's question, saying, yes, a loan would be nice, should he want to buy a crabbing boat, a good used one, and he appreciated the offer.

They discussed other topics, and after Aaron had two helpings of double-fudge ice cream, he said he was going to bed.

Two weeks later, Aaron went to work in the store. He'd helped by setting up strings of Christmas lights for the holidays. He looked forward to hearing from Deanna each evening. Then the letters stopped coming. He sensed something was seriously wrong. He dug out his wallet with the Lobster Pound business card. It was after midnight in Maine, but he knew he wouldn't sleep if he didn't find out.

Nobody answered. He called information for GB's phone number.

A voice answered on the second ring.

"Is this GB's wife?"

"Yes, and who is this?"

"Aaron Walker. I worked at the Pound for a while."

"Oh, yes. GB talked about you."

"I haven't heard from Deanna and need to know how Mick is doing."

"He's in the hospital, Aaron. GB stayed with him all afternoon, and Deanna is there now. I'll go in the morning."

"What's wrong?"

"Oh, I thought you knew. It's a bleeding ulcer, and he doesn't seem to be responding to treatment."

"What about the Pound?"

"It's closed down. They can't operate it without Mick."

Aaron felt fear for Mick, empathy for Deanna and Maddy. He should be there. They needed him. Even if nothing worked out between him and Deanna, he could do the work; he could scrub floors. They couldn't close the Pound indefinitely. If Mick was worried, that might be the reason he wasn't getting better. He hated hospitals. Aaron could hear him grumbling and complaining now. He needed something to look forward to, to see some hope on the horizon.

He had to go as soon as possible. Now came the part where he told his father. Leighton and Alice were at the table playing Scrabble.

"Dad, I don't know how to say this or to explain it, but I have to leave. They need me there. In Maine. I just don't know about the money to—"

"Don't worry about the money, Son. Alice said this would happen. I understand, really I do."

Aaron let out a whoop, leaned over, and hugged his father, then Alice. He ran down the stairs and packed in five minutes. Alice offered to drive him to Portland to catch the earliest flight out. One left for Bangor at 6:00 a.m.

Aaron said good-bye to Hannah's photo, hugged his father again, and followed Alice to the car. He looked out over Willapa Bay; the full moon shone out over the water. He would miss this place, but it wasn't as if he'd never be back. He would have the best of two worlds. God had seen to that.

"Thanks so much for driving me, Alice."

"Consider it an excuse for me to go into town and see that grandson." She smiled, then squeezed his hand. "It's going to work out, Aaron. When you put it all in God's hands, and I think you have, you will be blessed more than you can ever imagine."

They were far too early, but Aaron said he didn't mind waiting, that he'd catch a nap in one of the chairs in the lounge. He kissed Alice's cheek and thanked her again for loving his father. "I have never seen my father so happy. You are good for him, Alice."

"And he is good for me. I didn't realize what I was missing until he came into my life."

"And I leave this time knowing we've made peace and that there are no hard feelings."

"Isn't it a fantastic feeling?"

Aaron thought about that while he sat in the waiting area. Yes, it was fantastic. He was happy with his life. He had a purpose. He'd never felt committed enough to ask someone to date him exclusively and obviously had never asked anyone to marry him. He was young, after all. A lot of men and women, too, didn't marry this young. He had things to do yet. But try as he might, he couldn't think of what they were. He'd traveled, seen the country, and tried his hand at a host of different jobs. He was back to knowing that the bay was in his blood. It just happened to be a bay on the opposite end of the country.

When the boarding call came, Aaron slung his small backpack over his shoulder and went down the ramp. Deanna didn't know he was coming. He wanted to surprise her. He'd go to the hospital first, see Mick, and let him know he had not deserted them after all, that the Pound would stay open.

He slept off and on most of the way there. They had one layover in Minneapolis, but he didn't bother getting off the plane. It would be late when he arrived, but that was okay. He could find a bus or hitchhike to Belfast.

And if a store was open, he'd find something to take to Maddy. Being a father would mean doing and being a lot of things, but he felt he was ready for the responsibility.

It was eight when the plane landed. There were just four people getting off, and he and one other passenger were the only ones who were not met by anyone.

"Hey, do you have a ride to wherever you're going? My name's Larry." He held out a hand.

"Aaron." He looked at the man who had sat across from him. "I'm heading to Belfast."

"It's on my way."

"Are you sure? I need to stop at a store, if there's one still open," Aaron said.

The young man smiled. "I know of one. No problem. So you're going to Belfast. I'm just beyond about ten miles."

Aaron mentioned that his boss, Mick, was in the hospital.

"Sounds like you're returning just in time."

Larry chatted while they drove. At a discount store, Aaron found a teddy bear with a red coat and hat for Maddy. He then saw the carnations at the checkout stand and grabbed a bouquet.

Larry dropped Aaron off at the hospital at nine thirty, and Aaron offered to pay his friend for the ride, but he waved him away. "Like I said, I was going this way anyway. Hope your friend is going to be okay."

"Yeah, me, too. Thanks."

Aaron didn't expect to find Deanna still there. She sat in a chair pulled up next to the bed, and his heart pounded at the sight of her holding her father's hand, her head bent. Mick appeared to be asleep; maybe she was, too.

He stepped inside. She must have sensed his presence, as she glanced up and let out a squeal as she ran to him, the dark curls bouncing. "Aaron, oh, Aaron. I told Dad you'd come back. He just smiled and said, 'We'll see.'"

He pulled her out into the hall, not wanting to wake Mick. "How is he?"

"He's better; he comes home tomorrow. It's so wonderful to see you."

"You didn't call to tell me your father was in the hospital. I had to call GB's house."

"I didn't see any point in—"

"Why? Because you thought I didn't care anymore?"

Tears began to fill her eyes. "I knew how I felt but didn't dare hope. . ."

Aaron handed her the flowers. "For you. Red. Your favorite color. And I have something in the bag for Maddy. Where is she?"

"At Velma Cole's."

"In good hands, then."

"Aaron, you must be tired. I was getting ready to go home; it isn't as crucial as it was at first. He's going to be fine—just has to follow a better diet. No spices or fats."

He desperately wanted to kiss her, but dare he? He lifted her chin, and their eyes met and held. "Deanna, this isn't the time or the place, but I must tell you. I didn't come back just for Mick."

"Aaron." She shushed his words with her mouth, and he knew then how wonderful it was going to be. God must have had this in mind all along.

"I knew you were the right one after that first day," she said. "I prayed for God to send a soul mate my way. I wanted someone in my life and a father for my daughter."

"I wasn't praying, though."

"That's what's so neat. He answers one person's prayers, and the other one comes to realize that was what he wanted all along, too." She glanced in Mick's direction. "I'll tell the nurse I'm leaving and to call me if there's any problems."

They walked hand-in-hand to the car. The rain that had been more mist than true rain had stopped, and a fog now seeped over the area. Deanna glanced up but couldn't see the stars, though she knew they were there. It didn't matter. They'd be out another night.

"Tell me I'm not dreaming," she said, putting her head against his chest. "I don't want this to be a dream."

"It isn't a dream," Aaron said huskily. "It's for real, honey." He'd never called her "honey" before, and he liked the way it sounded.

She leaned up and pulled his face down again. "Call me 'honey' again," she murmured.

"Okay, honey."

"I like the way it sounds."

"Me, too."

"It's a good thing you have the cottage, and I have to stay at the house. . . ."

"You didn't rent out the cottage?"

"What do you mean, rent it out?" Then she saw that he was teasing, and she pulled his cap off and ruffled his hair. "You didn't get a haircut in Oysterville. And you've lost weight."

Aaron hadn't realized it until then. His pants did hang on him. "There are no barbershops in Oysterville."

"What's there, then?"

"A general store, post office, some houses, and a church."

"There must be a barber somewhere."

"Yes, but I decided to let it grow. Do you like it?"

She walked around and looked at the front, then the back. "It will do, but if you want to be a backwoodsman, you need to grow a beard."

"I just may do that."

"Just kidding!"

They stood and kissed, holding each other for a long moment before getting into the car. "This feels good and right."

"Hmmmm," she said in reply. "Next stop is to pick up a sleeping Maddy. I can't wait to see what she does when she sees you."

As they drove, Deanna looked over and grinned. He took out the harmonica and began playing "She'll Be Coming Around the Mountain When She Comes."

Deanna's clear alto voice sang the words while he played. "I didn't know you knew how to play a harmonica," she said after five verses.

"I found it in with Hannah's things."

"Oh."

Aaron reached over. "It's okay, Deanna. We'll talk about it sometime. I'm able to tell you now."

She took his arm again, saying nothing.

Velma Cole looked surprised to see the two on her doorstep so late. "The little one is asleep. You could leave her here for the night."

"No way," Deanna said. "I can't wait for her to see Aaron."

"She talked about you a lot," she said, nodding at Aaron. "I'm so happy you came back."

He hugged her and went to pick up the sleeping child.

"Mommy," she began, then opened her eyes. They sprang open, and she screamed out almost the same way her mother had at the hospital earlier, "Aaron!"

The three headed for home, thankful that the fog had lifted.

"The cottage is just as you left it."

"Good."

"You'll be up for breakfast?" she asked as he stood in the doorway.

"You bet."

"Bacon or ham?"

"It doesn't matter. Just give me anything."

As Aaron ran down the steps, Murph followed, as if he wasn't about to let him out of sight again.

"Hey, ol' boy, I missed you, too."

This time he let the black lab come with him down the familiar path to the cottage. One day soon he would carry Deanna over the threshold.

Epilogue

Aaron would have agreed to elope, as it would mean he would belong to Deanna that much sooner and she to him. He wanted to make her his wife, but he had to be patient. Mick was recovering; Leighton and Alice had made reservations to come east. Deanna bought a dress and planned a small wedding.

"I don't need a long white dress with a veil," she said. "I've been there, done that."

"But Aaron hasn't been married before," Pastor Neal said.

"I don't want a lot of expense," Aaron said. "We can get married by you before God and a few friends and family members and have a reception in the church fellowship hall."

Mick argued the point, though, which Aaron thought was strange. It was women who wanted big affairs, so why was Mick suggesting this now? Then Aaron realized that he had been both mother and father for many years. He was only trying to do what he thought was best.

Six weeks later, on one of the coldest days East Belfast, Maine, had seen in several years, with piles of snow on the ground and more expected by nightfall, Aaron and Deanna repeated their vows and exchanged rings.

"I love you already," Alice said, as she had agreed to be the matron of honor. "I can hardly wait for you to meet my Courtney."

"And I love Aaron with all my heart," Deanna said. "I never thought I could be this happy."

"Aaron is so settled. He has that look of contentment about him."

Deanna giggled as Alice checked the hem of her dress and made sure the bouquet was in one piece. She leaned over and hugged Maddy.

"I think it's cute that Aaron insisted you walk down the aisle and that your father said Maddy had to be a flower girl and ring bearer."

"And I have the rings right here on this white pillow," Maddy said. "It's so soft, I want to keep it."

"So you shall," said Alice. "I surely can't think of anyone I want to see have it more."

The entourage started: Madison Marie in her lilac gown with tiny rosebuds embroidered in the hem and neckline, then Alice with her dress of a deeper purple, and Deanna with a beige, long dress with scooped neckline and tiny seed pearls that had been carefully sewn in. Pearl buttons went to the waist, and she looked elegant in the straight skirt, carrying white lily of the valley and purple violets.

As they repeated their vows, Aaron's hand reached over for his Deanna's. He breathed a prayer to the Lord, who had made this day possible, the Lord who had loved him through it all.

"I now pronounce you man and wife," Pastor Neal said.

"And you get to kiss my mommy, Aaron," Maddy said, looking up with a smile on her face. Laughter sounded from the audience, then someone clapped, followed by another and another.

"And I get to kiss you, too," Aaron said, scooping the little girl into his arms and holding his two women close in a tight embrace.

DEANNA'S BANANA WALNUT PANCAKES

2 eggs, beaten
2 cups buttermilk
2 cups flour
1 tsp soda
1 tsp salt

2 tbsp oil
1 cup sliced bananas
  (about 2)
½ cup chopped walnuts

Beat eggs, add buttermilk. Add flour, soda and salt; mix well.

Fold in oil, then bananas and nuts. Drop by ¼ cup measuring cup onto a hot griddle.

Serve hot with real butter and Vermont maple syrup.

Woodhaven
Acres

To farmers everywhere,
who struggle to make a go of harvesting the land.
And special thanks to Polly,
who answered my endless questions about hazelnuts.

Chapter 1

Meredith circled an ad in the newspaper and handed it to her cousin, Cora. "There's no point in moping around. Leighton's married and that's that."

Cora set the paper aside. "How do you forget twelve years of your life?" Not counting her last job caring for an elderly woman, Cora had been housekeeper and nanny to the four Walker boys for nearly a decade. She'd fallen in love with Leighton, their father, and had stayed on as housekeeper/cook long after the boys were raised. She'd loved Leighton with all her heart, but he had not felt the same.

"You don't forget, but you move on." Meredith sounded emphatic as she passed a plate of cookies.

Cora took one and nibbled on it thoughtfully. "Hmm, these are different. What brand is this?" She knew they were her favorite pecan cookies, but they didn't taste right.

"Same cookie with less fat, less sugar."

Cora rolled her eyes. "Well, no wonder. If they take out all the good stuff, what's left?"

"Fewer calories."

Meredith refilled their cups with tea. "No sugar in this, either."

"What are you trying to do to me?"

"Get you to lose some weight."

Cora was twenty pounds overweight, but so was Meredith. However Meredith was tall and wore her weight better.

Cora sighed. "What's left to life if you can't eat?"

"Finding someone who cares about you and whom you care about in return. Marriage. Possibly a family."

"I'm forty-three, so we can forget the family part." Even as Cora said it, the pain started deep inside her. She had always wanted a baby. Did one ever get over that feeling? It was like a craving.

"It's never too late, Cora," Meredith went on. "I just read up on the latest medical facts on the Internet. Women are having healthy children later and later. I'll print out the article for you."

Cora cleared her voice. "I'd say that's putting the cart before the horse. Besides, why are you so worried about me? I don't see any guy in your life."

"I know, but I don't care, and there's the difference. You care. You want the home, the kids, and to make some guy happy."

Cora took the newspaper, but only because Meredith thrust it at her as she was leaving.

"Just look at it. Doesn't hurt to look, now does it?"

"No, but remember the first time I answered an ad and met a guy? I swore I'd never do it again."

"So? That's one time. There are lots of lonely men out there. It only takes one to make a match."

Cora headed for the car. She had no intention of reading any more personal ads, so she tossed the newspaper into the backseat. She may as well humor Meredith, though she wasn't sure why.

Ever since they were little, Cora had listened to Meredith, though Meredith was a year younger. Now here Meredith was, pushing at her from all angles: Lose weight. Exercise more. Read the ads and find someone.

Cora didn't want anyone if it couldn't be Leighton. Talk about crying at someone's wedding. She'd almost stayed home, but she'd relented at the last minute to make sure it was really happening. She had to admit that Leighton looked happy as the couple repeated their marriage vows, gazing into each other's eyes. Alice didn't seem to be his type, but how could one know?

Cora went home and bawled for a week. That was December, and it was now May. She had been busy with the job over in Naselle. Being a caregiver had buoyed her spirits. She felt needed and wanted. And then the poor woman died.

Cora drove down Stackpole Road toward town, fighting the urge to drive past Leighton's driveway. She could avoid his road by going another way. Sometimes she did; other times not. One night she'd awakened from a dream in which she'd become Mrs. Leighton Walker. The dream seemed so real, she couldn't move for a long moment. Then tears came.

At the last minute, Cora turned onto Sandridge. She could not see Leighton's house because it sat off the road and was surrounded by trees and brush, but she always thought she might catch a glimpse of him leaving or coming home.

Cora flipped on her favorite golden oldies station and hummed along with a familiar tune. She should have told Meredith about Gavin, whom she'd met in a chat room on the Internet. She wasn't worried about meeting him in person because he lived in Kansas. Meredith had once suggested that Cora should move away to get over Leighton. She now corresponded with someone from a far-off state. Cora was on the Long Beach Peninsula in the southwest corner of Washington State and had never ventured far. There had been a trip to Disneyland when she was eighteen and a cruise up the Northwest Passage with Meredith to celebrate her twenty-fifth birthday.

Cora saw a familiar car ahead and realized it was Alice, Leighton's wife. The pain cut deeper. She had all the things Cora wanted. It isn't fair, she'd railed at God more than once.

To love and lose two times was heartbreaking. Cora thought back to when she'd been engaged to Carson. She'd even bought the wedding gown. But it wasn't meant to be, and everyone consoled her when he ran off with a woman he'd met the week before.

"How could Carson do that, Mama? You know he can't know enough about her to break our engagement and run off to Reno to get married."

"Consider yourself lucky, Cora Jean. Think of what might have happened after you married him. Cheating. Flirting until it was embarrassing."

Cora had been thin then. Short and petite. Her size three wedding dress was sold later at a secondhand shop, though it definitely was not secondhand.

"Mama," Cora had cried out often. "I wish you were here to talk to. I know you'd understand." Her mother had died a year ago, and Cora missed her love and sage advice.

She stopped and chatted with one of her best friends where she cashiered at the local market. "How you doing, Cora Jean?" Frances, like Cora's mother, always called her by both names.

"You know, I think I need to get a new life, move somewhere, do something daring. Exciting."

"There you go!" Frances handed her the change. "Tell me when you're going to do it so I can go, too."

"You can't. What would you do about Bill and your kids?"

Frances shrugged. "Guess they'd figure something out."

Cora grabbed her small bag of fruit and waved over her shoulder. Somewhere between Meredith's house and the store, Cora decided she would cut back on eating. This time Meredith was right. She not only needed a new scene, but she needed a new body and hope for her future.

She hummed as she pulled into the driveway. She hesitated, then grabbed the newspaper from the backseat. It wouldn't hurt to read through the ads. Some were quite amusing.

Young farmer needs a cook/housekeeper/nanny for two girls. Full time. I offer a wage plus room and board, which is your own apartment separate from the house. Please call Dundee, Oregon, at. . .

A farmer? Cora had never lived on a farm, and the idea did not appeal to her. Two daughters would be different. Yes, she felt she could handle that with no trouble. And Dundee, Oregon, wasn't like going halfway across the country. Should she respond?

After dialing the number twice and hanging up twice, Cora finally let it ring. A man's voice answered on the third ring.

"My name is Cora Benchley. I'm calling about your ad for a housekeeper and nanny."

"What do you need to know?"

She liked his deep voice with its resonant tones. She pictured him as young and rugged and maybe in need of a wife. Not that she would ever think of him in a romantic way. She was through with those dreams. Obviously his girls needed supervision, and she felt confident about that.

"About the requirements, the duties."

"The ad said—"

"Oh, I read the ad, but I'd like to know what housework is involved and whether there is outdoor work, as well."

"No. Nothing like that. You clean and cook and spend time with the girls. I want this house to be a home again. It's as simple as that."

"I see."

"When could you start?"

"As soon as you need me. Until recently, I was a caregiver for an elderly woman who had cancer. She passed away, and now I need a job." *I also need to get away,* she thought.

"I'll need references."

"Of course." Cora gave him the pertinent details and phone numbers for her last employer and Leighton Walker. There should be no problem from either one, as Cora gave a job her all.

"If things check out, I'll need you immediately, but first you'll want to come to the farm to meet the girls."

"Sounds good." Cora's mind whirled as she wondered whether he had references, not that she was worried. She'd know after they met if she'd want to work there.

"I have references," he said, as if reading her mind.

"Okay." She had one more question. "How old are the girls?"

"Eight and eleven."

"A good age," Cora said, thinking there would be a lot of things they could do.

"Where and when would you like to meet?"

"If it's okay with you, I'd like to meet in Portland at the statue in Pioneer Courthouse Square. Say, noon tomorrow?"

"All right."

"Is that okay?"

"Of course."

Minutes later she jotted down her ideas: Woodrow Morgan would be in blue denims, a plaid shirt, cowboy boots, and he was probably six feet tall.

Cora hadn't told him what she looked like. It didn't seem necessary. She would look for him by the bronze statue of a man holding an umbrella. It was her favorite place at the square.

❧

"You what?"

"Meredith, you told me to get a life, to get out there and look for someone.

362

You even gave me the ad section."

"But I didn't think you'd do it. At least not this soon. And Dundee? Where is that?"

"In Oregon somewhere. Guess I'll find out soon enough."

"When are you going?"

"We meet tomorrow in Portland."

"You're crazy! Do you want me to come with you?"

"No. I can handle this by myself, but I do need you to take care of Keesy Kat and water my plants."

"Can do. That cat loves me."

Cora packed jeans as it was warmer over in the Willamette Valley as compared to the beach. She added to this a few tank tops and a couple pairs of shoes, just in case she decided to take the position. *God, You know I need something to do with my life, something that counts, and this may be it.* Cora slammed the trunk of her car. "Yes, this just may be the answer to my prayers."

Chapter 2

Dressed in faded jeans and a red and black plaid shirt, Woodrow Wilson Morgan III gazed out at the symmetrical rows of hazelnut trees. He hoped his forty-five-acre spread would produce a good harvest this fall. He had time to worry about that later, but what he needed now was someone to take care of the house, especially now with the girls here. Lacie, at eleven, could manage. She was sensible and wanted to please, but Mary Gray, who was eight, was a handful. She did not obey, and if he insisted she do something, she would not eat. That panicked him, and he always backed down.

If she didn't do her homework, she would have to repeat third grade. It seemed a simple deduction to him, but she'd gone through a lot this past year.

Woodrow thought about all the hazelnuts that had been gathered from these trees. His great-grandfather bought this parcel of land when he first arrived in Oregon. Back when he'd started the farm, the nuts were called filberts; now they were called hazelnuts. He was proud to carry on the family tradition and couldn't imagine doing anything else.

Woody, as friends and family called him, bent down and scooped up a handful of earth. It had been a dry year, but when harvesting started, the rains would come. It happened every fall.

He thought of the early mornings of harvest during his childhood. He had never known anything but the hazelnut business and was allowed to stay home from school helping with the harvest—school started earlier in the year back then. His staying home came with conditions: He had promised to keep up with his schoolwork, which meant doing lessons each night. He remembered the rainy days and coming in for lunch soaked to the skin.

"You get out of those wet clothes and warm up there by the woodstove," Freda, the Morgans' cook and housekeeper, called out, shaking her head. "Does the rain ever stop in Oregon?"

Freda had come west to live with a widowed sister and answered the first ad she saw. She'd never married, and she had loved Woody and his little brother, Hunter, as if they were hers. Even then their mother, Virginia, was often barely able to function. She planted asters and pansies each spring and on occasion dusted the furniture, but Freda had mothered the children, cooked the meals, and kept the house spotless.

Woody looked at the dried-up flower beds. Nobody had planted flowers after his mother went into the nursing home. She'd died there four months ago, and the memory of her was still vivid. Maybe he should spade up the earth and throw in a few seeds. Women usually took care of the flowers, but it looked like there would never be a woman in his life. If he did not marry, who would inherit the land and the sprawling farmhouse his great-grandfather built in the early nine-teen hundreds? Woody loved the house with its wraparound porch and spacious rooms. It was nothing like the tract homes he'd seen in one section of Dundee—people all cooped up in tiny bedrooms with one window. He thought of his two nieces. Would they want to take over the farm one day, harvest hazelnuts, and keep the family tradition going? Women were more into business these days, so perhaps one of them might.

How could life change so drastically in such a short time? His father and brother were killed in a tragic accident, and then Hunter's widow, Jenny, took the girls and left for her hometown in Montana. Six months later she returned and dropped them on his doorstep like orphans. Said she couldn't handle them. She had to find her life somehow. What about his life? Maybe he didn't need this responsibility right now.

Woody's attention was brought to the present with the sound of a truck rolling up the long driveway. It was probably his neighbor, Hoby. He lived on the adjoining acreage and had lost his wife two years before. Hoby was like an older brother, and lately they had become even closer what with Hoby offering his help and support when Woody lost his family.

"Hey, man, what are you doing out here, staring into space as if another day hasn't started?" The tall, ruddy-complexioned man walked forward. "How ya doing, anyway?" He took his hat off and wiped his forehead.

"Don't think it's going to rain," Woody said. "Kinda wish it would, to take care of the dust."

"Yeah, we sure could use rain, but I'd say that would be a miracle more than a blessing. Say, did anyone answer your ad for a housekeeper yet?" Hoby stuck his hat back on.

"One's coming today—meeting her in Portland. I hope the girls don't gang up on her like they did the last one. You know how Mary Gray is."

"Well, Mary Gray doesn't want someone around, telling her what to do."

"Yeah, tell me something I don't know."

"She just needs to meet someone as stubborn as she is."

"You're probably right." Mary Gray took after her father. Woody remembered how stubborn and determined his brother had been at that age.

The older man started off toward the old red pickup, then stopped. "Sure hope you get a good housekeeper this time."

"I hope so, too," Woody said. He stood on the porch, listening to the sounds of the girls in the background. They were supposed to be eating breakfast and then heading up the lane to catch the school bus.

"You two better hightail it or you'll miss the bus," he called into the house.

Lacie flounced out and reached up to give him a kiss. "I know, Uncle Woody. It's Mary Gray. She is the utterly slowest person that ever lived on this earth."

Lacie had the Morgan fair skin, the same gentle, hazel eyes of her father. Those eyes did not look gentle now, however.

"Mary Gray just keeps us on our toes." Woody chuckled, thinking of the younger girl. She had a name, that one—her grandmother's maiden name. It was ladylike, but there it ended. She was a tomboy, and if anyone would take over this farm someday, it just might be her.

The acreage had to be passed on. He realized that being a nut farmer did not hold the prestige it once had, but it was a good living. Most years. And yet, the day might come when some rich developer stopped by and offered him a fortune for his land to make a subdivision. It had happened to two of his fellow farmers. It would be hard to turn down a sure thing, but the thought practically tore his heart out.

"The bus!" Lacie tore up the road as Mary Gray ran out the door with shoes in hand, her backpack bobbing up and down.

The bus was at their stop. Woody knew the driver, and she always waited at least two minutes for the girls.

They needed a motherly hand—and supervision. The house needed to be a home, a godly home as it had once been. Woody thought of his mother again. Fragile, yet loving. Even when her mind wasn't right, she'd read her Bible—the same Bible Woody now had on his dresser. Not that he read it, but it was the first thing he saw each morning when he awoke and the last thing he saw before turning out the light. He could still say verses he'd memorized in Sunday school. But that's as far as it went now. Too much had happened, and it was as if God had closed the door on him. Nothing would ever be the same. It began changing when his mother began wandering off, and Woody's father did something he never thought he would have to do: found a good nursing home ten miles away. Until his death, he and Woody had visited every day.

A week ago Woody had placed an ad in the paper, knowing full well his chances of finding the "just right" housekeeper were slim. Still, he had to try something. Soon he would meet this Cora Benchley—whose references were impeccable—and she'd agreed to come on a trial basis. He had readied the spare apartment up over the garage where Freda had stayed. It had been vacant just two weeks since the last housekeeper left. He was thankful it was there now. It had a sitting room, kitchen, and bedroom, and it was far nicer than many of the high-priced apartments in Portland. Times were certainly changing, and he wasn't that old.

An hour later, Woody hopped in his truck and headed for Portland.

❧

Cora liked him the minute she saw him. And she knew it had to be Woodrow Wilson Morgan III. He was broad-shouldered and had a stance that showed authority. She wondered if she passed for what he thought a housekeeper/nanny looked like. Dressed in her favorite blue-striped top and jeans, she knew she looked casual, but that was her style. At least she'd had her hair cut last week. She reached up to check the short style that curled up just a bit on the ends. Her bangs were frizzy as always.

She stepped forward, speaking his name. "Mr. Morgan?"

He turned and flashed a warm smile. "Are you Cora Benchley?"

"Yes." She held out her hand. His handshake was firm. Another plus.

"Would you like some coffee? We can get some at the café over there." He pointed to the far end of the square.

"No, thank you. Perhaps I should follow you to your house, and we could discuss the details there." Cora looked away from his steady gaze. "If that's all right—"

"That's a good idea. The girls will be home early today. Some teacher conference thing." He smiled. "That could be the deciding factor for you."

What are the girls like? Cora wondered. *Is there something he hasn't told me?*

Cora followed Woody across town, onto the freeway and off, no easy feat since he knew where he was going and she did not. Finally they hit country roads and less traffic.

A wrought iron sign saying WOODHAVEN ACRES was at the end of a lane leading to an enormous house. The house was old, and Cora loved old. They had arrived none too soon as a school bus pulled up before she got inside.

Two girls trudged up the lane, the smaller one running ahead of the other.

Woody began introductions. "Mary Gray, this is Miss Benchley. She might be our new housekeeper."

Mary Gray gave Cora a scrutinizing look. Cora wondered if she'd made the wrong step or turned the wrong corner. What do you say to a scowling eight-year-old? Hold out your hand or just say hello? She decided to do both.

"Hello, Mary Gray, I'm—"

"Oh, yuck!" Mary Gray said, avoiding the proffered hand.

"Mary Gray!" Woody's face turned red. "Where are your manners?"

"They flew out the window," Lacie said, stepping forward. "Hello, I'm Lacie. Pleased to meet you."

Cora sighed inwardly. She knew when she was being patronized, and the older girl was good at it. She wondered what she was letting herself in for.

Woody seemed to have found his voice.

"These are my nieces, Miss Benchley."

"Nieces? Not daughters?"

"Our father died," Mary Gray offered. "And our mother doesn't want us—"

"She does so," Lacie interjected. "She has to find a job." Her voice trailed off.

"Your mother will come back one day," Woody added, as if wanting to smooth things over. "Miss Benchley will help us out in the meantime."

"Please, just call me Cora. I'm ready to do my best."

"My father and my brother died tragically last year," Woody explained, "but we're holding our own."

"Cora? Did you say your name is Cora?" Mary Gray asked. "That's a weird name."

For the second time, Woody shook his head. Cora tried to smile. It was clear that Mary Gray got away with a lot, including rude behavior.

"I never liked the name myself," Cora said. "I was named after an aunt."

"We cannot always choose our names," Lacie said. "You should know about that, Mary Gray. Uncle Woody," she said pointedly, "is this interview over? I have a bedroom to clean!"

Woody nodded and held an immense oak door open. Cora liked the large entryway and its colorful braided rug, which was obviously handmade. The house had been well cared for, an added bonus.

"The last two housekeepers did not work out, and I think the girls are afraid to trust anyone."

"I suppose you're looking for a Mary Poppins type?"

He laughed then. "Yes, that's about it. So, are you ready to see the apartment?"

Cora hesitated as she met his penetrating gaze. "If you don't mind, I'd like to know exactly what my duties are first." Cora had learned at an early age that it helped to look people in the eye. She had hoped Mr. Morgan might be short and stout, not tall and handsome with an engaging smile. *Steady*, she told herself. *Don't even start thinking such thoughts.*

"I mainly want someone to cook, to clean, and to be there for the girls. I'm not good at parenting, and they need someone who cares."

Cora nodded. "It'll take time. I'm sure you realize that. They seem determined not to like me. I sensed that right off."

"They can be incorrigible—"

"I assume I should discipline them, if necessary?"

Woody's face blanched. "I prefer to do the disciplining. If there's a problem, come to me. We'll work it out."

"Am I to see to their bedtime, help with homework, that sort of thing?"

Woody withdrew a sheet of paper from his shirt pocket. "This is a list. I believe it explains everything. I am a list person, as you'll notice. I have menus for breakfast and their lunches each day of the week."

Cora took the list and studied it for a minute. "I'm to follow the menu?"

"Yes, it's much easier that way." He leaned over and pointed at items under the girls' names. "I think you'll find it helpful."

Cora felt a funny knot in her throat, but surely it couldn't be too bad. She'd end up doing a lot of things her way, and Woody would see that it worked fine. She looked up again and met his gaze. There was something about those eyes. They were mesmerizing—no way could she let that thought continue.

"Come this way," Woody said. He led her through the large farmhouse kitchen. The old-fashioned dark table with carved legs and matching chairs were perfect for the room.

Cora loved the apartment, too. Someone had fixed it up nicely. The living room, or sitting room, as Woody called it, was small, but cozy enough with the love seat and matching recliner. The bedroom was painted a pale pink, and ruffled curtains fluttered in the afternoon breeze. She wanted to sit on the four-poster bed—complete with canopy!—but thought better of it.

Flowered chintz curtains fluttered beside the windows in the small kitchen. Cora didn't like the beige walls, but perhaps, if she stayed on, she could redecorate. The views of the hills to the north and the orchard to the south cinched the deal.

"It's not very big, but everything you need is here," Woody said.

"I love it. It's perfect!"

"The last housekeeper liked it, too, but she felt she could do a better job if she lived in the house."

"That won't be a problem. I'll get up as early as you need me."

Cora was comparing Woody to Leighton. Funny how she'd not thought of Leighton until just now. She was getting on with her life. She smiled. She felt good about this move. She knew the girls would be a definite challenge, but Woody and his lists might be even more so.

"This better work, because I need to concentrate on the orchard," Woody was saying.

Cora met his gaze straight on and nodded. "Yes, I understand all that."

He offered his hand. "If you want the job, it's yours." He grinned. "Trial basis, of course. Say, two weeks."

"Trial basis—two weeks," Cora repeated. *Yes, this is going to work out just fine. It has to.*

Chapter 3

Cora unpacked the smaller bag and went back to the house for the evening meal. Woody said dinner was promptly at six. She didn't need to cook this first day, as he'd picked up barbecued chicken and fruit salad at a deli. "It's the only kind of salad Mary Gray will eat," he'd explained.

Now he grabbed a tablespoon and stuck it in the fruit salad, dumped the chicken on a platter, and brought out bread and butter to round out the meal. The cookie jar was empty, so Cora would bake tomorrow.

"Do you live right on the beach?" Woody asked as he passed the chicken.

Cora looked up. "Do you suppose we could ask a blessing first?"

Woody appeared startled, but only for a moment. "Yes, of course. I'll say it." He uttered an awkward prayer and repeated his earlier question.

Cora took a thigh. "My little house, which was my grandmother's, is not on the beach. It's in a place called Oysterville. It's on the bay side. I'm close to water, but there's no view from my house."

"You left the beach to come here?" A look of disbelief crossed Lacie's face.

"Yes."

"The only water we have here is the pond over on the edge of my acreage," Woody explained.

"And we can't even swim in it," both girls chorused.

Cora turned to Mary Gray. "Would you please pass the butter when you're finished?"

Cora noted that the girls lacked even basic table manners when Mary Gray licked the butter knife. She wondered if Mr. Morgan—Woody, as he'd asked to be called—would mind if she tackled that problem. Woody. How could she ever call him Woody? Nicknames bothered her, especially between employer and employee. It had been different with Leighton.

Dinner finally ended with the girls squabbling, something Woody ignored. It made Cora's stomach churn. At least she ate less than usual, and there was no dessert. Now she wished she'd bought that package of chocolate-covered raisins at the store yesterday.

Both girls disappeared when Cora cleared the table, and a minute later the television blared from the den. Woody left out the back door. She wasn't surprised. Men could leave a situation; it was mothers, housekeepers, and nannies that bore the brunt of raising children. Why else would he have hired her? Two women had come and gone in the past few months, and she knew why now. Not many housekeepers would be willing to tolerate the girls' incessant bickering. They were rude. She scraped the chicken bones into the garbage can and rinsed the dishes before filling the dishwasher. The girls needed simple household chores. Responsibility built character, and what these girls needed was character. "But there is hope, Lord," Cora said. "Thank You for that."

After the kitchen was clean, the table wiped, and the sink free of dishes, Cora ignored the noise from the den and went out onto the porch. She'd noticed a porch swing right off as they drove up earlier. A slight breeze came from the south, and it would be nice to relax for a few minutes before going back to her apartment to arrange her belongings.

Woody was in the orchard. His red plaid shirt showed up in the growing evening dusk. She'd hoped to find him on the porch so they could talk about a few things.

The front door banged open, and Mary Gray stormed out. "Tell Lacie to leave me alone!"

Cora put a hand to her forehead, wondering if they ever stopped bickering. "What's the matter? Are you sick?"

"It's just a tension headache."

"Well, some good you're going to be if you get sick a lot."

"It's just been a long day. I sure would have appreciated some help with the dinner dishes."

Mary Gray backed up. "Oh, no. You're not going to make us do dishes. That's why Uncle Woody hired you. He wanted someone to cook and clean and maybe help me with my homework since I hate it so much."

Cora leaned forward. "Yes, I'm sure you're right, but young girls need to learn to cook and clean—"

"Where did you come from—the Dark Ages?"

"And how do you know about the Dark Ages?" Cora asked.

"Saw something about it on TV."

"I see. Well, perhaps I did come from the Dark Ages." Cora smiled. "And if that's the case, I certainly don't know any math or English."

Mary Gray rolled her eyes and stomped back into the house. Cora breathed a sigh of relief. Thankfully, they were still in school. A small reprieve until she had time to settle in.

Cora unfolded the list and saw that bedtime was at nine o'clock. That was in ten minutes. She'd get them started now, knowing there would probably be a battle.

She went back inside and entered the den. Cora reached for the remote control and muted the TV set.

"What're you doing?" Lacie looked up with a scowl.

"I just wanted to suggest that you start getting ready for bed since it's almost nine. Anything I can do to help?"

"You don't need to worry about that," Mary Gray said. "We do it ourselves."

"I see. Does your uncle tuck you in and listen to your prayers?"

Lacie shook her head. "Nobody tucks us in or listens to our prayers. That's for babies." She reached out, her palm up, indicating she wanted the remote back, but Cora held on to it.

"I'd like to see that you're safely tucked in, and if you don't want to say a prayer, I'll say it."

"That's not on the list," Mary Gray said.

"I know that." Cora smiled and handed Lacie the remote when the program resumed. "However, it's on my list."

"You have a list?" Mary Gray looked shocked.

Cora nodded. "Uncle Woody isn't the only one with lists." She paused in the doorway. "Turn the TV off when this is over, please."

True to their word, the girls took their time brushing their teeth and getting into their pajamas. Cora would ask Woody about getting them started earlier. Surely he couldn't argue with that.

She tucked Mary Gray in first and asked the Lord to bless her and keep her safe. Mary Gray said nothing and turned her head when Cora tried to kiss her cheek.

After facing the same difficulty with Lacie, Cora said an inner prayer as she walked back down the steps. *Lord, these girls need You. And I need Your help!*

The list of instructions said that once the girls were in bed, Cora was free to go to her apartment unless he'd specifically asked her to remain at the house longer. By nine o'clock Woody was either inside or near enough to the house that he would listen for the girls, himself.

Cora went through the house, out the back door, and around back where her apartment was. She might as well finish unpacking. It was obvious that Woody was not coming in anytime soon. She'd ask him tomorrow about bedtime. Meredith was probably right. This might not be the job for her.

≈

Woody enjoyed his evening strolls down through the hazelnut trees. The house was always noisy after dinner. The TV blared, though the girls rarely watched. When they weren't fighting with each other, they argued with him. Nothing he said or did seemed to change things. He wanted to love them, tried to feel empathy for his nieces who had not only lost their father, but their mother, as well. Jenny hadn't been able to control them, and he could see this new housekeeper— Cora—would have a problem, as well. She'd been quiet during the meal while the girls bickered—she'd hardly eaten a thing. He'd give her a few weeks before she turned in her notice, and then he'd have to place another ad. And yet. . .there was something strong about her—something he liked. She looked him in the eye when she talked. She also seemed to have definite ideas about things. He smiled, remembering how she'd looked aghast when he produced the list of her duties.

She seemed most disconcerted about the menus. He'd always written lists. How else did one finish anything? Hadn't his father done the same? Woodrow Wilson Morgan II, stern and unbending, had been the best teacher. And his mother always gave in to all demands. He supposed her life hadn't been easy. Funny, he'd never thought about that until now. He wondered if her bouts of illness had been an escape in the beginning.

Woody's thoughts returned to Cora. She might consider the job a challenge. And it wasn't as if she hadn't had practice. According to her first response, she'd taken care of a family of four boys for nearly ten years. Surely she could handle two feisty girls.

Suddenly Lacie barreled down the row in her pajamas, shouting at the top of her lungs.

"I need to take cupcakes to school tomorrow! I just remembered!"

"Cupcakes?"

"Yes. It's for a party, and I promised to bring some."

"It's too late—"

"You can go into town and buy some at the supermarket. Please say you will." She looked up at Woody with such a pleading expression, he knew he'd have to make the twenty-mile round-trip back into town, since the nearest store would be closed by now. If he didn't, he'd have no peace tonight.

"You could have mentioned it earlier—"

"I know, Uncle Woody, but I forgot."

"Okay. Okay." With shoulders hunched over, he followed her back up the row. He looked to see if Cora was still on the porch. Woody heard the door open earlier, and the swing creaked as he'd left for his evening stroll. He'd wanted to go back, sit on the steps, and talk as he used to do with his father. He missed those quiet times.

The porch swing was empty.

"What kind of cupcakes do you want?"

"Chocolate with chocolate icing."

He went inside and grabbed the truck keys. "Do you want to come with—"

"Me, too, me too!" Mary Gray called out.

When they both came along, they'd always find something to be disagreeable about. "No, you stay. You went the last time."

"Where are you going?" Suddenly Cora was there, looking from Lacie to Woody.

"To get some cupcakes for Lacie to take to school in the morning."

"You're going all the way back into town for that?"

"Not much else I can do about it."

"Maybe we could make some."

"I want ones from the store because they're all fancy and nice," Lacie interjected.

"We can make fancy cupcakes."

Mary Gray's eyes widened. "You know how to make cupcakes?"

Cora smiled. "I won a blue ribbon for my chocolate cake at the county fair year before last."

"Well, Lacie wants a special kind. We'll be back soon."

It was settled, but Cora felt rejected. Woody made rules and wasn't open to change; that was obvious. He'd never listen to any ideas she had.

There was a tug on her arm. "Would you make cupcakes now?"

Cora looked at the small, round face with those big, imploring eyes. Mary Gray was reachable; at that moment she knew she had an ally.

"I just looked, and there's no powdered sugar for frosting, so how about cookies? Let's hurry so we can surprise them."

"Oh, let's."

They decided on peanut butter cookies. "Because Uncle Woody likes peanut butter," Mary Gray said.

Cora breathed a prayer of thanks. Yes, Mary Gray was teachable. The fact that she thought of what her uncle liked, putting him before herself, was a good sign.

Soon the cookies were mixed, and Cora rolled them into balls while Mary Gray stamped them with a fork and sprinkled sugar on top.

Cora's arm slipped around Mary Gray's small shoulders as the first sheet went into the oven. It was going to be difficult with two foes in this house, but tonight she'd won over the youngest. At least for now.

Chapter 4

The next morning, Cora found a sobbing Lacie in the living room. The room, seldom used by Woody or the girls, was a typical old-fashioned parlor with heavy, dark drapes, a flowered carpet, and a couch and matching love seat. Lacie was sprawled across the love seat.

A photograph of Lacie's father, uncle, and grandparents hung above an old upright piano. Cora remembered the beautiful baby grand back at Leighton's where she'd worked so long. She wished again that she had taken lessons as a child and wondered if Woody or the girls could play.

Cora winced at the sight of Lacie's stooped shoulders. She understood heartbreak firsthand; Lacie needed comforting, but Cora doubted Lacie would respond to any attempts she made. The right words might help, but nothing would possibly make up for the loss of one's father. And at such a young age. Then to have the mother run off, leaving her daughters with her brother-in-law to raise. How could one treat the role of motherhood so lightly? She cleared her voice to let Lacie know she was in the room.

"You must miss him very much."

Lacie's head shot up. For one brief moment, she looked as if she wanted Cora to listen, but in the next second, her shoulders straightened and a look of disdain crossed her face. "You don't understand. I hate this farm! I hate my sister! I want to go live with my mother. She'll come for me soon. I know she will."

Cora nodded. "You're right. I don't understand. But I do know it's difficult to measure the sorrow felt by another. My father died in the Vietnam War when I was eight. I miss him to this day. If you ever want to talk, I'm available—"

"You're just saying that." Lacie nibbled her lower lip. "Did you really lose your father?"

"Yes. I could never lie about a thing like that."

Cora sighed, remembering the Walker children and how they had acted after their mother left. The children felt abandoned. They thought it was their fault.

"My mother sent me to my grandmother's for a few weeks after my father died," Cora said, "sort of like what your mother did. When I came home, it was never the same again. There was no laughter—my father was the one who smiled and joked. . . ." She choked at the memory.

Lacie's eyes widened. "It was that way at our house, too!"

"Time heals hurts, and prayer helps, too." Cora wanted to say more, something that would comfort the child's heart, but perhaps this was enough for now.

375

Lacie looked at her knotted hands, then moved past Cora. She hoped the young girl would know Cora would be there if she ever needed her. For now she'd planted a seed. Cora mouthed a quick prayer, asking for God's guidance. The rest was up to Woody.

Breakfast was expected in fifteen minutes. It was time to whip up the pancake batter. Or at least she thought this was the morning for pancakes. Woody's list made her cringe. What happened to the cook fixing what suited her at the time? And what was wrong with a bowl of cold cereal now and then? Not that she'd mind frying bacon and eggs for him, if he wanted them. At least she knew what was expected of her. That was a blessing, she reminded herself. She definitely needed to work on her attitude.

Lacie came in well after Woody had eaten his bacon and pancakes. Mary Gray, as usual, had slept in. She had a habit of grabbing a bit of whatever she could from the table, then dashing out the door when the bus honked at the foot of the driveway.

"Lacie needs your attention," Cora said, after the bus had come and gone. She poured second cups of coffee for both of them. Conversation definitely called for another cup. He said nothing.

"She was crying in the living room this morning and—"

Woody shook his head. "Girls cry a lot."

Cora counted to five before speaking. "Yes, girls cry a lot, but not without reason."

"How do you know?" His gaze met hers and held. "You don't even know these girls."

Cora was surprised at his brusqueness. "Lacie misses her father."

"And so do I. I lost a father and a brother—"

"But not at such a young age."

Woody looked pensive for a moment, then pushed his chair back. "I'm sure you're right on this, but I have nothing left to give."

"She's just a child."

"And I was left with a job to fulfill, one I did not ask for and was never coached in."

"She won't let me touch her."

"She doesn't let me get close, either."

"You could try again. Please."

He shook his head. "Are we going to have these conversations often? With you telling me all about what I should be doing and how I should improve the lives of two children who are not even my own?"

And are you going to run the house with an iron hand, going by lists and needs, never considering others' wants and desires? What's wrong with a little spontaneity?

"You're all they have," Cora finally said. "I know it's a full plate, but with God's help, you can handle it, one day at a time."

"One day at a time." Woody crossed his arms. "Hoby says that. He's been a good friend."

"He sounds like a wise man."

⁓

Long after breakfast, Woody was still out checking his trees. Cora went to the apartment, all the while wondering if he was a hopeless cause. Sure, she could cook, clean, offer support. . .but it was like the old adage: You can lead a horse to water, but you can't make him drink. Woody was set in his ways. There were rules and lists and the right way—his way—to do things. His nieces, though dear to him, were just getting in the way, hampering his farming—the one job he knew how to do, the one thing he felt confident about.

Cora had thought about asking Meredith to come and bring a few things she'd forgotten in her haste, but perhaps she should wait and see what transpired. She sensed that Woody did not like her, and she knew it was a hard call with the girls.

Now back in the kitchen, Cora looked at the list tacked to the bulletin board. Toasted cheese sandwiches and tomato soup. But there was leftover chicken, and chicken salad was always good. . .and with that she'd want a different soup. Dare she change the menu? Would Woody even notice, and if he did, would it matter that much?

He noticed. And it mattered.

"Chicken salad is fine," he said, setting his half-eaten sandwich down. "I also like mushroom soup, but I was hankering for a toasted cheese sandwich with tomato soup."

Cora said nothing as she grabbed a can of tomato soup and reached for a small pot. "Okay. That's what you'll have."

"No, it's all right. I can have it tomorrow, but that throws the menu off."

Cora plopped the soup into the pan and smashed the shimmering red tower with a large spoon. She didn't want him to feel as if she was running his life, but menus should be her concern. At least they always had been before. She swallowed hard. "Tomato soup coming up."

"I told you to forget the soup—"

"It's no trouble. You'll have tomato soup in five minutes. I add milk to it, like my mother always did. Or would you prefer water?"

"Milk," he said. "It is always going to be like this, isn't it," he stated bluntly.

"I can leave whenever you want," she wanted to say, but Cora liked the man in spite of his stubbornness. She wanted to succeed. One never liked to fail, did they?

Give it two weeks, she reminded herself. *That should be enough time. Yeah, enough time to either submit to his list or tear it up into itty-bitty pieces.*

"And one other thing," Cora said. "The girls need more discipline, especially about bedtime. And I'd get them up earlier in the morning. Another thing is chores. Children also need responsibility. I want to help with this since I'm supposed to be their nanny—"

Woody let the spoon fall back into his bowl. "I hear your concerns, but I think you're expecting too much. They've been through a lot, you know."

Cora poured herself a cup of water and reached for a tea bag. "I do understand that. I just want to help. I also think having a pet, especially a dog, helps teach children responsibility. I'm surprised that there are no pets on the farm."

"No pets." Woody scowled. "This is not an animal farm, or hadn't you noticed? I suppose you'll want chickens next and then rabbits."

"Not a bad idea."

"We've had them before," he went on, as if he hadn't heard Cora. "There simply isn't time for animals on a hazelnut farm."

"A dog would offer so much love. In this situation, it's worth a try."

"No." Woody pushed his chair back and rose to his feet. "No," he repeated.

"But—"

"What part of 'no' don't you understand?"

After Woody pushed his chair back and left the room, Cora felt tears threaten. He was disagreeable about everything! She reflected on the conversation. Was she being too harsh with Lacie and Mary Gray? Expecting too much too soon? This man had been running the orchard alone after losing his father and brother, then he had welcomed his nieces into his home when their mother couldn't cope with them. He wanted to hold the reins, and Cora was upsetting his plans, his list, his way of doing something. As she'd thought before, in many ways Woodrow Morgan III would be a bigger challenge, much more so than the girls, who were pliable. How willing was she to work at it? As his dark eyes penetrated her mind, she knew she was ready to take it as far as she could. And a dog was definitely worth fighting for.

Chapter 5

Cora was seething by the end of the first week. Her opinion of the girls from that first day had not changed. Mary Gray, who had seemed so cooperative while helping with the peanut butter cookies, now acted as if Cora was an interloper. Was it true that things got worse before they got better? What puzzled her was how Woody could be so oblivious to their behavior. Or did he just not care? Nothing seemed to matter but the farm. He and Hoby had checked for some kind of worm that was detrimental to the trees earlier that day. "It's an ongoing job," Hoby explained when Cora asked. "Always something to check for."

Cora liked the older man and suggested he come in for coffee and cookies. Of course he said yes. Once inside, he talked about the farms, the difficulty in getting a good price for the crops, and other things. He did like to talk. He also liked peanut butter cookies.

Cora's favorite time of day was when she came out on the porch and watched the sun dip behind a low range of mountains to the west. It was cooler here. She'd finished the dishes because both girls had homework. She often wondered if they were just saying that to get out of dish detail. She had done that when she was a child. *Some things never change,* she mused.

Woody was strolling down a row in the orchard, his eyes downcast. He seemed so lonely at times. She wished he could tell her what was on his mind, open up a bit, but most men weren't that way. Few seemed willing to divulge their worries or what lay in their hearts. Perhaps men saw it as a sign of weakness. Leighton had kept things bottled up inside him, too. Trying to get a man to talk was never easy. They usually walked away or turned the TV up. Either was an action that said far more than any words could.

Cora gently rocked the swing with one foot and tucked the other up under her. She'd been busy getting everything squared away, trying to overlook the girls' complaining and bickering and Woody's sighs and frowns. She'd been so involved with the three of them, she hadn't taken the time to notice how she felt. A job was a job, after all. But she liked it here in this peaceful spot. Sometimes Cora read a book out on the swing, but dusk was approaching fast, so tonight she sat and gave the swing an occasional push. Lost in her thoughts, she hadn't noticed Woody leaving the orchard, but then he was there, sitting on the top step, wiping perspiration from his brow.

"It's a nice night," he said, glancing in Cora's direction.

"A lot different from the coastal air," Cora said with a nod. "Most nights the fog creeps in, and you go inside because of the dampness."

"You miss it, don't you?"

"I—yes, I guess you could say that."

"Don't blame you. I'd certainly miss the farm if I ever moved away. I suspect they'll have to carry me off in a casket—"

"Uncle Woody! You're not going to die, are you?"

Both jumped and looked at Mary Gray in the doorway dressed in her night-gown. She was brushing her teeth, but the look on her face told all. Her father and grandfather both had died, and she'd lost a mother as a result of her father's untimely death. It was as if she couldn't bear to lose someone else.

"I'm not dying yet," Woody said, patting her on the back. "Now I think you'd better hightail it to bed, missy."

Missy. Woody sometimes called Mary Gray "Missy" and Lacie was "Miss Priss." Cora learned their father had started that, and sometimes Woody let the nicknames slip out.

Minutes later both girls came and hugged their uncle good night. Cora got up and followed them up the stairs. She heard the grumbles but ignored them. She wondered if she'd ever reach the status of deserving a hug.

"You don't have to see that we're in bed," Lacie said.

"I know you're big girls, but it's part of my job."

"You're just saying that," Lacie countered.

Cora smiled as she pulled back the covers. "No, I really like doing it."

Lacie crawled in and turned her face away from Cora. "I don't need you to say prayers."

"But I want to," Cora said. "And you are in my daily prayers. I just want you to know that."

Mary Gray faked being asleep when Cora entered her room, but Cora pulled the blanket up and prayed, "Lord, bless Mary Gray and keep her safe."

Minutes later, Cora went back outside and found Woody still sitting on the top step. She wanted to continue the conversation they'd had before Mary Gray interrupted.

"Of course we're all going to die sometime," Cora said. "Are you prepared?" she wanted to ask.

"Yes, we are." Woody glanced over, then looked away. Cora had some strange feelings, and she knew they were only her imagination. She'd had feelings like that with Leighton, and nothing had happened. Never again would she assume she knew what a look meant. Woody was grateful because she kept the house clean, cooked his meals, and helped with his nieces. And though he paid her a nice wage, she knew that to him she was simply a person doing a job, not someone who had a heart and feelings. And purpose. She wanted to ask him again about the girls helping with dinner and also about a dog. The time was right to bring it up, since Woody appeared to be in a good mood. Cora stopped rocking and cleared her throat.

"Is something wrong?"

"Yes." Cora started to cross her arms, then stopped. She'd read a book on body language and knew crossed arms could be construed as meaning anything from stubbornness to a semi-declaration of war, and she didn't want to portray that. "Each meal ends with plates left on the table and napkins wadded up on the floor. There's food to put away, the table to clear, and dishes to load in the dishwasher. It's important that Lacie and Mary Gray learn a few basic tasks."

"Those things are what I hired you to do."

"But," Cora sputtered, "if they don't learn now, what will they do when they're on their own? And their manners are dreadful. I take it their mother—"

"Leave Jenny out of it." Woody's tone was clipped. "All I ask is acceptance from you."

Cora should have let it go. One of her worst faults was always wanting to have the last word. "I'm sorry. I am trying to be accepting, Mr. Morgan, really I am."

"Maybe you could find it in your heart to try harder," Woody said. He got up from the step and headed toward the orchard.

Cora felt as if she'd been slapped. She stood, watching him disappear around the corner of the house. Why did any of this matter? Because she did care and she was a perfectionist. With a sigh, she fled into the house, letting the screen door slam behind her. Why not? Everyone else let it slam. Sometimes it seemed to be a contest where they worked at seeing who made the most noise. She went out the back door and headed for her apartment. A breeze picked up from the south, and it felt good to Cora's flushed face as she strode across the yard, still trembling from the sting of his retort.

Reaching the sanctuary of her own place, Cora smiled. It was quiet and perfect for one person. She liked the kitchen with its rose-patterned plates and odds and ends of other dinnerware. Woody had said his grandmother collected the same rose pattern, but over the years most had been broken with the exception of three plates. He apologized for the hodgepodge of dishes, but Cora liked it. It gave a set table a homey feel. Not that she'd be entertaining anyone, nor would she eat up here, but if there was another episode like last night, she might cook for them and then leave the table. Yes, that should get her point across nicely. "People can't stand to be ignored," her mother had told her once. "It's when you rant and rave that you lose the battle, and Cora, you rant and rave way too much."

Would her mother have considered that ranting and raving tonight? She really hadn't said as much as she wanted to, but perhaps it had been too much.

Cora sat in the darkness, watching moonlight and shadows dance across the walls. She felt weariness seep into her bones and decided to go to bed to read. She had just finished her Bible reading when there was a light tap at the door.

"Yes?" She presumed it was one of the girls because surely Woody would have knocked louder than that.

"Can I come in?"

Mary Gray. Her ally, if she had one.

Mary Gray bounced into the room. She never walked—she pranced like a young colt.

"I thought you were in bed."

Mary Gray grinned. "I like to slip out some nights. Uncle Woody never sees me."

"No wonder you don't want to get up in the morning. A night owl, huh?"

"Are you going to tell?"

Cora sighed. "I suppose not this time, but you can't go out wandering alone at night."

"Why not?"

"Because it's dangerous, you need your sleep, and I care what happens to you."

"You do?"

"Of course I do."

The small girl looked pensive. "Nobody else cares about me."

"I'm sure that's not true. Uncle Woody does and Lacie, too, even though she may not show it."

"I like this!" Mary Gray touched a throw on the back of the love seat. It was an assortment of cats on a deep blue background. It had been a birthday gift from Meredith.

"Do you like cats?"

"Oh, yes!" Mary Gray's face lit up, and Cora realized she really liked this child.

"Why don't you have a cat then?" Cora remembered what Woody had said about a dog or chickens, but cats took care of themselves.

Mary Gray plopped down on the love seat, her hand tracing the outline of a large yellow cat. "Uncle Woody hates 'em!"

Cora stood and took the girl's hand. "I think it's time for me to walk you back to the house."

"Do I have to go?"

"Yes, you do."

They chatted as they walked across the yard and into the house.

"Do you think we might pray about that?" Cora asked. Perhaps God would soften Woody's heart about pets.

Mary Gray hesitated for a long moment. "No. I think we'd better pray for a dog."

When they reached the bottom of the stairs, Cora stopped. "Mary Gray, I have a favor to ask."

The little girl turned. "What is it?"

"I need someone to set the table before dinner. Could you do that?"

"Sure. That's easy."

"Good. Thank you." Cora squeezed Mary Gray's hand. "And maybe Lacie can clear after dinner."

"I don't know about that." Mary Gray reached up and gave Cora a quick hug. "Can I come up to your apartment before bedtime tomorrow?"

"I don't know why not."

The warm night was bathed in moonlight, and Cora was glad she was here. It was going to work. With God's help, she would make it work.

Later, as she sat in her apartment, she thought of how easy it would have been to let Mary Gray stay. She was just more. . .likable, though Cora never tried to have favorites.

"Thank You, Lord," she murmured before turning the heat on under the kettle. It was time for a cup of tea.

Chapter 6

Woody had heard Mary Gray slip out the door, knowing she was probably heading for Cora's apartment. He had heard her leave the house before and wanted to say something, but as long as he knew her night wanderings were close to the house, he'd ignore it. As he sat watching the sky fill with stars, he wondered how Cora would handle it. Would she be angry with the child? She seemed to be harsh toward him, and he wasn't sure why. It seemed to stem from the list of duties. Yet, other housekeepers had found his list helpful.

Woody went into the house and sat in the den. It was quiet now—too early for the news, but he doubted he'd watch anyway. He enjoyed peace and quiet and agreed with Cora about that. How had this all happened to him, anyway? "Lord, are You really there? Do You really care about me? This farm? My nieces? I need a sign to help me believe again. I want to believe, but my heart seems all dried up. . . ."

Voices sounded, and soon Mary Gray and Cora entered the house. He heard Cora's request for help in setting the table. He thought about saying something, then felt the sudden desire to talk to Cora, but the moment passed. Soon Mary Gray's bedroom door closed, and Cora was gone.

Something was happening in this house. He didn't know what, nor did he know why he felt this way. But it was there. . .almost palpable. Cora was good for the girls. Could she also be good for his restless and hungry spirit? He wished he knew.

❧

Cora mentioned the dog again the next day after the girls left to catch the school bus—running as usual. Woody was enjoying his second cup of coffee while he pored over the morning paper. It probably wasn't the best time to ask, but she'd be gentle yet deliberate.

"About the girls and a dog. . ."

He glanced up with an annoyed expression on his face. "Again? Is this all we are ever going to talk about?"

Cora retreated and put the milk away. "It will wait."

Woody set the paper down. "No, you've broken my train of thought, so you might as well go on with it."

"I don't mean to anger you. I'm really trying not to overstep my bounds. In fact, I'm sorry we argued yesterday, and I truly don't want to start another argument."

Woody was silent for a moment, then nodded. "I agree. Seems we should be able to talk in a civil way. I want this to work, you know."

Cora felt her spirits lift. Was this the chance she had waited for? There was the matter of the bus waiting at the end of the lane each morning.

"I wanted to ask about alarm clocks. I don't think the bus driver should have to wait for them. Have you tried setting an alarm clock?"

"Once."

"Then we might try it. Maybe give the girls an incentive—"

Woody rolled his eyes as he finished his coffee and pushed the chair back. "You know I make the rules around here. That's an incentive for you to go by."

Cora realized she'd probably said enough but couldn't stop. "It's difficult to bring order to chaos without some rules and direction from authority."

"What do you mean?"

"You told me that first day that you wanted an orderly, even godly home."

Woody nodded. "Yes, I did say that."

"My comments and suggestions aren't intended to make you feel as if I'm trying to take over. I'm simply trying to give you what you asked for: an orderly and godly home. I've been praying with the girls, and last night I asked Mary Gray if she'd help me by setting the table tonight. I'd like to assign a few more chores for both girls. Perhaps you'd think about it, maybe even pray about it."

He cleared his throat. "All right. Just as long as you remember I'm in charge here."

"Oh, I quite agree." As with Lacie, she had planted the seed. He'd ponder and come back to her about this, probably tonight.

"I'm going over to Hoby's."

"Will you be back for lunch?"

He looked as if he couldn't believe she'd asked the question. "Of course." He strode from the kitchen and out the back door.

Cora finished kitchen detail and went upstairs to see if the girls had made their beds. Not that she would clean or bother anything. The list said each girl was responsible for cleaning her bedroom.

Clothes cluttered every space of the floor in Lacie's room. It looked worse than it had last night, but it surprised Cora. She believed that a bedroom was a child's domain, the one place they could retreat to. The one exception to the rule said they weren't allowed to leave food or dishes lying around.

Leaving Lacie's door semi-open, as she'd found it, she went into Mary Gray's room. The bed was hastily made and the floor was clutter-free, revealing the highly polished oak floors. Cora smiled at the poster of a huge calico cat.

She hesitated in the hall, then hurried down the steps, avoiding the temptation to look in the rest of the upstairs rooms. She would not invade Woody's privacy, though she was curious. During the few remaining morning hours, she dusted and vacuumed and made a few changes in the décor. She hoped Woody wouldn't mind that she changed the chairs in the TV room. If he did, she could always move them back.

The truck lumbered up the driveway at 11:35 sharp. Cora already knew that Woody would park in the same spot—back by the barn. He would also stay out there for several minutes, doing who knows what, then come inside, go straight to the small half bath off the kitchen, and wash up. This was Cora's cue to make the sandwiches and stir the soup on the stove. There was still coffee from breakfast. She'd never seen anyone consume so much coffee.

Woody came in but said nothing. Cora turned the heat up just a bit, since he liked his soup piping hot.

It was noon, straight up, when he came out of the bathroom and sat at the end of the table. Cora brought the food over and placed it in front of him.

He muttered "thanks" and grabbed a half sandwich without looking up from the paper he hadn't finished that morning.

Cora left before she could say anything she might regret. He wore the same scowl he'd worn earlier. They'd have the discussion later. There was something maddening about this man and his lists and habits. He was so systematic—he never did anything differently.

"Aren't you going to eat?" His loud voice followed her.

Cora looked around the corner. "No, I thought I'd leave you to your reading."

"I can read this later."

Was it a request for company? Could that be?

"I hadn't figured on eating with you. I have a lot of work to accomplish, but perhaps tomorrow."

Cora had mixed emotions as she left. Perhaps the work could have waited. Maybe Woody was genuinely trying to mend fences. Like the girls, he was obviously feeling pain. And she could commiserate. But therein would lie the danger. In knowing him better, she might care for him more deeply than she should, and she'd vowed never to get emotionally attached to an employer again.

Later, she walked down the lane toward the main road, enjoying the warmth of the sunny day. She thought again how nice it would be to have a dog to stroll along beside her. She missed having an animal. She wished she could have brought her cat, but Meredith was more than happy to take Keesy Kat.

Cora looked skyward. "Lord, help Woody to reconsider getting a dog. I think he might benefit from one, himself."

At four o'clock, the girls arrived. The bus ride was long, and they were the last to be dropped off. Soon noise filled the house, and Cora grew tense. If the TV wasn't blaring, the girls were arguing and hitting each other.

Mary Gray ran into the kitchen, her book bag bobbing. "I need to study for a spelling bee tomorrow. Will you help me with the words?"

Cora nodded. "Of course I will. You go study them now, and I'll quiz you after dinner."

❧

Woody was silent at the meal. If he liked the meat loaf, he never said. He heaped gravy on his mashed potatoes, then took seconds after finishing the first helping.

Lacie toyed with her food. "I don't like gravy," she said. "Uncle Woody can have my share."

Mary Gray was unusually quiet, and she ate everything on her plate. She'd set the table before dinner and now pronounced, to Cora's chagrin, that Lacie could clear the dishes. Cora should have realized that Mary Gray wouldn't wait for her to ask Lacie to help.

"I will not," Lacie declared. "I have to study for a test tomorrow."

"But that's the rules," Mary Gray said, jutting her chin out.

"I make the rules around here," Woody announced, pushing his plate back. "I guess we could all help out by taking our dirty dishes to the sink, however." He walked to the sink and placed his plate and silverware on the counter.

Lacie muttered something and followed suit, but Mary Gray stayed behind to clear the rest of the table. Not only had she set it, but she was clearing it voluntarily.

"That's okay, isn't it?" she asked, as if wanting approval.

"Yes, thank you, Mary Gray. But it would be best if you'd let me ask Lacie to help the next time, okay?"

"Okay."

The two worked side by side until the dishes were in the dishwasher and the table and counters clean.

"I'll get my spelling words."

Cora was pleased to see the little girl was a good speller. She missed only one and soon corrected herself.

"Is there anything else?"

"No. I don't need help with math." She opened her backpack and pulled out a math worksheet that appeared nearly finished.

"Then I suggest you do something you enjoy when you're done."

"Lacie's watching some stupid show, so I'm not going in there," she said as she worked the last problem.

"How about reading?" Cora asked once the child had put her homework away.

"Forgot my library book."

"Then maybe you'd like to do some handiwork."

"Handiwork? What's that?"

"I have an old loom my grandmother gave me and fabric loops in several colors. You place them on the loom, and when you're finished, you have a nice pot holder. You'll see."

"What about Lacie?"

"I'll see if she wants to come with us."

Lacie didn't look away from the program she was watching. "If you change your mind, come on up."

"I have homework, but this is my favorite show."

"Okay. We'll be back in an hour or so."

Soon Cora and Mary Gray were up in the apartment, and Cora handed Mary Gray the loom. She chose aqua and gray for her colors and in no time had a pot holder half-completed.

Cora picked up the crocheting she kept in a large basket. She'd started on an afghan a year ago.

"What do you call that?" Mary Gray asked.

"It's crocheting. Maybe you'd like to learn?"

"I would." Her eyes sparkled.

"Perhaps tomorrow," Cora said. "For now I think you should take your shower."

"But I always do that in the morning."

"I know, but if you did it tonight, you might be ready before the bus comes."

Mary Gray tilted her head. "That's a good idea. Then I won't have to wait for Lacie. She takes forever in the bathroom."

Cora laughed. "I know. Girls Lacie's age fuss with their hair a lot and probably change clothes at least twice."

"How did you know that?"

"Just a guess. I did it at her age."

Cora hugged the small girl. "Let's go back to the house now."

❧

Lacie was sprawled on the den floor, notebook open.

"Have you finished? It's almost bedtime."

"Ten minutes," Lacie said.

After Mary Gray's shower, Cora tucked her in and kissed her forehead. "No getting out of bed and wandering around in the middle of the night, you hear?"

"Okay," Mary Gray said reluctantly.

Lacie had not come upstairs yet, and it was past nine. Cora went back downstairs, but the girl wasn't in the den or kitchen. "Lacie?" she called.

The front screen door opened, and Lacie popped in. "Yes?"

Cora looked at her watch. "It's late."

"It's okay. I was talking to Uncle Woody."

Cora sighed. "All right, but you do need your sleep."

Lacie dallied around, but finally she was in bed. She'd asked Cora not to tuck her in anymore. "I'm not a baby. And I don't need prayers."

"I agree you're not a baby, but we all need prayers. Age doesn't matter." Cora clasped her hands and asked God to watch over Lacie and her mother.

Lacie shot up in bed. "You're praying for my mother?"

"Of course. Why not?"

"Because it won't do any good. I should know!"

"Prayers always do good. We just don't always know it."

Lacie lay back down, turning to the wall. "Good night," she said, as if dismissing Cora. Cora bent over and kissed her cheek.

"Sleep tight, Lacie."

Cora had the rest of the evening to herself, but Lacie's outburst tore at her heart. How could she help? She believed her prayer would be answered and one day Jenny would return.

She stood in the hallway, not wanting to be alone. More than anything she wanted to sit on the front porch and wait for the growing dusk. Woody was probably there. She wouldn't ask about the dog again, but maybe they could discuss something. Anything. What did he like besides hazelnuts?

Cora grabbed a sweater off the coat rack and opened the screen door.

The porch was empty. Where was Woody? She sat on the swing and pushed it gently.

The screen door opened minutes later, but Cora didn't look up.

Woody cleared his throat.

"It's such a nice evening," Cora said, turning to look at him. "Did you need something?"

"Yes, it is a nice night, and no, I don't need anything." There was a long, awkward silence. "I'll go back in. . .leave you with your thoughts."

But the door didn't close. "You don't have to leave," she wanted to say, but the words didn't come.

"About the girls. . . ," he said.

"Yes?"

Woody walked over and sat on the top step. "I appreciate your helping Mary Gray with her spelling."

"I told her I would earlier."

"It isn't on the list."

"Then it should be," Cora said. "I believe in helping when it's needed. I like to see a family come together, to blend, to get along, and I see lots of strife here. I also see girls who need attention, something you don't. . ."

Woody's eyes narrowed, but he said nothing.

Cora realized she was starting to overstep the line and soon they would be battling. She didn't want to do this. "Look, I'm sorry. I always say more than I should!"

He didn't acknowledge her apology. He stayed on the top step, his back to her.

Cora wanted to know about the farm, the history and caring for hazelnuts. Woody had said this piece of property had been in his family for the better part of a century. "I love this house," she said, breaking the silence. "Your grandfather built it?"

"Great-grandfather."

"And it's been in your family ever since."

"Yep."

Getting Woody to talk was apparently not going to happen. When she pressed the issue about the hazelnuts, he went into the house and came back a moment later, then handed her a book. "It tells about it here. The care, what we spray for, and all about the harvest."

Cora took the book and began reading. She hadn't realized there was so much to growing and maintaining a hazelnut orchard. Fertilizing, cultivating, leaf and soil analysis, and watching out for winter moth, aphids, leaf roller, worms, and moss and lichen. This was worse than harvesting oysters back home.

"I see there are some recipes in the back."

"Yeah. The idea is to get more people to buy and use filberts, I mean, hazelnuts." Woody explained how they'd been filberts when he was growing up, but the name had legally changed to hazelnuts in the midnineties. "It's an East Coast thing," he muttered.

"I can see it's an ongoing job. Maybe I can help?"

Woody stared as if he didn't believe she'd say such a thing. "I hired you for the house, not the grounds."

"I know."

Woody stood and humphed. "Yeah, well—"

Cora went inside and set the book on a table in the den. Why did he take things the wrong way? Usually folks tried to get acquainted pretty quickly in this sort of situation, but she still felt like a complete outsider. Perhaps that's the way he wanted it. Didn't he want her getting close to the girls? Was it because he couldn't? Or was there another reason? Perhaps he didn't want to get too close because he knew their mother would return and he'd have to give them up. But Cora knew he really did not want the responsibility of raising two girls. And if the girls were difficult now, what would they be like in a few years when they were both teens? Cora felt Lacie was already beginning that phase. It seemed some girls missed their childhood altogether.

It was late now, but Cora knew she would not be able to sleep. She had two choices. She could straighten the cupboards in the kitchen, which were a deplorable mess, or she could go up to her apartment and read or crochet. She chose reorganizing the cupboards.

The food cupboard was the easiest. She placed fruits on one shelf, vegetables on the next, flour and sugar and such on another. She left the cereal and oats on the middle shelf. She tackled the pots and pans next and had a pile of pans and lids on the floor when Woody came in for another cup of coffee.

"What's all this?"

"I can't stand disorganization," Cora said, not looking up.

"But working at this hour?"

"Everything will be back in tip-top condition in no time."

"I hope so. Seems it was okay for the last two housekeepers."

"I'm persnickety about the kitchen," Cora said. "I need organization in order to work efficiently."

"Humph!" Woody said again and left the room.

Cora soon learned that "humph" was his favorite word. And his favorite gesture was removing his cap, then wiping his brow. Sometimes he tapped it on his knee, especially when he was sitting. His favorite cap was the beige one that had Hazelnut Farmer sewn in red above the bill. Some days he wore a tattered straw hat that was on the verge of falling apart. He definitely liked old.

Cora wondered what her unconscious habits were. Her mother used to say it was frowning.

She went to her apartment and lay on the love seat and closed her eyes. She reached for the cat throw to cover her legs, repeating the words of Philippians four, verse thirteen. "I can do all things through Christ which strengtheneth me."

She thought about the man who couldn't be pleased. Tonight his gaze was almost hateful. This was not going well, and she prayed things would improve soon. She just had to watch her tongue and trust God for the rest.

Chapter 7

Cora woke the next morning with a crick in her neck, and her legs were cramped from being scrunched up on the love seat all night. She couldn't believe she hadn't wakened and gone to bed.

She stretched, but her back had spasms, and she tried to move slowly and relax. She took two aspirin and saw it was already six o'clock—and she liked to be in the kitchen by now. She hadn't showered, but it would have to wait.

Cora threw a fresh change of clothes on and hurried down the steps. Woody was in the kitchen, putting water in the coffeepot. He grumped a "good morning," and Cora nodded.

"Here let me do that."

"About last night. . . .I was rude. Of course the kitchen should be your domain."

Cora felt her insides turn. She didn't feel like a discussion this early. She needed time alone to start breakfast preparations.

"We can discuss this later, if you don't mind, Mr. Morgan."

"Woody. I asked you to call me Woody."

"Woody."

"Okay. Let me know when the coffee's done."

"Of course." Her neck hurt when she turned back to the stove to get the bacon frying.

Minutes later, Mary Gray was the first to come for breakfast. "I'm sure glad I showered last night."

Cora beamed. "Good for you. Do you want to butter the toast?" Cora knew she might be pushing it, but she could use some help, and if the little girl was willing, why not?

"Sure!"

Woody came into the kitchen to find his niece setting bowls and plates on the table and actually smiling. He scratched his head. "Mary Gray? You're up and ready for school already?"

"Yep. I showered last night so I'm all ready!"

"Well, if I didn't believe in miracles before, I certainly do now."

"It was Cora's idea."

Cora didn't want to take credit for it; she didn't need praises, but maybe this would work in spite of her own shortcomings. If Woody knew that his niece was trying to do better, maybe he would become receptive about a dog.

"Thank you, Cora," he said, pulling out his chair. "It seems you have some good ideas."

Cora brought the pot of oatmeal and raisins and dished some into his bowl. "Thank you," she murmured.

When Lacie came in, her eyes widened. "Mary Gray is up already?"

The younger girl just smiled as she took the stack of toast to the table.

When the blessing had been asked, Cora excused herself, saying she wasn't feeling well. She knew they were puzzled, but she had to go stand under the hot water in the shower and see if it would ease the stiffness in her neck. She half-expected Woody to say something, but he just poured milk on his oatmeal. At least one thing had been accomplished. Better yet, he'd noticed and was pleased. *A step at a time,* she reminded herself.

Woody was gone all morning, helping Hoby with some tree inspection, he'd said. After lunch he said he had to go pick up a few things from the co-op. He'd be back in time for dinner. Cora wondered what he'd be doing all afternoon but didn't ask. He was so private about everything, something she was trying to get used to. She knew he was concerned about the trees, but she didn't understand why. They looked perfectly healthy. She wondered if walking through the rows was when he pondered things. Everyone had a place to do that. Cora's thinking spot was a bench overlooking the bay. She often sat watching the shimmering water as the tide came in or gazing at the mud flats when the tide was out. She missed it, but her apartment had taken its place for now. It wasn't as if she couldn't return home for a visit. She might even ask to take the girls there one Saturday.

Cora cleaned and looked through a paint chart she'd had in her craft supplies. The kitchen needed a fresh coat of paint. It needed a lot of things, but she'd start with paint. Soon it was four o'clock, and Woody hadn't returned. Where was he? The girls were due any moment.

She heard the bus but no other sounds until the door opened and closed.

"Hello?" Mary Gray called.

"Hi," Cora called out. "I'm in the kitchen. Where else? Wait until you see. . ." She stopped. "Where's Lacie? Lagging behind?"

"Nope! She wasn't on the bus."

"Not on the bus?" Cora felt a thread of panic rippling through her. "Why not? Did you see her at all?"

Mary Gray shook her head. "She wasn't where she always is."

"Did you ask someone?" Cora went on. What could she do? She knew none of Lacie's friends or their phone numbers. She hadn't thought to ask Woody if he had a list of them. "What's that one girl's name she mentions a lot? Kathi?"

"No, she wasn't on the bus, either. I think she got into trouble and had to stay after."

"Trouble? What kind of trouble?"

"Sixth graders can't be tardy to class. If they are too many times, they stay after for an hour. That's what I heard."

"I'd better call the school."

⋘⋙

"Lacie was kept after for detention because she's been late to class all week," a voice explained.

"But she rides the school bus," Cora protested.

"We realize that."

Cora soon discovered she was speaking to the vice-principal of the elementary school. "Parents need to make other plans when things come up, or a student can ride home on the sports bus."

Sports bus?

"I'm the new housekeeper. I didn't know anything about this. Where is she now?"

"In the office waiting for a ride."

"What will you do when the school closes for the day?"

"Relax, Miss—uh, what did you say your name was?"

"Benchley. Cora Benchley."

"Lacie was going to call."

Cora felt anger taking over. "And if I didn't have a car, since her uncle is not home, what then?"

"I suppose one of us would have to take her home."

"I'm coming after her. Don't close down yet." Cora didn't wait for an answer. She and Mary Gray hopped into the car, and Cora drove toward the school. It was only ten miles away, but it was the principle of the thing.

They arrived in under fifteen minutes in spite of the commuters beginning to wend their way home.

Lacie was not waiting outside as Cora hoped she would be. Nor was she in the office.

Mrs. Burns, the secretary, looked up from a folder. "Miss Benchley?" she asked.

"Yes," Cora answered. "I just called."

"I know. I looked in Lacie's folder, and there is no authorization for anyone other than her legal guardian to pick her up."

"I'm the new nanny and housekeeper."

"I suggest you ask Mr. Morgan to fill out a new authorization form," she said, handing Cora the form.

"Where is Lacie?"

"I believe she got a ride with a friend's mother."

"And that's okay?"

"If we know the student and the parents."

Cora turned and hurried out of the office before she said any more. She was nearly in tears as she pulled out of the U-shaped drive and drove back toward the farm. She prayed Lacie would be there when they arrived.

❧

Lacie was already in her bedroom when Cora and Mary Gray went in the house.
"Lacie!" she called.

Music pounded upstairs.

"Will you go tell her I want to speak to her?"

Minutes later, Lacie stood looking Cora in the eye. "I missed the bus."

"Because you were held after for detention," Cora said.

"So?"

"We need to discuss why you've been late to class and what to do about it."

"You're not my mother," Lacie said. "I don't have to listen to you."

"When your uncle isn't here, I'm responsible for you. I need to know where you are and that you're safe. And—"

"I have homework to do." Lacie turned and walked away.

Cora wanted to say something, but she decided she'd better count to ten—at least three times.

❧

Woody didn't need another confrontation when he got home. He was already feeling down after hearing at the co-op that the price for hazelnuts had dropped. "Less than last year," the owner said. "Things are tough all over."

❧

Woody had pressing expenses. He had counted on a bumper crop this fall, money that would help him get current with his bills. Now this. And the Social Security checks for the girls' support had not been sent as usual. He could press Jenny about it—if he knew where she was. He should call the government and find out what happened. With or without the girls' monthly support checks, he might need to take on an extra job as Hunter had done.

All he wanted now was a cup of coffee and to go out in the barn while waiting for dinner. The barn was his thinking place. He'd find something to tinker with, or he'd oil the old steam tractor. It was ancient—an antique, Hoby had said once. "You ought to sell that thing. It'd bring you a pretty penny."

"Nah, can't sell it. It's something I want to hang on to."

Hoby knew about the finances. He might have had a problem, but his house was paid for, and he only had to keep up on the taxes. That was another thing. Taxes went up every year, but the prices for hazelnuts didn't, though the demand was good.

Woody parked his truck in the usual spot and decided to forgo the coffee and go in the barn for a while, but Mary Gray ran outside, shouting.

"Uncle Woody, you gotta come in the house! Cora's really mad at Lacie!"

Woody shook his head. That was another thing. He was tired of Cora saying the girls needed chores and were unmannerly. And that thing about the dog. What had he gotten himself into? She wasn't going to work out at all, and yet,

Mary Gray was the first one up this morning and was out the door and waiting before the bus came. He'd never seen that happen before.

He put an arm around her shoulders and walked with her into the house.

❧

"So what's this about Lacie?"

Cora explained the circumstances, saying that she couldn't have picked up Lacie if she wanted to. "Here's a form for you to sign."

Woody held up a hand.

"I'm the guardian here, not you."

"I know, but shouldn't I have the authorization to pick her up, if necessary?"

Lacie and Mary Gray looked from their uncle to Cora and back again. Cora thought she detected a smirk on Lacie's face.

"All kinds of things could have happened to her," Cora went on. "I think the school shouldn't keep kids who ride the bus after school unless they inform their guardians ahead of time so they can make other arrangements."

"Cora, it's okay. I'll sign the form and call the school tomorrow to straighten it out." He turned to Lacie. "And what do you have to say about all this? I thought it was Mary Gray who had the problem with being on time. It should be a simple matter to make it to class before the tardy bell."

Lacie looked a bit chagrined but not enough for Cora's liking. "I'm sorry, Uncle Woody. I'll try to make it to class on time."

"Seems there should be more than a sorry here," Cora mumbled under her breath as she started dinner. It would be late, very late, and she wasn't even going to worry about it. They'd have leftover macaroni cheese and salad, whether Woody liked it or not.

He said nothing about the sparse dinner, but she noticed he ate lots of bread and butter and grabbed a handful of cookies. After taking his plate to the sink, he headed out the back door. Cora was glad she'd put the paint chart away. Somehow she didn't think this was the best time to bring up painting the kitchen. Not a good time at all. Something else was bothering Woody, but she had no idea what.

Chapter 8

Cora called Meredith the next day. "I need to see a friendly face. Besides, I need my favorite boots, just in case it rains. It's going to be awfully mucky here when it does."

"Can do." There was a pause. "Things aren't working out as well as you hoped?"

"Why do you say that?"

"I can tell by your tone of voice."

"Well, it could be better."

"I told you not to take another job where there were kids. None of them mind anymore. Remember my experience with teaching?"

Cora bristled. Meredith thought she knew so much, but she had never married, never had children, and couldn't understand why Cora liked kids. The way things were going, Cora was beginning to wonder about that herself.

"Hey, I'm just kidding," Meredith said. "Sure, I can come. Been wanting to see the big city, anyway. Saturday okay?"

"It's great."

Cora looked around her apartment and wondered what Meredith would say. Her cousin was often outspoken and would probably have some negative comment. Now that she thought about it, she realized Meredith was often negative, even back when they were kids. Cora knew she, too, had been negative. She'd blamed everything and everyone for Leighton finding Alice and marrying her. She remembered reading a book by Oswald Chambers. He said: "You can't enjoy the mountaintop unless you've been through the valley."

She'd gone through the valley, prayed, and found God again. The moment had been awesome.

It was now being reinforced, as Woody was teaching her without knowing it. No matter what, you went on. You put one foot in front of the other and held your head high. "Life is for living, no matter what hand you've been dealt."

Those words were Woody's answer to her question of how he had coped with both his father and brother dying. Cora had lost her father and then her mother a year ago, but she hadn't lost them both at the same time.

"Surely their mother will come back one day," Cora had suggested that first day.

"Don't count on it. Jenny is spoiled. My brother never admitted it, but down deep, he knew."

Cora gazed out the window and over at the acres of trees, thinking it would be wonderful for the girls to be able to grow up in a beautiful, sparsely populated area like Dundee.

She made her bed and set the coffee cup in the sink. She was lingering this morning, but that was because it was Saturday and the girls could sleep in, if Woody allowed it.

The chintz curtains fluttered in the early morning breeze. After breakfast, she'd shop for a roast for tonight's dinner. Woody didn't seem to mind that her cousin was coming for the weekend.

Mary Gray accompanied Cora to the grocery store. They'd dropped Lacie off at her friend's, with a promise that she'd be picked up in two hours. Cora also needed to stop at the discount store and buy more yarn. She'd decided to start another afghan. She chose red, black, and a soft gray, then found a suitable design called Basket Weave in a crochet book. It looked masculine and would be perfect for Woody. Just last night something her mother used to say came to mind. "When you have an enemy, make a friend." And she wanted to be friends with Woody. She'd also buy a crochet hook for Mary Gray.

"I get to pick out the colors I want?"

Cora nodded. "Of course."

She selected blue, aqua, and lavender. "This will be so pretty. Are you sure I can learn?"

"Positive."

Cora enjoyed crocheting, especially in the summer when there was nothing but reruns on the TV.

After picking up Lacie, Cora pulled into a drive-in, and they ordered hamburgers and fries. "Just this once won't hurt."

When they arrived home, Cora couldn't believe her eyes. Woody had found leftovers to eat, and his plate and bowl were in the dishwasher.

Cora got out the makings for piecrust and began cutting lard into the flour.

"What are you making?" Mary Gray asked.

"Lemon meringue pie."

"Why are you making a lemon meringue pie?" Mary Gray asked as she grabbed a pinch of pie dough.

"Because it's Meredith's favorite dessert. Do you like lemon pie?"

Mary Gray shrugged. "Don't think I've ever had it."

Cora was aghast. "Never ever?"

"Never ever, what?" Lacie entered the kitchen, a book in one hand and a cookie in the other.

"Are you eating between meals?" Cora asked.

Lacie rolled her eyes. "Yes, and so?"

"I wish you wouldn't," Cora said, "not after our heavy lunch."

"If wishes were horses, beggars would ride," Lacie said, a glint in her eyes.

Cora remembered talking one night about sayings she'd learned as a child, and the adage had been mentioned. Now it would come back to taunt her.

"So what is it that you've never eaten, Miss Mary?"

Mary Gray knocked the last bite of cookie from Lacie's hand.

"Oh, you little brat!" Lacie reached over and hit her sister's arm.

"Girls! That's enough! I'm cooking. I have lots to do, and since nobody is helping, scram, and I mean it!"

"Scram?" Lacie said from the doorway. "That's what you tell cats and dogs."

Cora dropped the piece of crust from the table knife. "I cannot work in a kitchen with chaos, and bickering is chaos."

"I won't fight," Mary Gray said, grabbing the crust off the floor. "See? I even helped."

"You may stay. One at a time," Cora said. "That's it."

"Okay," Lacie said. "I know who your favorite is." She dashed out of the room and stomped up the stairs.

Cora sighed heavily. She tried not to play favorites, but she couldn't change the fact that Mary Gray wanted to learn to crochet and cook and Lacie had declined every invitation Cora extended.

"I want to see how you make lemon meringue pie," Mary Gray said, breaking through Cora's thoughts.

"First we must bake the crusts, and since it's silly to heat the oven up for just one, I'm making three. I can put one or two crusts in the freezer for later use."

"You like to cook," Mary Gray said, pulling the stool over. "I can tell."

"And you do, too."

Mary Gray snitched another piece of dough.

"That might give you a bellyache," Cora said. "That's what my mother always said."

"Why?"

"Not sure. It was probably so I'd stop eating it." She chuckled.

"I like it."

"Well, no more or I won't have enough to make a sugar pasty."

Of course she knew there would be the question about the sugar pasty. Cora explained how to roll the scraps of dough into a circle, butter them, and sprinkle sugar and cinnamon on top. "You eat them right out of the oven when they're nice and hot."

While the piecrusts were baking, Cora showed Mary Gray how to separate eggs and let her do the last one.

"You can't get yolk in the white or it won't beat up."

"Why?"

"Because the yolk keeps it from beating into a white froth."

"You sure know a lot of things."

"Did you know I cooked for a family for many years? Those boys liked to eat!"

And so did their father, she wanted to add, but that would only elicit more questions from the inquisitive Mary Gray. Cora pushed the thought of Leighton aside. It all seemed so long ago now. She wondered if Woody liked lemon meringue pie and found herself hoping he did.

"Why did you leave that job?" Mary Gray asked, stabbing the egg yolks with a fork.

"I knew you'd ask that."

"And?"

"The man of the house married, so he no longer needed a cook or housekeeper."

"And the kids?"

"They are grown now."

"Do you miss them?"

Cora nodded. "I do. Very much. But I can see them again when I go back to Oysterville."

"Oysterville. That's a funny name for a town."

"Not really. It was founded because of the oysters."

Soon Cora was explaining how oysters grew and how plentiful clams and fish were where she was from.

Lacie stood in the doorway again. "Mary Gray, you're a pest, and I think you should come play a game with me."

"I want to help Cora."

"And I want you to come play with me." She grabbed Mary Gray's arm and pulled.

"Lacie, if you want to stay to watch, that's fine, but you're not going to tell Mary Gray what to do or pick a fight with her. If it were up to me, I'd give you a chore because I think you're bored. A busy child is a happy child, as my mother used to say."

"You're always spouting off something your mother said!" Lacie's eyes smoldered, and Cora realized that "mothers" was another subject to stay away from. The girls' mother was a touchy subject, and Cora's comments were like pouring salt on an open wound.

"Uncle Woody said I didn't have to work, that school is work."

"I know."

Cora started whipping the egg whites into a wild froth. Maybe Lacie would let it go if Cora didn't push the issue. It was worth a try. It was sure going to be nice to have Meredith here, have an adult to talk to for a change.

"Here, I want to do that." Mary Gray grabbed the mixer and, before Cora could caution her, had lifted it. Egg whites splattered on her hair, the table, on Cora's face, and even on the floor.

"Oh!" Mary Gray cried. She dropped the mixer and ran from the room.

Later Cora went to her room and tapped on the door.

"What do you want?"

"To talk."

"I don't want to talk."

"Okay."

Seconds later footsteps pounded on the floor, and the door opened. "I changed my mind."

Cora went in and sat on the edge of the bed.

"It's okay about the egg whites. I just used more. It's not worth getting upset over."

Mary Gray began pacing between the nightstand and the door. "It was stupid. Lacie says I always do stupid things!"

"Everybody makes mistakes. It's okay to make mistakes."

Cora reached out to pull the small child close, but Mary Gray shrank back. She expected that from Lacie, but not Mary Gray. She'd hugged Mary Gray many times, but that was over something happy, not something upsetting. Things were tenuous, and she must wait for the girls to make the first gesture. She couldn't be a mother when they already had one, but it was difficult not to mother them.

Mary Gray sat next to Cora on the bed. "I like to help in the kitchen," she said. "I think it would be nice if I could make things by myself."

"You can help me anytime you want. And I know some easy recipes you could try on your own sometime."

"And Lacie has to stay out?"

"She can have a turn another time if she wants to."

⁓

Two pies were soon finished, the meringue a golden brown with high peaks. Mary Gray looked at them in awe. "I even helped put the meringue on."

"Yes, you did."

Cora had been so busy she'd forgotten the time. It was two o'clock. Hadn't Meredith said she was leaving early and would be here by one? As if in answer, the doorbell rang. Mary Gray ran to the door.

"Cora! It's your cousin!"

Cora patted her hair in place and ran to the door.

Meredith grabbed her in a quick hug, and they started talking, each interrupting the other.

"Oh, you look so good, a sight for sore eyes," Cora said. "I can't believe you're actually here." She stepped back. "Have you lost weight?"

Meredith brushed the hair off her shoulders. "Been working at it."

"That's great."

"This is way out in the pucker brush, as Mama used to say."

"Your mother had lots of sayings, too?" Lacie had come into the living room and stared.

"That's because our mothers were sisters."

"Like me and Mary Gray."

"Yes."

"And did they fight?" Mary Gray asked.

"I don't know," Meredith said. "I don't remember them talking about it."

"All sisters fight," Lacie said in that know-it-all tone. "It's just the way it is."

"They don't have to," Cora said. "If I'd had a sister, I would have wanted to be best friends with her."

"You say that because you never had one. If you had, you would be sick and tired of her, too," Lacie said, squaring her shoulders.

Mary Gray started to reach over to hit her but suddenly stopped. She looked back at Cora and smiled. "It's okay. Someday she will like me."

"In your dreams," Lacie yelled, flouncing from the room.

Meredith rolled her eyes. "Phew! I see what you mean."

"Come on in and look around. I can make you a cup of tea."

"I stopped at a darling little café and had a latte. One of those with soy milk that's supposed to be so good for you."

"Then you can save room for dinner; we're having pot roast," Cora said. "Woody has a menu tacked to the kitchen bulletin board. For breakfast and lunch. Dinner is my choice."

Meredith paused, a puzzled look crossing her face. "A menu? Something you follow every day?"

Cora nodded. "Yes, it's one of many rules."

Mary Gray stood on the sidelines, as if waiting to hear more. "Are you going to stay up in Cora's apartment?"

"Yes. She's going to take the bed, and I'll sleep on the recliner," Cora said, remembering her night on the love seat. "In fact, let's just take your stuff up there now before I start the roast."

"We have a surprise," Mary Gray said. "Something you'll like."

Cora shrugged. "Well, maybe not now that you're watching your calories."

"Let me guess," Meredith said. "My cousin makes the best lemon meringue pie ever! Did I guess right?"

"Wow, I guess she does know you," Mary Gray replied before turning back to Meredith. "That's what it is, and I helped make it."

"Ooh, I can hardly wait."

"Can I help carry something?" Mary Gray asked.

"You can carry my overnight bag; thank you," Meredith answered.

Lacie reappeared and followed Cora, Meredith, and Mary Gray up the steps, and Cora invited both of them in.

"This is wonderful, Cora!" Meredith trilled. "I love it! It's bright and cheerful."

"It's just right for one," Cora added.

The girls sat on the floor, and Cora put the teakettle on. They chatted, and Meredith answered questions about mutual friends and caught Cora up on the latest news.

"Of course it isn't the same with you gone."

"It's not as if I'll never be back—"

"But you like it here, right, Cora?"

Cora smiled then. "Yes, I do."

"Except when we fight," Mary Gray said.

"Aaron and Deanna are expecting a baby. Remember, they went back to Maine."

"Don't they have a little girl?"

"Sure do. Deanna has a girl from her first marriage—her husband died at sea. This is a boy she's carrying."

"Died at sea?" Lacie asked. "Do you mean he drowned?"

"Yes," Meredith answered.

"Who is Aaron?" Mary Gray asked.

"He was the youngest of the four boys I took care of," Cora answered.

"Would I like him?" Mary Gray looked at Meredith.

"Oh, Mary Gray, stop asking such stupid questions," Lacie said.

"It's okay," Cora said. "Asking questions is how we learn."

"Seems everyone is getting married and having babies but us," Meredith added.

"You can marry my uncle," Mary Gray said. "He needs to marry someone!"

"Mary Gray!" Lacie pulled her sister's arm and scowled. "You don't need to be saying stuff like that. Uncle Woody is happy without getting married!"

"Well, I certainly should hope so," Meredith said then. "No way would Cora ever want to live here the rest of her life!"

"And what's wrong with here?" Lacie's tone was cold.

"Oh, nothing, darling." Meredith looked stricken, apparently realizing what she'd said. "I'm sure this is a wonderful place to live—I certainly like your house—I just meant that Cora is from the beach, and once you have sand in your shoes, you can never get it out."

"That sounds uncomfortable to me!" Mary Gray piped up. "I wouldn't want sand in my shoes!"

Both Cora and Meredith laughed, but when Cora saw the hurt look crossing the little girl's face, she added that it was just a saying.

"I like it here, too," Lacie added. "I don't like sand in my shoes, either. You can have all the sand you want." And with that she turned and ran out the door and down the steps.

Cora watched Mary Gray retreat, also, just as the whistle sounded on the stove. She shook her head as she poured water into their cups. "Don't worry about them. They're a bit touchy. I told you their father died and their mother left them, so it's just been their uncle, and of course they are going to defend the only home they remember."

They chatted until the dinner bell sounded, and Cora jumped. It was three o'clock, and she'd told Mary Gray she had to get the roast started at three. How had the time gotten away?

"What's the bell for?"

"I'm sure it's Mary Gray. She's my helper in the kitchen. Has a mind as sharp as a tack, as Mama used to say." They laughed as Cora led the way back down the stairs.

"Woody just pulled in. Come meet the man of the house, the owner of Woodhaven Acres. He's really quite handsome, even if he acts like a bear."

"I can hardly wait," Meredith said with a smile as she followed Cora across the backyard.

Chapter 9

Woody came in the back door and took his cap off. "Hello," he said. "You must be Cora's cousin." He offered his hand. "Glad you could come."

"Woody, this is Meredith."

"I love your house, Woody. It's quite elegant."

"Built in 1910. It's housed a lot of people over the years."

"I should think so."

Meredith could be charming when pressed into it, and she seemed enthralled with Woody for some reason. Yes, Woody was handsome, but because Cora saw and faced the inner turmoil every day, she tended to forget his good features. Besides, Meredith could flirt.

"How long are you staying?" Woody asked.

"Just tonight. Must head back tomorrow. Job, you know."

"And what do you do?"

"I keep books for a local plumber."

Cora turned back to the roast and set it in the pan to brown. It sizzled, and Mary Gray came to see what was happening.

"It's always better to brown both sides of the beef first," she explained. "Then I put sliced onions on top, add just a bit of water, and let it simmer and make its own juices."

Meredith followed Woody out of the kitchen and out the front door. Cora felt miffed. Why was he talking to her as if she were an old friend? Cora couldn't get him to say more than two words, and when she'd wanted to know more about growing hazelnuts, he'd handed her a book!

A few minutes later, Cora turned the burner on low, stuck a lid on, and went to join her cousin and her boss. Mary Gray sat at the far end of the porch. Lacie was obviously in her room listening to music, as the sound traveled down the stairs and out the open door.

"Yeah, I've been thinking about getting a dog—"

"Uncle Woody!" Mary Gray ran over and threw her arms around his neck. "You really mean we can have a dog?"

Meredith looked from the child and met Cora's gaze. Cora felt stunned. She hadn't even brought it up again, and here he was saying it was okay. So God was answering her prayers. She and the girls had prayed that God would change Woody's heart about getting a dog, and Cora had included them in her personal prayers each night.

Woody glanced in her direction and smiled. "Thought you might want to go to the shelter and pick out one tomorrow."

Mary Gray turned and now hugged Cora tight. "Oh, can I go, too?"

"We'll go after church, and I wouldn't dream of going without you, Mary Gray." Cora had not attended church since coming to Dundee, but she had noticed a community church in town the day she went to pick up Lacie from school. Now if she could convince the girls to go with her. . .

"But I don't think I like church."

"I think you will," Cora answered, "and I just bet there will be someone there you know."

"I gotta tell Lacie," Mary Gray said. She opened the screen door and let it bang hard behind her. Meredith jumped. Cora laughed, remembering how much the girls' constant noise bothered her at first.

"I better check the roast." Woody followed her in, his empty coffee cup dangling from a finger.

"You look surprised. . .about the dog."

"You said no."

"I've been thinking about it. Mary Gray's made such a turnaround, I can't believe it." Woody stopped when he saw the pie. "Is that lemon meringue pie?"

Cora nodded. "You never have it, Mary Gray tells me."

"It's been a long time," he said. "My grandma made the best pies ever."

"I'm sure my pie won't measure up to hers," Cora said and then stopped, realizing how negative that sounded.

"And I'm just as sure it will."

"Thank you. Mary Gray helped with the meringue."

"She's becoming quite a cook." He paused in the doorway. "And your cousin is nice."

Unlike me? Cora wondered. She peeled carrots and then potatoes to put around the roast. She knew Woody would like her pot roast; everyone always raved over how tender the meat was and the way the potatoes and carrots browned in the liquid.

When she went back outside, the porch was empty. Meredith was off in the orchard with Woody, examining the hazelnut trees. His arm shot out, and she knew he was explaining how they grew, how they were harvested, and other bits of information, and Meredith was hanging on every word. A funny, unexpected feeling crept through her, something she couldn't quite put her finger on. Why did she care what Woody did? Why did she care what he said or how he felt toward her? This was a job, and if it didn't work, it didn't work, and soon she'd be packed up and on her way. But was that what she wanted? Seeing him with Meredith made her realize she did care about the enigmatic man. She wanted to please him with her work, but most of all she wanted to make him happy. She wanted to see him smile as he had in the photo with his father and brother as they stood over a piece of machinery, beaming over their latest buy. It reminded her of home and the proud expression fishermen wore after the catch of the day.

"Cora!" Meredith called as she came around the side of the house. "Let's take the girls shopping after dinner! What do you say?"

Cora looked up from the paper she was reading. Woody stood on the bottom step, his hand touching the railing. Cora's heart squeezed nearly shut. Why did this feeling hit now? Was it because he was something she knew she couldn't have?

"Did you enjoy the tour?" Cora asked, suddenly realizing how curt she sounded.

"What's wrong?" Meredith asked, looking from Cora to Woody. Then she smiled and took her cousin's arm. "Don't you think the girls would like to go to Portland to shop?"

"That's thirty miles away," Woody said.

"I know, but I need to do some serious shopping."

Woody smiled, and Cora saw the way he looked at Meredith. Was it with interest? Curiosity? Or what? Whatever it was, Meredith was wrapping him around her finger, and Cora wondered if it had been a good idea to invite her cousin for a visit.

"We could all go, but five wouldn't fit in my truck or either of your cars."

"I'll stay home," Cora offered.

"Don't be silly," Woody said. "I was just kidding. You don't think I'm going shopping with four women, do you?" They laughed, and the tension was broken.

⁓

Dinner was a smashing success, the trip was fun, and the girls each bought a new pair of shorts for summer. Meredith bought skirts, dresses, and denim pants. "I've gone down two sizes, dear heart, and couldn't wait to shop."

When they got back, Meredith followed Cora up the stairs to her apartment, arms laden with shopping bags. "I can't wait to try them all on again."

Cora sat back, watching the fashion show, wishing she had slender curves like Meredith's. She knew she could if she worked at it, but she liked to eat too much. She thought of the refrigerator magnet she'd seen in the novelty store tonight: Never trust a skinny cook.

"You like?" Meredith asked when she came out in a hot pink skirt and a rose satin top with a scooped neckline. She put her hands on her hips and shook her head.

"Sure. It's great if you have someplace to wear that sort of thing."

"What's wrong?"

"Nothing." Cora looked away.

"You're not falling for this guy—"

"What are you talking about? You know my pact." Cora held the afghan she was making for Woody, studying it, afraid to meet Meredith's gaze.

"You know what I mean, Cora Jean. I've been your cousin too long for you to think you can fool me about something."

"Woody drives me nuts—"

"That's exactly what I mean."

Cora sat up straighter, leaning on the armrest. "Explain yourself, if you don't mind."

"I saw how you looked at him—"

"And I noticed how he looked at you," Cora shot back. "I'm not blind, you know."

"And you think I'd want to move here? Get real, girl."

"Well, I sure don't want to live on some nut farm!"

Meredith laughed. "Nut farm. Good one, Cousin!"

Cora pushed the afghan aside.

"I saw a look in your eyes that can only mean one thing. It's called interest. Infatuation. Something."

"We argue. About everything. We're as bad as the girls."

Meredith grinned. "That's how some relationships go in the beginning—"

"And it's how some go all the time. That's not for me."

"You want someone to come along riding a white horse, sweep you into his arms, and ride off into the moonlit night."

"Speaking of moonlight, did you notice we have a full moon tonight?"

"Yes, and stop changing the subject."

"He wouldn't agree to getting a dog until today. Figure that one out, if you can."

"Men must be in control. It's that simple."

Meredith went back to the bedroom and came back with a black, lace-trimmed silk caftan. "This is for lounging on a cruise, if ever I go on one again."

"Take me with you when you go."

"You'll be too busy here."

"No, I won't," Cora said.

"Tell me, dear cousin, do you ever think about Leighton?"

Cora said nothing. Of course she did. She'd loved him for so long and had been so hopeful that someday he might return that love, but she'd come to accept that it wasn't God's will for her life.

"I see you aren't going to answer my question, but that's okay. You don't get over someone in the blink of an eye. The time will come when he's just a dim memory."

Cora leaned forward. "How is he? Do you know?"

"I hear that he and Alice are very happy. Now, let's change the subject. Sorry I brought it up."

Cora got the pecan cookies, though they didn't need more sweets, considering the pie. One pie had disappeared immediately, and she wondered if Woody would have another piece before going to bed. Meredith brought out her latest photos of a family gathering, then slipped into her nightclothes.

The moonlight streaming through the window in the living room made Cora realize this was where she was meant to be for the present time. Meredith had exposed Cora's feelings, which she had denied vehemently; but now that they had risen to the surface, she knew her cousin was right. She had feelings for Woodrow, which terrified her. Terrified the breath out of her.

"Mer, what about that guy you were dating a year or so ago?"

"Jerry?" Meredith shrugged. "He moved on. Left one night—called me from Billings."

"Montana?"

"One and the same."

"But you didn't love him."

"No, but he was a guy, and we had dinner dates, and I had someone to go to the movies with. Speaking of. . ." Meredith took a video from her bag. "I brought that romantic comedy we both wanted to see last summer. You'll love it, and it'll show you there is hope for us. We just have to change. That's why I went on this diet program with several ladies from church. The focus is on prayer."

"I'm glad you brought a movie, and I'm happy that you're losing weight. You really look great." Cora thought about all the diets she'd tried, but nothing ever worked for long. Maybe she should look into this new program.

Meredith removed the cookies. "You need to change, Cora."

"Change?"

"Yes." Meredith raised her eyebrows. She wrote "change" in big block letters on a tablet. Her enormous bag contained all sorts of intriguing objects. A small clipboard was one such item. She brandished a half-empty bag of sunflower seeds. "Dry roasted. They're good for you."

"What does the 'change' stand for?" Cora asked.

"It's a heading. Now we add to it."

Cora shook her head. "I've never been much for change."

Meredith pointed her pen at Cora. "Oh, no? What're you doing in Dundee, Oregon, then? We change every day without realizing it."

"But what? How?"

"Physical appearance is a beginning. In that category are weight, muscle tone, hairstyle, makeup, and dress."

Cora ran a hand through her hair. She'd wanted a hairstyle change for a long time. Makeup: almost nil. She'd been telling herself the natural look was in, but was it?

"Inner being is next," Meredith said. "Attitude. The positive nature God wants you to have. As His children, we are made in His image." Meredith tore off the sheet of paper and handed it to Cora. "Think about these, Cora Jean. Change your life. Start now. Today."

"This movie brought about all this?"

"Some of it. But most is from the group. We talk about how God is there to lean on, to guide us, if we let Him."

"Wow, I am impressed." Cora curled her feet up under her. "Let's watch the movie."

Meredith was right. Cora laughed as the plain girl became a ravishing beauty. The script was good, and she found herself wondering if Woody would enjoy the movie. Probably not. It was more of a woman's flick. A Cinderella story. She figured he probably liked action-packed movies, though she was only guessing. Suddenly she wanted to know that about him.

❧

Woody sat on the porch, sipping a cup of coffee, eating another slice of pie. Maybe he shouldn't have, but it was good, and it had been so long since he'd had lemon meringue. He could have ordered it when he went out, but whenever he had, the crust was never right, nor was the filling. Cora knew how to cook; that was one of her best points. But her attitude, her coming down on the girls frustrated him. It was his job, so why did she insist on correcting them? They'd been over this more than once. And yet, there was something that drew him to her. He wasn't sure what it was, and he had no desire to find out. Women! He intended to remain a bachelor all his life. There was nothing wrong in that, was there? He didn't need children. He had his nieces, and they were a handful. Cora was right about that.

Woody thought back to how he used to fight with his brother. It was all in good fun, or so he thought, but his father often sent them to their rooms. And if they dared to talk back or argue with him, he spanked them. Woody rarely argued, but Hunter did nearly every time and would get five swats. Woody would count them and hide his head. Perhaps it was that memory that kept him from spanking or punishing his nieces. They'd gone through a lot. They couldn't help how they acted, going around with chips on their shoulders, especially Lacie. He hoped Cora was right about the dog. He didn't know what had made him suddenly announce it earlier tonight. There'd be no backing out of it now.

He thought again of how he liked the evenings when Cora sat on the porch with him, and suddenly he wished she were here. They'd had some interesting conversations, and he wanted to tell her how each year they hoped and prayed that the price for hazelnuts would be higher than the year before. It was a lot of work for a small profit, but he wouldn't trade jobs for all the money in the world. This was what he was meant to do, and he would continue working, planting, hoeing the fields, spraying in the spring, and examining the nuts each summer, hoping there'd be no blight.

Woody set the empty plate on the floor and got up from the swing. He liked to stroll on moonlit nights. Just him and the earth and the moon. He couldn't help glancing up at the apartment over the garage, wondering about the two women. The light was still on, and on occasion he heard laughter. Wild, raucous laughter. What could they be up to?

Chapter 10

Bright sunshine came through the window, wakening Cora with a start. Had she overslept? Thankfully it was Sunday, and the rules were more lax. For that she was thankful. She looked forward to attending the community church. Meredith had said she would drive her car, too, and then leave from there, insisting she had to get back to Oysterville early. "Besides, we've done all our catching up, and I think you're looking better already."

Meredith called, "Good morning," when Cora stepped out of the shower.

"Good morning, yourself."

Cora chose a dark skirt and short-sleeved baby blue sweater.

"Wow, did I ever sleep good."

"Must be the farm air," Cora said, drying her hair. "Are you really sure you have to leave already? You could help us pick out a dog."

"No, I can't. I need to get back, but it's been great fun."

When Cora arrived at the house minutes later, leaving Meredith behind to shower, both girls met her at the door.

"When are we going to get our dog? I looked on the Internet," Lacie said, "and the shelter in Portland opens at noon. If we find one we like, we can take it right then!"

Woody was in the kitchen, perusing the Sunday newspaper while drinking his coffee. Obviously he'd been up for a while.

"I want a collie."

"A collie?" three voices chorused.

"Yeah."

"Uncle Woody, we just want a nice dog," Mary Gray said. "We don't care what kind—do we, Cora?"

"Sometimes collies are adopted by families and never get to the shelter. I know it's common with basset hounds and golden retrievers."

"Collie," Woody said, pouring another cup of coffee.

"A mixed breed is okay, right?"

"Has to look like a collie, though."

Cora wasn't sure that was possible. The main thing was to find the best dog for a family. She had a retriever in mind as they were good with kids, and she hoped there were good mixes at the shelter.

"You could come with us," Cora suggested.

"Can't take the time."

"Yes, Uncle Woody, come with us!" both girls chorused.

"Oh, go ahead and get what you want." He tossed the paper on the table and headed out the door.

❧

Cora fixed thick slices of ham, whipped up an omelet, and asked Meredith to butter the toast. Soon they had eaten, though Woody said nothing after the short blessing. He was clearly not going to talk about the dog again.

It was a short drive to church, but it seemed longer with the girls grumbling all the way.

"I don't like church," Lacie said.

"When was the last time you attended?" Cora asked.

"A long time ago," Mary Gray said. "I can hardly remember."

"Uncle Woody doesn't go," Lacie said. "That's why I don't think I should have to go."

"Fine," Cora said. "We'll just turn around and go back home."

"And not get our dog?" Mary Gray looked stricken.

Cora shrugged. "That's the way I see it."

"It's blackmail," Lacie said. "Don't think I don't know what you're up to."

Cora smiled. "Well, here we are, and there's Meredith. Are you coming with me?"

The girls went in reluctantly, but just as Cora had predicted, they both found kids they knew from school and asked to sit with them.

Cora liked the small church. They played piano because they had no organ. They also played two of her favorite hymns, and she sang them with gusto.

After the service and a quick handshake from the pastor, Meredith hugged Cora and both girls and waved good-bye from her small sports car.

It would be a long drive into town, and Cora disliked the heavy traffic. "I rather enjoyed the service. How about you?" she asked.

"I don't like church," Lacie said. "It isn't fun."

"Having a good time isn't the focus of why we go to church," Cora said. "It's a chance to learn about God's love. We'll have this discussion later on."

They were only a mile from the shelter, according to the directions they had obtained from the Internet.

"Stop hitting me!" Lacie, always the loudest, turned and glared at her sister. The girls were taking turns riding in the front seat. Mary Gray's turn was to be on the way home.

"I didn't hit you!"

"And who was it, since nobody else is in this car!"

"Girls!" Cora's voice rose. She was afraid of missing the exit from the freeway, and the noise didn't help her concentration.

"I hate sisters," Lacie declared.

"You should never say 'hate,'" Cora cautioned. "It's a terrible word and once said, you can't take it back."

"Who'd want to take it back?"

"You will one day—"

"Won't!"

"Will!" shouted Mary Gray.

The voices grew louder as Cora exited the freeway. She turned right onto a road not quite so heavy with traffic, pulled onto the shoulder, and stopped the car.

"Is this the place?" Lacie looked around. The only thing on the corner was one service station and a quick mart on the opposite side.

"No," Cora said, "it isn't."

"Why are we stopping?"

"Because I refuse to drive with all this noisy bickering going on. It's distracting, and I don't want to have an accident because I'm distracted."

"Oh, sure," Lacie said. She mumbled and Mary Gray mumbled back. Cora knew she was supposed to like the lower volume.

Cora did not move.

"We're quiet. Can't we go on to get our dog?" Mary Gray's voice had a tremor.

"It isn't quiet yet," Cora said. "I'm not driving until you two promise to behave and have apologized to each other."

"What?" Lacie's shrill voice filled the car.

Cora said nothing more and still didn't start the car. Lacie apologized to Mary Gray, who then apologized to Lacie.

When they reluctantly promised to behave, Cora thanked them and smiled as she started the ignition. *Well, it's a good beginning,* she thought. She half-expected the girls to start squabbling again before they got to the shelter. She had barely gotten the car up to speed when she saw the shelter just ahead of them.

The shelter was crowded, and a variety of noises filled the halls.

"We have an overabundance of cats right now," the young woman at the counter said. Her name tag identified her as Sharon. "Are you sure you don't want a cute, playful kitten?"

"We need a dog," Cora said. "We have a farm."

"Oh, I see."

"A collie would be great."

Sharon shook her head. "Collies aren't in demand as they once were. But we have some nice retrievers and labs; they make wonderful pets and like having the run of several acres. You know, we don't let our animals go to just anyone. We have to be sure they will have a good home."

"Oh, we will give a dog a good home. Definitely," Cora said as the girls nodded.

Soon the three followed Sharon down one corridor. Cora tried to ignore the meowing and barking. There was even a potbellied pig.

"People don't realize how much work pets are and often bring them back."

Mary Gray stopped to talk to a cat. "He's cross-eyed," she declared. "See!"

Sharon stopped and nodded. "Yes, he is part Siamese, and it's quite common to find Siamese cats that are cross-eyed. I call that one Clancy."

"I want him," Mary Gray said. "He looked at me, and he's so cute."

"We're here for a dog," Lacie said authoritatively. "We're not getting a cat."

The next cage held a dog that was at least part golden retriever, and its tail had a friendly wag. It nosed up to the cage. Lacie reached out and it licked her hand.

"All our animals have had shots and are free to go with a small adoption fee," Sharon continued as they moved on.

"Adoption!" Mary Gray said. "I thought only people were adopted."

"We like to think we're a family here."

They continued past more cages. Some dogs leaped up and wagged their tails, as if begging for the trio to stop. Others stayed in corners and barely looked up. When they got to the end cages, Mary Gray burst into tears. "I don't see any I like!"

"You don't?" Cora asked.

"Well, I did," Lacie said. "That one golden-looking dog didn't wag his tail that much, but he had the saddest eyes I've ever seen."

Lacie directed them back to the cage and pointed. "See, isn't he cute?"

"That's a female, one year old, and she's been spayed."

"Spayed?" asked Mary Gray. "What—"

"It means she can't have puppies."

"Oh."

"Does she like children?" Cora asked.

"Yes," Sharon said. "She came from a family, but they had to move and couldn't take her. She's moped around ever since they left her here two days ago. I feel so sorry for her."

"See? That's why she has such sad eyes!" Lacie said. "Oh, please, Cora, don't you like her?"

"Your uncle wants a collie, so I don't know what to do."

"Call him."

"He wouldn't answer. He and Hoby were going to be outdoors all day, remember?"

"I'm sorry we have no collies, and this one isn't a purebred golden retriever, but she has the markings of one."

"I don't know what to say. If only your uncle had come. It certainly would have helped make the decision. What do you think, Mary Gray?"

"I like her. I think she's had a sad life, and if we can make her happy again, we should do it!"

"She's in good health and is well groomed as you can see," Sharon said. "In fact, I think we have her picture on the Internet. We change it every other day. It would be nice to write 'adopted' across her photo."

"What's her name?" Mary Gray asked.

"Rosie, they said when they brought her in."

"Your uncle says we must name our dog Queenie."

"But we can't change her name now," Lacie interjected. "How do you think I'd feel if suddenly you said I had to be Lisa or Madison or Riley?"

"Yes, I get your point," Cora said with a sigh. They followed Sharon back to the counter to fill out the necessary paperwork and pay the fee. Woody had given her money, saying he knew that dogs were not free anymore.

"I think Uncle Woody will like her," Lacie said, "and he'll understand about her name."

"I do hope so."

Rosie was leashed, and Lacie took hold of her while Mary Gray hugged her neck.

"I know you'll be happy with your choice."

The girls waved, but Rosie looked straight ahead, as if she knew she was about to start a new adventure.

They stopped at a pet store and bought a dog bed and food and water dishes. Cora also bought a huge sack of the recommended dog food. "Wow, this is costing more than your uncle figured. I hope he doesn't mind."

Soon they were on the freeway and heading home. Cora felt like a chauffeur, as both girls wanted to sit in the back with Rosie.

Rosie didn't bark, but she kept licking and smiling—if a dog can really smile. Cora was glad she'd asked, glad she'd pressed the issue, and really glad that they'd found a good, gentle dog. Woody's reaction was her major concern. She took the Dundee turnoff and headed the last ten miles to home. Home to Woodhaven Acres. Funny, but in spite of the problems, she was beginning to think of it as home. And the fact both surprised and pleased her.

Chapter 11

Rosie bounded out of the car the second the door was open. Lacie, still holding the leash, nearly flew through the air behind the big dog.

"Rosie!" Cora yelled. Rosie stopped momentarily and then kept on running. Lacie had to let the leash go or be dragged wherever the strong canine wanted to go.

"Where is she going?" Mary Gray asked.

Cora laughed. "I have no clue. Looks like she's headed for the field. Oh, I see why. There's your uncle coming in. She knows who the important member of this family is!"

"How would she know that?" Mary Gray looked puzzled.

"Because dogs are smart and very sensitive."

"I just hope Uncle Woody likes her."

"He will learn to love her. Trust me on this."

"Whoa!" Woody yelled as if he was talking to a horse, but Rosie jumped up and licked his face. Both girls clapped and called for Rosie to come back, but she ignored them. Woody held the leash and walked the exuberant dog out of the orchard toward the house.

Lacie frowned. "I don't think Uncle Woody likes a dog to jump on him—"

"She can be trained," Cora said. "My friend Tina back home trains dogs, and I'll get some tips from her."

Woody stopped in front of the trio, took his cap off, and wiped his brow. Rosie stood at attention, as if waiting for him to lean down and pet her again.

"So this is Queenie."

"Rosie," both girls chorused.

"Rosie?"

"Uncle Woody," Lacie began to explain, "she already had a name, and we didn't think we should confuse her."

"There were no collies at the shelter," Cora added.

Rosie licked his hand as if to say she was as good as a collie any old day.

"She likes you," Cora said. "That's a good sign."

Woody turned toward the house. "She's the girls' dog, remember?"

Cora hurried to fix sandwiches but didn't make soup. Woody said it was fine this once. She added a plate of sliced pickles and a few radishes. Woody looked over at the dog sitting in the doorway of the kitchen.

"Never had a dog in the house before. Mom wouldn't allow it."

"I've never had a dog that didn't come into the house," Cora said.

"What's it going to be next? She gets to sit at the table with us?"

Mary Gray giggled. "That would look funny."

"I know. It was an exaggeration," Woody said.

"Can she sleep with us?" Mary Gray asked.

"Yes," Lacie picked up the argument. "That's okay, isn't it?"

"Perhaps just for the first night or two, until she gets used to her new home," Woody said.

Cora looked at Woody and met his gaze from across the room. She thought she saw a twinkle in his eye. She trembled unexpectedly. His comment surprised her. She sensed he was beginning to understand more about the girls and how they needed certain things. It was a good thing, and it amazed her at how happy she suddenly felt.

The girls drew straws to see who would have Rosie the first night. Lacie won, which Cora was grateful for. If she hadn't, she might have griped for hours whereas Mary Gray was more apt to give in.

"I still don't know if this is a good idea," Woody stated. "How do we know the dog is house-trained?"

"The young woman at the shelter assured us she is."

Both girls took Rosie outside to walk her around the farm.

"Thank you, Woody," Cora said. "I promise you won't be sorry. She's a good dog, and today you gave a homeless animal a family to love."

He scowled for a moment. "Why don't I feel benevolent, then?"

Cora ignored the question as she put a clean cloth on the table. "You'll grow to like her. She already likes you; that's pretty evident."

Soon it was dinnertime, and Rosie sat in her spot just inside the doorway. The girls downed their food in order to have one last romp before bedtime.

That night Lacie turned to face Cora as she started to pray.

"You were right."

"I was? About what?"

"You prayed every night that we could get a dog, and here we have one."

At the mention of the word "dog," Rosie came over and nudged Lacie's arm.

Cora smiled. "God doesn't always answer prayers in the way we want, but this time He did."

Later as Cora went out the back door, across the yard, and up the stairs to her apartment, she breathed a prayer of thanks. A milestone had been reached today. She looked around, remembering how cozy it had been last night with Meredith here. She saw the light go on in the upstairs bedroom. Woody was probably going to bed.

Cora read a few chapters, and then went back to the house, which was now dark. She wanted that last sliver of lemon meringue pie. She should have taken it with her earlier. Cora turned off the kitchen light and headed for the door when she heard a sound behind her. Startled, she whirled around to find Woody there. Even in the dark, she sensed he was frowning.

"I heard someone prowling around down here and came to investigate."

"Just came for a snack. . . I'm on my way back to my place."

"Cora?"

Cora turned and waited, her hand on the doorknob.

"Thanks for getting the dog. I'm sorry I opposed it for so long. I think she's a wonderful dog, and she seems to like the farm."

"You're welcome. I think she's a good dog, too."

Not knowing what else to say, Cora opened the door and said good night.

"I appreciate all you do for us," he said to her retreating back.

Cora paused and glanced over her shoulder, not quite able to meet his gaze. She nodded and smiled, then made a hasty exit. In truth, she wanted to stay, wanted to hear more, but she wasn't good at accepting compliments. For now she'd let it ride. Tomorrow was another day, and with her success rate, she was pretty sure she'd do something wrong.

❧

Over the next few days, Cora wondered several times how they'd ever lived without a dog. Both girls were content to take turns having Rosie sleep in their rooms.

"I thought it was just for a night or two," Woody said. He squared his shoulders and stood with that authoritative stance, eyebrows raised. The girls usually didn't argue when they saw his firm stance, but this was different. Mary Gray begged and cried and finally he relented. "Queenie sure never came into the house."

"But Queenie was a collie, and I believe collies prefer the outdoors," Cora said in the girls' defense.

"Besides, Uncle Woody, she would be so lonely and cry like a puppy," Lacie argued.

"Yeah, she'd keep us up all night," Mary Gray added.

"And what about the doghouse Hoby gave me this morning?"

The girls and Cora looked at the doghouse that badly needed paint. Cora supposed it would be a good project for the girls to work on.

Rosie looked at Woody. She went over and licked his hand, as if begging to stay in the house.

Cora's gaze met Woody's and lingered for a long moment. She saw a smile transform his face and knew they had won him over. Different dog. Different name. New rules. They had won, but it had all been democratic.

That night after the girls had settled in—it was Lacie's turn again—Cora tidied up the kitchen, then went out to enjoy the evening sunset. She lifted her face to the sky and thanked God for being here, for loving and protecting her, for Meredith's visit, and most of all for the lovable dog now residing in the Morgan household. Things were looking up.

The door opened, and Woody stood in the doorway, hands folded. "I don't suppose you'd like a dish of ice cream. . . ?"

Cora thought about the diet she wanted to go on, but ice cream sounded wonderful, so she nodded. "Yes, I would like a small dish. Thank you."

Minutes later, Woody reappeared with two bowls of vanilla ice cream with fudge topping.

They sat communicating in silence while the streaks of pink disappeared from the evening sky.

"You know, I often wonder," Cora began, breaking the quiet, "how people cannot believe in a superior being when there is so much beauty surrounding us. How can one deny God's existence?"

Woody rocked the swing, pushing it absentmindedly. "Yeah, you're right, but where was He when I needed Him a year ago? Why did I have to lose both my brother and father?"

"He has plans, Woody. We don't always know what they are, but He does. He was there where He's always been. Just waiting for you to lean on Him, to acknowledge Him. . ."

Cora stopped, sensing Woody's shoulders raring back. When would she ever learn that one word could do the work of two, that one sentence was better than three?

"I cannot know your pain, Woody, and I'm sorry if I sounded preachy. . . ."

He stared straight ahead, as if not hearing her, but he didn't get up and go inside or walk down the rows of the orchard.

"I had someone once," he said then. "I loved Helen and thought she loved me, but she didn't like the idea of farming. . .wanted to live in the city. I'd die in the city. It would be stifling and—well, I knew I couldn't do it, so it ended. I can still see her walking down the path toward her car. She waved as she drove up the lane."

Cora thought about her major disappointment with Carson. Keeping the engagement ring and later giving it back because she didn't want the reminder. . .

"I've been there, too."

"You?"

"Well, yes. Did you just think of me as an old maid?"

"No, it isn't that." He hesitated. "Guess I hadn't thought about it."

"I'm forty-some, you know." She was hedging a bit, but he didn't need to know her exact age.

"I'm almost there. So I guess you'd consider me an old bachelor set in my ways."

Cora said nothing, for Woody had hit the proverbial nail on the head. Of course she was set in her ways, too. It just seemed to happen to people.

"I decided then that I could go it alone, that I didn't need a wife or kids. And now I wonder if it was God's way of saying He'd give me kids—my two nieces to raise. Do you think that's what God had in mind all along?"

He turned, and Cora met his steady gaze. She trembled when she saw the glint of tears. She so longed to take his hand, but wouldn't he construe it to mean the wrong thing? And yet, to give comfort to someone hurting could never be wrong, could it? She reached over and touched his hand.

"I think God sends joy our way in ways we could never imagine."

He grasped her hand and held it for a long moment before releasing it. "I. . .I don't have any answers. Seems I'm always seeking."

Cora nodded, knowing the discussion had ended. Woody was a quiet, introspective man, and she had heard far more from him tonight than the entire time she'd been at Woodhaven Acres.

"Cora. . ." He hesitated. "The trial period is over. Had you realized that?"

She felt her insides coil. "Yes, I thought of that earlier today."

"What do you think?" His gaze held hers.

"About staying?" She looked away. "I think it's your call."

"Yeah, I guess it is, at that."

She waited for what seemed like an eternity. Did he want her to stay? There was no way of knowing, but she knew in the deepest part of her being that she wanted to. Yet she could not tell him so.

"Yes," he finally said. "I'd like you to stay."

"Then I will."

"I'm going in now."

He bent down to retrieve his bowl, but Cora took it from him, adding it to her own. "I'll rinse these out."

She listened while his footsteps clomped up the stairs, and her heart gave that funny lurch again. How could she feel this way? How could she even allow it? Nothing could come from it. Woody was four years younger. He would never return her feelings, and yet, she thought of the list Meredith had tacked on the bulletin board in the kitchen of her apartment.

"All things through Christ are possible. . . ."

She rinsed the bowls and put them in the dish drainer. She had never looked in on the girls before, but she felt compelled to see how Rosie was doing.

The big dog lumbered over to the door when she peeked in. Lacie lay on top of the covers, her hair fanning out on the pillow. She looked so angelic, so peaceful. How could one little girl think of so many mean things to do to her sister?

Cora ruffled the dog's ears and felt the warm lick on her hand. Closing the door, she breathed a short prayer before heading back down the stairs.

Just as she got to the landing, she turned toward the sound at the end of the hall and saw Woody standing in the open doorway of his bedroom.

"Cora? Is something wrong?"

She trembled. "I. . .just wanted to see how Rosie was doing."

"Oh, yeah. I'm sure everything is fine."

Cora nodded and hurried down the steps and out the back door. The apartment would be a welcome sight. She climbed the steps and tried to silence her pounding heart. She couldn't let him know how she felt right now. There was no way he could ever know. Leaning against the closed door, she felt tears slipping down her cheeks.

Three times, Lord, she thought later as she snuggled under the goose down cover. *I've fallen in love three times.* She stopped. Fallen in love? How could she even think it? What made that thought enter her head? She'd pray for it to leave her mind and heart right now. It was the only way.

Cora slipped back out of bed and knelt on the furry rug. "Lord, I am Your child, and I know You love me and care about me. Help me to remember that when things seem bleak."

She got into bed again and pulled the covers up under her chin, thinking of how Woody's hand had felt. Warm. Reassuring. And there had been kindness, if only for one short moment. Most important, she was going to stay on.

Chapter 12

Things continued to be better. Lacie was less argumentative, and Woody was smiling more. Cora and Mary Gray continued to work on their crocheting projects in the evening. The young girl learned fast.

At the end of May, Cora read about a baking contest in the newspaper. Something simple was the key. She had read the hazelnut cookbook Woody had on the shelf. The recipes looked good but sounded complicated. Hazelnut piecrust, cheesecake, bars, and even a pudding. Cora wanted a quick recipe that anyone could make and present to company an hour later.

Cora loved the old stand mixer at the end of the counter. She'd used it several times now and figured she was the first one to use it in a very long time. There was nothing like a large mixer to cream butter and sugar, then add eggs until you had a frothy mixture.

She removed the skins from the hazelnuts and ground the nuts in a grinder she'd found in a cupboard. Pressing the batter onto a cookie sheet took the longest. The bars were cooling when Hoby stopped by to chat.

"Checking for suckers tomorrow. . ." He saw Cora and removed his hat. "Mornin', Cora."

"Good morning." Suckers. Cora remembered reading about them in the book Woody gave her. Suckers were secondary shoots near the base of the tree that had to be cut back to keep the tree in good shape.

"What's that incredible smell?" Hoby asked.

"A new recipe I made up," Cora said.

"Do we have coffee?" Woody asked.

"I can't stay for coffee," Hoby said. "Just stopping for a sec."

"Of course you can stay for coffee," Cora said. "You have to be my taster."

Hoby frowned. "Taster?"

"It's a recipe I made up, and I'm entering it in a contest. I need two tasters—well, make that five, counting the girls and myself."

"Hey, okay."

Hoby followed Cora into the kitchen and sat at the large oak table. Cora set the coffeepot on the table, then cups, spoons, milk and cream, and a plate of what she called Cookies Delicious.

Hoby took one, then another. "Hey, I think you're on to something here. These are delicious!"

Woody agreed as he took a third.

"Good. I'm sending the recipe in tomorrow. I may experiment with a few other ideas."

"You like to cook?" Hoby asked, pouring a second cup of coffee. "Cuz if you do, and you ever get tired of this place, I'd hire you in a minute."

Cora felt her cheeks flame as she turned back to the counter, where she began putting the rest of the cookies in the cookie jar.

"She's staying right here," Woody said. "You find your own cook!"

The men left and stood chatting out in the driveway by Hoby's truck. They seemed comfortable, and Cora noticed that Woody almost smiled while talking with his friend. She wanted him to feel comfortable around her, and things were looking better.

Hoby left, and Cora finished cleaning the kitchen. She had time before the girls came home so she went out the back door and across the yard to her apartment. A voice called out, stopping her stride.

"Thanks for making those cookies and being kind to Hoby. He's the best friend I have."

Cora hadn't expected to see Woody here. She thought he'd probably gone out to the orchard to finish hand cultivating. He tried to keep the rows clean so they'd be ready for harvest. It seemed to be an ongoing job, from what Cora read in the book. Tending forty-five acres of established orchard was a lot of work for one man.

Woody stood next to the oak, which held a tire swing in one of its massive branches. His arms were crossed as he nodded.

"You're welcome, but it's just my job."

"Not in the job description, not on the list," Woody said before turning and heading south to his trees. Had she caught a glimmer of a smile? Her heart soared as she headed to her apartment.

Cora dug the journal out of the smaller bag she kept sitting beside the bed. She'd brought it along, but so far hadn't written a thing other than her first impressions.

"I think I scored a point," she wrote with flourishes and scrolls. When she felt good, she wrote fancy; when she was depressed, the words were so small, she could barely read them later.

"Mr. Morgan, that is, Woody, is hard to figure out, but maybe I'm not supposed to do that. . . ."

An hour later, the girls got home, and neither wanted to try the new cookies. "I hate hazelnuts," Mary Gray said. "I don't like any kind of nuts."

"How can you say that," Cora asked, "when this is your uncle's livelihood?"

Lacie shook her head as the book bag slipped from her shoulders. "I don't like 'em, either."

So Cora had to send the recipe in with just three tasters' approval, but they were discerning tasters, and she felt good about it. What if she won the contest? Wouldn't that surprise and please Woody?

Chapter 13

Cora hummed as she dried her hair and dressed for the day. Everything had been going smoothly; she was almost afraid to take a breath. Yet, that was negative thinking, and she was working diligently on that part of her life. She reread the daily devotional and the accompanying paraphrased scripture. "In all things, give thanks."

The sun was rising over the hill to the east. Cora took a deep breath and headed for the house.

◦❦◦

"Where's Rosie?" Mary Gray asked, brushing her hair from the kitchen doorway. "I opened my door and she went out."

"Mary Gray, please don't brush your hair in the kitchen."

"I'm clear over here, away from the food—"

"Just stay out in the hall, please." Cora flipped the pancakes on the griddle. "As for Rosie, I have no clue."

Woody had risen early, as he always did, so Cora imagined the dog saw a chance to escape outdoors. She liked walking along with him and seemed obedient, but Woody acted sometimes as if she was interfering in his orderly life. Cora couldn't believe it. She knew of other people who hadn't wanted a pet in the family but soon loved it and became devoted entirely. Men were that way about babies, too, so she'd heard. Not that she'd ever find out.

Lacie clomped down the stairs in the blocky, high-heeled shoes she insisted on wearing. She was usually more demure about things, but not in the morning. Mornings often found both girls contentious. Lacie swirled into the room in one of her dramatic stances. "Did you let Rosie out?"

Cora piled another stack of pancakes on the platter. The sausage continued sizzling in the fry pan. "No. I didn't."

"She's gone."

"She's probably outside with your uncle."

"Uncle Woody doesn't like her following him in the morning. You know that."

Cora sighed. "I'll ring the dinner bell! and let him know breakfast is ready, and we'll see if she's with him."

"Why do you call it a dinner bell when it's breakfast time?" Mary Gray asked.

Cora shrugged. "Breakfast bell sounds weird, I guess."

She wondered if Mary Gray would ever run out of questions. It seemed Cora was constantly bombarded with "why this" and "why that." She'd never known a child who needed so many details.

The girls went back upstairs to get their backpacks. The back door opened, and Woody began removing his boots. There was no sign of a dog, no wagging tail.

"Good morning. I assumed Rosie was with you."

"Mornin'. No. Haven't seen her."

"Oh, no. Here, sit. Say your blessing, and I'll go call her. She's not in the house, and I know the girls will want to look for her."

"How did she get out?"

"Good question." Cora put the sausage, bacon, stack of pancakes, and a variety of syrups and jams in front of Woody.

"Dogs are more trouble than they're worth," Woody mumbled, holding his cup for a refill.

"I don't know why you say that. The girls love Rosie. She's brought happiness and laughter into this household. Now, if you'll excuse me."

"Girls, come eat first," Woody called from the bottom of the stairway.

"But, Uncle Woody," Mary Gray protested, halfway down the steps. "Rosie is lost. We must find her."

Cora started to say something but closed her mouth.

"I can't eat a thing until I know Rosie is safe," Lacie added.

"Woody." Cora found her voice. "Please. If all three of us look, it will go faster. And of course the girls have school."

Woody shook his head, as if knowing he'd lost the battle. "Okay. Go search, but count me out."

"We'll call her first," Cora said. "You go out back, Mary Gray. Lacie, you go toward the orchard, and I'll go down the road."

"She's never run off before." Mary Gray was close to tears. "If she went to the road, she'll be hit by a car."

"I know." Cora took off on a run, praying inwardly that the big dog was not on the road and that she had stayed on the farm. Cora had no idea if she was street-smart. Some dogs instinctively avoided cars and vehicles on the road. Was Rosie one of them? She couldn't remember if the young woman at the shelter had mentioned it.

Cora heard the girls' shouts behind her as she got to the end of the driveway. Which way to go first? She didn't have tennis shoes on, so it would be hard walking in her slip-ons. But she had to do it.

Hoby's farm was closest, and she headed that way. Perhaps he could help in the search.

⤜⤝

Sure enough, Rosie was in his yard. Hoby had his hand on her and waved when Cora nearly stumbled down his driveway.

"Rosie!" she cried. "Bad dog! What are you doing over here?"

Hoby didn't look too happy. "She chased my cat up a tree, and I have no idea what happened to my outdoors boots. I leave 'em here on the porch."

Cora clung to the dog's fur and shook her head. "Has she been over here before?"

"Not that I know of."

"The girls are worried to death. I've got to get back. I'll buy you a new pair of boots since she must have taken them."

"It's okay." Hoby smiled. "C'mon, get in the truck. I'll drive you back over."

Rosie jumped into the pickup bed as if she'd ridden there all her life.

Cora tried to bite back sudden tears as she hopped in beside Hoby. "Woody didn't want a dog; you probably knew that."

"Yeah, I heard him say something about the girls clamoring for one, and there was no talking them out of it with you on their side."

"Rosie's been a good dog. I don't think we should get too angry over one wrongdoing."

"Tell Woody that."

Cora stared at the outline of Hoby's face. He was a kind man, a good neighbor, and he would give you the shirt off his back, as the saying went. But he, like Woody, had definite ideas about things.

"When you run a farm, you can't be bothered by runaway dogs or animals who dig up the yard."

"Rosie hasn't dug up the yard."

"No? I heard she did. And it was that old dead rosebush."

"Dead rosebush?" Cora was perplexed. "If it was dead, seems it wouldn't matter."

"It did, because his grandmother planted it years ago. When it died, he couldn't dig it up; he just left it there."

"Oh, I know where you mean." An idea started formulating in Cora's mind. Perhaps if she planted a new one in its place, that would make Woody happy. It was worth a try.

Hoby put the truck in gear and rolled off down his driveway. "Woody said he found her digging a hole in the orchard, burying a bone."

"He never told me about it."

"I'd say he's going to advise you to get rid of the dog."

"But he can't. It would break the girls' hearts." Cora sat upright in the seat, again fighting back tears. Maybe Hoby was right. Maybe they needed to get another dog, a smaller dog that wouldn't want to roam and wouldn't dig holes.

Woody stood on the porch, arms folded, in the stance Cora had come to know meant he was angry. Not that he ever said anything, but the look said it all.

Cora got out, thanking Hoby for the ride. Rosie had already jumped out of the back of the truck and ran to Mary Gray, who was crying. Hoby parked the truck, got out, then ambled over to Woody.

"Now, Woody, the dog has never come to my place before. I don't think she'll do it again."

"Could have been killed on the highway."

"I know that."

"Don't need another worry on my mind just now."

Hoby put a foot on the bottom step and nodded. "Know that, too."

Cora listened as the girls hugged the lovable dog. Why was Hoby changing his mind now? Men. It was just as well that she stay an old maid. At least she wouldn't have to try to figure some man out.

"You missed the bus," Woody said to the girls.

"It's Friday," Lacie said. "We don't do as much on Fridays—"

"Hey, I can take them in. Got to go to the store and run a few errands." Hoby walked toward his truck. "Get your books and gear and we're off."

"But they haven't had breakfast," Cora interjected.

"We can do without breakfast," Lacie said. Was she already starting to worry about putting on an extra pound?

"Absolutely not!" Woody said. "You'll eat, and Cora can write an excuse and take you in herself."

Hoby grinned. "Okay. That's fine, but I don't mind."

"Have you had breakfast yet, Hoby?" Cora asked. "Because if not, I know there is a stack of pancakes and plenty of bacon and sausage. And I can make a fresh pot of coffee."

"Yeah." Woody clapped his friend on the back. "C'mon in and eat. Cora makes enough to feed ten people!"

"But I don't waste anything," Cora said, coming to her own defense. And she didn't. She would heat leftover pancakes in the microwave for a snack for the girls. Sometimes she rolled them up with jam and whipped cream inside, then sprinkled powdered sugar on top. Her pancakes were thin, almost like crepes, so it worked well.

"It wasn't a criticism," Woody muttered under his breath. Cora heard and kept her mouth shut. With Hoby here, she didn't feel the need for further comment.

The girls drank their orange juice, and Lacie took one pancake and a piece of bacon. She looked over as if to see if Cora was watching, which she was. Cora often said that both girls needed more protein.

Cora smiled as she sat at one end of the table. The pancakes were not as warm as she liked them. Putting them in the oven, Woody's idea, was okay in a pinch. She'd much rather serve them steaming hot from the griddle. Hoby didn't seem to mind as he took five and buttered each one.

"These are good, Cora. Just like my wife used to make."

Rosie found her spot on the kitchen floor, on a strip of old rug Cora found in the shed. She lay down, eyeing everyone, and put her head on her paws. Cora didn't feel like eating, so she just filled glasses with milk and cups with coffee and cooked the last of the batter.

Ten minutes later, Hoby pushed his chair back and reached for his hat. "Now, let's get you two to school."

Cora hastily wrote notes for both girls. "Here. This will explain."

Long after the thanks for breakfast and the return thanks for the ride for the girls, Woody eyed Rosie, still lying obediently on her rug.

"I know you'd be too upset to send her back to the shelter, but she can't go wandering off like that. Next time she could get hit, and we don't need that."

"That's true." Cora busily removed plates from the table, stacking them in the sink. "Guess we'll have to keep a closer eye on her. Or maybe build a small pen."

"No fence or pen," Woody said. "Ruins a dog. I won't keep a dog that way."

He opened the back door and looked at the dog for a long moment before slamming the door behind him. Cora breathed a prayer of thanks. Rosie would stay. Just like kids, dogs got into trouble, and Rosie was barely over being a pup. Cora hoped this would be her last escapade and knew she had to make sure nothing else happened. Woody had a lot on his mind right now, and worrying about a dog should not be one of his concerns.

Cora went over and patted Rosie's head. "You know what's going on, don't you, girl? No more running off. This is your home, and you're supposed to protect it." As if in answer, Rosie licked Cora's hand and put her head down on her paws again. It was something she did often, and Cora smiled. Dogs were smarter than humans gave them credit for. She didn't think Rosie would run off again.

And she didn't. Fortunately, there were no more holes dug in the orchard or the flower beds. Cora remembered about the rosebush and decided to go to town.

Cora had never been able to grow flowers or keep plants alive inside the house. She didn't know why. Some people had a green thumb, but not Cora. She tried to make up for it in the kitchen and knew she had succeeded there. Woody had not once complained since the afternoon when she'd made the wrong soup and sandwiches. She'd learned that one did not fight Woody over a list. His lists and schedules were important, and he checked them several times a day. It would have driven her crazy, but she could see the reasons for them.

She selected a rosebush with beautiful, pale orange flowers. Ned, the nurseryman, assured her it was hearty, and she could hardly do a thing to hurt it, unless she forgot to spray for aphids or didn't water during the dry summer months.

"Water thoroughly once a week, especially after planting." He smiled. "I assure you, Woody will love the gorgeous color and sweet fragrance. And later I'll show you how to prune, but you don't need to worry about that yet."

Cora dug a hole and carefully planted the rose, and then turned the hose on and let a trickle cover the ground with dampness.

"Uncle Woody will like this, Cora," Mary Gray said when she got home from school. "I'm sure he will."

Cora pointed the trowel at Rosie. "You do not dig here or close to here anymore!"

Rosie looked away as if she understood, and Mary Gray put an arm around the dog. "She didn't mean to be bad."

That evening Woody looked at the rosebush, read the tag, and said nothing.

"It's okay, isn't it?" Mary Gray was the first to speak.

"Sure."

"But Uncle Woody, is that all you're going to say?"

"My grandmother's rose was yellow," he finally muttered.

"Well, I can get a yellow rose to put over there. . . ." Cora pointed to a spot nearby.

"Roses take too much time. It'll never live."

It was that declaration that made Cora determined that as long as she lived here on Woodhaven Acres, the rosebush would survive. If it died suddenly, overnight, she would replace it before Woody knew. The rosebush had to live.

Chapter 14

Cora fertilized the rosebush, checked for aphids daily, and enjoyed the sweet fragrance, even if Woody didn't. She'd put a fence around it to protect it from critters and Rosie.

Cora kept the house clean and did the girls' laundry twice a week. Woody still took care of his own clothes, in spite of her saying she didn't mind. Sometimes she didn't understand that man. What did she mean—sometimes? She never understood him at all.

The girls would be out of school in another week. Cora decided they might enjoy a trip to Portland, to see Pioneer Courthouse Square, go shopping, and have lunch in one of the quaint little cafés. Of course she'd have to get Woody's permission. He was so protective of them. She knew he loved them, even if he never said so. It showed in his expression when he thought no one was looking. And Hoby had him figured out right.

"You're doing fine, Cora," he'd said that morning he took the girls to school. "Woody is an okay guy. . .just hard to understand at times."

In her spare moments, she wrote in her journal. Random thoughts. Frustrations. Surely there was someone, somewhere who would appreciate her. But there were the girls. They'd wound their way into her heart, and she worried about them. And Rosie. How could anyone not love Rosie?

Mary Gray taught her to hold up a paw when she wanted attention, which was most of the time. They also taught her to sit and speak, and there was no more running off or digging holes.

There were letters to and from Meredith. Cora wished she had her own computer so they could e-mail, but it wasn't her top priority right now. In fact, she didn't know what her top priority was. Girls. Dog. Woody. The house he loved more than life itself. What if something happened to the farm or to the orchard? It would kill him, she knew. He had already lost so much, and she had to remind herself of that every time he seemed moody, unapproachable, or argumentative. That was how she would describe their relationship.

Not that they had a relationship. But it was just business, and Cora had always prided herself in getting along with people. The thing with Leighton had tripped her up, and she'd behaved stupidly, but that was behind her now. She found she had no residual feelings about him now, and that pleased her immensely. Now there was Woody to think about.

And think about him she did, though she tried hard not to. What possible good would it do? She had too many strikes against her. Her age. Her figure. Her nature.

"One day I may find someone who cares about me passionately," she jotted in the journal. "In the meantime, God is teaching me patience. Patience that things will work out for the best. They always do."

Cora thought about the many Bible verses that talked about patience. Ecclesiastes 7:8 said it was better to be patient in spirit than proud in spirit. And Luke 8:15 mentioned bringing forth fruit with patience. Could that also mean hazelnuts?

Cora had not been patient a day of her life, she now realized. It had taken her reaction to Leighton's marriage to turn her around, to make her a viable person again, to allow her to see there was good in her, and that she could make children happy. Maybe not a man, but she loved children, and somewhere there would always be children who needed her.

Since that first morning in the parlor, Lacie had gone to Cora for advice, but not often. Reserved like her uncle, she never brought up how much she missed her father again. Cora knew it still pained her—how could it not—but Lacie was brave and good at putting up a front. If only their mother would contact them. Jenny could phone, write a letter. . .something to let the girls know she was alive and well. How could she ignore these two beautiful girls? Cora asked herself repeatedly. Why did God give some women children and others not? Leighton's first wife had been like that, too. Cora simply did not understand it. Would she always be the one to come along to help get a family back on track?

Cora found Woody cultivating in the middle of the orchard. He glanced up when she said hello. She'd told Rosie to stay behind, and she'd obeyed as if she understood.

"Is something wrong?" Woody asked, squaring his shoulders.

"No." *Does something always have to be wrong?* Cora found herself wondering. "I need to go into town, so I wanted to tell you that the soup is ready to heat up, and I made two sandwiches for your lunch. Is there anything you need at the store?"

"Nope." His face looked downcast more than usual, and she couldn't help wondering why.

"Now it's my turn to ask you. Is something wrong?"

Woody shook his head.

Cora knew so little about growing hazelnuts, but she wondered why he was cultivating when everything looked fine. There must be a lot to learn. If only Woody would tell her more about his concerns in caring for the crop.

"Can I help you with this—flailing, don't you call it?"

"Yes and no." A grin started to play at the corners of his mouth.

"Yes and no?"

"Yes, it's called flailing, and no, you don't need to help. The job description—"

431

"Doesn't call for working in the orchard," Cora interrupted, finishing his sentence. She turned, thrust her chin forward, and headed back toward the house. So he didn't want her help. She could understand that, as she wouldn't know what she was doing, but suddenly the idea appealed to her, working alongside him, accomplishing the task. . . . Cora smiled, remembering the half grin on Woody's face. It hadn't lasted long, but it was a grin nevertheless. With renewed determination and thanking God for helping her to say the right thing, Cora got in the car and headed to town to do grocery shopping.

Woody sensed that something really was wrong, but he couldn't even guess what it might be. It was just a feeling. Cora had interrupted his reverie earlier that day, and while she and the girls chatted at the table, he had kept quiet. He wondered what it would be like to be alone with complete silence, yet sometimes he liked hearing laughter in the house. And Cora sure knew how to cook. He'd never deny that.

It was late now, and he reached for the old leather volume. His mother's Bible. It sat in a strategic spot on his dresser, but he hadn't looked at it in months. Cora had asked him to attend church with her, but he'd refused. He hadn't made the girls go, though they'd gone the Sunday they found Rosie. That thought bothered him now. He had shut God out of his life, yet in one tiny corner of his mind he knew one did not, could not, shut God out indefinitely. Not when you've accepted the Lord and asked Him to forgive your sins, as Woody had done when he was fourteen. They'd all prayed around the kitchen table, holding hands as his father's voice filled the room.

Woody went to youth meetings and camp each summer. His father thought camp was nonsense and that his sons were old enough to help more, but Virginia Morgan remained firm on this one issue.

His father ran the hazelnut farm. His word was law. Many other growers in the area sought his opinion. Woody remembered attending meetings while farmers discussed their crops, the blight that sometimes threatened, and the harvesting. Woody also remembered picking hazelnuts, though they called them filberts then, from the ground after the trees were shaken. It didn't matter if it rained, and it always did, as they gathered the nuts—leaves and all. A machine sorted the debris from the actual nut, and soon it was on its way to the drying station.

Woody had earned spending money by working the harvest each fall. He had bought his first car, complete with mag wheels, with his earnings. He drove it to high school with fierce pride. And though lots of girls liked him, he pretty much ignored them. His life was busy with the farm. What spare time he had, he spent going out for sports. Nothing in the fall, but he loved baseball in the spring. For years he had coached Little League. Lacie had not been interested, though girls were on the teams now. And Mary Gray had been too young, but perhaps now she'd consider it. He wished he had a son he could take to a ball game.

Put that thought out of your mind.

He thought of Cora and how she had fit into the family from that first day. Not that there hadn't been problems. He imagined there would always be problems with Cora. She was what his father used to call his brother: headstrong. Yet there was a kindness about her, and she believed in fighting for what she thought was right. The dog was a case in point. The other was in getting Lacie and Mary Gray to help with the chores—which they actually seemed to enjoy. He still wasn't sure how she'd managed that, but she had. And he was glad for the changes, though he'd never admit it.

He supposed that made him headstrong, too.

He turned to Psalms because they were short and easy to read. David, the shepherd boy, had taken care of the sheep, so Woody identified with him. And David had his trials with God, yet he'd had a contrite heart, and God always forgave him. Just as God was ready to forgive Woody now. But Woody couldn't pray. Other than the blessings before meals, he hadn't prayed in so long, he didn't feel comfortable thinking about it. Cora said what she called "sentence prayers"— praying for the day, the moment. She was a good woman. He knew that.

Cora. Why had her face popped into his mind again?

She was easy to talk to, but unlike a lot of women, she always listened, and he'd observed her listening to the girls on several occasions. She was bringing them around to her camp; oh, he had noticed all right. Soon all three would be against him, just like with the dog. What would it be next time?

Does there have to be a next time?

Why had he brought up Helen the other night? His heart had healed from the hurt, so why even mention her? Yet it had been good to discover Cora'd had heartbreaking experiences, too. He guessed it happened to most people. Not his brother, though.

He'd had a wife, two girls, and the farm to support him. Hunter had a good life and future, yet he had died. And why? For what reason? He could accept his father's death; he'd had a long, full life. But Hunter had so many years left, girls to raise. . . It didn't seem fair. Woody remembered a pastor saying that many things in life didn't make sense; you just had to trust God for the reasons and the answers. Was he ready to do that? And what about these feelings for Cora? He tried to ignore them, but they were there, coming back again and again.

Woody's eyes misted over as he looked at the highlighted verse: Psalm 46:10. "Be still, and know that I am God. . . ." He was sure his mother had marked it.

Was God testing him? Maybe that's what it was. You just thanked and praised Him anyway, trusting Him to work things out.

What about the girls? He'd tried holding them at bay, for that was better than becoming attached and then having Jenny come back for them. And she would one day. She needed time to sort through things, but one day she would return to being a mother. It was just a matter of time.

The room was stuffy. Woody opened a window. A full moon filled the night sky. His mother used to say she thought the moon was winking at just her. Was it? He hadn't noticed a full moon in ages, but moon glow filled the bedroom, and he knew he wouldn't be able to sleep. There must be peanut butter cookies in the kitchen. A glass of warm milk, a remedy his father believed in, was his for the taking.

Rosie moved and sniffed at Lacie's bedroom door as Woody walked by. The last thing he needed was to have a dog watch him eat.

The kitchen light went on, and he found a few cookies in the old Red Riding Hood cookie jar his mother had inherited from her mother. Cora said it was an antique and they should put it on display and use something else to hold cookies, but it had held cookies since he could remember, and he couldn't bear to think of using anything else.

Woody paused at the hallway. Maybe he should let the dog join him. Perhaps it was time they got better acquainted.

He set the plate and glass on a hall table and tiptoed back up the steps. Opening the door just a crack, he called softly, "Rosie, do you want to go for a walk?"

Rosie bounded to the door and pushed it open enough to get out. Woody ruffled the thick hair and got a wet kiss for his efforts.

"C'mon, let's go see what we can find to do."

❧

Cora worried when she looked over and saw the house lit up, until she remembered that Woody didn't know how to use just one light. He turned every light on and left them on when he left the room. Hence this particular night the hall, kitchen, dining room, and his upstairs bedroom lights blazed.

She stepped into her jeans, pulled a sweatshirt over her head, then padded down the steps. As she rounded the corner of the old farmhouse, she heard a voice. Moments later she saw Woody and Rosie walking out toward the orchard. She swallowed at the sight. She knew he'd come around; she just didn't know when. Woody needed a dog, too, though he'd never admit it. He needed something to love, to lean on. But what would happen in the event that someday the girls' mother came for them? Rosie was the girls' dog, and of course they would take her with them. Wouldn't they?

Cora headed back to her place, feeling warm and good inside. Morning would come sooner than she wanted it to. But it would be a morning of promise. Tonight had proven that. She'd known that getting the dog was one step in the right direction, and even though it seemed that they took two steps back, she could see a change. Tomorrow she'd ask about the painting project.

Chapter 15

After lunch, Cora brought up the subject of painting. "What this house needs is fresh paint. Inside that is." The girls were in school. She didn't need anyone to chorus an agreement, and painting a room would be something they'd agree on.

"Paint?" Woody stared at Cora as if she'd suggested a complete remodeling job. "Where?"

Cora shrugged. "The kitchen for one, the girls' bedrooms, maybe the hall. . . It's pretty dingy in spots."

"I don't think—"

"And you might consider modernizing the kitchen just a bit," Cora went on. "A double sink is much handier than a single one."

Woody's face was a mask now. "The kitchen stays as it is. Some people like old-fashioned."

Cora swallowed. She wasn't getting anywhere. "Okay, no major overhaul in the kitchen, but couldn't I paint just a few things? And the girls would love to paint their rooms—"

"No painting."

Cora poured more coffee. Woody was finished, meaning the discussion was closed. Then she got it. He probably thought she wanted someone to come in to do the job, but she would do it herself. She and Meredith had painted lots of times, changing the décor of their homes every other year. And since she already had the paint. . .

"Woody, I'd do the painting my—"

"No."

"What about the apartment?"

He sighed audibly. "I thought you loved the apartment. Weren't those your exact words?"

"It's just the kitchen. I would like a different color." She had seen an article about sponge painting and wanted to try it. Lacie and Mary Gray could help, and with school being out soon, they needed a project or two.

"Okay!" He pushed his chair back. "Just the apartment."

"I thought it would give the girls something to do when school's out."

"They're going to camp for two weeks the end of June."

"They are?"

"Yes. Paid for months ago. It's a day camp, so they'll be home at night."

"Well, I think that's a great idea. What will they learn?"

Woody sighed again. "Forgot what the brochure said, but it's a variety of camping, cooking, and studying butterflies, that sort of thing."

"Mary Gray will love it, but I'm not sure about Lacie."

"She's going anyway."

"About the painting. . .sorry I brought it up."

"You can do what you want with the apartment. Just don't burn it down."

It was Woody's attempt at being humorous, and Cora smiled. She was thankful she'd purchased the colors she wanted in the kitchen. And there was plenty of time to paint before camp. It would be an afternoon project.

❦

"You mean I get to help?" Mary Gray said on Friday when Cora showed her the paint.

"Yes. I'll paint the first coat, which will be a lime green, then you and Lacie can sponge on the second coat if you'd like. That's a darker green. It's really pretty. You'll like it."

"Sponge?" Lacie asked. "You sponge on paint?"

"Yes. I cut the instructions out of a magazine. I'll show you when we get back."

"Does Uncle Woody know about this?" Lacie asked.

"He does and he approves."

"That's weird."

"When do we start?"

"Tomorrow. Right after lunch."

❦

The girls chatted about the upcoming paint job at the dinner table. Cora shot a warning look, but it was too late.

"Do you suppose we could have some peace and quiet around here?"

Lacie pushed her plate back. "I'm not hungry."

"Me neither." Mary Gray followed suit.

"I suppose you're not hungry, either," Woody said, staring at Cora. "You seem to have a way of getting things going in this household." He set his fork down. "I'll be in the orchard, should you need me."

"I thought you said he approved," Lacie said as she cleared the table.

"He did." Cora felt bad. This wasn't supposed to happen. "Your uncle is under a strain right now. Be patient."

"Are we still painting?"

Cora nodded. "Maybe we should wait for a few days. I don't want to go against his wishes."

"But we want to paint," both girls chorused. They were clearly disappointed, as was Cora, yet she couldn't go ahead with it. Not now.

"I know, and so do I. We'll find another project to work on."

Woody tromped over the paths, cutting across the rows of trees. Why did some people keep things stirred up? He thought back to the end of the two-week period. The girls were doing better, getting their homework done before bedtime, and he did enjoy Cora's cooking. They'd agreed she would stay. Now it was time for another evaluation. Yet there was a hollow feeling when he thought about it.

Stopping, he looked at the top of one of the trees. The breath caught in his throat. He reached up and examined the branch halfway up the tree. Was that a cankering of the wood? He shook his head. It couldn't be. He and Hoby sprayed and checked the trees constantly for any problems, but this looked like the Eastern filbert blight, and it was too late to spray again. He'd have to look to see if it had spread. If so, the orchard could be doomed, or at least part of it. If you didn't destroy the blight, it spread like wildfire. It had destroyed Washington State's crops a few years ago. It was too late to inspect further. With a heavy heart, he trudged back to the house.

It was quiet. No TV, no arguing. He imagined they were in Cora's apartment, moving things around so they could paint. Such silliness, but he didn't care. He also knew they were working on some surprise, as Mary Gray called it, telling him it was a secret.

Woody paced across the porch, sat on the swing, and hopped up again. He would call Hoby, but it was his bowling night. Tomorrow they would inspect the entire orchard and look for more infected trees. They would need to prune, although he'd probably wait until after harvest. He'd move the branches out of the orchard and burn them. There would be many more hours of labor.

Why this now? He didn't need problems. He still had some money in the bank, and he could hear his father's voice: "Son, you always must have a reserve for those lean years, and come they will." But money wasn't everything. Money was nothing to Woody. Never had been. As long as he could pay his bills, he was happy. Satisfied. After a full day's work, especially during harvest, he was more than happy. He was ecstatic. Now he had this worry, along with Cora. Cora. How could one woman come along, worm herself into his thoughts, anger him until he stalked out the door, and still make him like her? And she had made the house a home with her incredible cooking and way of getting to know the girls. With them, she was kind. With him, abrasive. Why did it matter if she painted? It didn't matter if she spruced things up a bit. The only thing that mattered was the blight, if indeed it was. He looked skyward and asked for help.

He paced again and decided to call the number in the grower's handbook. It was for the president of the Grower's Association, who would probably come out to look tomorrow. No answer, so he called Jeff, the county extension agent. No answer there, either, so he left a message.

Cora woke early. It had been a fitful night with her worrying about the orchard.

She'd been in the kitchen when she overheard Woody leave a message for someone about it, and the problem sounded serious. It wasn't her concern, but she couldn't stop thinking about it.

Hoby had just returned from town and was unloading supplies from his truck when Cora walked into the yard.

"Hey! Good to see you." He paused, setting a sack down. "Is something wrong?"

"It's Woody."

The older man frowned, took his cap off, and put it back on his head. "I assume it isn't an emergency, or you'd look different."

"It's the orchard, Hoby. Something about blight. He found something on one of the trees down on the south side last night. He called someone about it. Do you know anything about blight?"

"Sure do." Hoby picked up his sacks, motioned for Cora to get the other bag, and hurried up his steps. "We sprayed, but I've checked most every day for the telltale signs."

"Why does it happen if you've sprayed?"

"Things come in with the wind; there's no guarantee of catching it all or not getting it again. That's why I'm entertaining the idea of selling out. There's a developer coming around, and he wants to buy my place. I'm just getting too old for this, anyway."

Cora shivered suddenly, though the early morning sun shone out of a denim blue sky. "Does Woody know about this developer? You know he won't sell."

"Yeah, he knows. You're right. He doesn't want to sell, but he may be forced to." Hoby put the grocery bags on the table and motioned for Cora to sit in a chair. "He just got the same offer. The developer wants both of our properties—wants to make a compound of row houses. What do you think of that?"

"And the farmhouse?" Cora knew Woody would never agree to sell it.

"That, too. Sometimes one has to go along with progress. I'm considering it because I'm due for retirement; maybe I'll take that cruise I've always wanted to take." Hoby hesitated for a moment. "If Woody sells, he'd never need to worry about making a living as a hazelnut farmer. There are others who can provide the country with all the hazelnuts they will ever need. Our little nut is a rarity, it seems, but definitely not a favorite. Now take peanuts. . ." He turned the burner on under an ancient coffeepot. "There's where the money is, but we can't grow them here. Just too wet."

"Woody won't sell," Cora said again. "I know he won't. I guess they'll build houses all around him, but he will keep doing what he loves to do. I can't imagine him doing anything else."

Hoby turned the heat down before answering. "I see how it is."

"Well, you know that for a fact, Hoby. You've known him a lot longer than I have."

"I don't mean that." The older man poured coffee into a cup that looked as if it hadn't been washed in years. He offered her a cup, but Cora declined. "I'm talking about you."

"Me?"

"Yes, you. It's great. I'm all for it."

Cora swallowed. "I don't know what you're talking about."

"You love the guy, don't you." It was a statement, not a question.

Cora's face reddened. "How could you think that? I'm just concerned about a person who likes what he's doing and wants to keep doing it. Is that so wrong?"

"You're fighting for him, and if Woody ever needed someone on his side, it's now. It's been rough since his father and Hunter died. He needs you, Cora."

She felt tears close to the surface for the second time that day. "I don't think Woody needs anyone, or he's not ready to admit it if he does," Cora finally blurted. "But how did you notice?"

"I've lived a good many years, my dear, and I notice a lot of things." He drained his cup, making Cora wonder what kept him from scalding his mouth. "Those girls are doing so much better since you came," Hoby continued, "and Woody has got to notice that. He never says a thing to you, I know, but he notices all right."

"And the dog?"

"He didn't want to let himself get attached to another animal. Lost his collie in a horrible accident when a tractor backed over her."

Cora shuddered. "That must have been awful for him."

"Yes, it was. See, I knew him when he was just a kid, so I've seen him grow up. Seen his mother get all sick inside the head and things—seen how the old man came down hard on his boys. Hunter fought the rules, but Woody never did. Hunter would have sold out to a developer in a heartbeat because Jenny would have talked him into it. Then Woody would have had a problem keeping the place. See, it's all in the timing. The good Lord knows what He's doing; we just don't know and worry needlessly."

"Do you think Jenny will come for the girls someday?"

Hoby poured another cup of what looked like mud to Cora. "Yes, I do."

"Lacie has been praying for it."

"But she won't keep the girls."

"Why not?"

"She has wild oats to sow. You've heard that saying about young boys, well sometimes it's that way for young girls. Those two married young, and Jenny has had her fling now. I doubt she'll take the girls permanently from their uncle."

"I want what's best for the girls, and I hope you're right for his sake." Cora stood. "Now about Woody, can you come over and talk to him?"

Hoby laughed. "Sure will, but there's not much we can do. He won't listen to me. He knows my decision to sell out, and he's mad as a hornet about it. I told him I'd sell him my equipment, and he can pay me what he can, when he can."

"But will he accept those terms?"

"It's his choice."

Cora walked toward the door. "Thanks for talking to me, and I guess what happens happens."

"No, we're not giving up. I didn't mean to imply that. I'll be over in a bit, assess the situation. Not that I know any more than Woody, cuz I don't, but I know the bigwig from the Hazelnut Association will come out and take a look."

"Really?"

"They like to keep up with these things, make reports and such."

When Cora started for home, Rosie greeted her halfway down the Morgan driveway, her tail wagging, as always.

"Hey, Rosie, things aren't going so well. You better be a good dog. More trouble is something we don't need right now." Cora scanned the horizon but couldn't see Woody. When he was out on the acreage, there was no way she could see him. Finding him was pure guesswork, a waste of time—yet something compelled her to look. She wished he'd come in, get a cup of coffee, and at least talk to her. She found she wanted to talk to him, to hear his voice, and the thought scared her. How could she care about him when it was pointless? She found herself caught up with him, the problems of the farm, and wanting to solve everything. What was in her nature that caused this? She knotted her hands and looked at the ground. She'd never understood how people could be tied to the land, but suddenly she was understanding. And her heart was breaking for Woody and his determination to keep his hazelnuts, to eke out a living as his ancestors had done.

Cora looked at the house and the rosebush she'd planted. Sudden tears filled her eyes. It was so gorgeous. She sniffed a bloom, thanking God for the rose's beauty. There was nothing she could do to help. She wouldn't even try. Leave it to Hoby to talk to Woody about the blight. Perhaps that would help, but down deep she knew it wouldn't. Times were changing all over for farmers, and Oregon was no different. With so many people out of jobs, Cora knew it had to be difficult for the hazelnut farmer. Was Woody prepared for what might happen? Did he lean on God in prayer? It was a question she couldn't ask. Then she got an inspiration. She would plant flowers. What better way to show that the farm was going to stay the same for a good long time to come? Nobody planted flowers if they were moving, did they?

The girls were in the kitchen squabbling over the last pancake.

"Good morning!" she called out.

"And where have you been?" Lacie asked.

Cora sighed. "Something's come up and I need your help. It means a trip to town."

"To shop?" Lacie's face lit up. "I need some stuff for school."

"To the nursery," Cora said.

"Nursery!" both chorused. "Why there?"

"Because we're going to get some bedding plants and fix up the old flower garden."

"Why are you planting stuff?" Lacie asked.

"It's to cheer your uncle up."

"What's wrong with Uncle Woody?"

"He's worrying about the hazelnuts, and I realize now we should have been praying for the farm and the crop."

"We prayed and got Rosie," Mary Gray spoke up.

"But our mother hasn't come back or even called," Lacie said, her face downcast.

"It doesn't mean He isn't answering your prayer," Cora said, slipping an arm around the older girl's shoulder. She pulled away, and Cora smiled in spite of the rejection.

"Well," Lacie said, putting her plate in the sink, "considering how he didn't say much about the rosebush, I doubt he's going to notice any flowers we plant."

"He might," Mary Gray said.

The girls reluctantly got into the car, not wanting to give up painting Cora's kitchen, but Cora assured them it would be done, perhaps tomorrow after church.

"We don't have to go to church, you know," Lacie said.

"Yes, I know, but I thought you might be eager to see your friends there."

"I'll go," Mary Gray said. "It wasn't as bad as I thought it would be."

"Good for you," Lacie shot back. "You do that then."

"Okay." Cora gripped the steering wheel, grateful the nursery was close.

"I want purple flowers," Mary Gray said.

"Yellow for me," Lacie said.

❧

"Hey," Ned called, walking out to greet them. "Looks like you have a crew with you today."

Cora nodded. "Yeah. Ned, these are my helpers, Lacie and Mary Gray."

"What can I do you for?"

"Bedding plants," Cora said. "Lots and lots of them."

Soon they had petunias, pansies, and primroses.

"You won't need to nurture these; they'll just bloom their hearts out," Ned said. "How's the rosebush doing?"

"Great!" Cora said, adding scarlet snapdragons to the mix. "I think that's it."

"How about fertilizer?"

Cora bought fertilizer and some compost stuff Ned said was necessary. Soon the trunk and floor of the backseat were filled with pinks, purples, and yellows. It would take all afternoon, but she was determined to have everything potted or planted before Woody and Hoby returned.

They drove back to Woodhaven after buying Lacie's notebook for a final project, and the girls chatted amicably.

Hoby's truck was still in the driveway, and Woody's was still gone.

Cora and the girls were soon busy planting the flowers. There would be two pots on the front porch and one on the steps. She liked seeing a burst of color as she came up to the house. The flower beds were now full, and Cora put the white plastic picket fence around them to keep Rosie out. The dog sat watching, waiting for someone to throw the ball that was at Mary Gray's feet.

Cora's hands were dirty and a couple of fingernails were broken, but she loved the feel of the earth, tapping the soil around each plant. Like kneading bread dough, this felt good, too. Lacie had gone inside after declaring she didn't like the dirt, but Mary Gray stayed and soon had smudges on both cheeks.

"Well." Cora stood, surveying their work. "I say we did a good job."

"Will Uncle Woody notice?"

"Oh, I'm sure he will. Let's go wash up. I've got to start thinking about dinner."

Pork chops were on the menu for the evening meal, and Cora was glad it was one of Woody's favorites. She always mashed potatoes and made gravy and served a salad or vegetable. Tonight there would be yeast rolls, too.

Woody and Hoby were late. They didn't come in but went straight to the orchard, and Cora turned the burners off and put the lid on the chops.

Still they didn't come. Should she go out to see what was going on? Hoby's old truck started up, then Woody clomped up the back porch steps. She turned the burner back on low and listened for the thump of his boots as they hit the floor. The door finally opened. It had taken longer than usual.

When Woody came in, Cora turned to say something, but the look of defeat on his face made her stop. Everything depended on the land, the harvest, and it went on year after year. And in that instant she knew she must have been feeling the anxiety farmers' wives felt. They wanted what their husbands wanted, prayed for rain, prayed for the harvest, prayed for good prices. The realization stunned Cora as she glanced away.

"I'm hungry," he said. "Be back as soon as I wash up."

"No problem," Cora finally said.

She went to find the girls, not resorting to the dinner bell, not wanting to hear the loud, abrasive sound.

"Did he notice the flowers?" Mary Gray asked, bending down to pat Rosie.

"No, I don't think so, but I'm certain he'll notice them tomorrow. Don't say anything." Cora hugged the small girl close. She knew Lacie would sense his mood and not talk, but Mary Gray often chattered at the dinner table.

"Okay," she said, crossing her fingers.

The food was on the table, and the rolls were barely warm, but it couldn't be helped. Cora passed the chops, then remembered they hadn't offered a blessing yet.

"I want to pray tonight, if that's okay."

Woody nodded without looking up.

"Dear Lord, we thank You for this food and for this day You have given us. Please help us to know the right thing to do, guide our paths, and I pray for the trees. In Your name, amen."

Woody humphed as he slipped two chops off the platter onto his plate. He then reached for the milk carton. "I've come to a decision today," he said finally, after all the food was on his plate.

"Oh?"

"There's no sense in holding out. A developer wants this property, and since Hoby's selling out, I may as well go that way, too. It's too hard keeping the orchard going with Dad and Hunter gone. I just can't do it alone."

He sighed audibly, and Cora swallowed hard. It was a long speech for Woody to make. It was also a concession, giving up something he loved, and it was tearing him apart. Cora knew he didn't want to do it. How could he let Hoby talk him into it? It was all because of the blight; just one more thing to worry about. She had hoped Hoby would offer to help and talk Woody into staying or convince him to hang in there. But he had apparently done the opposite, and Woody was convinced he had to sell the farm.

"But what about us?" Mary Gray wailed. "We love this farm. And Rosie loves the farm. We can't just move."

"Of course we can," Lacie said. "People move all the time."

Cora knew then that the person Woody had hoped would carry on the tradition of growing hazelnuts had never been Lacie, but would have been Mary Gray. Her heart was heavy now, as she knew Woody's was. Could she do something to make a difference? Maybe not, but she could pray about it, and this would be added to her prayer list. The farm couldn't be sold. It was that simple.

Chapter 16

Things went on as before with Cora preparing three meals a day. The girls attended church with Cora on Sunday, and Lacie was invited to spend the afternoon with a friend, but she turned it down, preferring to go back and help with the painting. Woody had said they should go ahead with the project.

Cora had painted the first coat that morning, and the girls sponged on the second color. It looked cheery, and Cora loved it, but Woody's silence troubled her and took the joy away.

On Monday, Cora received a letter from Meredith.

> *There is a new business opening up on the peninsula.*
> *The manager came from Portland. She recognizes the need for better*
> *elder care, and since she's been advertising for people to work short-term jobs,*
> *I thought of you. Would you be interested?*
> *You'd be assisting people who live alone and can't manage their meds,*
> *meals, and so forth. . . .*

Cora slipped the handwritten note back into the blue envelope. It was good to know she'd have a job if she returned to Oysterville, but a sudden uneasiness hit her. Did she want that? Here was the chance to return to her hometown, but she knew she didn't want to go. *I belong here. I'm needed here.* She would miss Woody, Lacie, and Mary Gray.

"You're so intense," Meredith often said. And perhaps she was right. She gave her work her all and came to love the people she worked and cared for. Now she was caught up in another situation. How could this be happening? She'd approached this job with clarity. No way would she fall in love again. Some people were not meant to marry. She'd accepted that fact. Why and how had she let her guard down?

Cora stuck the letter in her bag and got out the ingredients for peanut butter cookies. When she was troubled, it helped to create something in the kitchen. Perhaps it was the enjoyment others received from her baking that prompted her on. She wasn't sure, but it didn't matter. As she placed the dough on the second cookie sheet, she thought of a book she had read that spoke of the potential she had as God's child. If she thanked God for her life and noticed one thing to be thankful for, perhaps she could help instill this in Lacie and Mary Gray. What better job could anyone have than that?

She picked up both cookie sheets and turned to set them on the counter until the oven had preheated.

"I believe in God's goodness, and I know He can work in all situations," she said.

"How's that?" a woman's voice asked.

Cora jumped and nearly dropped the cookie sheets. She hadn't heard the door or footsteps. While Cora was lost in her reverie, someone had slipped in.

She looked up to see a woman in brown suede with matching boots, and they weren't cowboy boots. A tam covered a mass of blond curls. There was something familiar about her, but what?

"I'm Jenny." She smiled. "The girls' mother. I didn't mean to startle you."

"I'm Cora. Lacie looks just like you."

Jenny smiled. "Yes, we've heard that before. Tell me, how are the girls? Are they doing okay?"

The oven's preheat signal dinged, startling Cora again, but she was glad for the distraction. She put the cookie sheets in the oven, then set the timer. How was she going to answer the question? Dare she tell her about Lacie crying for her mother? How she knew Jenny would be back for them? What would Woody have said?

"Did you speak to Woody yet?"

"Not yet. I figured he's out in his orchard, and I didn't want to get my boots all dusty."

"Yes, well. The girls are fine, and I'm sure they'll be happy to see you. They get home at four, but you probably already know that."

Jenny looked around the kitchen and laughed. "Sure looks better than when I last saw the old place."

Cora's mind whirled with questions. What was Jenny doing here now? Had she come merely to see her daughters, or was she going to take them with her?

"We could ring the dinner bell, and Woody'd come in."

"No, that isn't necessary. I came to get the girls, so as soon as they can pack, we'll head back to the city."

Cora felt as if someone had punched her in the stomach. Yet hadn't Lacie prayed every night that her mother would return one day? And now her prayers had been answered. What better proof was needed that God listened to a young child's plea? Jenny's return had been inevitable. Even Hoby thought so.

"Woody will need to see you before you leave." Cora wiped her hands on a dish towel. "I can go get him for you."

There was a sound of boots on the back steps, and a second later Woody entered the room, his gaze taking in the scene.

"Well, how about that. Didn't recognize the car, Jenny. Thought it was someone else."

Jenny went over to hug her brother-in-law, but he stepped back.

"I suppose you're here to take the girls."

It was out. Blunt as only Woody could be.

Cora motioned to a chair. "Why don't you sit and I'll bring you some tea or coffee." She tried to smile. "And the cookies will be done soon. Mary Gray loves warm cookies."

"No, thanks. I haven't had a cookie in two months! Diet, you know."

Cora nodded. "A cup of coffee or tea then?"

"Gave that up, too." Jenny laughed. "Aren't you the typical housekeeper?"

Woody hadn't moved. His eyebrows were still raised. "I repeat, have you come for the girls?" His deep voice filled the kitchen. Woody loved the girls. He didn't want them to go in spite of what he'd said when she first came.

"You are surprised to see me. How is the orchard doing, Woody?"

"You haven't answered my question, Jenny."

Jenny tossed her head back. "Well, of course I came for my girls. Why else would I come back to this place with its memories and sadness?"

Cora noticed Jenny's mouth quiver momentarily.

"Where have you been all this time?" Woody asked. "With no calls, no letters to let us know you were okay? Do you realize how selfish that is?" His face was a dark mask.

Jenny nodded. "I know I've been selfish, but things have changed now. I left Montana, moved back to Portland, and I have a good job. I want the girls with me. I'm going to sit out on the porch and wait for the bus."

Woody poured himself a cup of coffee, saying nothing. Cora thought about Lacie and Mary Gray, believing that there was nobody like a real mother to care for a child.

"I knew she'd do this," he said, heading toward the back door. "She just better make it work this time."

Cora sat at the far end of the table, wanting to say words of comfort to his retreating back, but the door slammed shut. She wondered what would happen when the girls arrived home. She didn't have long to wait.

Screams of "Mom!" filled the air as Cora removed the second sheet of cookies. She had just one more sheet to bake—glad to be busy in the kitchen so she wouldn't have to see their faces. Yet she wanted to know. If Jenny was taking them, that meant Cora's position was over. Woody didn't need her just to cook. He could do it himself or have someone come in once a week to clean and cook up a few things.

The door banged open, and seconds later Mary Gray appeared in the kitchen. She dropped her backpack and sweater on the table.

"My mother's here."

"I know. I met her."

Mary Gray grabbed one of the cooler cookies. "Does this mean I'm going to live with her?"

Cora looked up and saw tears in the dark eyes. Were these tears of joy or tears of regret?

"What do you think?" Cora asked, placing the last cookie sheet in the oven.

"I suppose so. That's the way it usually works."

Crumbs covered her shirt and the corners of her mouth. Cora handed her a napkin. "What do you want?"

"To stay here."

Her answer surprised Cora, yet looking back, Cora realized Lacie was the one who spoke of her mother the most. She had missed a mother's help and love far more than Mary Gray, who was younger, more pliable, and had settled into living with her uncle.

"Things work out for the best, Mary Gray. There's a scripture I think of often. It's Romans 8:28. 'We know that all things work together for good to them that love God, to them who are the called according to his purpose.'" Cora stacked the cooler cookies into the cookie jar.

"I don't want to go," Mary Gray said. Her head bowed, she began to cry. Cora took the small child into her arms and just held her.

"You can come back for visits, and we can go see you." But even as she said it, she wasn't so sure. She doubted that Woody would go for a visit. And if he had his say, he'd keep them, but he wouldn't say it. The thought of the girls leaving felt like a knife in her heart.

"But we can't take Rosie," Mary Gray said, wiping her face with the tissue Cora handed her.

"Why not?"

"My mother doesn't like dogs. She says they shed too much."

"I think you should go sit with your mother on the porch, see what her plans are."

Mary Gray left, but not with her usual bounce. Surely Jenny could make room for a dog, unless she lived in an apartment complex that didn't allow animals.

Cora followed Mary Gray out to the porch just as Woody came from the side yard.

"I'm going over to Hoby's for a minute," Woody said.

"You're walking?" Lacie asked.

"Yes."

❧

Woody felt he should leave Jenny alone with the girls and decided the walk was just what he needed. No reason not to. It wasn't raining, and he felt like walking. Sometimes he could think things through better that way.

Sure, he'd expected Jenny to come someday, but she looked so different. This wasn't the sobbing Jenny who had begged him to take the girls. Fortunately, they had stayed in the car when Jenny came to the house and asked him to help her out. She'd been thin, much too thin, and her eyes looked bleak. Today Jenny looked like she'd stepped out of a fashion page. What happened to her faded jeans and blue denim shirt? He didn't like the fancy suede suit. Besides, it was almost summer, not winter. She must have met a man. He hadn't asked and wondered now why he hadn't.

Was he ready to give up the girls? Of course it didn't matter now. Now that he had decided to sell. Where would he go, though? What would he do? And Cora? What about her? Now where had that come from? He paused and looked back at the house. He'd always liked the view from the road. It was the typical old farmhouse, but they'd kept it up, and the gleaming white paint with dark blue trim looked sharp. The picket fence around the small flower garden Cora and the girls made set it off nicely, adding a splash of color it had missed for so long. And the rosebush she'd planted. So it wasn't yellow, but orange was a good color, and it smelled heavenly. He swallowed. He hadn't even thanked her for her efforts.

Hoby invited him in for coffee. "Just brewed a fresh pot. Where's the truck?"

"Felt like walking." Woody removed his cap. "Jenny's back."

"Oh, yeah?"

Woody pulled a chair out and sat down. "You're not surprised, are you?"

"She certainly took her time."

"I know."

Hoby handed him a cup of steaming black coffee. "What did the girls say?"

"Lacie's ecstatic, but Mary Gray just went into the kitchen and helped Cora with the cookies."

"It figures." The older man looked over and nodded. "She was hurt, but she can't let on, so it's easier to remove herself from the situation."

"When did you become a psychiatrist?"

"Oh, I've been watching this great guy on TV every day. Used to take a short nap around that time, but now I have to see what pearls of wisdom he's going to dish out."

"You're kidding!" Woody took a big gulp of coffee and almost spat it back out.

"It just came off the stove. Ain't no lukewarm stuff like you get with those drip coffeepots. I like the old percolator better."

"What do I do, just let the girls go and wait patiently for the next time she gets tired of them?"

"They are her daughters."

"But I'm not sure it's what's best for them. If Jenny has someone, well, you know how stepfathers can be."

"It isn't your problem, Woody. You did what you could. And now with selling the house and property, it's probably all for the best."

"And Cora?"

"What about Cora?"

"No point in her staying now. I hate to let her go. She's the best cook and housekeeper I ever had."

"Is that all she is?" Hoby asked, refilling his cup.

Woody felt his face turn red. "There's been nothing going on. You know me better than that, Hoby."

"I wasn't inferring there was, but I'm thinking you might be thinking about her that way."

"Hoby! I don't need a woman in my life, so just forget it."

"Of course you don't," Hoby said, acting as if he hadn't heard his friend. "I think Jenny might have hoped at one time that you'd offer to marry her."

Woody rolled his eyes. "Do you know how crazy that sounds? Jenny and me? No way. You should see her, Hoby. She isn't the farm girl she was when she left. She's got fancy boots, not cowboy ones, and her outfit looks like it's suede with a silly-looking fur collar."

"Hmm. Maybe she's got herself a good job."

"I think she's found a man."

They avoided discussing the farms, and finally Woody pushed his cup back. "Thanks. See you later."

Hoby walked him to the door. "I'd hang on to Cora awhile longer. Even if the girls do go with their mother, it might not last. Jenny could decide it wasn't working out, and there you'd be."

"Yeah. There I'd be."

"I'll tell you what." Hoby crossed his arms. "I might hire Cora if you decide to let her go."

Woody looked startled. "You said that before, but I didn't think you meant it. Why would you hire Cora?"

"You know how I hate cooking and cleaning. I'm from the old school that says it's woman's work."

"But you're moving."

"Yeah, but that ain't 'til after the harvest. Could use someone now."

"Hire someone then. You can't have Cora." Woody couldn't believe he'd said it. The words just rolled right off his tongue so easy-like.

Hoby laughed. "Guess that settles that."

Woody knew as he walked toward his place that Cora wouldn't want to stay if the girls weren't there. And Rosie. Oh, what would happen to the dog? She was too big for city living, but the girls were so attached to her. He knew they shouldn't have gotten a dog. Why had he let Cora talk him into it? And now here she would leave and go back home, the girls would be with their mother, and since she didn't like dogs, he'd be stuck with a dog he hadn't wanted in the first place. He'd grown fond of Rosie, though he hated to admit it. There was something about a dog walking to the orchard with you, patiently waiting for pats on the head, never demanding, never cross. His thoughts turned to Cora and how they'd argued about things in the beginning. She'd managed to get inside his heart, and he wondered if this was part of God's plan all along.

Rosie saw him coming down the driveway and trotted up to join him. "Hey, girl, how's it going?"

∽

Woody and Rosie walked to the porch where Cora sat on the swing.

"They're up packing clothes."

"That quick, huh?"

"And they are taking the dog. Temporarily, Jenny says. I don't think she wants to, but Lacie and Mary Gray insisted."

"Does she have a house?"

"No. It's an apartment, and they have to pay extra for having a dog there."

"Rosie won't like it."

"I know that and you know that, but you can't tell the girls that."

Woody sat on the top step, and Rosie ambled over and licked his hand. "Why do I think things are going to work out? They never do."

Cora took a deep breath. There was a time when she'd believed that, too. But she'd found hope in her daily Bible reading and prayer. God was there to lean on. Had Woody ever leaned on Him? Sought His advice?

"Like I told Mary Gray earlier, things do work out according to God's plan. I believe that, Woody. I hope you can see that, too."

Woody looked away. "I believed once, but things just keep happening, and I don't see God working in my life at all."

Cora wanted to tell him he was wrong, that God did care about him, cared about the orchard, but voices sounded down the stairs and soon the trio was out onto the porch. Lacie had her arm around her mother.

"Mom says that school is out in the city, but they'll transfer our records for next year."

Woody nodded. "Yeah, that's right. You go longer here because school starts later due to the harvest season."

Jenny stood, running a hand through her blond hair. "I should have called, I know, Woody, but I just couldn't wait a minute longer."

"Is this going to work?" Woody removed his cap, then stuck it back on. "I mean, remember last time?"

Jenny shot him a warning look and then smiled. "I have a boyfriend now, and that makes all the difference. I feel I can handle anything."

"Even a dog?"

She grimaced. "That might take some doing, but we'll manage."

Soon the girls were hugging Cora, then their uncle. Minutes later, Jenny backed the car up, and Woody loaded the trunk with suitcases, the dog's bed and dishes, and the sack of dog food.

It hurt, but Cora watched for a moment, then turned and went inside. If she could just believe it was for the best, but somehow she didn't think so.

She fixed a cup of tea, listening to the sound of the car fading away into the distance. Tomorrow was another day, but what sort of day would it be? And wouldn't Woody tell her he didn't need her anymore? With the girls gone, he could go back to being a bachelor as he'd done before. She'd bring it up soon.

The occasion arose the next morning after breakfast.

"I suppose I should be moving on now that you don't need me to be the girls' nanny," Cora said. The house was so quiet. The one thing she had prayed for now bothered her.

"Not yet," Woody said, not quite meeting her gaze. "I want you to stay for a few more days, if that's all right."

"Whatever you think." She didn't dare hope that he needed her for her, not her cooking or cleaning. Yet there had been no indication. Patience, God seemed to be telling her. Patience, Cora.

∽

It was strange cooking for two. Now she had enough casserole, chowder, and pie to last an extra meal. Not that the girls had been hearty eaters, but she couldn't get used to cutting down.

She missed them. Both of them. They were the cement that kept the family together, and she knew they kept Woody going. He'd had a special purpose with parenting his nieces, and though he rarely hugged them, they sensed his love. He had so much to give. If only he'd open up a bit. He made her think of Captain Von Trapp in *The Sound of Music* when Maria came to be their governess. No life in him. She realized, too, that she had seen him laugh. She remembered making it Number One on her list: Make Woody Laugh. She smiled. Maybe it was more of a goal. There had to be something that would make him respond. She wondered if he'd had fun in childhood, if he'd laughed then. She supposed Hoby might know. He seemed all-knowing and wise about things that went on at Woodhaven. She'd ask him the next time she saw him.

Then there were the lists. If Woody had lists, Cora's lists topped his. They were carefully written in her journal.

Self-improvement list (working on)
Ways to win the girls over (succeeded to some degree)
How to change and improve the farmhouse (nada)
And now: how to make Woody laugh (yes, finally!)

The memory returned as she reflected on that day.

It was a knock-knock joke Mary Gray had heard at school. Woody'd had his usual "oh, no" expression as she began.

"Knock, knock."

"Who's there?" Cora asked.

"Orange."

"Orange who?" Lacie said.

"Orange you going to come out to play with me?"

Woody thought for a second, then out came a deep belly laugh. The girls looked at him and over at Cora. Cora started laughing, then Mary Gray, and finally Lacie.

Cora knew she'd have that memory forever. She glanced at the finished afghan she'd thrown over the table. It was error-free, something she rarely accomplished. Her hand smoothed out the stitches. The basket weave design was a good one. She wanted to give it to Woody now. Maybe it would cheer him up, but what would he think?

She opened a magazine and flipped through the pages. Fashions didn't interest her but recipes did. She clipped a few to try. Maybe, just maybe Woody would let her experiment with a few new tastes for breakfast. The cheese soufflé sounded good. Peach pancakes topped with whipped cream and a sprinkling of chopped hazelnuts. Would Woody stand still for such?

Cora stood and looked out the window. She missed Rosie, too, almost as much as she missed the girls. She considered asking Woody about getting another dog or looking in the ads for a collie. Surely they had them. Border collies were plentiful, she knew, but he wanted the regular old-fashioned collie. What if she surprised him with one? But what if the girls returned? According to Hoby, they would, and when they came back, Rosie would be with them, and she suspected two dogs were more than Woody could take.

◦◦◦

Woody hadn't realized how much he would miss the girls. What happened to his earlier complaints, his wish that Jenny would come for them? He thought of Mary Gray and how she'd hugged him good night. She had been the most difficult at first but had wound her way into his heart. He missed Lacie, too, with her airs, worrying about how her hair looked, acting like a teen, more like a city girl, like her mother. He also thought of Cora's faith that things worked for good, according to God's purpose. He wanted to have his own faith again, wanted to believe that everything would work out, but he kept thinking of his losses, the things that had gone wrong. He wished now that he had attended church with Cora and the girls.

While Cora was up in her apartment, Woody went to the office. Now that it was a sure thing that they wouldn't get top dollar for their crops, he had to go to Plan B. He bent over the figures, adding the expenses, the debits in the left column. The debts far outweighed the assets. He couldn't come close to making all his payments. He'd have to secure another loan, but he hadn't paid back the last one. Surprisingly, his father had not had a large life insurance policy, and Hunter had none, so most of the life insurance money went for funeral expenses. He'd put the rest in the bank. It had been eaten up gradually by various expenses that came along. If he stayed with his intentions of selling, it wouldn't happen until after harvest. Should he take out a third mortgage on the house and property? He didn't like that idea, either. He set the pen down and leaned back in his chair. Times were hard—worse than he ever remembered.

The office, a small room off the kitchen, was the only one in the house without a window, and he found he wanted to look out a window now. He wanted to look out over the orchard to the south, the driveway and cedars that lined it as it led out to the main road, the backyard with the barn and shed—both buildings he didn't need. His great-grandfather had no one to help him, and everything was done manually back then, the slow way. If Grandpa Woodrow had hung in there, so could he. What was a little blight?

He looked at the last expense in the debit column. Cora. Cora was dispensable. He could go back to baching it, especially now that the girls were gone. Might as well get used to it since he intended to remain a bachelor forever. He had decided to let Cora go a week ago, but something wouldn't let him. He had this same empty feeling again as he thought about her and how much help she'd been to him. How could he tell her?

He couldn't. Or wouldn't. There was no explanation for the hollow feeling he felt when he thought about losing her. She had that look in her eye when she meant business. He had noticed it the first time they argued. He remembered the stubborn thrust of her chin, the way her mouth went all firm and determined. But it was her eyes that he recalled now. Their look was unwavering, strong, one of confidence. That look had stayed with him. Woody was never one to reason things out. Something either was or was not. You did what you had to do. If you had to sell a car, you sold it. If a loan was possible, you procured one. But he knew it was different for women. Women thought and deliberated and looked at things from all angles. He'd never been more aware of this than when Cora came to work. Jenny had gone along with Hunter and never argued. And his mother. . . Tears came to his eyes as he thought back to the early days when his mother would come to tuck him in, listen to his prayers, and smooth the hair back from his forehead. "My firstborn," she whispered, "you will always be special." Those were the words Woody clung to when his father seemed distant and often critical.

Sometimes his mother would read a story, usually from the Bible, the same Bible that sat on his dresser.

Later when he was in his twenties, his mother's mind began to get fuzzy, and Woody was the first to mention that something wasn't right with Mama.

His father ignored all signs, refusing to believe anything was wrong. "It's her way of getting attention." Hunter backed his father, so Woody had to bear the burden alone. He watched her retreating more into her shell. She disliked noise and family get-togethers. Then one day she'd wandered off, and the sheriff found her a mile away, sitting by a small creek that ran through a friend's property. She didn't know anyone. From then on she was watched, still nothing was said, nor was she taken to a doctor for evaluation. Woody missed the person she'd been, her kind, gentle ways. And he missed his father far more than he would have thought possible.

Woody picked up a family photo, one taken the last Thanksgiving they'd all been together. Hunter, looking so like the Morgan side of the family. . . Woody looked more like his mother's side. Jenny with her petulant smile, and Lacie, not frowning, but not smiling, either. Mary Gray with that impish grin, as if she was just waiting to get into trouble. His mother was missing in the picture because she had gone to a home the previous month, all because their doctor intervened and said she needed twenty-four-hour care, not just in the daytime. It tore his father's heart out, but Woody was at peace with it. He knew the person looking at him with the blank stare was hidden deep inside, yet there was always the hope that she would come out again.

Woody stopped daydreaming and looked back at the figures. Cora's name leapt off the page again. And once again, he got the feeling that he wanted to protect her. Protect her? Cora? The thought was ludicrous. If anyone needed protecting, it certainly wasn't her. What made him think that?

He doodled in the margin of the ledger. And he found his pencil writing Cora's name, over and over. Woody leaned back again as he remembered the first disagreement, all over the lunch she'd prepared. It wasn't on the menu. And she'd insisted on making the tomato soup, moving like a robot, as she dumped the contents into a pan. He'd said no, but she hadn't listened. Next it was about the girls and their lack of discipline and manners. And then it was the dog.

He jumped to his feet and began pacing, which wasn't his nature at all. Rosie. He missed her, but he'd never admit it, and he had scoffed when Cora suggested they look in the classifieds for a collie. He did not need a dog, not even a collie.

He heard sounds in the kitchen and was glad he'd closed the door. He didn't want Cora looking in on him. She was probably preparing something for lunch, though it was only ten thirty. She liked bustling around in the kitchen. At first he didn't like extra items added to the menus, but now he looked forward to her latest recipe.

Sitting down again, he tapped the pencil on the desk. "Not to decide is to decide," his father always said. Woody heard his father's loud voice projecting as if he were in the room, looking over his shoulder. Make a priority list. Write out all possible solutions. Go from there.

It was back to Cora, the one expense he could do away with.

❧

Cora had come in from outdoors with fresh flowers for the vase on a shelf over the sink. She loved having flowers there. They cheered her as she worked. Mary Gray used to bring wild daisies from the meadow with short stems, so Cora had one vase for that and one for the wild arrangements she made. Wild wheat, purple foxglove, and whatever greenery she could find.

It was then she noticed the closed door. Woody must be in there doing the books. He was quiet, but that was his way. Was he reconsidering his idea to sell the farm? Was there another struggle? The lower price for hazelnuts must be hard to take. And then to find the blight. Just yesterday Woody mentioned selling the old steam tractor in the barn. There was also an old trunk. Even if he sold those things, would it be enough to sustain the place?

She visualized him, shoulders slumped, poring over figures as he sat at the old rolltop desk. He could get a good price for the desk—it was at least two hundred years old—but she knew he couldn't part with it.

After arranging the flowers and setting them on the shelf, Cora put the teapot on. When she had to think, a cup of tea always helped. Perhaps she should make fresh coffee and offer Woody a cup. He definitely was not a tea drinker.

The coffee finished and the soup in a pan, though it was too early, she tapped on the door. "Do you want a fresh cup of coffee?"

The chair creaked and footsteps came across the floor, then the door opened. He could have said "come in," but he hadn't.

He stood mere inches from her, and that odd look he'd had once before swept across his face. Cora met his gaze and didn't waver. She was the first to speak.

"I thought if you were working hard, fresh coffee might be appreciated, but if I disturbed your figuring, I apologize." Suddenly he reached out and pulled her close. Cora, stunned, met his gaze again. There was another look this time, one she had not seen before.

"I—"

He cut off her words with a sudden brush of his mouth against hers. Just as quickly, he stepped back, visibly shaken.

"I'm through with the figures," he said, his back to her now. "Thanks, and I'm sorry for. . ." He did not finish his sentence, but moved past her and out the back door.

Cora was wordless, and she'd never been without words a day of her life. Woody had held her in an embrace, if only for a moment, and kissed her lightly. She'd wanted to pull him back and kiss him again, but the moment was gone.

She shouldn't have looked at the ledger, but it was open and she had to look. Her name was at the bottom of the list of expenses. But it was the doodles in the margin that caught her eye. He must have realized that he had to let her go. Cora was one expense he couldn't justify.

Cora felt her heart lurch as she ran from the room, out the back door, and up the stairs to her apartment. Frantically, she grabbed a suitcase and started pulling clothes from the closet. The time had come to move on. She'd return to Oysterville. Take that job Meredith talked about. She'd save Woody the problem of telling her.

Cora packed the suitcase in five minutes, tossing things in as fast as she could. She didn't take time to roll anything as she had done with Lacie's clothes. It didn't matter if stuff got wrinkled. Who cared?

Suddenly it was as if her mother were in the room with her, scolding her. "Cora Jean, what are you doing? Why do you always jump to conclusions?

Remember what happened in the past when you did that? You assume too much and just let yourself in for disappointment."

Cora stared at the sponged walls she'd done with the girls' help. It had been a good project and such fun. Even if she was let go, she knew it wasn't because of failure. She hadn't failed this job at all. She'd given it her all, and that was all anyone could expect. God had buoyed her spirits on more than one occasion, and He would again.

Closing her eyes, Cora prayed for guidance and for help in going back to the house to finish making the lunch she had begun as if nothing at all had happened.

She stood and just as fast as she'd packed, she put clothes back on hangers and the clothes in the chest drawers that gaped open and empty.

After washing her face, she brushed her hair and pulled it back behind her ears. It was time for a haircut. She'd make an appointment tomorrow. Tomorrow. Whatever came tomorrow, she was more than ready.

⁓

Woody headed for the barn, his thinking spot. What had ever possessed him to grab Cora like that and then, to top it off, kiss her?

And Cora. He felt the lift to his spirit as he recalled how she'd felt for that brief moment. She seemed to fit against his chest so well. And she hadn't pulled back. His hopes soared. If she hadn't wanted it to happen, wouldn't she have pulled away, perhaps even slapped him? That's what they did in the movies.

And she had kissed him back. He'd never been more sure of anything. Then he'd acted stupid, like a bashful schoolboy, and run out the door.

He paced and thought and paced some more. If he sold, the old barn would be torn down. Demolished. Developers came in and bulldozed barns, garages, sheds, and houses. How could he let it happen? He thought about the book of Matthew and verses pertaining to farming. Working the land, harvesting, and not worrying about what one should wear. But the verses that spoke to him now, Matthew 6:19–21, said: "Lay not up for yourselves treasures upon earth, where moth and rust doth corrupt, and where thieves break through and steal: But lay up for yourselves treasures in heaven, where neither moth nor rust doth corrupt, and where thieves do not break through nor steal: For where your treasure is, there will your heart be also."

Woody felt as if lightning had struck him. His treasure wasn't here at Woodhaven Acres. It was in heaven. He'd known that all along, but somehow he'd lost his way. And God had tried to tell him to hang on, to believe things would work out, jus. as it had for his ancestors. They'd struggled, but had they given up? No, and neither would he. God hadn't promised that life would be easy, just that He'd be there to lean on.

Woody walked around inside the old barn, remembering his father replacing the roof the year before the accident, remembering oiling and starting up the old steam tractor just as his father had. He knew it ran well. There couldn't be a rusty spot on it. Wouldn't it be better to sell a few items than to sell everything?

He hummed while he looked over the contents in the barn. An old hand cultivator. . . A well-worn saddle hung from a peg. It had been years since there had been a horse on the Morgan farm, but the saddle was well preserved. The story going with it made it special: His father had won top prize bulldogging in a rodeo. He could get a handsome price for most of this stuff. He'd never realized that collectors went in for the old stuff until Hoby mentioned it that day. There were also old coffee cans, glass insulators, and glassware. His father had never thrown a thing out, and Woody had followed in his footsteps. If he sold these antiques, he could make that balloon payment due the end of the month.

Cora came into the house with a renewed feeling. Woody couldn't pay her; that was the problem. But she knew in her heart of hearts that he wanted her to stay. Maybe his actions surprised him, but there had been emotion in that embrace, feelings in the kiss. And she had kissed him back.

She turned the heat on under the pan, assuming Woody would be in for lunch, made just two sandwiches, deciding she couldn't have eaten a sandwich if her life depended on it, and put a cup of coffee in the microwave to heat.

Twelve came, and then twelve thirty. Twice Cora looked at the dinner bell but didn't ring it.

She turned the stove off, wrapped the sandwiches, and left the kitchen. He knew where everything was. He'd find his lunch when and if he decided to come in.

Cora did not go back to her apartment. She felt like walking through the orchard. It might be the last time she did so. Even as she thought it, she knew she'd come back to see the girls. It wouldn't be here, but she'd go to Portland, find Jenny's apartment, and visit. She loved them. They had wound themselves into her mind and heart. Through them she would hear about Woody and the farm or wherever he went if he did sell the place.

When she returned, the message light on the answering machine was flashing. She pushed the button.

"Uncle Woody? Cora? If someone is there, please pick up."

It didn't sound like Mary Gray. The voice was thin and didn't have its usual lilt.

"I want to come home!" She realized the child was in tears, then she heard a click.

Cora's heart picked up a beat. If Mary Gray wanted to come home, Woody would surely say yes. And Cora could help. She so longed to hold the child tight, braid her hair again, and listen to her prayers. She hadn't mentioned Rosie, but she was sure Mary Gray would not come back unless Rosie accompanied her.

She wrote a note to Woody and propped it up on the table where he'd be sure to see it.

Mary Gray wants to come home. Listen to her message. She sounds so homesick.

Cora went back to her apartment to think things over. She could say nothing, pretend the kiss had not happened, repack her clothes, and just leave without saying good-bye. That seemed childish and cowardly, so she doubted that she would do that. Or she could drive into Portland—she had gotten Jenny's address so she could write to them—and bring Mary Gray back. She knew that Woody detested driving in the city and had so much work to do, so she could do this for him, couldn't she?

Cora heard the dinner bell and jumped about a foot. Not once had she heard Woody use the dinner bell. She hurried down the steps and toward the house.

"Is something wrong?" she asked, not quite meeting his glance.

"Yes."

"You mean about Mary Gray?"

"That and other things."

"What other things?"

"You know what I'm talking about."

"I do?"

"You know what happened before—"

"Oh, that. It's okay. I've already forgotten about it." *Liar, liar, pants on fire,* rang through her head. It was an old ditty her cousin had chanted more than once when they were kids.

"If Mary Gray returns, I want you to stay."

"I wondered about that, but if you sell the farm—"

"I'm not selling the farm!" He dropped his hat on the table, and Cora jumped.

"I thought. . .well, you said. . ."

"I say a lot of things, but what I do is more important. I'll take on another job, if necessary."

"You don't need to pay me." The words were out before Cora had assimilated them. She couldn't believe she'd even said that.

"Of course I'll pay you, but it may be a bit less until I secure a loan."

Cora didn't dare look at him. If she did, she might make a move in his direction and that definitely could not happen. She walked to the kitchen and opened the refrigerator.

"I appreciate all you do here."

Cora tried to swallow past the lump in her throat.

"Cora. . ." His tone was pleading.

"I know you do," she said, still not looking at him.

"I want you to stay always."

She swallowed for what seemed like the tenth time. Always? Had she heard right?

"Cora," he said again as his footsteps came closer. Her hands knotted at her sides, and she dared not turn or look in his direction. He touched her shoulder, and she felt herself melting. Slowly he turned her around until she faced him, then his big, rough hand lifted her face so she had to meet his gaze.

"I am not good with words—surely you know that—but I want you to stay, and I want us to be a family. You, me, Mary Gray, and the dog."

Had she heard right? Could Woody really mean it? He wanted her to stay? He wanted her to be part of his family?

The bubble burst as quickly as it rose. He hadn't said he loved her. His gaze hinted at it, but she needed to hear the words. She needed to know that he wanted her to be his helpmate. . .that he wanted to cherish and protect her. And all those other wonderful words that were repeated in the marriage vows. . .

"I have to think." She moved away from him.

He sat at the table in silence, and she wanted to ask—hoped that he did love her—but his shoulders had slumped over again, and she didn't know what to do.

"I'll go after Mary Gray this afternoon if you want," Cora offered.

"No, no, that's okay. I can go, but first we better call Jenny. See what's going on."

Minutes later, Woody hung up the phone. "No answer. I'm going to see what this is all about."

"You haven't eaten lunch."

"I know."

"I'll get the sandwiches."

Woody came toward her, pulling her around. "You will stay?"

"Yes."

"I'm going after Mary Gray now."

Cora gazed out the window, watching the man she'd grown to love. He held his head high, shoulders back. Her heart soared. She hadn't wanted to love him. She'd given up on the idea of finding someone and had fought the feeling for several weeks now. But there it was.

The truck pulled around from the back, then stopped at the end of the walk. Woody jumped out and ran inside and grabbed her in a quick embrace. "I'll hurry back."

Chapter 17

After Woody left, Cora looked out over the acres of hazelnut trees, trying to imagine what it was like when Woody's great-grandfather first came to Oregon. It had to be backbreaking work then. And probably they had fought blight of some kind, and no doubt some years were good, some not so good. Always there would be good and bad when it came to farming anything. She wondered why men stuck with it. It seemed to be in their blood. They had to farm. They had to carry on the tradition. To expect Woody to be any different was ludicrous.

Cora tried to write in her journal, but her hand was shaky. Could this be happening? She wasn't sure when she first started falling in love, but it had happened. Meredith had pointed it out, and Hoby had noticed, also. Yet she'd never dared believe. She was too old, too set in her ways. They fought at first, and Cora realized, looking back, that she had tried to take control and had wanted to discipline children that weren't hers. Could it work? She knew there were marriages for the sake of convenience. Is that what this would be? He hadn't said he loved her, yet there was a look of caring in his eyes.

Cora recalled one night when they'd sat on the porch. Woody in the swing, she in the comfortable ladder-back chair. It was dusk, and they had listened to the crickets chirp. They had eaten popcorn until the chill of night hit. No words were spoken. They didn't need to talk.

She opened the journal and read a line from last month.

> *I thank God for giving me this time with Woody and the girls. It's been a good time. I've come to face many things, to understand that life is so short— too short to pine over things that might have been.*

Woody sang as he headed north, then east toward the freeway. He never sang. His voice was flat; it was one thing his mother had told him. But he sang anyway, and the sound carried out the truck window into the traffic. Cora said she would stay. He had so feared she would not. She didn't love him, but she loved Mary Gray and Rosie, and they would keep her here.

He felt sudden exhilaration. He'd never imagined that he'd want the girls back. He had always wanted Jenny to fetch them, make a home for them again. That's what Hunter would have wanted. Yet, they added something to his life, something he'd been afraid to admit before.

Girls? But what about Lacie? Was she coming back, too? He doubted it. She seemed more cut out for city life. No, Mary Gray was the farmer. She had the spunk to fight the problems, the work. Soon he would know.

Cora went to the apartment to fetch the afghan. The time had come to give it to Woody. Not that he'd need it these warm July days, but he would soon enough. He would enjoy it in the evening while sitting to watch one of his favorite TV shows. She could see him now, feet up on the footstool. His cap would be off and his hair a bit mooshed down on top. It was a picture she would carry in her heart always.

A car pulled into the driveway, and before it stopped, barking erupted from inside. Cora watched as a door opened and a familiar dog bounded out and ran in circles, then back and forth in the front yard. Rosie! But the car wasn't the one Jenny had come in the day before. A man crawled out from behind the wheel, then the other three doors opened. They had come, not knowing that Woody was on his way to Portland!

Mary Gray ran up the steps into the house, yelling. Lacie, wearing new boots, hip-hugger jeans that looked like they hadn't been washed in a week, and a V-neck top, emerged. She paused beside her mother before going up the steps. The man stood, stretching and looking around, as if he'd never been to the country before. Cora wondered if he appreciated the clean, fresh air.

Cora walked away from the window, set her cup in the sink, and was just about to go down when she heard the clattering of footsteps on the stairs. Mary Gray. Nobody else moved quite like her.

"Cora! Are you in there?" She thrust the door open, not waiting for an answer. "Oh, you are!" Mary Gray came over and threw her arms around Cora. "I missed you!"

Cora hugged her back. "And I missed you and Lacie and Rosie."

"We've come back!"

"We got your message, and your uncle went to town after you."

"He didn't!"

"Afraid so."

"He'll be back when he finds us gone."

"I'm sure he will."

Mary Gray's cheeks were a hot pink as she clasped her hands. "I hate the apartment, and since my mother is getting married, and I don't like Jeff, and he doesn't like me or Rosie, I asked if I could come back here," she said all in one breath. She then stood back as if waiting for Cora's answer.

"Lacie's not staying," Mary Gray said then, as if anticipating Cora's next question. "She wants to live with Mom and Jeff."

"Oh."

"I was worried that you had gone because we weren't here, and Uncle Woody wouldn't need you."

Cora swallowed. "Well, he asked me to stay and I agreed." She felt the lift to her heart at the memory of his penetrating gaze, the words spoken.

"I'm so glad!" Mary Gray hugged her again.

"I think we should go downstairs. I'll meet Jeff, say hello to Lacie and your mother, and maybe we can make a pot of coffee or tea for our guests."

A light misty rain had started, touching Cora's cheeks and eyelashes. She didn't look forward to meeting Jeff nor seeing Jenny. She had seemed so artificial the last time they'd met. Cora couldn't fathom the young woman ever living on the farm, helping with the harvesting, or making lunches for the workers.

Jenny and Jeff sat in the parlor since the weather wasn't conducive to sitting on the porch. Cora entered the room and held out a hand to Jeff.

"I'm Cora. Chief cook and housekeeper and former nanny." He was young with deep blue eyes in a baby face, high cheekbones, and a mesmerizing smile.

"Pleased to meet you." He took Cora's hand and gripped it for a minute. Football player. Wrestler? She guessed he had been a jock in school.

"Where's Lacie?"

Jenny cleared her throat. "She's gone off to her room to get a few things." Jenny hesitated. "She's coming to live with me permanently. I'm sure Mary Gray has already told you that she wants to stay here with the dog. See, we cannot have a dog in our new apartment, and Rosie needs the outdoors."

"Of course," Cora said.

"And Mary Gray loves that dog. Do you think it will be all right with Woody?"

Jeff never said a word, but looked in adoration at the woman he was going to marry. She looked like a high school cheerleader in a denim skirt and matching top.

"I know it is, because Woody went to Portland to get her when he couldn't reach you after we heard her phone message."

"Phone message?" Jenny looked perplexed.

"She called earlier asking to come back, and he decided to go see what it was about."

"I had no idea. I'm sorry for the trip."

"Well, I need some tea. Anyone for tea? Coffee? Lemonade?"

"Nothing for us," Jeff said. "We really need to drive back. We have appointments at the gym where we work out every day."

"I'll go up to help speed things along," Cora said.

Lacie had all her clothes out of the closet and tossed on the bed. Mary Gray had a suitcase open and was looking from the pile of clothes to the suitcase, shaking her head. "They ain't going to fit, Lacie."

"Aren't," Cora corrected.

"Aren't," Mary Gray said, not looking up.

"We can hang some from the hooks in the backseat. We'll have lots more room now without you and Rosie."

Mary Gray looked away for a minute, and Cora knew what she must have been thinking. The sisters had never been separated. Lacie seemed to look forward to the move, while Mary Gray looked sad. Reflective.

Cora began rolling the clothes to fit into the suitcase. "It isn't as if Lacie is moving across the country. We'll see her. I'll even take you there some Saturday."

Lacie nodded. Then, as if realizing how her little sister felt, Lacie stopped and threw her arms around her. "You'll always be my sister, and there won't be any more because Mom and Jeff don't want any kids." She paused and chewed her bottom lip. "In fact, I'm not sure they really want me!"

"You always have a home here, I'm sure," Cora said. "This big old house has missed the laughter, the running on the stairs, and, yes, even the constant bickering."

She heard the sound of a familiar truck in the driveway, and Cora knew Woody would come barreling inside any moment. She looked out and saw him park the truck in front, something he hadn't done since she lived here, and run up the steps.

"Lacie! Mary Gray!" Woody's voice boomed from the bottom of the stairs. Mary Gray was out of the room in a flash, shouting as she went. Lacie set a sweater down and left the room. Cora finished packing what could fit into the medium-sized flowered suitcase. Maybe she could offer the use of one of her suitcases. That would ensure a trip into town to visit Lacie.

"Of course you can stay," Woody was saying, his voice louder than usual. Cora smiled. Maybe it was the tone, the decibel of his voice that showed his emotion. She'd never thought about it before. Loud meant he was happy. Low and quiet meant he was worried or angry. Now if she and Mary Gray could just make him laugh more. She snapped the suitcase closed and carried it down the steps. When she got to the next to last step, Woody turned and looked at her. It wasn't a passing look, but a lingering one, and she trembled unexpectedly.

"Cora. You already know what's happening?" He still hadn't taken his gaze from her face.

She nodded. "I do. I've packed one suitcase, and I'll loan Lacie mine so she can get the rest of her stuff—"

"She doesn't need everything," Jenny interrupted. "I'm sure we'll be buying new clothes and belongings." She looked over at Jeff, taking his hand, as if asking for his approval. He nodded but said nothing.

Cora went to the kitchen, just to get out of the way. Woody followed her, and she trembled again.

"You're so calm about all of this," he said, suddenly at her side.

"What else can we do?"

"Do you think it's a good thing for them to be separated?"

Cora reached up and smoothed the wrinkle lines on his brow. He took her hand and held it. "You didn't change your mind?"

"No, never." Woody showed concern for her like he showed for his trees, his orchard, and the big, old house. The icy interior had started to melt just a little, and Cora liked the new Woody.

"I've got to go say good-bye."

Cora listened to the sounds from the other part of the house—then heard the screen door open and shut with a bang. She knew she had to hug Lacie good-bye. She hoped with all her heart that it would work out with Lacie and her mother.

Lacie was on the porch, suitcase in hand. Cora held her arms out. "I came to tell you good-bye, and. . .well, I'm going to miss you. We're all going to miss you."

The girl looked stunned for a moment, then dropped her suitcase and put her arms around Cora. "I never thought you liked me," she said quietly. "You always liked Mary Gray the best."

Cora's hand smoothed back the blond hair. "I'm sorry if it seemed that way, Lacie. You are a special person, and I want you to always remember that. God go with you, sweetheart."

Moments later, the car left, and Lacie waved from the back window. Cora held back tears as she went inside. Like Woody, she worried about Lacie, but she was in God's hands now. If need be, she knew Woody would open his arms again to Lacie, just as he had to Mary Gray. Yes, he had missed them much more than he would ever admit.

Chapter 18

Woody didn't say anything about the dinner. He ate in silence, and Mary Gray kept watching him. Rosie lay in her favorite spot. Everything was as it had been with the exception of Lacie being there.

"You're sure you want to stay?" Woody asked suddenly. "Seems you'll miss Lacie."

Mary Gray's eyes clouded over. "I would miss Rosie more. Nothing was right, and she hated it there. When I took her out for a walk, I couldn't go anywhere except around the block. Rosie didn't like all those sidewalks and the noisy cars."

"It isn't as if we can't visit," Cora said, "and I've suggested to Mary Gray that we might take an overnight trip to Oysterville, if you don't mind."

"That would be a fun thing to do."

Cora nodded. "You are welcome to come, too. Might be nice to get away."

Woody looked pensive for a moment. "I'll think about it."

Cora wanted to show Woody where she'd lived all her life, thinking that he'd enjoy it, too.

After Woody left to check on the orchard, Cora asked Mary Gray what she wanted to do. She knew the little girl needed to get her mind off of Lacie's leaving. "Is there a friend from school you'd like to see?"

Mary Gray wrinkled her nose. "No, I don't think so."

They ended up making cookies together, and Mary Gray got out her loom and finished a pot holder in no time.

"I missed you, you know," Cora said.

"I missed you, too. I didn't think I would so much."

Rosie inched her way closer to where they sat at the table.

"But now you'll miss Lacie."

"But not Jeff. He ignores me."

"It takes awhile to get used to having kids around. The main thing is that he and your mother are happy."

"She won't be."

"Why do you say that?"

"She complains a lot."

"That's too bad," Cora said. "Does she go to church?"

Mary Gray shook her head. "She doesn't believe in Jesus. She told me so."

"Maybe that's something we should pray about."

Mary Gray was wise for her years. She knew her home was here, and she

465

wasn't looking for some pie-in-the-sky solution, as Cora's mother called it. Cora had been seeking unrealistic goals for a long time. She'd matured in the past year, for which she was grateful.

Cora wondered if Woody was going to say anything about the situation and if he would make his intentions known. So far Cora was staying on as housekeeper and nanny. She hadn't heard a proposal, only that he wanted them to be a family, and she wasn't sure he really loved her. Yet she knew he was busy getting things ready for the upcoming auction. He had high hopes of bringing in top dollar for several items.

The next day he asked Cora to help him carry a trunk into the house. When he opened it, they were surprised to see how tight the seal was. It had no musty smells, and the contents seemed well preserved.

"Would you go through this and see what all is in here? I'll probably take most of it to the auction, depending on the condition."

"Whose is it?" Cora asked.

"I'm not sure. It's just stuff my mother kept and probably her mother before her—"

"Woody, these would be family heirlooms. You can't just sell things like that. You want to pass them down to family members, don't you?"

"Well, I don't have any kids." He stopped and grinned. "Not yet, that is."

Cora met his gaze and smiled. Not yet, but soon, she hoped. Very soon.

There were postcards from all over. The writing was surprisingly legible, and Cora read a few. She now could put the words with the face in the round oval frame in the parlor. She set some of the postcards aside.

A white christening gown wrapped in some kind of burlap material was at the bottom of the trunk. Cora held it up, noticing the dainty stitches, the bits of lace around the collar, the hem, and on each sleeve.

Woody's face was white as his big, clumsy fingers touched the fragile dress. "It's my mother's. I remember her showing it to me once, back in the days when she was well."

"Did you and your brother wear this at your christenings?"

"I don't know."

"I'd think there would be photos somewhere." Cora shook her head. "Woody, you can't sell this," she repeated.

"I know." He stalked over to the stove, poured a cup of coffee, and came back. "I've had an offer on the old steam tractor. It was way more than I hoped to get." He grinned. "You know what that means."

"I do?"

He grabbed her and pulled her close. "Do you want to marry me?"

Cora felt his closeness and met Woody's gaze. "I do if you do."

"I do," he murmured. "The sooner, the better."

"Do you think Mary Gray will approve?" Cora teased.

Woody smoothed the bangs back from Cora's forehead. "Oh, yes. She loves you, you know."

The telephone rang and Woody answered. A moment later he held the receiver out to Cora. "For you. Someone from the newspaper." He shrugged.

"Hello?"

"Cora Benchley?"

"Yes."

"Do you remember submitting a recipe to our contest?"

"Yes, I do."

"I'm calling to inform you that you're our First Prize winner!"

"I won?"

"Yes, you did. We liked your recipe because it used a product Oregon is famous for: hazelnuts! The check's in the mail."

"What did I win?"

"One hundred dollars and a romantic getaway on the Oregon coast!" The voice hesitated. "Well, make that a getaway, in case you're not married."

Cora felt sudden happiness bubbling inside. It would be perfect for a honeymoon. "Thank you so much!"

"The recipe, along with the photo you sent, will appear in next Tuesday's paper."

Woody whooped after Cora reminded him about the recipe contest. "I'd forgotten all about that," he said.

"So did I." She decided not to tell him about the romantic getaway. Not yet.

Mary Gray ran downstairs to see what had happened.

"I won, I won!" Cora said, waltzing around the room. "Mary Gray, would you please go to my apartment and get that special surprise gift in the living room?"

"Okay!"

"You're going to have to enter more cooking contests, I guess."

Cora just laughed and reached over and hugged him hard. "Yes, maybe you're right."

When Mary Gray came back, she had her hands behind her back. "It's something for you, Uncle Woody. From Cora." She held the afghan out.

Woody unfolded it, looking pleased as he held it up. "You made this, Cora?"

"Yes. I wanted to wait for your birthday, but I'll get something else for you then."

"Do you like the colors?" Mary Gray asked.

Woody grinned. "It reminds me of my favorite plaid shirt."

"The one you wore the day we met," Cora said.

Woody leaned over and kissed Cora's cheek. "You know I've just got to tell her—"

"Tell who?" Mary Gray asked.

"It's something that will make you happy."

"You love Cora?"

Woody looked stunned. "Did Cora tell you already?"

Mary Gray shook her head. "No."

"Well, how did you—"

"I knew it would happen because I prayed it would."

Woody slipped an arm around Cora and pulled Mary Gray into the circle. "Cora has made me very happy and I. . ."

"And what?" Cora looked up and met his steady gaze. Was he going to say it—the words she so longed to hear?

"And I love you."

Cora closed her eyes, basking in the moment. "And I love you, Woodrow Wilson Morgan. You're stubborn and worry too much, but I love you anyway."

Mary Gray clapped. "I knew it! I just knew it!"

"This calls for a celebration," Cora said. "Let's have Hoby come for dinner. We'll have a pork roast and a special treat with the fresh peaches I bought. Better call him before he makes something for dinner."

"You are the bossiest woman," Woody began, but there was a twinkle in his eyes as he said it.

Hoby had no plans for dinner and said he'd be there by five.

"And I have something to do," Woody said, "something I should have done a long time ago."

"What's that?" Cora asked.

"You'll see." He started up the stairs, and while she and Mary Gray looked at each other, wondering what it could be, Woody came back down with the old Bible in his hands. "This book belongs in the parlor where my mother used to keep it. I want it on display so everyone knows this is a house where God resides."

"Oh, Woody." Cora leaned over and hugged him. "That's wonderful."

"This is a book to be used, not to sit on the dresser gathering dust."

❧

Later, Cora set the table for guests. She liked putting out placemats and added a bouquet of wildflowers to the center of the table. Pork roast, potatoes and carrots, gravy from the drippings, and baking powder biscuits rounded out the meal.

Mary Gray helped with the biscuits. She cut them out, placing them in the pan to bake. "I missed all of this when I was at Jenny's."

"Why do you call her Jenny?" Cora asked.

"She prefers that over 'Mom.' "

"I see."

Cora had never understood why mothers would want their children to call them by their names. She remembered a friend in Oysterville who wouldn't let her grandchildren call her "Grandma." She supposed they didn't want to admit to getting older. Cora knew she was getting older, but the only time it bothered her was when she thought about the babies she'd never have.

Dinner went well, with Hoby doing most of the talking. Cora remembered that about him. Conversation never lagged when Hoby was around. But it was good and just what they all needed.

When she brought peach ice cream out, Woody jumped up to remove the lid from the old-fashioned ice cream freezer. "I don't even remember the last time anyone used this."

Cora smiled. "That's what I thought."

"This is the best meal I've had in ages," Hoby said. "If you ever want to come cook for me, the door is open," he added. "Not that you don't know that already."

Mary Gray tapped her foot several times. "Aren't you going to say something?"

Hoby looked from Woody to Cora and back to Mary Gray. "What's there to say?"

Woody stood and walked over to Cora. "I've asked Cora to marry me, Hoby."

The older man pushed his chair back. "I wondered when you were going to wake up, my friend."

"Of course, that is, if we can get along."

"I have a solution," Cora said. "I boss on Mondays, and you can have Tuesdays."

Mary Gray giggled. "Sounds okay to me. Can I have Wednesdays then?"

"When's it happening?" Hoby asked.

"Soon as we can find a preacher who will do the job. Will you be my best man?"

"What? And get a tuxedo and all that?"

"No, nothing like that," Cora said. "Just a small gathering. You wear any old thing you want. I'm not one for frills."

They walked Hoby to the door, then he stopped. "Hear you're selling that tractor."

"Yeah. And?"

"I want to buy it."

Woody looked puzzled. "Why would you buy a tractor when you're selling your place?"

"Because I changed my mind."

"You did?" three voices echoed.

"Well, yeah. Can't a fellow change his mind?"

"You bet he can!" Woody said. "I just can't believe it."

"If I go moving to town, I'll be miserable. And how could I leave my friends?"

"You can't," Cora said.

Hoby got as far as the porch before he stopped. "Remember what I said that morning—that I hoped this housekeeper would work out?"

"Sure do," Woody said.

"Well, I never dreamed this would happen."

"Neither did I," Woody said.

Epilogue

It was an August wedding. A garden wedding. They'd rented a plastic covering for the ground and extra chairs. An orange rosebush was in one corner, and a few potted plants sat off to one side. The orchard was in the background, making a perfect backdrop for the celebration.

Meredith, Cora's maid of honor, wore her best dress—a long, rose-colored silk gown with cap sleeves and a scoop neckline. Its straight skirt accentuated her slim figure.

Mary Gray and Lacie wore long, garnet-colored silk gowns, something Jenny had insisted on paying for. She was getting ready to leave for Boston, where Jeff had a job waiting, and Lacie would not be going with them. But Lacie didn't look too disappointed as she held her sister's hand and watched her uncle wait for her aunt-to-be to step off the porch. Even Rosie wore a bright scarlet ribbon and bow.

Woody and Hoby wore dark suits, white shirts, and cowboy boots. Garnet red ties, the only new purchases, completed their attire. Hoby's suit smelled like mothballs, but Cora reassured him nobody would notice at an outdoor wedding.

Woody didn't know what Cora would be wearing. Nor did Meredith and the girls. She said it was to be a surprise and that she had sewn it herself. Being practical, she wanted something she could wear later. She also had made the tiered wedding cake: banana-filbert with cream filling and white icing.

Lacie's boom box belted out one of Cora's favorite romantic songs as Cora, holding her bouquet of yellow roses, walked off the porch.

Her two-piece dress of white linen had an empire waistline and was set off with a short bolero jacket. She tried to bite back the sudden tears, but they came anyway as she walked toward Woody.

The preacher held Woody's old Bible and turned to the couple.

"To honor, to love, to cherish. . ."

Rosie barked and trotted over to the couple.

"Through sickness and health. . ."

"Rosie," Mary Gray hissed, reaching down for the dog, who ignored her.

"Let her stay," Hoby said. "After all, it was Rosie that helped bring these two together."

Cora reached down and patted the dog's head.

"Do we have tokens of this love?" the preacher went on.

Meredith handed over a ring, a simple, golden band.

Cora felt the tears again and held tighter to Woody's hand. Their eyes met,

471

and it was as if he said, "It's going to be all right."

Cora had realized the dream she'd had for so many years now. She had let go and let God take over her life, and in so doing, He had given her the desires of her heart. Woody, though he didn't say the same thing, had agreed that it was God who led him to put the ad in the Portland newspaper for a housekeeper. He'd been ready to give up but felt the nudge to try at least one more time.

Now she could tell him about the surprise she'd kept to herself the past two months.

"We're going to the beach for a romantic getaway," she murmured.

"We are?"

She grinned. "It was part of the prize when I won the cooking contest."

"Well, what do ya know."

❧

A year later, Woodrow Wilson Morgan IV was born. His father had to leave the harvest, but neighbors chipped in to help, for that's what friends do.

As Cora held the precious bundle close, she looked at Woody. His dark eyes told her all she needed to know. Woody loved her. He cherished her. She'd never been cherished before. Her husband showed her, in so many ways, that he loved her with all the love God gave to a man to have for his wife.

The following day, Cora, beaming and full of pride, put her new son in the infant carrier, and they drove home from the hospital. God had indeed blessed her and Woody. The orchard was faring well; the girls were settled in and eagerly looking forward to helping with their new baby cousin. Soon Woody and Cora would adopt them. And now there was a new child to raise, a new life to fill their lives with more joy than they could have ever imagined.

"Yes, God doesn't take away without giving an even bigger blessing than you could have hoped for," she said. Woody squeezed her hand in agreement.

COOKIES DELICIOUS

Cream together: 1 cup butter (2 sticks) and 1 cup sugar
Add: 1 egg yolk to mixture (reserve the white)
Mix in: 2 cups flour with 2 tsp. cinnamon

Spread mixture evenly on lightly greased cookie sheet.
Brush top of mixture with the stiffly beaten egg white.
Sprinkle with chopped hazelnuts.

Bake 30 minutes in preheated 325°F oven.
Cut into squares while hot.
Cool thoroughly before removing
the squares from the cookie sheet.

A Letter to Our Readers

Dear Readers:

In order that we might better contribute to your reading enjoyment, we would appreciate your taking a few minutes to respond to the following questions. When completed, please return to the following: Fiction Editor, Barbour Publishing, Inc., P.O. Box 719, Uhrichsville, OH 44683.

1. Did you enjoy reading *Oregon Breeze*?
   ❏ Very much—I would like to see more books like this.
   ❏ Moderately—I would have enjoyed it more if _____
   _____
   _____

2. What influenced your decision to purchase this book?
   (Check those that apply.)
   ❏ Cover   ❏ Back cover copy   ❏ Title   ❏ Price
   ❏ Friends   ❏ Publicity   ❏ Other

3. Which story was your favorite?
   ❏ *Finding Courtney*   ❏ *Ring of Hope*
   ❏ *The Sea Beckons*   ❏ *Woodhaven Acres*

4. Please check your age range:
   ❏ Under 18   ❏ 18–24   ❏ 25–34
   ❏ 35–45   ❏ 46–55   ❏ Over 55

5. How many hours per week do you read? _____

Name _____

Occupation _____

Address _____

City_____ State_____ Zip_____

E-mail_____

If you enjoyed

Oregon Breeze

then read:

ALABAMA

Southern Charm Reigns in Four Inspiring Romances

by Kay Cornelius

Politically Correct
Toni's Vow
Anita's Fortune
Mary's Choice

If you enjoyed
Oregon Breeze
then read:

Virginia

FOUR INSPIRING STORIES OF
VALOR, VIRTUE, AND VICTORY

by Cathy Marie Hake

Precious Burdens
Redeemed Hearts
Ramshackle Rose
Restoration